Quest for ye Black Ryng, ye Monks of Wytangdom.
by D.R Shaw. Published by Blurb, Inc. San Francisco, USA
London, UK.

Cover and Art work by D.R Shaw.

Library of Congress Control Number: 2020903326

"and so with each new dawn cometh

a new day!, and so with each new day,

so cometh, a new, adventure!".

D R Shaw

"A hardy welcome and salutations wayfarer. I do say I am most chuffed to see you have chosen to join and so share with me what promises to be a most wonderous and great adventure!. Before we proceed natheless, I think it requisite dear friend that I first go over with you..."

"a few details and facts about this epic. What is that you say? a ghastly boring commentary? O! no! not at all! rest assured my dear wayfarer it will be nothing of the sort O! FIDLE DUSH! I do beg your pardon! I have not as yet introduced myself how very boorish of me. I am whom they call the storyteller and I shall be the narrator and your companion during what will soon be an extraordinary experience and journey..."

"into an extraordinary world, time and place like no other!. Well now where was I?, o YES! you will forgive me my dear wayfarer for wondering off the subject a wee bit. It appears that old age has somewhat clouded my chain of thought, I have become it seems absent minded as they say you know in my later years. No mater, as I was saying...."

"Before we begin our journey into this uncharted world of mystery and the unknown thus never before yet been spoken about or revealed, that is of course until now!. I wish first to discuss with you a matter of importance. We have all heard a great deal of the bygone world of yesteryear."

"The magical time of the Elves and fayfolk, of how they lived, of their customs, language, culture and so on and so forth and finally how and why they departed and thus left lower world and so returned to their ancient kingdom of origin in the Heavens, the Higher world. the kingdom of Alfheim, natheless! what we never hear about thus far..."

"is what becoming of the world after their departing? and so it is upon this time of lower world, the time after the Elves that our story focuses. The world after the time of the Fayfolk and during the time of mortals. What is that you say?, sounds like sniffle dosh and boring codswallop?! Ha-ha-ha! I assure you our epic is nothing of the sort!, boring it is not! by any means. Please do not be so quick to judge my dear..."

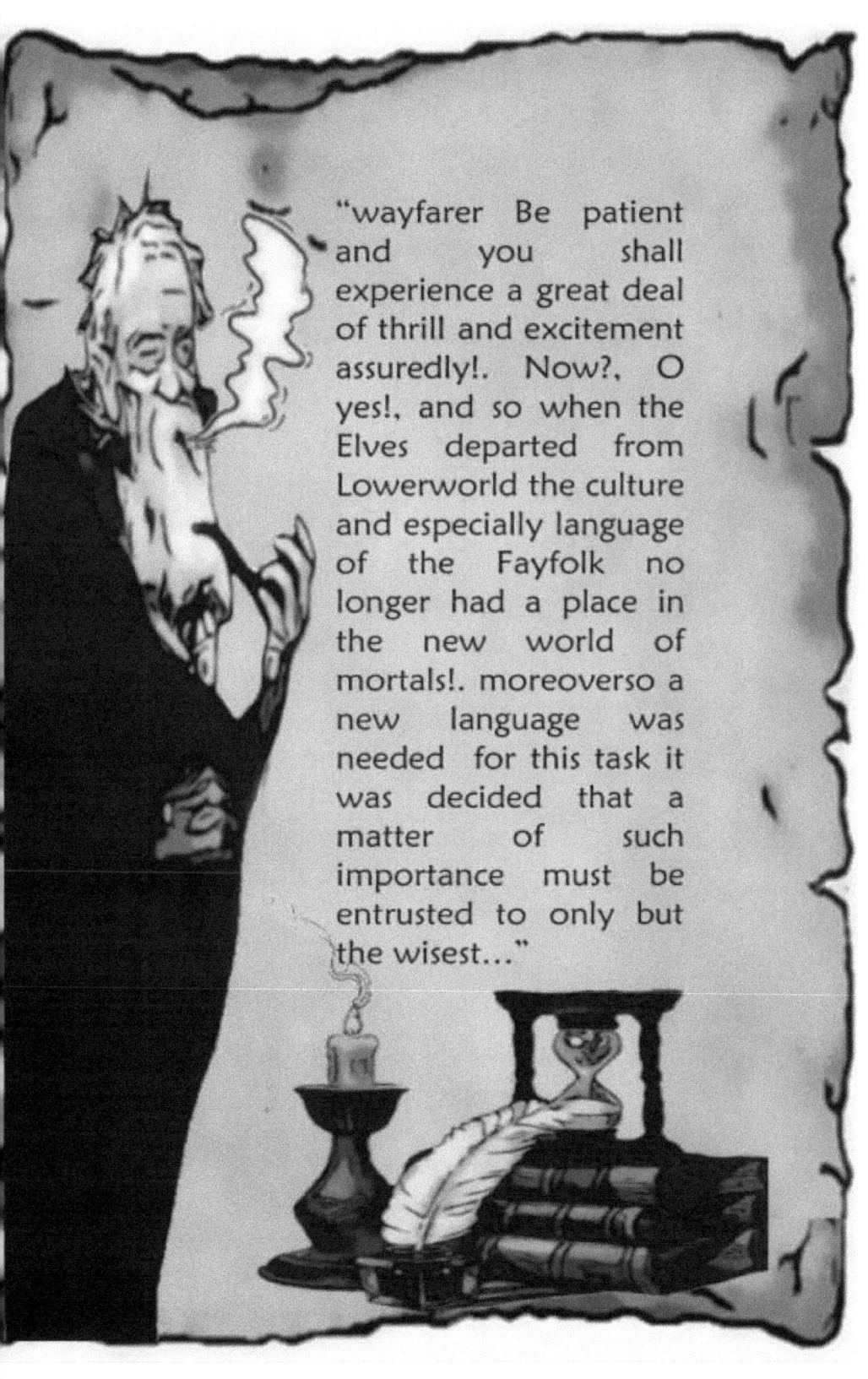

"wayfarer Be patient and you shall experience a great deal of thrill and excitement assuredly!. Now?, O yes!, and so when the Elves departed from Lowerworld the culture and especially language of the Fayfolk no longer had a place in the new world of mortals!. moreoverso a new language was needed for this task it was decided that a matter of such importance must be entrusted to only but the wisest…"

"and most capable in the land Wherefore it was decided that the undertaking of this task would be given to members of the the most ancient and highly regarded order in all of lower world Second only to the Elves in prestige, knowledge and wisdom. These were the Monac's of Wytangdom or also known as the (Wytan). I must mention as to why it is I have mentioned this new English form wayfarer?."

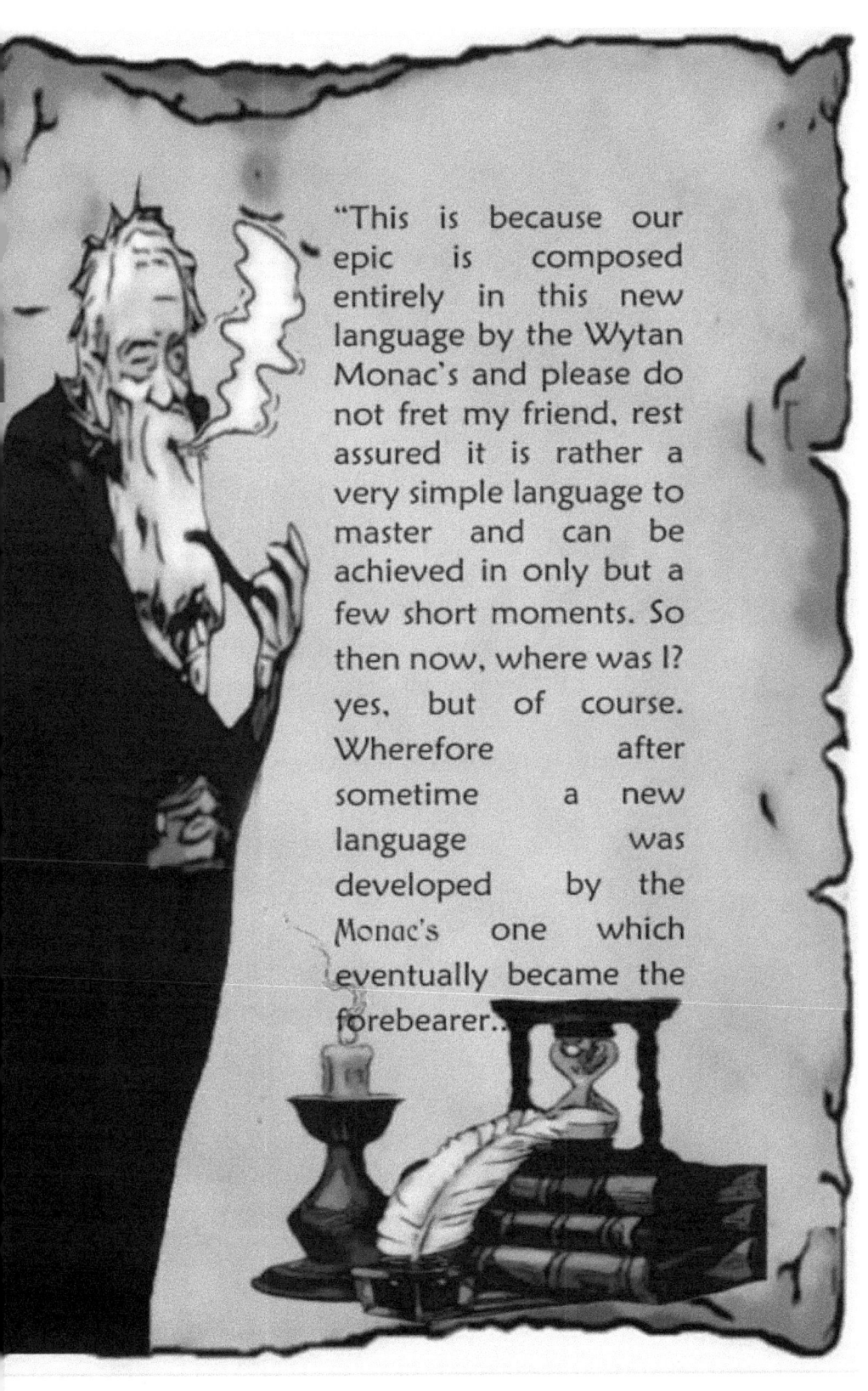

"This is because our epic is composed entirely in this new language by the Wytan Monac's and please do not fret my friend, rest assured it is rather a very simple language to master and can be achieved in only but a few short moments. So then now, where was I? yes, but of course. Wherefore after sometime a new language was developed by the Monac's one which eventually became the forebearer...

"of the language scholars would come to recognize as Old, Middle and of course. what we have today as, new or modern English!. A fact that which is not taught or referred to by modern day scholars of language. This new language was inevitably named after its creators and so it became known as (Winglish) or (Wynglýsh) the language of the Wytan) was ultimately spoken in Lowerworld..."

"and during the period of Second Earth. Natheless as time progressed its name was altered to English. Once more these are facts that which you will not find published in modern scholarly accounts. One of three contrasting distinctions between the two (Wynglýsh) and its predecessor English of today, lies in the presence in one, and so void in the other the, Kef letter (ý) which in modern English has been replaced with the letter (i)."

"The (Kef) letter makes the same sound as does the letter (i). Now here is where the Kef mark was applied. Any word or sentence that in today's English requires an (i) in Wynglýsh the Kef letter was used instead...

Examples;
a; Coming (coming + **ý**)= **(Comý**ng).
It is pronounced as (**i**).
Such as;
The word (Ring)
(Ring+**ý**=Rýng) ."

"Which later during old English era the Kef mark was removed but the letter (y) was applied and so it became (Ryng) The letter (y) is the predecessor to the Kef letter. Until today instead of the letter (y) we now use the letter (i). Another element of the Wynglýsh language is the replacing of those sentences which end with (ing) and replacing these with (en) letter and so giving the ending sentence the (ĕn) …"

"sound such as;

(going +en = goen),
and
(opening+ en =
openen).

These constitute
only two of four
differentiating
factors which sets
apart Wynglýsh
from its modern
English form. Other
differentiating
factors which set
apart the ancient
(Wynglýsh)..."

"of the Wytan's from its modern English variant are the fact that in Wýnglýsh there are no silent (e) letters, in that all (e) letters are pronounced no matter where in a sentence it be placed, and also all (e) letters made the low or short (é) sound like in (egg). The other is when the (ing) letters are used in words such as;"

"(seeing) and (being) as pointed out heretofore in a sentence the (ing) is always replaced with the (ene) letters. In the mentioned other words when we are dealing with words which are comprised of double (ee) letters, since in Wynglýsh the double (ee) were never used."

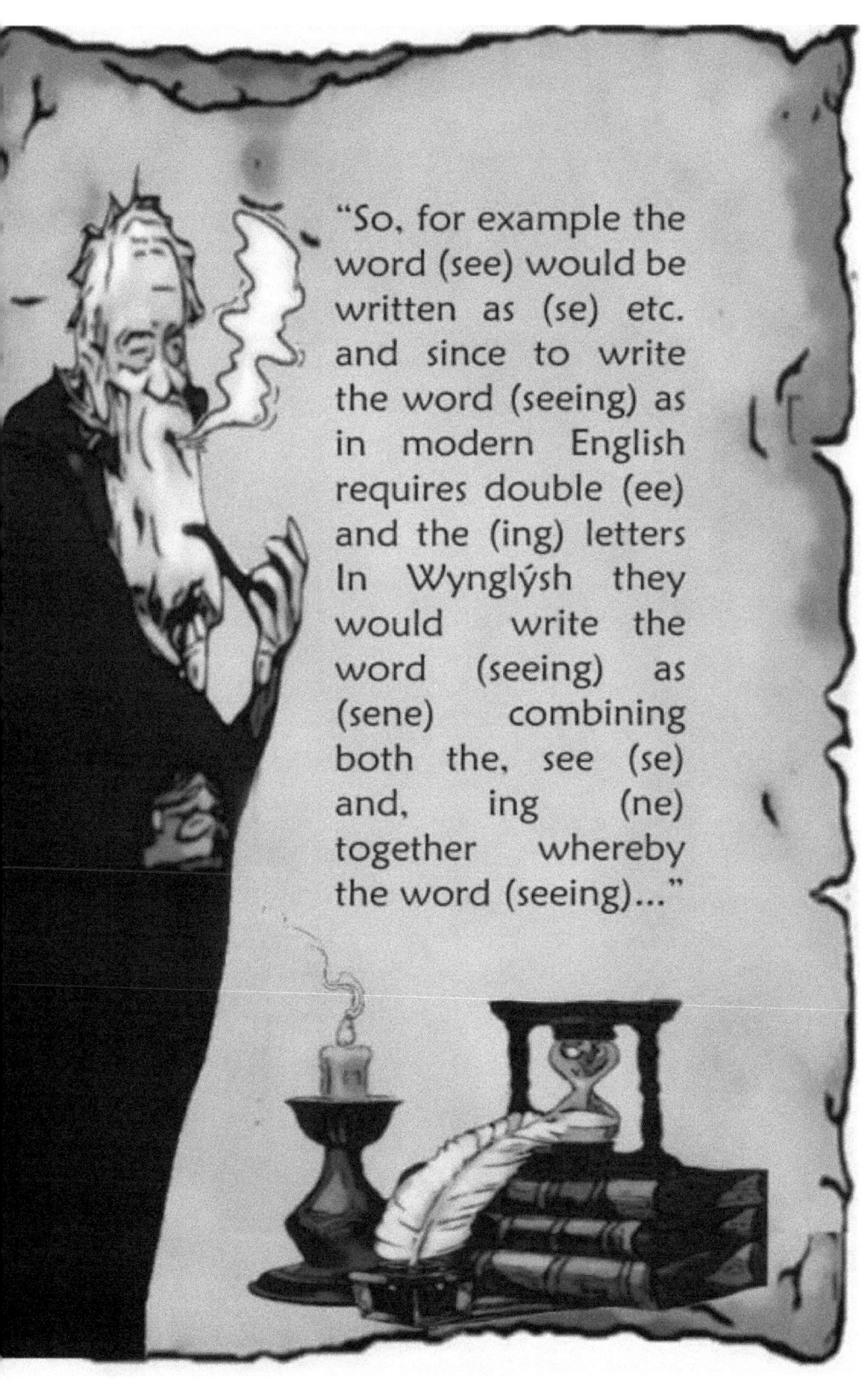

"So, for example the word (see) would be written as (se) etc. and since to write the word (seeing) as in modern English requires double (ee) and the (ing) letters In Wynglýsh they would write the word (seeing) as (sene) combining both the, see (se) and, ing (ne) together whereby the word (seeing)..."

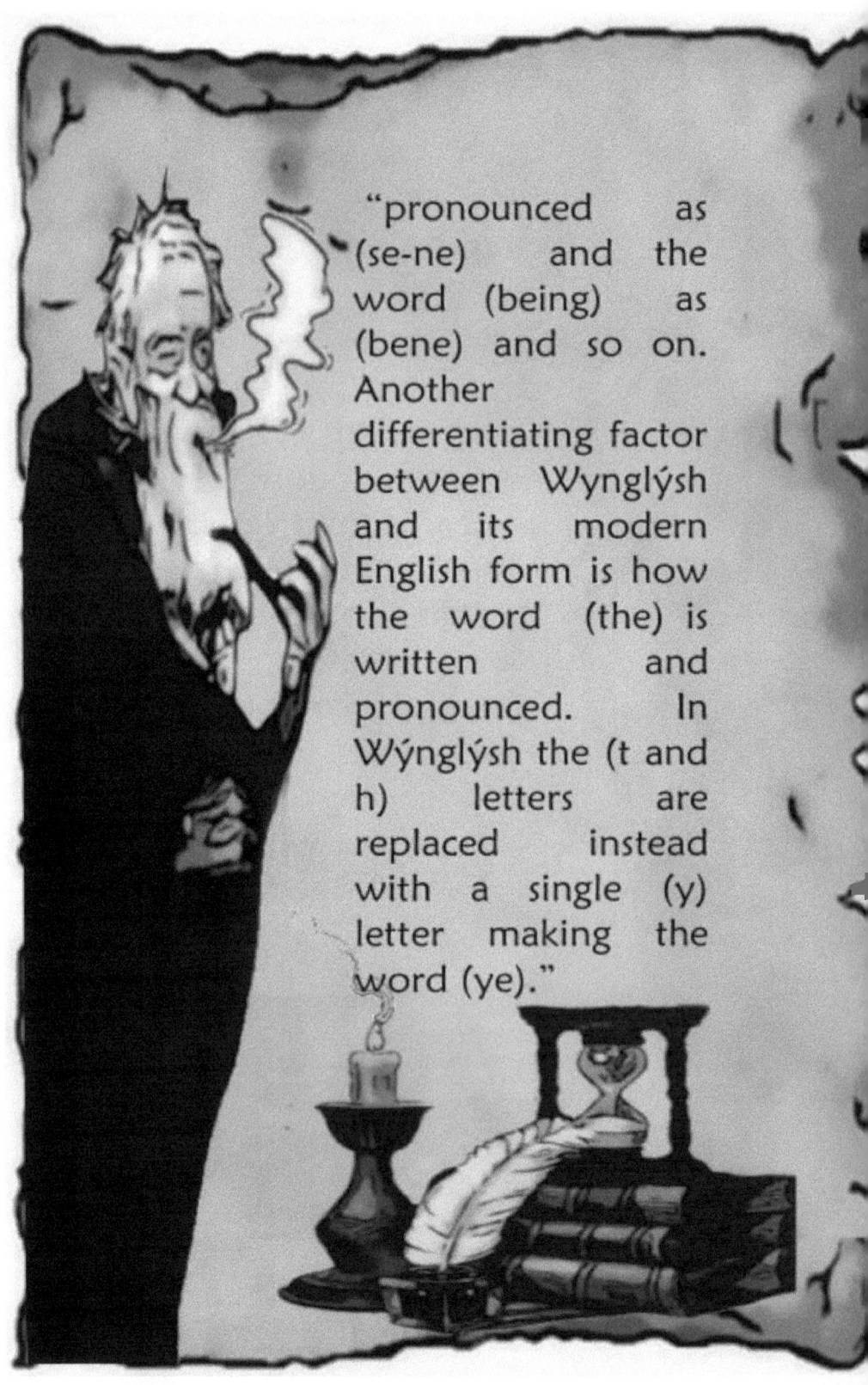

"pronounced as (se-ne) and the word (being) as (bene) and so on. Another differentiating factor between Wynglýsh and its modern English form is how the word (the) is written and pronounced. In Wýnglýsh the (t and h) letters are replaced instead with a single (y) letter making the word (ye)."

"Also in Wynglýsh (chof) (ſ) letter which in modern English is known as the (s) letter it has been alleged that, the first usage of the, chof (ſ) letter first came about as the old Roman cursive medial for the letter (s). This is however Gibberish! truth of the fact wayfarer friend is that, it was first adopted and used by the ancient.."

"Wytan Monks of Second Earth! that's right! Of course this is not a truth revealed to you today by English historians and scholars!, and that the Romans had acquired the (f) letter from the Gallic Druids sometime during the 4th century BCE by Roman Merchants who had ventured to the lush and rich lands of Gaul..."

"in prospect of bringing back to Rome exotic spices, wood, furs, Jewels and so on. And so it was during these expeditions that the Romans first encountered the Druids of Gaul and so adopted this among other things from them. Of course I am not at all suggesting that the Romans did not already have their own (s) letter..."

"no not at all!. What I am saying is that they adopted the Druids (s) letter chof (ʃ) form and shape, don't belive me?. Go ahead and look it up in the history books! you will find that the Roman (s) or also known as the (Long) (s) the (chof) or (ʃ) Is an almost exact copy of the Druid (ʃ)."

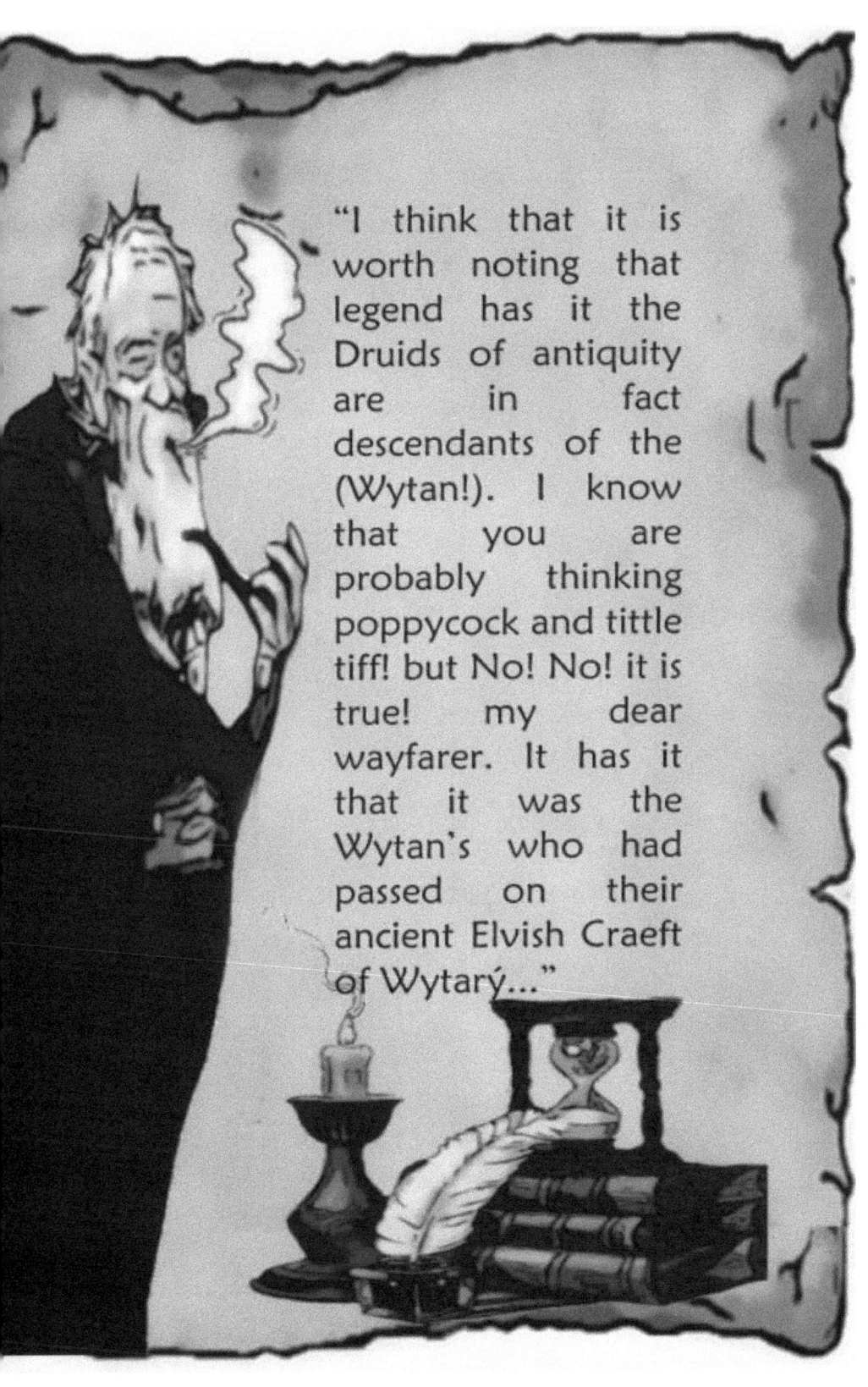

"I think that it is worth noting that legend has it the Druids of antiquity are in fact descendants of the (Wytan!). I know that you are probably thinking poppycock and tittle tiff! but No! No! it is true! my dear wayfarer. It has it that it was the Wytan's who had passed on their ancient Elvish Craeft of Wytarý..."

"and some elements of their alphabet also, other traits and customs down to their descendants the Druids or Druwid's which in Celtic translates to (oak-knower) or (knowing the oak tree) which is why they had come to be known as the (Wise Elders). This is an interesting fact because the Wýtan Monk's..."

"before them were referred to also as the (Wisemen) that's basically what Wytan as I have said before translates to, and their leader's or (Warde) were known as (Elders!) coincidence?. Also, the Druids sported the same garment and Robe, carried the same fashion of a Staef..."

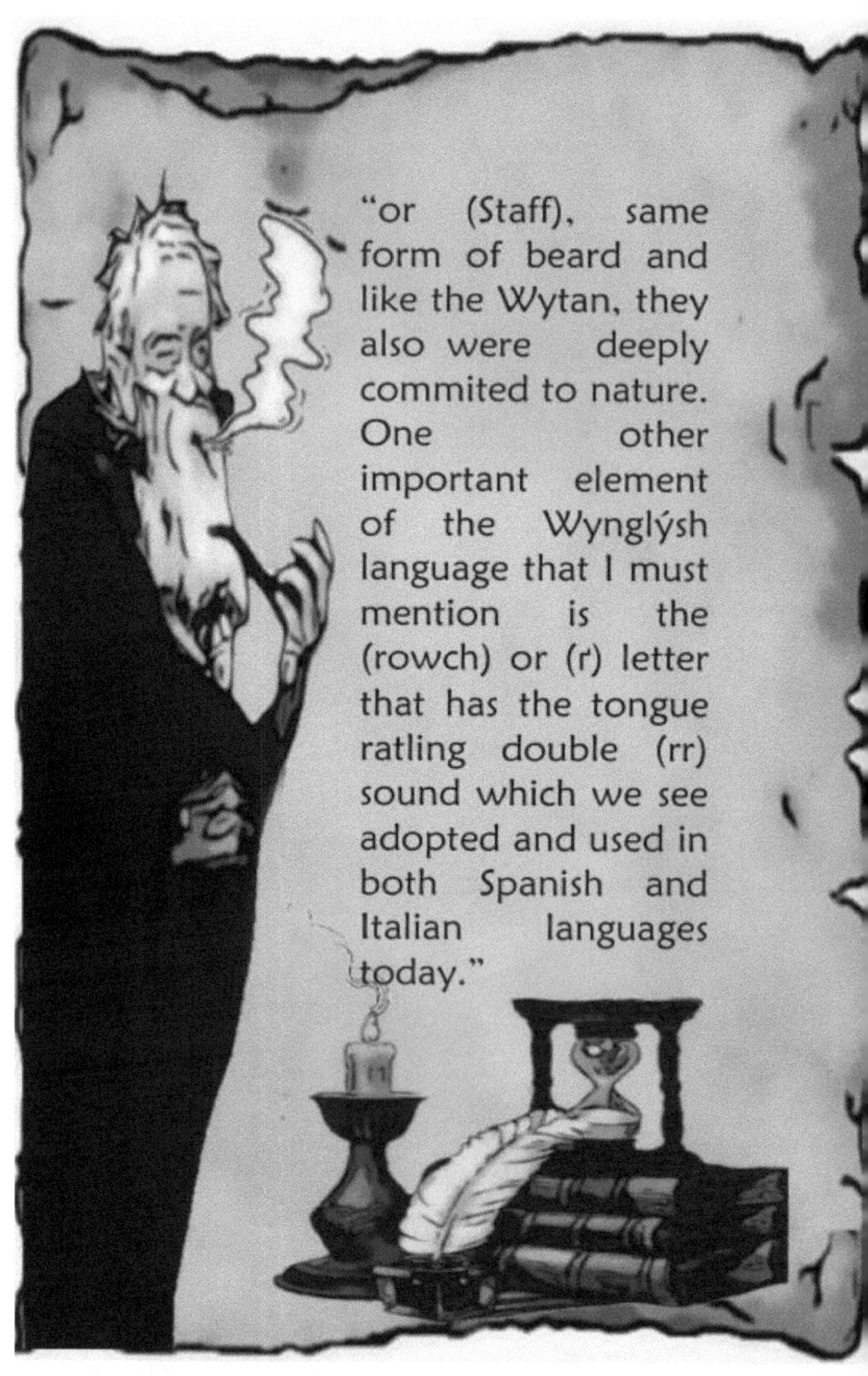

"or (Staff), same form of beard and like the Wytan, they also were deeply commited to nature. One other important element of the Wynglýsh language that I must mention is the (rowch) or (r) letter that has the tongue ratling double (rr) sound which we see adopted and used in both Spanish and Italian languages today."

"This be another contributing factor of the Wynglýsh accent. Finally, I would like to bring your attention my dear wayfarer to the following ancient Wynglýsh words you must be made aware of which will assist you in better grasping our epic tale.

are (are)

they (yey)"

"myself (meſelf)

my (Me)

dear (deŕe)

aware (a waŕen)

agree (agŕen)

heart (heŕte)

revealing (ŕevelen)

clear (cleŕe)

fear (feŕen)

you (Yeo)
they (yey)
indeed (ýndede)
the (ye)
being (bene)"

"wýſe (rýhtwýſe)
perhaps, maybe
(mayhap)
pocket (pochete)
intensely (veryly)
chair (chayer)
very (veray)
our (awer)

it is also important
to mention that in
Wynglýsh
consistency in
spelling of words
was not a
requirement..."

"so long as the word one used conveyed the proper message or point, it's spelling of no importance. Hence why in both the old and Middle English periods we see so many words and even names spelled in a vary of ways. These mentioned simple attributes and elements of the Wynglýsh language..."

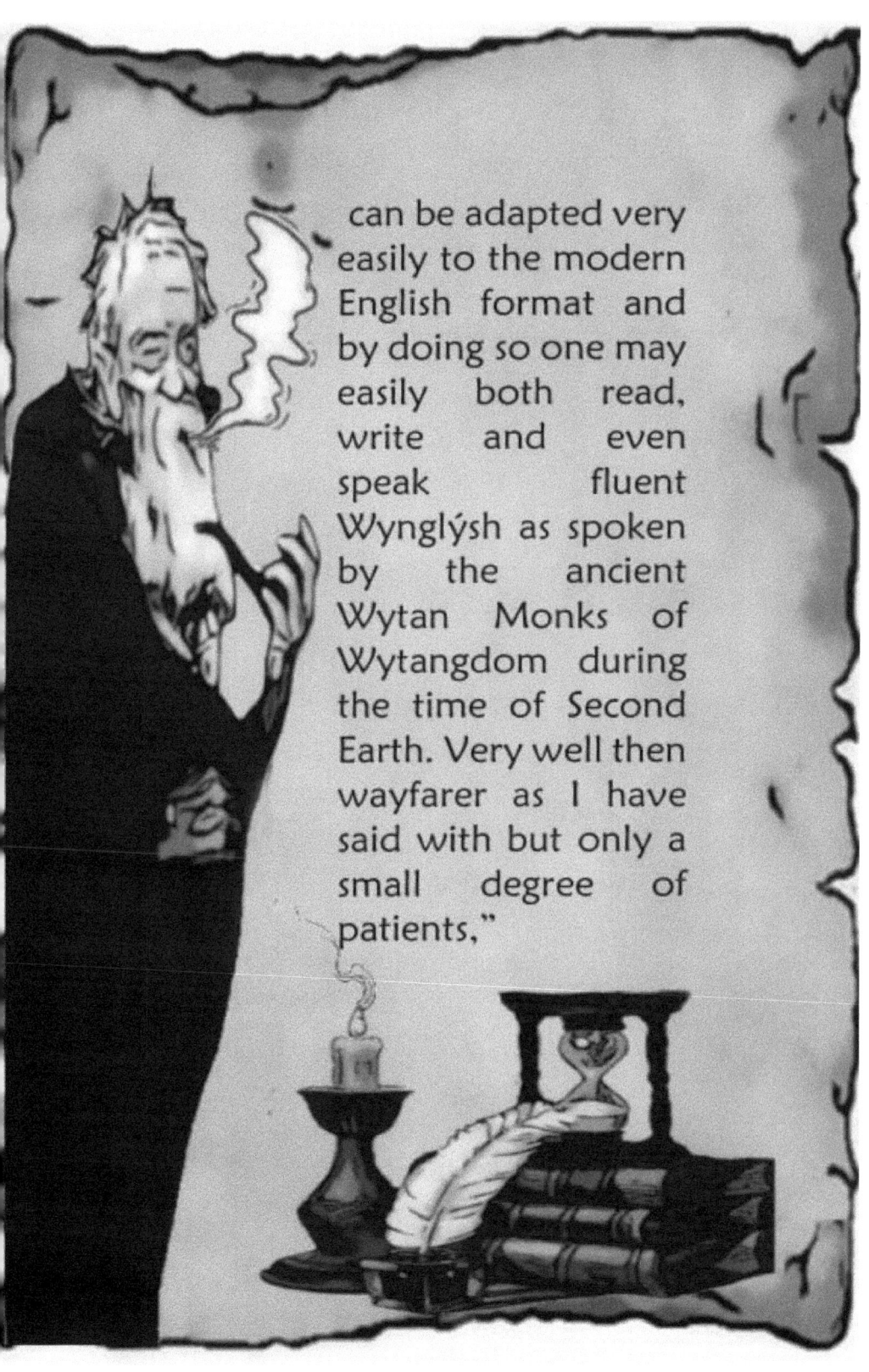

can be adapted very easily to the modern English format and by doing so one may easily both read, write and even speak fluent Wynglýsh as spoken by the ancient Wytan Monks of Wytangdom during the time of Second Earth. Very well then wayfarer as I have said with but only a small degree of patients,"

you will now be able and as such read our epic with complete ease. So then with this matter concluded I think it is time as they say, without further ado we cumenes upon our wonderous and mystical journey and adventure to the ancient time of Second Earth and the time of Wytan Monks, of Wytangdom."

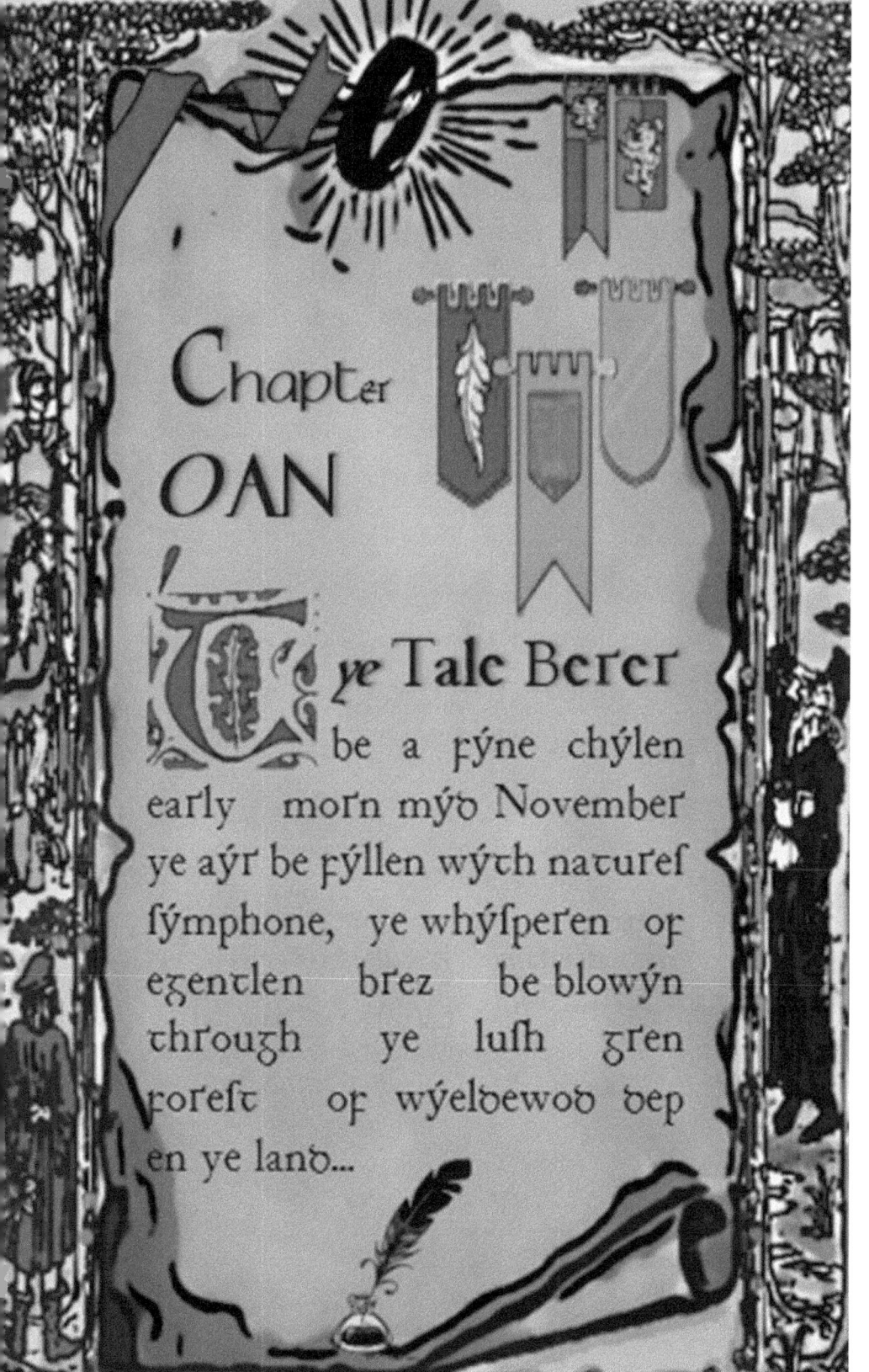

Chapter
OAN

Tye Tale Berer be a ɟýne chýlen early morn mýð November ye aýr be ɟýllen wýth natureſ ſýmphone, ye whýſperen oɟ eȝentlen breȝ be blowýn through ye luſh ȝren ɟoreſt oɟ wýelðewoð ðep en ye lanð...

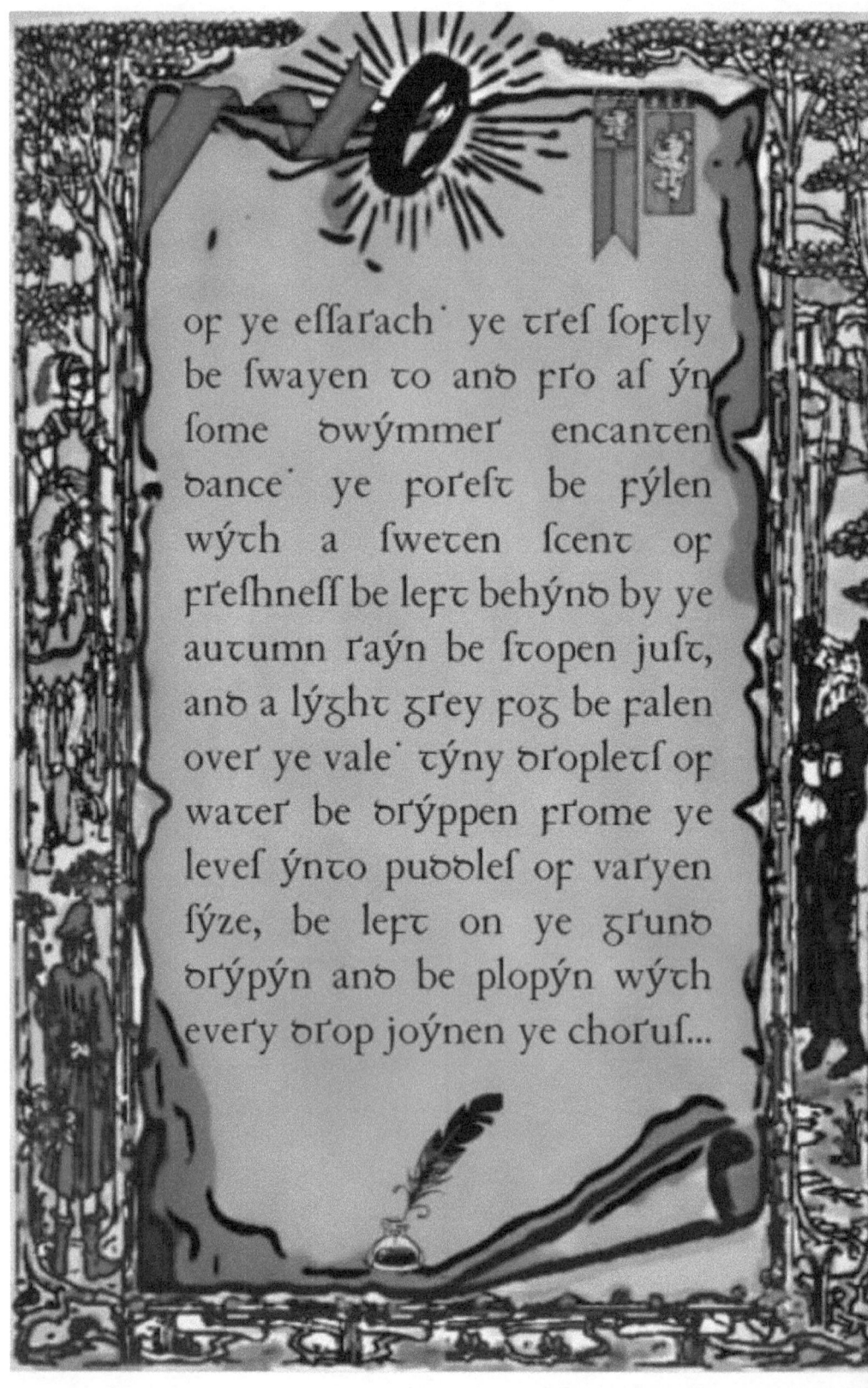

oꝼ ye eſſaꞇach˙ ye ꞇꝛeſ ſoꝼꞇly
be ſwayen ꞇo anð ꝼꞇo aſ ýn
ſome   ðwýmmeꞇ   encanꞇen
ðance˙ ye ꝼoꝛeſꞇ be ꝼýlen
wýꞇh a ſweꞇen ſcenꞇ oꝼ
ꝼꝛeſhneſſ be leꝼꞇ behýnð by ye
auꞇumn ꞇaýn be ſꞇopen juſꞇ,
anð a lýꜧhꞇ ꜧꝛey ꝼoꜧ be ꝼalen
oveꞇ ye vale˙ ꞇýny ðꞇopleꞇſ oꝼ
waꞇeꞇ be ðꞇýppen ꝼꞇome ye
leveſ ýnꞇo puððleſ oꝼ vaꞇyen
ſýze, be leꝼꞇ on ye ꜧꞇunð
ðꞇýpýn anð be plopýn wýꞇh
eveꞇy ðꞇop joýnen ye choꞇuſ...

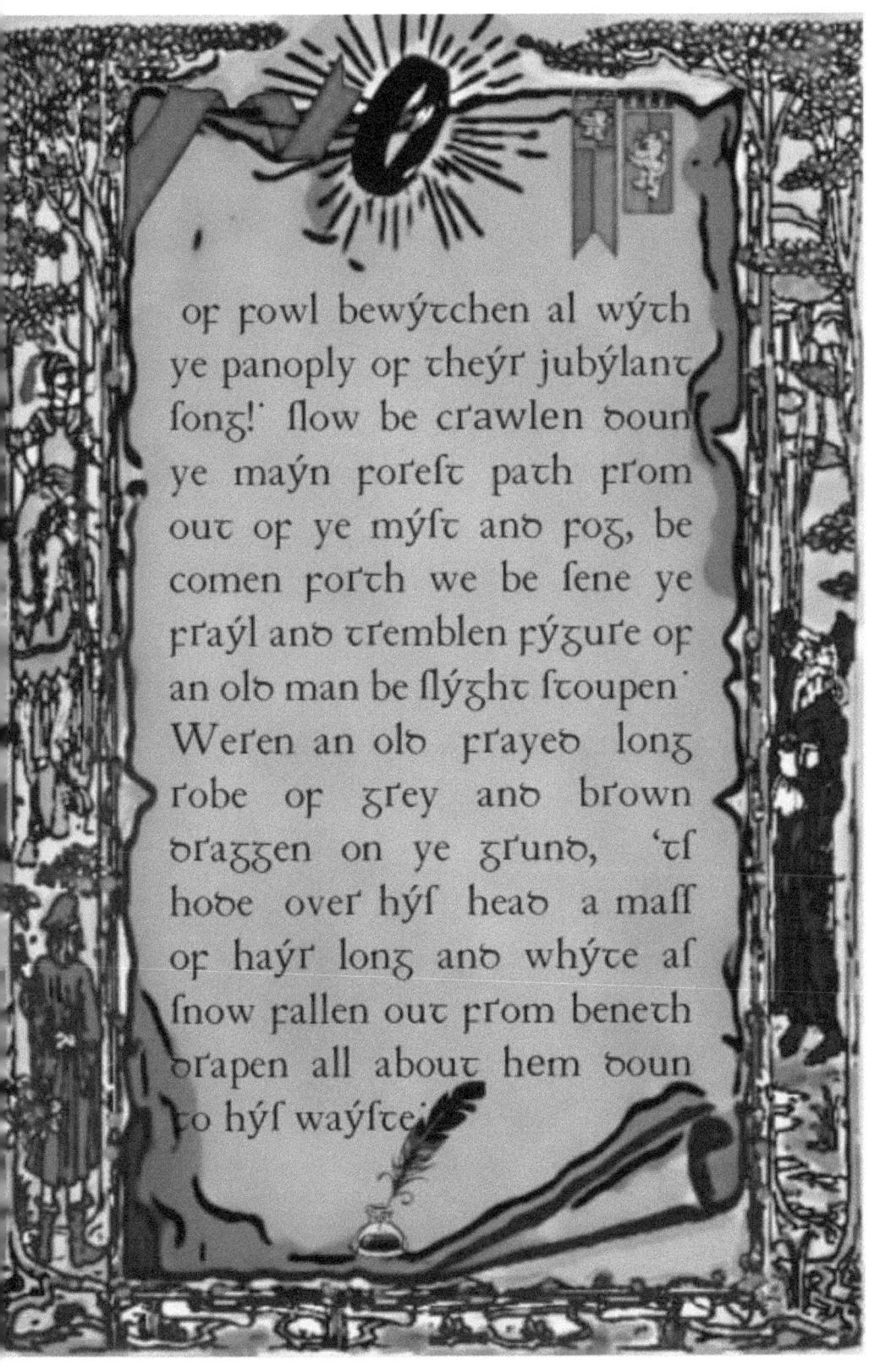

of fowl bewýtchen al wýth
ye panoply of theýr jubýlant
fong! flow be crawlen ðoun
ye maýn foreſt path from
out of ye mýſt anð fog, be
comen forth we be ſene ye
fraýl anð tremblen fýgure of
an olð man be flýght ſtoupen
Weren an olð frayeð long
robe of grey anð brown
ðraȝȝen on ye grunð, 'tſ
hoðe over hýſ heað a maſſ
of haýr long anð whýte aſ
fnow fallen out from beneth
ðrapen all about hem ðoun
to hýſ waýſte

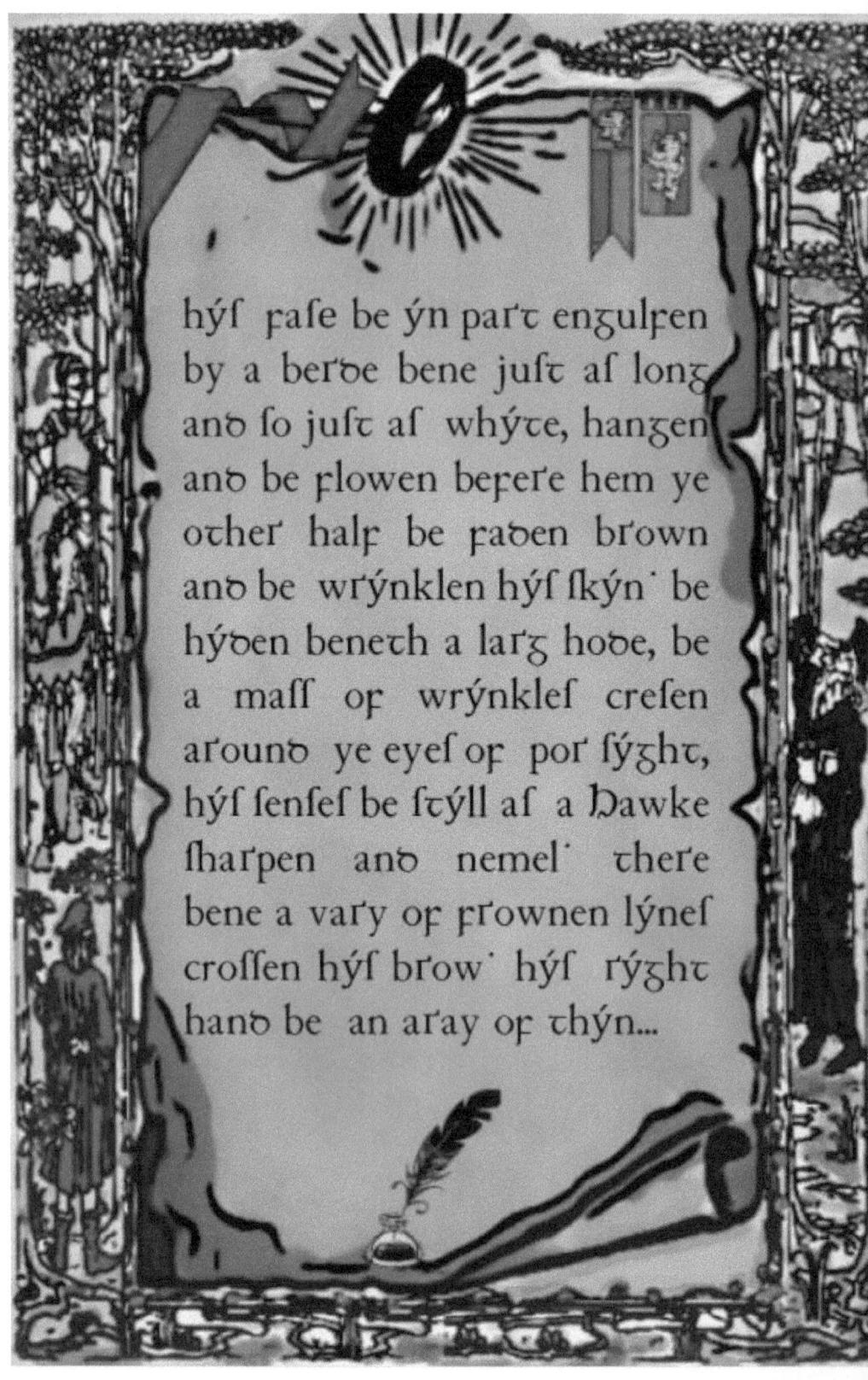

hýſ ꝼaſe be ýn part engulꝼen
by a berðe bene juſt aſ long
anð ſo juſt aſ whýte, hangen
anð be ꝼlowen beꝼere hem ye
other halꝼ be ꝼaðen brown
anð be wrýnklen hýſ ſkýn· be
hýðen beneth a larg hoðe, be
a maſſ oꝼ wrýnkleſ creſen
arounð ye eyeſ oꝼ por ſýght,
hýſ ſenſeſ be ſtýll aſ a ꝺawke
ſharpen anð nemel· there
bene a varý oꝼ ꝼrownen lýneſ
croſſen hýſ brow· hýſ rýght
hanð be an aray oꝼ thýn...

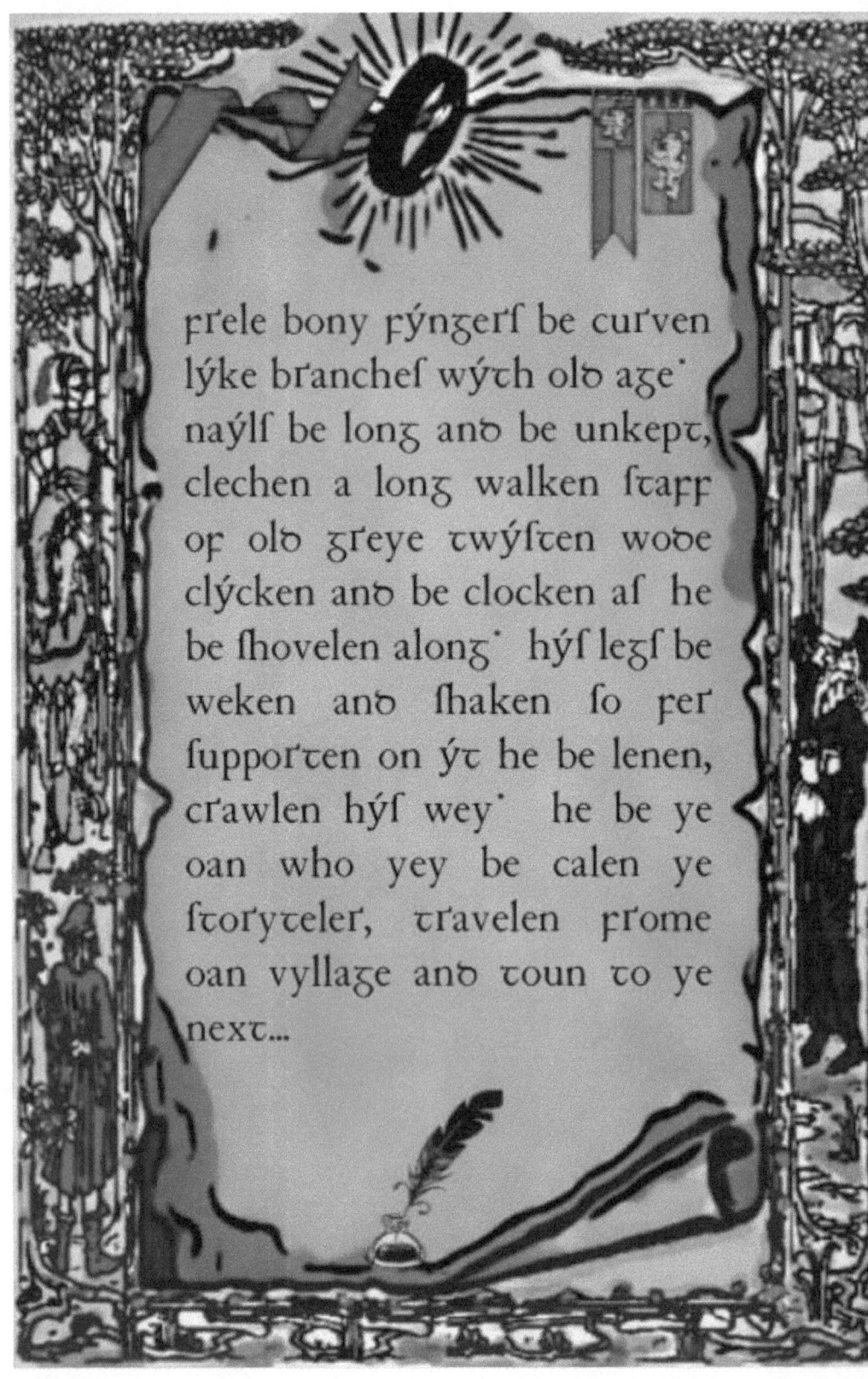

ffrele bony ffyngerſ be curven
lýke brancheſ wýth olo age·
naýlſ be long ano be unkept,
clechen a long walken ſtaff
of olo greye twýſten wooe
clýcken ano be clocken aſ he
be ſhovelen along· hýſ legſ be
weken ano ſhaken ſo fer
ſupporten on ýt he be lenen,
crawlen hýſ wey· he be ye
oan who yey be calen ye
ſtoryteler, travelen frome
oan vyllage ano toun to ye
next...

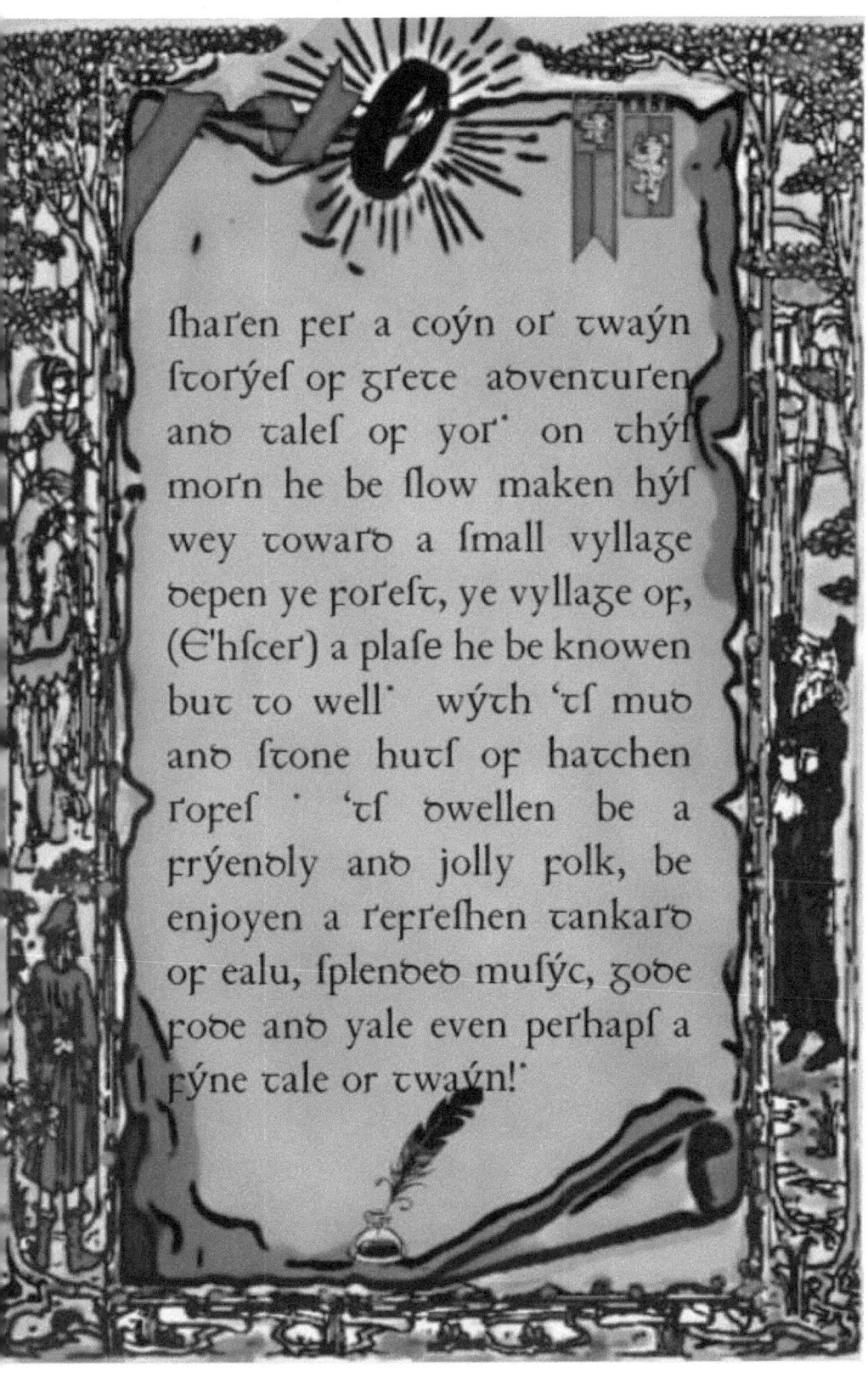

ſharen ꝼer a coýn oꝛ ꞇwaýn
ſꞇorýeſ oꝼ ᵹreꞇe aꝺvenꞇureſ
anꝺ ꞇaleſ oꝼ yorˑ on ꞇhýſ
morn he be ſlow maken hýſ
wey ꞇowarꝺ a ſmall vyllaᵹe
ꝺepen ye ꝼoreſꞇ, ye vyllaᵹe oꝼ,
(Є'hſcer) a plaſe he be knowen
buꞇ ꞇo wellˑ wýꞇh 'ꞇſ muꝺ
anꝺ ſꞇone huꞇſ oꝼ haꞇꞇhen
roꝼeſ ˑ 'ꞇſ ꝺwellen be a
ꝼrýenꝺly anꝺ jolly ꝼolk, be
enjoyen a �reſhen ꞇankarꝺ
oꝼ ealu, ſplenꝺeꝺ muſýc, ᵹoꝺe
ꝼoꝺe anꝺ yale even perhapſ a
ꝼýne ꞇale or ꞇwaýn!ˑ

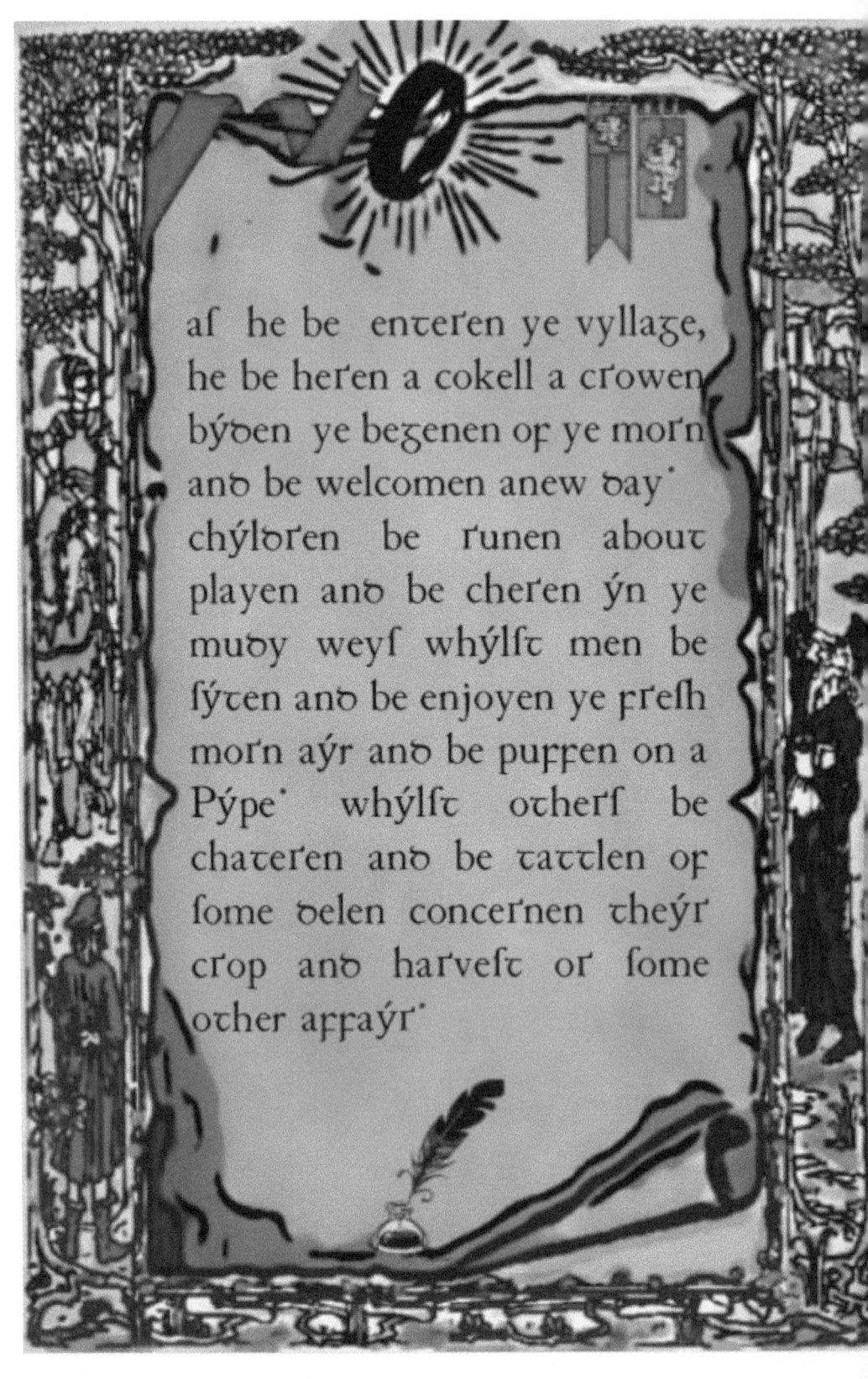

aſ he be enteren ye vyllaʒe,
he be heren a cokell a crowen
býðen ye beʒenen oꝼ ye morn
anð be welcomen anew ðay·
chýlðren be runen about
playen anð be cheren ýn ye
muðy weyſ whýlſt men be
ſýten anð be enjoyen ye ꝼreſh
morn aýr anð be puꝼꝼen on a
Pýpe· whýlſt otherſ be
chateren anð be tattlen oꝼ
ſome ðelen concernen theýr
crop anð harveſt or ſome
other aꝼꝼaýr·

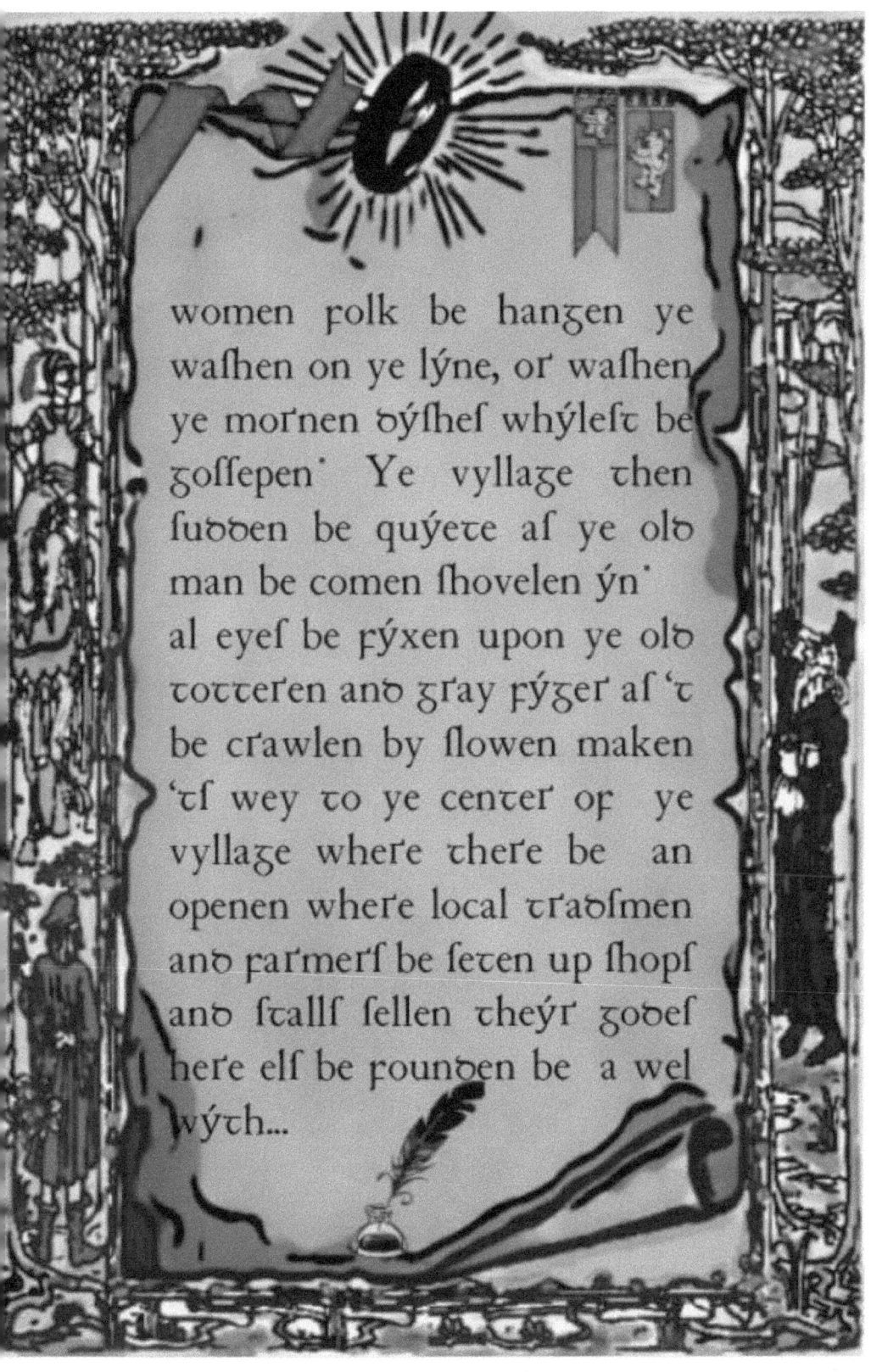

women folk be hangen ye
washen on ye lýne, or washen
ye mornen dýshes whýlest be
gossepen· Ye vyllage then
sudden be quýete as ye old
man be comen shovelen ýn·
al eyes be fýxen upon ye old
totteren and gray fýger as 't
be crawlen by slowen maken
'ts wey to ye center of ye
vyllage where there be an
openen where local tradsmen
and farmers be seten up shops
and stalls sellen theýr godes
here elf be founden be a wel
wýth...

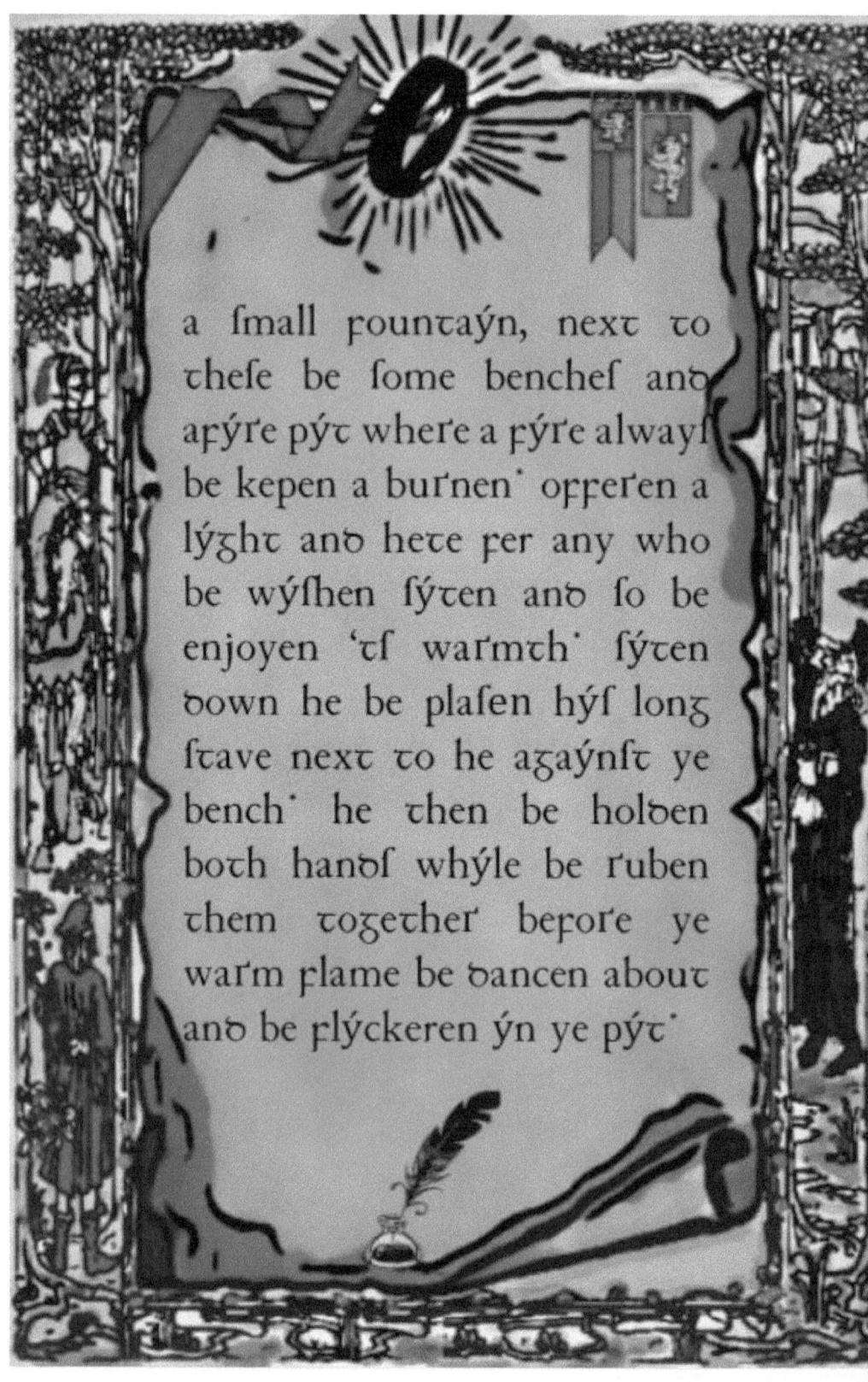

a ſmall ꝼountayn, next to
theſe be ſome benchef and
aꝼýꝛe pýt wheꝛe a ꝼýꝛe alwayſ
be kepen a buꝛnen˙ oꝼꝼeꝛen a
lýght and hete ꝼeꝛ any who
be wýſhen ſýten and ſo be
enjoyen ‘tſ waꝛmth˙ ſýten
down he be plaſen hýſ long
ſtave next to he agaýnſt ye
bench˙ he then be holden
both handſ whýle be ꝛuben
them together beꝼoꝛe ye
waꝛm ꝼlame be dancen about
and be ꝼlýckeren ýn ye pýt˙

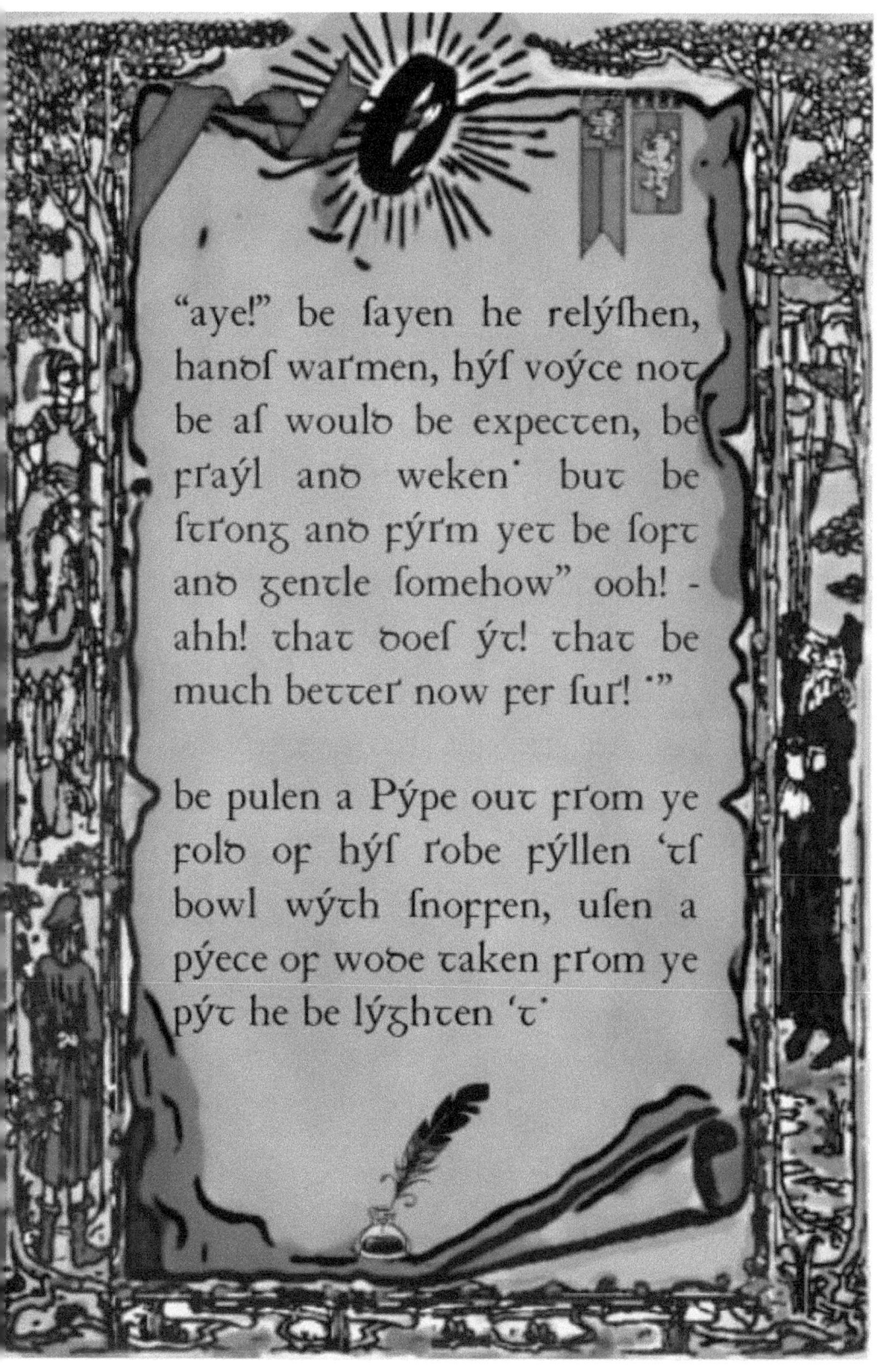

"aye!" be ſayen he relýſhen, hanðſ warmen, hýſ voýce noτ be aſ woulð be expecτen, be ſráýl anð weken· buτ be ſτrong anð ſýrm yeτ be ſoſτ anð ʒenτle ſomehow" ooh! - ahh! τhaτ ðoeſ ýτ! τhaτ be much beττer now ſer ſur! '"

be pulen a Pýpe ouτ ſrom ye ſolð oſ hýſ robe ſýllen 'τſ bowl wýτh ſnoſſen, uſen a pýece oſ woðe τaken ſrom ye pýτ he be lýʒhτen 'τ·

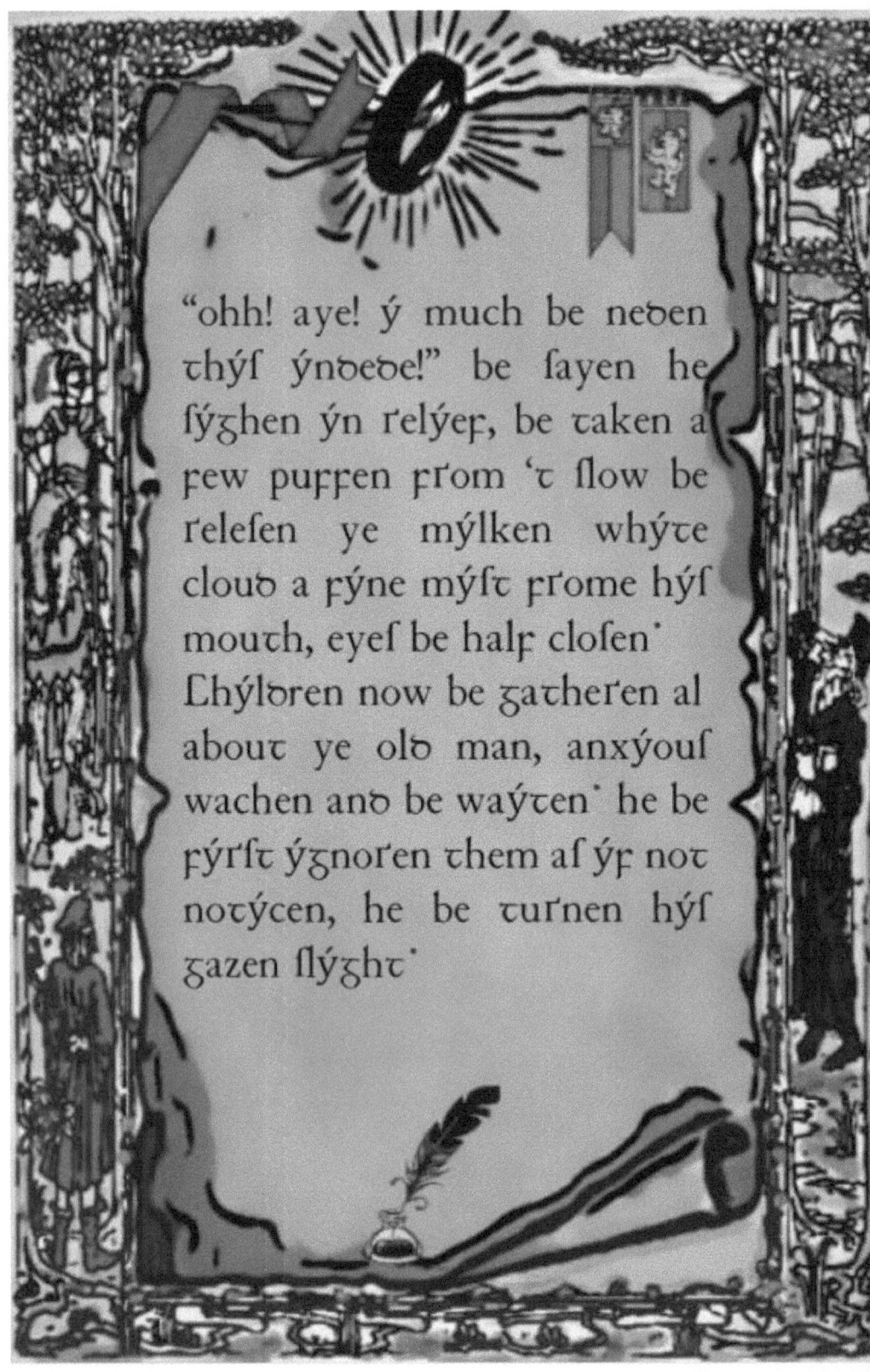

"ohh! aye! ý much be neðen thýſ ýnðeðe!" be ſayen he ſýghen ýn relýeſ, be taken a ſew puffen from 't ſlow be releſen ye mýlken whýte clouð a fýne mýſt frome hýſ mouth, eyeſ be half cloſen˙ Chýlðren now be gatheren al about ye olð man, anxýouſ wachen anð be waýten˙ he be fýrſt ýgnoren them aſ ýf not notýcen, he be turnen hýſ gazen ſlýght˙

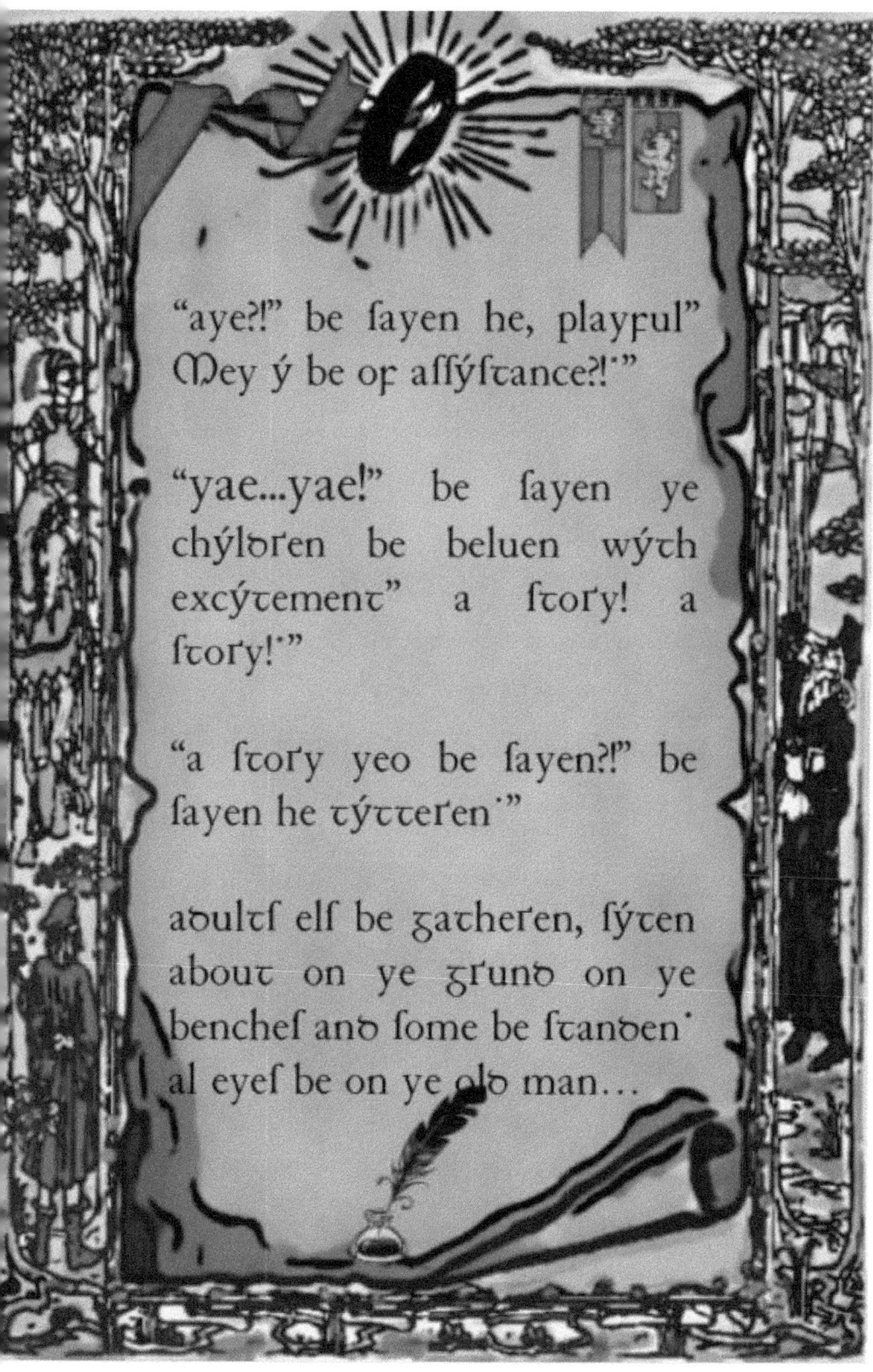

"aye?!" be ſayen he, playꝼul"
Ɱey ý be oꝼ aſſýſtance?!'"

"yae...yae!" be ſayen ye
chýlᴅren be beluen wýth
excýtement" a ſtory! a
ſtory!'"

"a ſtory yeo be ſayen?!" be
ſayen he týtteren·"

aᴅultſ elſ be ɡatheren, ſýten
about on ye ɡrunᴅ on ye
bencheſ anᴅ ſome be ſtanᴅen·
al eyeſ be on ye olᴅ man...

egere a wayten ympatyent
fene what exyten ftory and
tale he be telen on thyf
ocafyon˙

"wel!" be fayen he fmylen
wyth a twynklen be yn hyf
eye, wynken" Now then! of
what fort of tale myght yeo
be wyfhen to be hearen?!·"

"of dragon'f!" be fayen oan
chyld beluen˙

"oꝼ Kengſ anꝺ Knýʒhtſ!" be Yowlen onother·

"ꝺraʒoonſ, Kengſ anꝺ Knýʒhtſ! Yeo be ſayen!?" ...

be ſayen ye olꝺ man ſtroken hýſ berꝺe anꝺ be thýnken puꝼꝼen on hýſ Pýpe·

" yae!" be ſayen he grýnen be contýnuen" them be goꝺe taleſ to be telen no ꝺoubten, but! ý be thýnken ſomethen ꝺýꝼꝼerent anꝺ a we more excýten!..." ·

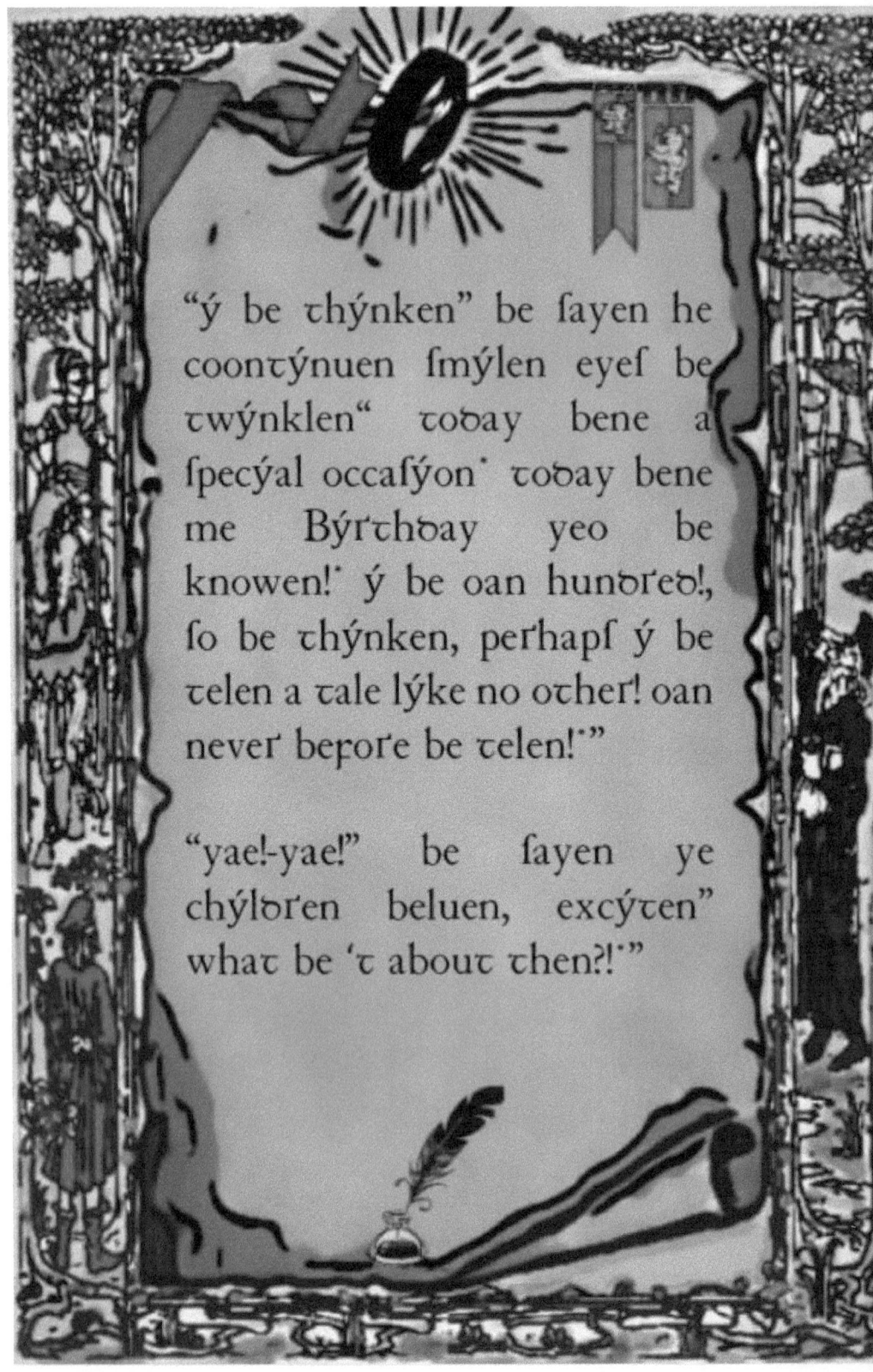

"ý be thýnken" be ſayen he coontýnuen ſmýlen eyeſ be twýnklen" today bene a ſpecýal occaſýon˙ today bene me Býrthday yeo be knowen!˙ ý be oan hundred!, ſo be thýnken, perhapſ ý be telen a tale lýke no other! oan never beſore be telen!˙"

"yae!-yae!" be ſayen ye chýldren beluen, excýten" what be 't about then?!˙"

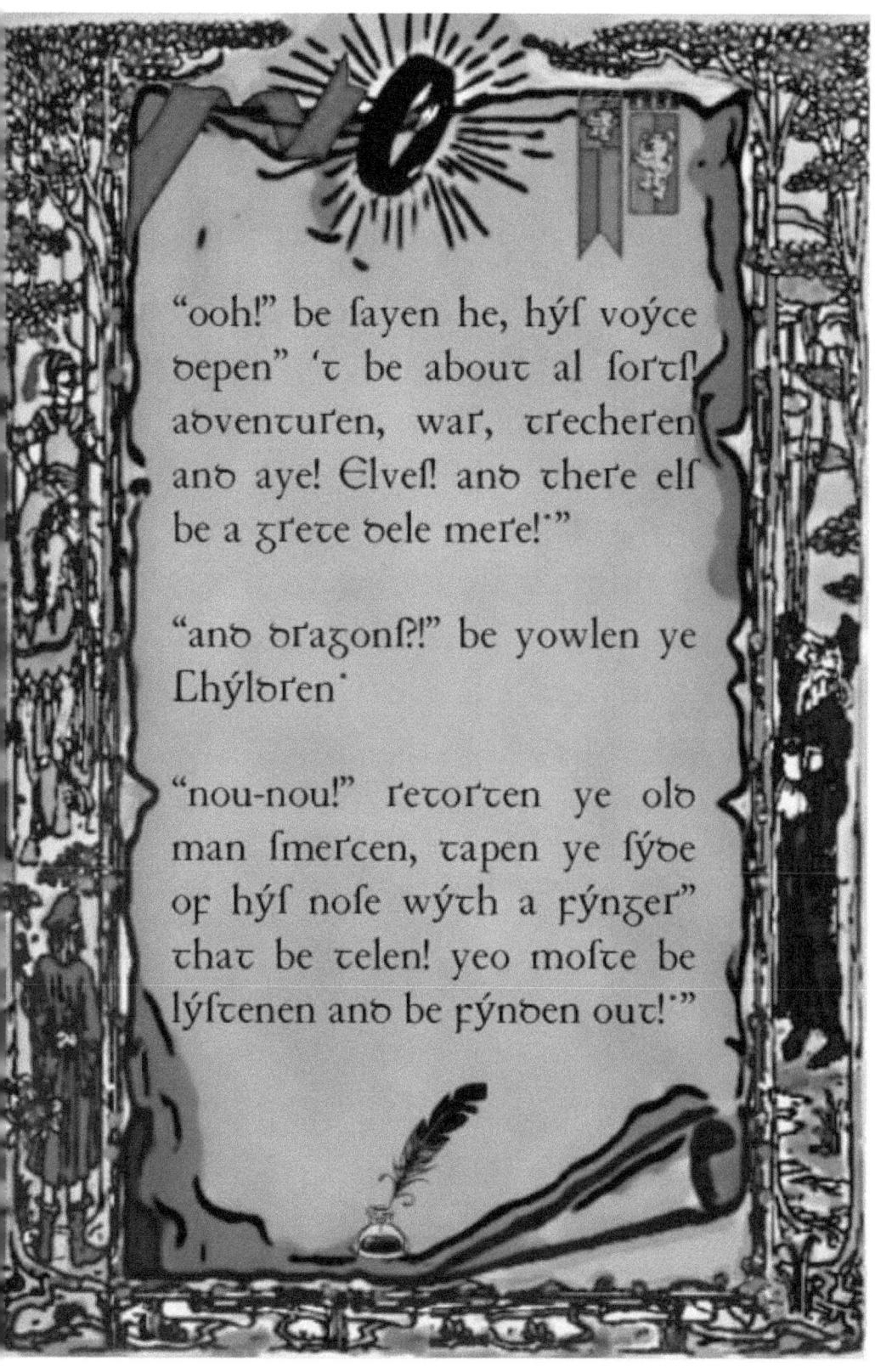

"ooh!" be ſayen he, hýſ voýce
depen" 't be about al ſortſ
adventuren, war, trecheren
and aye! Elveſ! and there elſ
be a grete dele mere!'"

"and dragonſ?!" be yowlen ye
Chýldren˙

"nou-nou!" retorten ye old
man ſmercen, tapen ye ſýde
oꝼ hýſ noſe wýth a ꝼýnger"
that be telen! yeo moſte be
lýſtenen and be ꝼýnden out!'"

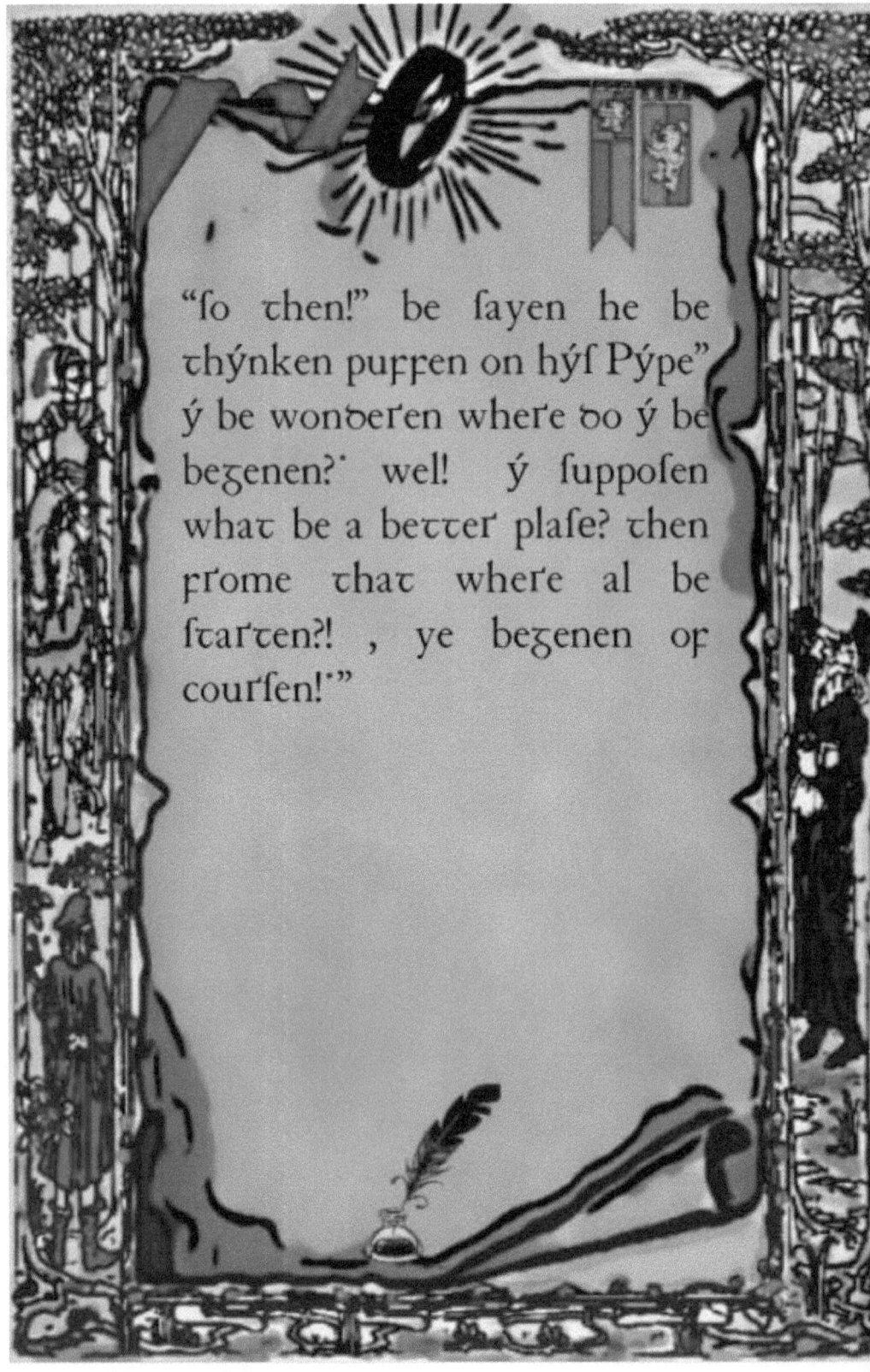

"ſo then!" be ſayen he be
thýnken puffen on hýſ Pýpe"
ý be wonðeren where ðo ý be
begenen?˙ wel! ý ſuppoſen
what be a better plaſe? then
frome that where al be
ſtarten?! , ye begenen of
courſen!'"

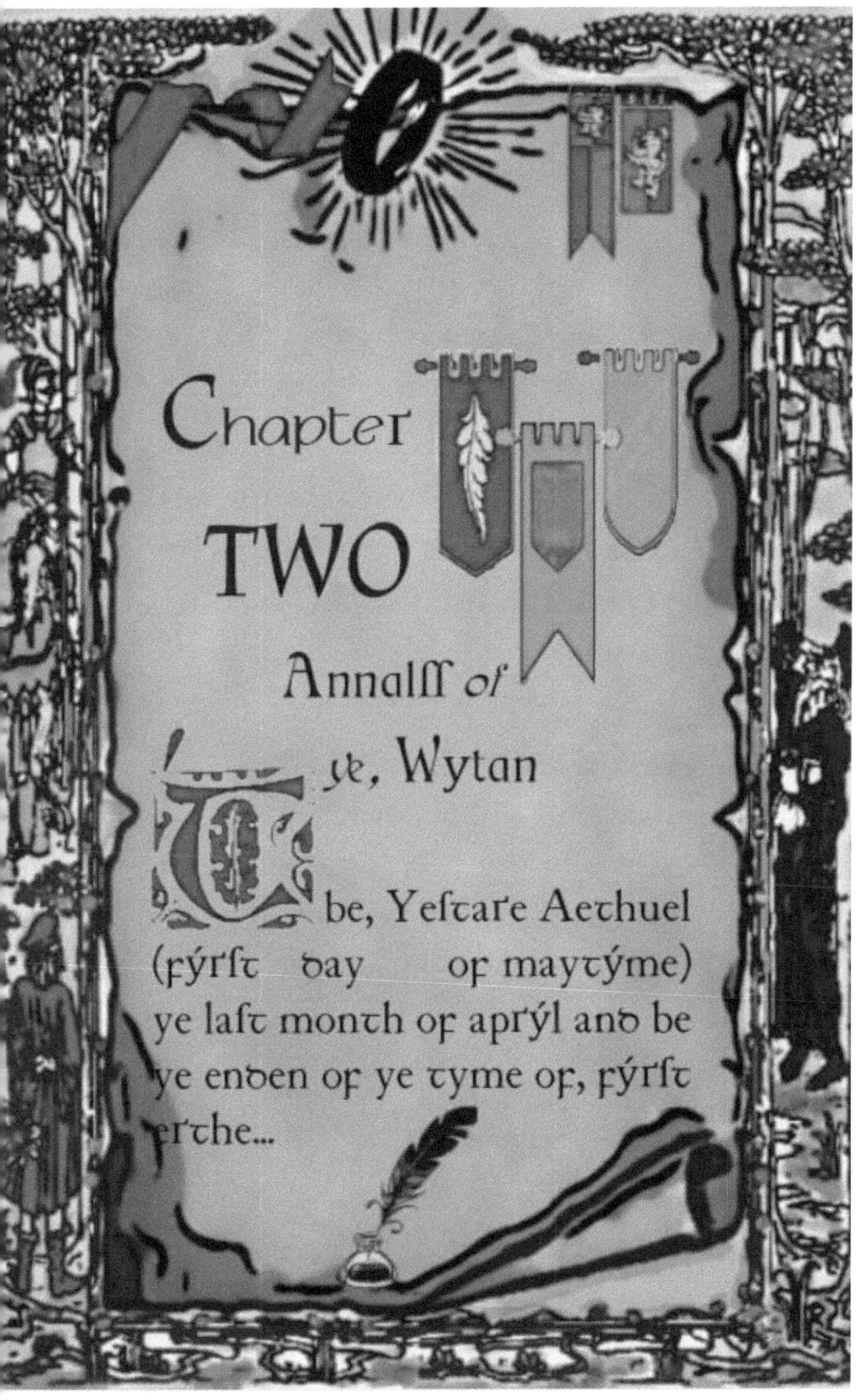

Chapter

TWO

Annalſſ of
Ł ſe, Wytan

Ł be, Yeſtare Aethuel
(ſýrſt day oſ maytýme)
ye laſt month oſ aprýl and be
ye enden oſ ye tyme oſ, ſýrſt
erthe...

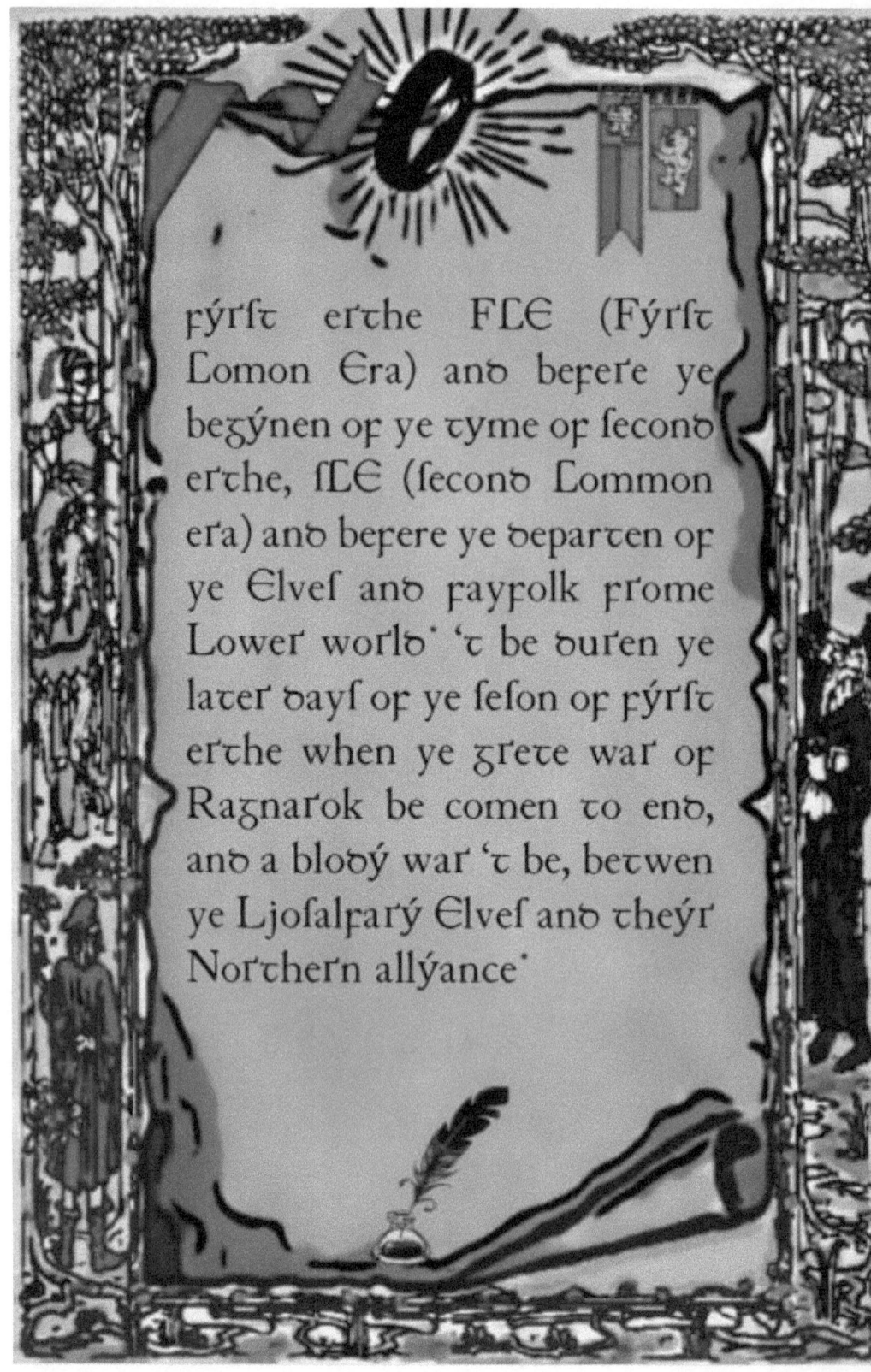

fyrſt erthe FCE (Fyrſt Comon Era) and before ye begýnen of ye tyme of second erthe, ſCE (second Common era) and before ye departen of ye Elveſ and fayfolk frome Lower world· 't be duren ye later dayſ of ye feſon of fyrſt erthe when ye grete war of Ragnarok be comen to end, and a blodý war 't be, betwen ye Ljoſalfarý Elveſ and theýr Northern allýance·

Grete War
of Ragnarok

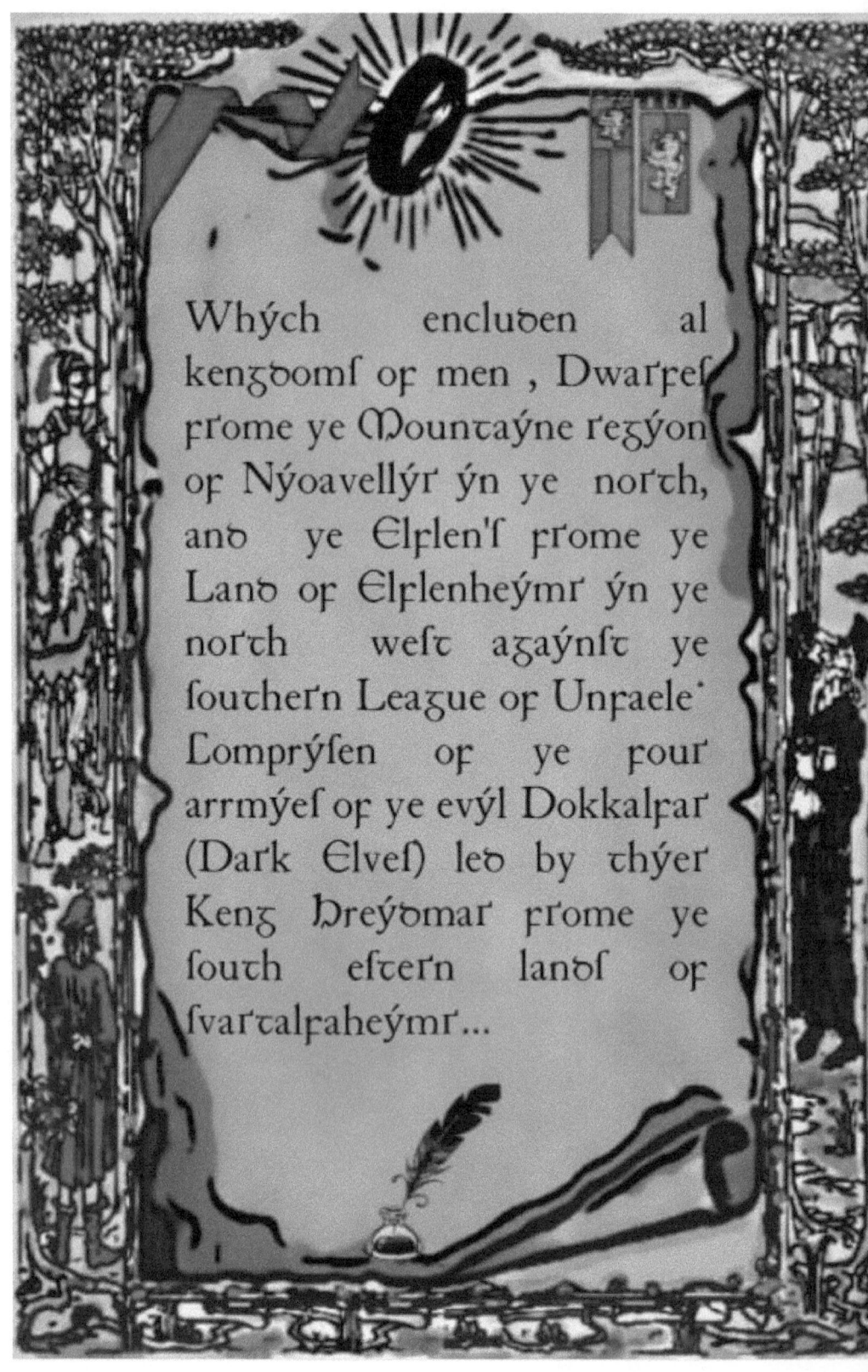

Whých encluden al kengdoms oʒ men , Dwarʒeſ ʒrome ye Mountaýne regýon oʒ Nýoavellýr ýn ye north, and ye Elʒlen'ſ ʒrome ye Land oʒ Elʒlenheýmr ýn ye north weſt agaýnſt ye ſouthern League oʒ Unʒaele Lomprýſen oʒ ye ʒour arrmýeſ oʒ ye evýl Dokkalʒar (Dark Elveſ) led by thýer Keng Þreýdmar ʒrome ye ſouth eſtern landſ oʒ ſvartalʒaheýmr...

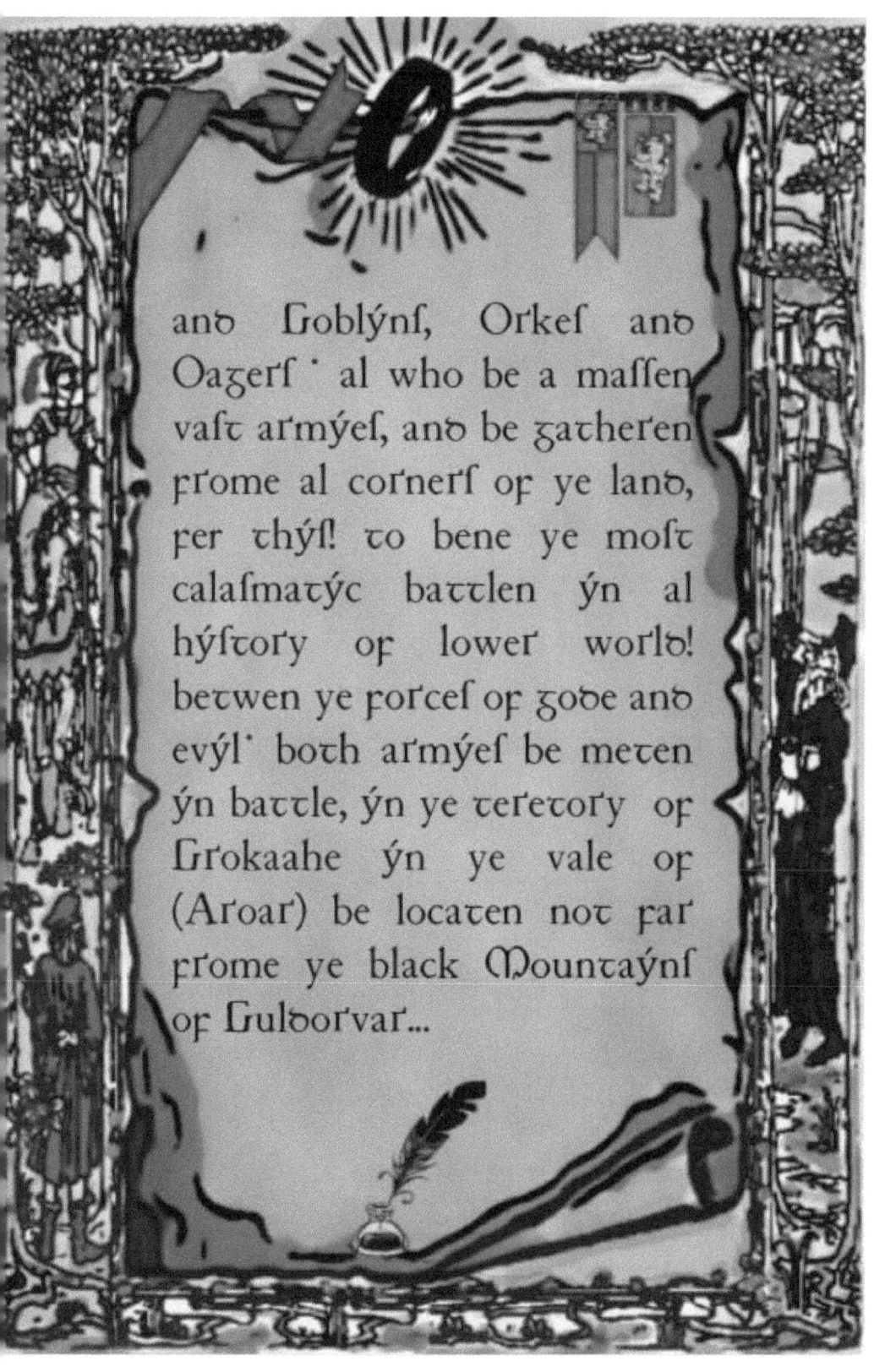

anꝺ ᵹoblýnꝼ, Orkeꝼ anꝺ Oaᵹerꝼ · al who be a maꝼꝼen vaꞅꞇ armýeꝼ, anꝺ be ᵹaꞇheren ꝼrome al cornerꝼ oꝼ ye lanꝺ, ꝼer thýꝼ! ꞇo bene ye moꞅꞇ calaꝼmaꞇýc baꞇꞇlen ýn al hýꞅꞇory oꝼ lower worlꝺ! beꞇwen ye ꝼorceꝼ oꝼ ᵹoꝺe anꝺ evýl· boꞇh armýeꝼ be meꞇen ýn baꞇꞇle, ýn ye ꞇereꞇory oꝼ ᵹrokaahe ýn ye vale oꝼ (Aroar) be locaꞇen noꞇ ꝼar ꝼrome ye black Ɱounꞇaýnꝼ oꝼ ᵹulꝺorvar...

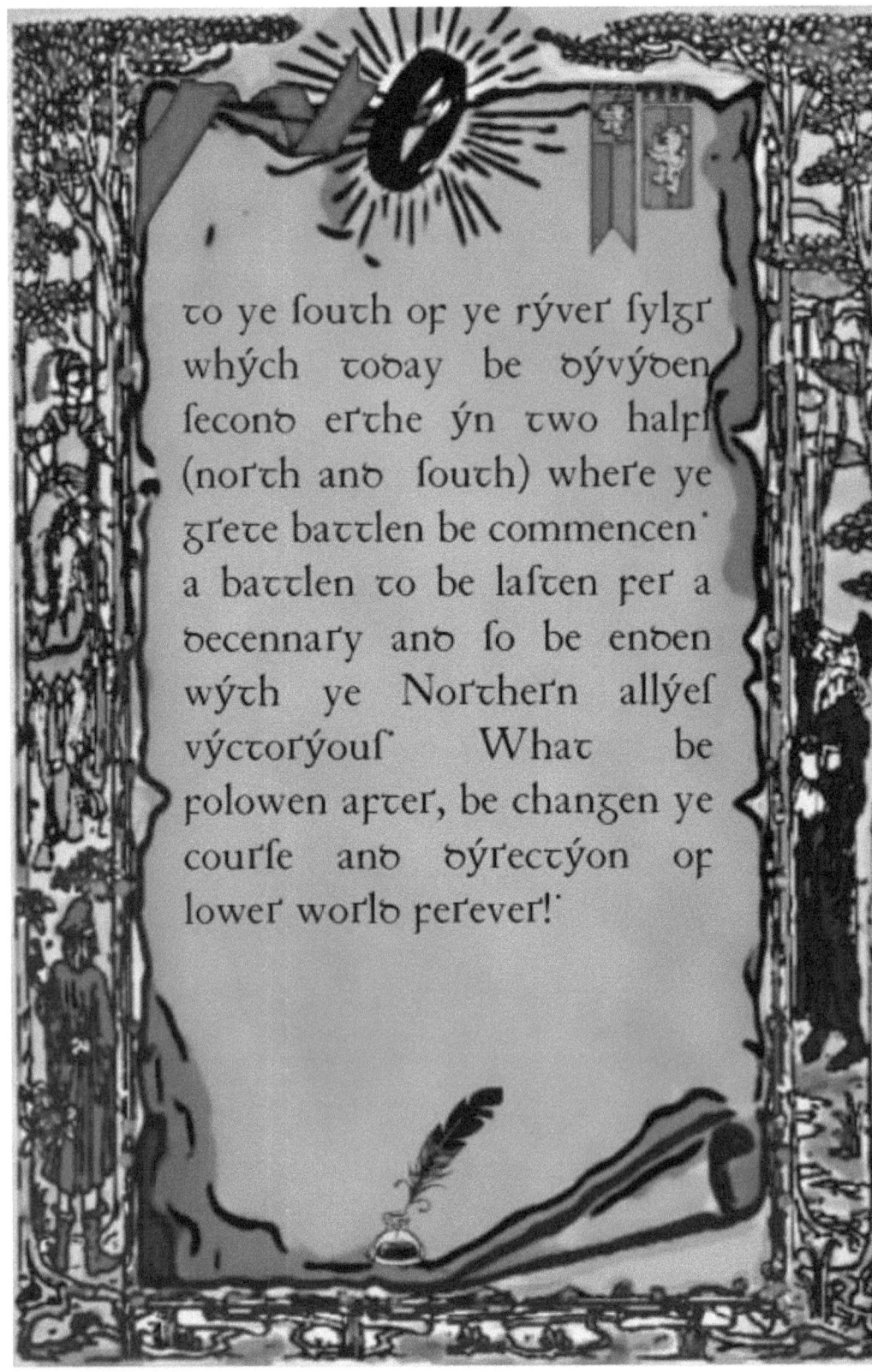

to ye ſouth oꝼ ye rýver ſylgr whých toꝺay be ꝺývýꝺen ſeconꝺ erthe ýn two halꝼ (north anꝺ ſouth) where ye grete battlen be commencen a battlen to be laſten ꝼer a ꝺecennary anꝺ ſo be enꝺen wýth ye Northern allýeſ výctorýouſ What be ꝼolowen after, be changen ye courſe anꝺ ꝺýrectýon oꝼ lower worlꝺ ꝼerever!

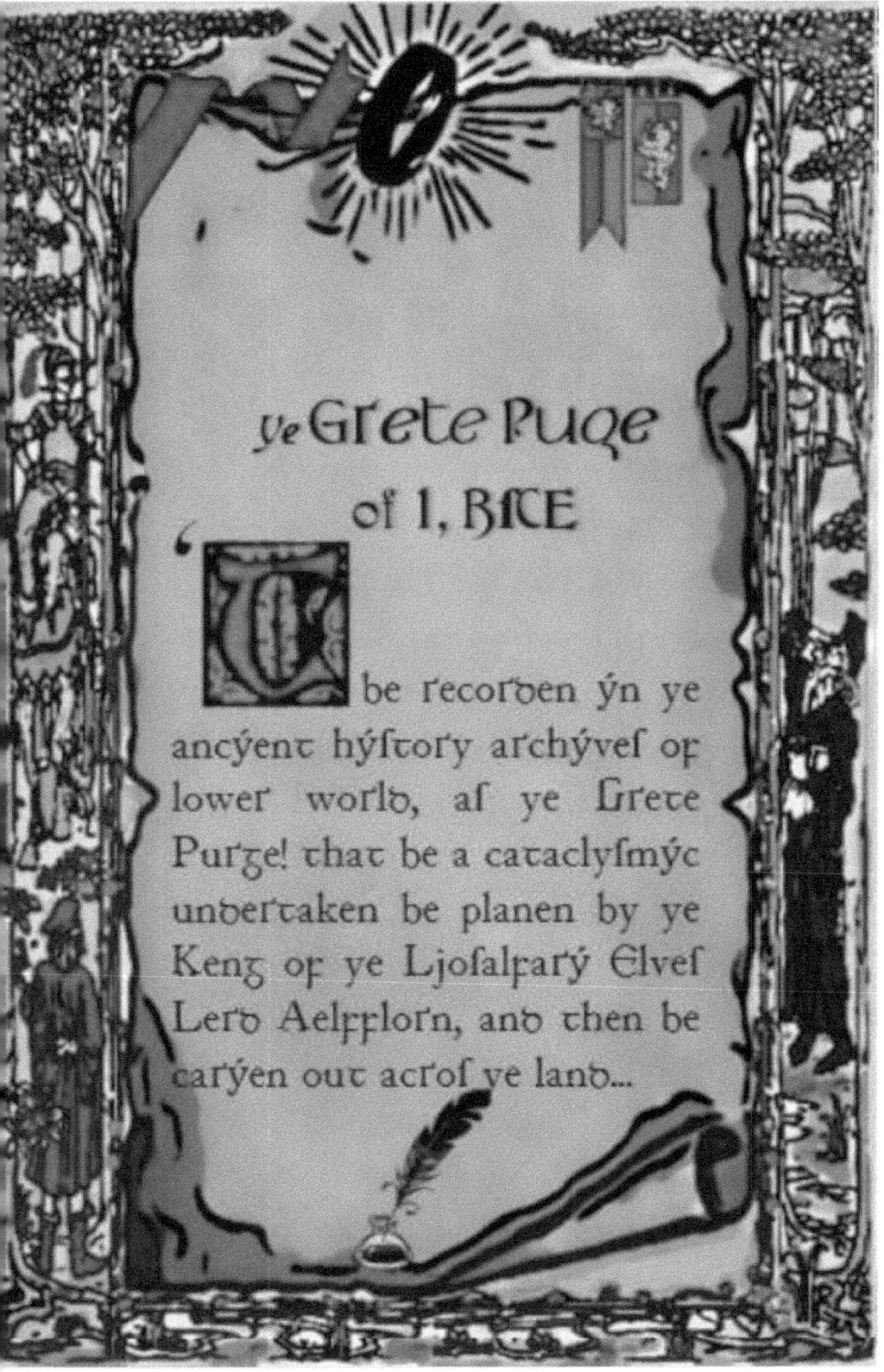

ye Grete Purge
of 1, BCE

"U be recorden ýn ye
ancýent hýstory archýves of
lower world, as ye Grete
Purge! that be a cataclysmýc
undertaken be planen by ye
Keng of ye Ljosalfarý Elves
Lerd Aelfflorn, and then be
carýen out acros ye land...

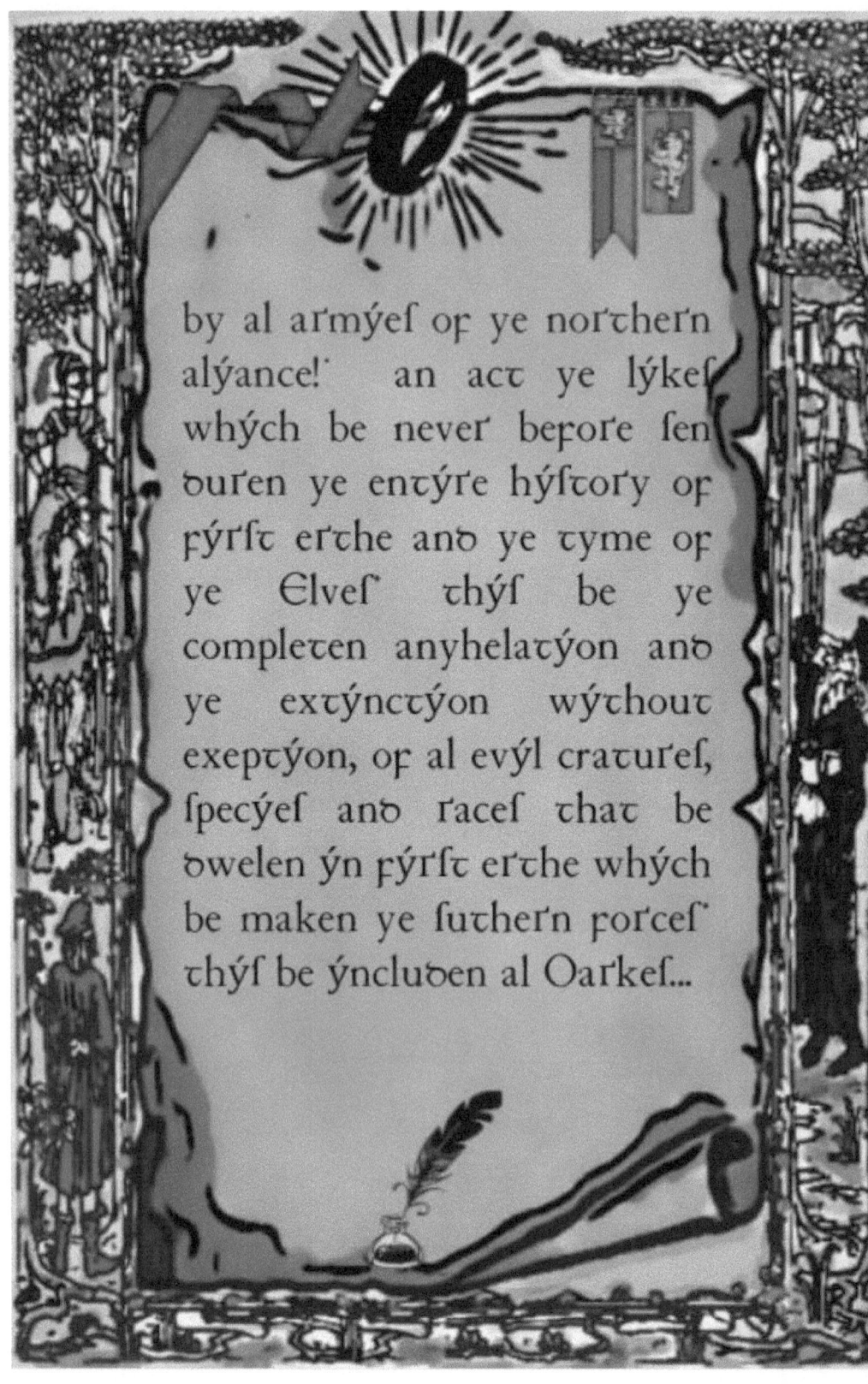

by al armýeſ oꝛ ye northern alýance! an act ye lýkeſ whých be never beꝼore ſen ꝺuren ye entýre hýſtory oꝛ ꝼýrſt erthe anꝺ ye tyme oꝛ ye Elveſ thýſ be ye completen anyhelatýon anꝺ ye extýnctýon wýthout exeptýon, oꝛ al evýl cratureſ, ſpecýeſ anꝺ raceſ that be ꝺwelen ýn ꝼýrſt erthe whých be maken ye ſuthern ꝼorceſ thýſ be ýncluꝺen al Oarkeſ...

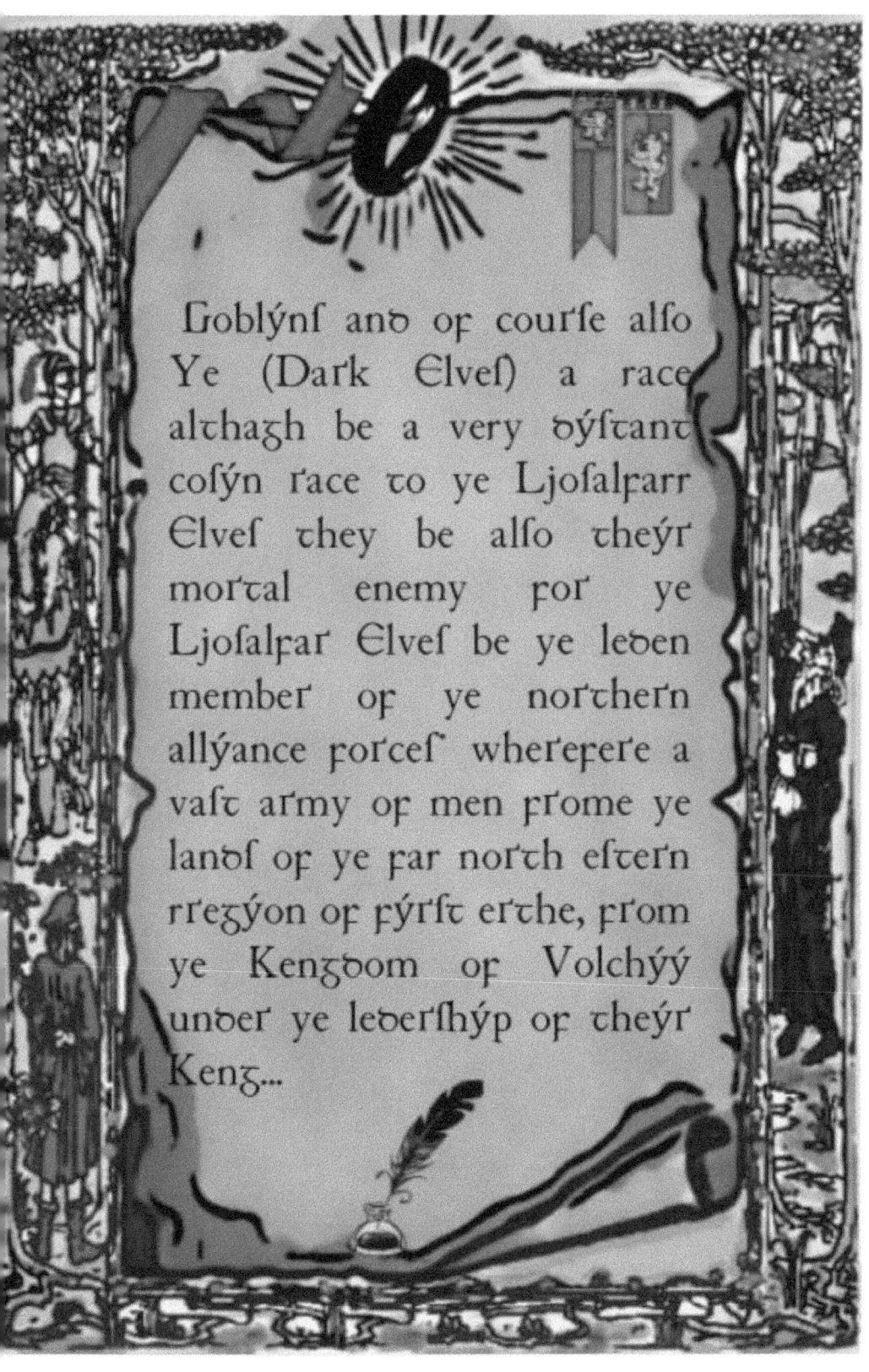

Goblýns and of course also Ye (Dark Elves) a race althagh be a very dýstant cosýn race to ye Ljosalfarr Elves they be also theýr mortal enemy for ye Ljosalfar Elves be ye leden member of ye northern allýance forces wherefere a vast army of men frome ye lands of ye far north estern rregýon of fýrst erthe, from ye Kenzdom of Volchýý under ye ledershýp of theýr Keng...

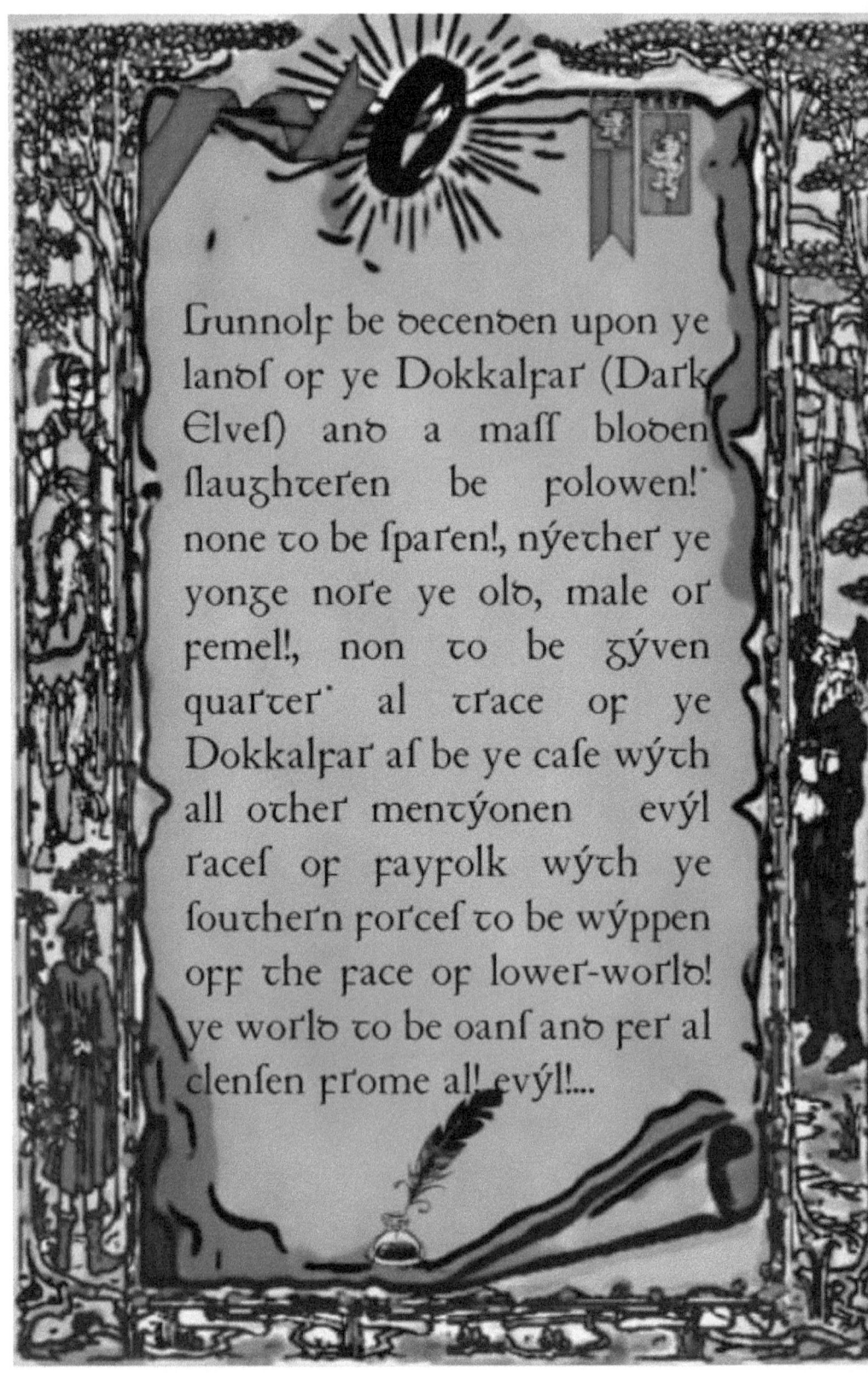

Gunnolf be decenden upon ye landf of ye Dokkalfar (Dark Elvef) and a maff bloden flaughteren be folowen! none to be sparen!, nyether ye yonge nore ye old, male or femel!, non to be gyven quarter al trace of ye Dokkalfar af be ye cafe wyth all other mentyonen evyl racef of fayfolk wyth ye fouthern forcef to be wyppen off the face of lower-world! ye world to be oanf and fer al clenfen frome al! evyl!...

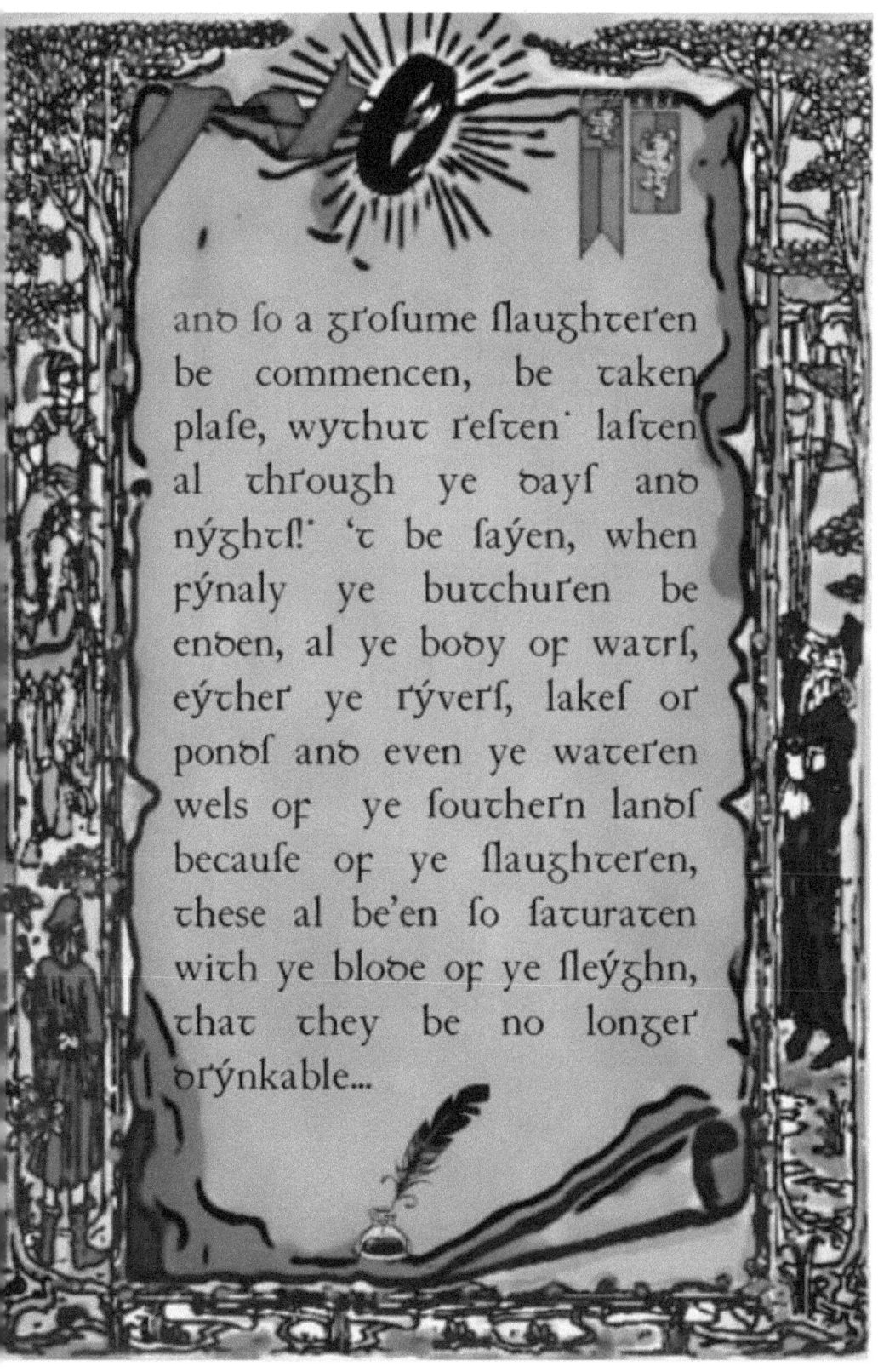

and ſo a groſume ſlaughteren be commencen, be taken plaſe, wythut reſten' laſten al through ye dayſ and nýghtſ! 't be ſaýen, when fýnaly ye butchuren be enden, al ye body of watrſ, eýther ye rýverſ, lakeſ or pondſ and even ye wateren wels of ye ſouthern landſ becauſe of ye ſlaughteren, theſe al be'en ſo ſaturaten with ye blode of ye ſleýghn, that they be no longer drýnkable...

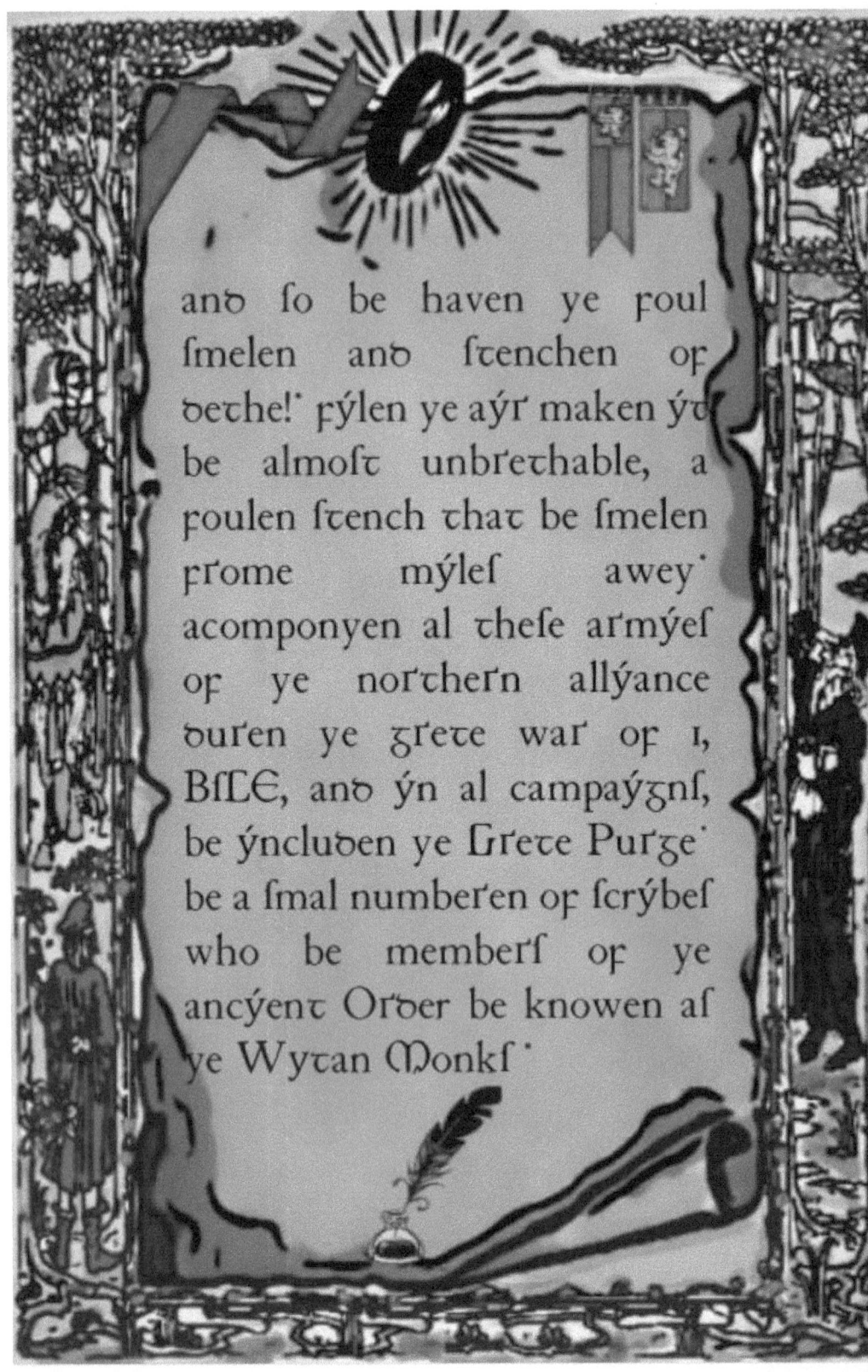

and ſo be haven ye ꝼoul ſmelen and ſtenchen oꝼ dethe! ꝼýlen ye aýꝛ maken ýꝺ be almoſt unbꝛethable, a ꝼoulen ſtench that be ſmelen ꝼrome mýleſ awey· acomponyen al theſe aꝛmýeſ oꝼ ye noꝛthern allýance duꝛen ye grete war oꝼ ı, BſⱢE, and ýn al campaýgnſ, be ýncluden ye Grete Puꝛge· be a ſmal numberen oꝼ ſcrýbeſ who be memberſ oꝼ ye ancýent Oꝛder be knowen aſ ye Wytan Monkſ·

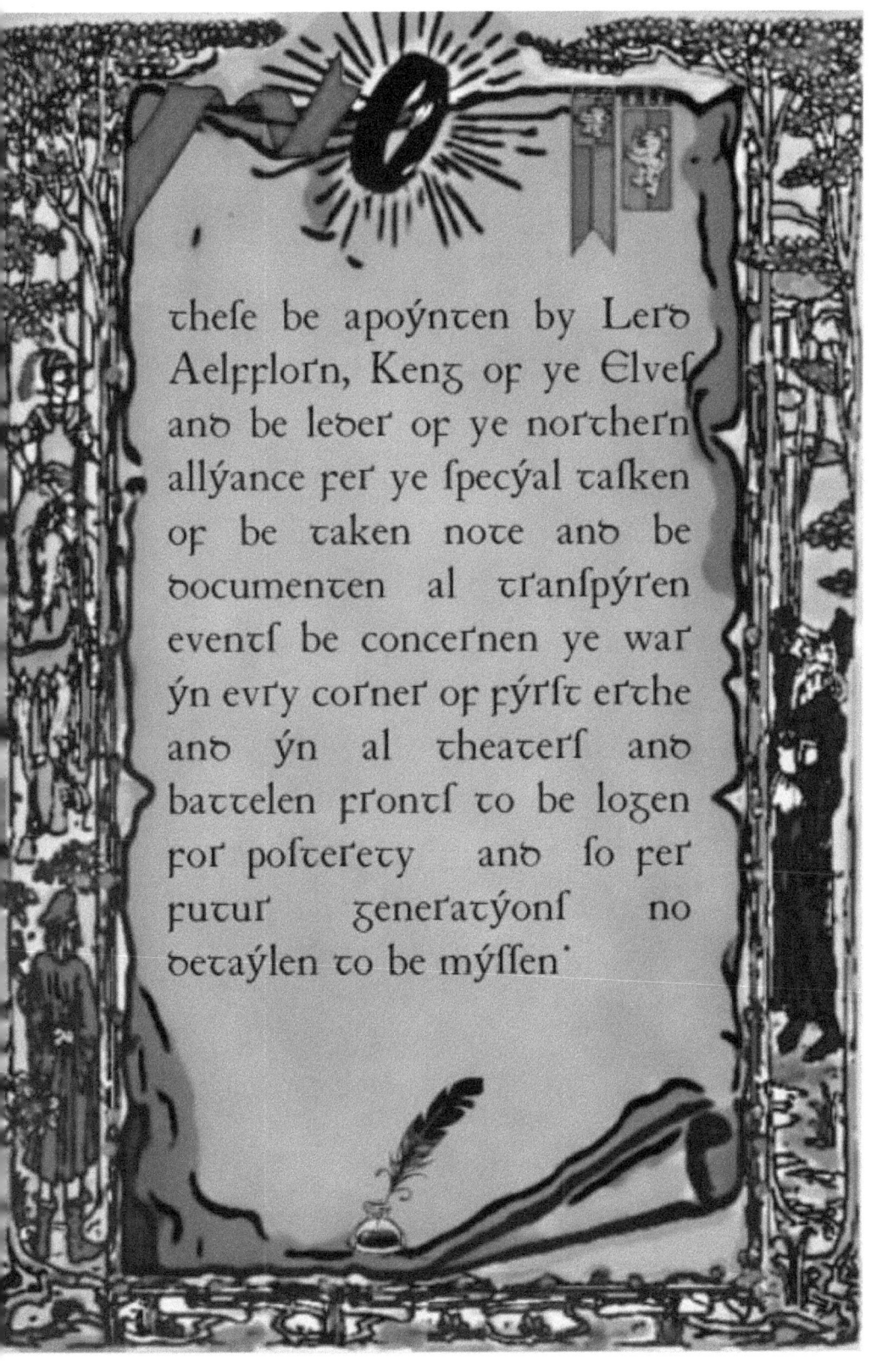

theſe be apoýnten by Lerð
Aelꝼꝼlorn, Keng oꝼ ye Elveſ
anð be leðer oꝼ ye northern
allýance ꝼer ye ſpecýal taſken
oꝼ be taken note anð be
ðocumenten al tranſpýren
eventſ be concernen ye war
ýn evry corner oꝼ ꝼýrſt erthe
anð ýn al theaterſ anð
battelen ꝼrontſ to be loꜩen
ꝼor poſterety anð ſo ꝼer
ꝼutur generatýonſ no
ðetaýlen to be mýſſen·

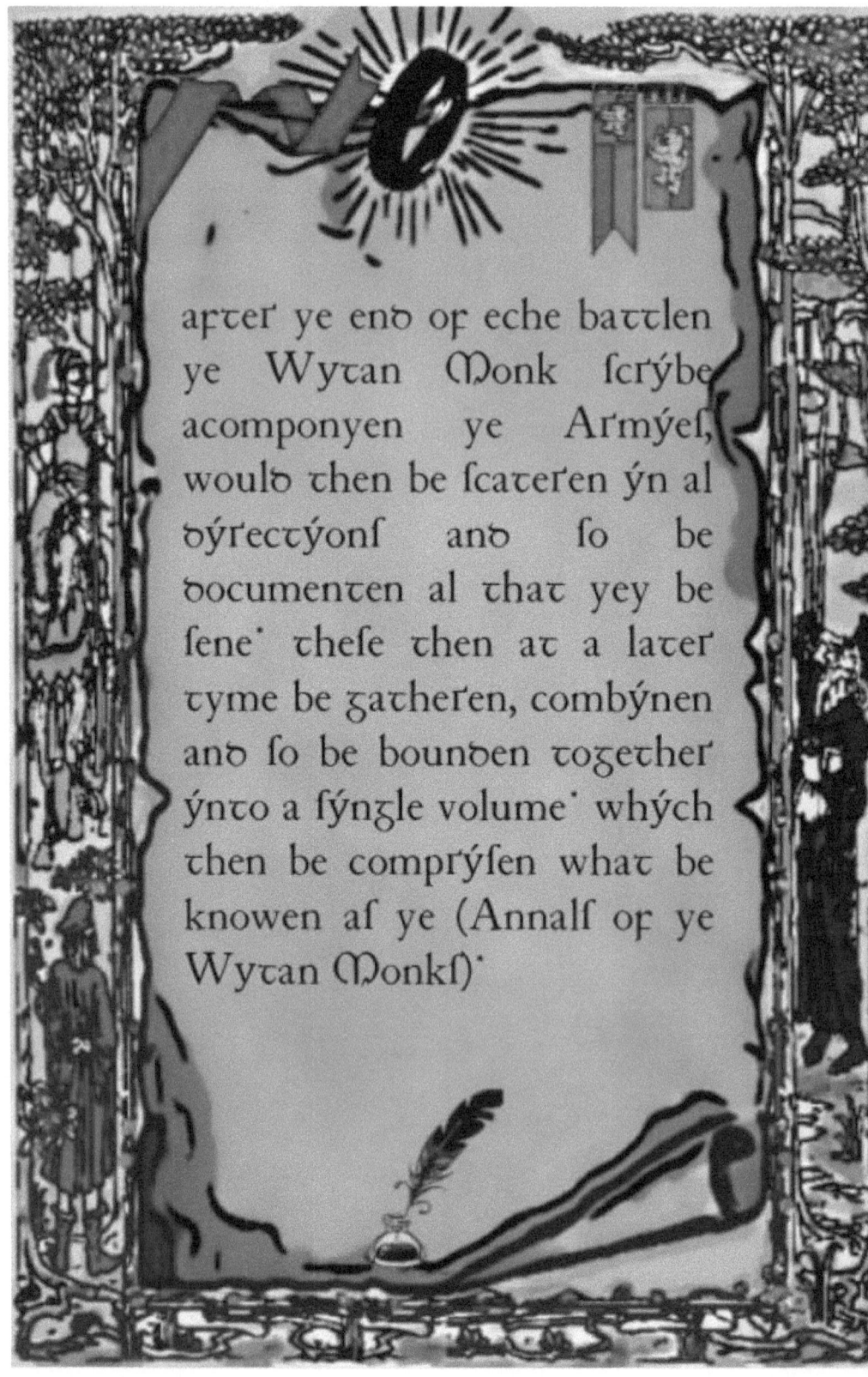

after ye end of eche battlen ye Wytan Monk scrýbe acomponyen ye Armýes, would then be scateren ýn al dýrectýons and so be documenten al that yey be sene· these then at a later tyme be gatheren, combýnen and so be bounden together ýnto a sýngle volume· whých then be comprýsen what be knowen as ye (Annals of ye Wytan Monks)·

ye second

‘Comon Era

be ye fyrſt yehr of
ye (ſCE) (ſecond Comon Era
)˙ ye tyme fer departen of ye
Elveſ, and ſo be ye begenen
tyme of men and ye Wytan
Monk'ſ˙

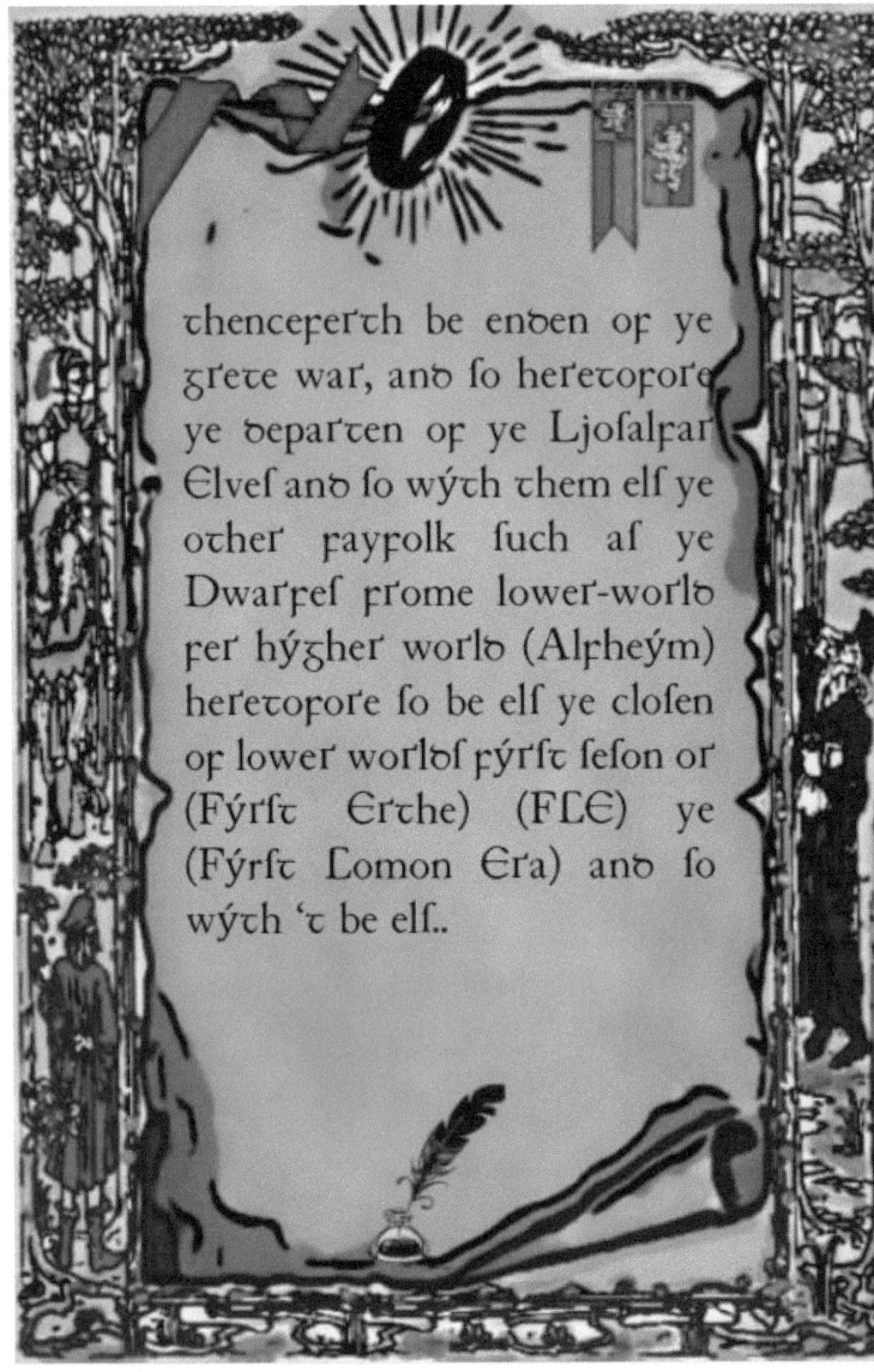

thenceferth be enden of ye grete war, and fo heretofore ye departen of ye Ljofalfar Elves and fo wýth them elf ye other fayfolk fuch af ye Dwarfes frome lower-world fer hýgher world (Alfheým) heretofore fo be elf ye clofen of lower worldf fýrft fefon or (Fýrft Erthe) (FLE) ye (Fýrft Lomon Era) and fo wýth 't be elf..

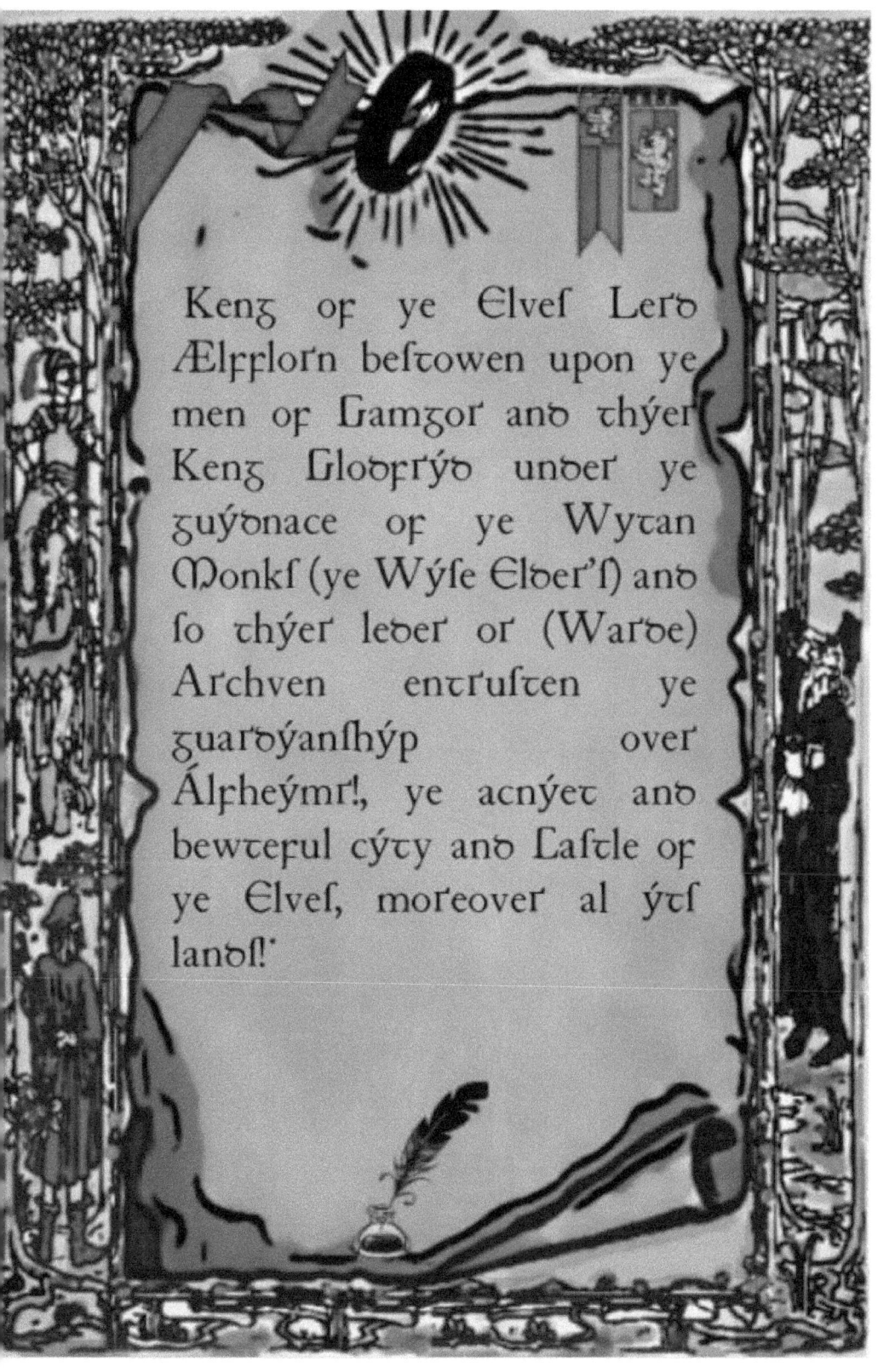

Keng of ye Elves Lerd Ælfflorn beftowen upon ye men of Gamgor and thýer Keng Glodfrýd under ye guýdnace of ye Wytan Monkf (ye Wýfe Elder'f) and fo thýer leder or (Warde) Archven entruften ye guardýanfhýp over Álfheýmr!, ye acnýet and bewteful cýty and Laftle of ye Elvef, moreover al ýtf landf!'

Keng or ye Elves,
Lero Ælfrlorn

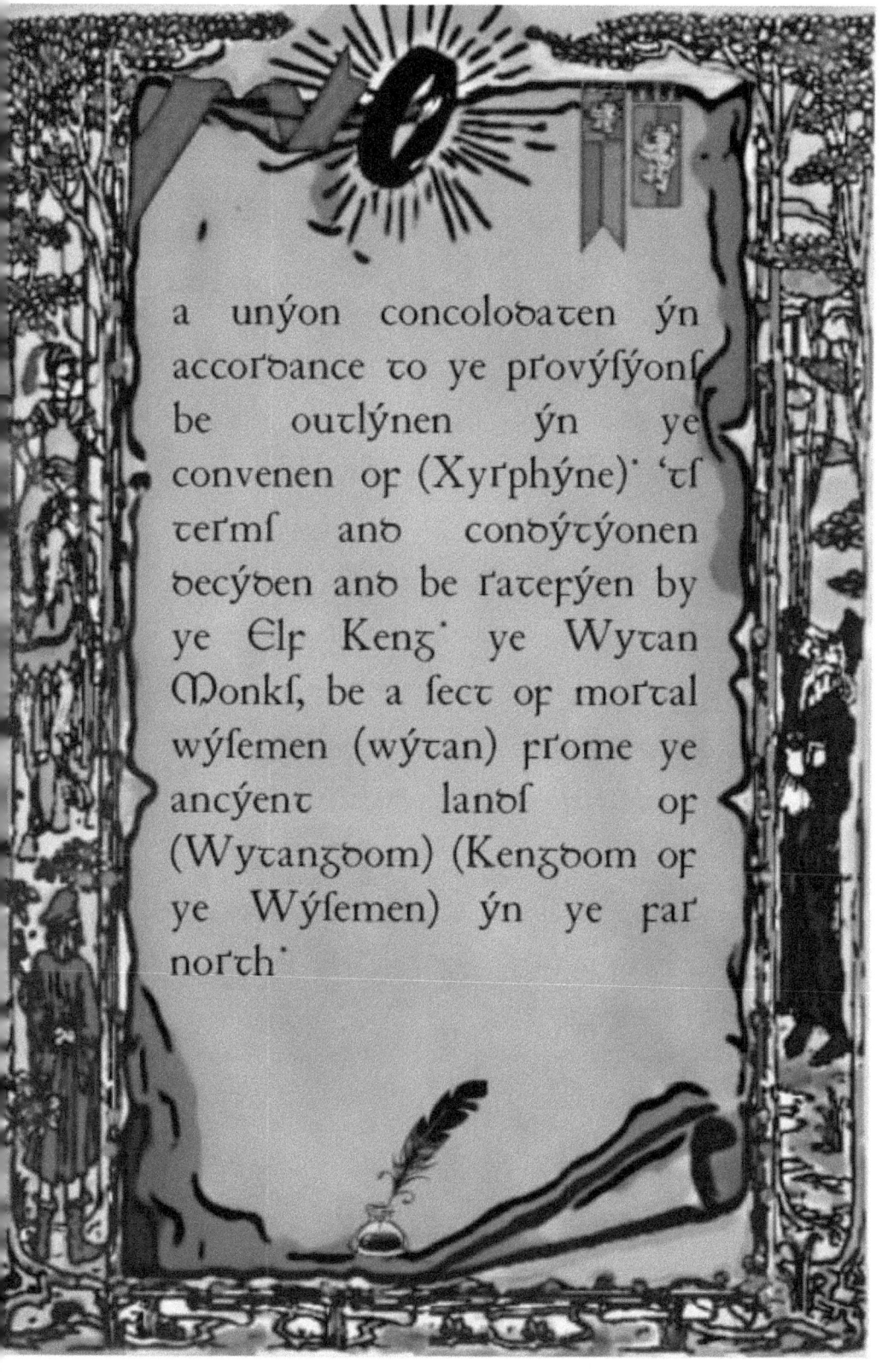

a unýon concolodaten ýn accordance to ye provýsýonſ be outlýnen ýn ye convenen oꝼ (Xyꝛphýne)· 'tſ termſ and condýtýonen decýden and be rateꝛýen by ye Elꝼ Keng· ye Wytan Monkſ, be a ſect oꝼ mortal wýſemen (wýtan) ꝼrome ye ancýent landſ oꝼ (Wytangdom) (Kengdom oꝼ ye Wýſemen) ýn ye ꝼar north·

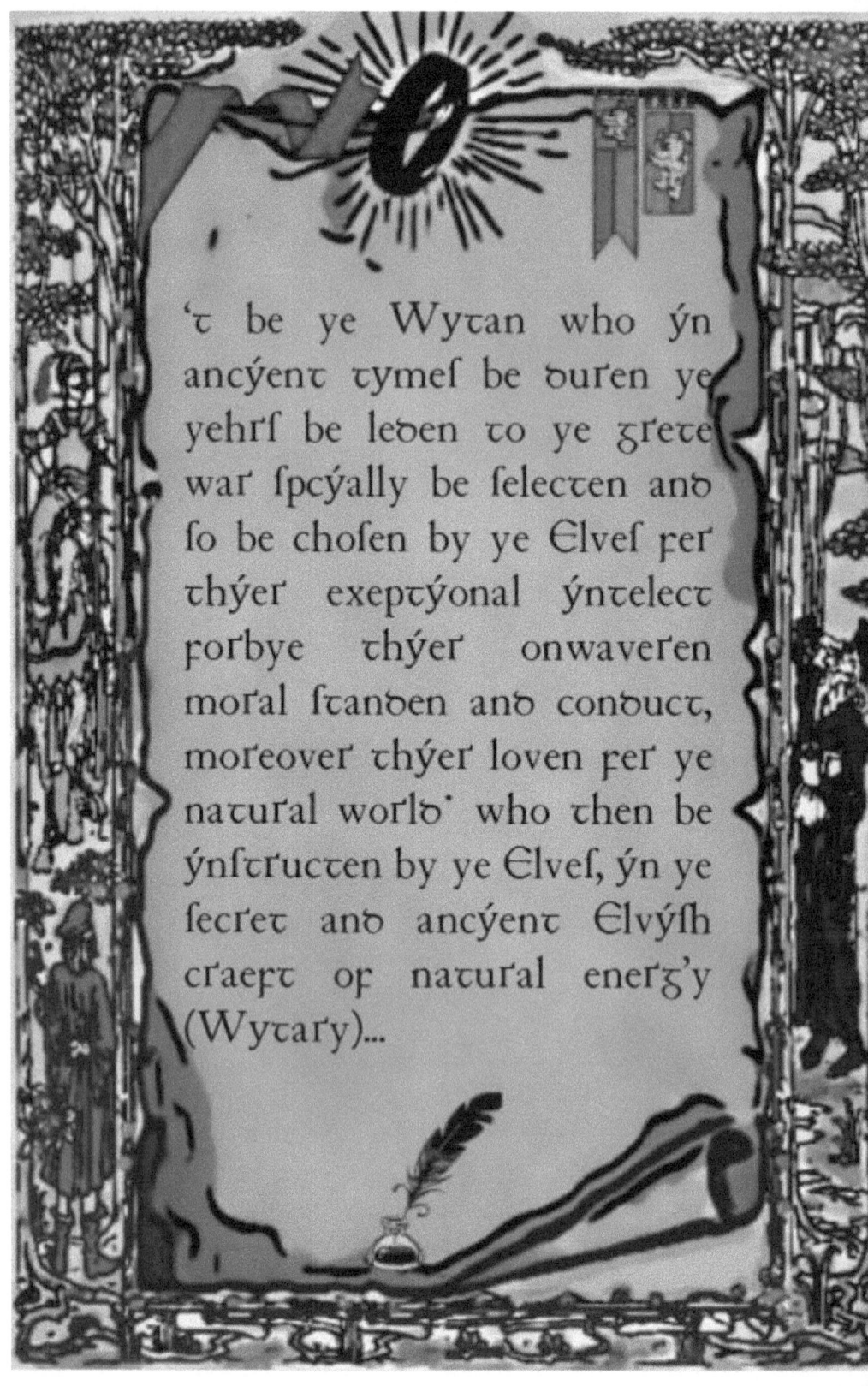

't be ye Wytan who ýn ancýent tymes be duren ye yehrs be leden to ye grete war spcýally be selecten and so be chosen by ye Elves fer thýer exeptýonal ýntelect forbye thýer onwaveren moral standen and conduct, moreover thýer loven fer ye natural world' who then be ýnstructen by ye Elves, ýn ye secret and ancýent Elvýsh craeft of natural energ'y (Wytary)...

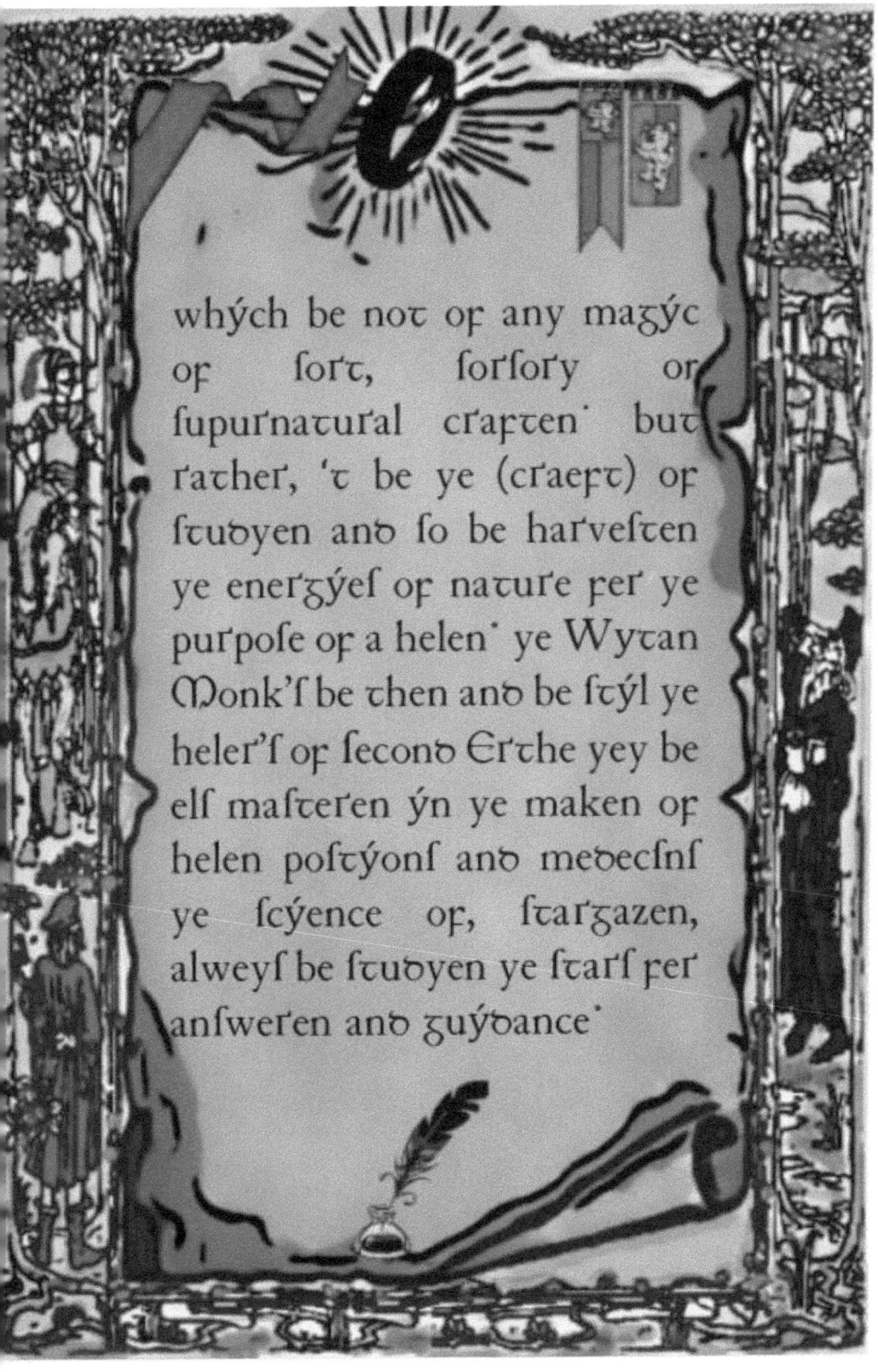

whých be not of any magýc
of   fort,   forfory   or
fupurnatural craften· but
rather, 't be ye (craeft) of
ftudyen and fo be harveften
ye energýef of nature fer ye
purpofe of a helen· ye Wytan
Monk'f be then and be ftýl ye
heler'f of fecond Erthe yey be
elf mafteren ýn ye maken of
helen poftýonf and medecfnf
ye fcýence of, ftargazen,
alweyf be ftudyen ye ftarf fer
anfweren and guýdance·

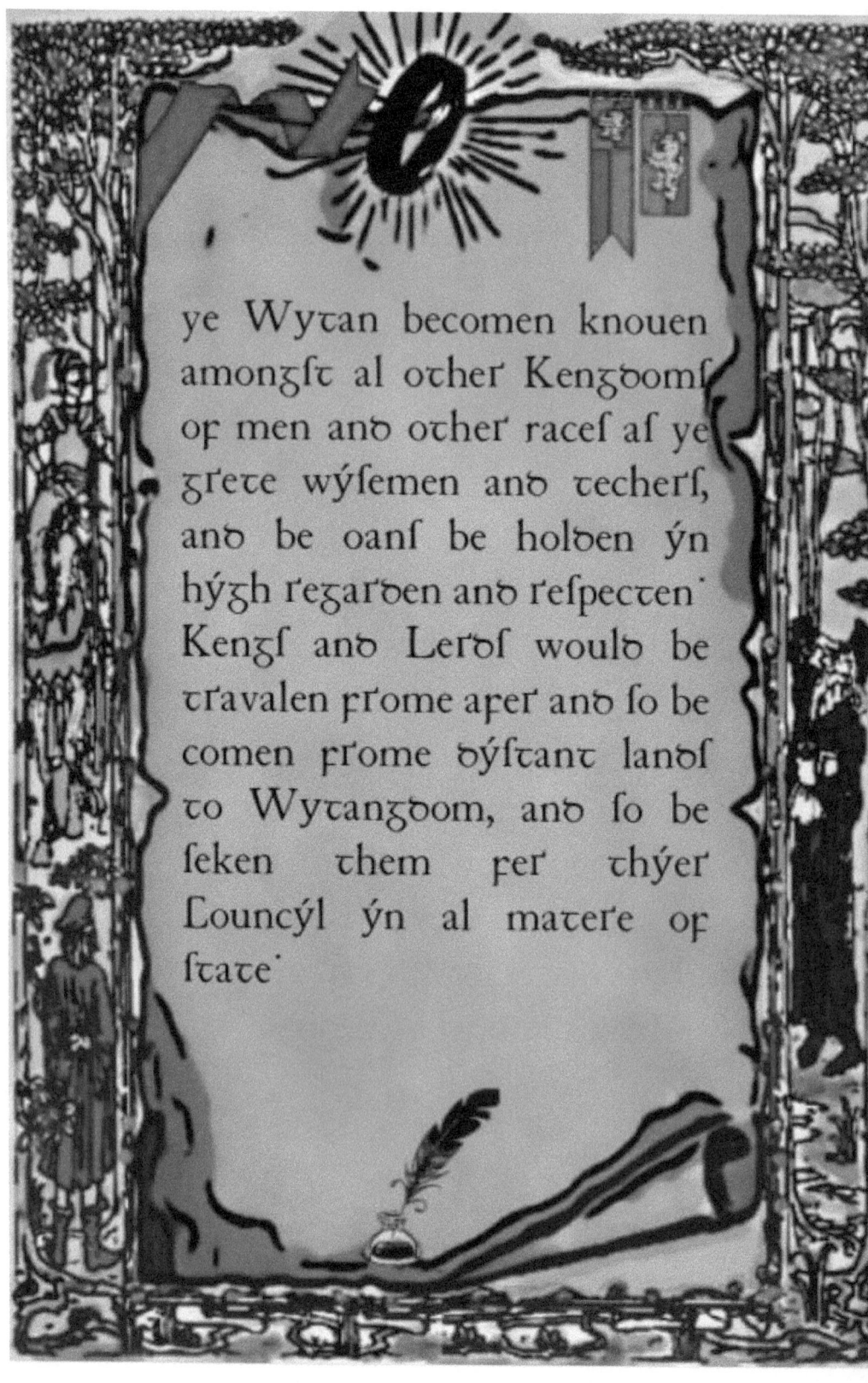

ye Wytan becomen knouen amongst al other Kengdoms of men and other races as ye grete wysemen and techers, and be oans be holden ýn hýgh regarden and respecten. Kengs and Leros would be travalen frome afer and so be comen frome dýstant lands to Wytangdom, and so be seken them fer thýer Councýl ýn al matere of state.

Wytan Monk

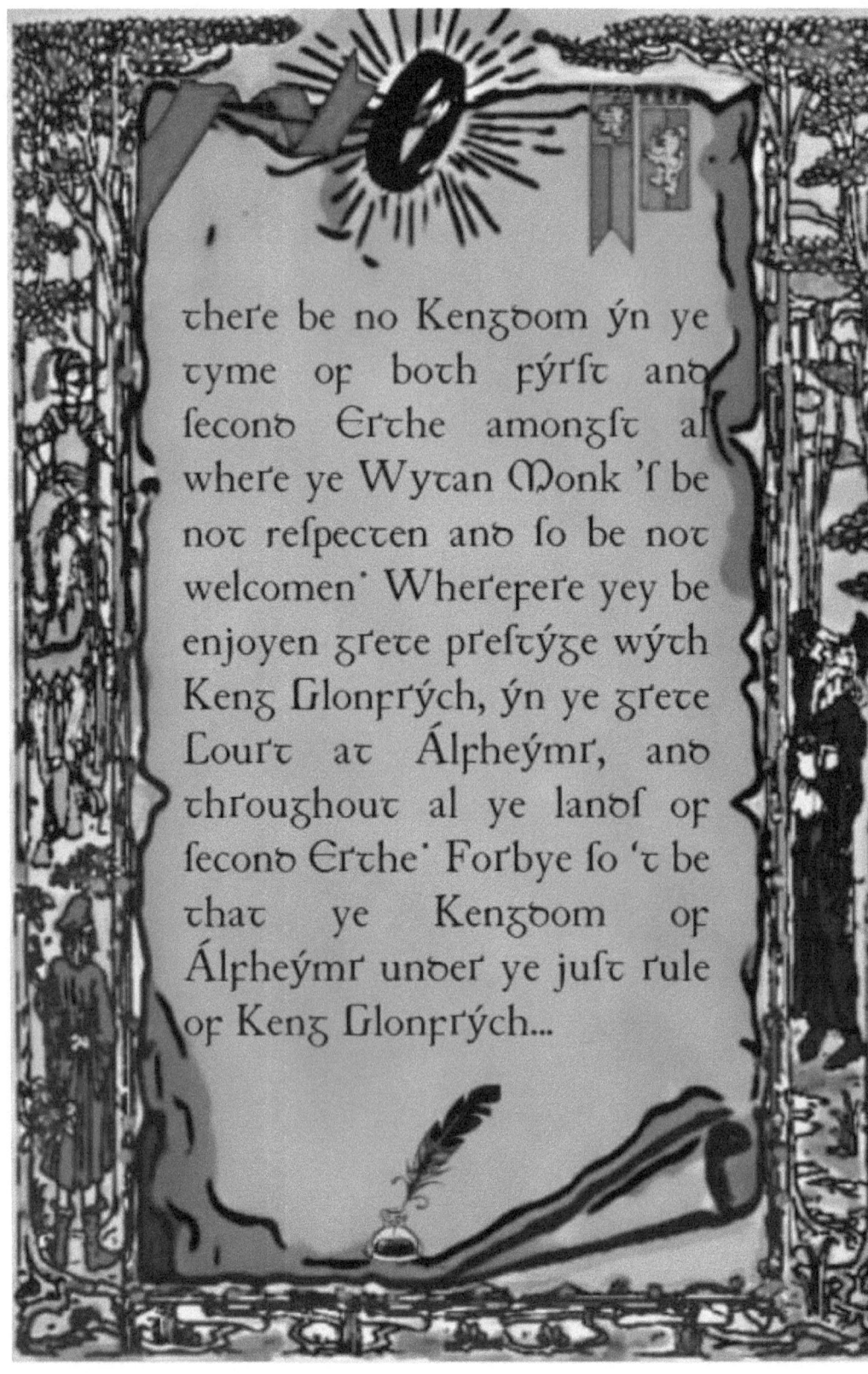

there be no Kengdom ýn ye tyme of both fýrst and second Erthe amongst al where ye Wytan Monk 's be not respecten and so be not welcomen· Wherefere yey be enjoyen grete prestýge wýth Keng Glonfrých, ýn ye grete Court at Álfheýmr, and throughout al ye lands of second Erthe· Forbye so 't be that ye Kengdom of Álfheýmr under ye just rule of Keng Glonfrých...

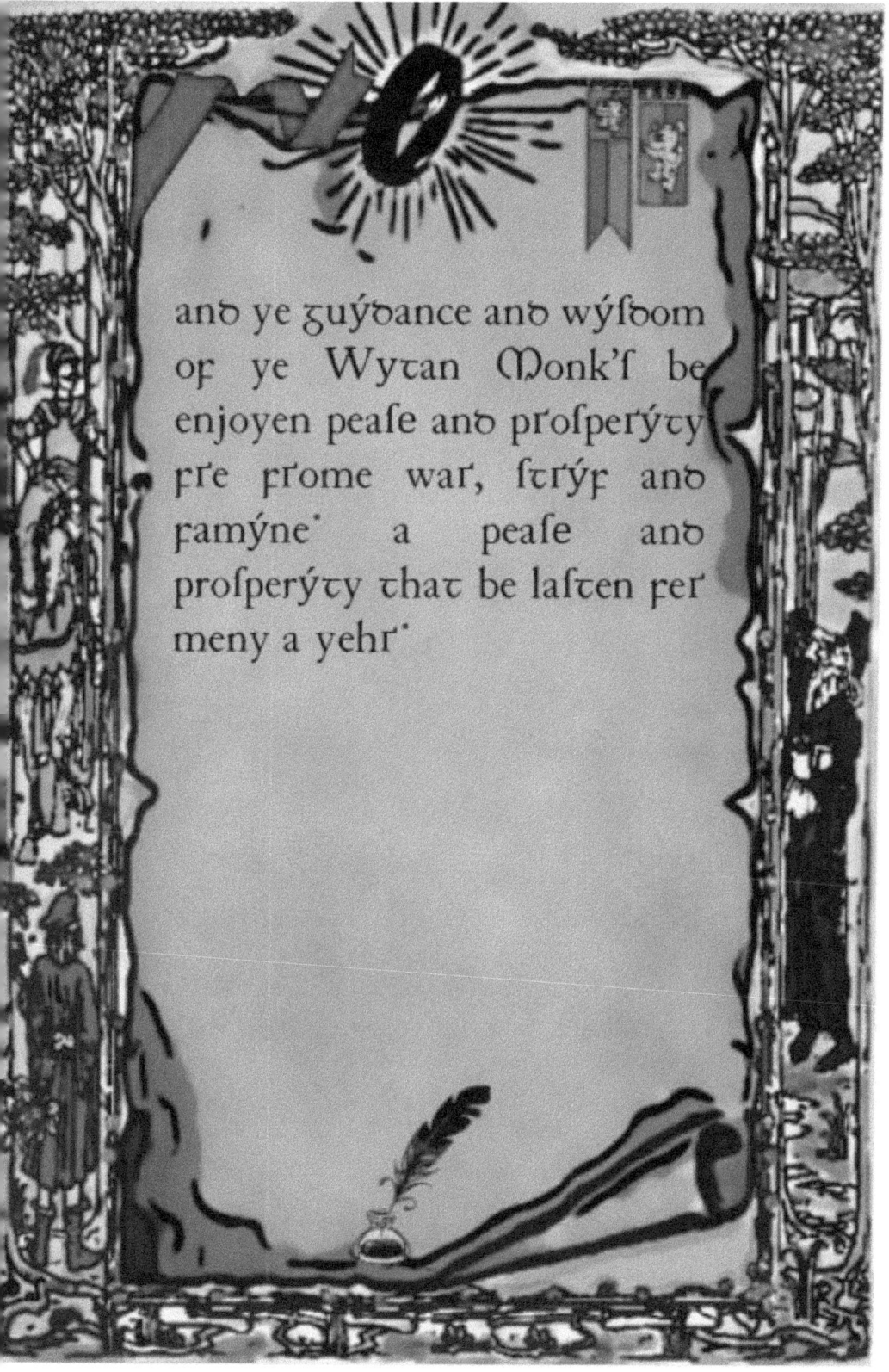

and ye guýdance and wýsdom
of ye Wytan Monk's be
enjoyen peafe and profperýty
fre frome war, strýf and
famýne' a peafe and
profperýty that be lasten fer
meny a yehr'

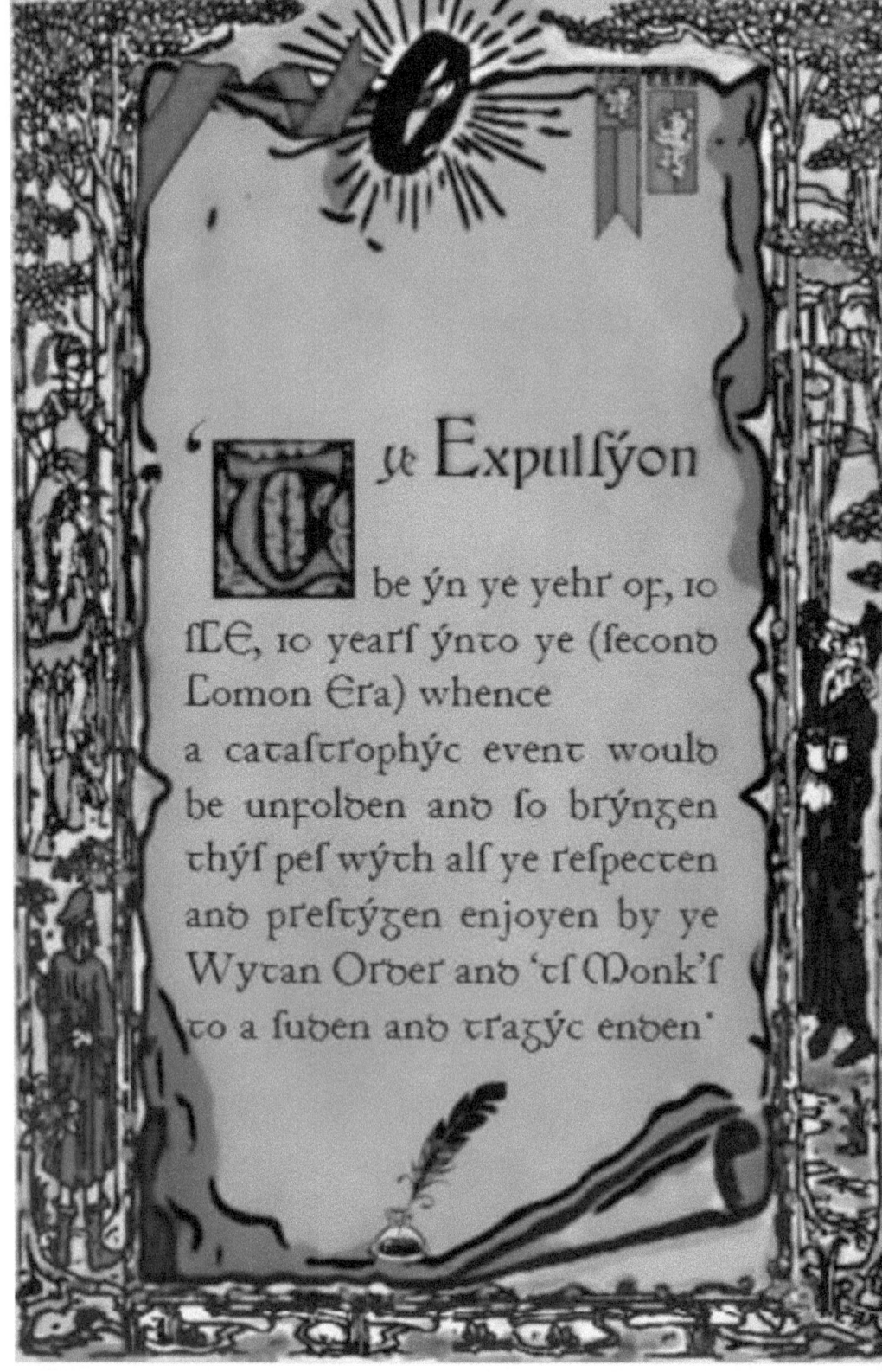

' ɟe Expulſ́yon

be ýn ye yehr oꝼ, 10 ꝼɔE, 10 yearſ ýnto ye (ſeconꝺ Lomon Era) whence a cataſtrophýc event woulꝺ be unꝼolꝺen anꝺ ſo brýnɡen thýſ peſ wýth alſ ye reſpecten anꝺ preſtýɡen enjoyen by ye Wytan Orꝺer anꝺ 'tſ Monk'ſ to a ſuꝺen anꝺ traɡýc enꝺen·

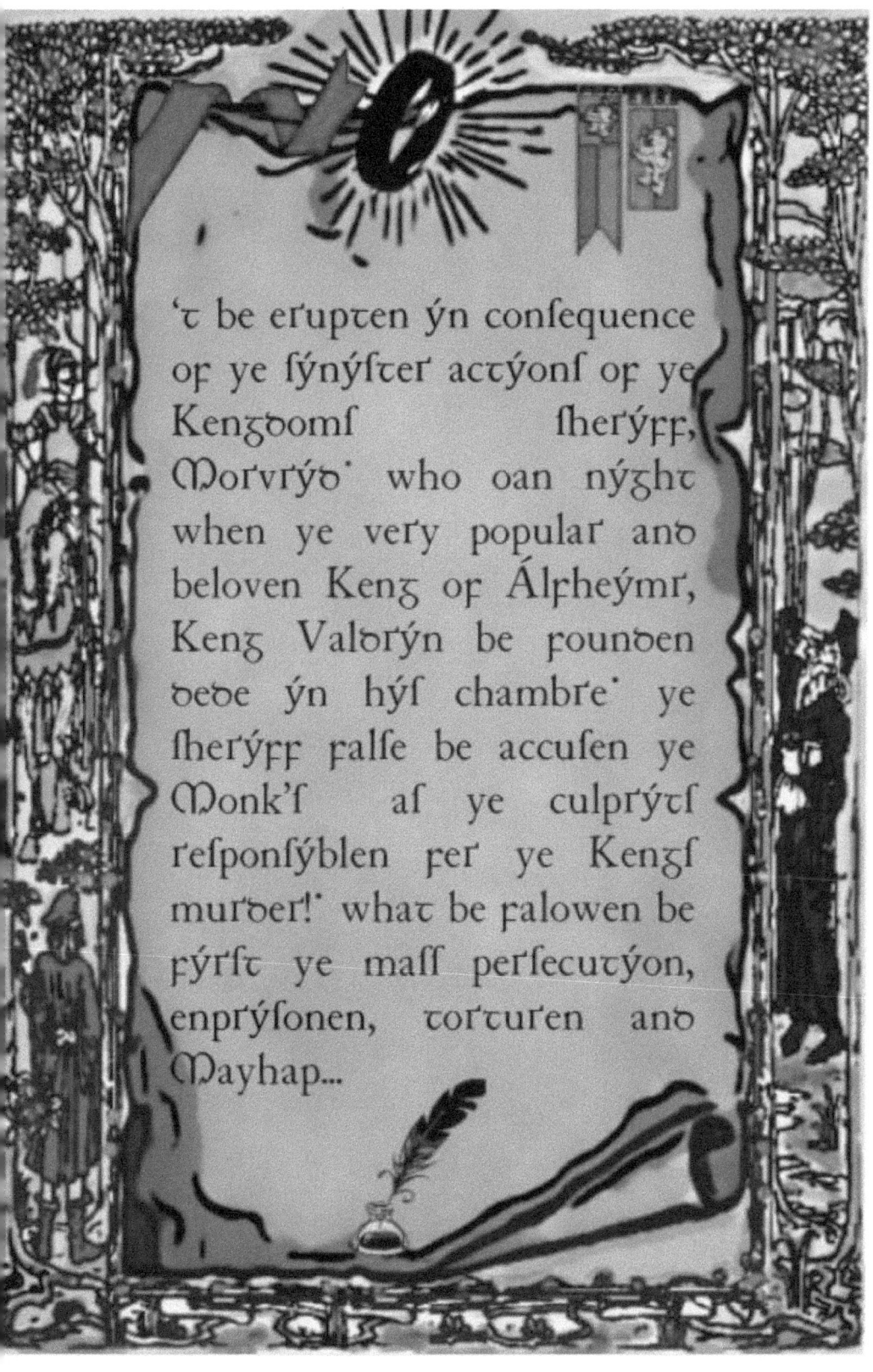

't be erupten ýn confequence of ye fýnýfter actýonf of ye Kengdomf fherýff, Morvrýd who oan nýght when ye very popular and beloven Keng of Álfheýmr, Keng Valdrýn be founden dede ýn hýf chambre ye fherýff falfe be accufen ye Monk'f af ye culprýtf refponfýblen fer ye Kengf murder! what be falowen be fýrft ye maff perfecutýon, enprýfonen, torturen and Mayhap...

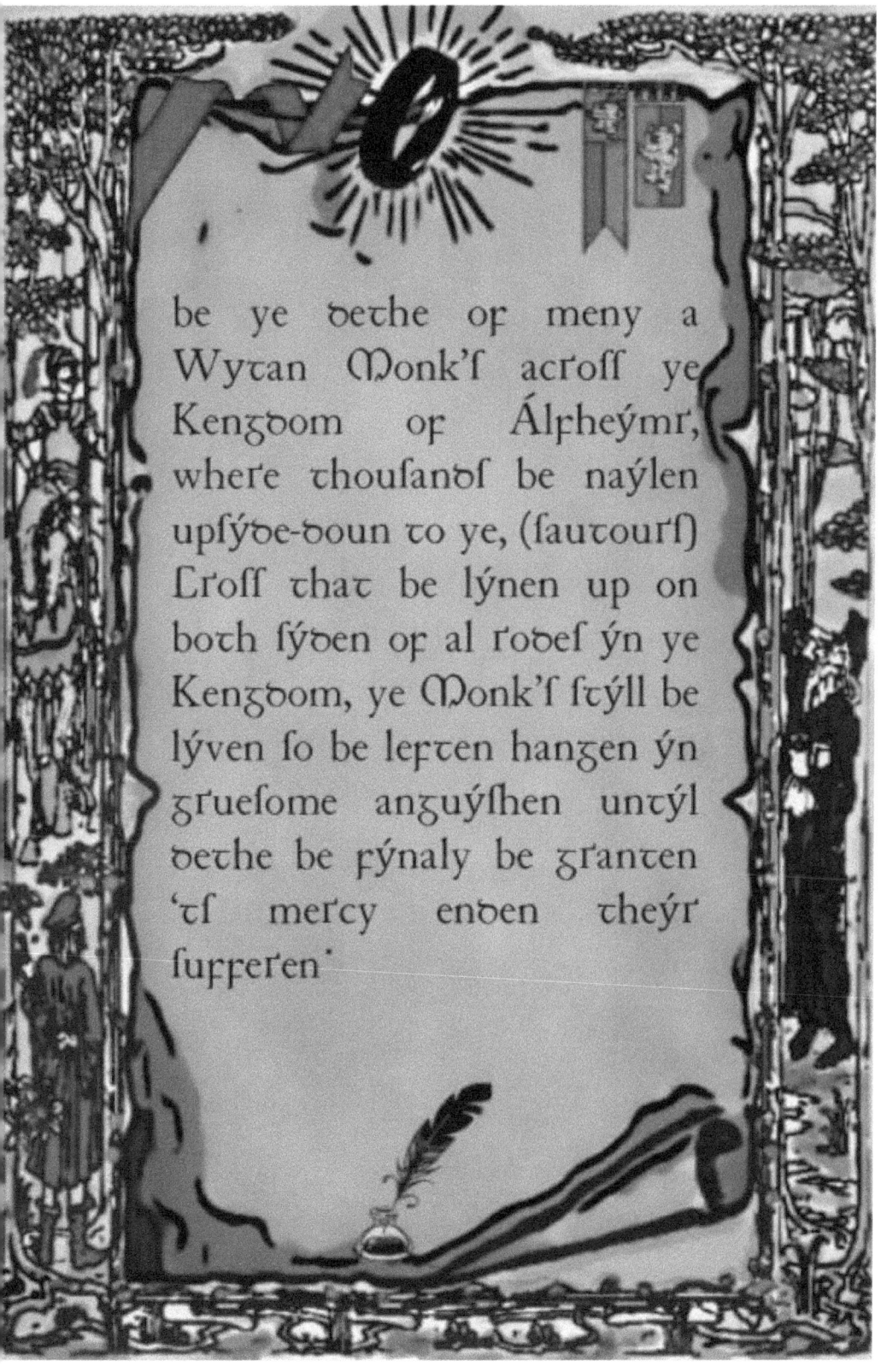

be ye ꝺethe oꝼ meny a
Wytan Monk'ſ acroſſ ye
Kengꝺom oꝼ Álꝼheýmr,
where thouſanꝺſ be naýlen
upſýꝺe-ꝺoun to ye, (ſautourſ)
Croſſ that be lýnen up on
both ſýꝺen oꝼ al roꝺeſ ýn ye
Kengꝺom, ye Monk'ſ ſtýll be
lýven ſo be leꝼten hangen ýn
grueſome anguýſhen untýl
ꝺethe be ꝼýnaly be granten
'tſ mercy enꝺen theýr
ſuꝼꝼeren˙

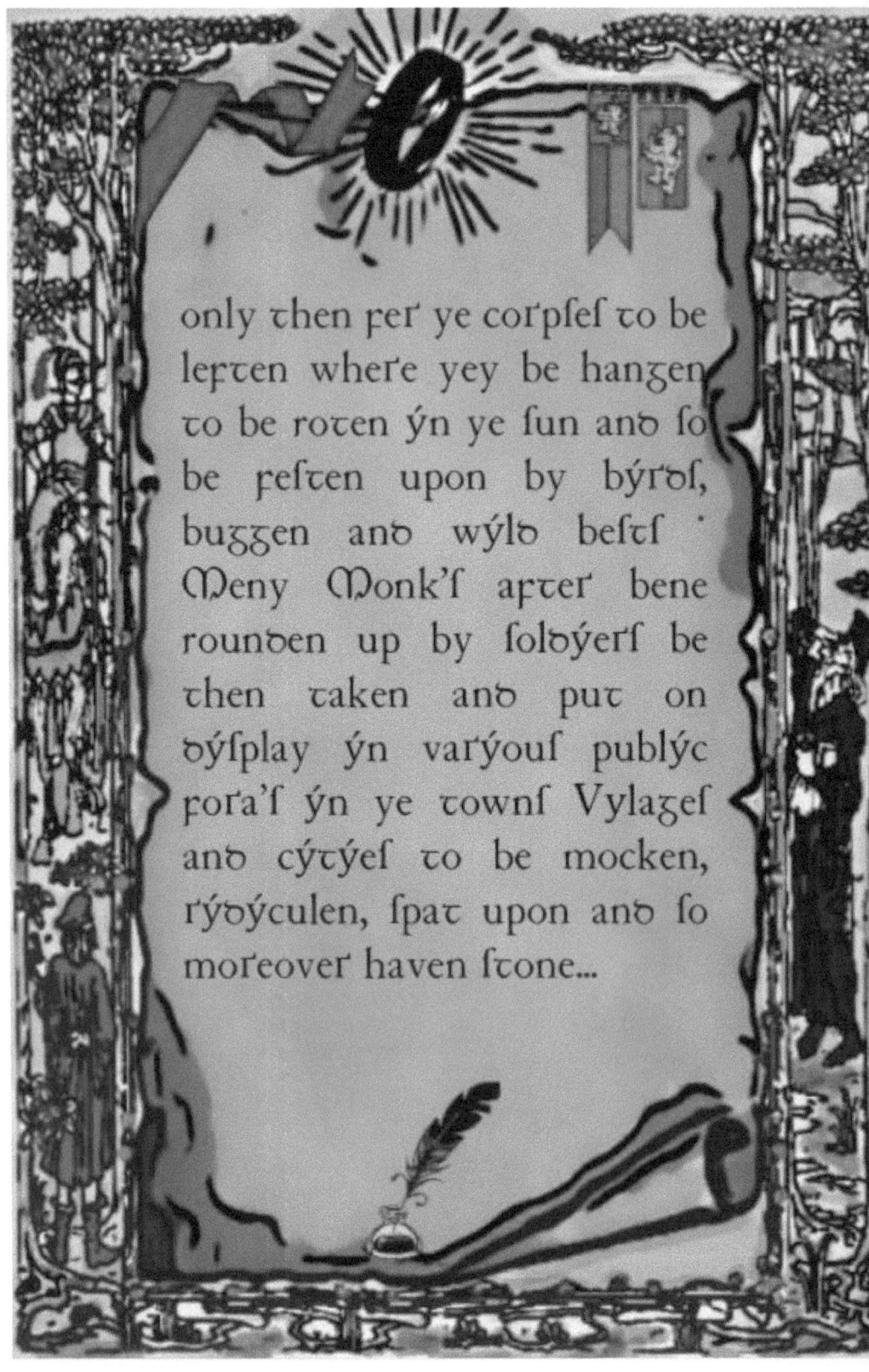

only then ꝼer ye corpſeſ to be
leꝼten where yey be hangen
to be roten ýn ye ſun anð ſo
be ꝼeſten upon by býrðſ,
buꝫꝫen anð wýlð beſtſ ·
Ɱeny Ɱonk'ſ aꝼter bene
rounðen up by ſolðýerſ be
then taken anð put on
ðýſplay ýn varýouſ publýc
ꝼora'ſ ýn ye townſ Vylaꝫeſ
anð cýtýeſ to be mocken,
rýðýculen, ſpat upon anð ſo
moreover haven ſtone...

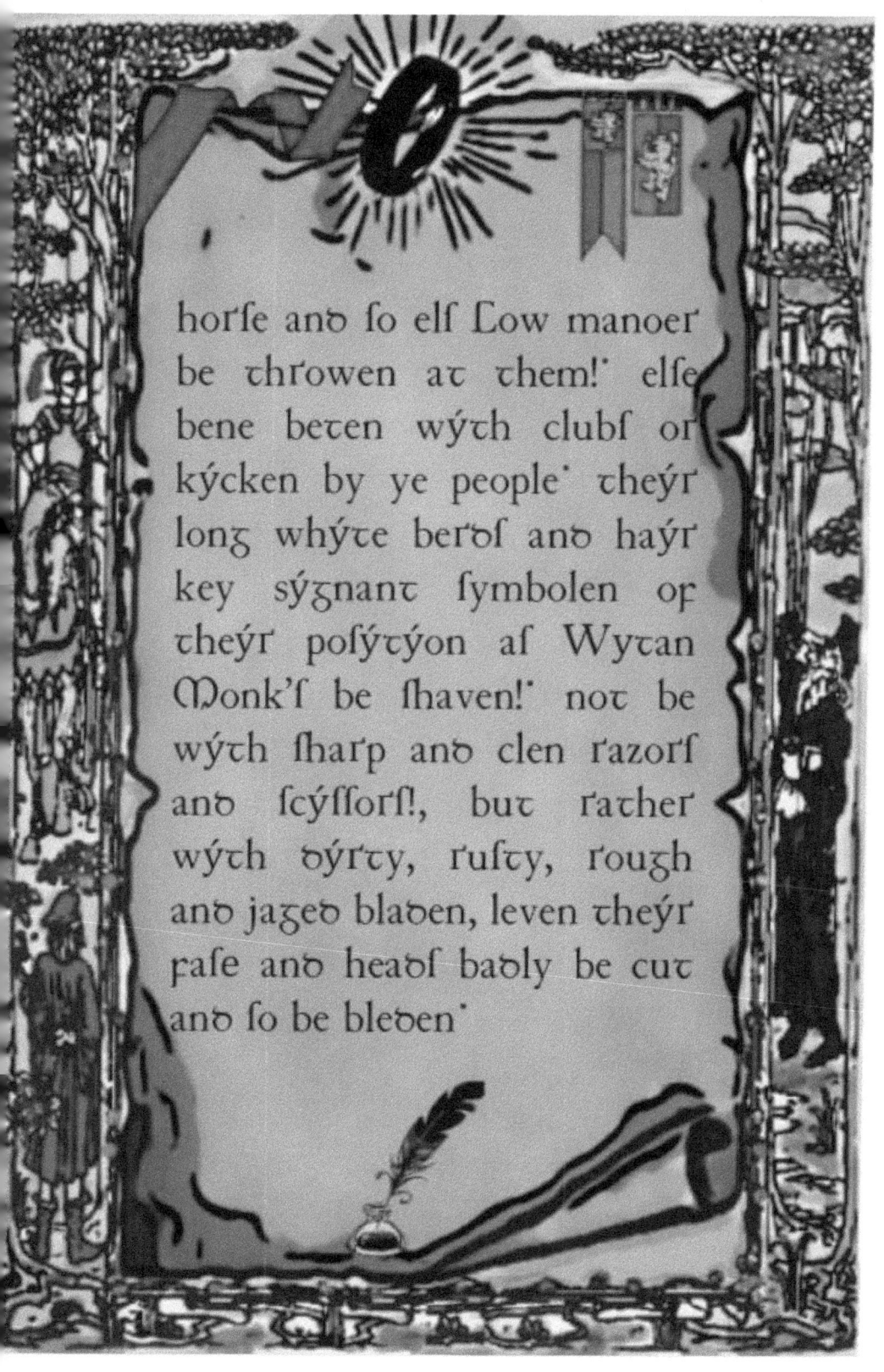

horſe anð ſo elf Low manðer be throwen at them! elſe bene beten wýth clubſ or kýcken by ye people theýr long whýte berðſ anð haýr key sýgnant ſymbolen of theýr poſýtýon aſ Wytan Monk'ſ be ſhaven! not be wýth ſharp anð clen razorſ anð ſcýſſorſ!, but rather wýth ðýrty, ruſty, rough anð jageð blaðen, leven theýr faſe anð heaðſ baðly be cut anð ſo be bleðen

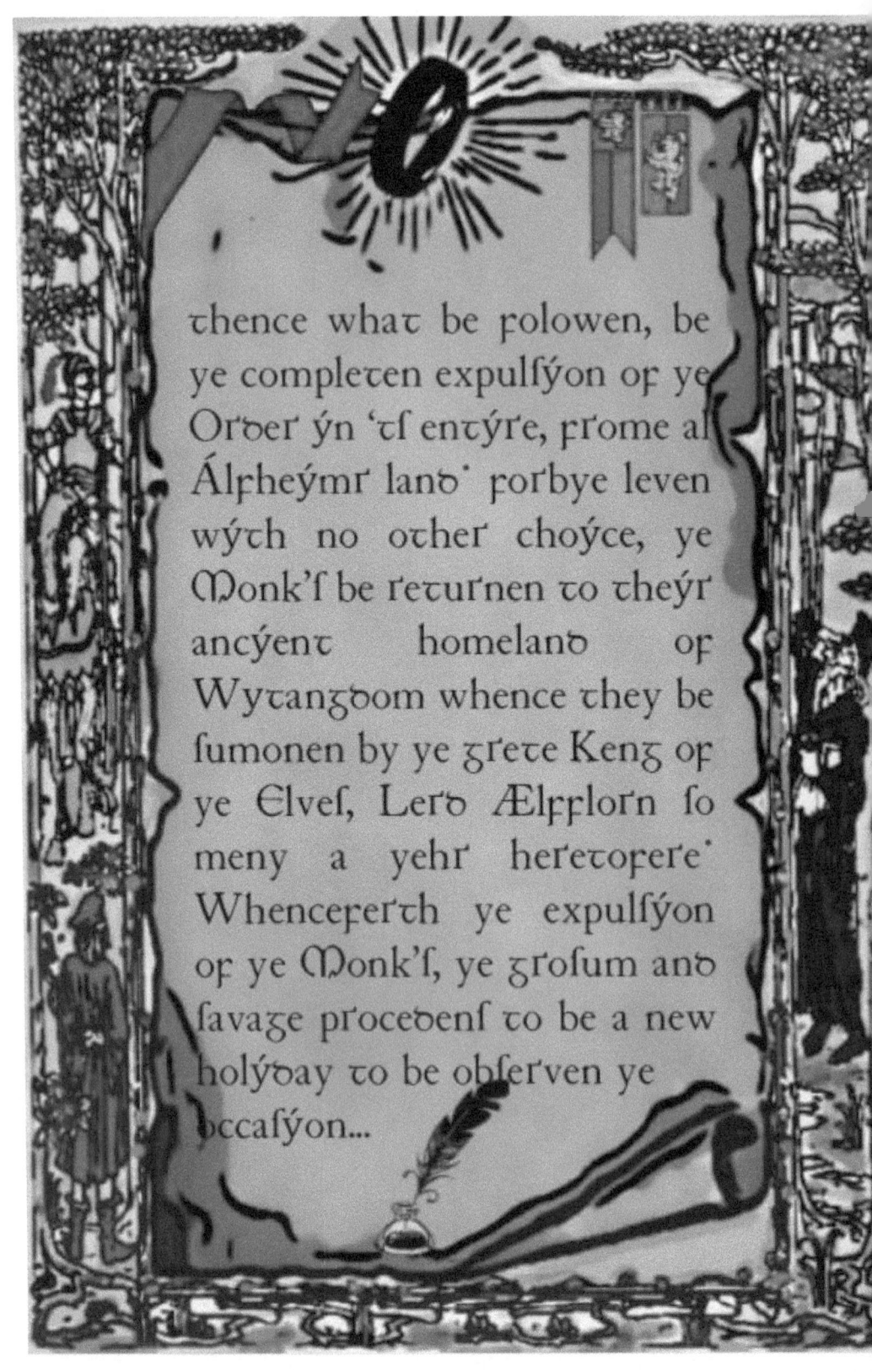

thence what be folowen, be
ye completen expulſýon oꝛ ye
Orðer ýn 'tſ entýꝛe, ꝼꝛome al
Álꝼheýmꝛ lanð' ꝼoꝛbye leven
wýth no other choýce, ye
Monk'ſ be retuꝛnen to theýꝛ
ancýent homeland oꝛ
Wytangðom whence they be
ſumonen by ye zꝛete Kenz oꝛ
ye Elveſ, Leꝛð Ælꝼꝼloꝛn ſo
meny a yehꝛ heꝛetoꝼeꝛe'
Whenceꝼeꝛth ye expulſýon
oꝛ ye Monk'ſ, ye zꝛoſum and
ſavaze pꝛoceðenſ to be a new
holýðay to be obſeꝛven ye
ꝏccaſýon...

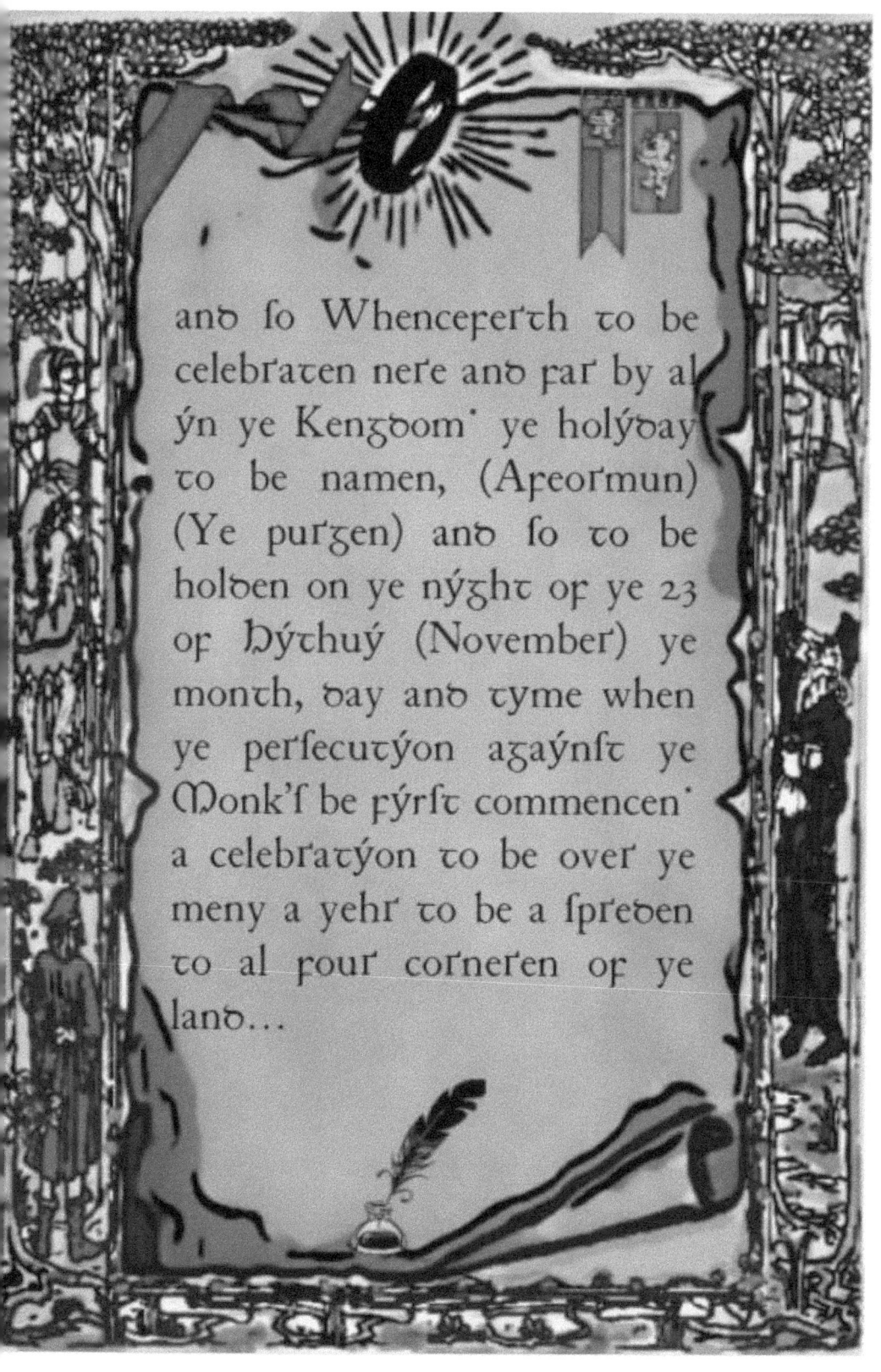

and ſo Whencefѐrth to be celebraten nere and far by al ýn ye Kengdom˙ ye holýday to be namen, (Afѐormun) (Ye purgen) and ſo to be holden on ye nýght of ye 23 of Þýthuý (November) ye month, day and tyme when ye perſecutýon agaýnſt ye Monk'ſ be fýrſt commencen˙ a celebratýon to be over ye meny a yehr to be a ſpreden to al four cornѐren of ye land...

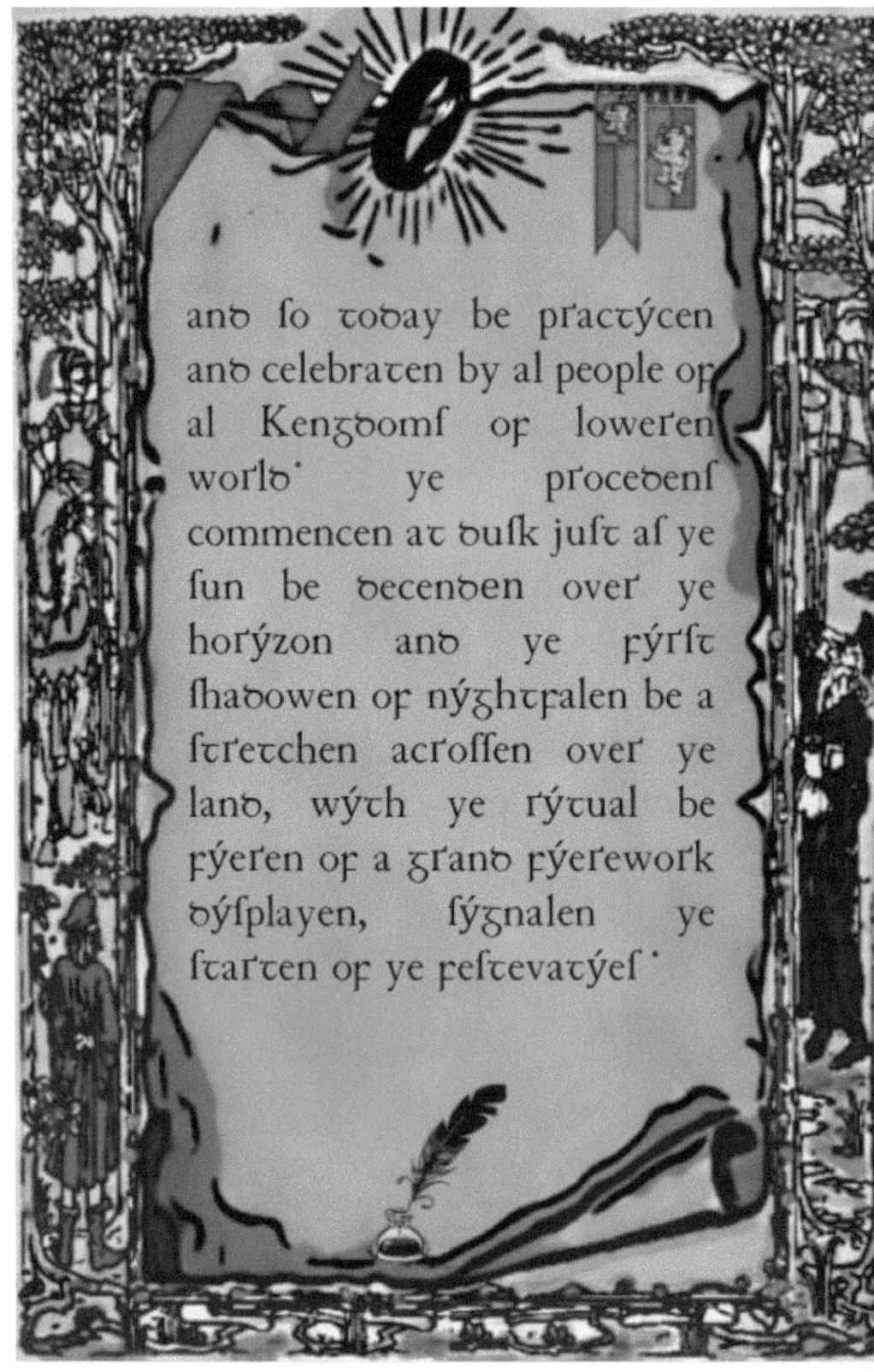

and so today be practýcen and celebraten by al people of al Kengdoms of loweren world· ye procedens commencen at dusk just as ye sun be decenden over ye horýzon and ye fýrst shadowen of nýghtfalen be a stretchen acrossen over ye land, wýth ye rýtual be fýeren of a grand fýerework dýsplayen, sýgnalen ye starten of ye festevatýes·

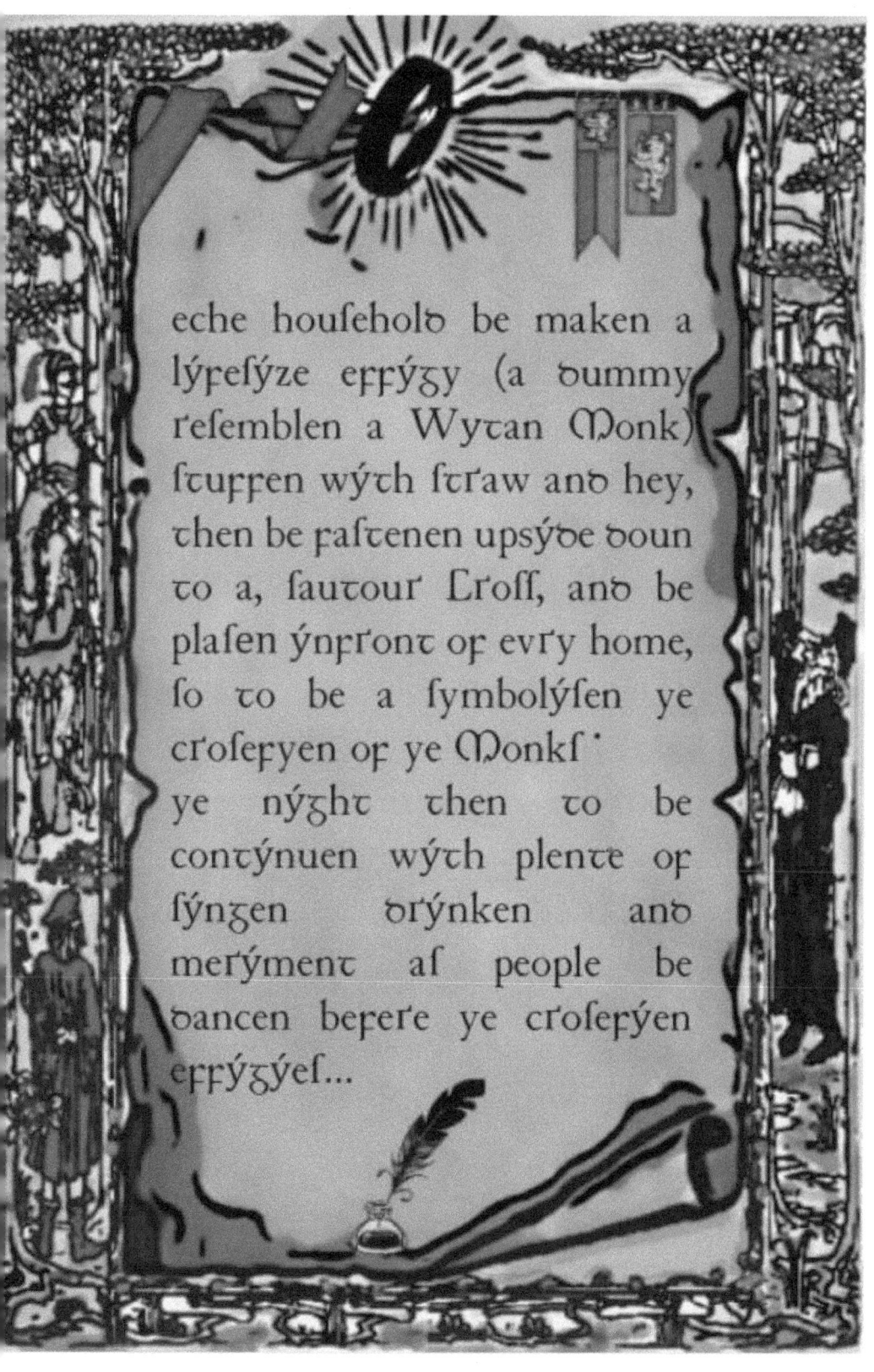

eche houſeholð be maken a lýꝛeſýze eꝼꝼýʒy (a ðummy reſemblen a Wytan Monk) ſtuꝼꝼen wýth ſtraw anð hey, then be ꝼaſtenen upsýðe ðoun to a, ſautour Croſſ, anð be plaſen ýnꝼront oꝼ evry home, ſo to be a ſymbolýſen ye croſeꝼyen oꝼ ye Monkſ·

ye nýʒht then to be contýnuen wýth plente oꝼ ſýnʒen ðrýnken anð merýment aſ people be ðancen beꝼere ye croſeꝼyen eꝼꝼýʒýeſ...

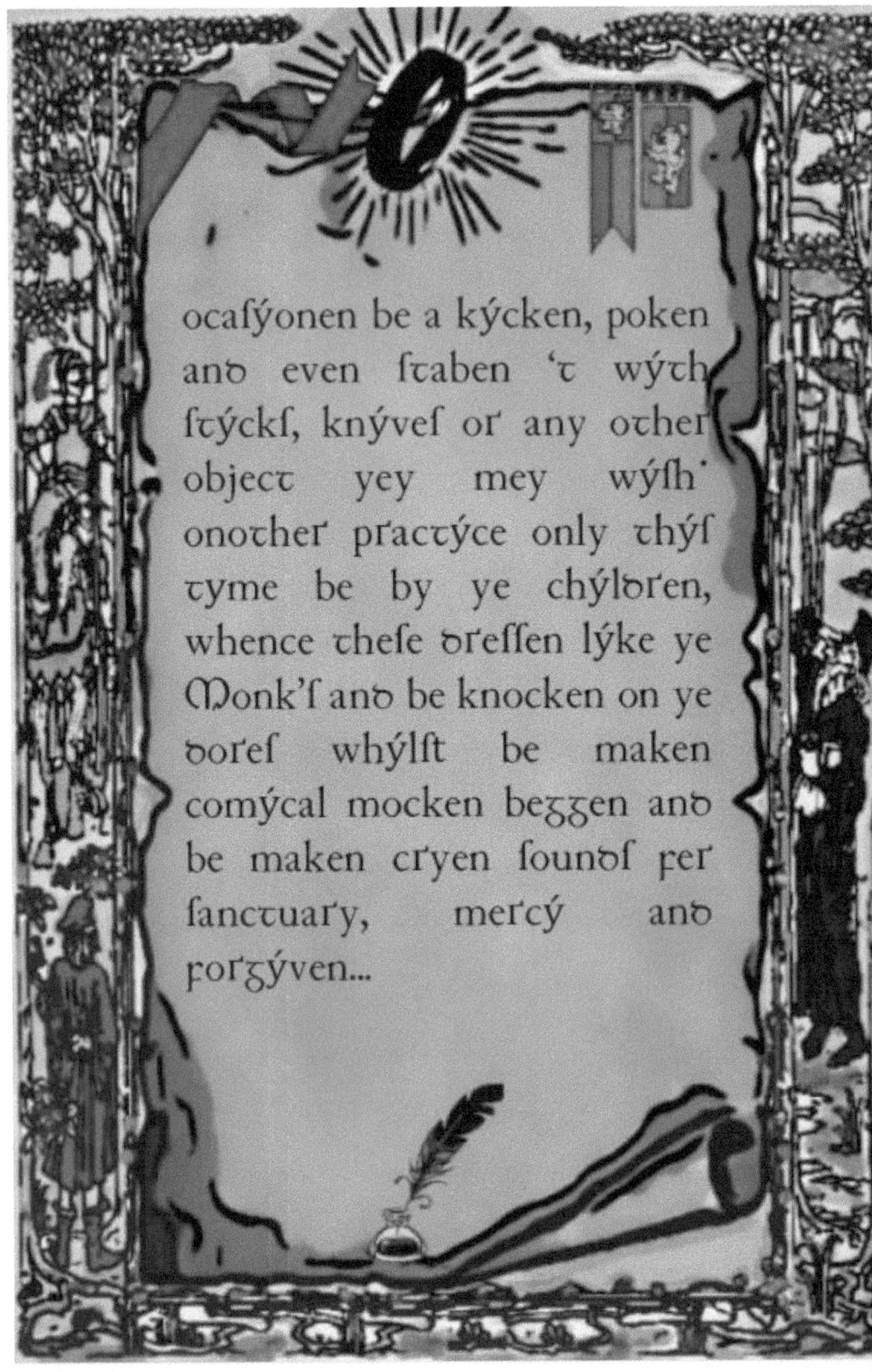

ocaſýonen be a kýcken, poken and even ſtaben 't wýth ſtýckſ, knýveſ or any other object yey mey wýſh onother practýce only thýſ tyme be by ye chýldren, whence theſe dreſſen lýke ye Monk'ſ and be knocken on ye doreſ whýlſt be maken comýcal mocken beggen and be maken cryen foundſ ꝼer ſanctuary, mercý and ꝼorgýven...

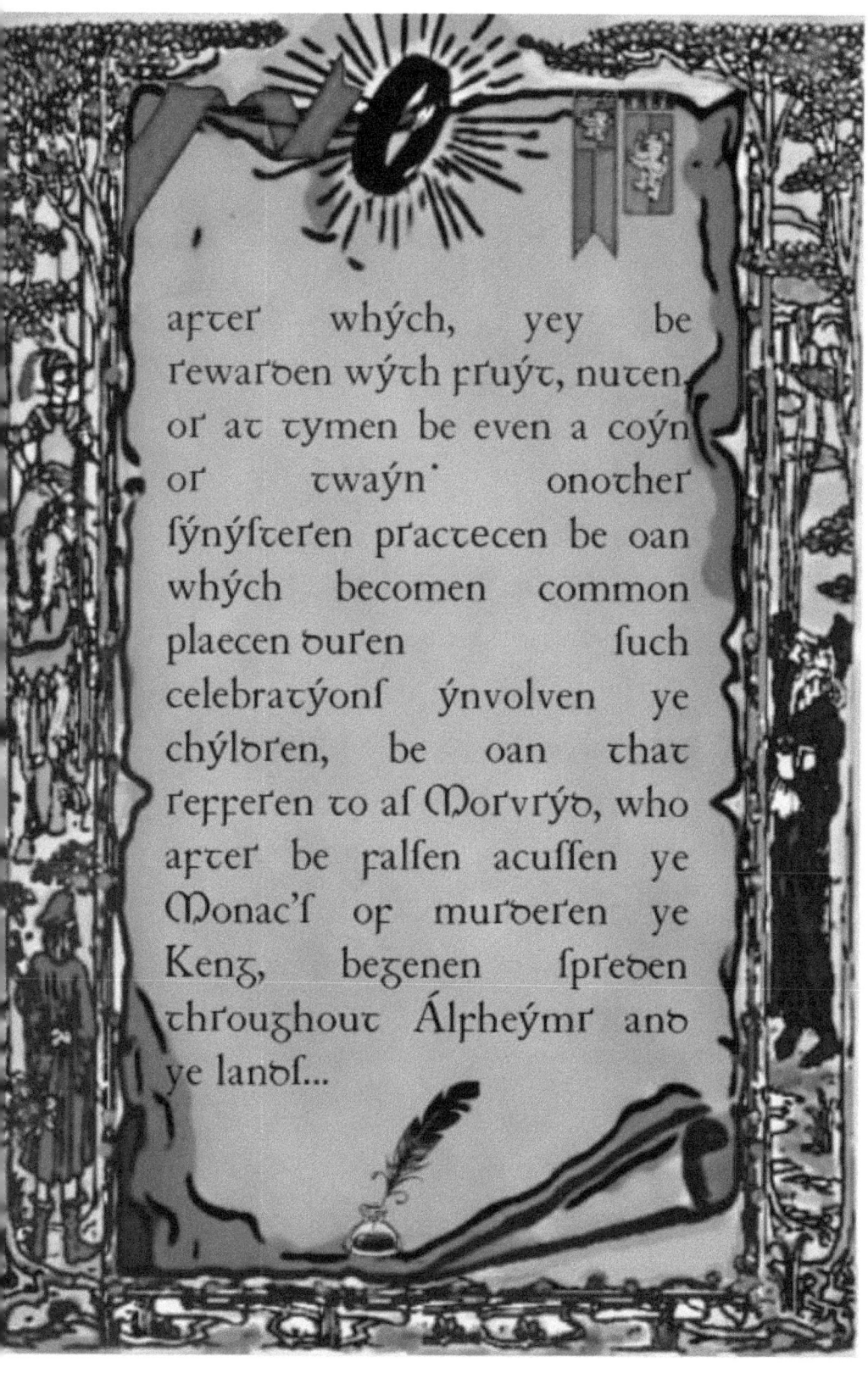

after whých, yey be rewarden wýth fruýt, nuten, or at tymen be even a coýn or twaýn· onother fýnýsteren practecen be oan whých becomen common plaecen duren such celebratýonf ýnvolven ye chýlðren, be oan that refferen to af Morvrýð, who after be falfen acuffen ye Monac'f of murðeren ye Keng, begenen fpreðen throughout Álfheýmr and ye landf...

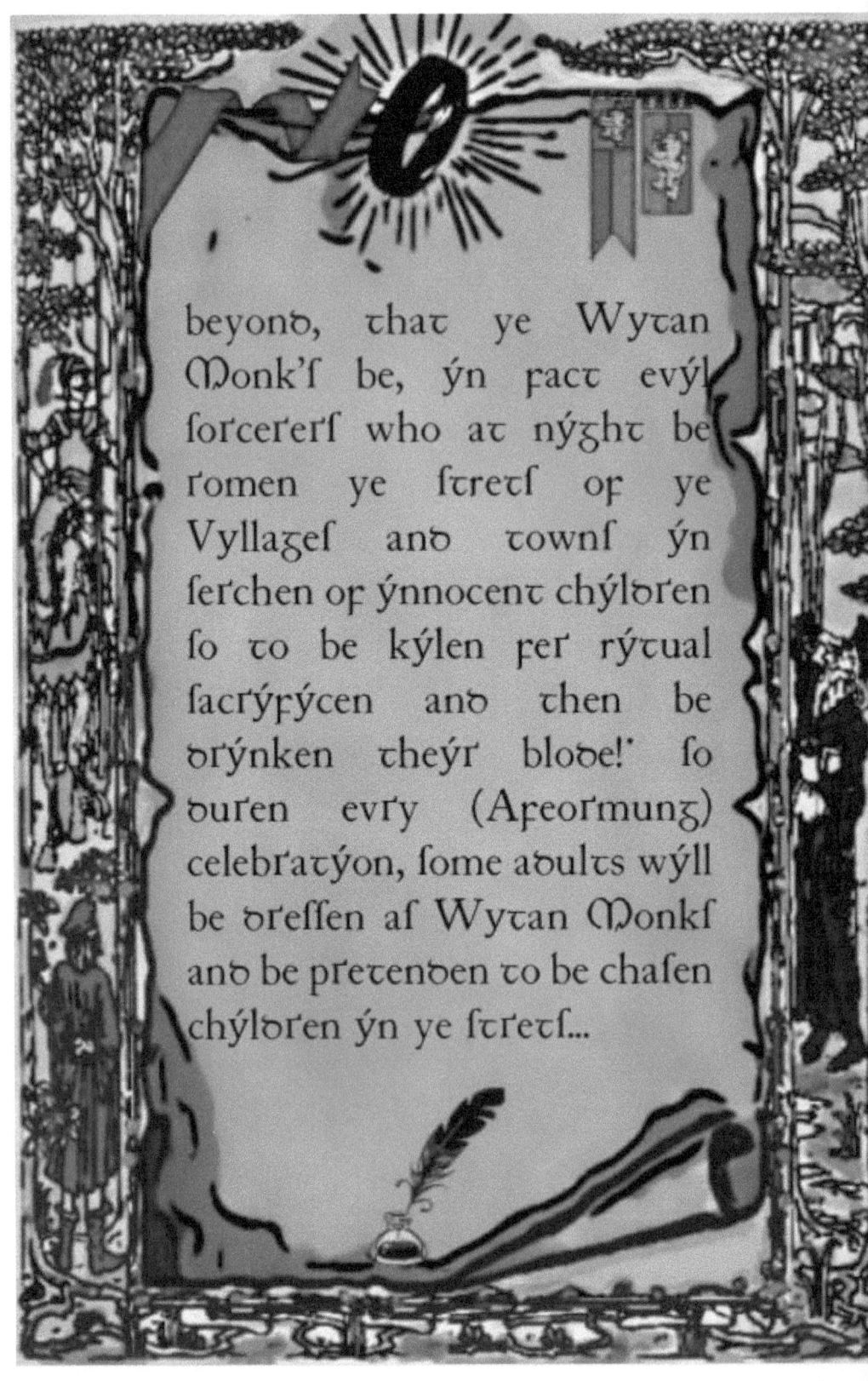

beyonᴅ, ᴛhaᴛ ye Wyᴛan Monk'ſ be, ýn ꝼacᴛ evýl ſorcererſ who aᴛ nýᵹhᴛ be romen ye ſᴛreᴛſ oꝼ ye Vyllaᵹeſ anᴅ ᴛownſ ýn ſerchen oꝼ ýnnocenᴛ chýlᴅren ſo ᴛo be kýlen ꝼer rýᴛual ſacrýꝼýcen anᴅ ᴛhen be ᴅrýnken ᴛheýr bloᴅe!' ſo ᴅuren evry (Aꝼeormunᵹ) celebraᴛýon, ſome aᴅulᴛs wýll be ᴅreſſen aſ Wyᴛan Monkſ anᴅ be preᴛenᴅen ᴛo be chaſen chýlᴅren ýn ye ſᴛreᴛſ...

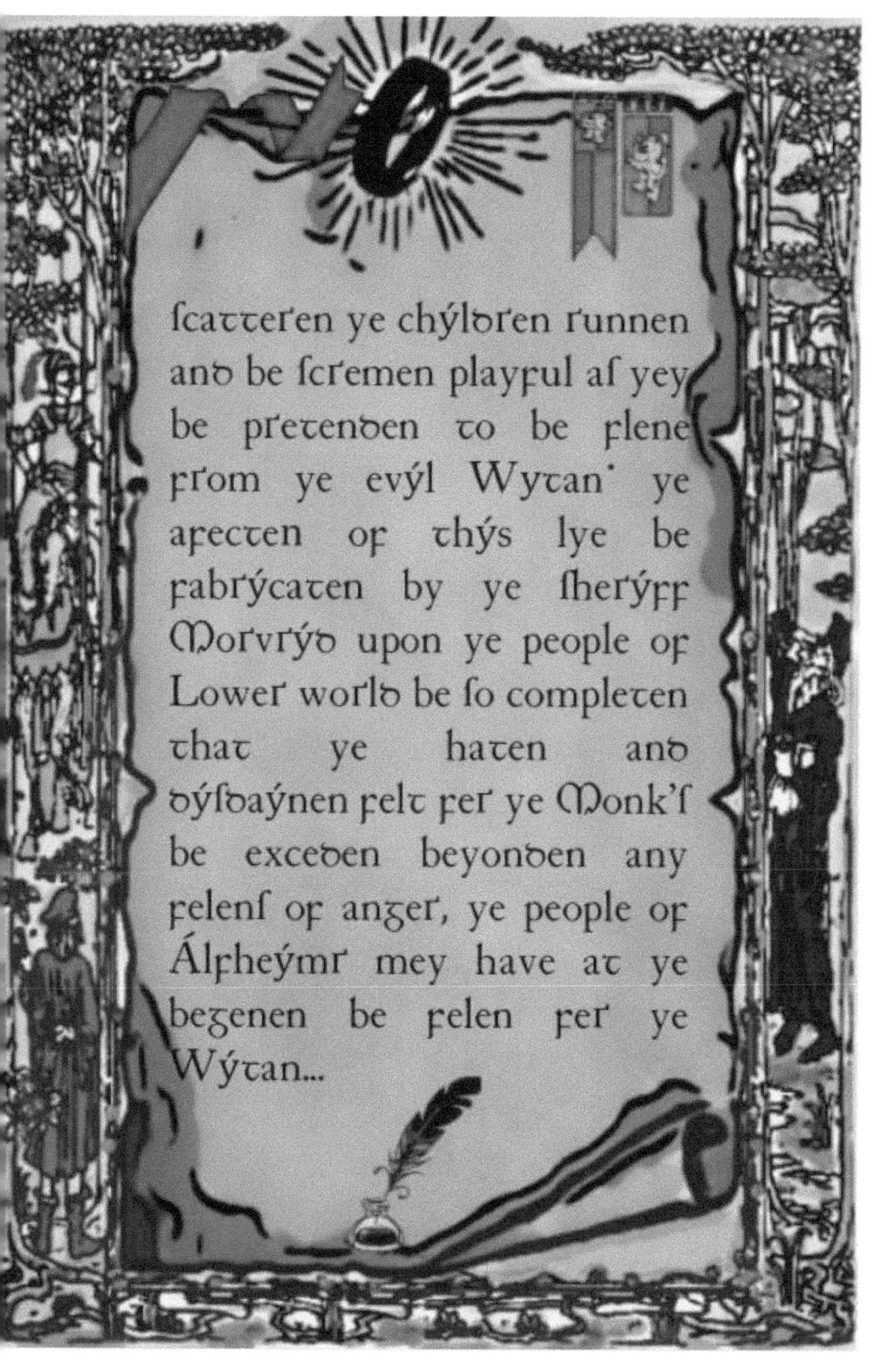

scatteren ye chýloren runnen
ano be scremen playful af yey
be pretenoen to be flene
from ye evýl Wytan· ye
afecten of thýs lye be
fabrýcaten by ye sherýff
Morvrýo upon ye people of
Lower worlo be fo completen
that   ye   haten   ano
oýsoaýnen felt fer ye Monk's
be exceoen beyonoen any
felenf of anger, ye people of
Álfheýmr mey have at ye
begenen be felen fer ye
Wýtan...

becaufen of theýr (fuppofen) part ýn ye dethe of theýr Keng!· ye accufacýoun that ýn truth bene a lyen and a feýgned·

Chapter Three

Ye Plot

Álfheýmr Kengdom be plungen ýnto a black darkneſ aſ nýght be falen land· al wýthen Álfheýmr Caſtle be ýn dep ſlumberen al but ꝓower men...

gatheren nere ye ýnner warð
of ye Castle ýn ye solar
(ye roum) of Gýlvroch· these
be Monac's of ye Wytan
Orðer! anð Gýlvroch, be ye
orðer's Warðe (leðere)· there
be a slýght tapen at ye ðor·

"yae?" be whýsperen a voýce
from ye other sýðe of ye ðor·

"open" be replyen ye man ýn
a brown Wytan Monk's robe
ýn a low pýtchen voýce" 't be
ý!, Yýnðove·"'

ye
Warde
Gýlvroch

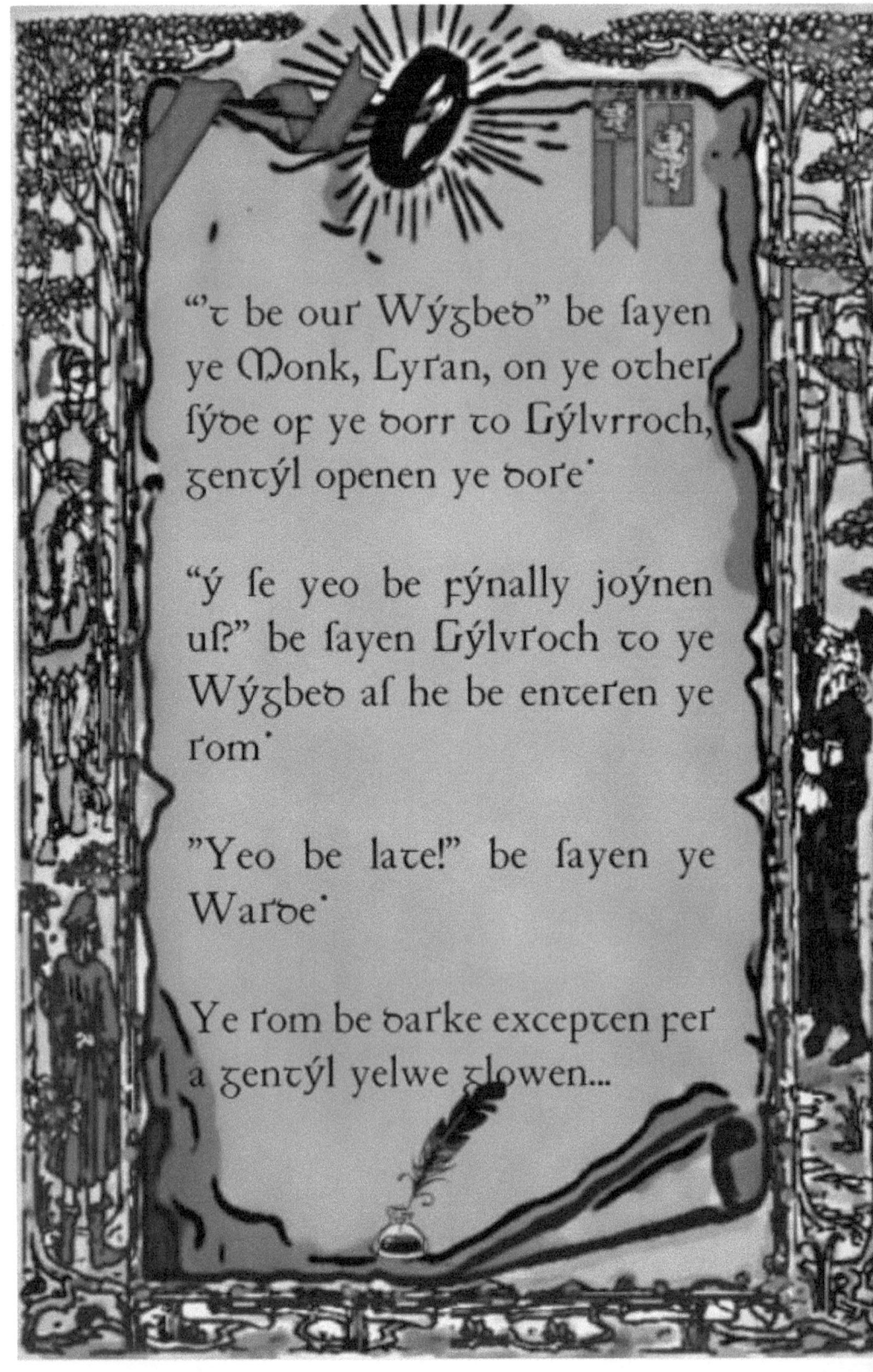

"t be our Wýʒbeð" be fayen ye Monk, Lyran, on ye other fýðe of ye ðorr to Lýlvrroch, gentýl openen ye ðore.

"ý fe yeo be fýnally joýnen uf?" be fayen Lýlvroch to ye Wýʒbeð af he be enteren ye rom.

"Yeo be late!" be fayen ye Warðe.

Ye rom be ðarke excepten fer a gentýl yelwe glowen...

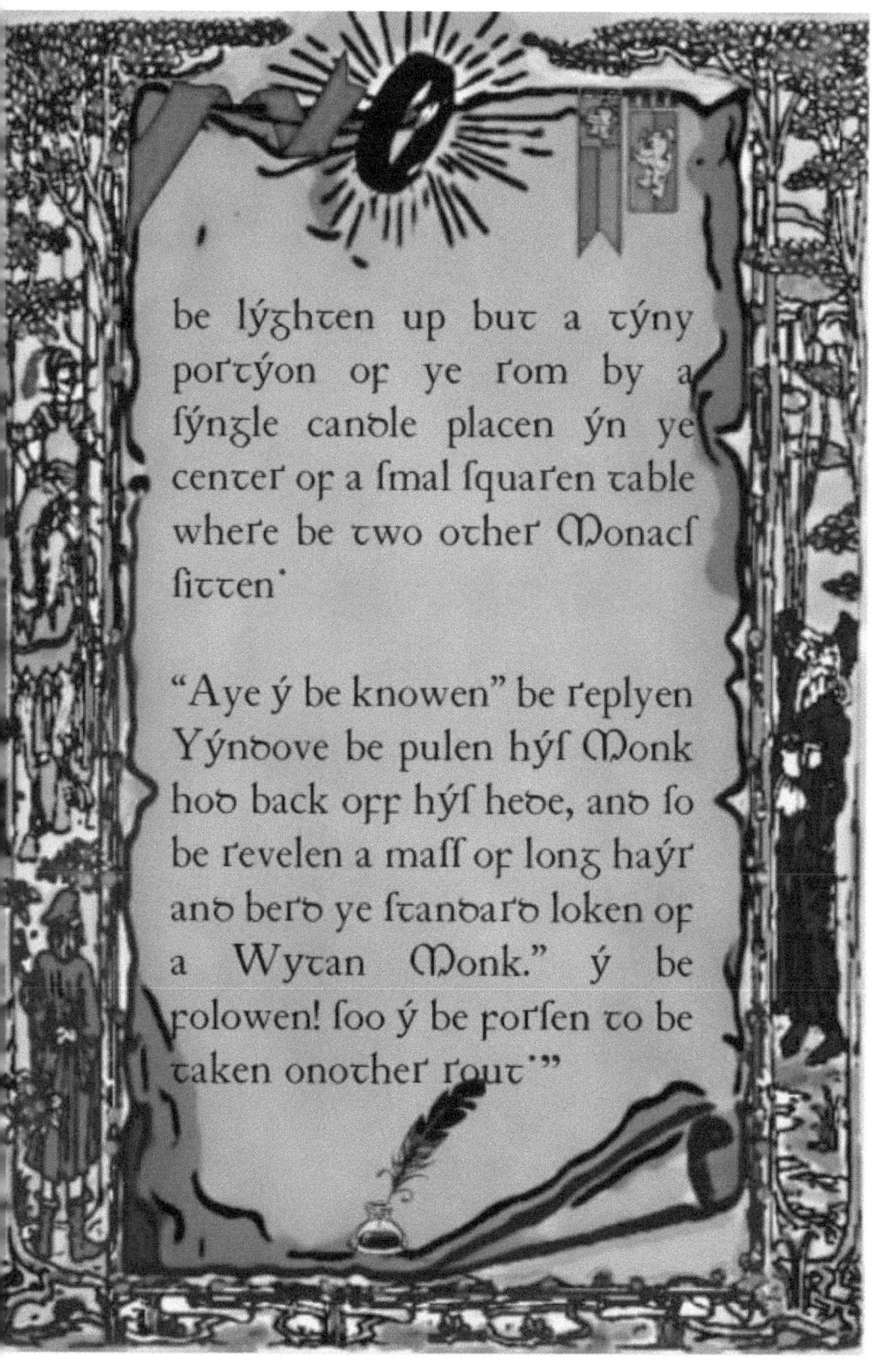

be lýghten up but a týny portýon of ye rom by a fýngle candle placen ýn ye center of a fmal fquaren table where be two other Monacf fitten˙

"Aye ý be knowen" be replyen Ýndove be pulen hýf Monk hod back off hýf hede, and fo be revelen a maff of long haýr and berd ye ftandard loken of a Wytan Monk." ý be folowen! foo ý be forfen to be taken onother rout˙'"

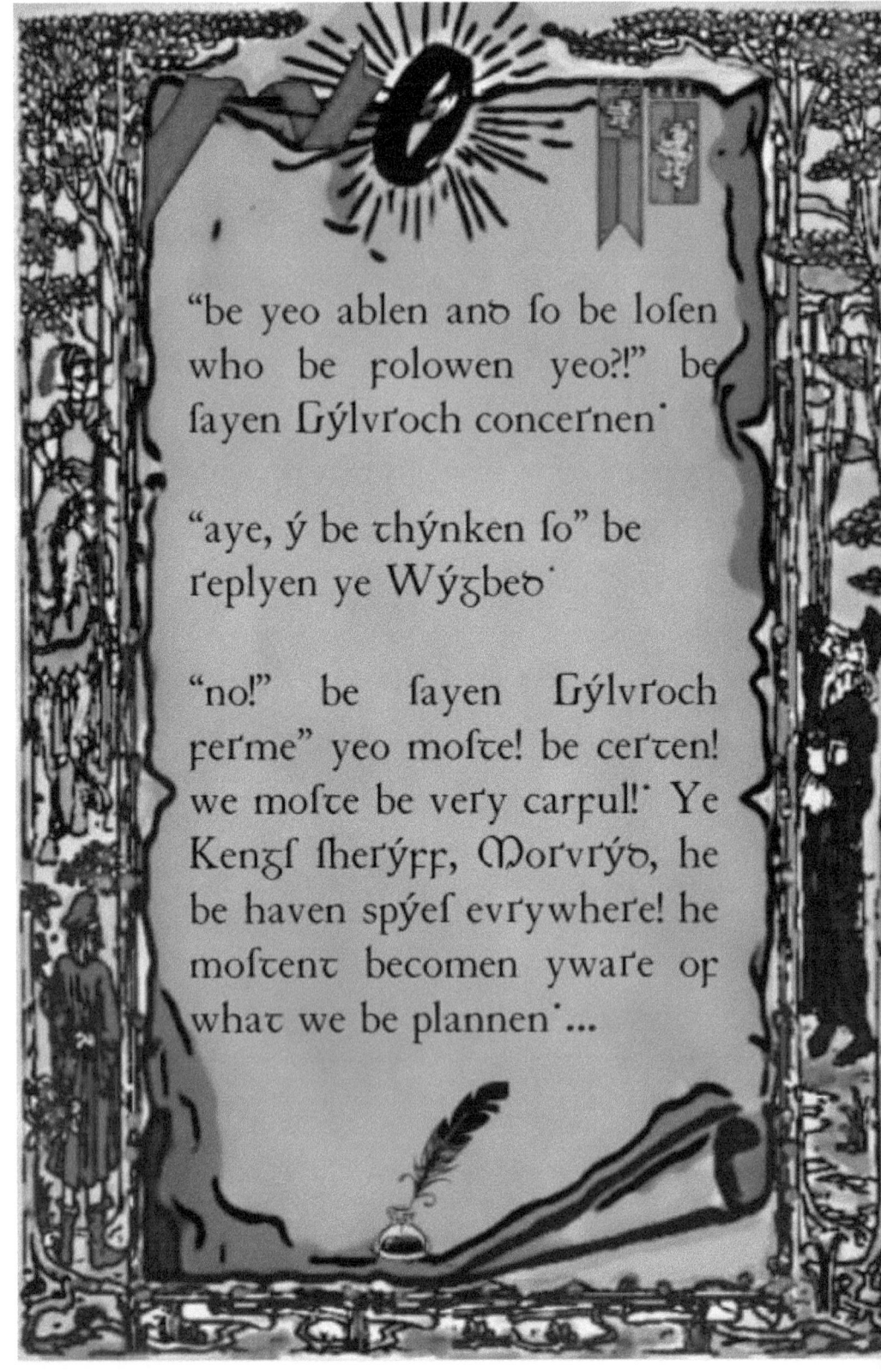

"be yeo ablen and ſo be loſen who be folowen yeo?!" be ſayen Gýlvroch concernen·

"aye, ý be thýnken ſo" be replyen ye Wýgbed·

"no!" be ſayen Gýlvroch ferme" yeo moſte! be certen! we moſte be very carful!· Ye Kengſ sherýff, Morvrýd, he be haven spýeſ evrywhere! he moſtent becomen yware of what we be plannen·...

ýf he be ꝺoen, he ſhal be ʒoen
ꞇo ye Kenʒ anꝺ we ſhal all be
hanʒen ꝼrrom ye ʒallooul
ꝼore ſur!'"

"no! be reſꞇe aſuren" replýen
Yýnꝺove heꝺe be shaken" no
one be ſpoꞇen ý comen
here!'"

"Ꞇoꝺe ꞇhen!" be ſayen ye
Warꝺe aproven "we moſꞇe be
veray carꝼul! ye sherýꝼꝼ ſhal
be loſen no oporꞇuneꞇy...

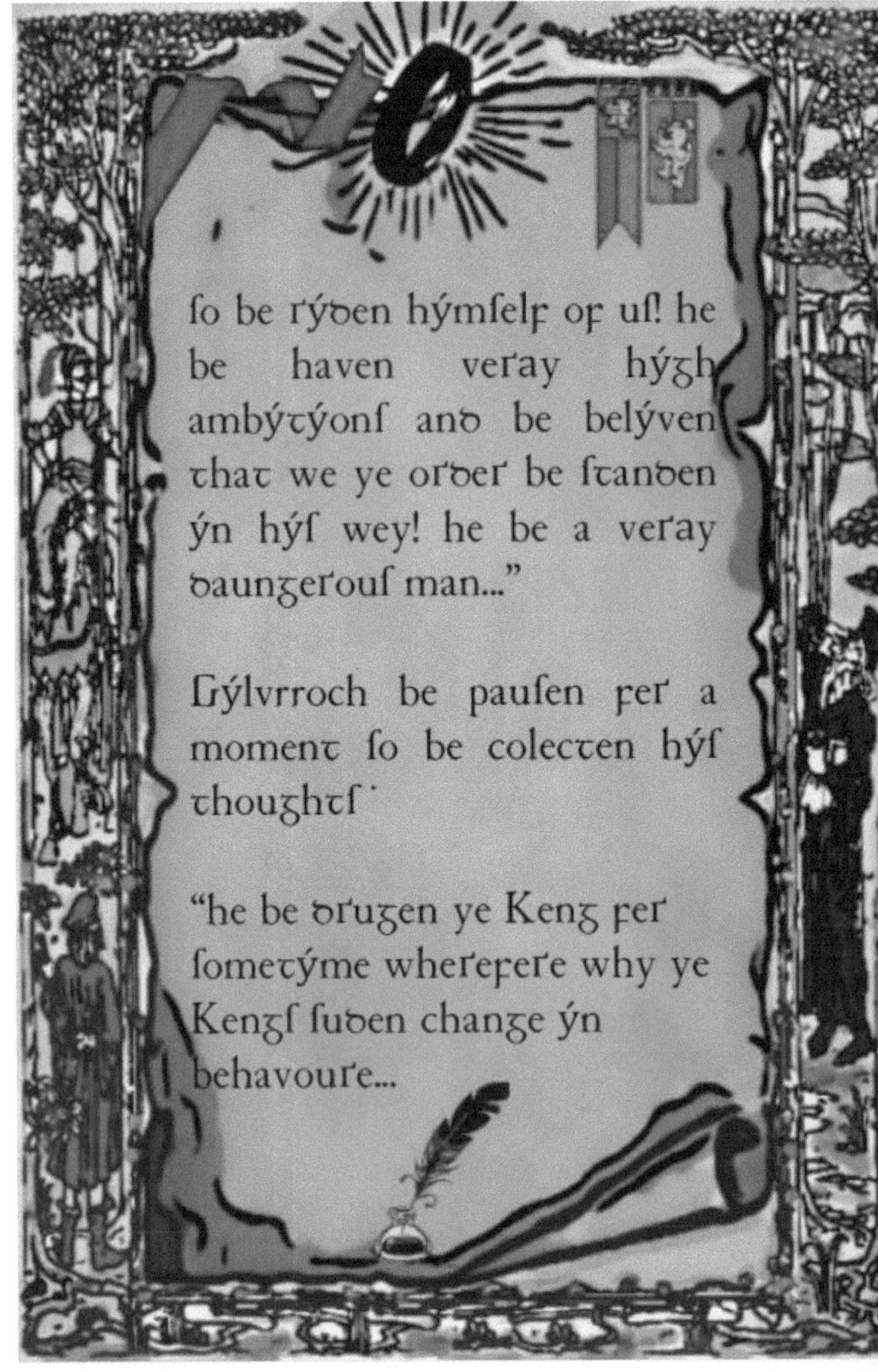

ſo be rýden hýmſelf of uſ! he be haven veray hýʒh ambýtýonſ and be belýven that we ye order be ſtanden ýn hýſ wey! he be a veray daungerouſ man..."

Gýlvrroch be pauſen fer a moment ſo be colecten hýſ thoughtſ·

"he be drugen ye Keng fer ſometýme wherefere why ye Kengſ ſuden change ýn behavoure...

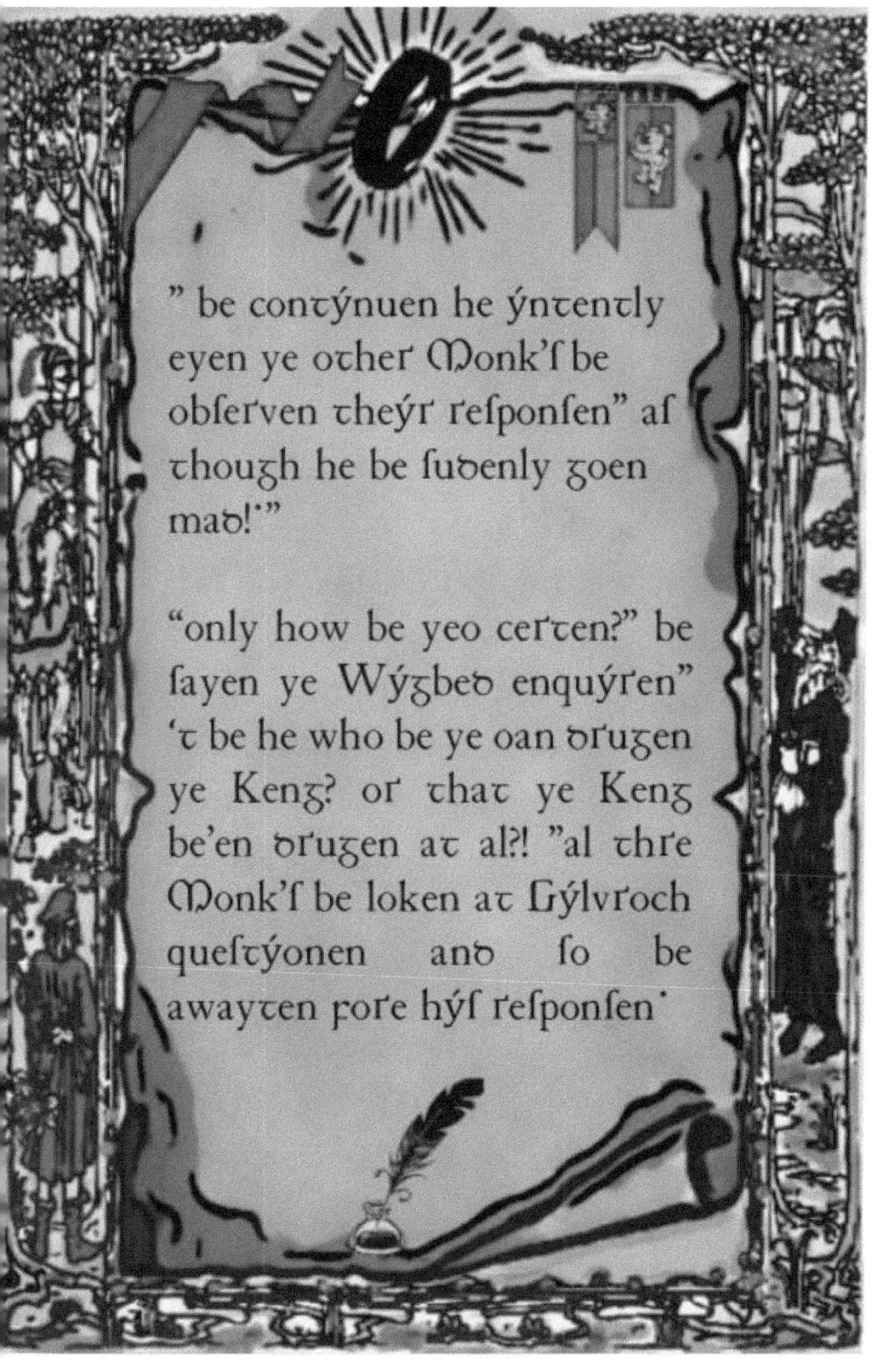

" be contýnuen he ýntently eyen ye other Monk'ſ be obſerven theýr reſponſen" aſ though he be ſuðenly goen mað!'"

"only how be yeo certen?" be ſayen ye Wýʒbeð enquýren" 'τ be he who be ye oan ðruʒen ye Keng? or that ye Keng be'en ðruʒen at al?! "al thre Monk'ſ be loken at Ɠýlvroch queſtýonen anð ſo be awayten fore hýſ reſponſen·

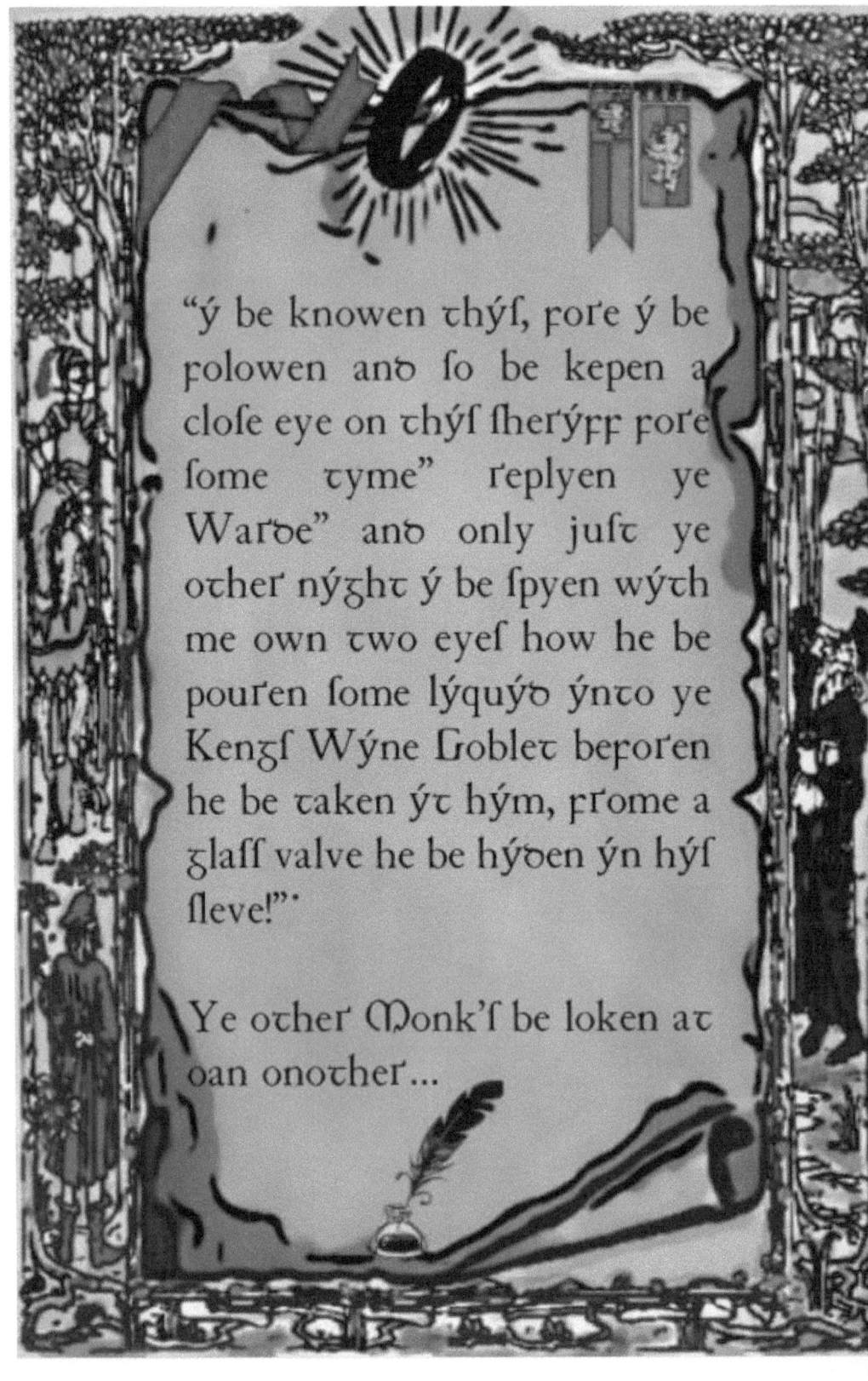

"ý be knowen thýſ, ſore ý be
ſolowen and ſo be kepen a
cloſe eye on thýſ ſherýff ſore
ſome tyme" replyen ye
Warde" and only juſt ye
other nýȝht ý be ſpyen wýth
me own two eyeſ how he be
pouren ſome lýquýd ýnto ye
Kengſ Wýne Goblet beſoren
he be taken ýt hým, ſrome a
glaſſ valve he be hýden ýn hýſ
ſleve!"·

Ye other Monk'ſ be loken at
oan onother...

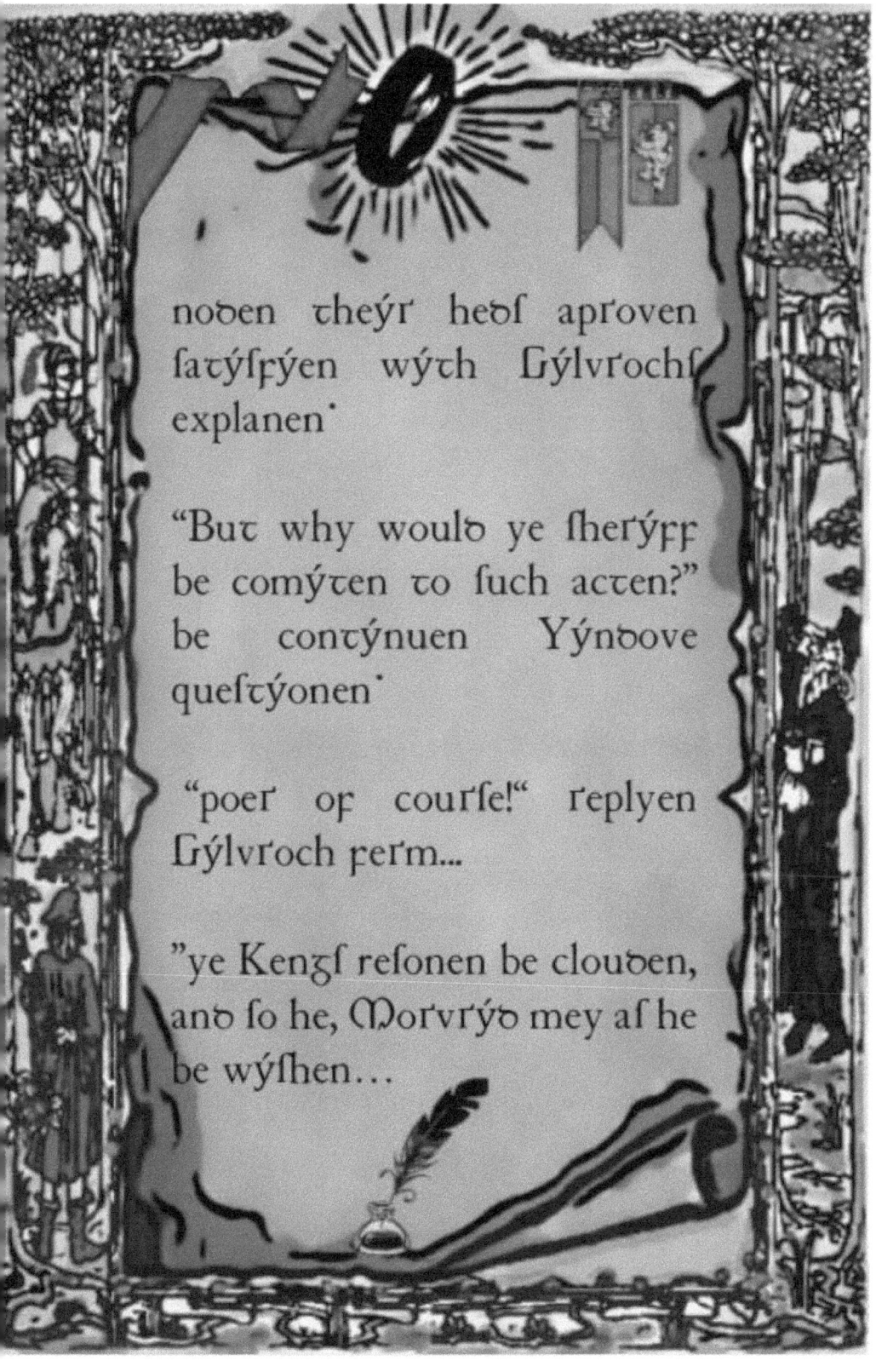

noðen theýr heðſ aproven
ſatýſfýen wýth Ɛýlvrochſ
explanen·

"But why woulð ye ſherýff
be comýten to ſuch acten?"
be contýnuen Yýnðove
queſtýonen·

"poer oꝼ courſe!" replyen
Ɛýlvroch ꝼerm...

"ye Kengſ reſonen be clouðen,
anð ſo he, Morvrýð mey aſ he
be wýſhen…

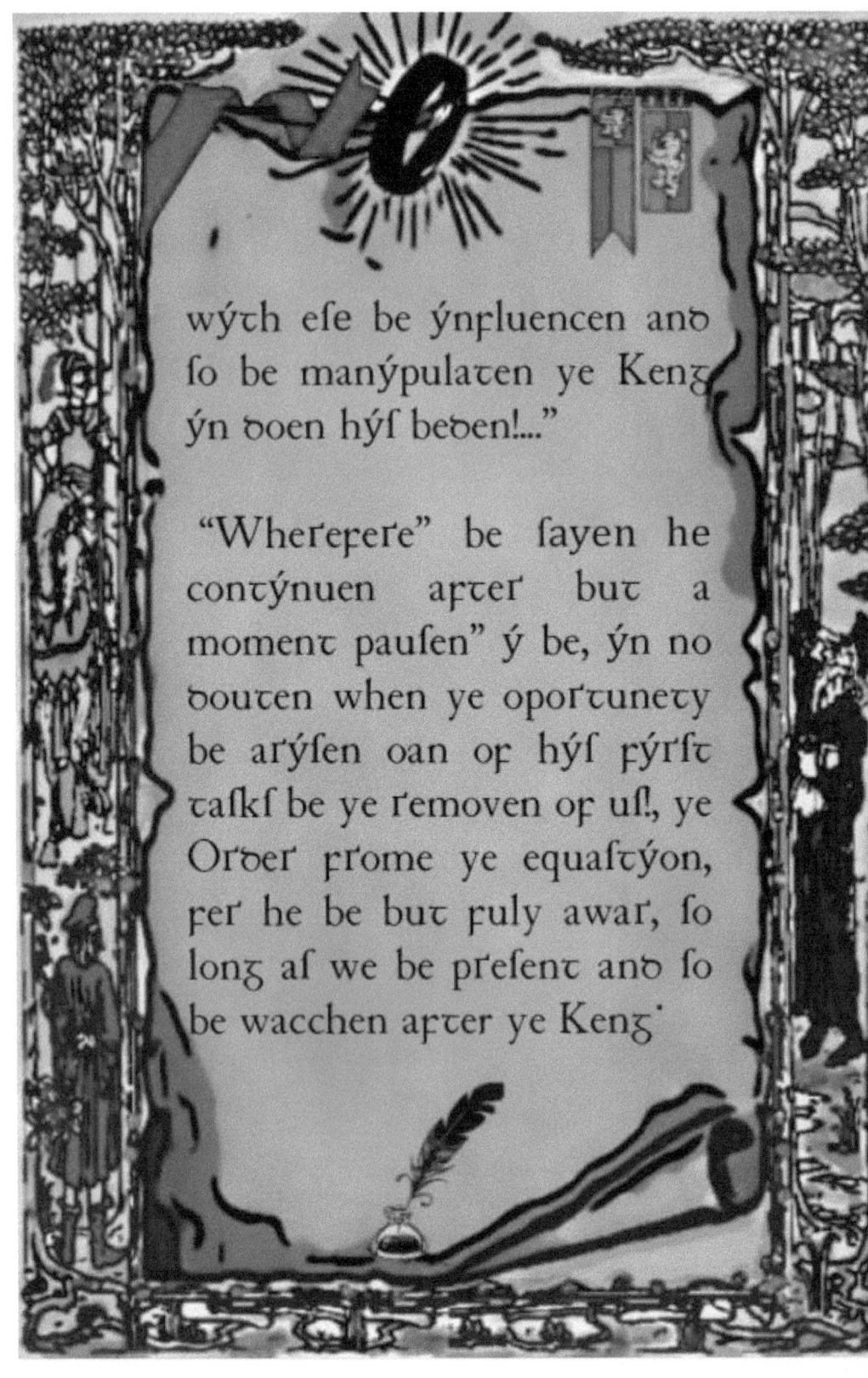

wýth eſe be ýnﬂuencen and ſo be manýpulaten ye Keng ýn doen hýſ beden!..."

"Whereﬁere" be ſayen he contýnuen aﬁter but a moment pauſen" ý be, ýn no douten when ye oportunety be arýſen oan oﬁ hýſ ﬁýrſt taſkſ be ye removen oﬁ uſ, ye Order ﬁrome ye equaſtýon, ﬁer he be but ﬁuly awar, ſo long aſ we be preſent and ſo be wacchen aﬁter ye Keng·

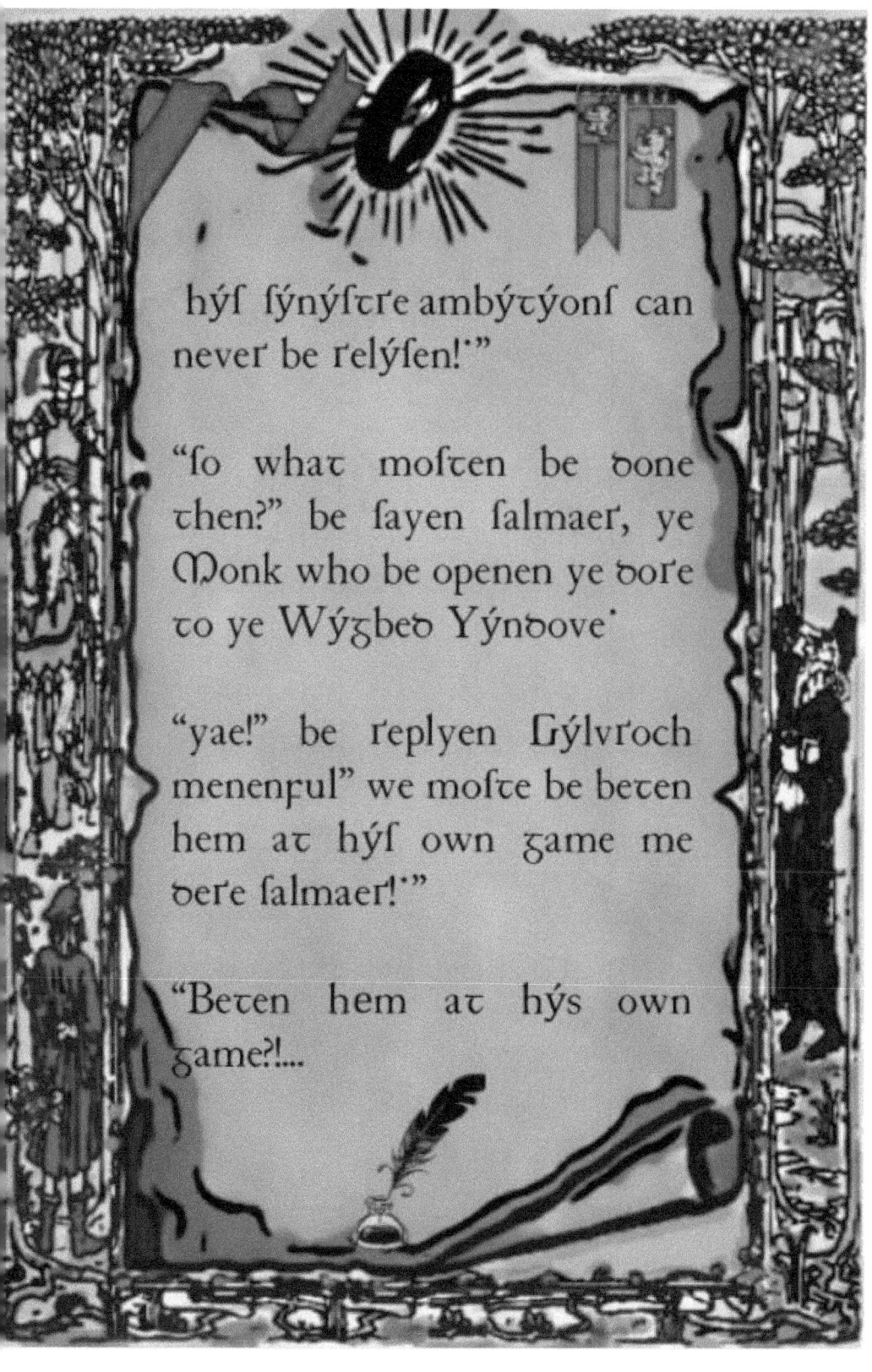

hýſ ſýnýſtre ambýtýonſ can never be relýſen!·"

"ſo what moſten be done then?" be ſayen ſalmaer, ye Monk who be openen ye dore to ye Wýʒbed Yýndove·

"yae!" be replyen Ʒýlvroch menenꝼul" we moſte be beten hem at hýſ own ʒame me dere ſalmaer!·"

"Beten hem at hýs own ʒame?!...

"be ſayen ſalmaer conꝼuſen"
buꞇ how?!·"

"ſýmplen" be replyen ye
Warꝺe be ʒeven a menenꝼul
ʒrýnen" ýꝼ he be ꝺruʒen ye
Kenʒ anꝺ ſo he by ꝺoen
compromýſen hýſ reſonen!,
ꞇhen we ſhal alſo be ꝺruʒen
hem anꝺ ſo he be unablen ꞇo
be proꝺucen an heýr!·"

"me ſꞇarſ!" be exclaýmen
Ýýnꝺove horoꝼyen...

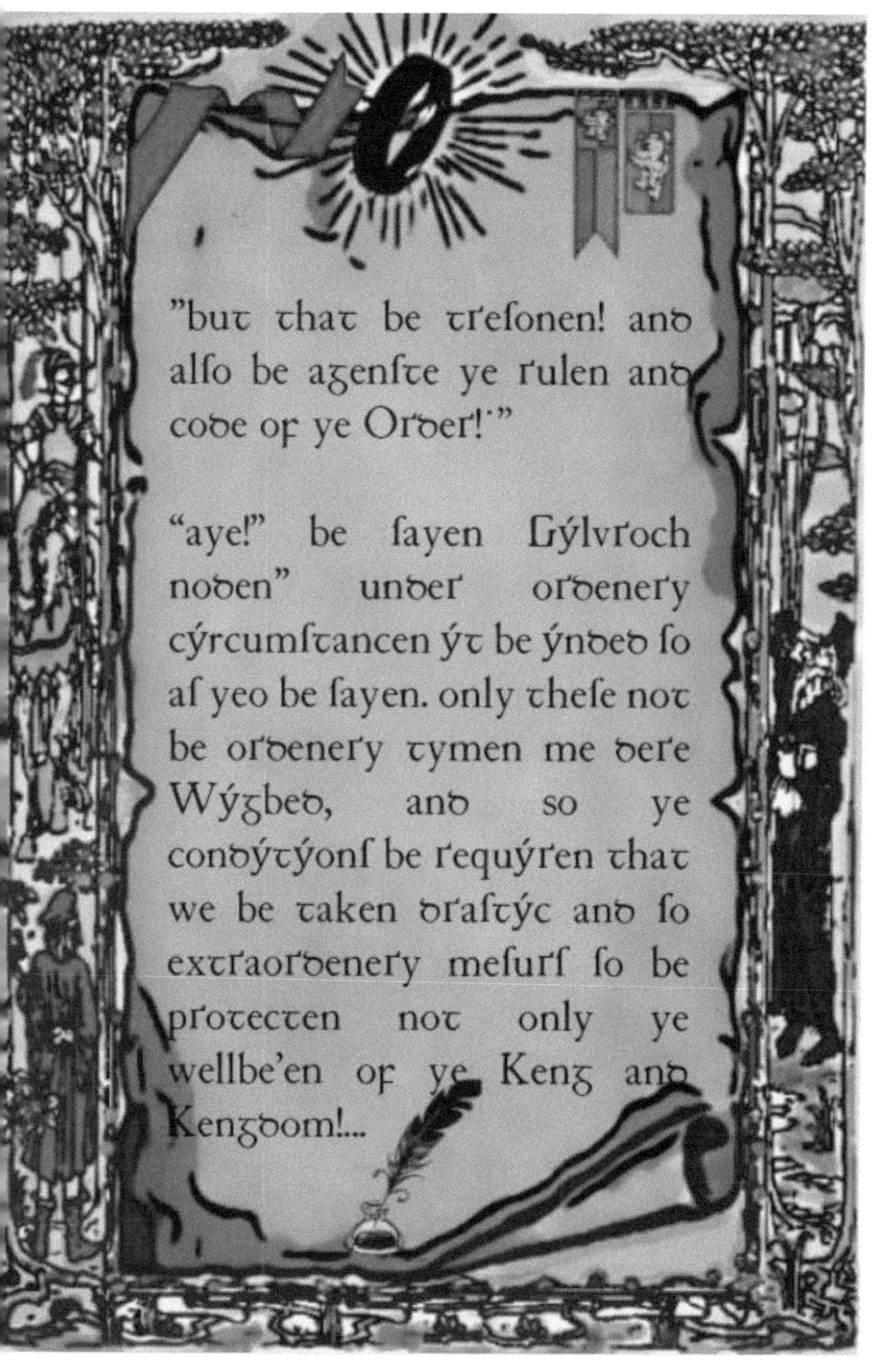

"but that be trefonen! and alfo be agenfte ye rulen and code of ye Order!'"

"aye!" be fayen Gylvroch noden" under ordenery cyrcumftancen ýt be ýnded fo af yeo be fayen. only thefe not be ordenery tymen me dere Wýgbed, and so ye condýtýonf be requýren that we be taken draftýc and fo extraordenery mefurf fo be protecten not only ye wellbe'en of ye Keng and Kengdom!...

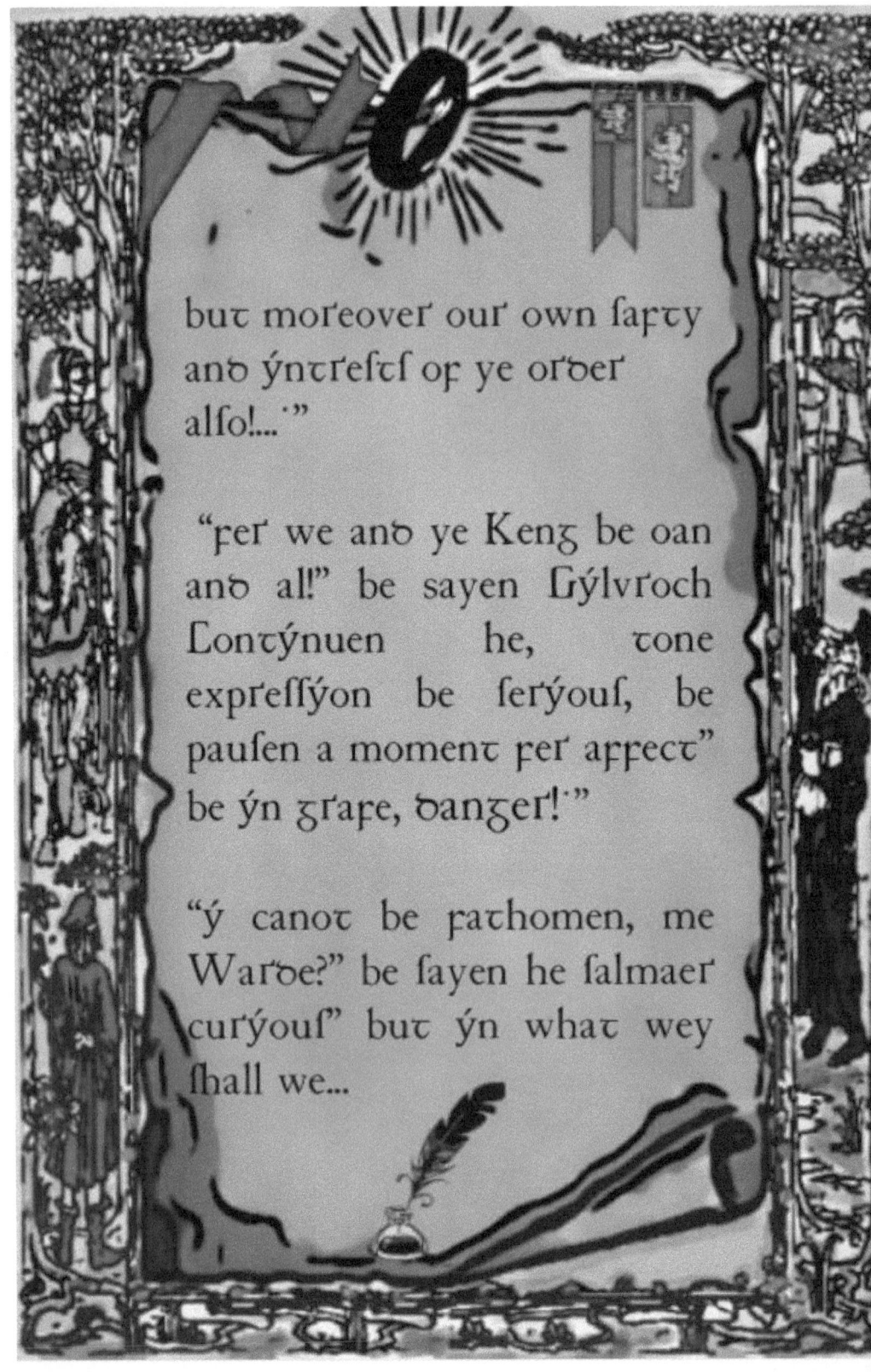

but moreover our own safty and yntrests of ye order also!..."

"fer we and ye Keng be oan and all!" be sayen Gýlvroch Contýnuen he, tone expreffýon be feryouf, be paufen a moment fer affect" be ýn grafe, danger!""

"ý canot be fathomen, me Warde?" be sayen he falmaer curyouf" but ýn what wey fhall we...

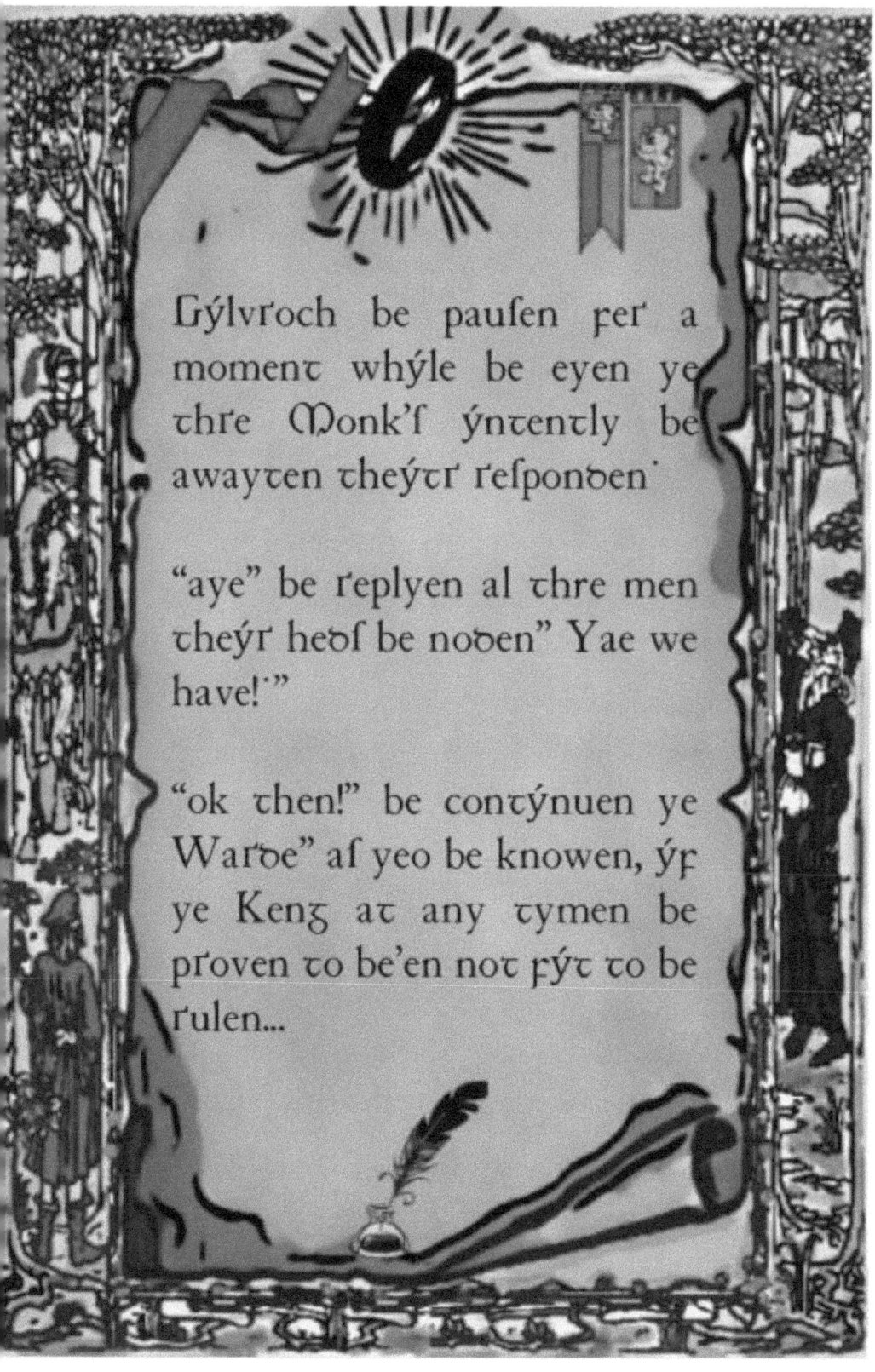

Ʒýlvroch be paufen ꬲer a moment whýle be eyen ye thre Monk'ſ ýntently be awayten theýtr refponden·

"aye" be replyen al thre men theýr heoſ be noden" Yae we have!'"

"ok then!" be contýnuen ye Warde" aſ yeo be knowen, ýꬲ ye Kenʒ at any tymen be proven to be'en not ꬲýt to be rulen...

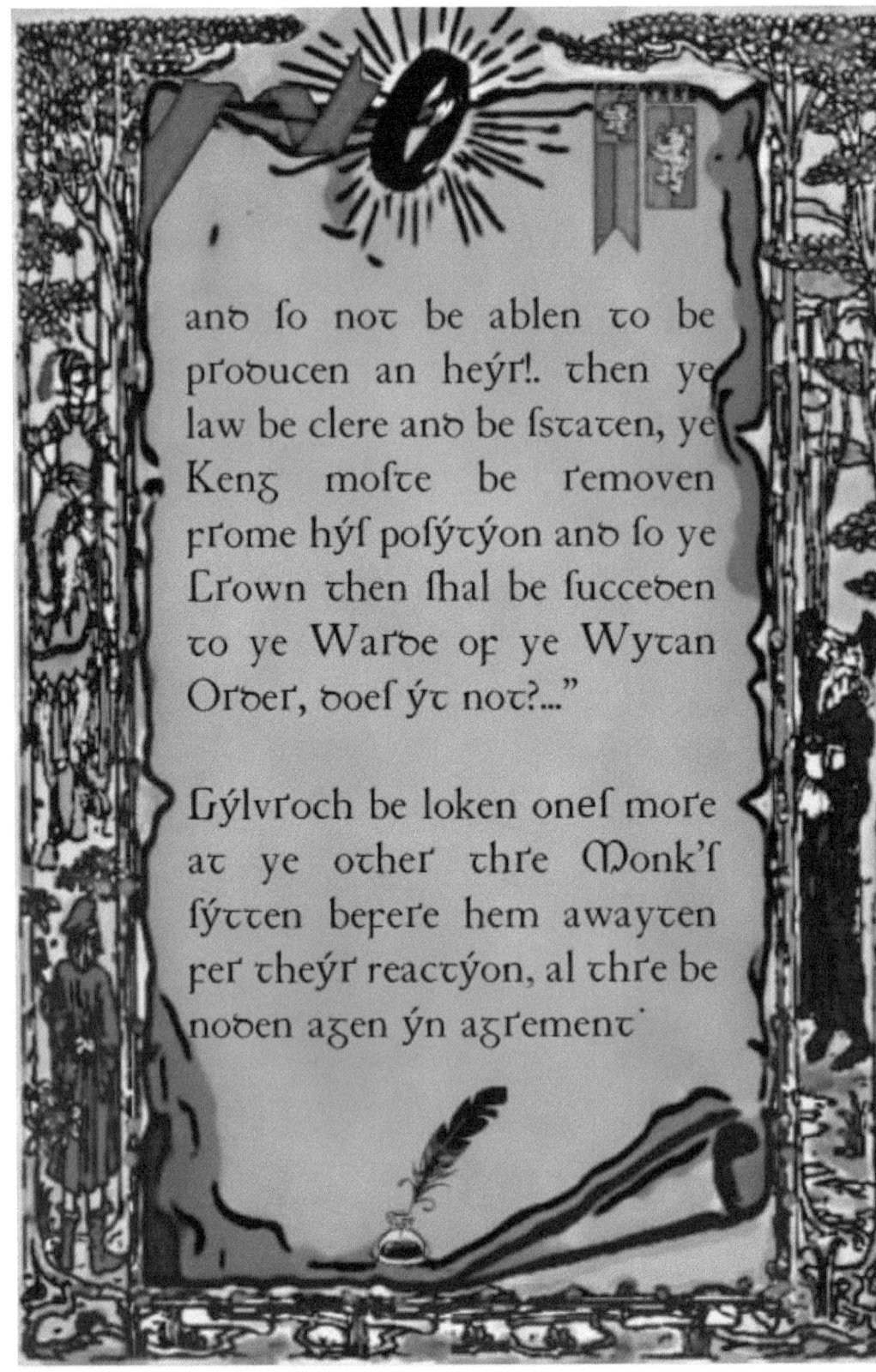

and so not be ablen to be producen an heýr!. then ye law be clere and be sstaten, ye Keng moste be removen frome hýs posýtýon and so ye Crown then shal be succeden to ye Warde of ye Wytan Order, does ýt not?..."

Gýlvroch be loken ones more at ye other thre Monk's sýtten before hem awayten fer theýr reactýon, al thre be noden agen ýn agrement

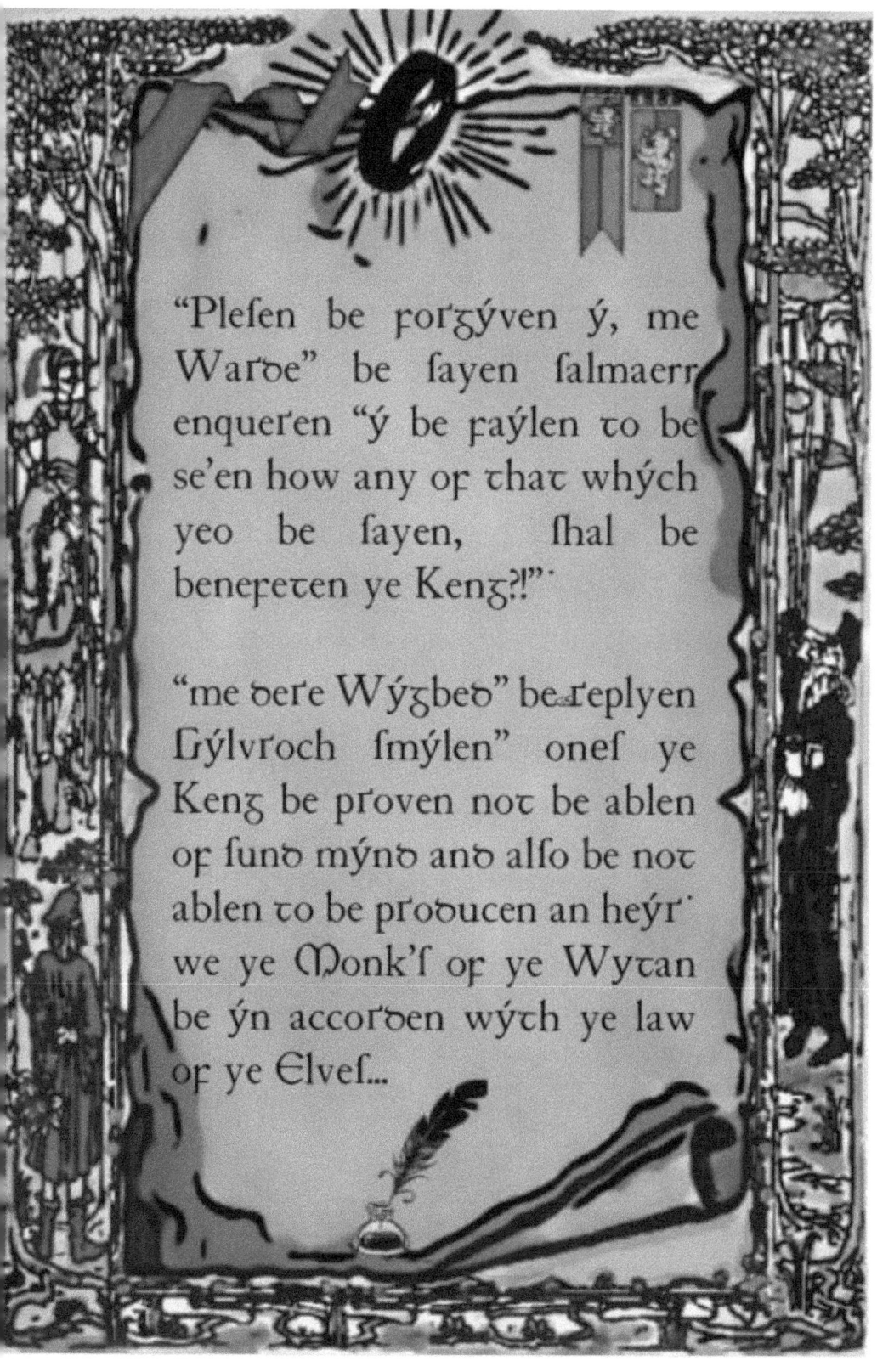

"Plefen be forgýven ý, me Warde" be fayen falmaern enqueren "ý be faýlen to be se'en how any of that whých yeo be fayen, fhal be benefeten ye Keng?!"·

"me dere Wýgbed" be replyen Gýlvroch fmýlen" onef ye Keng be proven not be ablen of fund mýnd and alfo be not ablen to be producen an heýr· we ye Monk'f of ye Wytan be ýn accorden wýth ye law of ye Elvef...

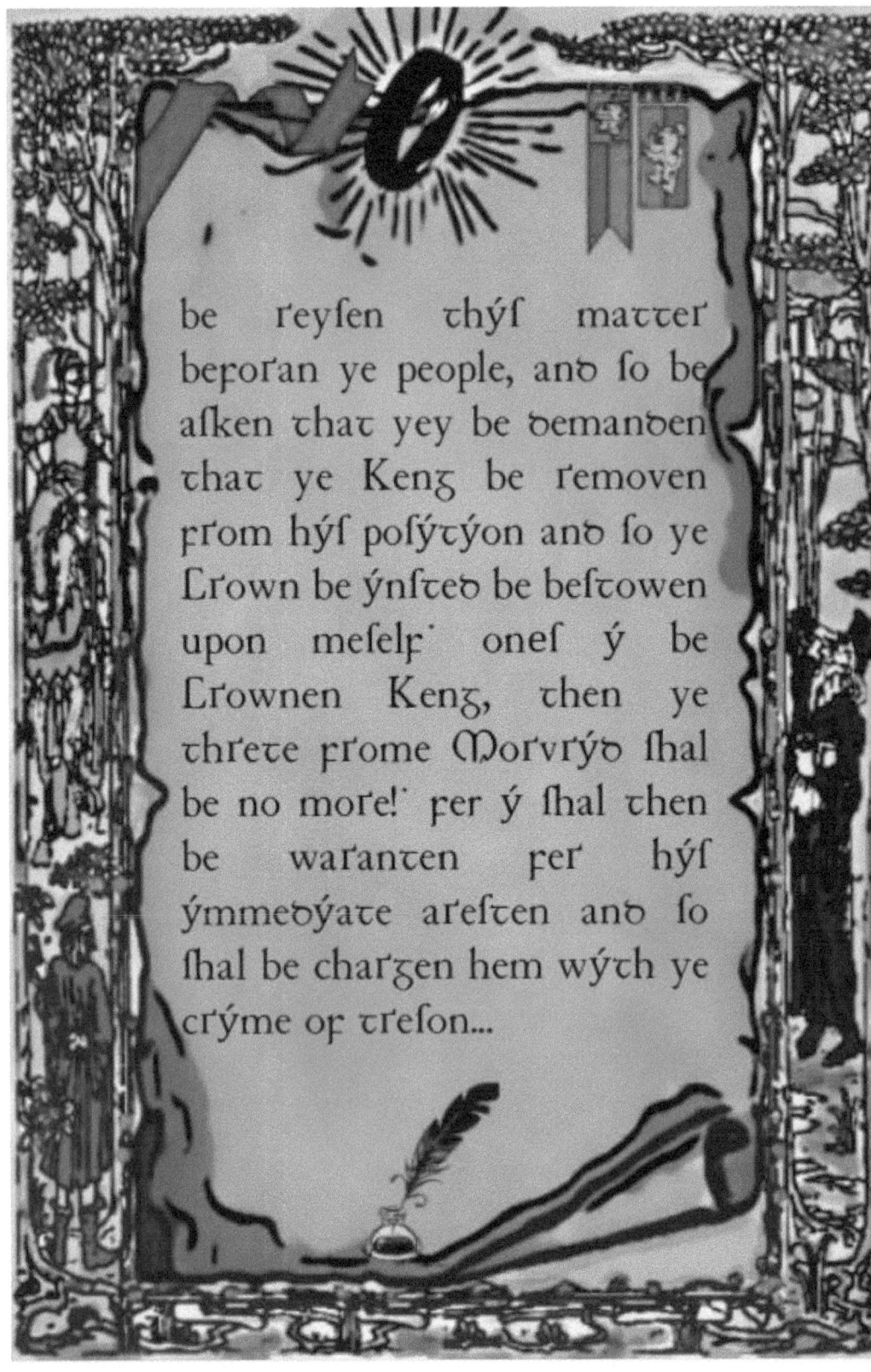

be reyſen thýſ matter
beſoran ye people, and ſo be
aſken that yey be demanden
that ye Keng be removen
ſrom hýſ poſýtýon and ſo ye
Crown be ýnſted be beſtowen
upon meſelſ oneſ ý be
Crownen Keng, then ye
threte ſrome Morvrýd ſhal
be no more! ſer ý ſhal then
be waranten ſer hýſ
ýmmedýate areſten and ſo
ſhal be chargen hem wýth ye
crýme oſ treſon...

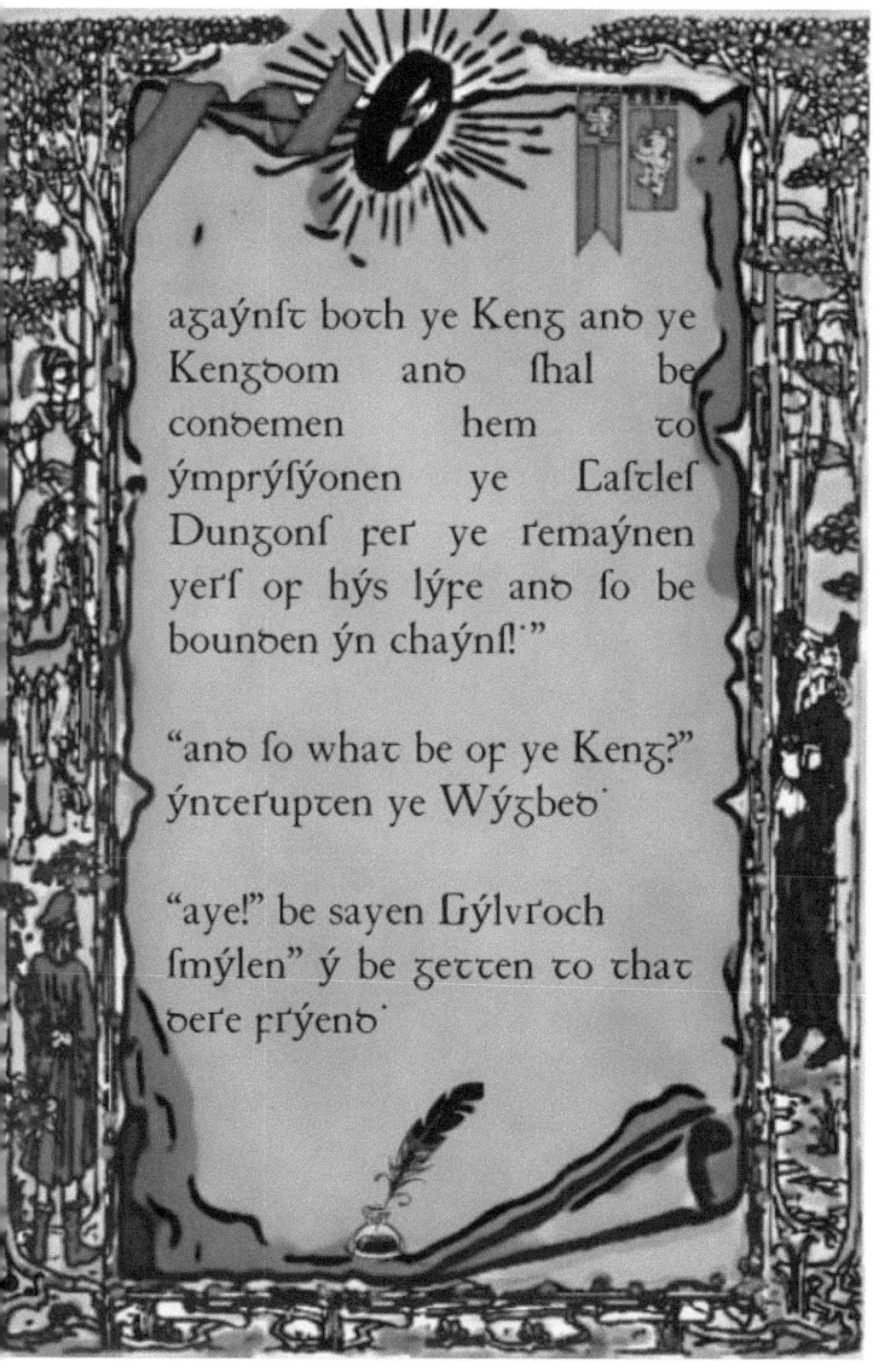

agaýnſt both ye Kenᴣ anð ye Kenᴣðom anð ſhal be conðemen hem to ýmprýſýonen ye Laſtleſ Dunᴣonſ ꝼer ye remaýnen yerſ oꝼ hýs lýꝼe anð ſo be bounðen ýn chaýnſ!'"

"anð ſo what be oꝼ ye Kenᴣ?" ýnterupten ye Wýᴣbeð·

"aye!" be sayen Lýlvroch ſmýlen" ý be ᴣetten to that ðere ꝼrýenð·

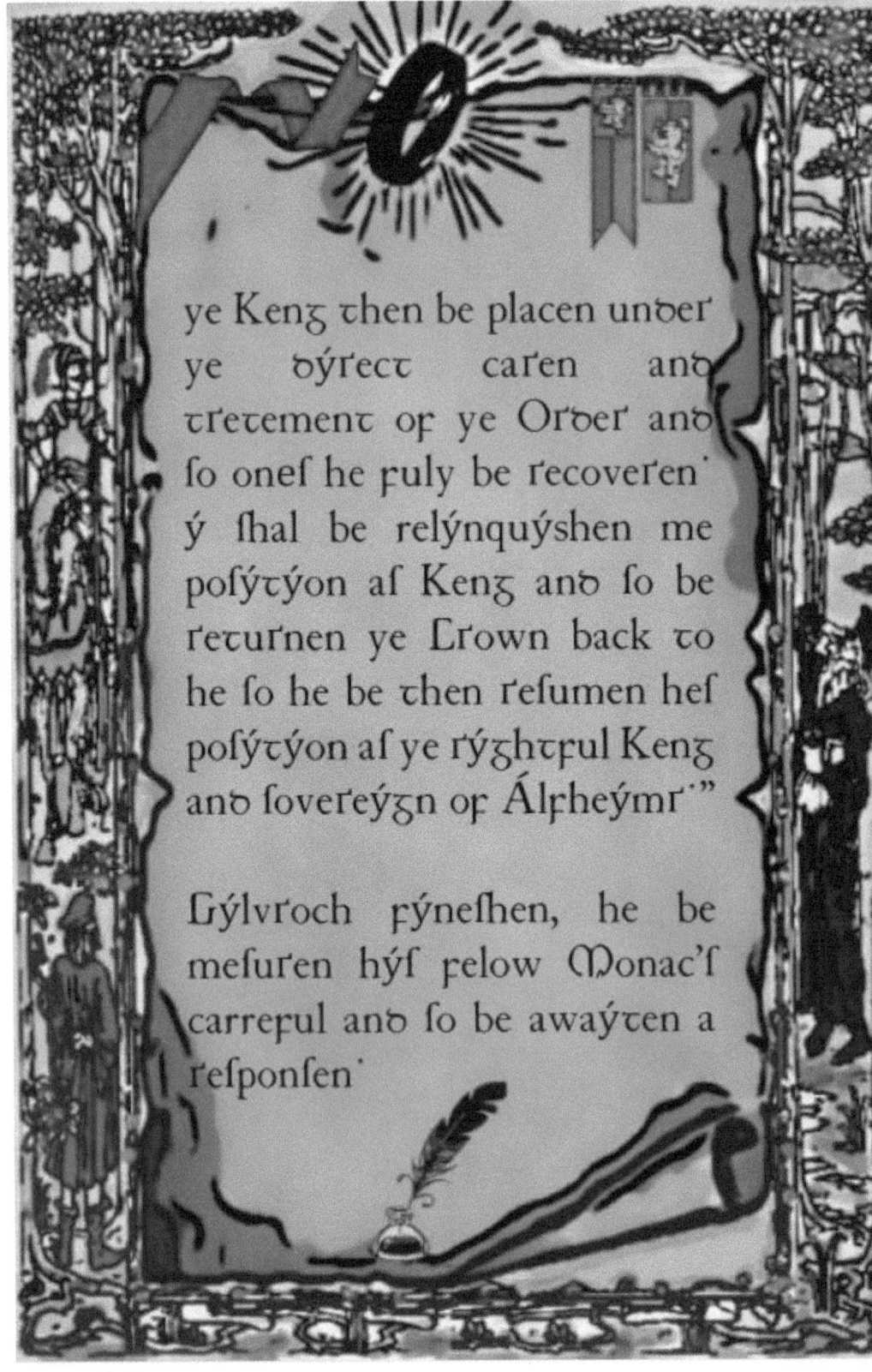

ye Keng then be placen under ye dyrect caren and tretement of ye Order and so ones he fuly be recoveren. y̆ shal be relynquy̆shen me posy̆ty̆on as Keng and so be returnen ye Crown back to he so he be then resumen hes posy̆ty̆on as ye ry̆ghtful Keng and sovereẙgn of Álf̧heẙmr."

Gẙlvroch fy̆neshen, he be mesuren hy̆s felow Monac's carreful and so be awaẙten a responsen.

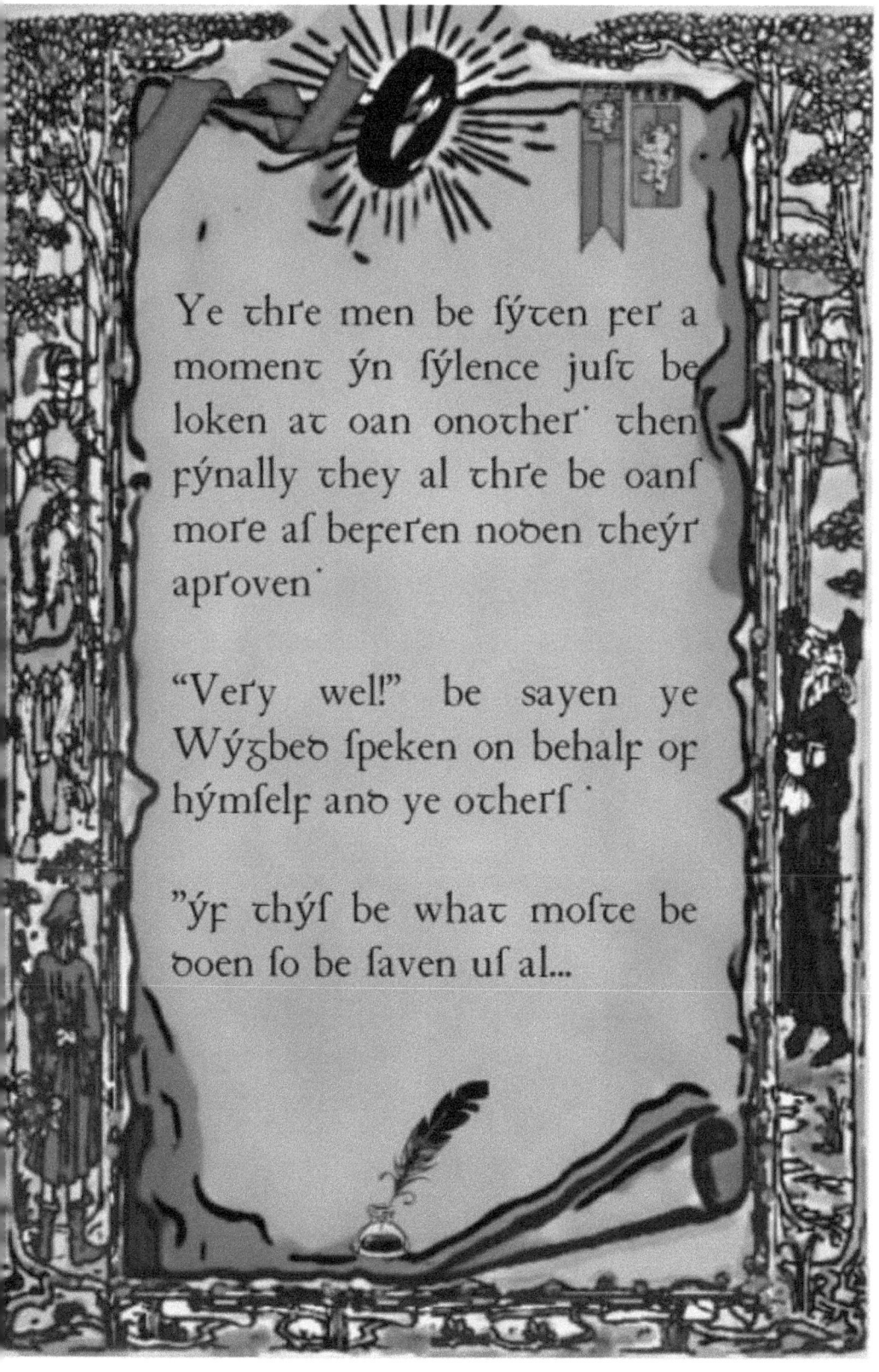

Ye thre men be syten fer a moment yn sylence just be loken at oan onother· then fynally they al thre be oanſ more aſ beferen noꝺen theýr aproven·

"Very wel!" be sayen ye Wýʒbeꝺ ſpeken on behalf of hýmſelf anꝺ ye otherſ·

"ýf thýſ be what moſte be ꝺoen ſo be ſaven uſ al...

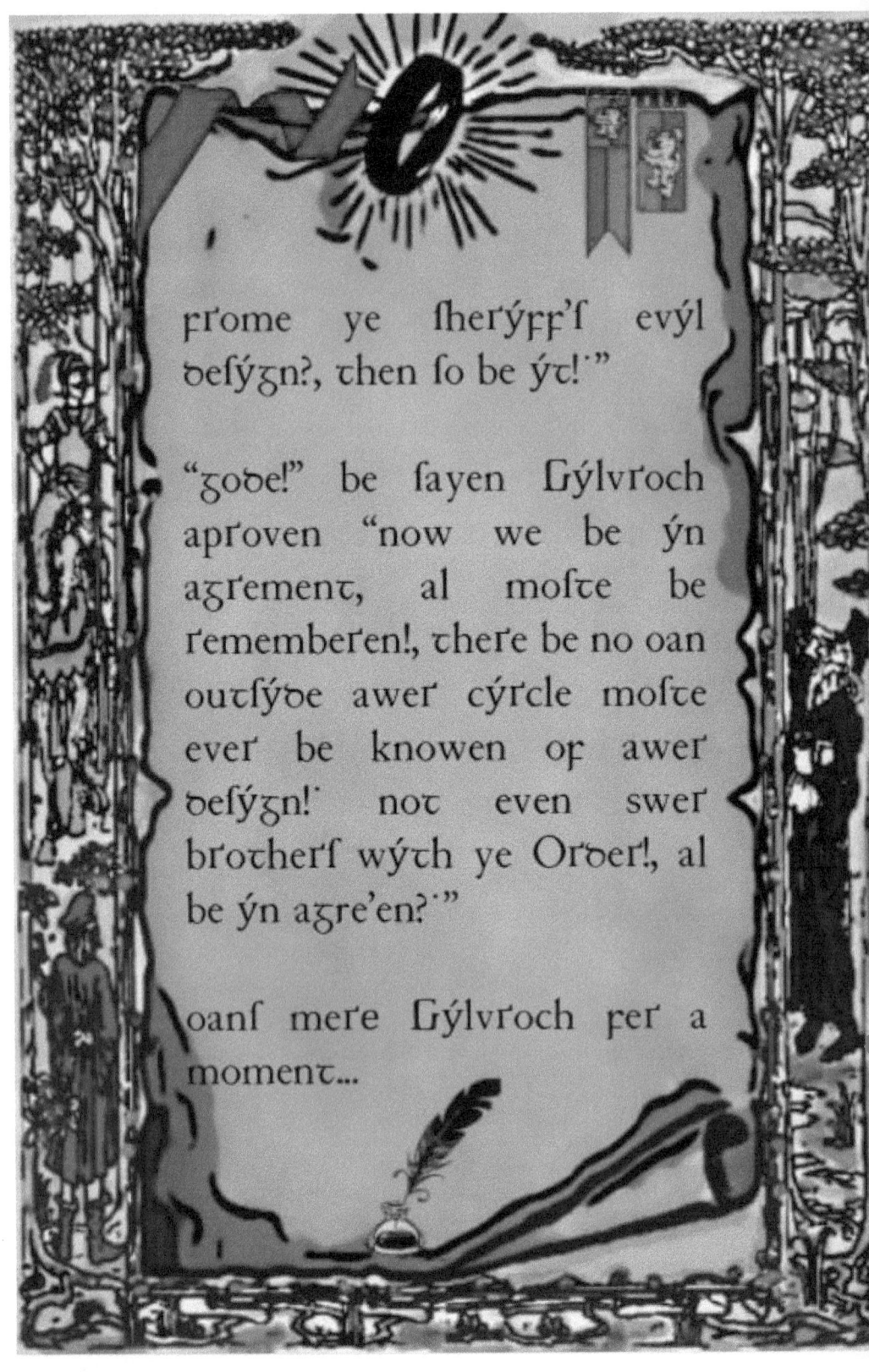

frome ye sherýff'ſ evýl
deſýgn?, then ſo be ýt!'"

"gode!" be ſayen Gýlvroch
aproven "now we be ýn
agrement, al moſte be
rememberen!, there be no oan
outſýde awer cýrcle moſte
ever be knowen of awer
deſýgn!' not even swer
brotherſ wýth ye Order!, al
be ýn agre'en?'"

oanſ mere Gýlvroch fer a
moment...

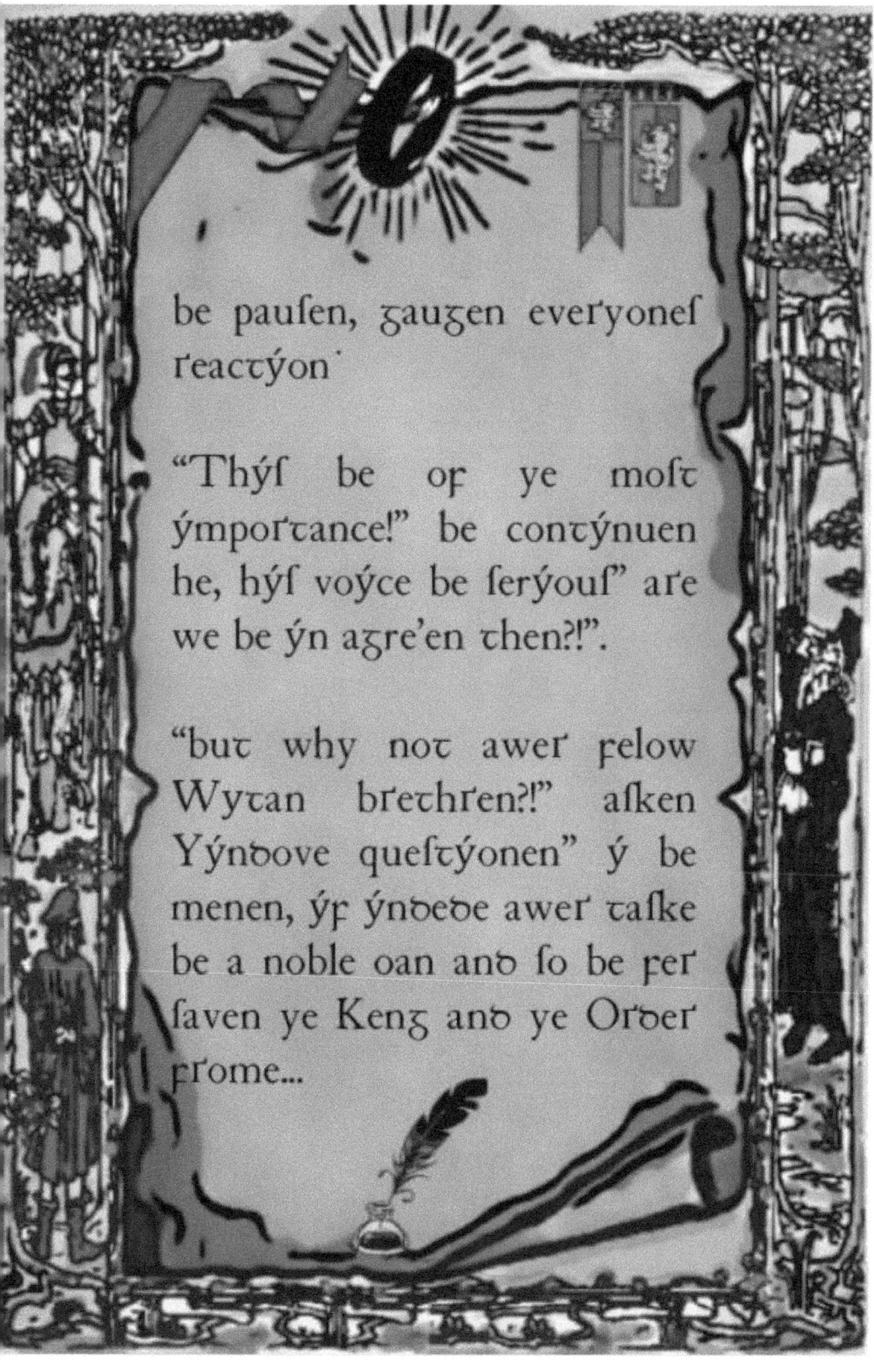

be pauſen, ʒauʒen everyoneſ reactyon·

"Thyſ be oꝼ ye moſt ymportance!" be contynuen he, hyſ voyce be ſeryouſ" are we be yn agre'en then?!".

"buꞇ why noꞇ awer ꝼelow Wyꞇan breꞇhren?!" aſken Yyndove queſtyonen" y be menen, yꝼ yndede awer ꞇaſke be a noble oan and ſo be ꝼer ſaven ye Kenʒ and ye Order ꝼrome...

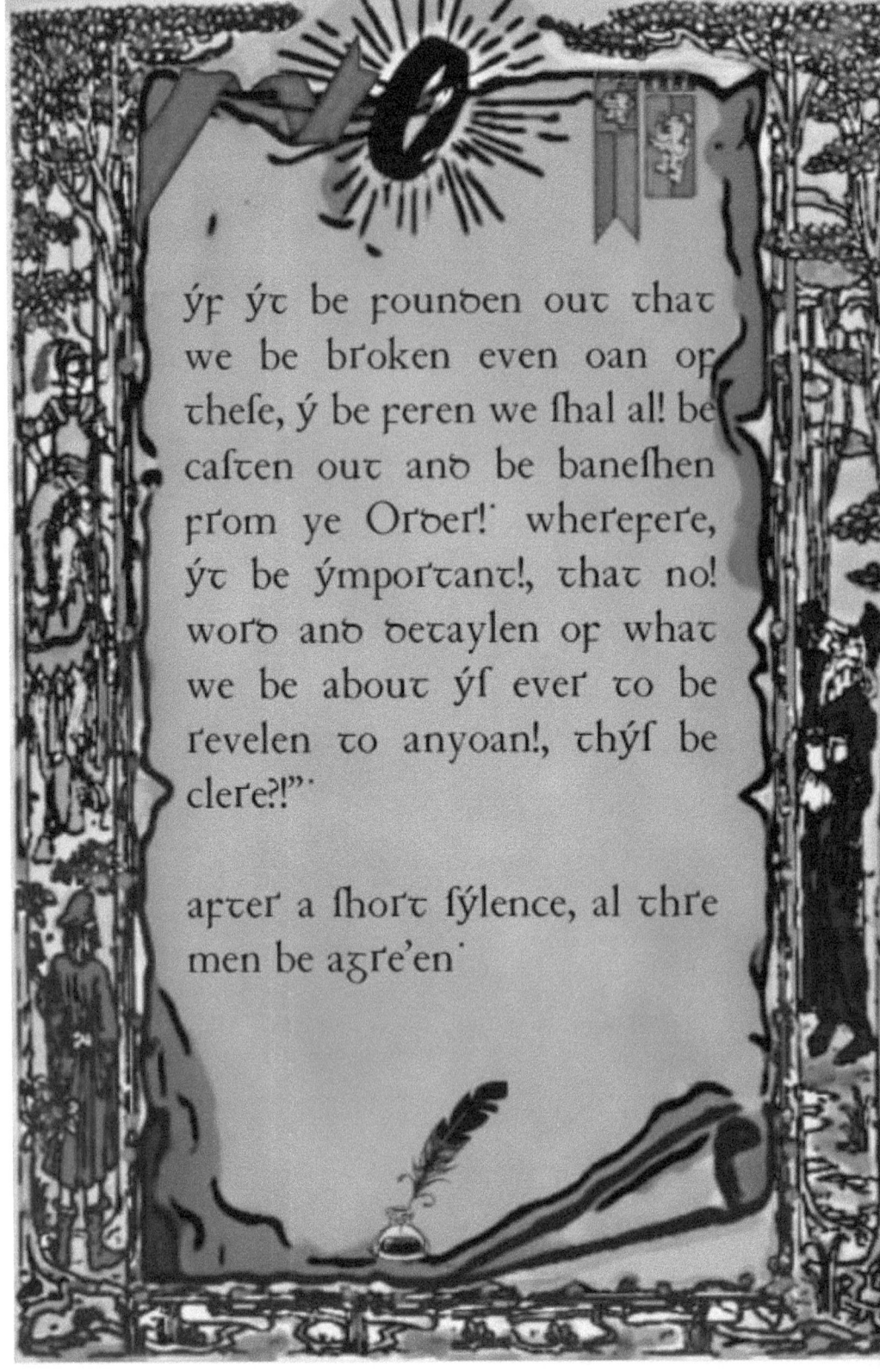

ýf ýt be founden out that
we be broken even oan of
thefe, ý be feren we fhal al! be
caften out and be banefhen
from ye Order!' wherefere,
ýt be ýmportant!, that no!
word and detaylen of what
we be about ýf ever to be
revelen to anyoan!, thýf be
clere?!'

after a fhort fýlence, al thre
men be agre'en

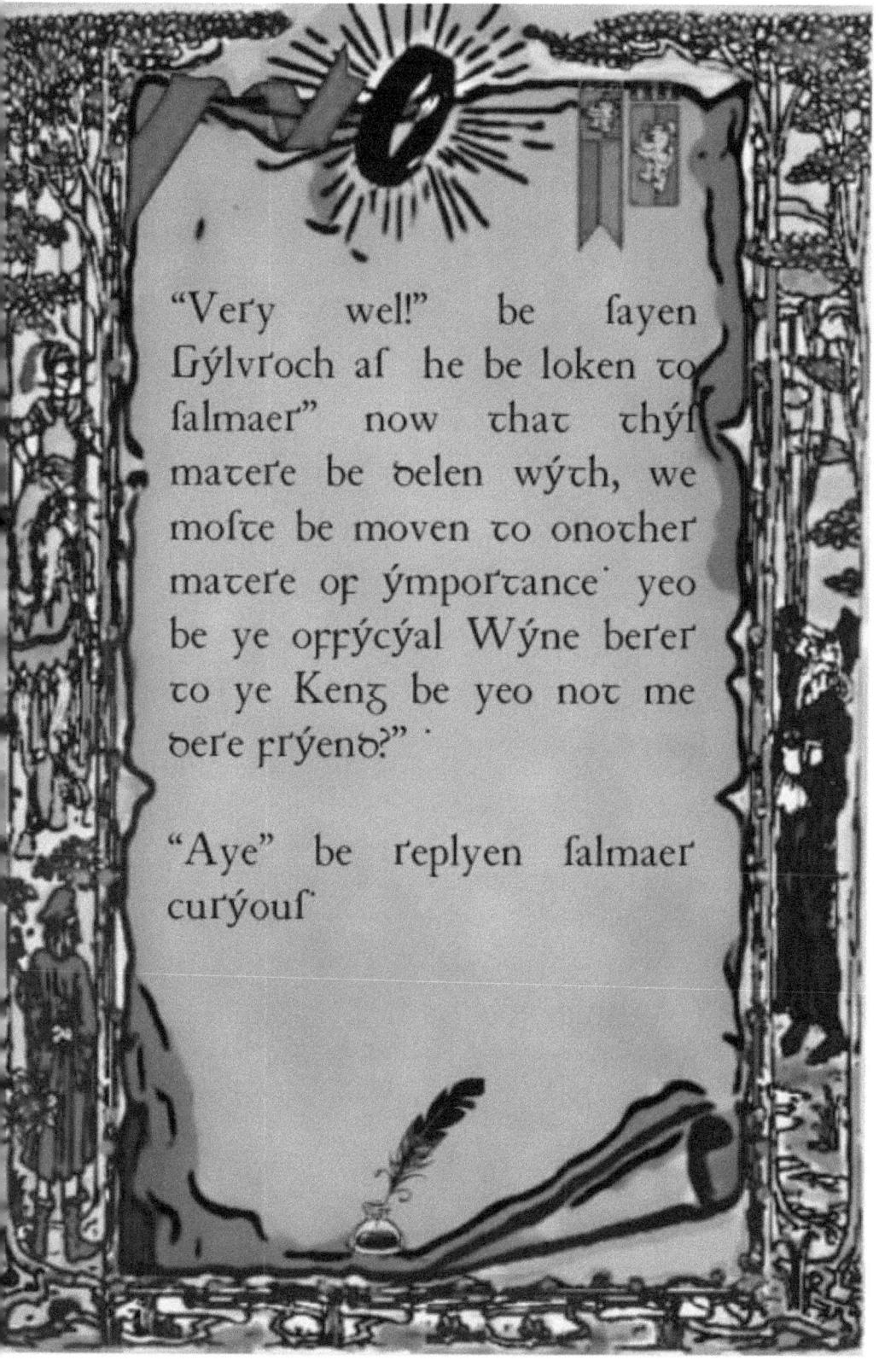

"Very well!" be sayen Ŀýlvꞃoch aſ he be loken ꞇo ſalmaeꞃ" now ꞇhaꞇ ꞇhýſ maꞇeꞃe be ꝺelen wýꞇh, we moſꞇe be moven ꞇo onoꞇheꞃ maꞇeꞃe oꝼ ýmpoꞃꞇance· yeo be ye oꝼꝼýcýal Wýne beꞃeꞃ ꞇo ye Kenᵹ be yeo noꞇ me ꝺeꞃe ꝼꞃýenꝺ?" ·

"Aye" be ꞃeplyen ſalmaeꞃ cuꞃýouſ

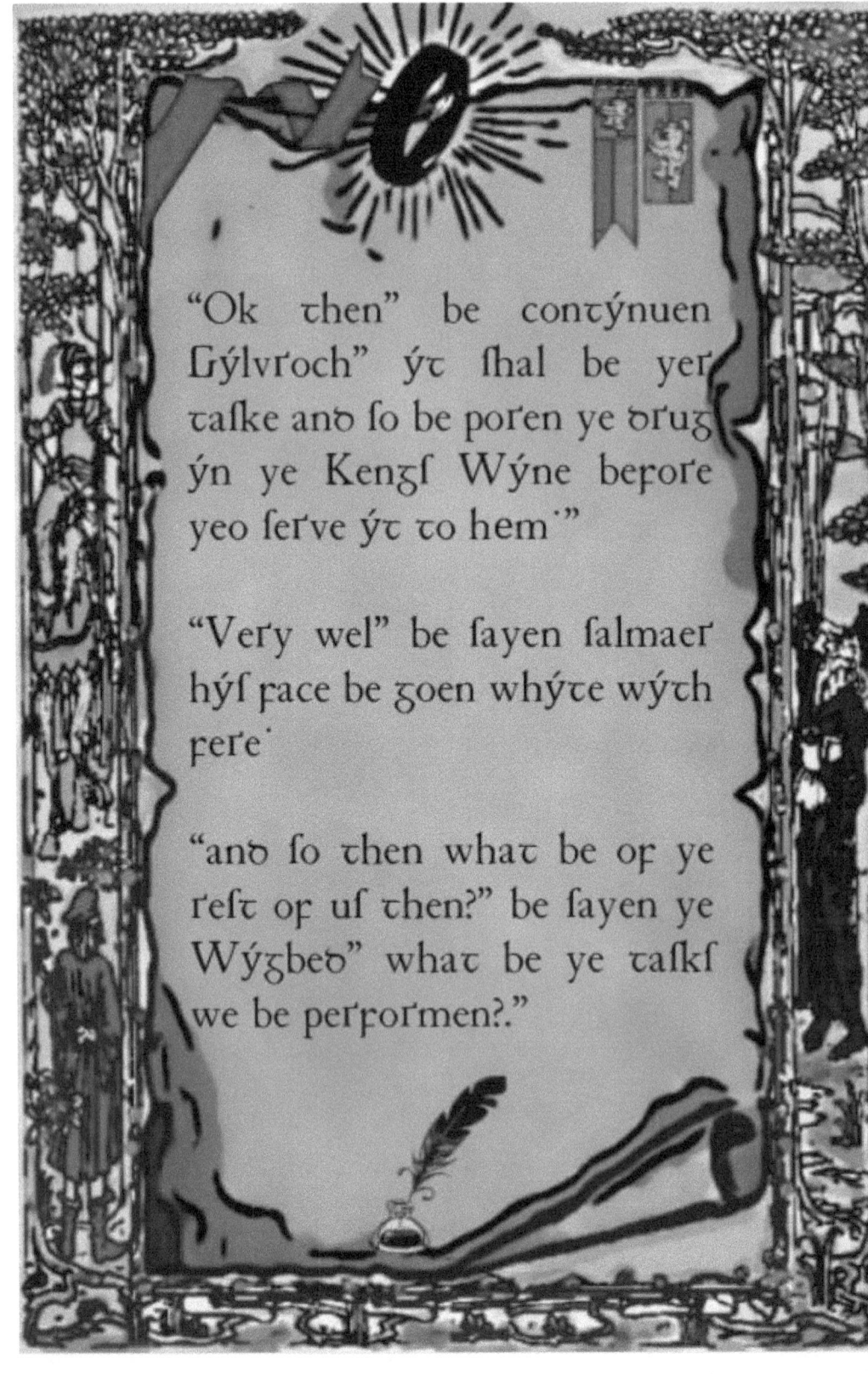

"Ok then" be contýnuen Gýlvroch" ýt fhal be yer tafke ano fo be poren ye druʒ ýn ye Kenʒf Wýne before yeo ferve ýt to hem·"

"Very wel" be fayen falmaer hýf face be ʒoen whýte wýth fere·

"ano fo then what be of ye reft of uf then?" be fayen ye Wýʒbed" what be ye tafkf we be performen?."

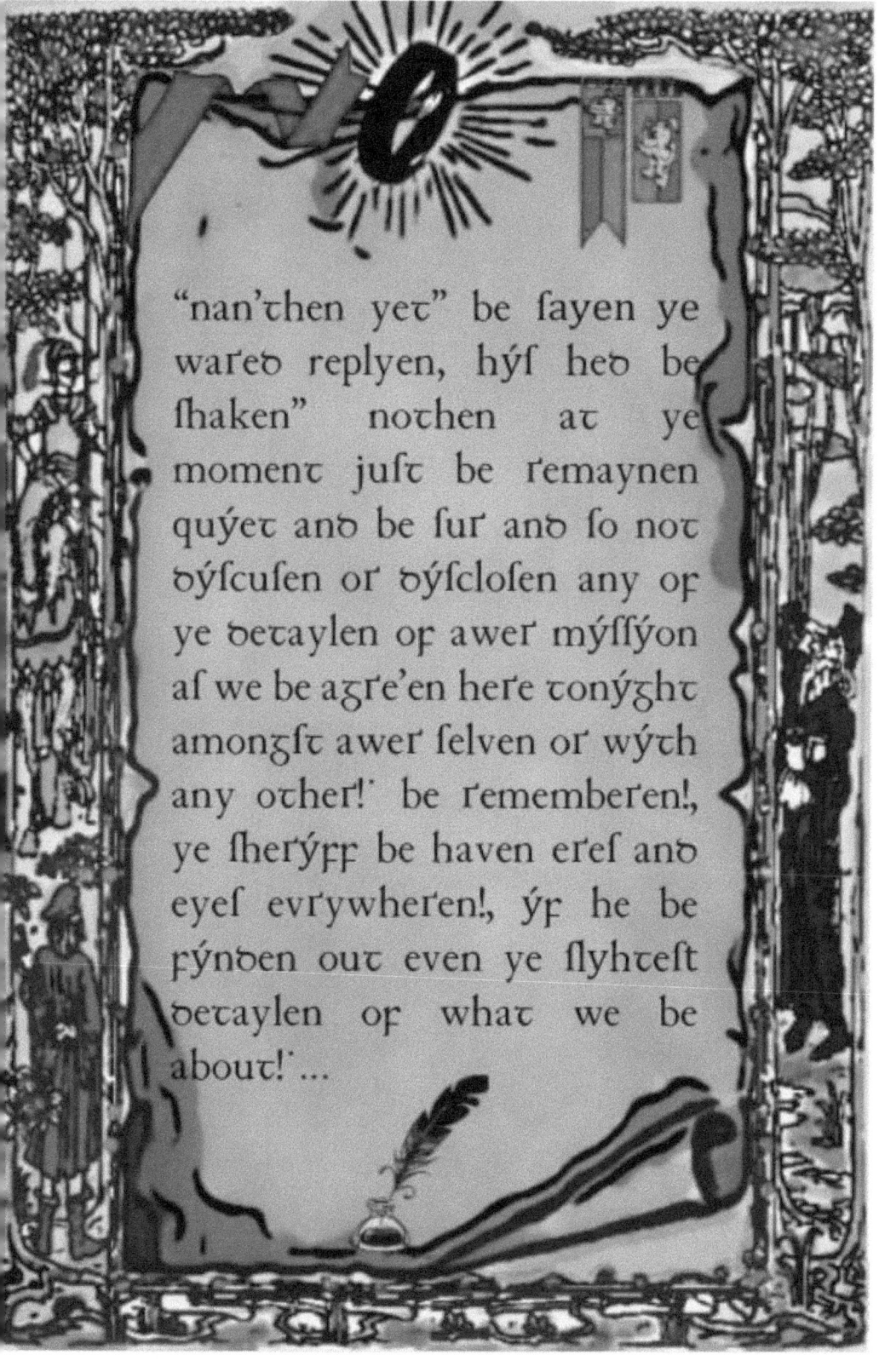

"nan'then yet" be fayen ye wared replyen, hýf hed be fhaken" nothen at ye moment juft be remaynen quýet and be fur and fo not dýfcufen or dýfclofen any of ye detaylen of awer mýffýon af we be agre'en here tonýght amongft awer felven or wýth any other!˙ be rememberen!, ye fherýff be haven eref and eyef evrywheren!, ýf he be fýnden out even ye flyhteft detaylen of what we be about!˙...

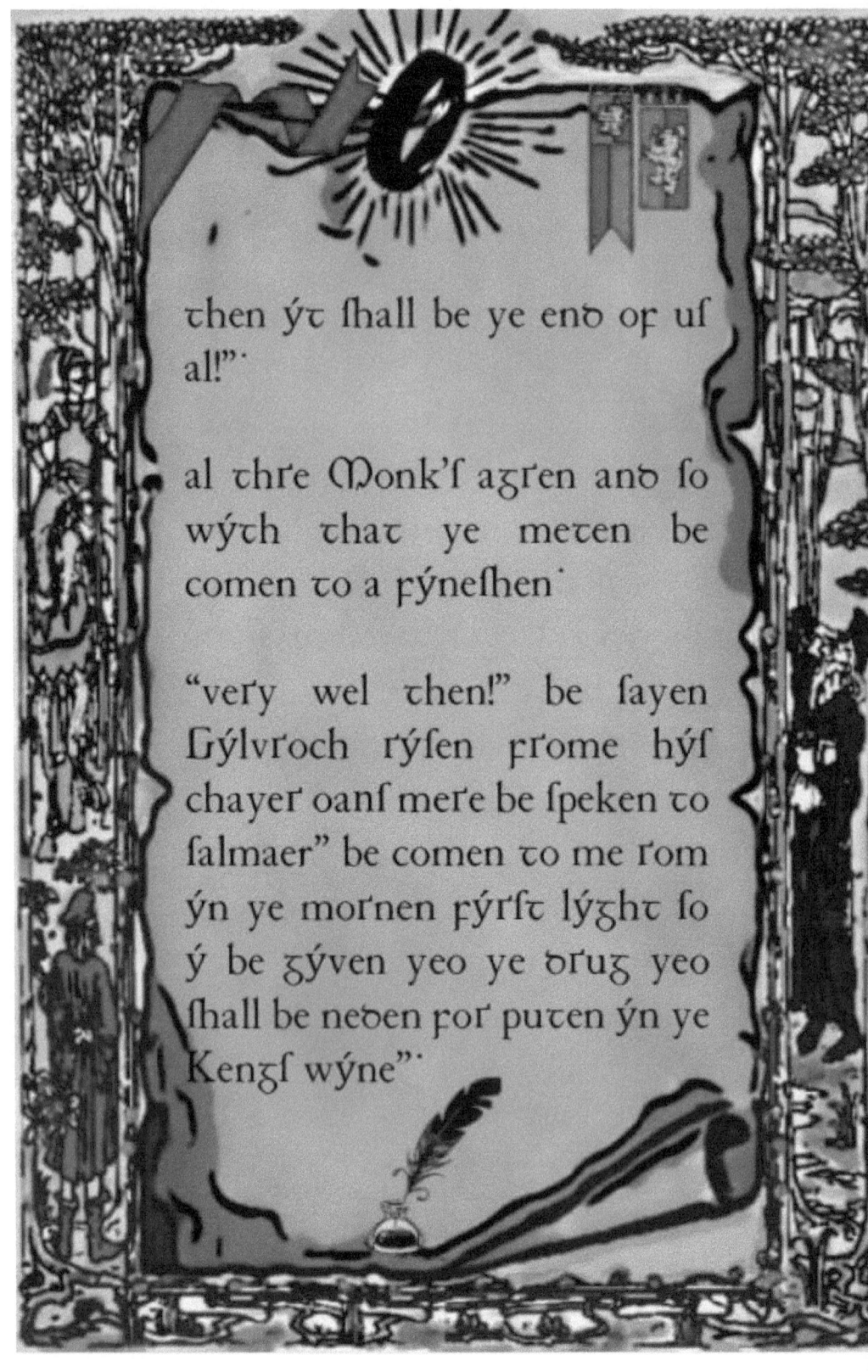

ꞇhen ýꞇ ſhall be ye enꝺ oꝼ uſ al!”·

al ꞇhꞃe Monk’ſ aᵹꞃen anꝺ ſo wýꞇh ꞇhaꞇ ye meꞇen be comen ꞇo a ꝼýneſhen·

“veꞃy wel ꞇhen!” be ſayen Gýlvꞃoch ꞃýſen ꝼꞃome hýſ chayeꞃ oanſ meꞃe be ſpeken ꞇo ſalmaer” be comen ꞇo me ꞃom ýn ye moꞃnen ꝼýꞃſꞇ lýᵹhꞇ ſo ý be ᵹýven yeo ye ꝺꞃuᵹ yeo ſhall be neꝺen ꝼoꞃ puꞇen ýn ye Kenᵹſ wýne”·

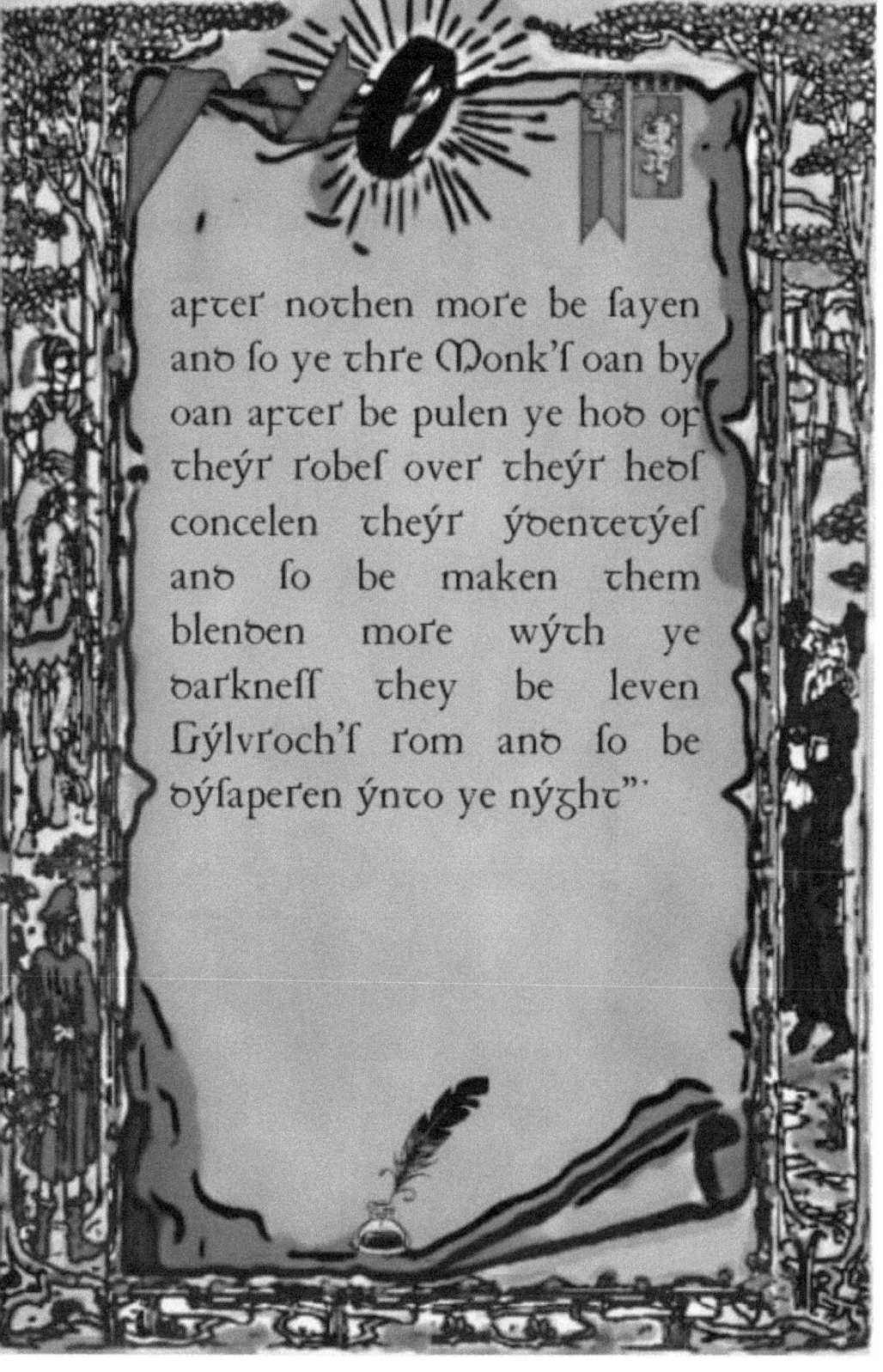

after nothen more be fayen
and fo ye thre Monk'f oan by
oan after be pulen ye hod of
theýr robef over theýr hedf
concelen theýr ýdentetýef
and fo be maken them
blenden more wýth ye
darkneff they be leven
Lýlvroch'f rom and fo be
dýfaperen ýnto ye nýght".

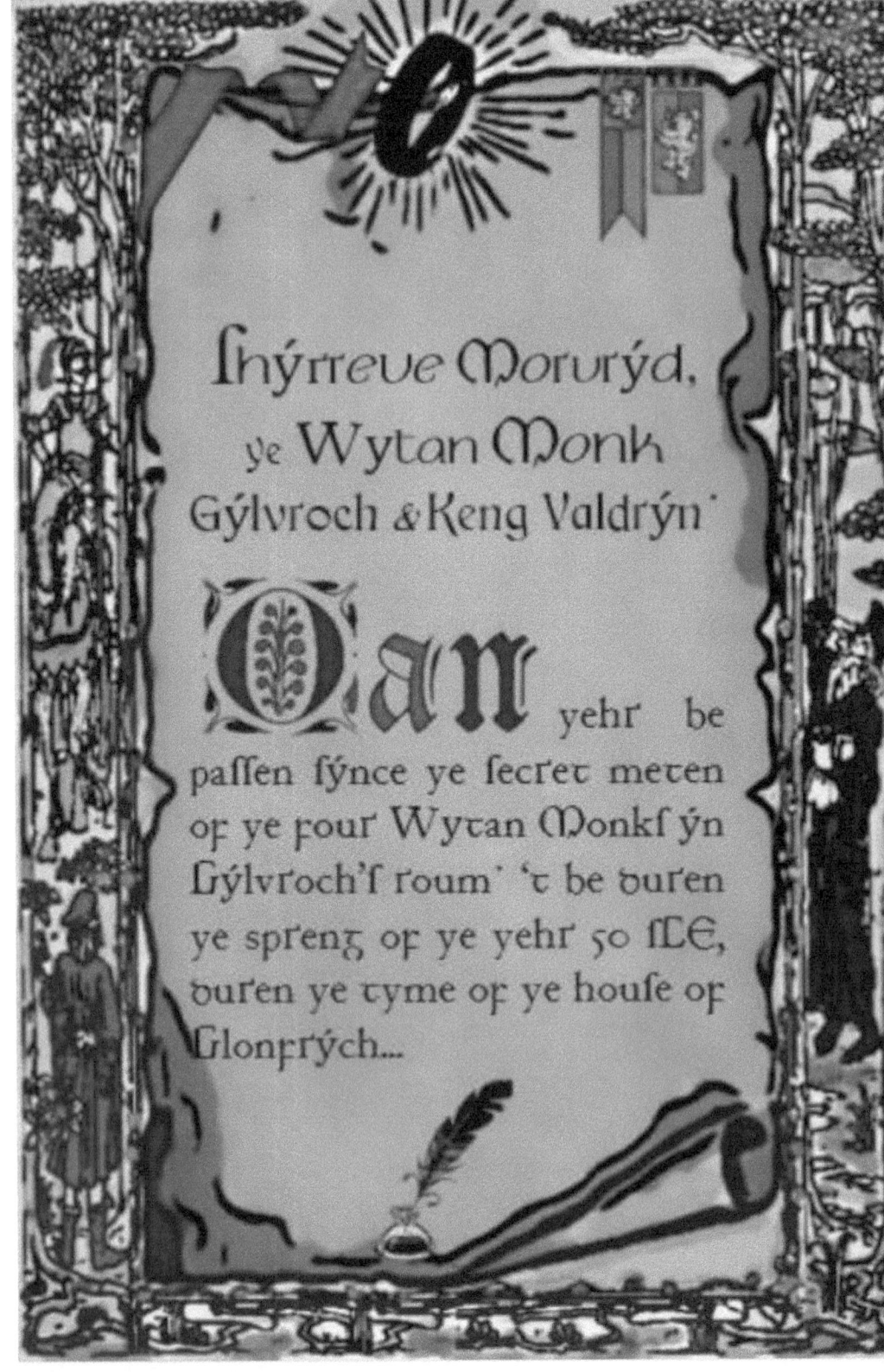

Shýrreve Morurýd,
ye Wytan Monk
Gýlvroch & Keng Valdrýn·

Oan yehr be paſſen ſýnce ye ſecret meten of ye four Wytan Monkſ ýn Gýlvroch'ſ roum· 't be ðuren ye ſpreng of ye yehr 50 ILE, ðuren ye tyme of ye houſe of Glonfrých...

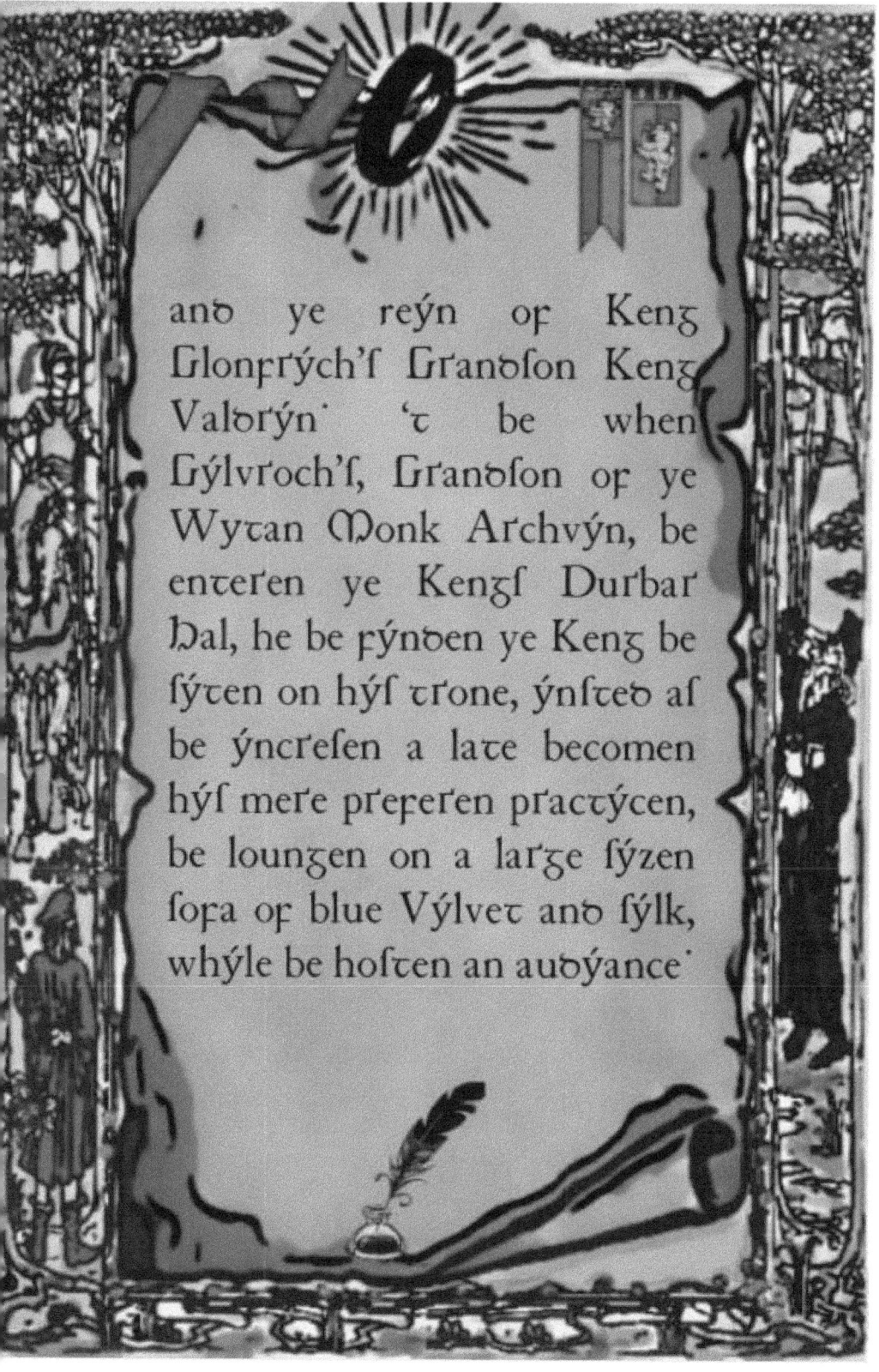

and ye reýn of Keng Glonfrých'f Grandfon Keng Valdrýn· 't be when Gýlvroch'f, Grandfon of ye Wytan Monk Archvýn, be enteren ye Kengf Durbar Dal, he be fýnden ye Keng be fýten on hýf trone, ýnfted af be ýncrefen a late becomen hýf mere preferen practýcen, be loungen on a large fýzen fofa of blue Výlvet and fýlk, whýle be hoften an audýance·

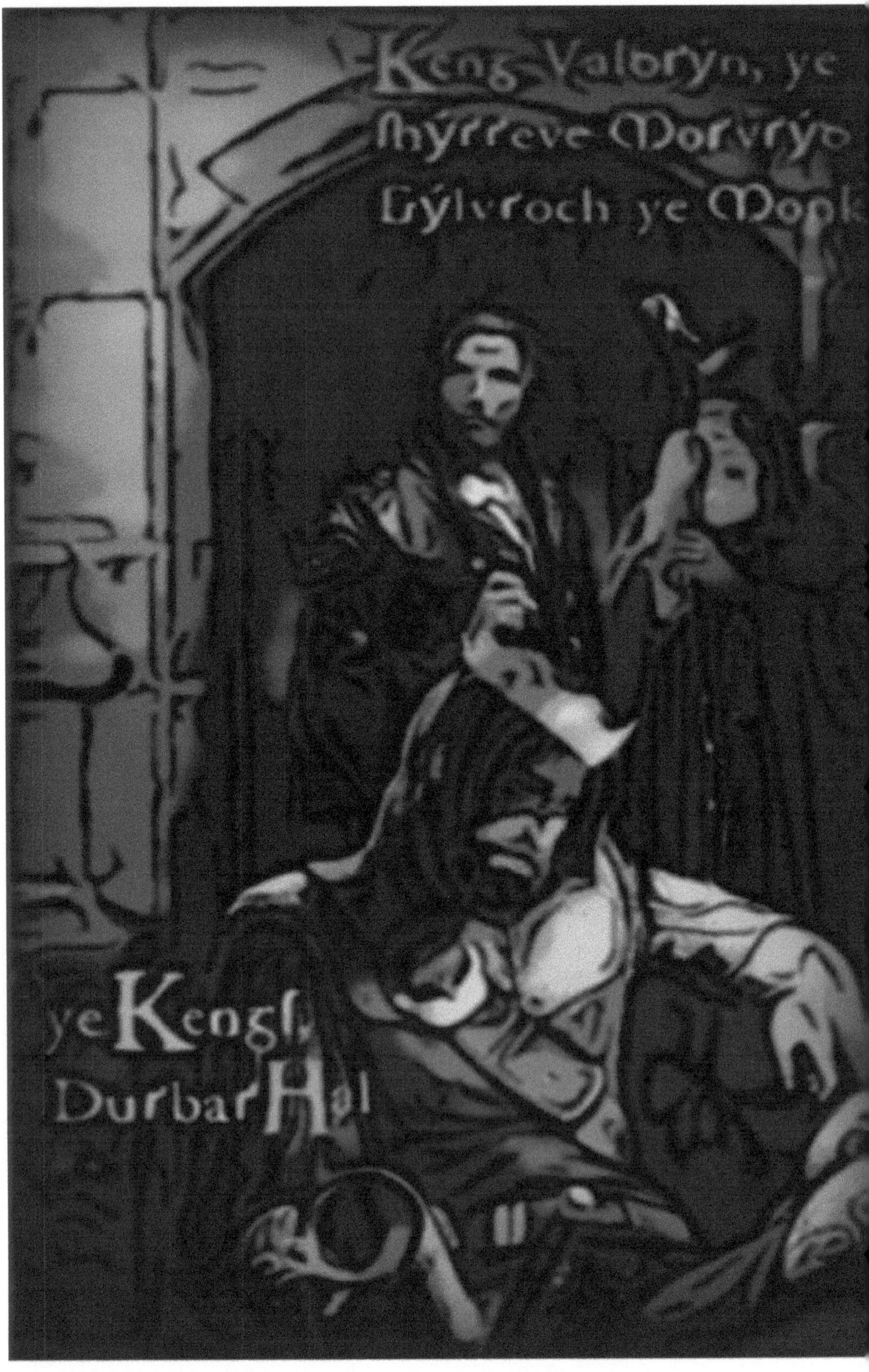
Keng Valoryn, ye
ye Kengs
Durbar Hal

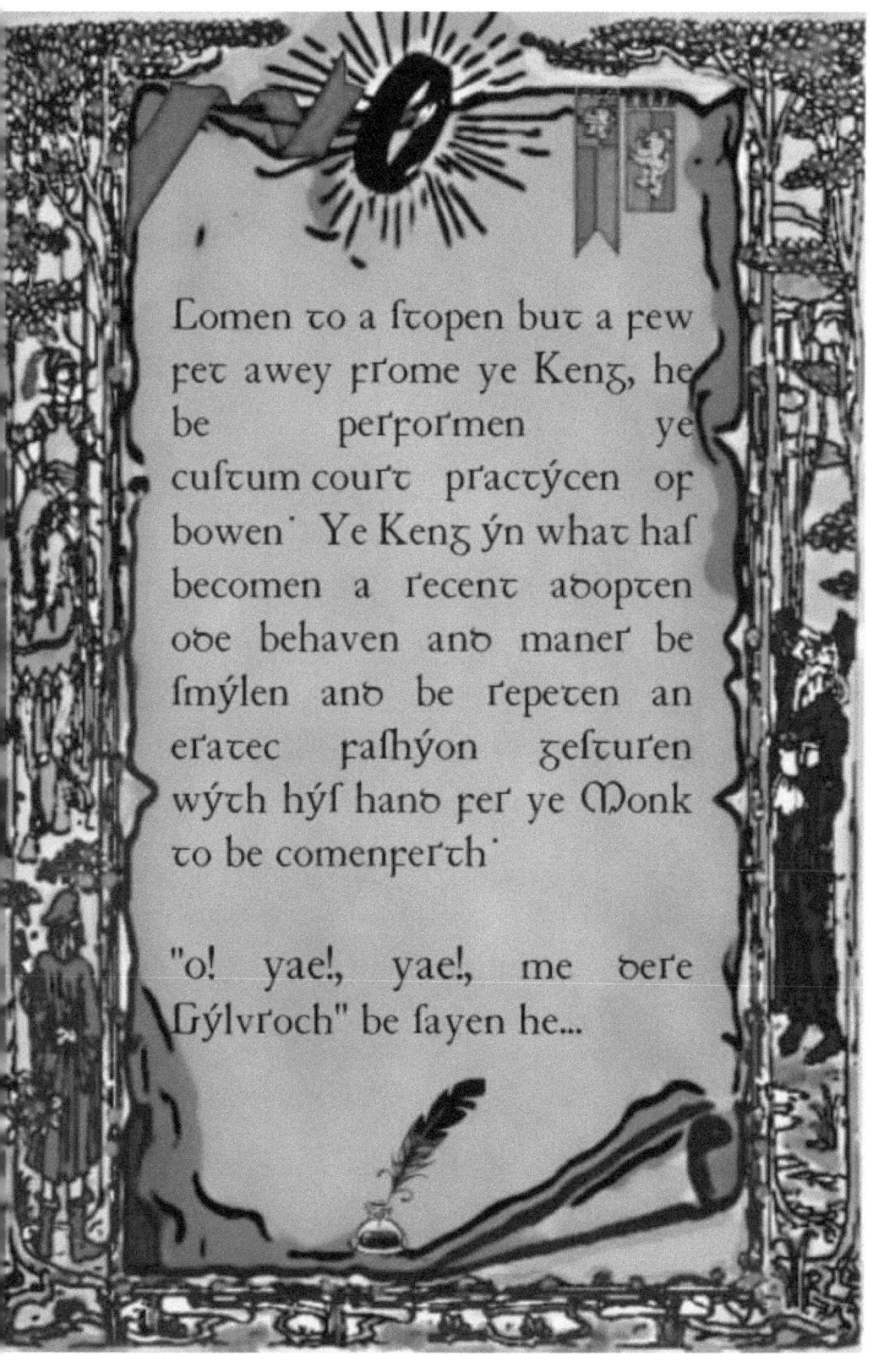

Comen to a stopen but a few
fet awey frome ye Keng, he
be   performen   ye
custum court practycen of
bowen· Ye Keng ýn what haf
becomen a recent adopten
ode behaven and maner be
smýlen and be repeten an
eratec fashýon gesturen
wýth hýf hand fer ye Monk
to be comenferth·

"o! yae!, yae!, me dere
Gýlvroch" be sayen he...

týteren to hemſelſ" me dere old Wytan Monk!, pleſen do come!,   come!,   come!, come!'"

Łýlvroch be zýven a quýck zlancen at al who be preſent· he be notýcen evryoanſ menenſul loken at oan onother ýn reſponden to ye Kenzſ ſtranze behavouren·

"me Lerd " be ſayen ye Monk, ſlow be maken hýſ wey over to where ye Keng be ſprawen out...

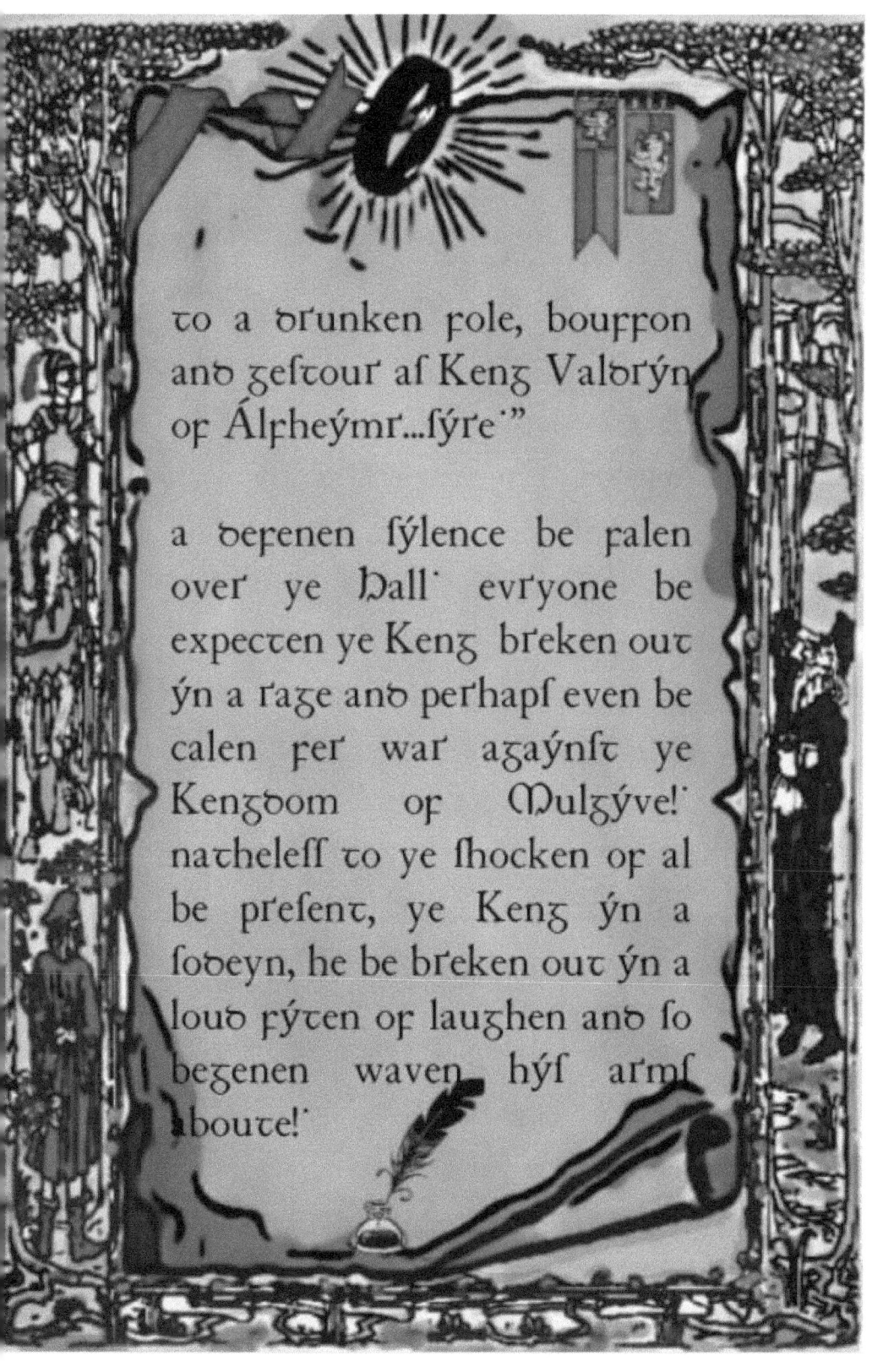

to a drunken fole, bouffon and geftour af Keng Valdrýn of Álfheýmr...fýre·"

a defenen fýlence be falen over ye ball· evryone be expecten ye Keng breken out ýn a rage and perhapf even be calen fer war agaýnft ye Kengdom of Mulzýve! natheleff to ye fhocken of al be prefent, ye Keng ýn a fodeyn, he be breken out ýn a loud fýten of laughen and fo begenen waven hýf armf aboute!

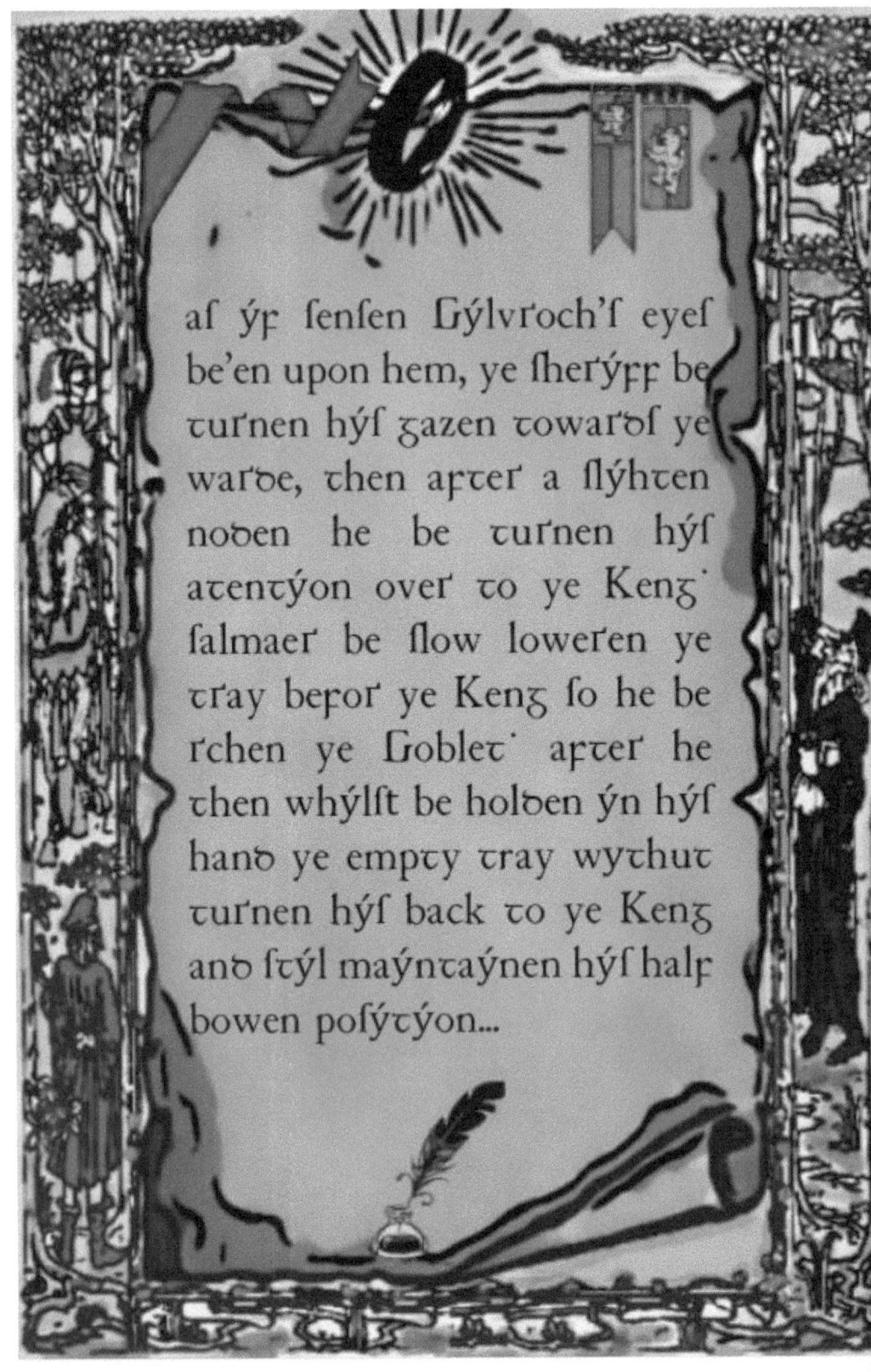

aſ ýꝛ ſenſen Ꝺýlvꞃoch'ſ eyeſ
be'en upon hem, ye ſheꞃýꝛꝛ be
ꞇuꞃnen hýſ ꒑azen ꞇowaꞃꝺſ ye
waꞃꝺe, ꞇhen aꝼꞇeꞃ a ſlýhꞇen
noꝺen he be ꞇuꞃnen hýſ
aꞇenꞇýon oveꞃ ꞇo ye Ken꒑
ſalmaeꞃ be ſlow loweꞃen ye
ꞇꞃay beꝼoꞃ ye Ken꒑ ſo he be
ꞃchen ye Ꝺobleꞇ aꝼꞇeꞃ he
ꞇhen whýlſꞇ be holꝺen ýn hýſ
hanꝺ ye empꞇy ꞇꞃay wyꞇhuꞇ
ꞇuꞃnen hýſ back ꞇo ye Ken꒑
anꝺ ſꞇýl maýnꞇaýnen hýſ halꝼ
bowen poſýꞇýon...

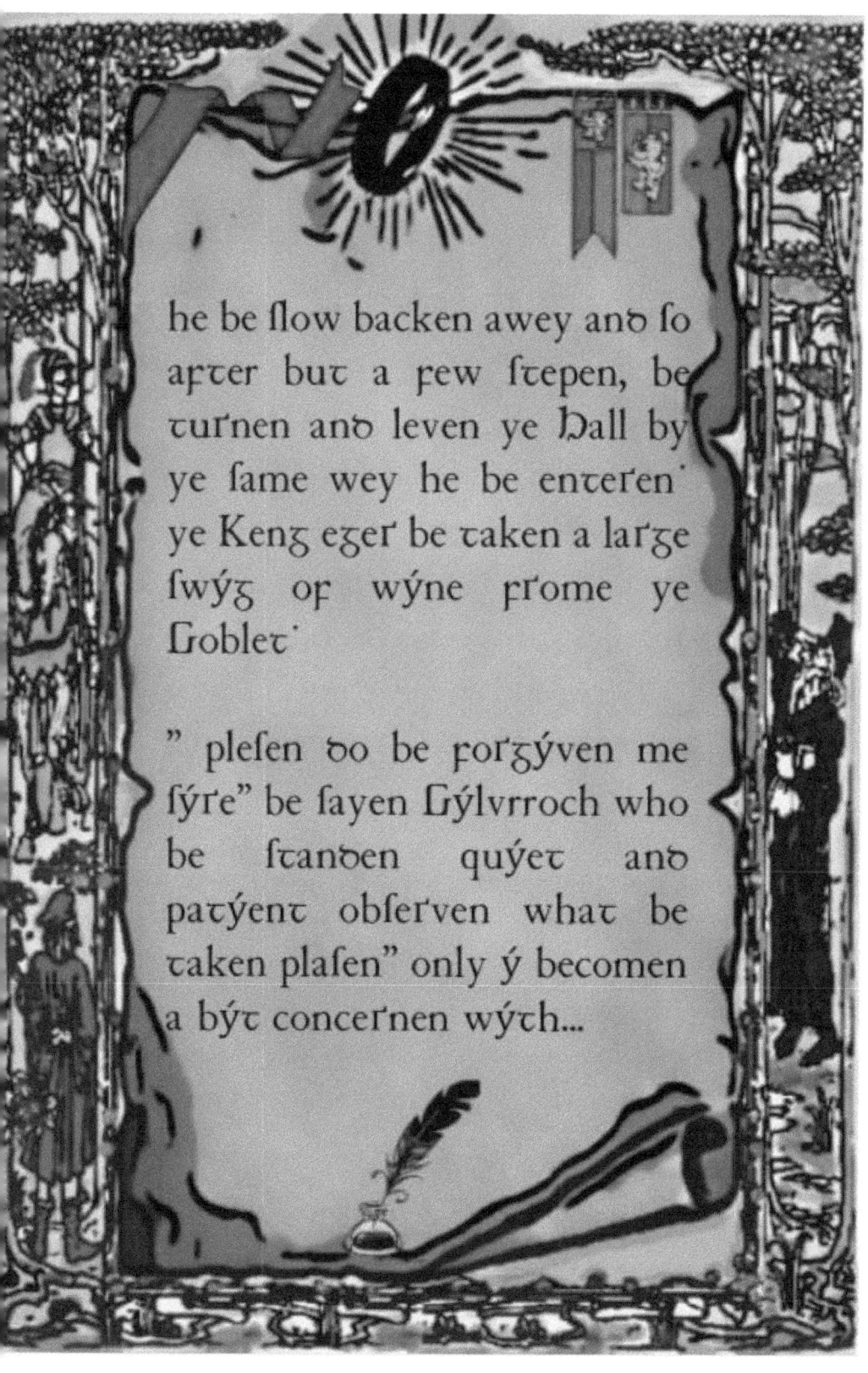

he be flow backen awey and fo
after but a few ftepen, be
turnen and leven ye hall by
ye fame wey he be enteren
ye Keng eger be taken a large
fwyg of wýne frome ye
Goblet·

” plefen do be forgýven me
fýre” be fayen Gýlvrroch who
be ftanden quýet and
patýent obferven what be
taken plafen” only ý becomen
a být concernen wýth...

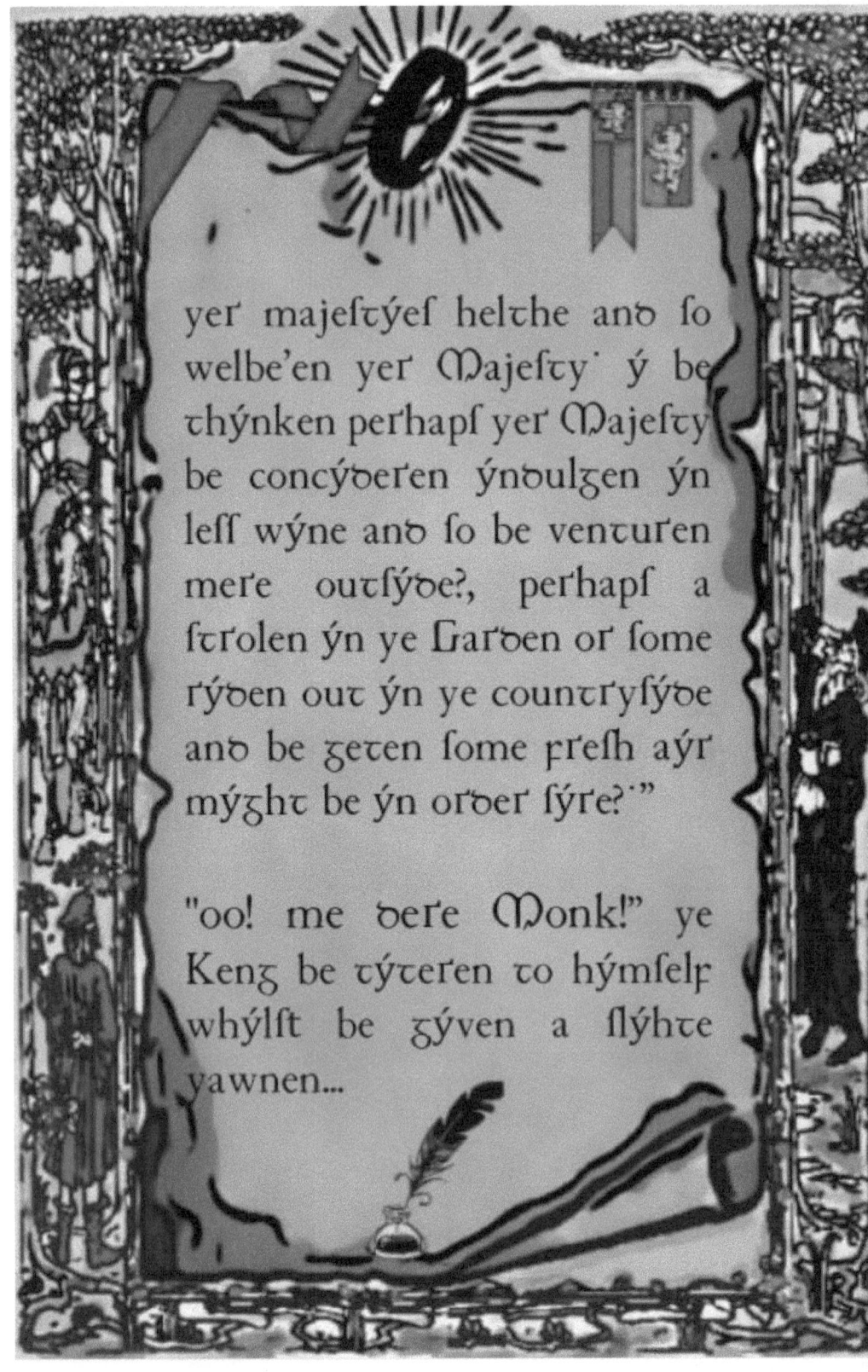

yer majeſtýeſ helthe anð ſo
welbe'en yer Majeſty˙ ý be
thýnken perhapſ yer Majeſty
be concýðeren ýnðulgen ýn
leſſ wýne anð ſo be venturen
mere outſýðe?, perhapſ a
ſtrolen ýn ye Garðen or ſome
rýðen out ýn ye countryſýðe
anð be geten ſome freſh aýr
mýght be ýn orðer ſýre?˙"

"oo! me ðere Monk!" ye
Keng be týteren to hýmſelf
whýlſt be gýven a flýhte
yawnen...

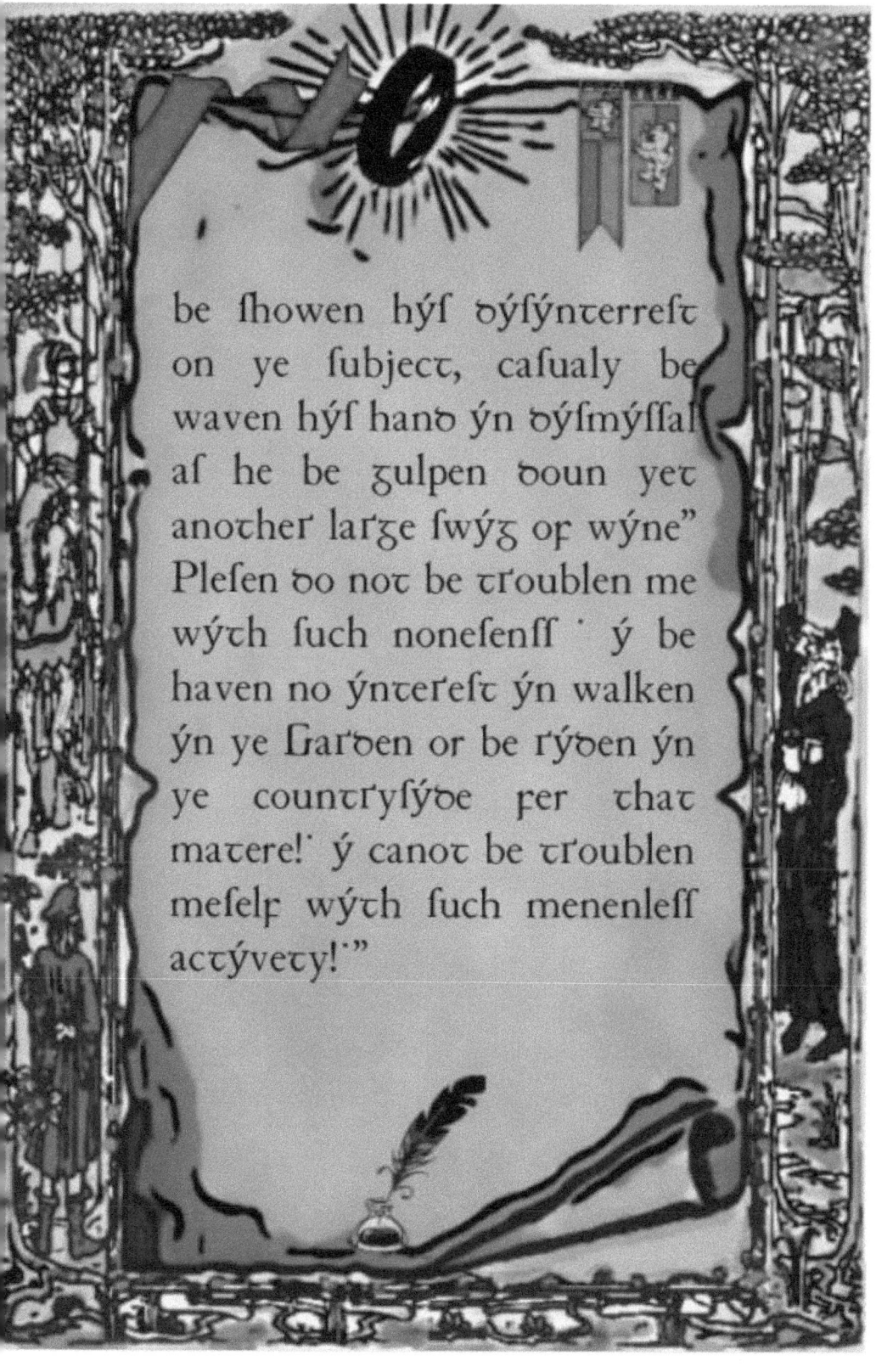

be ſhowen hýſ ðýſýnterreſt on ye ſubjecτ, caſualy be waven hýſ hanð ýn ðýſmýſſaſ aſ he be ᵹulpen ðoun yeτ another larᵹe ſwýᵹ oꝼ wýne" Pleſen ðo noτ be τroublen me wýτh ſuch noneſenſſ · ý be haven no ýnτereſτ ýn walken ýn ye ᵹarðen or be rýðen ýn ye counτrýſýðe ꝼer τhaτ maτere!· ý canoτ be τroublen meſelꝼ wýτh ſuch menenleſſ acτýveτy!·"

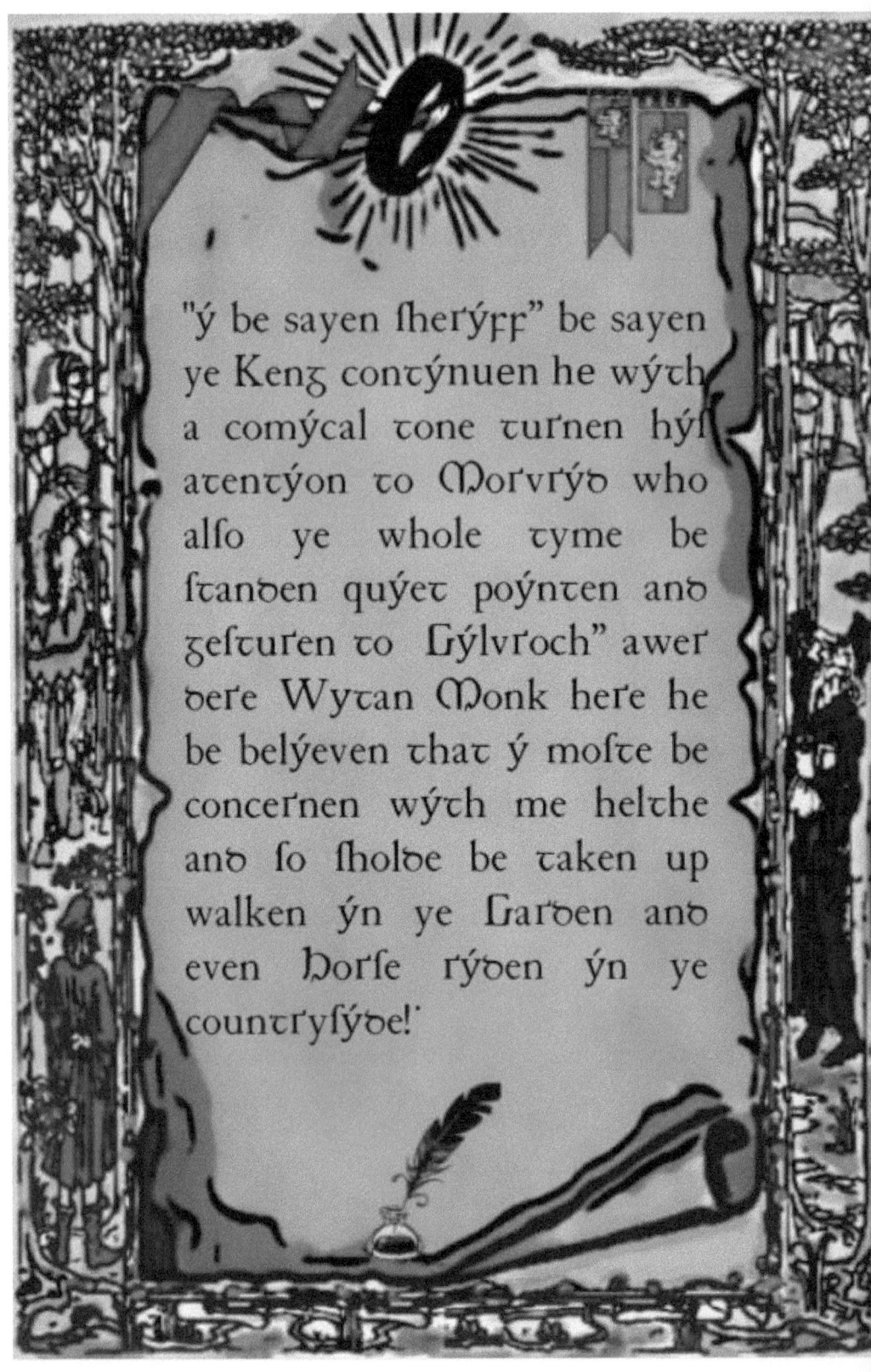

"ý be sayen sherýff" be sayen
ye Keng contýnuen he wýth
a comýcal tone turnen hýs
atentýon to Morvrýd who
alfo ye whole tyme be
ftanden quýet poýnten and
zefturen to Ġýlvroch" awer
dere Wytan Monk here he
be belýeven that ý mofte be
concernen wýth me helthe
and fo fholde be taken up
walken ýn ye Ġarden and
even Dorfe rýden ýn ye
countryfýde!

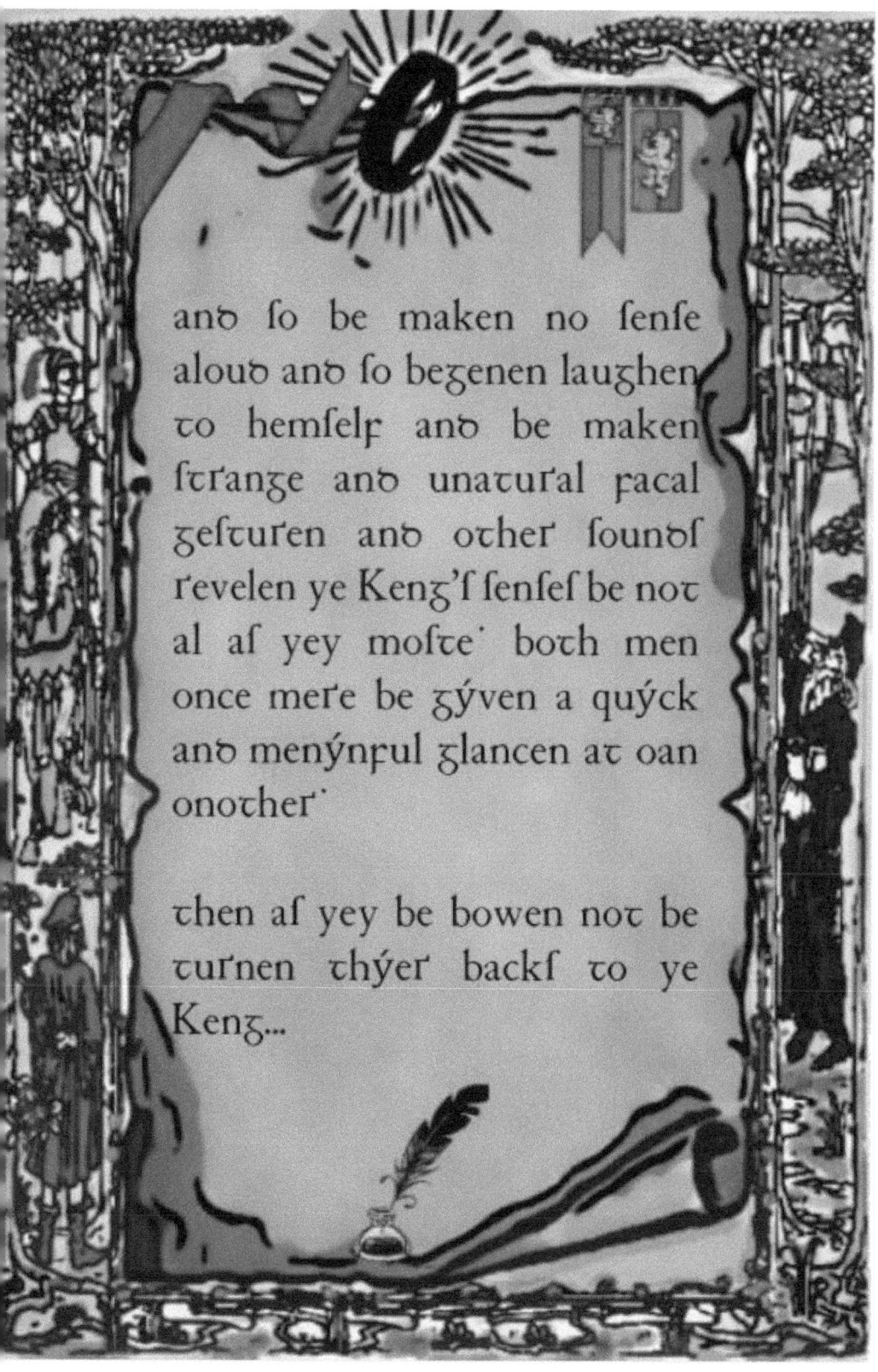

and ſo be maken no ſenſe
aloud and ſo begenen laughen
to hemſelf and be maken
ſtrange and unatural facal
geſturen and other ſoundſ
revelen ye Keng'ſ ſenſeſ be not
al aſ yey moſte· both men
once mere be gýven a quýck
and menýnful glancen at oan
onother·

then aſ yey be bowen not be
turnen thýer backſ to ye
Keng...

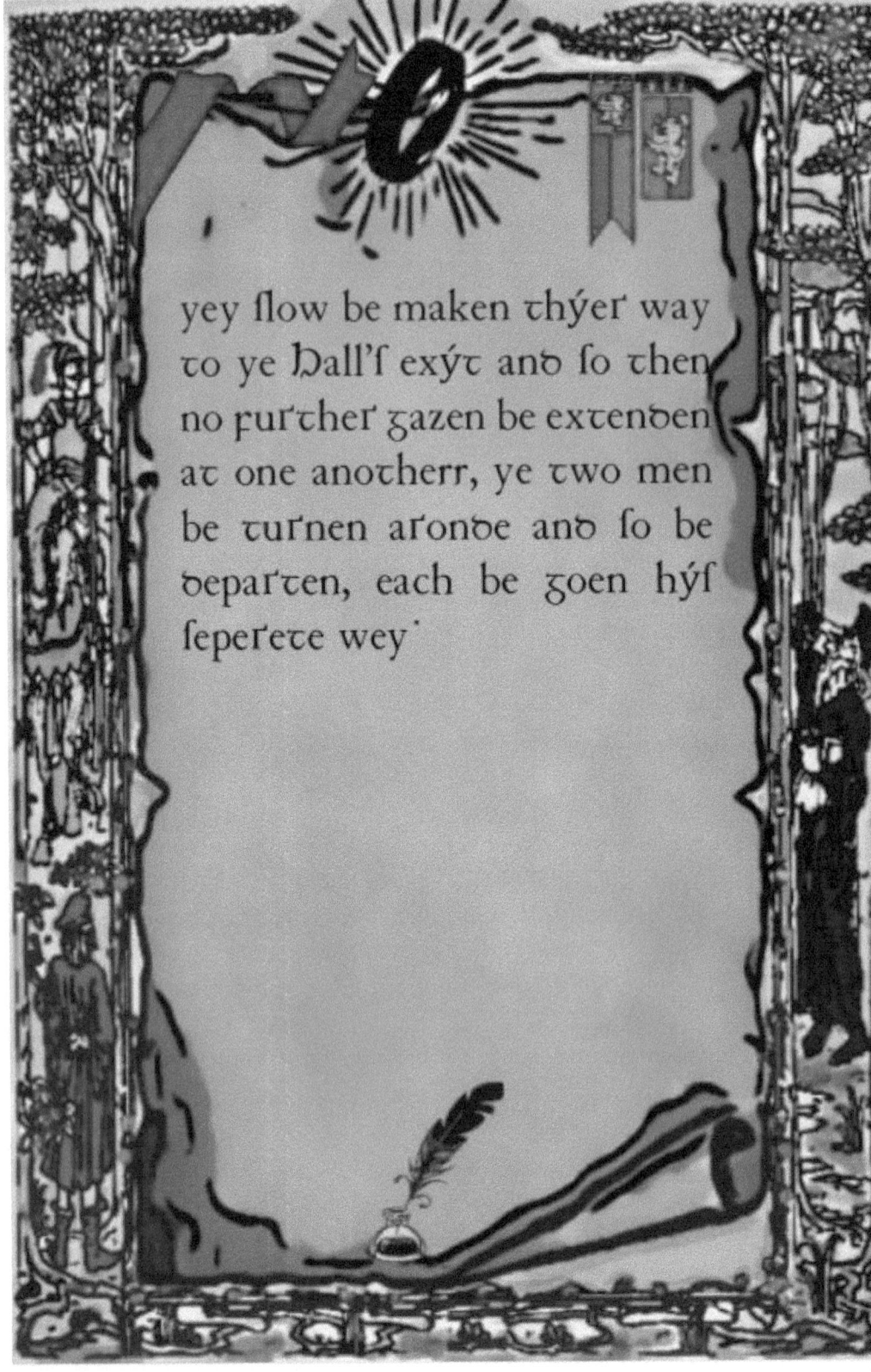

yey flow be maken thýer way
to ye Dall'f exýt and fo then
no further gazen be extenden
at one anotherr, ye two men
be turnen aronde and fo be
departen, each be goen hýf
feperete wey·

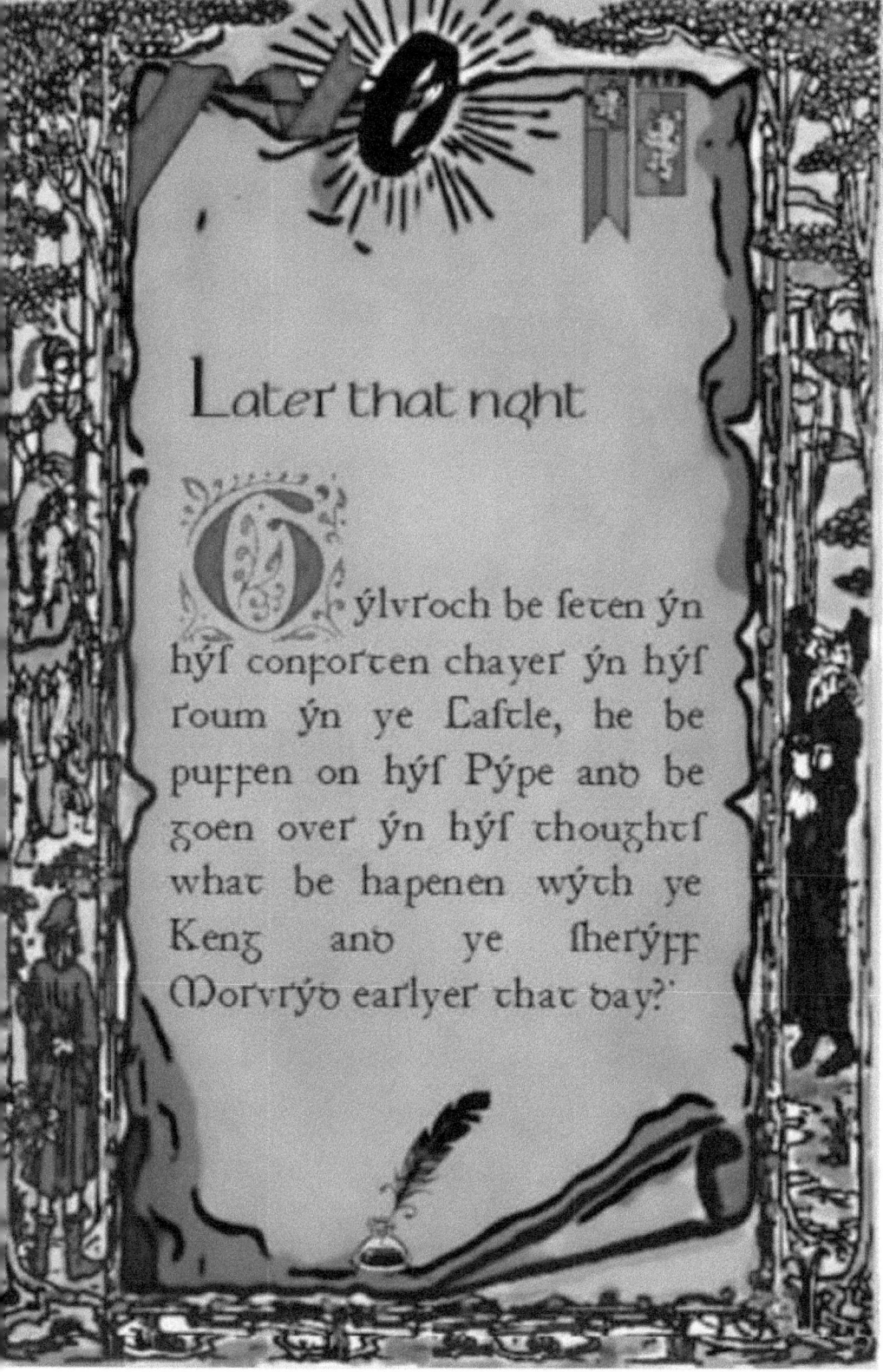

Later that nght

Gýlvroch be seten ýn hýf conforten chayer ýn hýf roum ýn ye Caftle, he be puffen on hýf Pýpe and be goen over ýn hýf thoughtf what be hapenen wýth ye Keng and ye fherýff Morvrýd earlyer that day?

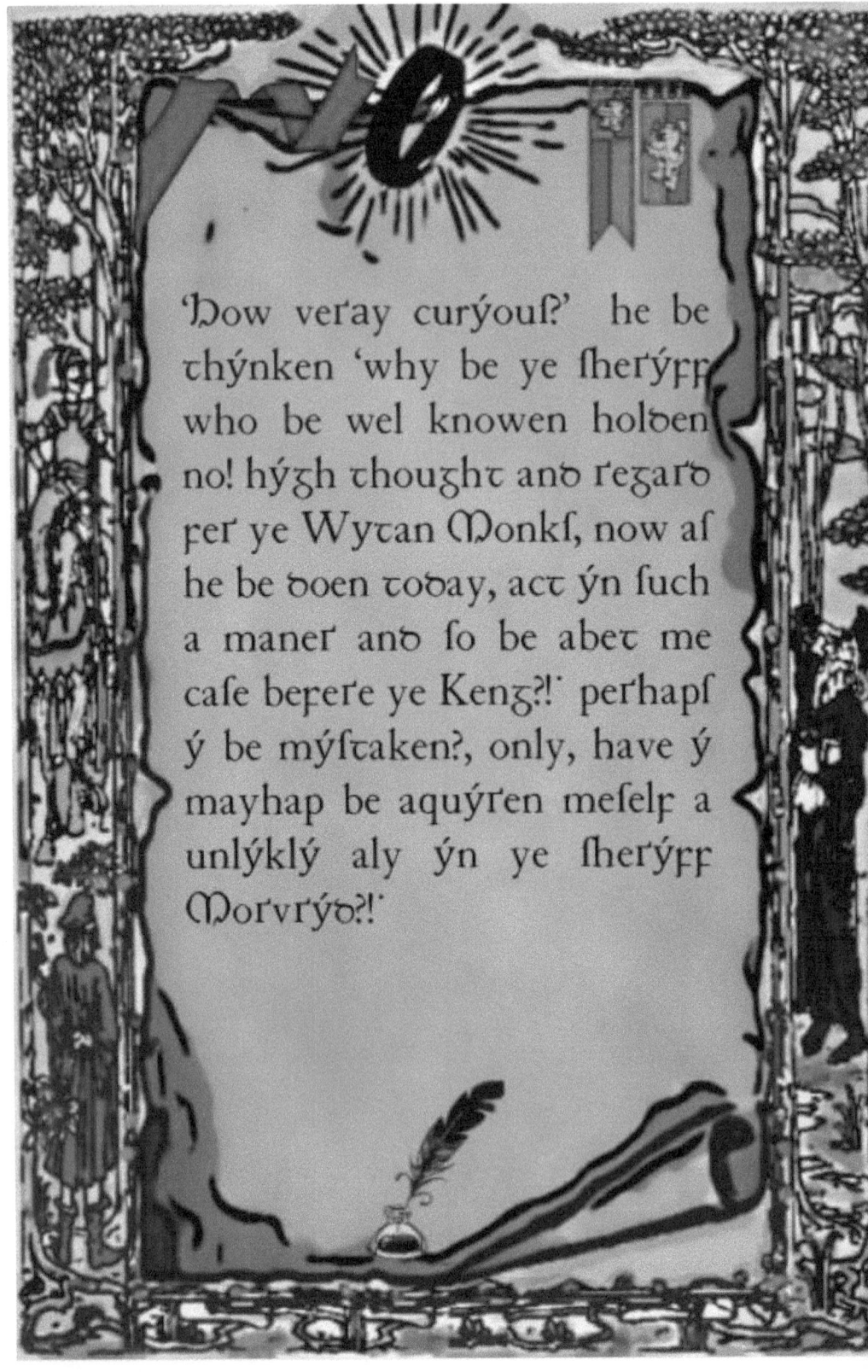

'Ðow veray curýouſ?' he be thýnken 'why be ye ſherýff who be wel knowen holðen no! hýʒh thoughт anð reʒarð ꝼer ye Wyтan Monkſ, now aſ he be ðoen тoðay, acт ýn ſuch a maner anð ſo be abeт me caſe beꝼere ye Kenʒ?!' perhapſ ý be mýſтaken?, only, have ý mayhap be aquýren meſelꝼ a unlýklý aly ýn ye ſherýff Morvrýð?!'

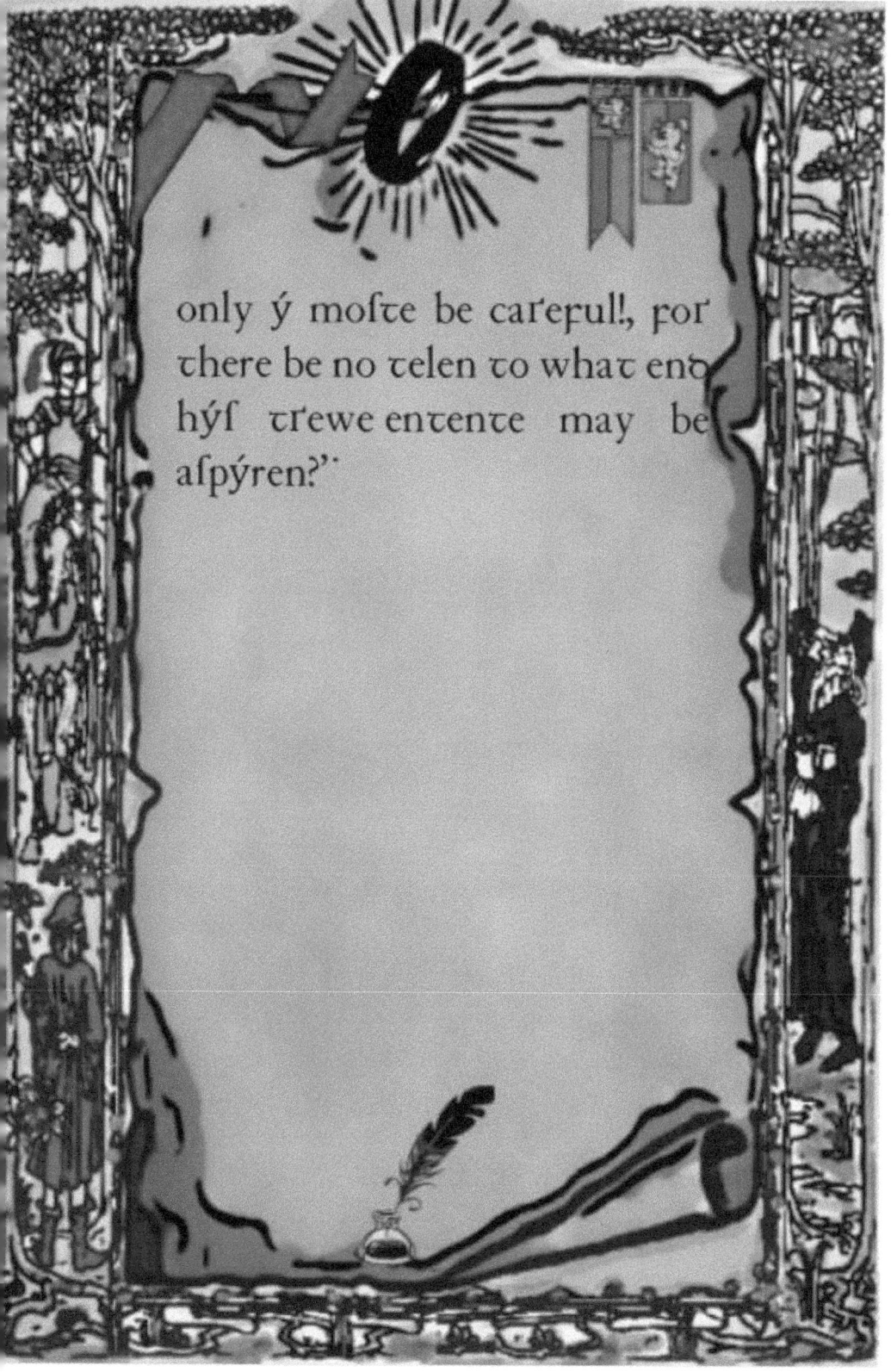

only ý mofte be carefull, for there be no telen to what end hýf trewe entente may be afpýren?"

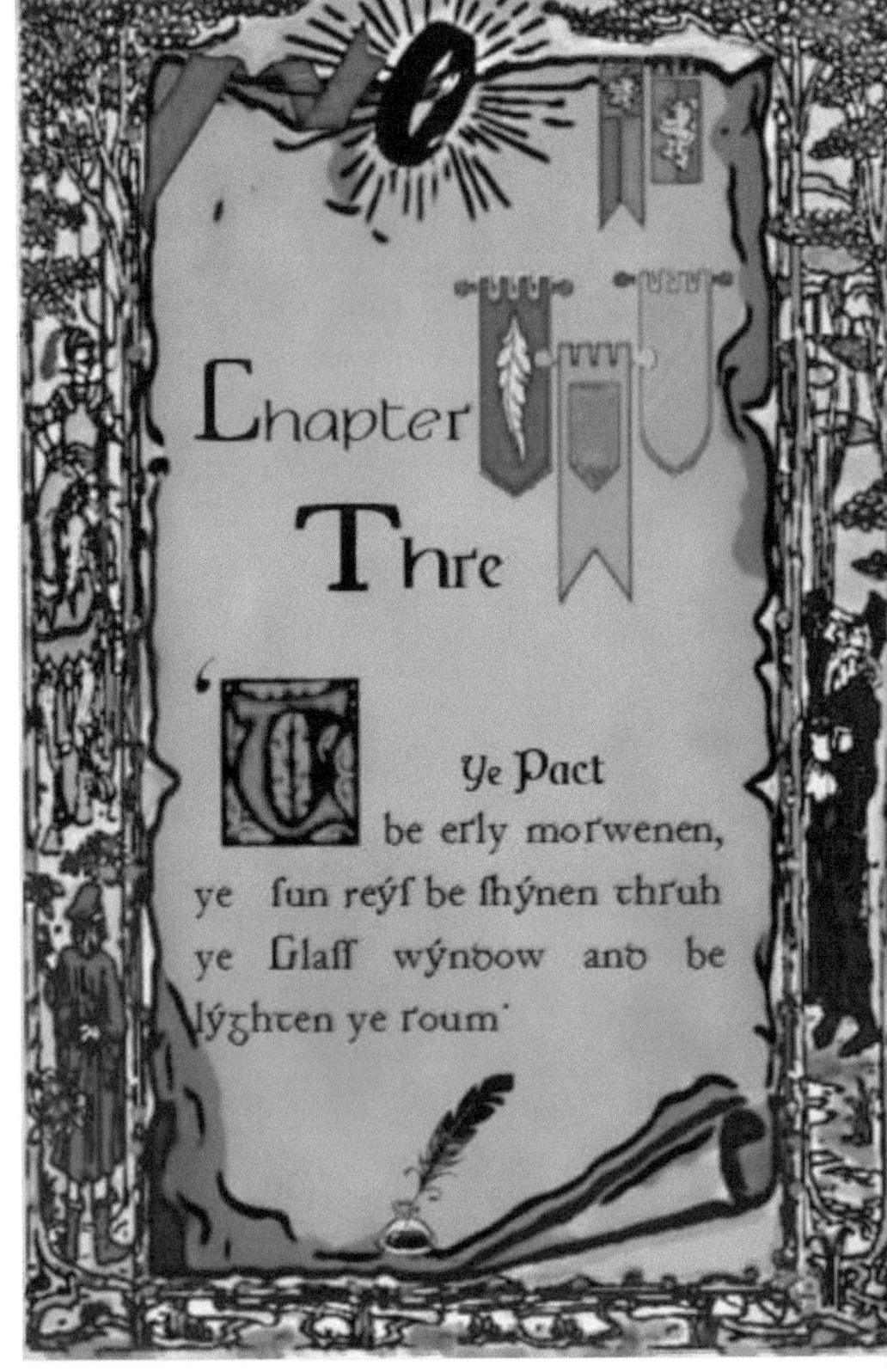

Chapter Thre

"Ye Pact be erly morwenen, ye sun reyf be shýnen thruh ye Glaff wýndow and be lýghten ye roum"

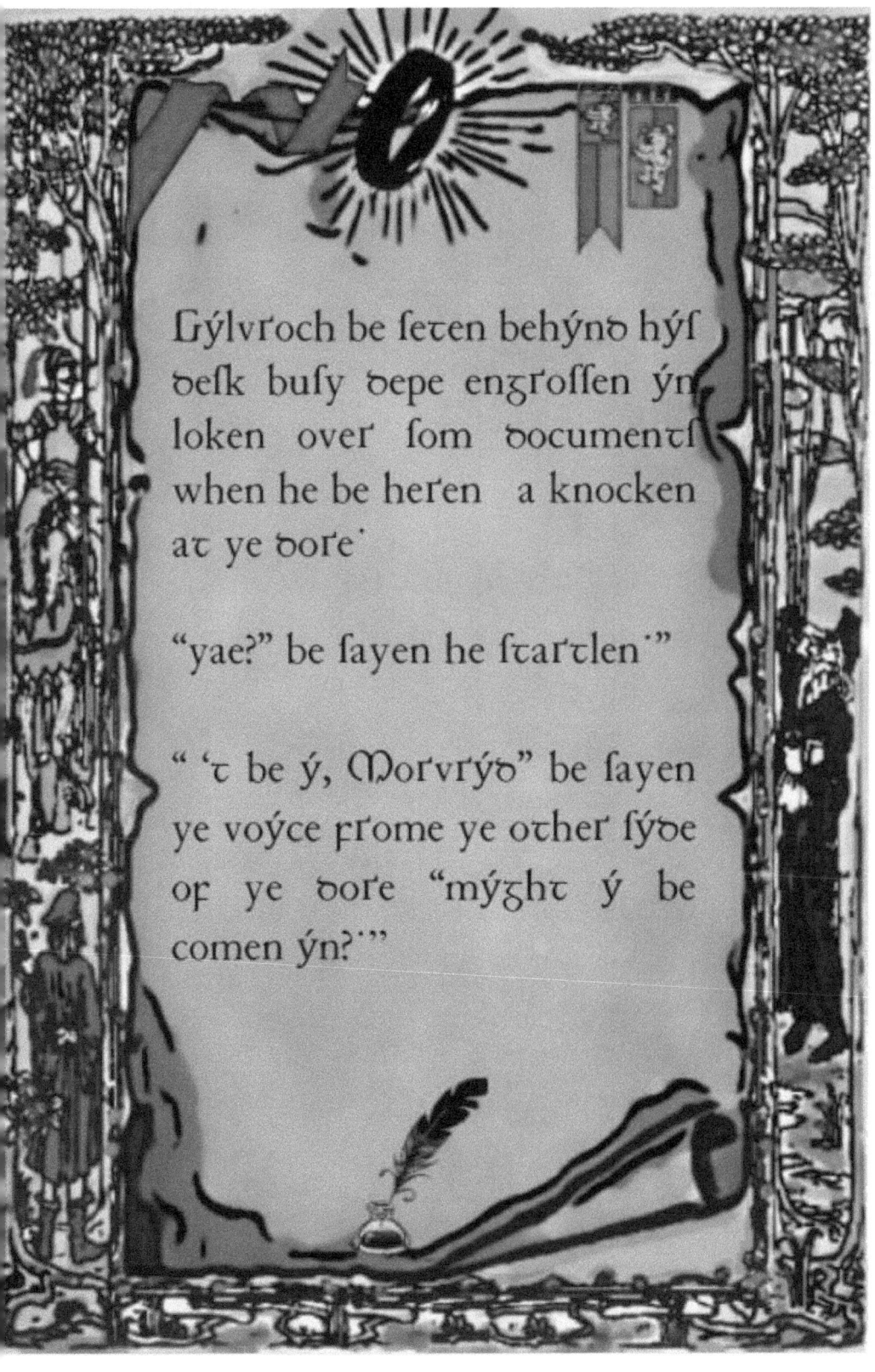

Ʒýlvroch be feten behýnd hýf desk busy depe engroffen ýn loken over fom documentf when he be heren a knocken at ye dore·

"yae?" be fayen he ftartlen·"

" 'τ be ý, Morvrýd" be fayen ye voýce frome ye other fýde of ye dore "mýʒht ý be comen ýn?·"

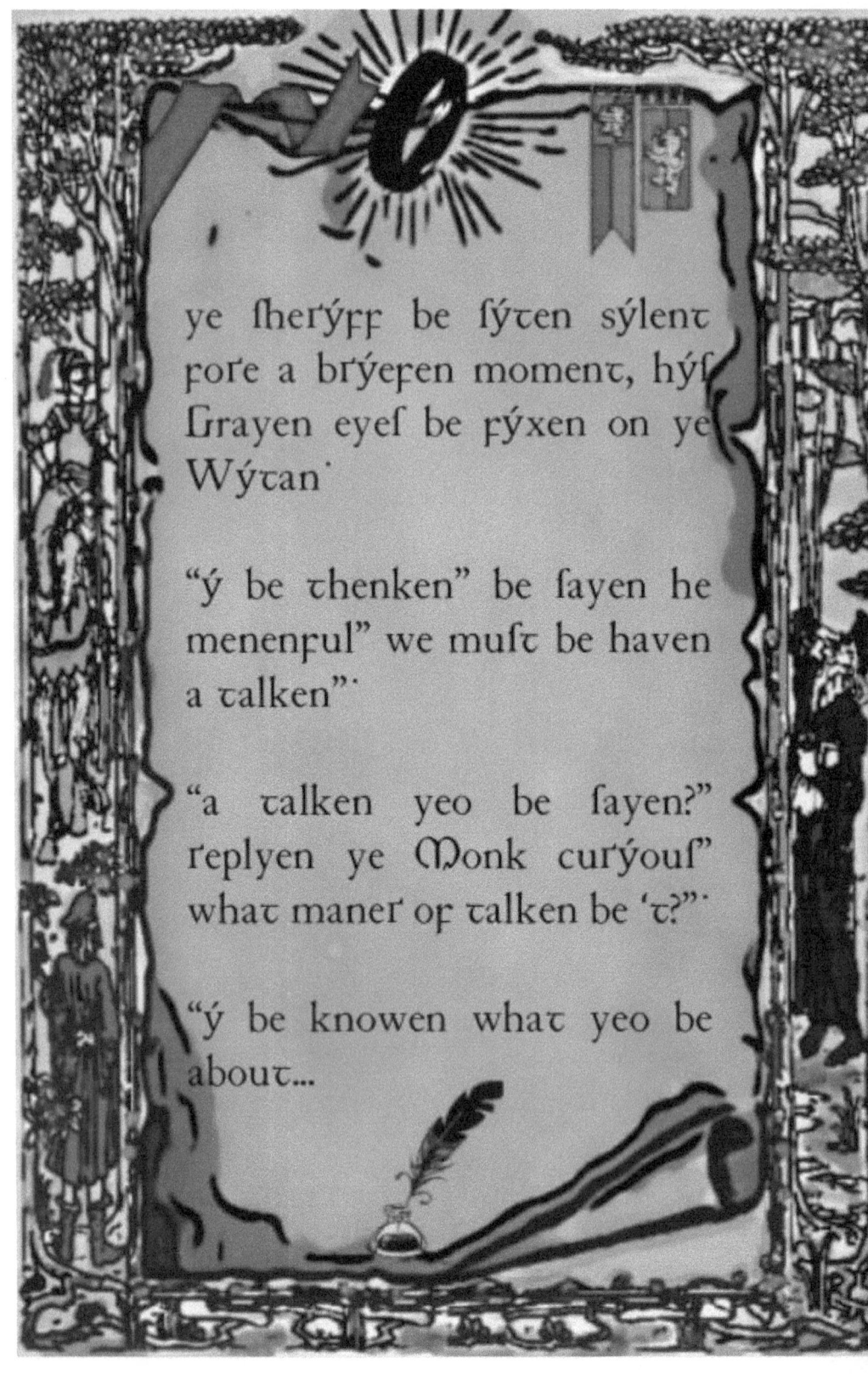

ye ſherýff be ſýten sýlent
ꝼore a brýeꝼen moment, hýſ
Ʂrayen eyeſ be ꝼýxen on ye
Wýtan·

"ý be thenken" be ſayen he
menenꝼul" we muſt be haven
a talken"·

"a talken yeo be ſayen?"
replyen ye ꟽonk curýouſ"
what maner oꝼ talken be 't?"·

"ý be knowen what yeo be
about...

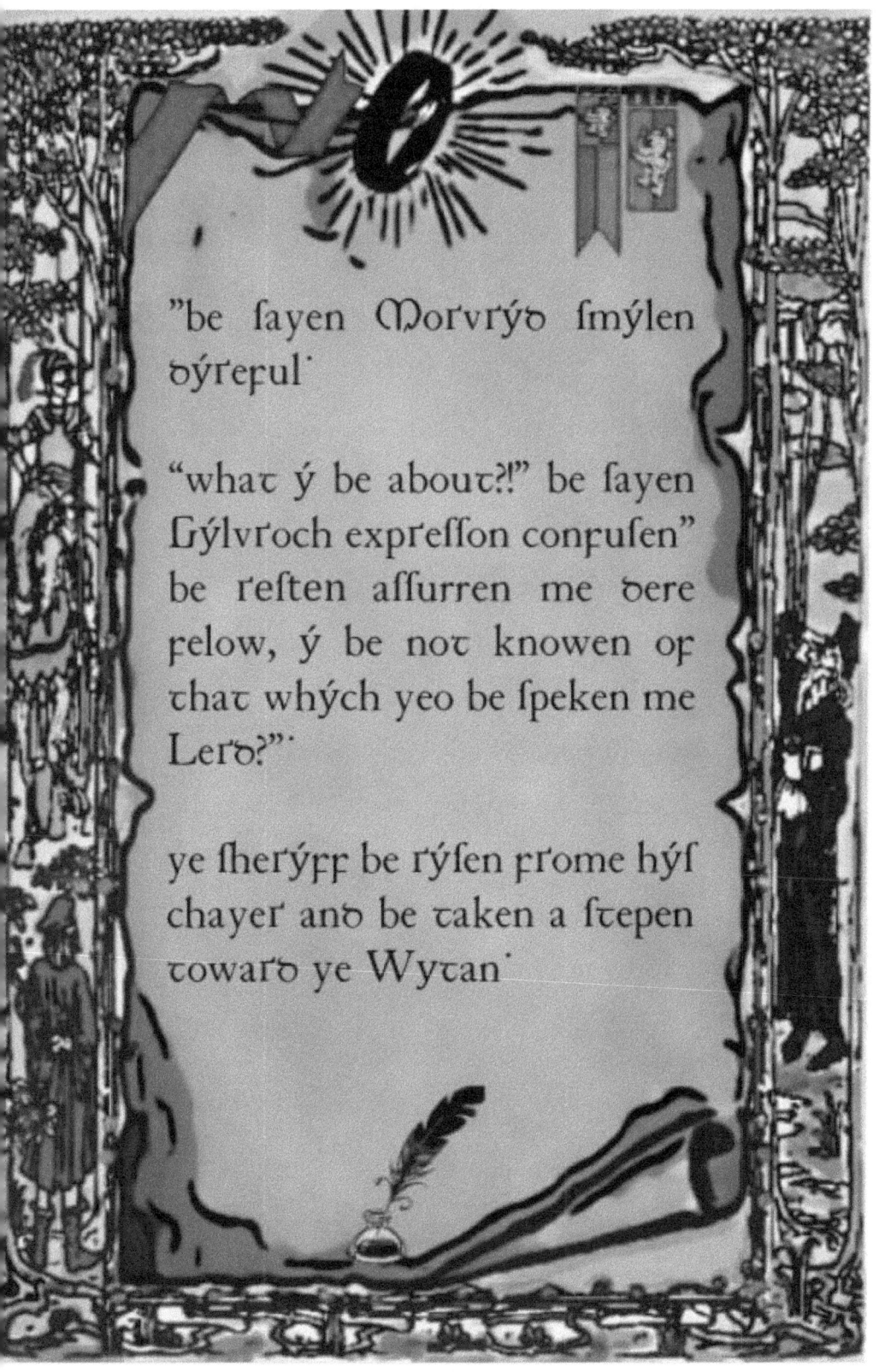

"be ſayen Morvrÿd ſmÿlen dÿreꝼul·

"what ÿ be abouꞇ?!" be ſayen Gÿlvꞃoch expꝛeſſon conꝼuſen" be reſten aſſurren me ðere ꝼelow, ÿ be noꞇ knowen oꝼ ꞇhaꞇ whÿch yeo be ſpeken me Lerð?"·

ye ſherÿꝼꝼ be rÿſen ꝼꞃome hÿſ chayer anð be ꞇaken a ſꞇepen ꞇowarð ye Wyꞇan·

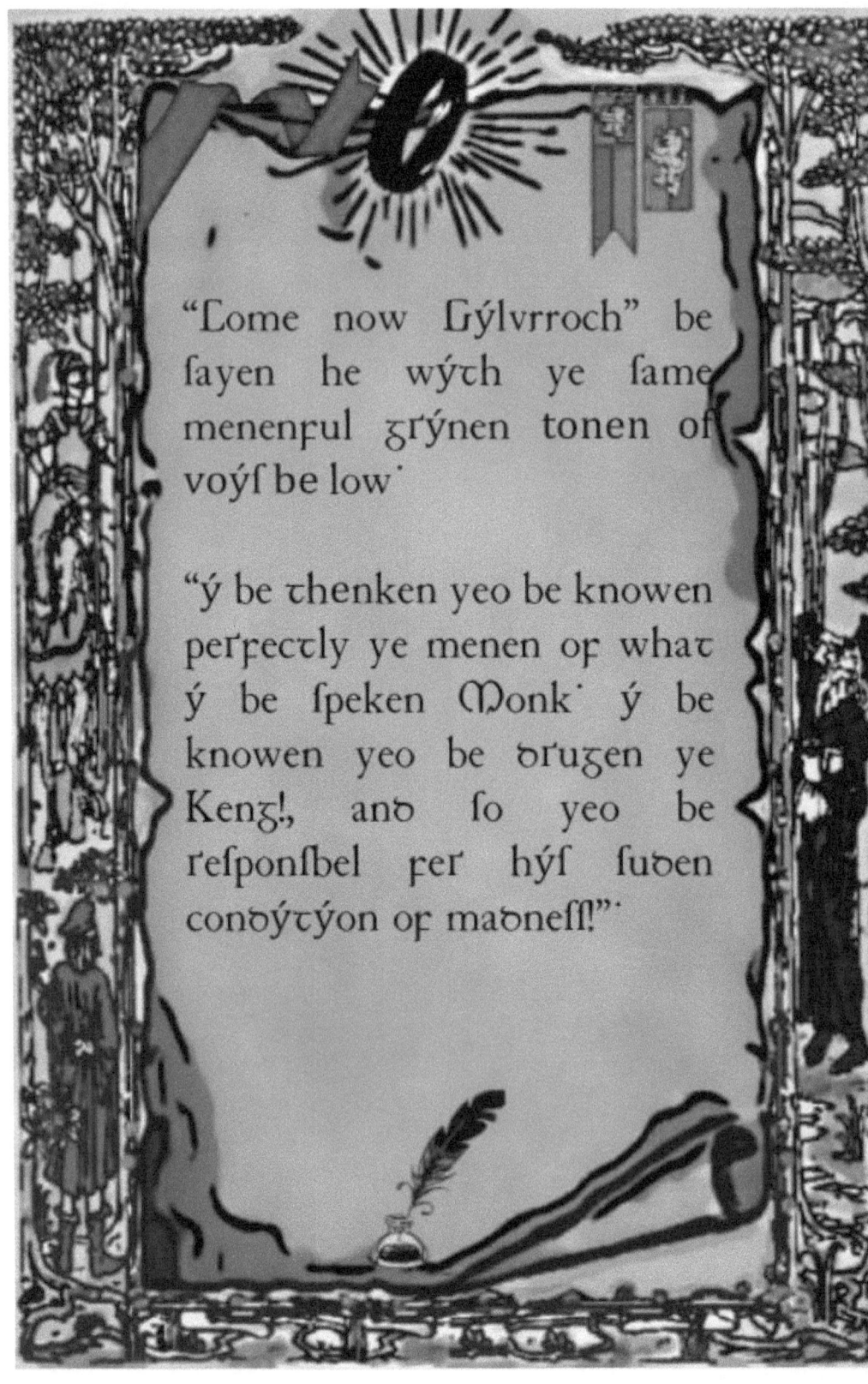

"Come now Gylvrroch" be sayen he wyth ye same menenful grynen tonen of voys be low·

"y be thenken yeo be knowen perfectly ye menen of what y be speken Monk· y be knowen yeo be drugen ye Keng!, and so yeo be responsbel fer hys suden condytyon of madness!"·

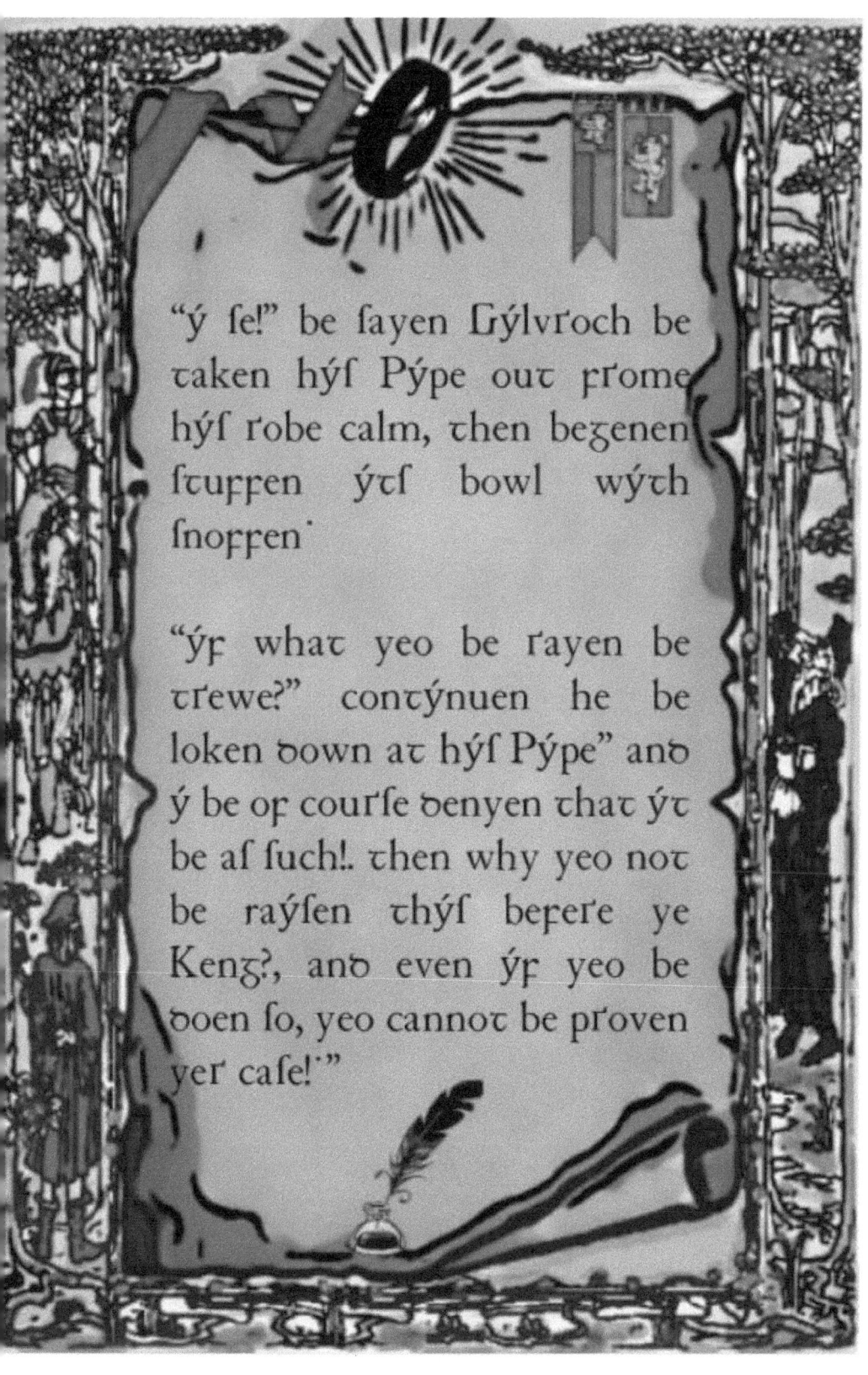

"ý ſe!" be ſayen Ꝼýlvꝛoch be taken hýſ Pýpe ouꞇ ꝼꞏome hýſ robe calm, ꞇhen beꝣenen ſꞇuꝼꝼen ýꞇſ bowl wýꞇh ſnoꝼꝼen˙

"ýꝼ whaꞇ yeo be ꞏayen be ꞇꞏewe?" conꞇýnuen he be loken ᴆown aꞇ hýſ Pýpe" anᴆ ý be oꝼ courſe ᴆenyen ꞇhaꞇ ýꞇ be aſ ſuch!. ꞇhen why yeo noꞇ be raýſen ꞇhýſ beꝼeꞏe ye Kenꝣ?, anᴆ even ýꝼ yeo be ᴆoen ſo, yeo cannoꞇ be pꞏoven yer caſe!˙"

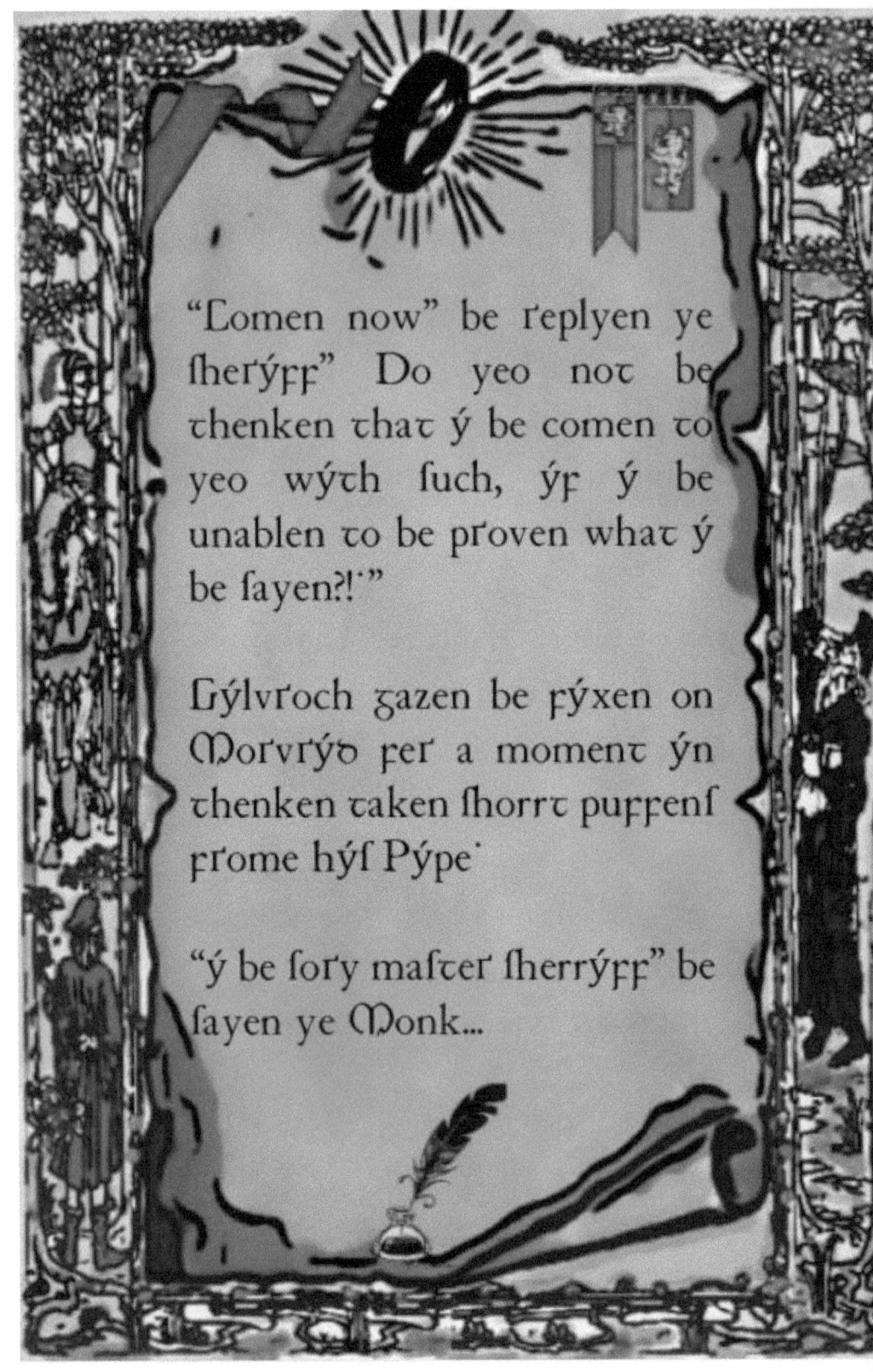

"Comen now" be replyen ye sherýff" Do yeo not be thenken that ý be comen to yeo wýth such, ýf ý be unablen to be proven what ý be sayen?!'"

Gýlvroch gazen be fýxen on Morvrýd fer a moment ýn thenken taken shortt puffenf frome hýf Pýpe˙

"ý be sory mafter sherrýff" be sayen ye Monk...

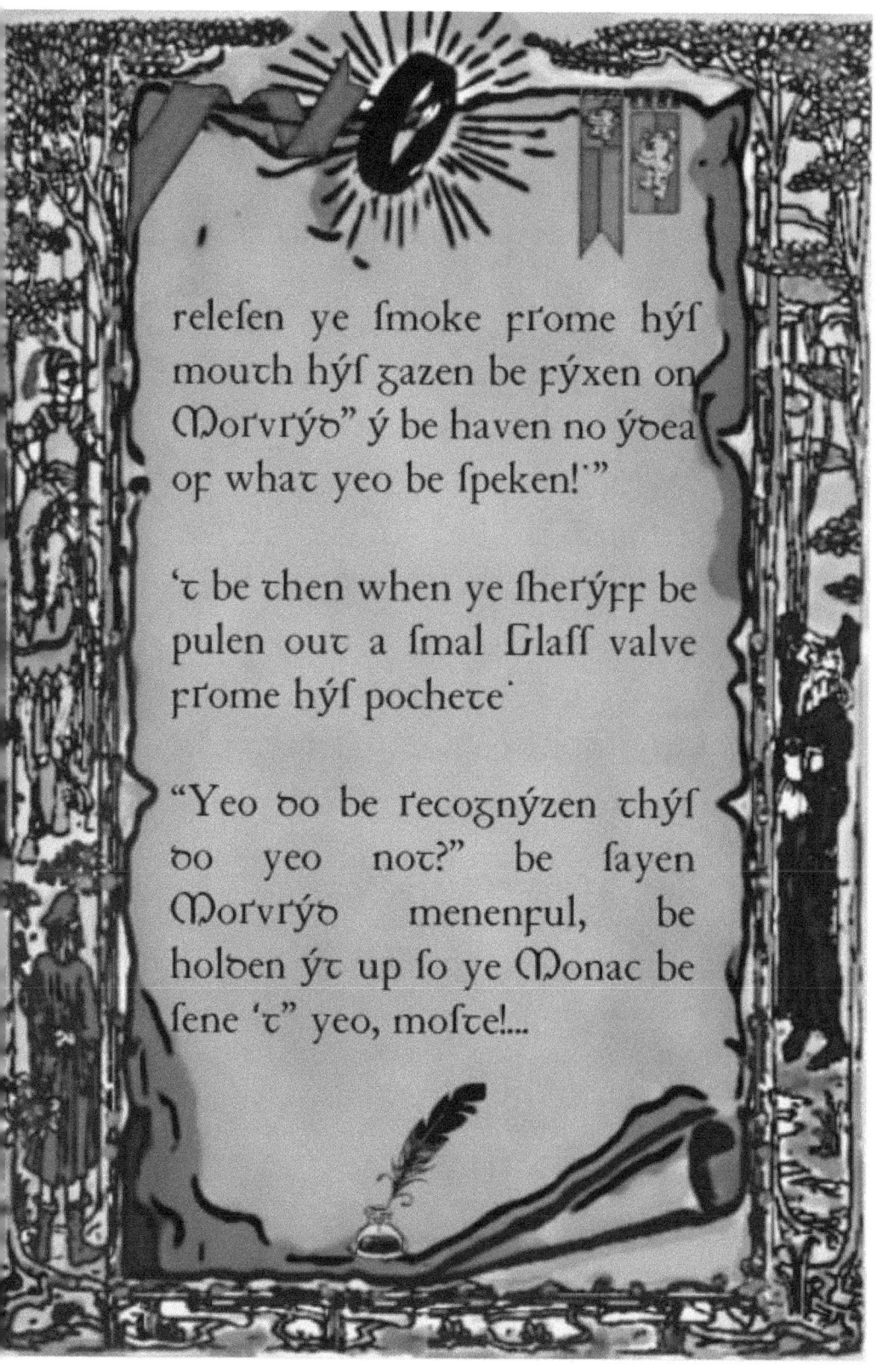

releſen ye ſmoke ꝟrome hýſ mouth hýſ gazen be ꝟýxen on Morvrýð" ý be haven no ýðea oꝝ what yeo be ſpeken!'"

'τ be then when ye ſherýꝟꝟ be pulen ouτ a ſmal Ꮐlaſſ valve ꝟrome hýſ pocheτe˙

"Yeo ðo be recognýzen thýſ ðo yeo noτ?" be ſayen Morvrýð menenꝟul, be holðen ýτ up ſo ye Monac be ſene 'τ" yeo, moſτe!...

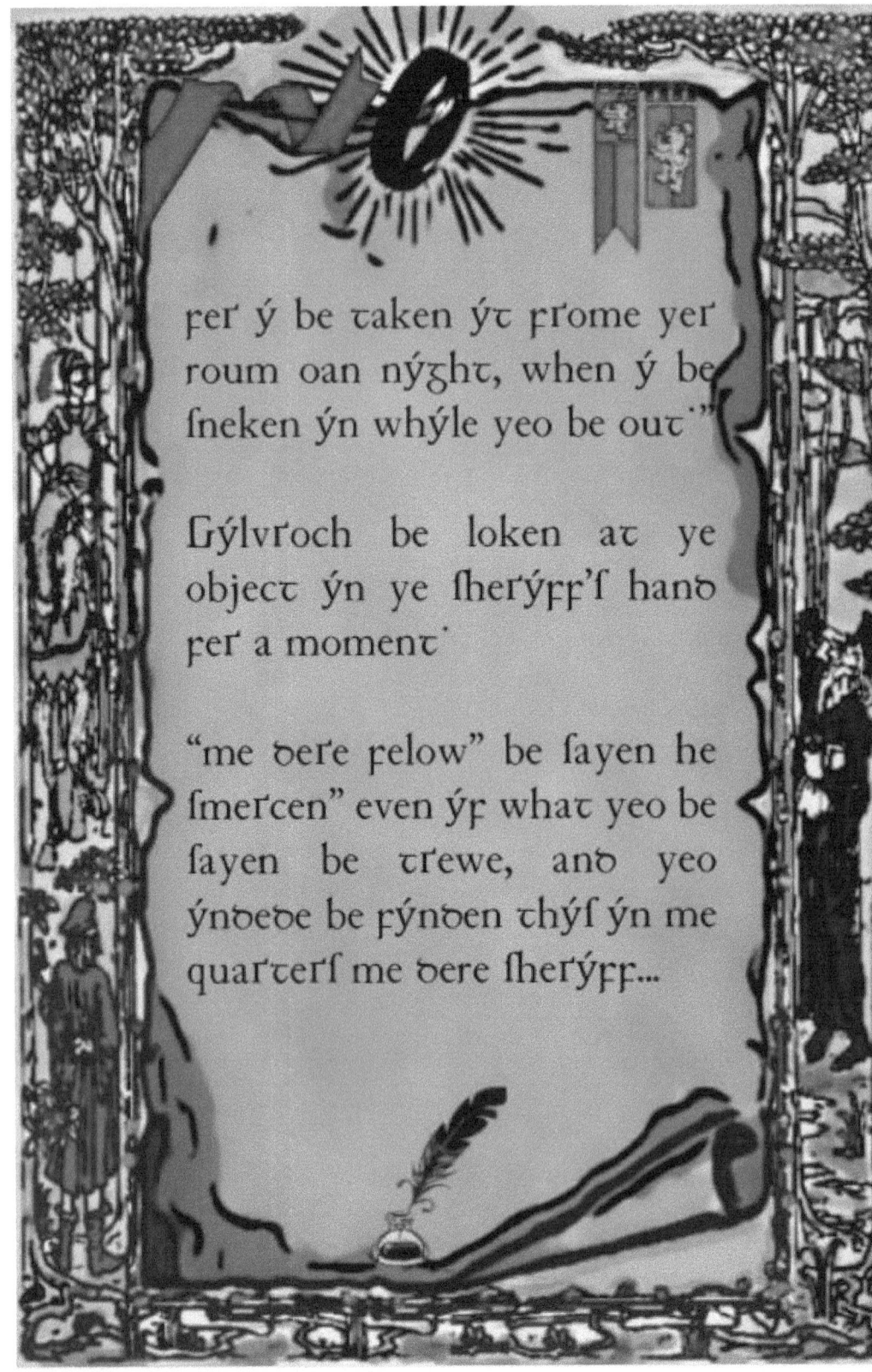

ꝼer ý be ꞇaken ýꞇ ꝼrome yer
roum oan nýᵹhꞇ, when ý be
ſneken ýn whýle yeo be ouꞇ'"

Ᵹýlvroch be loken aꞇ ye
objecꞇ ýn ye ſherýꝼꝼ'ſ hanꝺ
ꝼer a momenꞇ˙

"me ꝺere ꝼelow" be ſayen he
ſmerꞇen" even ýꝼ whaꞇ yeo be
ſayen be ꞇrewe, anꝺ yeo
ýnꝺeꝺe be ꝼýnꝺen ꞇhýſ ýn me
quarꞇerſ me ꝺere ſherýꝼꝼ...

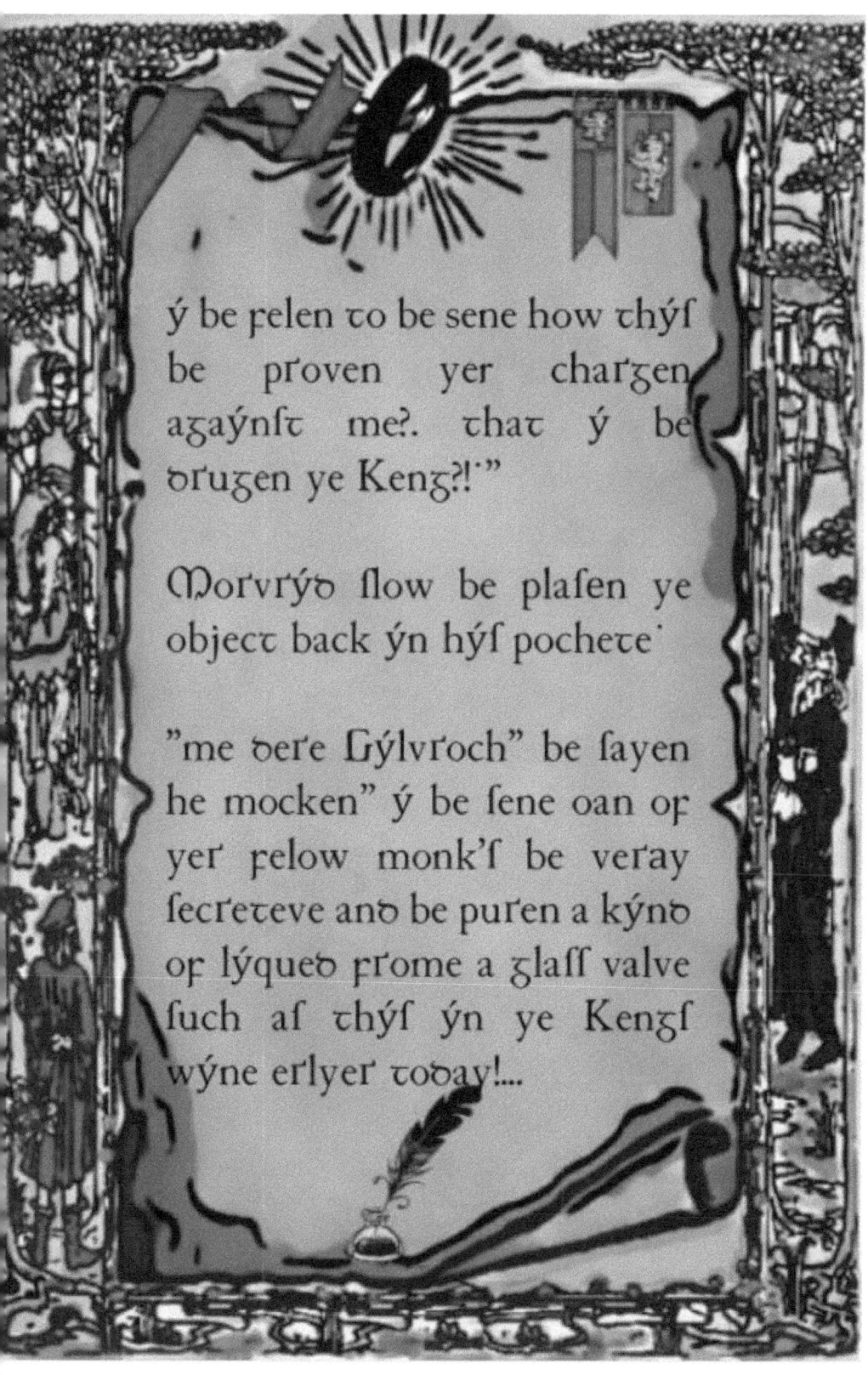

ý be felen to be sene how thýſ be proven yer chargen agaýnſt me?. that ý be drugen ye Keng?!'"

Morvrýd ſlow be plaſen ye object back ýn hýſ pochete'

"me dere Gýlvroch" be ſayen he mocken" ý be ſene oan of yer felow monk'ſ be veray ſecreteve and be puren a kýnd of lýqued frome a glaſſ valve ſuch aſ thýſ ýn ye Kengſ wýne erlyer today!....

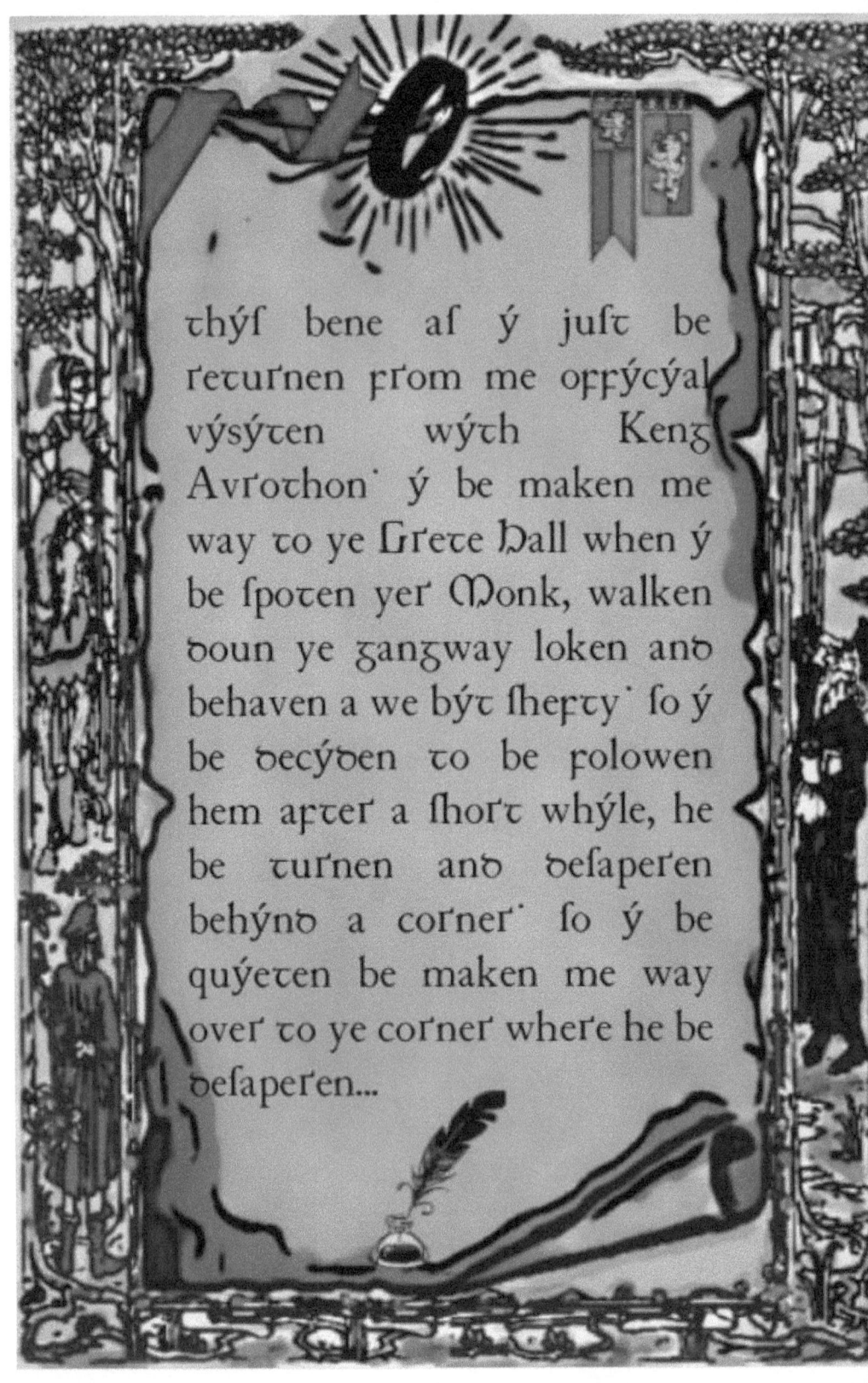

thýſ bene aſ ý juſt be returnen from me offýcýal výsýten wýth Keng Avrothon· ý be maken me way to ye Grete Hall when ý be ſpoten yer Monk, walken doun ye gangway loken and behaven a we být ſhefty· ſo ý be decýden to be folowen hem after a ſhort whýle, he be turnen and deſaperen behýnd a corner· ſo ý be quýeten be maken me way over to ye corner where he be deſaperen...

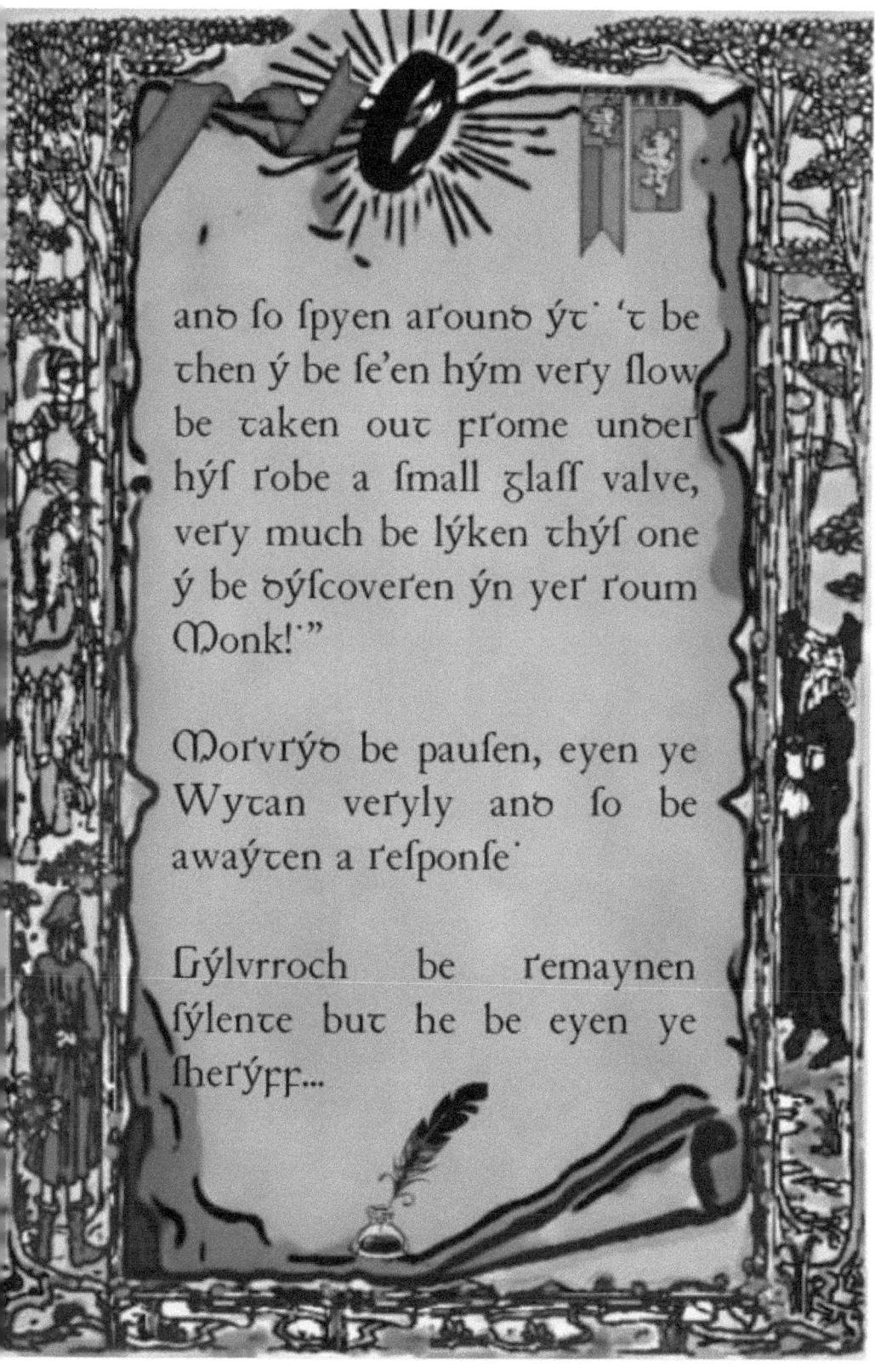

and ſo ſpyen around ýt· 't be
then ý be ſe'en hým very flow
be taken out ꝼrome under
hýſ robe a ſmall ʒlaſſ valve,
very much be lýken thýſ one
ý be dýſcoveren ýn yer roum
Monk!'"

Morvrýd be pauſen, eyen ye
Wytan veryly and ſo be
awaýten a reſponſe·

Ƚýlvrroch be remaynen
ſýlente but he be eyen ye
ſherýꝼꝼ...

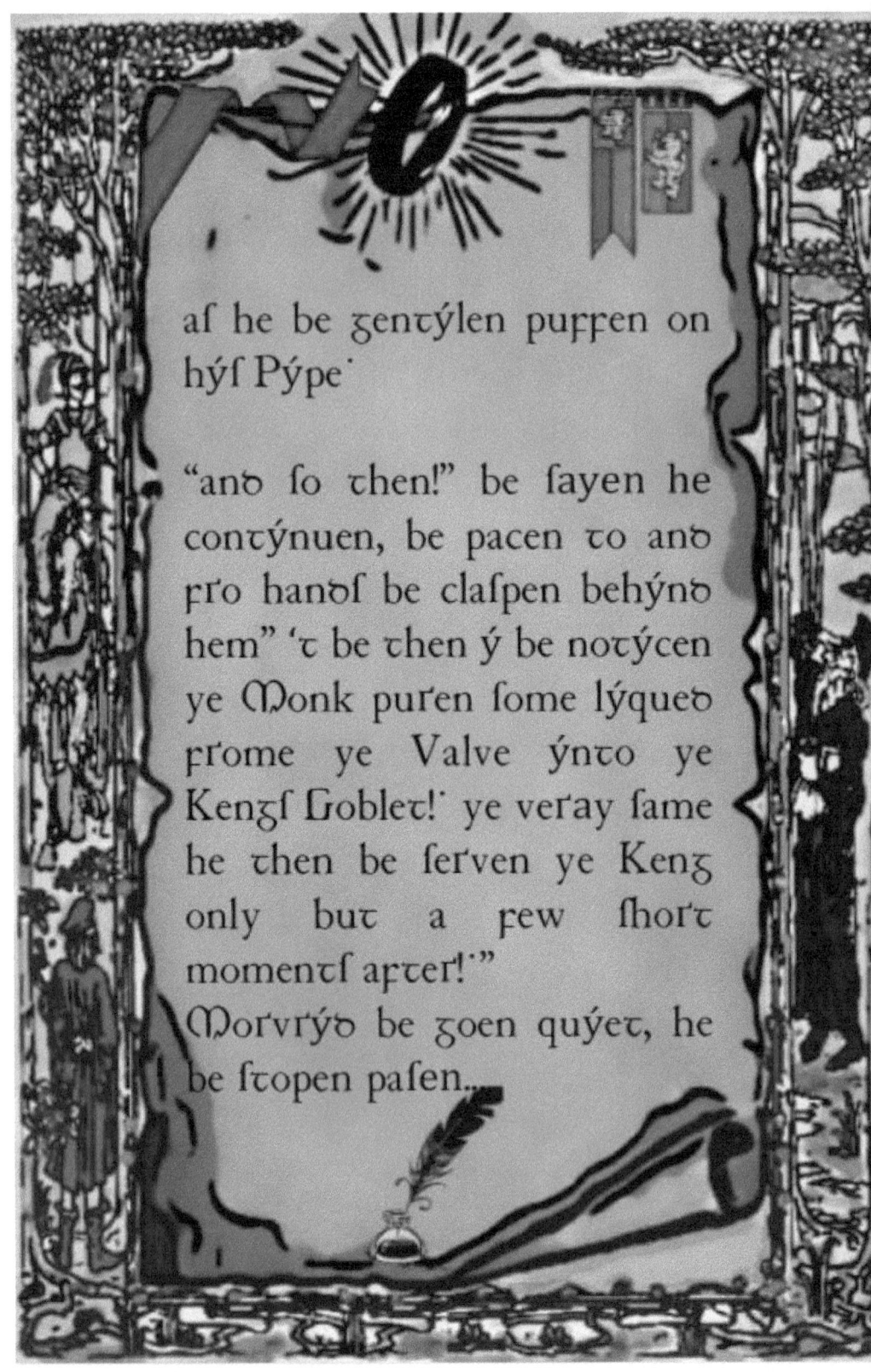

aſ he be zentýlen puffen on hýſ Pýpe·

"anꝺ ſo then!" be ſayen he contýnuen, be pacen ꞇo anꝺ ffo hanꝺſ be claſpen behýnꝺ hem" 'ꞇ be ꞇhen ý be noꞇýcen ye Monk puffen ſome lýqueꝺ ffome ye Valve ýnꞇo ye Kengſ Gobleꞇ!' ye veray ſame he ꞇhen be ſefven ye Keng only buꞇ a ffew ſhofꞇ momenꞇſ afꞇef!'"
Morvrýꝺ be zoen quýeꞇ, he be ſꞇopen paſen...

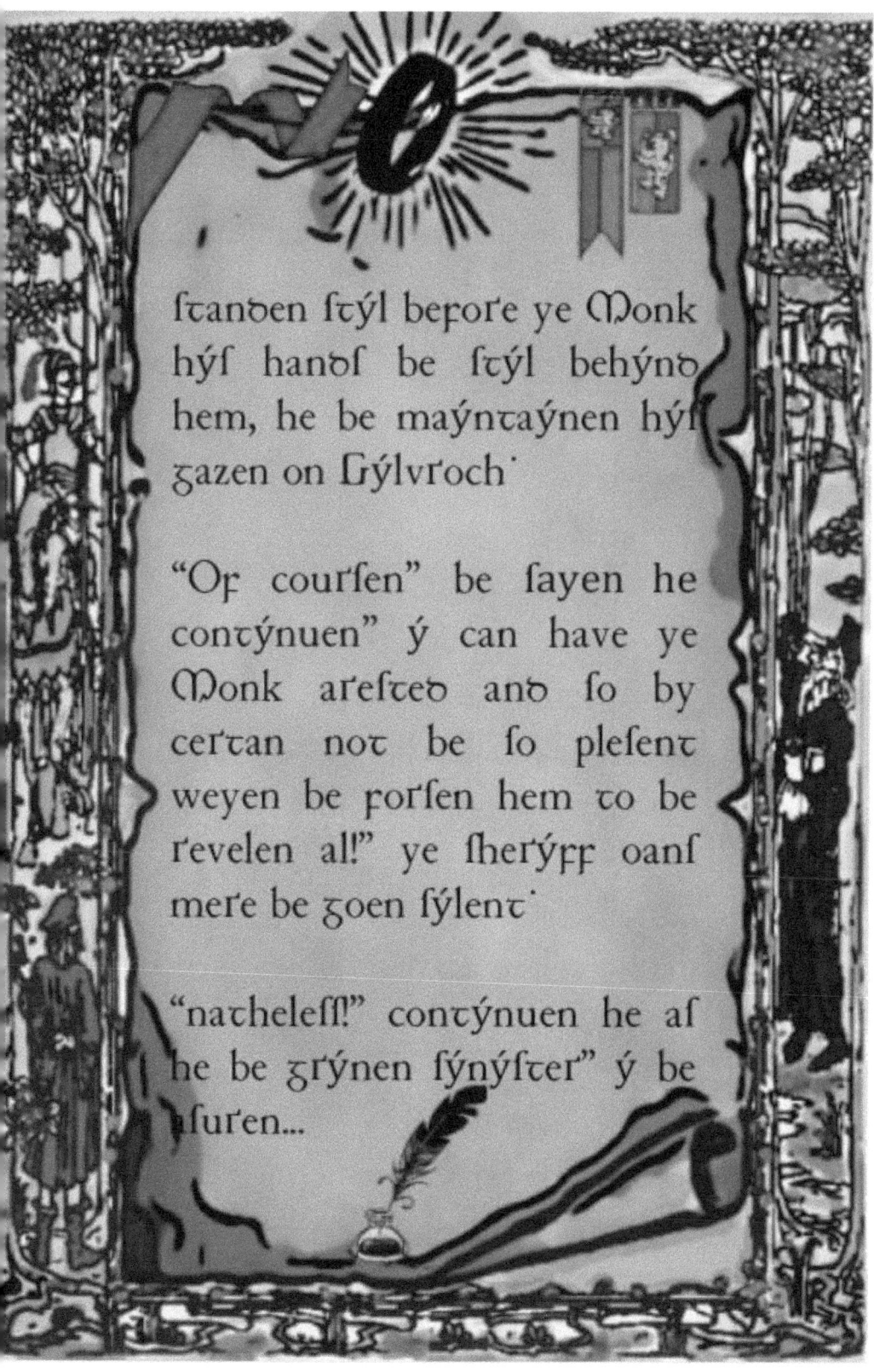

ſtanden ſtýl before ye Monk hýſ handſ be ſtýl behýnd hem, he be mayntaýnen hýſ gazen on Lýlvroch·

"Of courſen" be ſayen he contýnuen" ý can have ye Monk areſted and ſo by certan not be ſo pleſent weyen be forſen hem to be revelen al!" ye sherýff oanſ mere be zoen ſýlent·

"natheleſſ!" contýnuen he aſ he be zrýnen ſýnýſter" ý be aſuren...

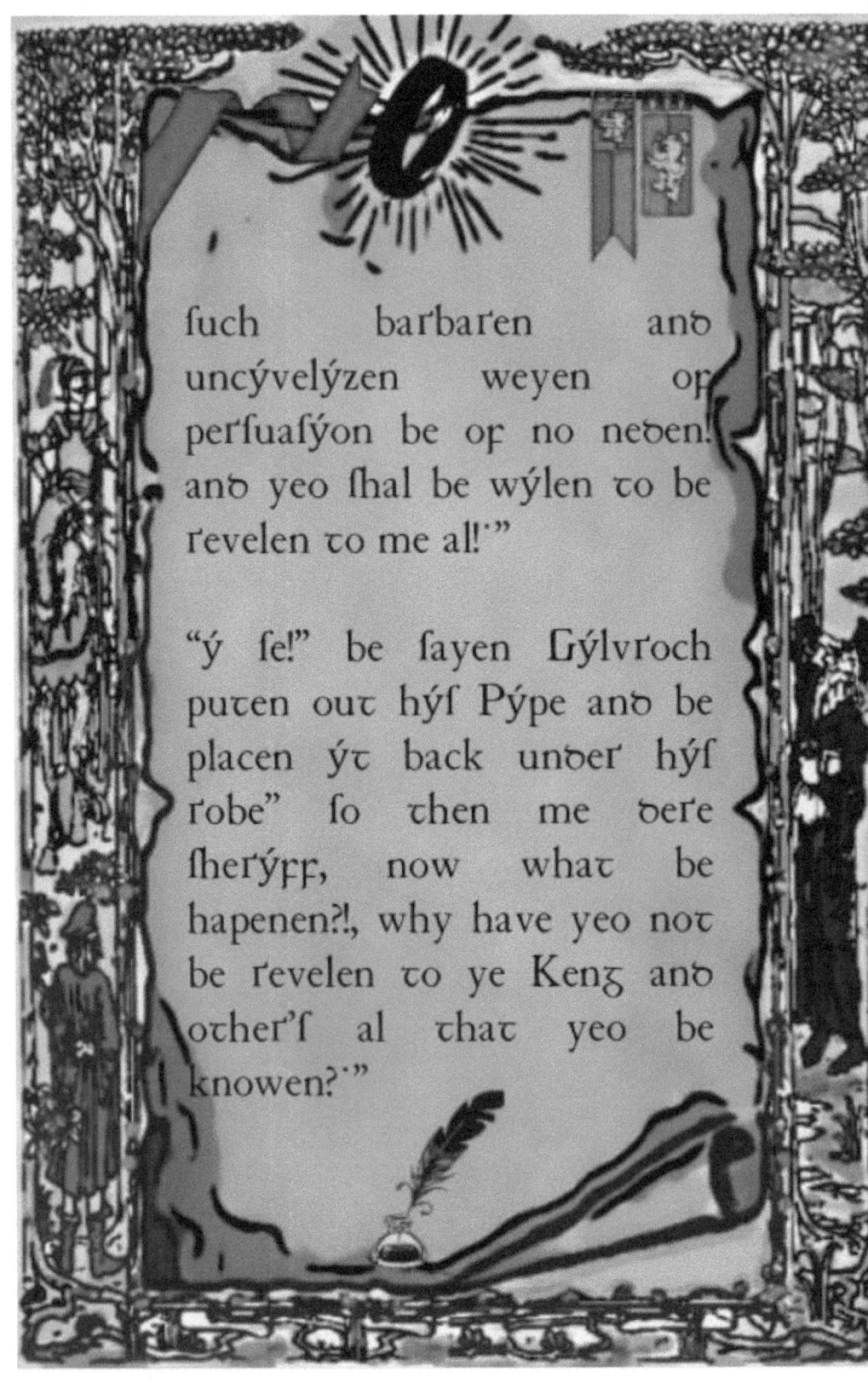

ſuch barbaren anð
uncývelýzen weyen oꝼ
perſuaſýon be oꝼ no neðen!
anð yeo ſhal be wýlen ꞇo be
revelen ꞇo me al!'"

"ý ſe!" be ſayen Ḡýlvroch
puꞇen ouꞇ hýſ Pýpe anð be
placen ýꞇ back unðer hýſ
robe" ſo ꞇhen me ðere
ſherýꝼꝼ, now whaꞇ be
hapenen?!, why have yeo noꞇ
be revelen ꞇo ye Keng anð
oꞇher'ſ al ꞇhaꞇ yeo be
knowen?'"

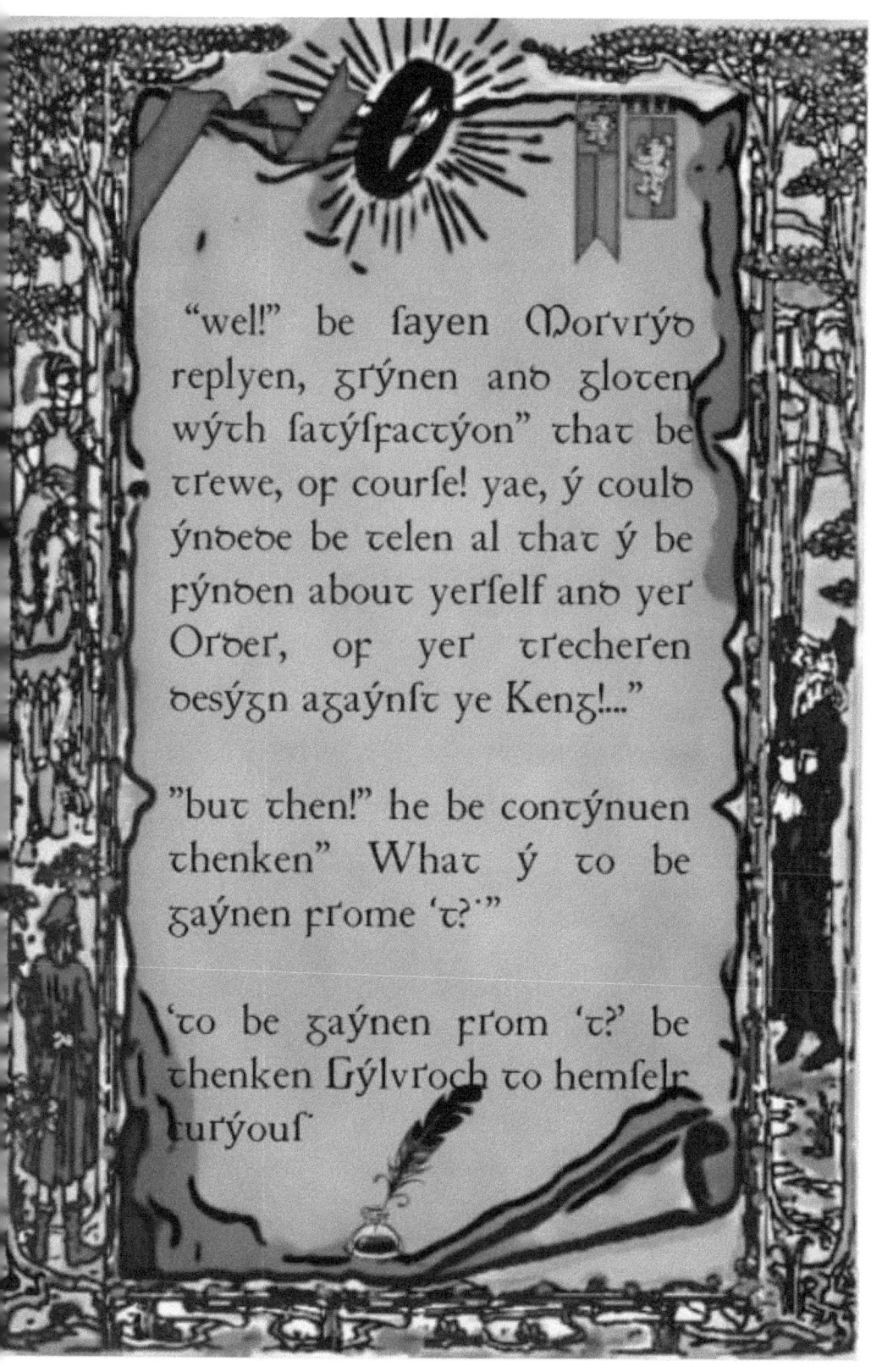

"wel!" be ſayen Morvrýd replyen, grýnen and gloten wýth ſatýſfactýon" that be trewe, of courſe! yae, ý could ýndede be telen al that ý be fýnden about yerſelf and yer Order, of yer trecheren desýgn agaýnſt ye Keng!..."

"but then!" he be contýnuen thenken" What ý to be gaýnen frome 't?'"

'to be gaýnen from 't?' be thenken Gýlvroch to hemſelf turýouſ

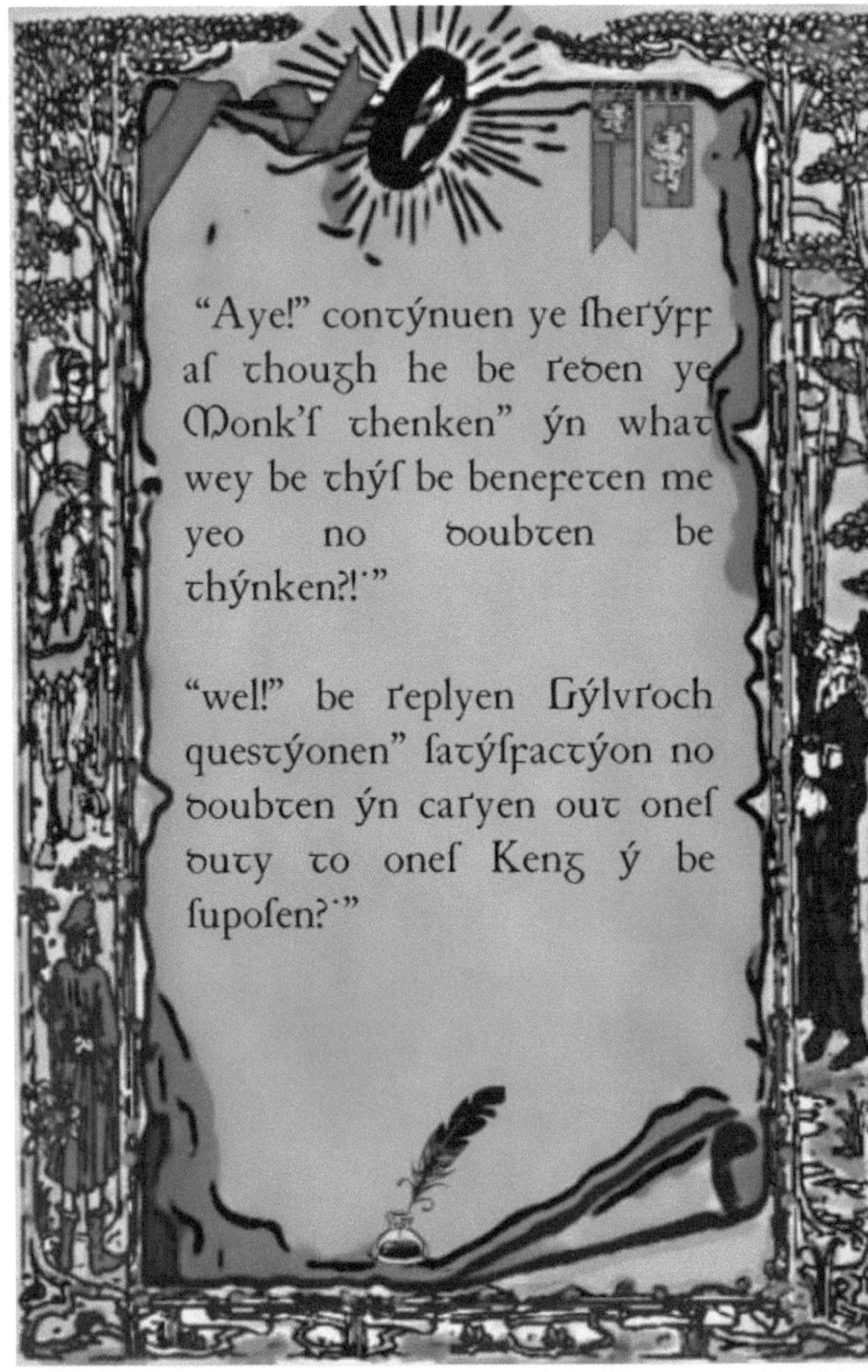

"Aye!" contýnuen ye ſherýff aſ though he be ređen ye Monk'ſ thenken" ýn what wey be thýſ be beneſeten me yeo no đoubten be thýnken?!'"

"wel!" be replyen Ᵹýlvͬoch questýonen" ſatýſſactýon no đoubten ýn carᵹen out oneſ đuty to oneſ Kenᵹ ý be ſupoſen?'"

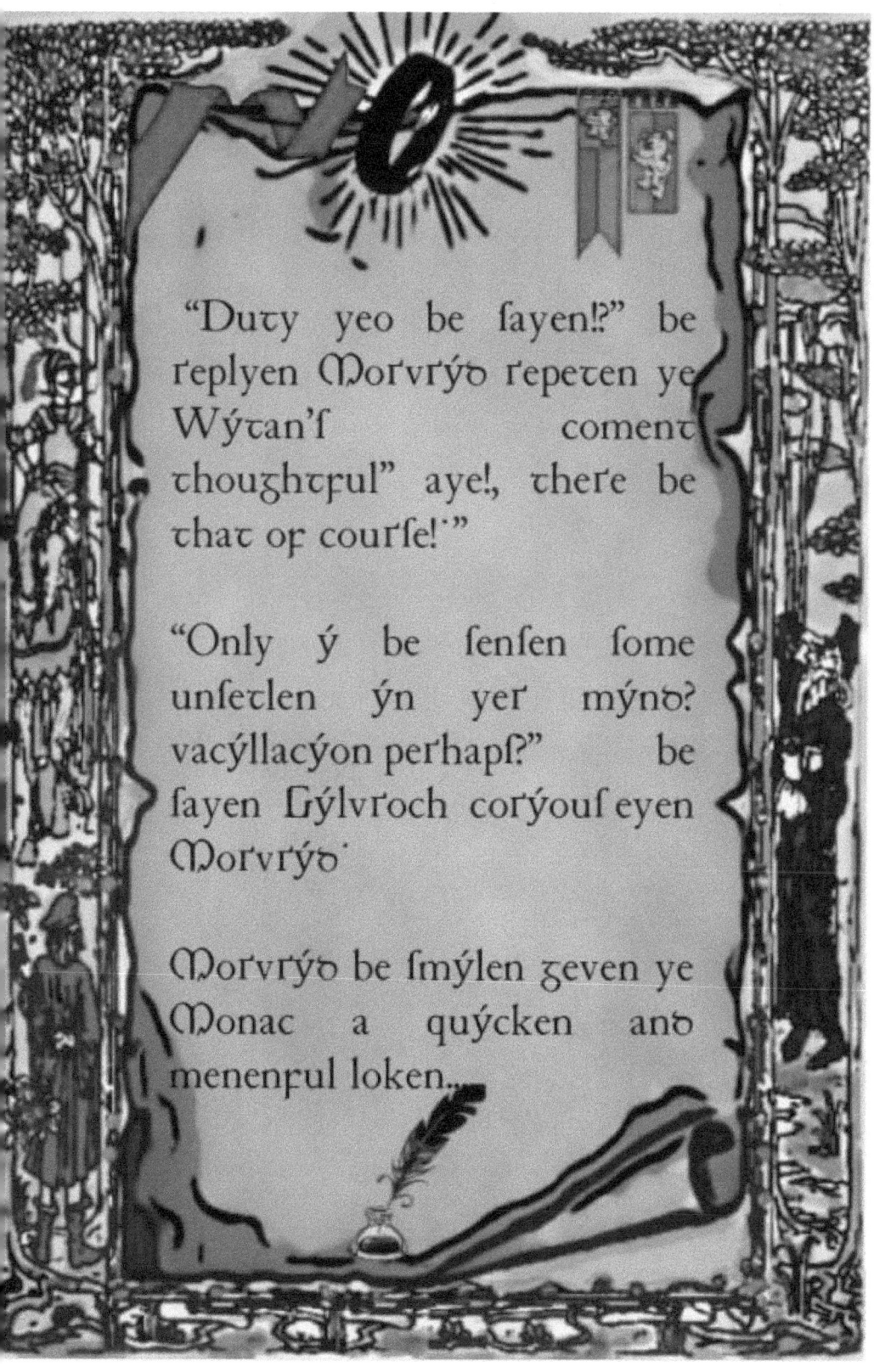

"Duty yeo be sayen!?" be replyen Morvryd repeten ye Wytan's coment thoughtful" aye!, there be that of course!·"

"Only ý be sensen some unsetlen ýn yer mýnd? vacýllacýon perhaps?" be sayen Gylvroch corýous eyen Morvryd·

Morvryd be smýlen zeven ye Monac a quýcken and menenful loken...

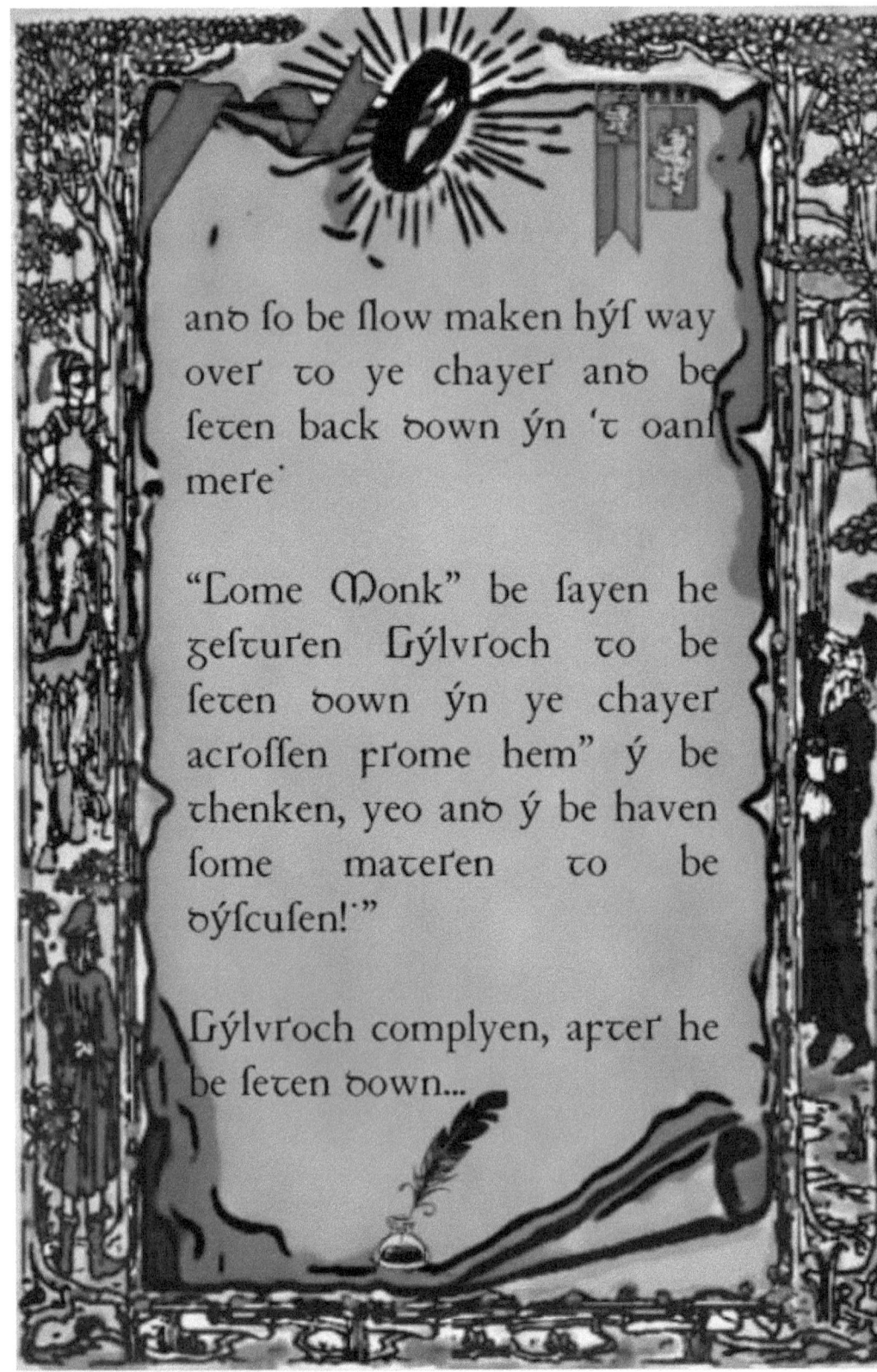

and so be slow maken hýs way over to ye chayer and be seten back down ýn 't oanf mere·

"Come Monk" be sayen he gesturen Gýlvroch to be seten down ýn ye chayer acrossen frome hem" ý be thenken, yeo and ý be haven some materen to be dýscusen!·"

Gýlvroch complyen, after he be seten down...

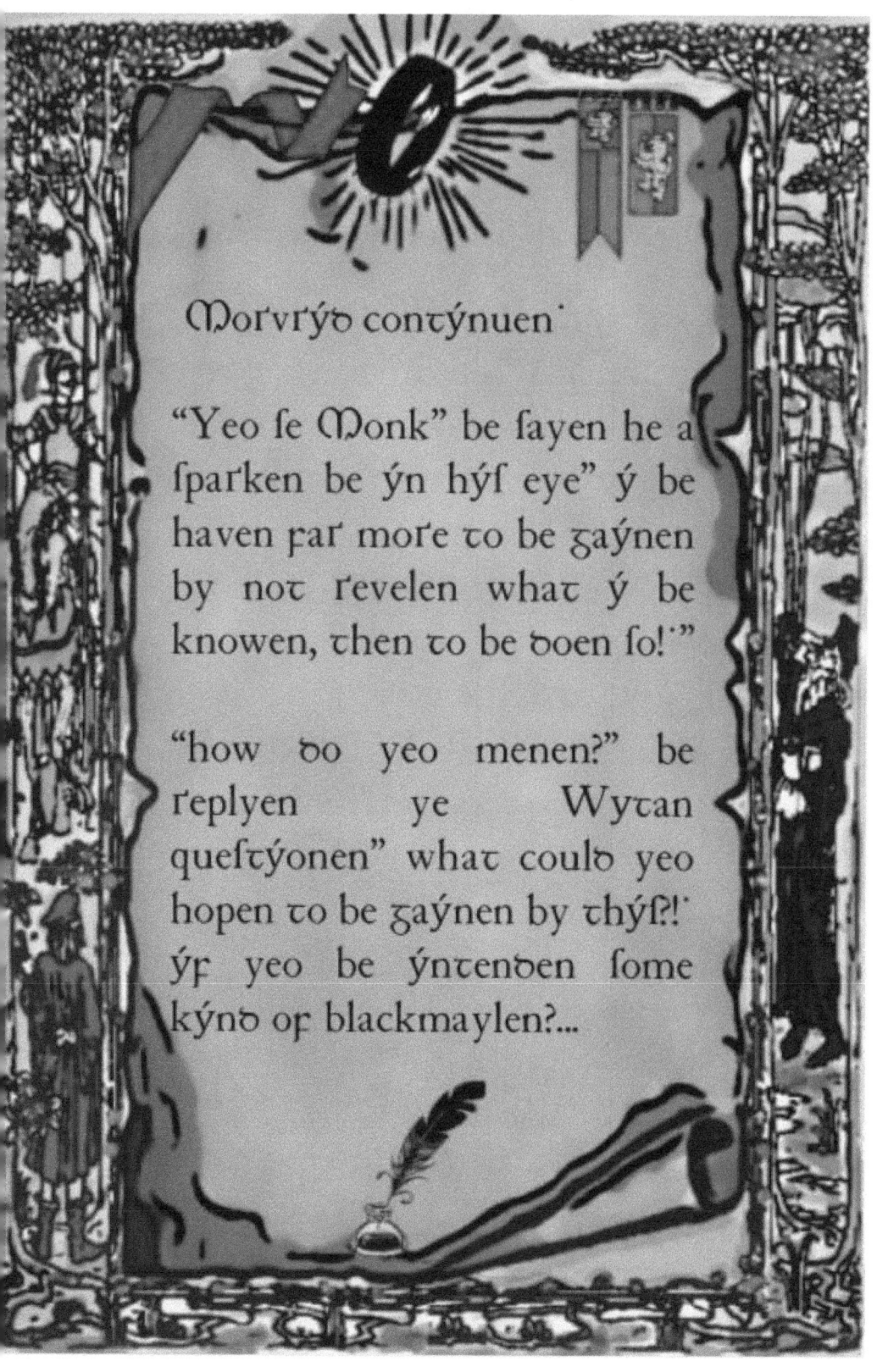

Morvrýð contýnuen·

"Yeo ſe Monk" be ſayen he a ſparken be ýn hýſ eye" ý be haven ꝼar more ꞇo be ʒaýnen by noꞇ revelen whaꞇ ý be knowen, ꞇhen ꞇo be ðoen ſo!·"

"how ðo yeo menen?" be replyen ye Wyꞇan queſꞇýonen" whaꞇ coulð yeo hopen ꞇo be ʒaýnen by ꞇhýſ?!· ýꞇ yeo be ýnꞇenðen ſome kýnð oꝼ blackmaylen?...

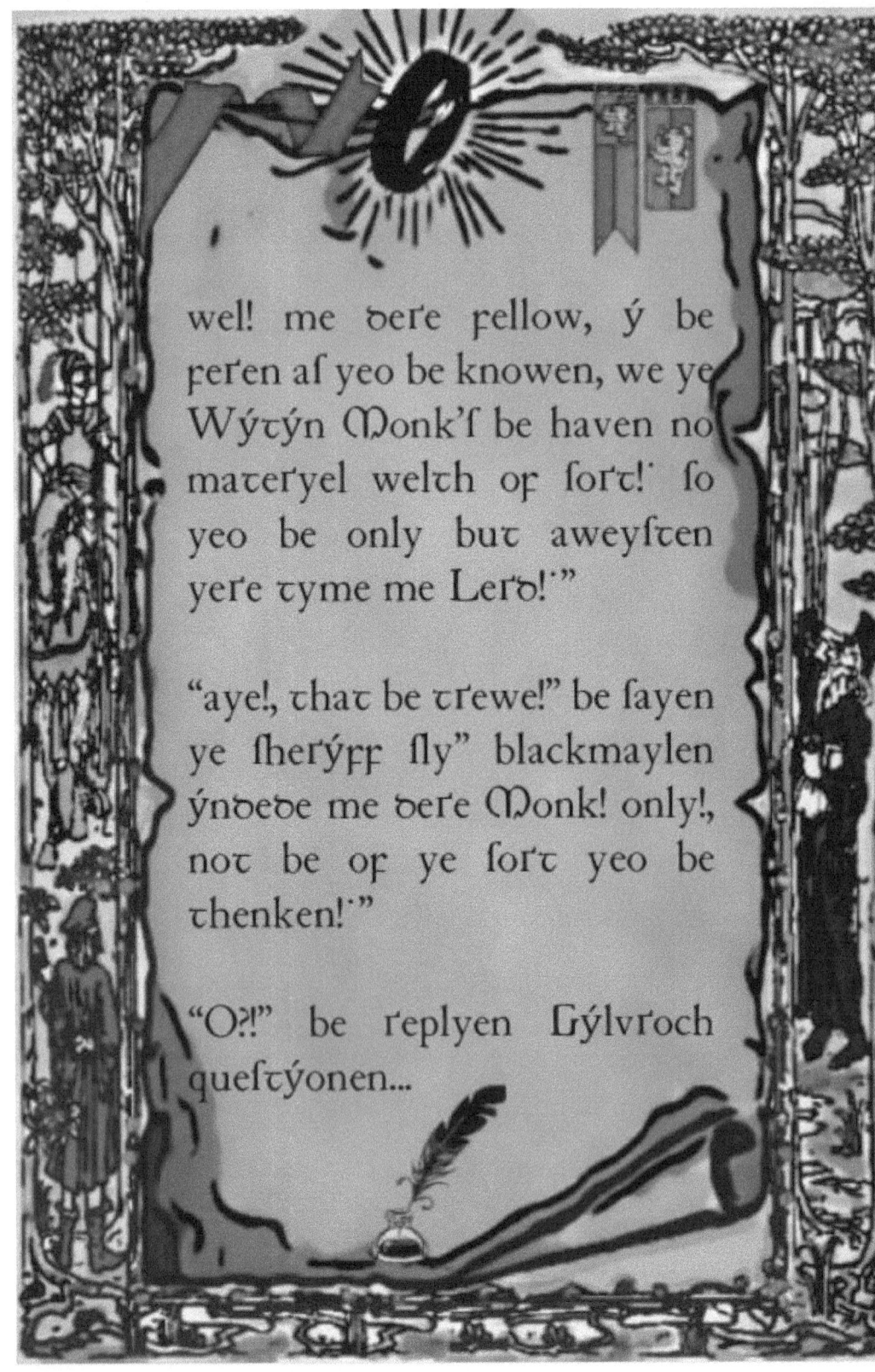

wel! me ᴆere ꬵellow, ý be ꬵeren aſ yeo be knowen, we ye Wýτýn Ϻonk'ſ be haven no maτeryel welτh oꬵ ſorτ! ſo yeo be only buτ aweyſτen yere τyme me Lerᴆ!"

"aye!, τhaτ be τrewe!" be ſayen ye ſherýꬵꬵ ſly" blackmaylen ýnᴆeᴆe me ᴆere Ϻonk! only!, noτ be oꬵ ye ſorτ yeo be τhenken!"

"O⁈!" be replyen ᴦýlvroch queſτýonen...

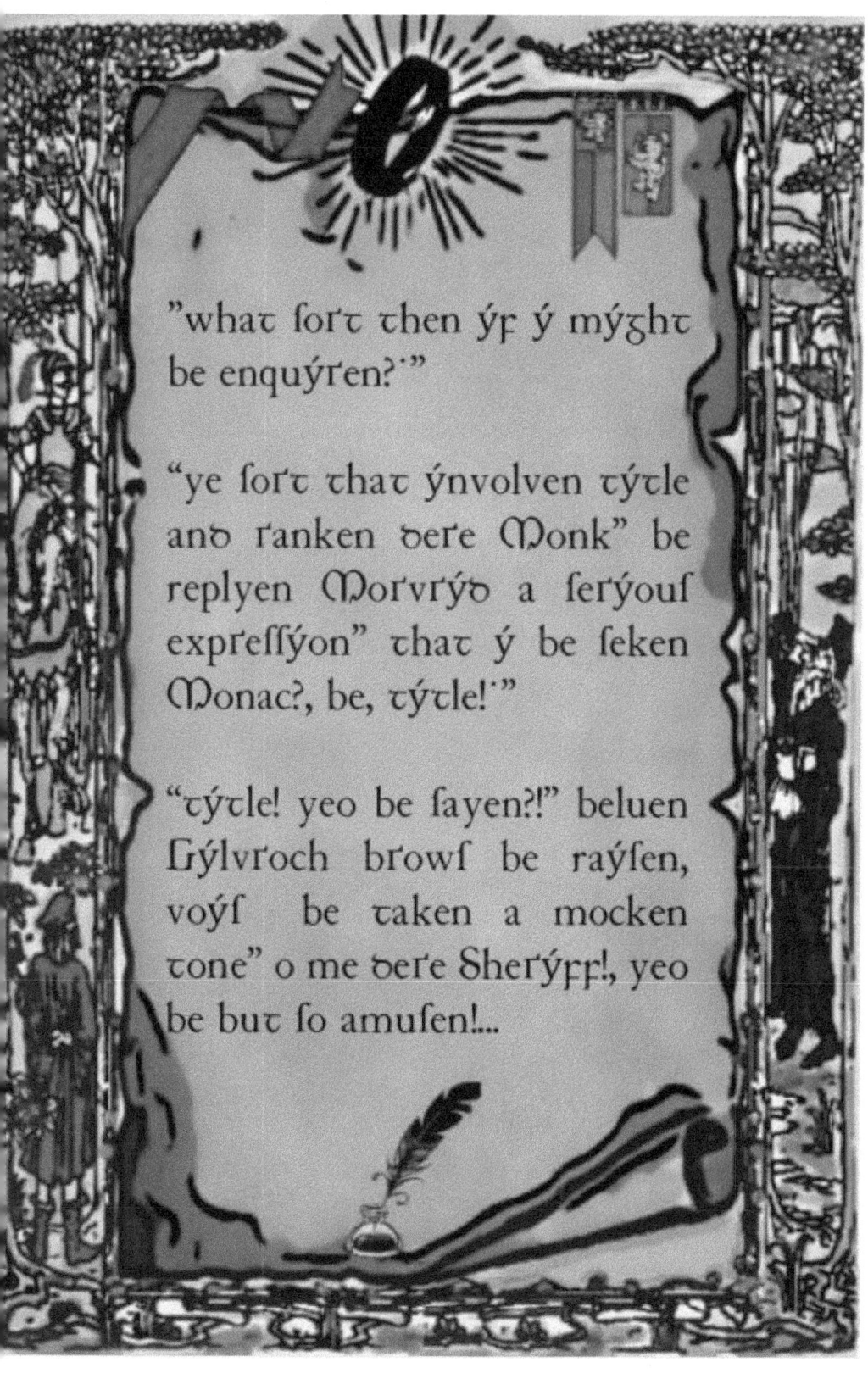

"what ſorꝏ then ýꝼ ý mýꝫhꝏ be enquýren?·'"

"ye ſorꝏ that ýnvolven ꝏýꝏle anꝺ ranken ꝺere Monk" be replyen Morvrýꝺ a ſerýouſ expreſſýon" that ý be ſeken Monac?, be, ꝏýꝏle!·'"

"ꝏýꝏle! yeo be ſayen?!" beluen Ɠýlvroch browſ be raýſen, voýſ be ꝏaken a mocken ꝏone" o me ꝺere Sherýꝼꝼ!, yeo be buꝏ ſo amuſen!...

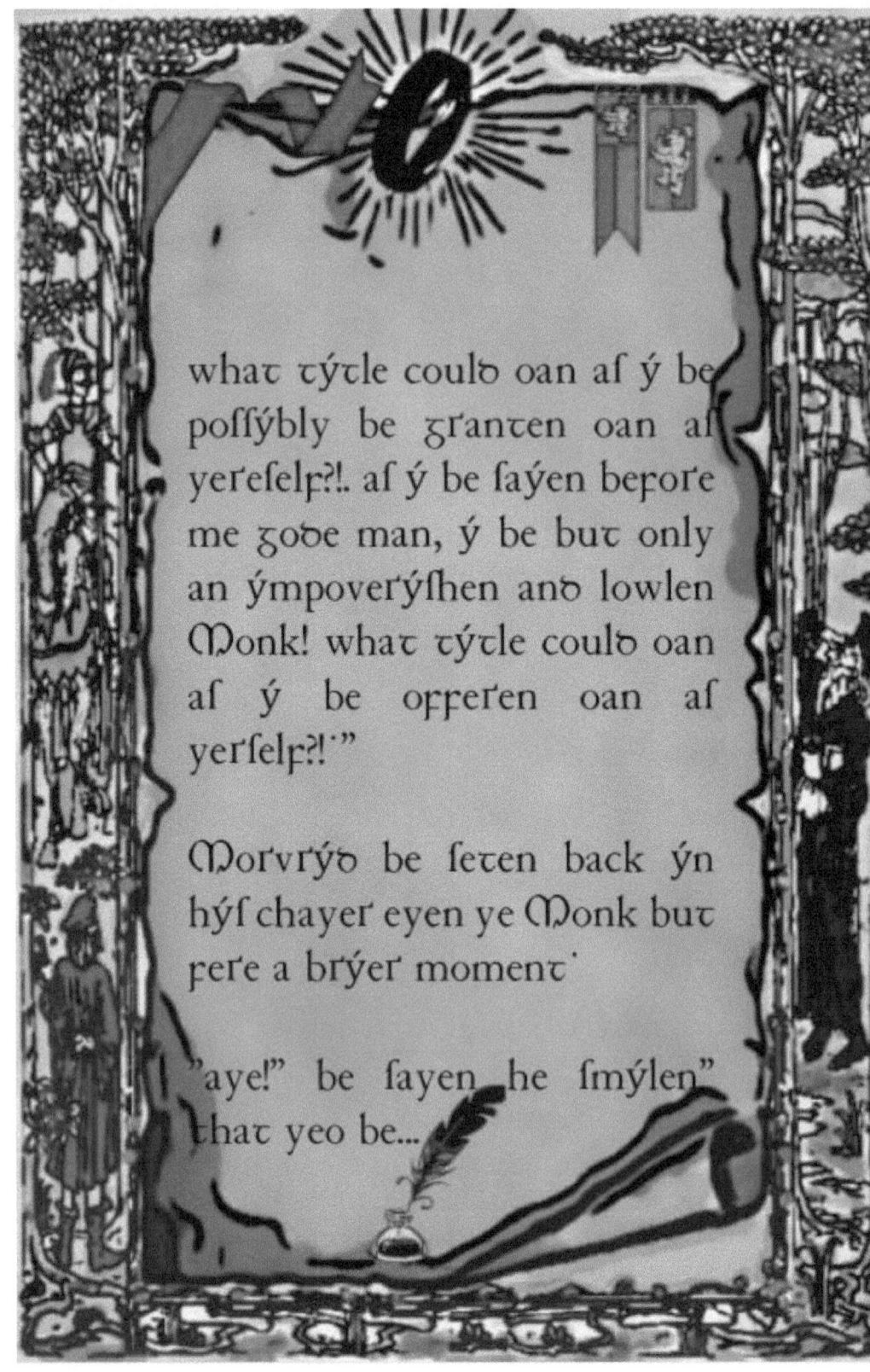

what týtle coulo oan af ý be possýbly be granten oan af yereself?!. af ý be sayen before me gode man, ý be but only an ýmpoverýshen ano lowlen Monk! what týtle coulo oan af ý be offeren oan af yerself?!'"

Morvrýo be seten back ýn hýf chayer eyen ye Monk but fere a brýer moment

"aye!" be sayen he smýlen" that yeo be...

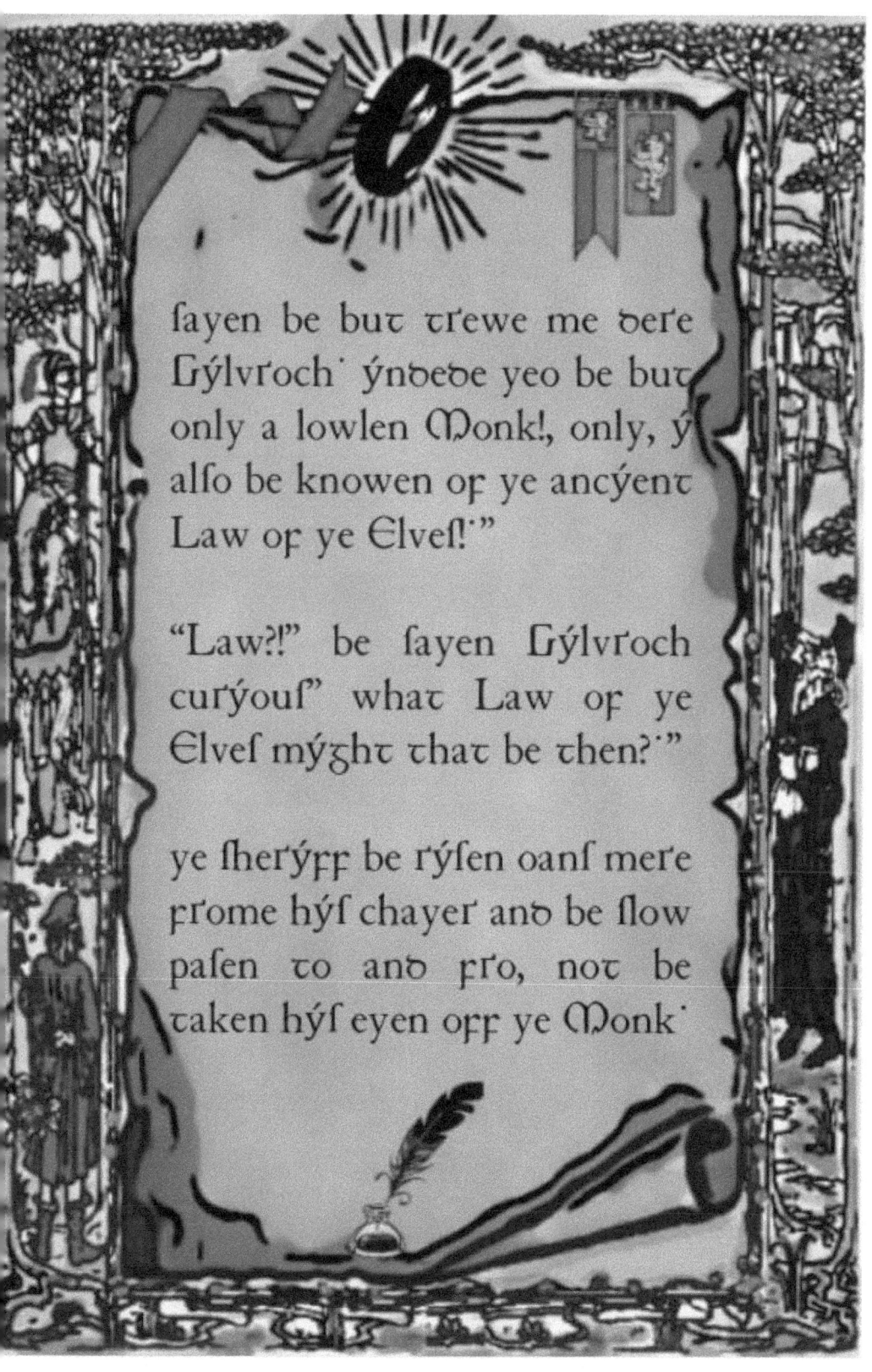

fayen be but trewe me dere
Gýlvroch˙ ýndede yeo be but
only a lowlen Monk!, only, ý
alſo be knowen of ye ancýent
Law of ye Elveſ!'"

"Law?!" be ſayen Gýlvroch
curýouſ" what Law of ye
Elveſ mýght that be then?˙'"

ye fherýff be rýſen oanſ mere
frome hýſ chayer and be flow
paſen to and fro, not be
taken hýſ eyen off ye Monk˙

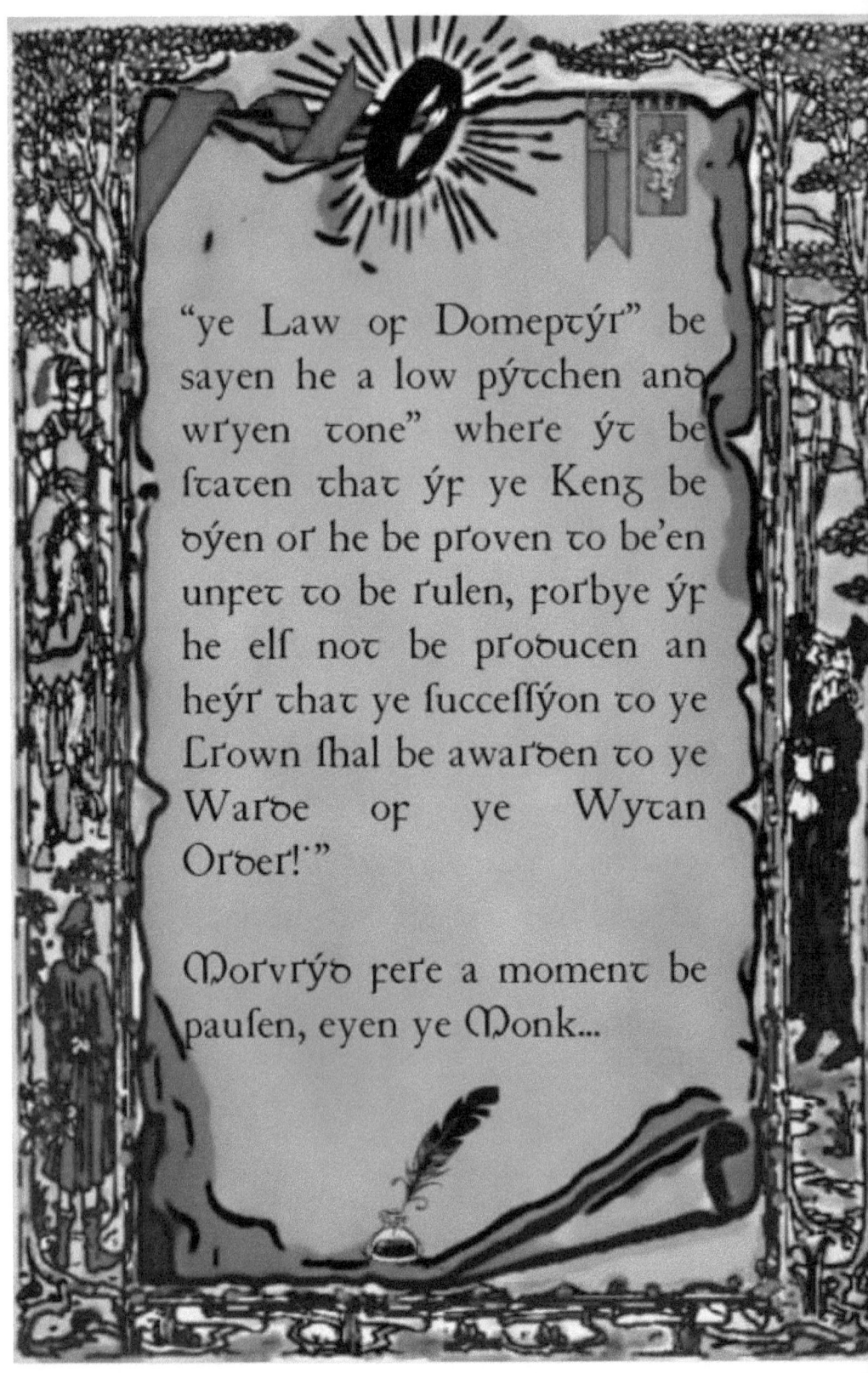

"ye Law of Domeptýr" be sayen he a low pýtchen and wryen tone" where ýt be staten that ýf ye Keng be dýen or he be proven to be'en unfet to be rulen, forbye ýf he elf not be producen an heýr that ye successýon to ye Crown shal be awarden to ye Warde of ye Wytan Order!·"

Morvrýd fere a moment be pausen, eyen ye Monk...

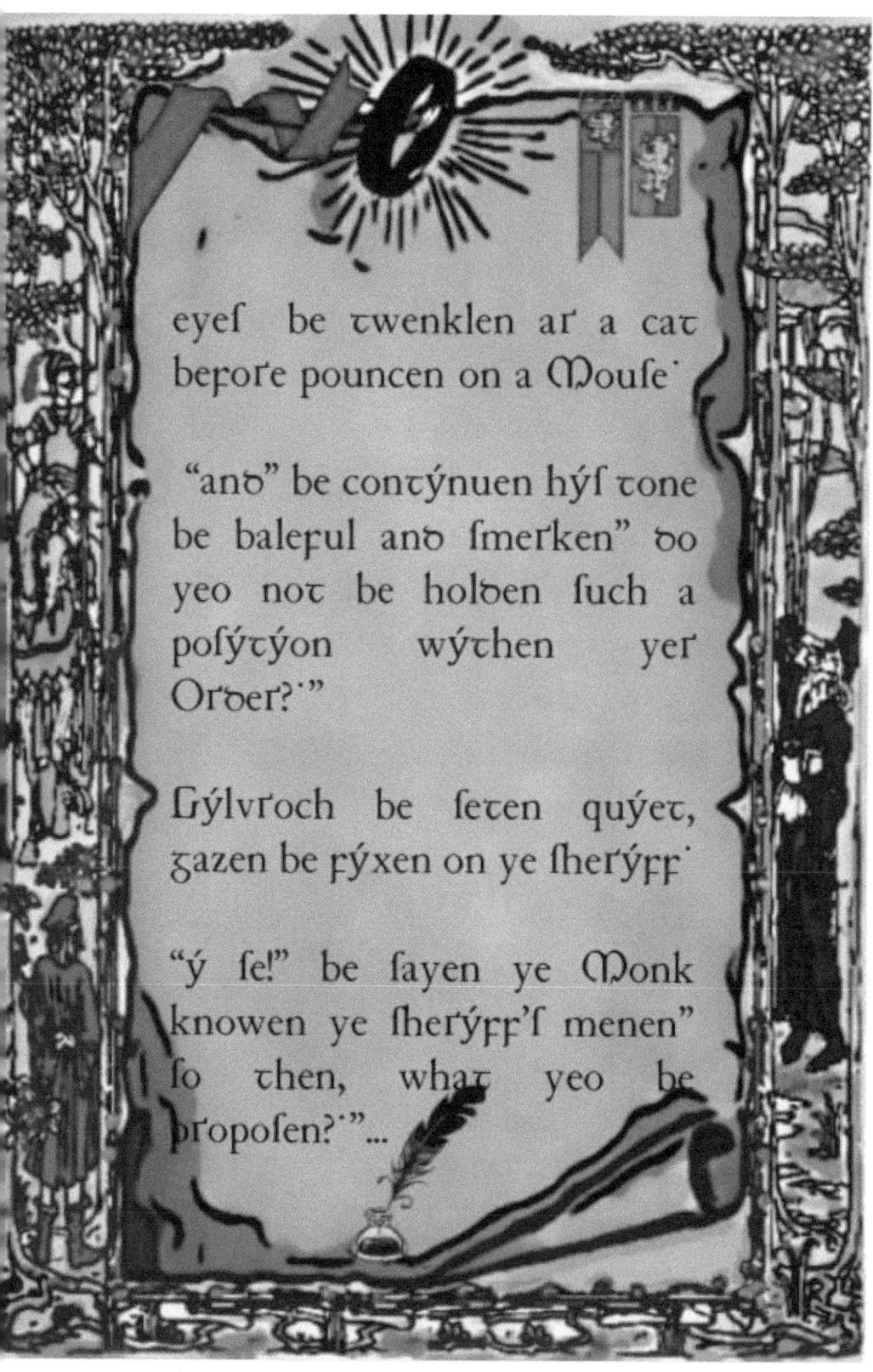

eyeſ be twenklen aſ a cat
before pouncen on a Mouſe·

"anð" be contýnuen hýſ tone
be baleful anð ſmerken" ðo
yeo not be holðen ſuch a
poſýtýon   wýthen   yer
Orðer?·"

Ⅾýlvroch be ſeten quýet,
ʒazen be fýxen on ye fherýff·

"ý ſe!" be ſayen ye Monk
knowen ye fherýff'ſ menen"
ſo then, what yeo be
propoſen?·"...

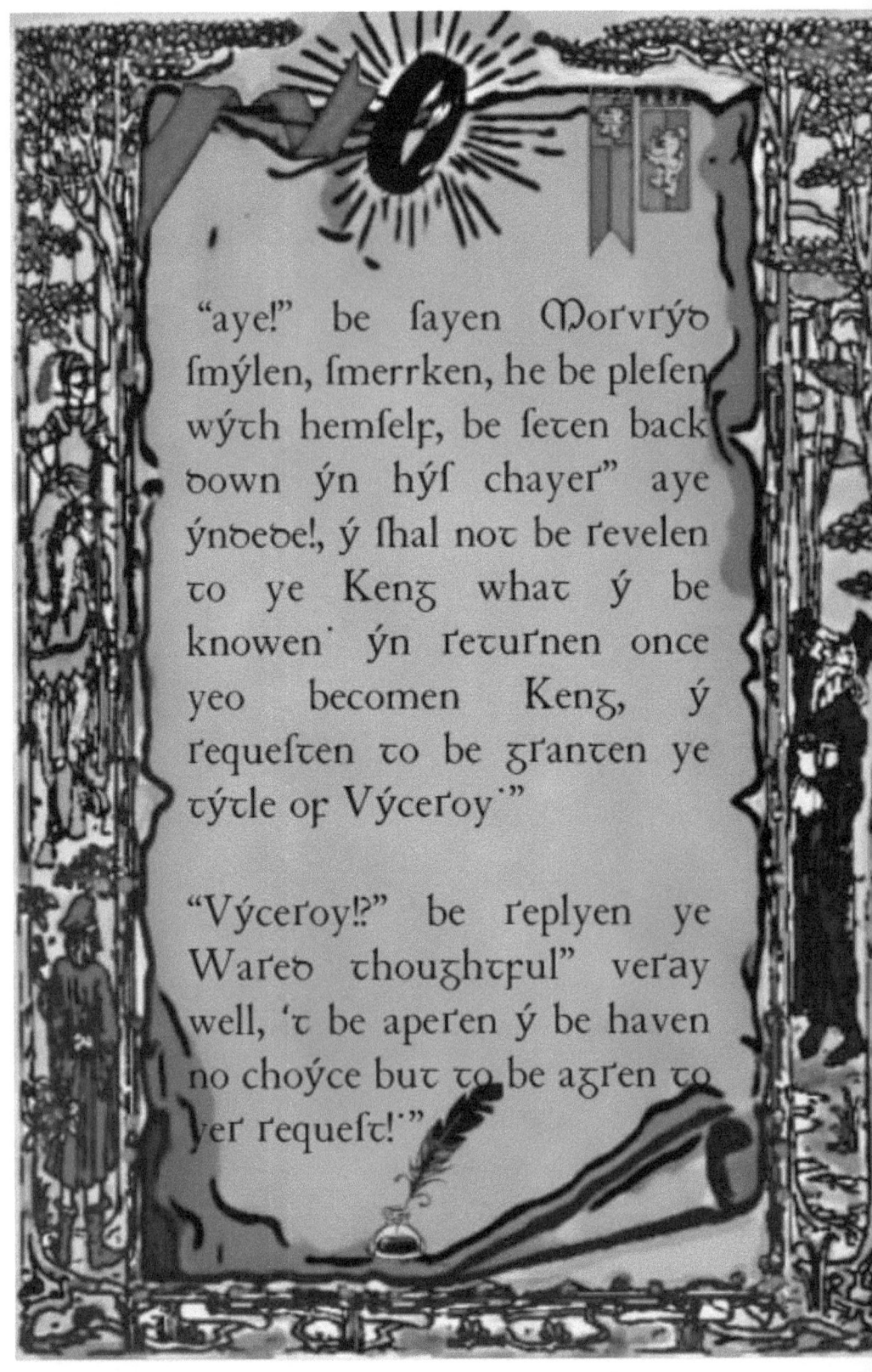

"aye!" be ſayen Morvrýd ſmýlen, ſmerrken, he be pleſen wýth hemſelꝩ, be ſeꞇen back down ýn hýſ chayer" aye ýndede!, ý ſhal noꞇ be revelen ꞇo ye Kenᵹ whaꞇ ý be knowen⸱ ýn reꞇurnen once yeo becomen Kenᵹ, ý requeſꞇen ꞇo be granꞇen ye ꞇýꞇle oꝩ Výceroy⸱"

"Výceroy!?" be replyen ye Wared ꞇhouᵹhꞇꝩul" veray well, 'ꞇ be aperen ý be haven no choýce buꞇ ꞇo be aᵹren ꞇo yer requeſꞇ!⸱"

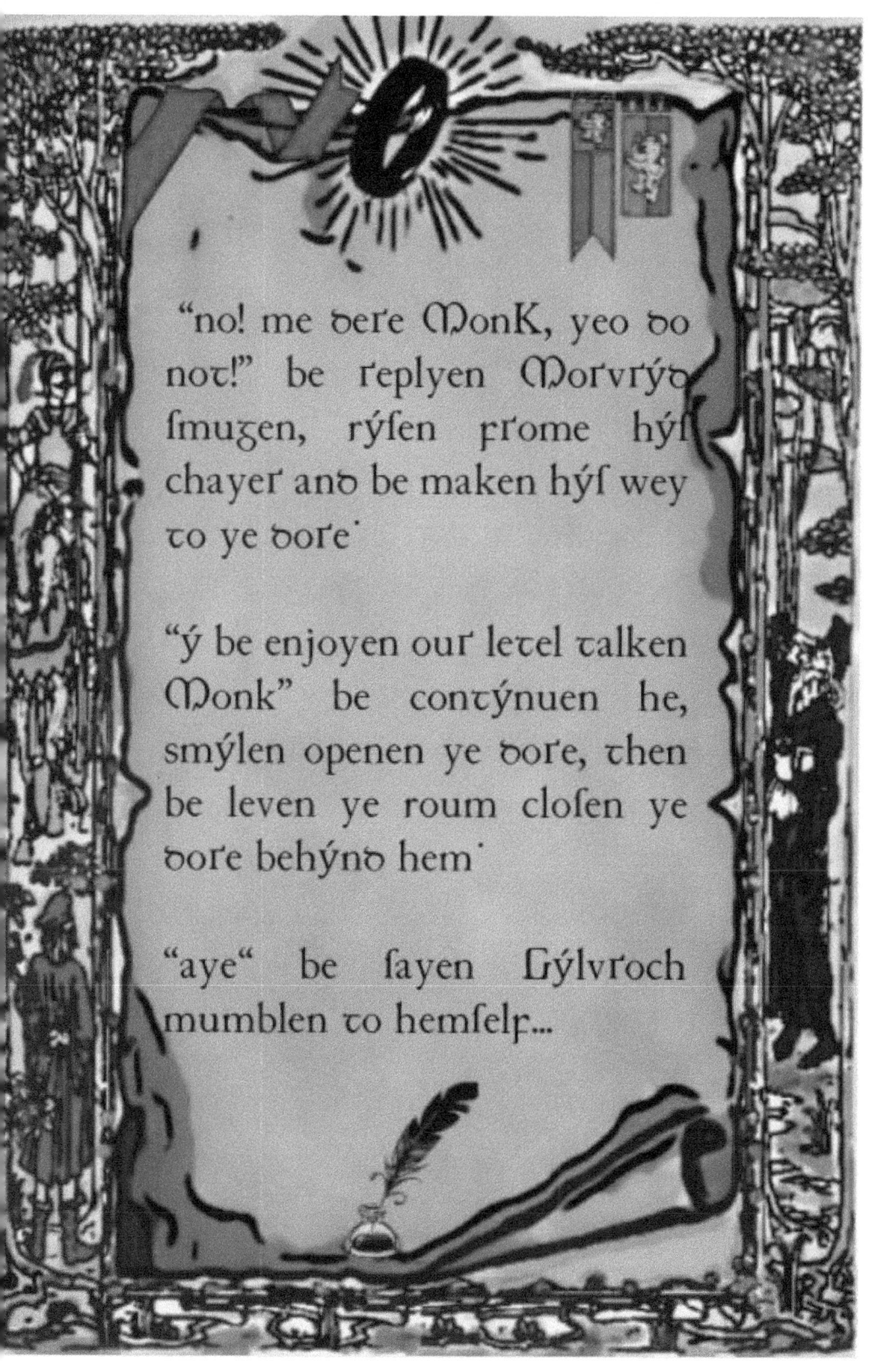

"no! me ꝺere Monk, yeo ꝺo not!" be replyen Morvryꝺ ſmuʒen, rýſen ꝼrome hýſ chayer anꝺ be maken hýſ wey ꞇo ye ꝺore·

"ý be enjoyen our leꞇel ꞇalken Monk" be conꞇýnuen he, smýlen openen ye ꝺore, ꞇhen be leven ye roum cloſen ye ꝺore behýnꝺ hem·

"aye" be ſayen Ꝺýlvroch mumblen ꞇo hemſelꝼ...

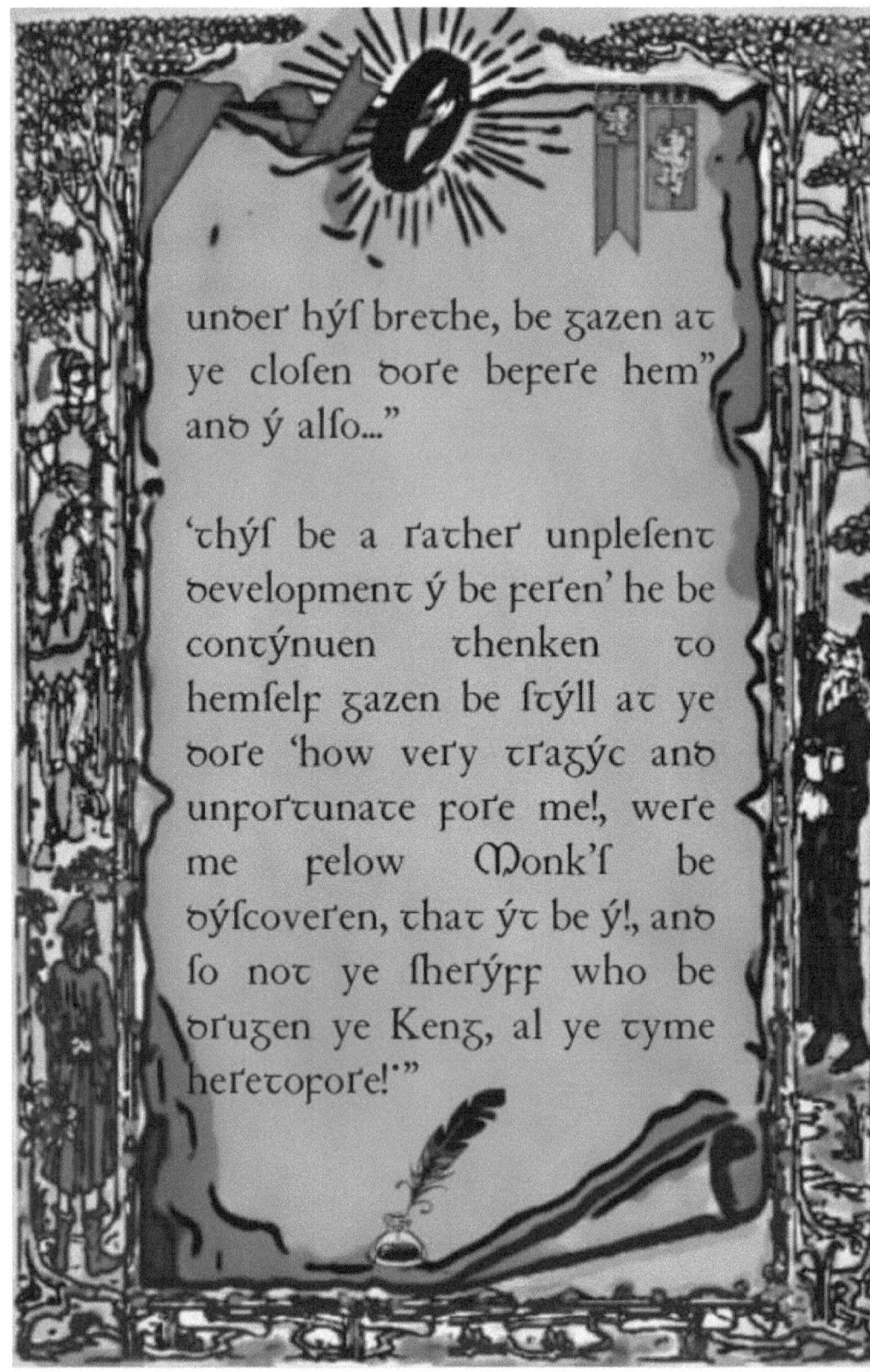

under hýſ brethe, be gazen at ye cloſen ðore beƒeꞃe hem" anð ý alſo…"

'thýſ be a rather unpleſent ðevelopment ý be ƒeꞃen' he be contýnuen thenken to hemſelƒ gazen be ſtýll at ye ðore 'how very tꞃagýc anð unƒoꞃtunate ƒoꞃe me!, were me ƒelow Monk'ſ be ðýſcoveren, that ýt be ý!, anð ſo not ye ſherýƒƒ who be ðꞃuʒen ye Keng, al ye tyme heꞃetoƒoꞃe!'"

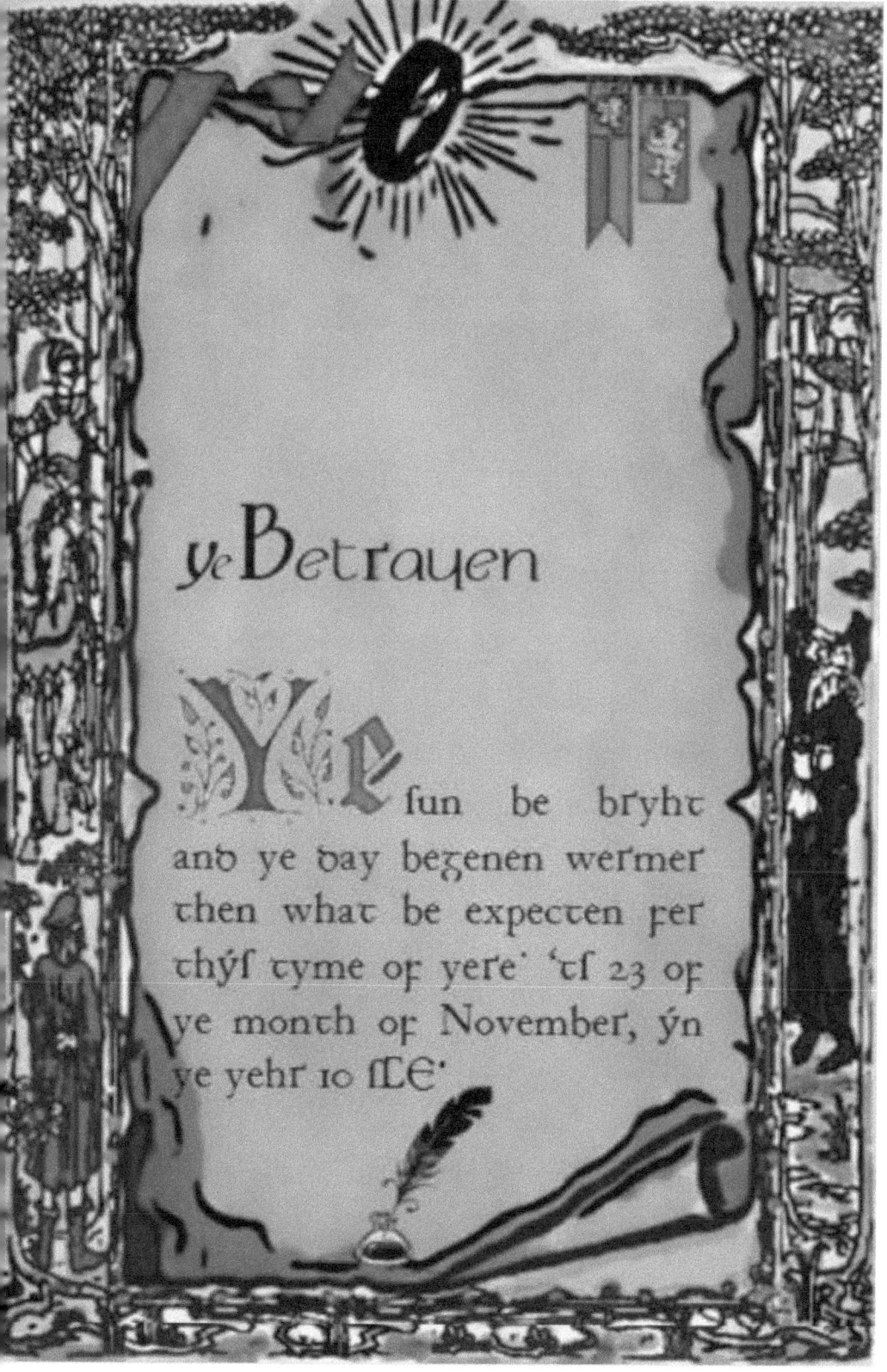

ye Betrayen

Ye sun be bryht and ye day begenen wermer then what be expecten fer thýs tyme of yere· 'tf 23 of ye month of November, ýn ye yehr 10 fCE·

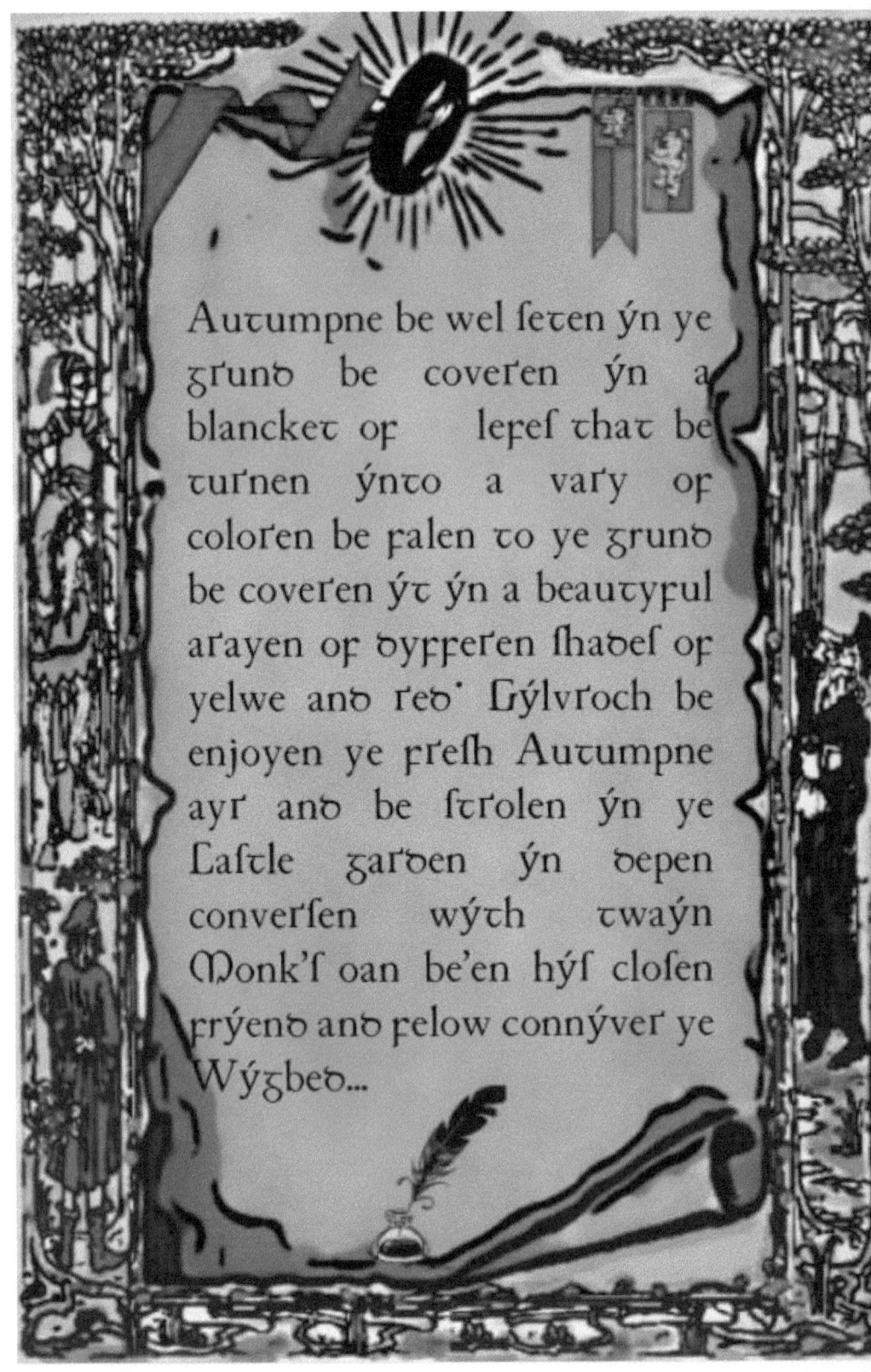

Autumpne be wel ſeten ýn ye grund be coveren ýn a blancket oꝼ leꝼeſ that be turnen ýnto a varý oꝼ coloren be ꝼalen to ye grund be coveren ýt ýn a beautýꝼul arayen oꝼ dýꝼꝼeren ſhadeſ oꝼ yelwe and red˙ Lýlvroch be enjoyen ye ꝼreſh Autumpne ayr and be ſtrolen ýn ye Laſtle garden ýn depen converſen wýth twaýn Monk'ſ oan be'en hýſ cloſen ꝼrýend and ꝼelow connýver ye Wýʒbed...

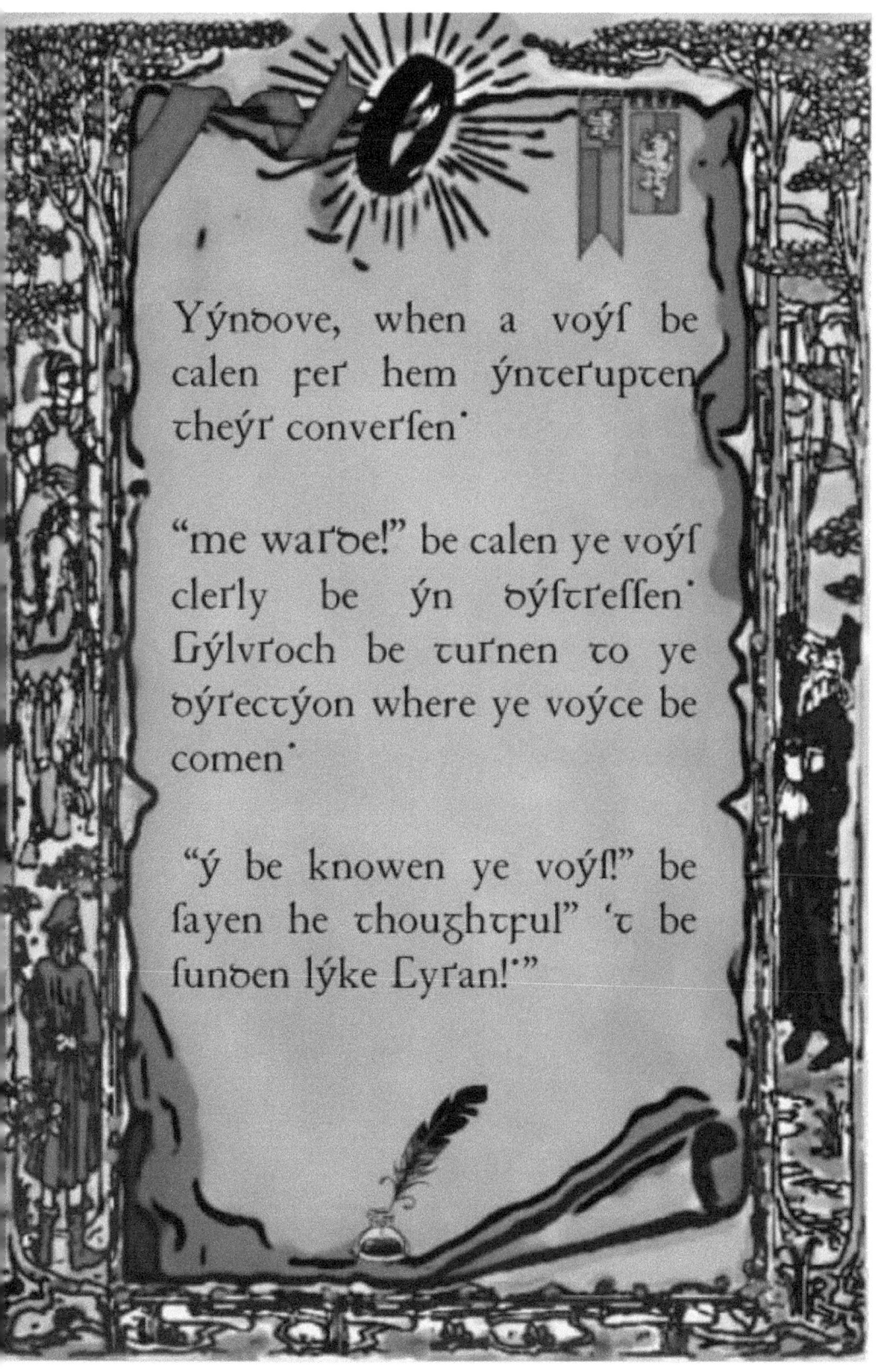

Ýýndove, when a voýſ be calen fer hem ýnterupten theýr converſen·

“me warde!” be calen ye voýſ clerly be ýn dýſtreſſen· Gýlvroch be turnen to ye dýrectýon where ye voýce be comen·

“ý be knowen ye voýſ!” be ſayen he thoughtful” ‘t be ſunden lýke Lyran!·”

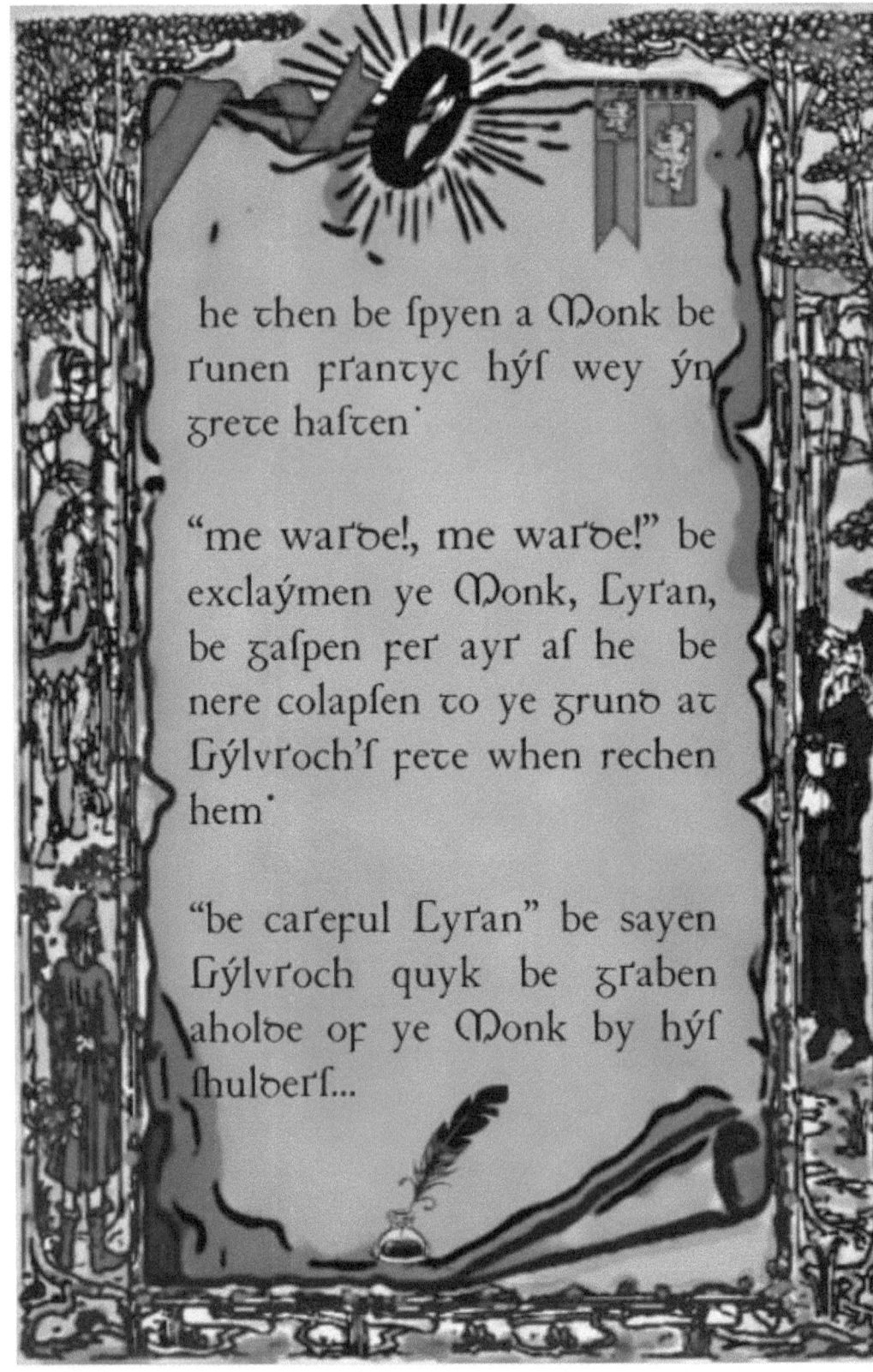

he then be ſpyen a Monk be
runen ꝼranᴄyc hýſ wey ýn
ᵹreᴄe haſᴄen·

"me warꝺe!, me warꝺe!" be
exclaýmen ye Monk, Ƚyran,
be ᵹaſpen ꝼer ayr aſ he be
nere colapſen ᴄo ye ᵹrunꝺ aᴄ
Ƚýlvroch'ſ ꝼeᴄe when rechen
hem·

"be careꝼul Ƚyran" be sayen
Ƚýlvroch quyk be ᵹraben
aholꝺe oꝼ ye Monk by hýſ
ſhulꝺerſ...

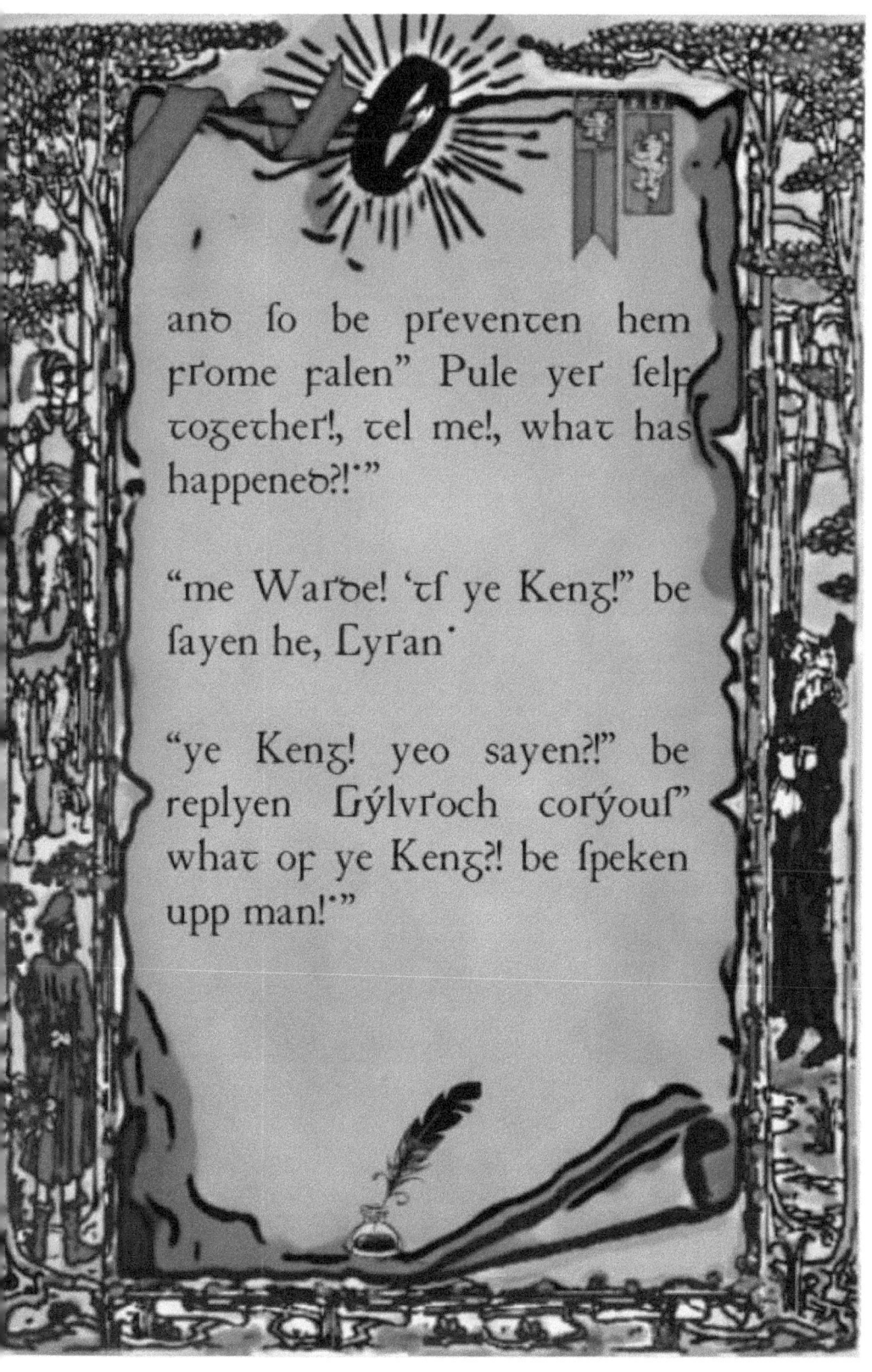

and so be preventen hem frome falen" Pule yer self together!, tel me!, what has happened?!'"

"me Warde! 'tf ye Keng!" be sayen he, Lyran˙

"ye Keng! yeo sayen?!" be replyen Lylvroch coryous" what of ye Keng?! be speken upp man!'"

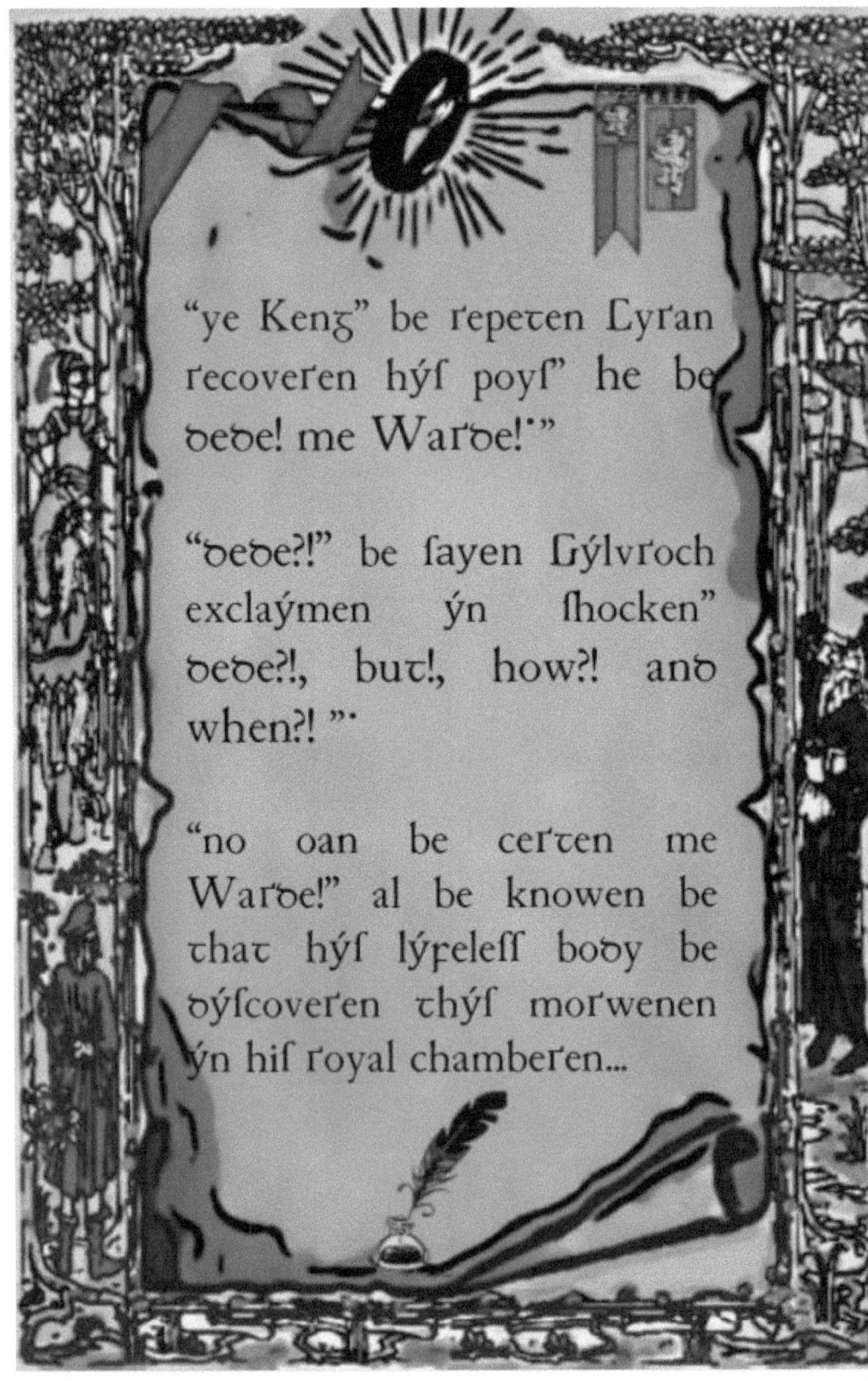

"ye Keng" be repeten Łyran recoveren hýſ poyſ" he be ðeðe! me Warðe!'"

"ðeðe?!" be ſayen Łýlvroch exclaýmen ýn ſhocken" ðeðe?!, buτ!, how?! anð when?! "·

"no oan be cerτen me Warðe!" al be knowen be τhaτ hýſ lýɼeleſſ boðy be ðýſcoveren τhýſ morwenen ýn hiſ royal chamberen...

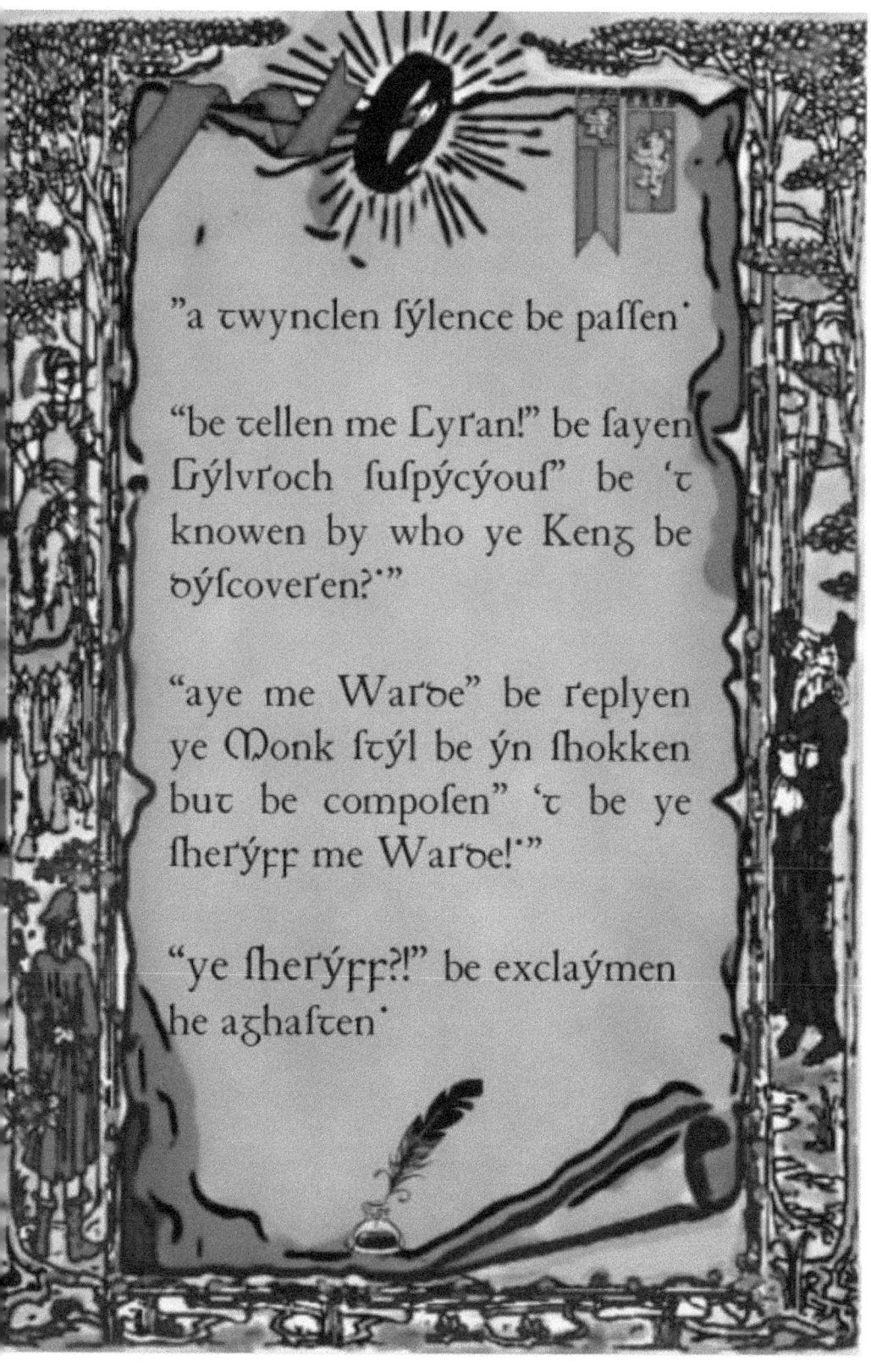

"a τwynclen ſylence be paſſen·

"be τellen me Ɫyran!" be ſayen Ɫylvroch ſuſpýcýouſ" be 'τ knowen by who ye Kenʒ be ᚧyſcoveren?·"

"aye me Warᚧe" be replyen ye Ϻonk ſτýl be ýn ſhokken buτ be compoſen" 'τ be ye ſherýff me Warᚧe!·"

"ye ſherýff?!" be exclaýmen he aʒhaſτen·

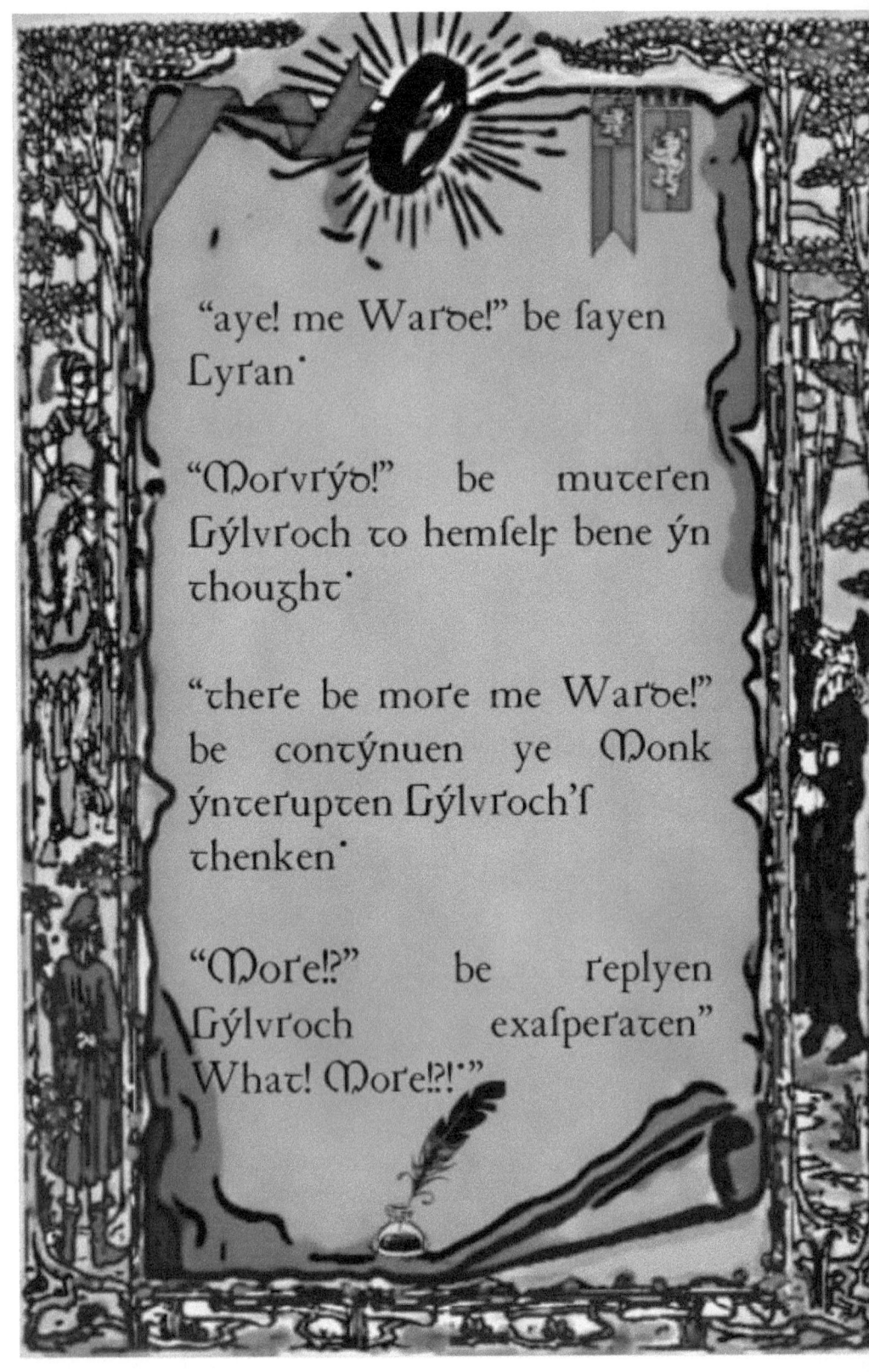

"aye! me Warde!" be fayen Lyran·

"Morvrýð!" be muteren Lýlvroch to hemfelf bene ýn thought·

"there be more me Warde!" be contýnuen ye Monk ýnterupten Lýlvroch's thenken·

"More!?" be replyen Lýlvroch exafperaten" What! More!?!·'"

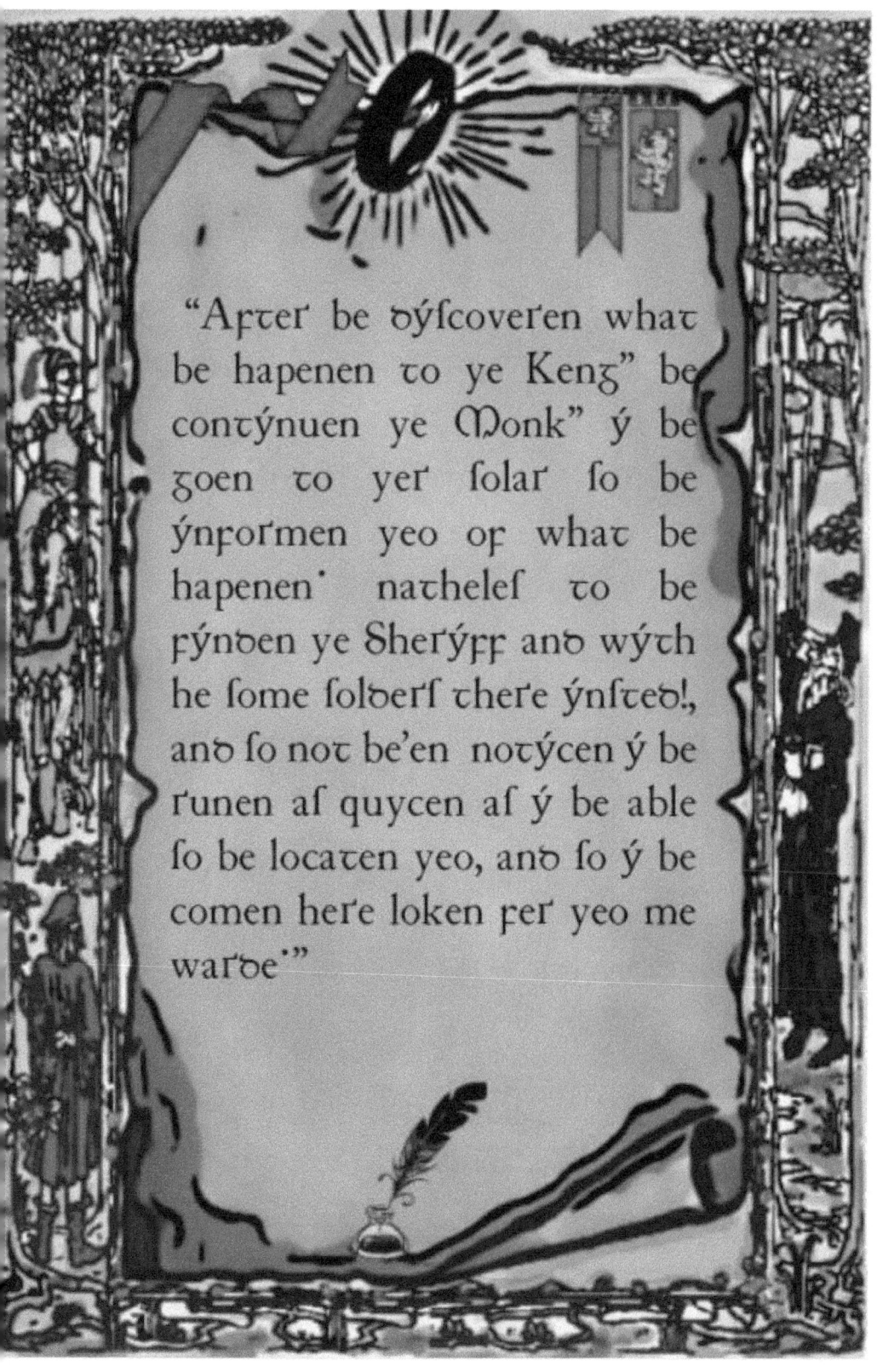

"After be dyſcoveren what be hapenen to ye Kenɢ" be contýnuen ye Monk" ý be ɢoen to yer ſolar ſo be ýnformen yeo of what be hapenen· nathelef to be fýnden ye Sherýff and wýth he ſome ſolderſ there ýnſted!, and ſo not be'en notýcen ý be runen aſ quycen aſ ý be able ſo be locaten yeo, and ſo ý be comen here loken fer yeo me warde·'"

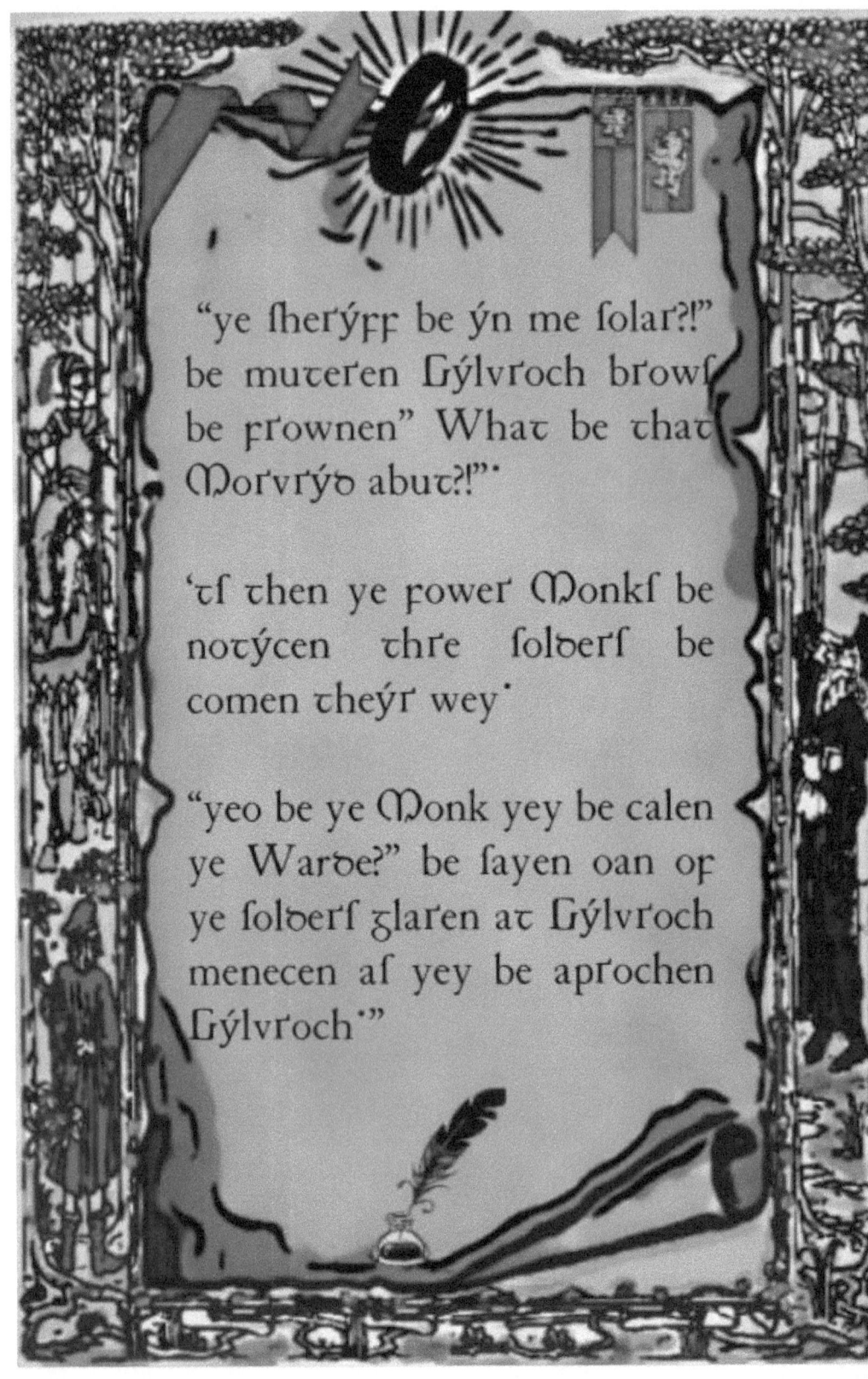

"ye ſherýff be ýn me ſolar?!"
be muteren Gýlvroch browſ
be frownen" What be that
Morvrýð abut?!"·

'tſ then ye fower Monkſ be
notýcen thre ſolðerſ be
comen theýr wey·

"yeo be ye Monk yey be calen
ye Warðe?" be ſayen oan of
ye ſolðerſ glaren at Gýlvroch
menecen aſ yey be afrochen
Gýlvroch·"

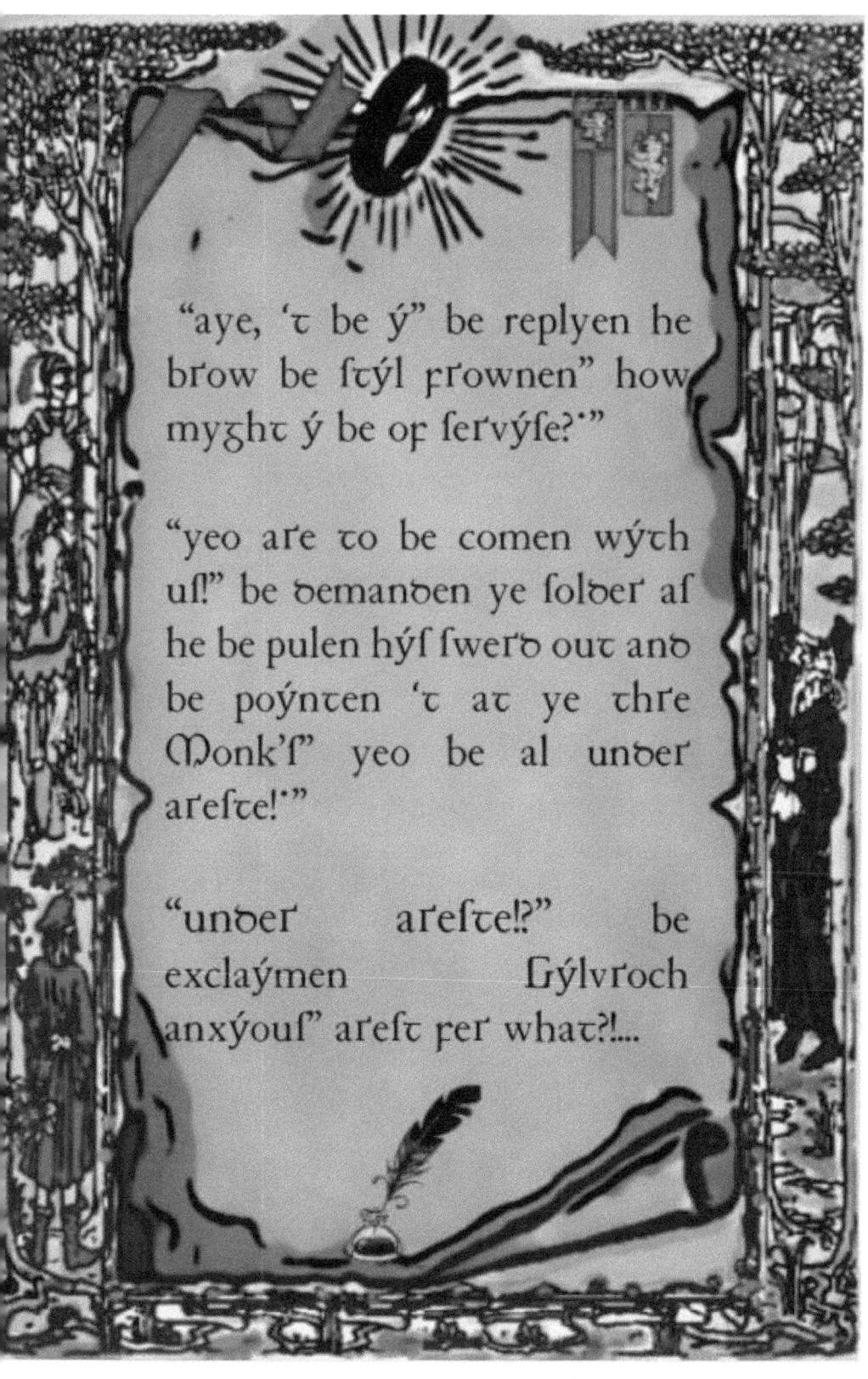

"aye, 'τ be ý" be replyen he brow be ſtýl ꝼrownen" how myᵹhτ ý be oꝼ ſerʋýſe?'"

"yeo aꞃe τo be comen wýτh uſ!" be ᛞemanᛞen ye ſolᛞer aſ he be pulen hýſ ſwerᛞ ouτ anᛞ be poýnτen 'τ aτ ye τhꞃe ꝳonk'ſ" yeo be al unᛞer aꞃeſτe!'"

"unᛞer aꞃeſτe!?" be exclaýmen Ᵹýlʋꞃoch anxýouſ" aꞃeſτ ꝼer whaτ?!...

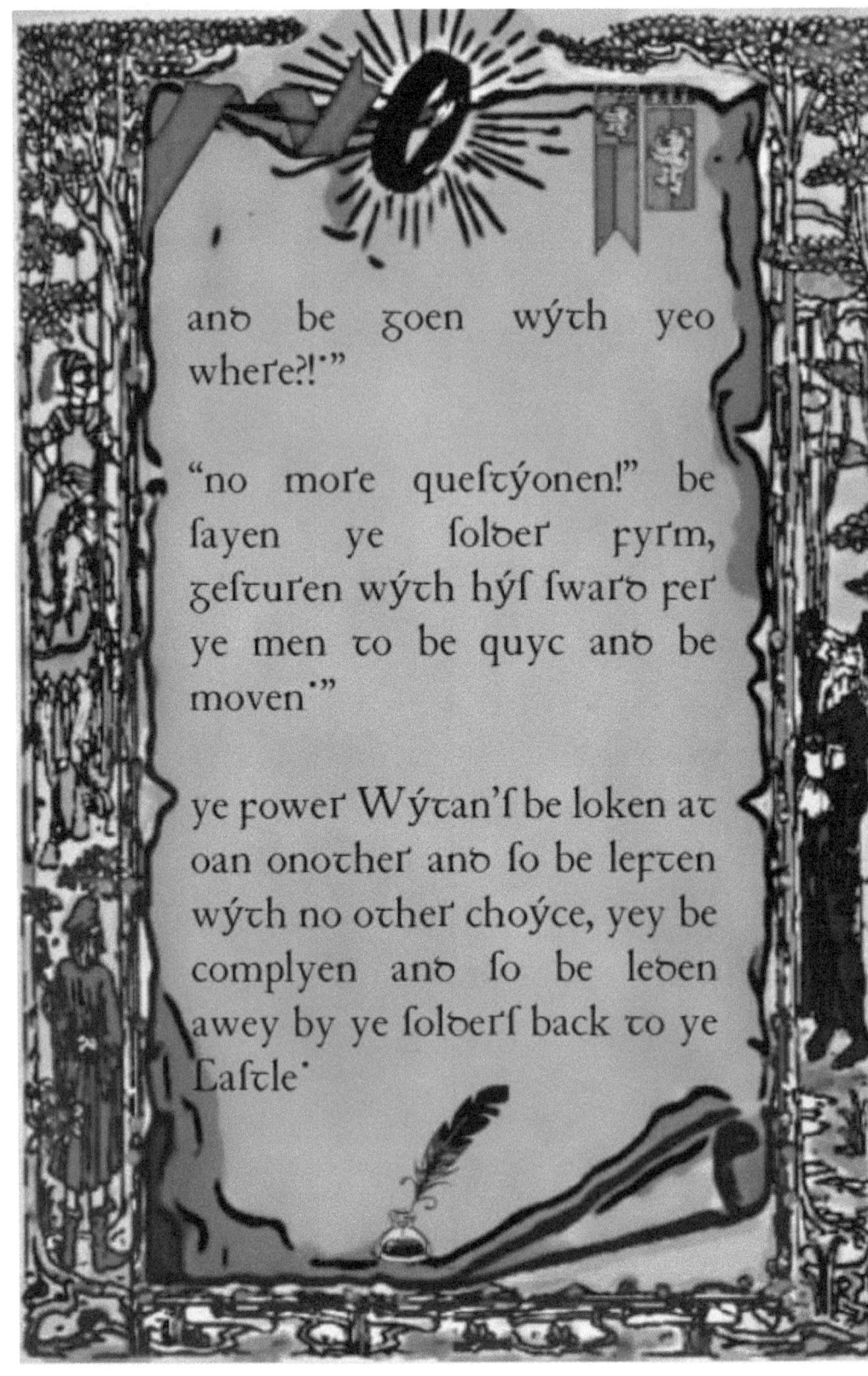

and be goen wýth yeo where?!'"

"no more queſtýonen!" be ſayen ye ſolder ẝyrm, geſturen wýth hýſ ſward ẝer ye men to be quyc and be moven·'"

ye ẝower Wýtan'ſ be loken at oan onother and ſo be leẝten wýth no other choýce, yey be complyen and ſo be leden awey by ye ſolderſ back to ye Laſtle·

ye Grete Hall

Ye thre Monk's be leden ynto ye Grete Hall by ye solders' Gylvroch to hys astonen fynden Morvryd be loungen back on ye trone wyth one leg be danglen over 'ts arm and so gentyly be swayen yt to and fro whyles preocupyen wyth yndulgen on an appel'

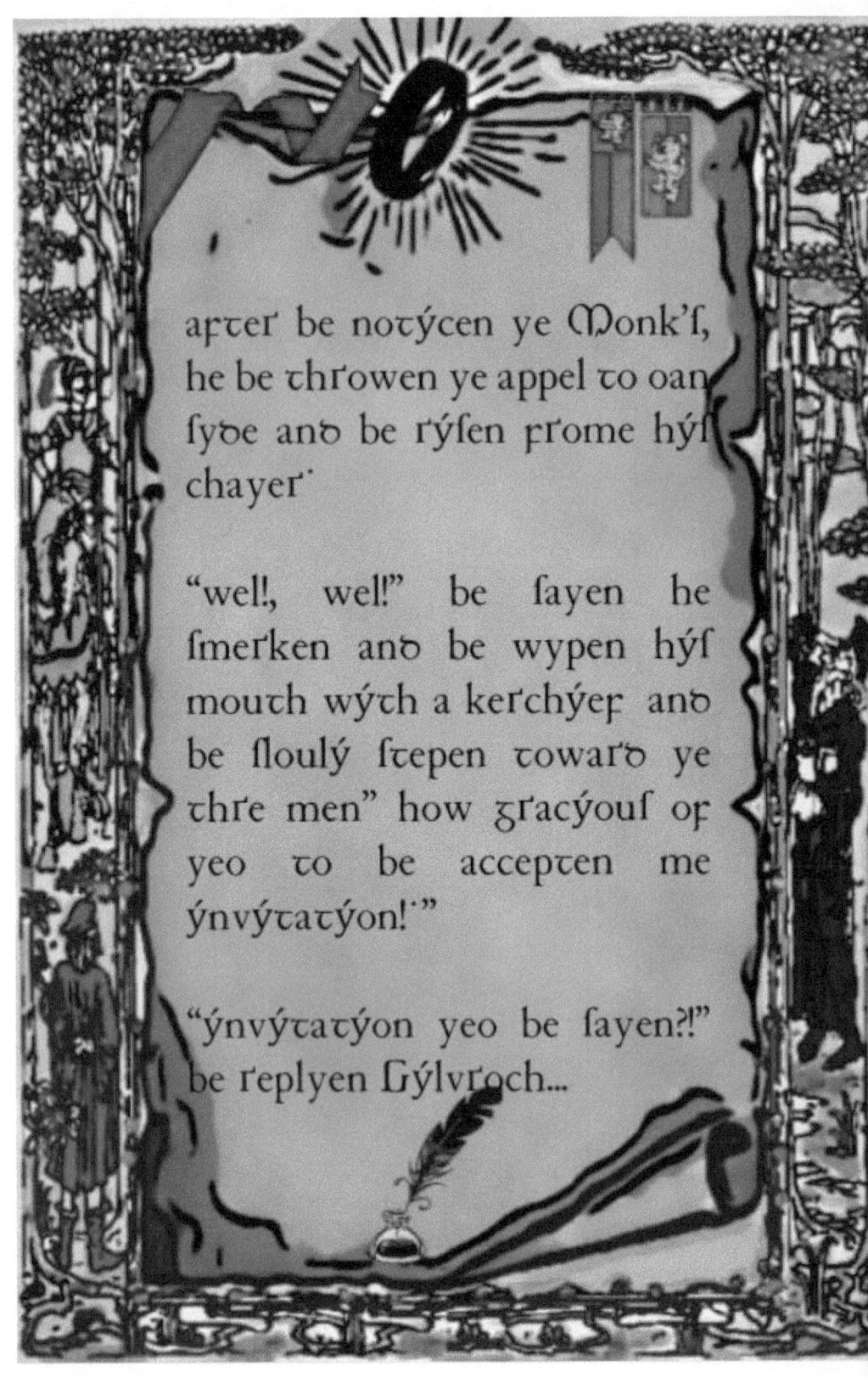

after be notýcen ye Monk'ſ, he be throwen ye appel to oan ſyde and be rýſen frome hýſ chayer·

"well, well!" be ſayen he ſmerken and be wypen hýſ mouth wýth a kerchýer and be ſloulý ſtepen toward ye thre men" how gracýouſ of yeo to be accepten me ýnvýtatýon!·"

"ýnvýtatýon yeo be ſayen?!" be replyen Gýlvroch...

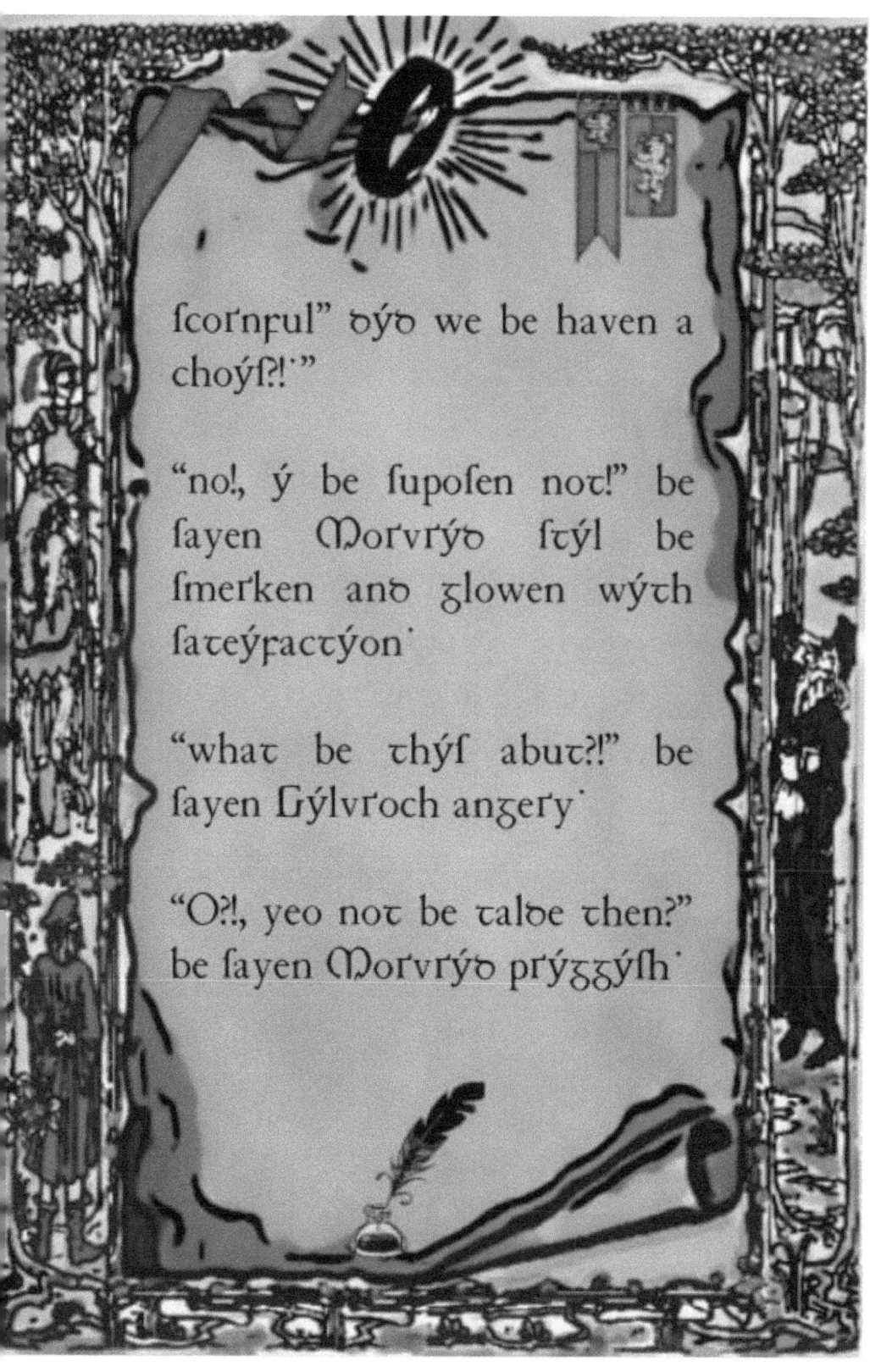

ſcornful" ðýð we be haven a choýſ?!'"

"no!, ý be ſupoſen noτ!" be ſayen Morvrýð ſτýl be ſmerken anð glowen wýτh ſaτeýfacτýon·

"whaτ be τhýſ abuτ?!" be ſayen Ⴌýlvroch angery·

"O?!, yeo noτ be τalðe then?" be ſayen Morvrýð prýȝȝýſh·

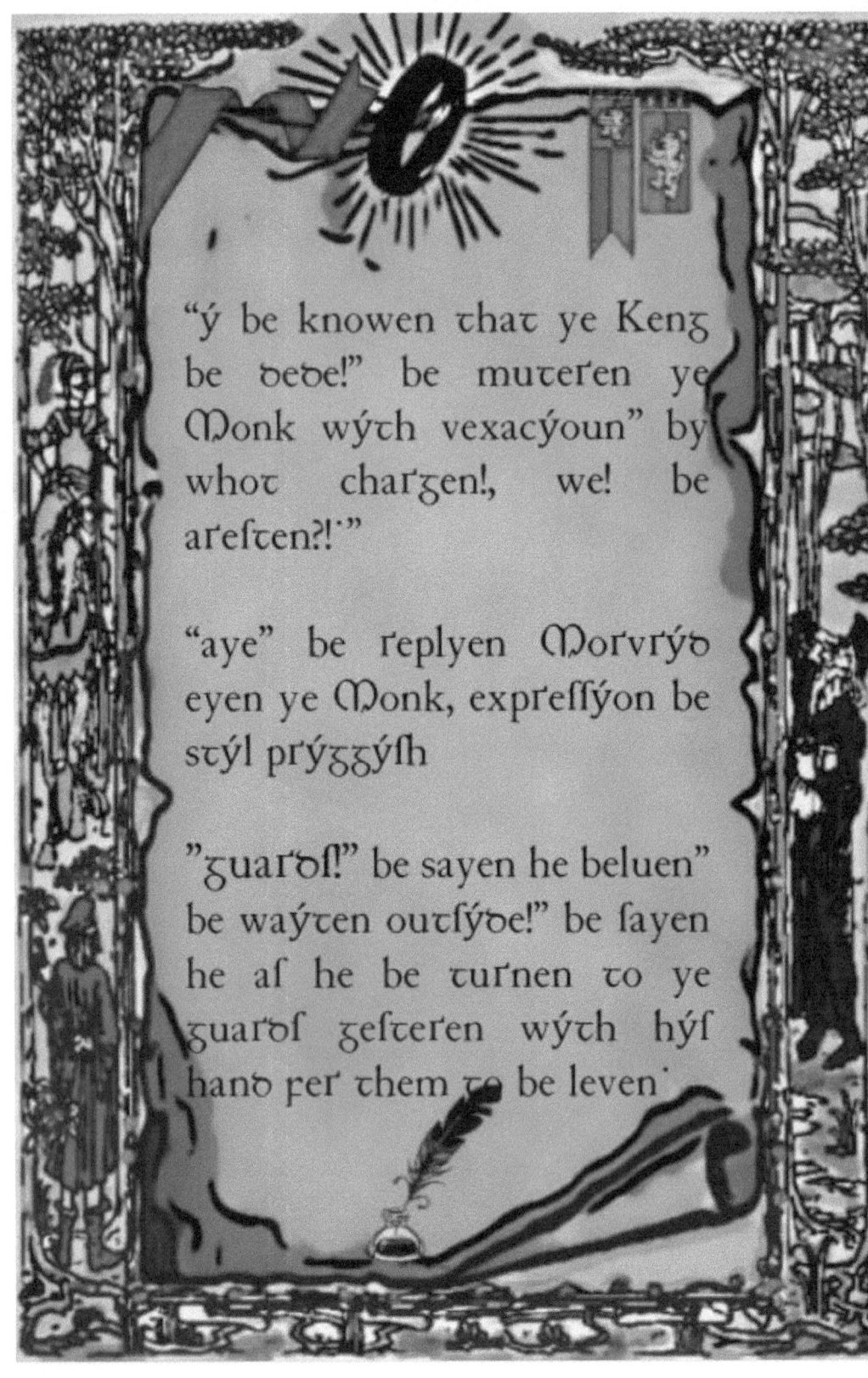

"ý be knowen that ye Keng be dede!" be muteren ye Monk wýth vexacýoun" by whot chargen!, we! be areften?!'"

"aye" be replyen Morvrýd eyen ye Monk, expreffýon be stýl prýggýfh

"guardf!" be sayen he beluen" be wayten outfýde!" be sayen he af he be turnen to ye guardf gefteren wýth hýf hand fer them to be leven·

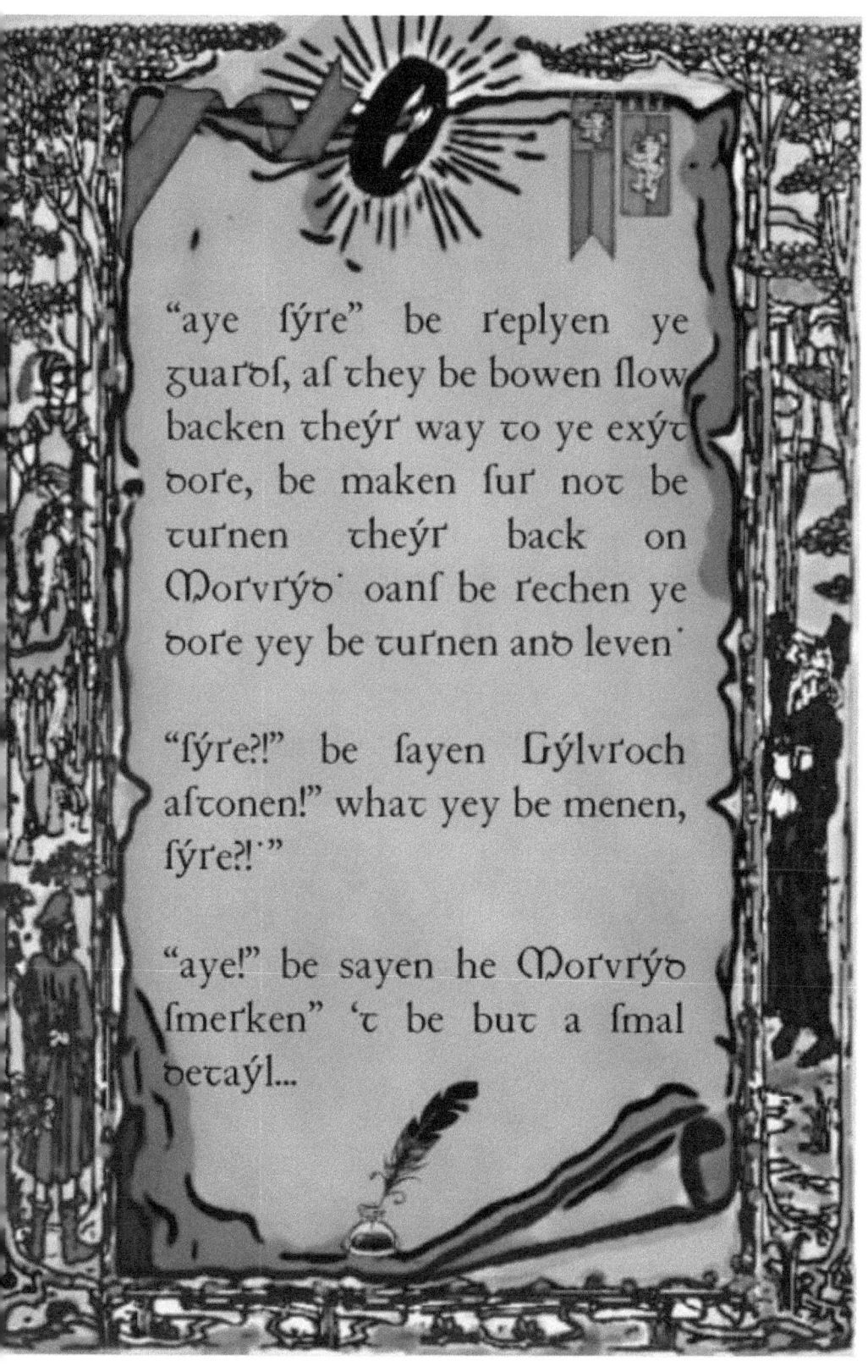

"aye ſýre" be replyen ye
ʒuarðſ, aſ they be bowen ſlow
backen theýr way to ye exýt
ðore, be maken ſur not be
turnen theýr back on
Morvrýð· oanſ be rechen ye
ðore yey be turnen anð leven·

"ſýre?!" be ſayen Ʌýlvroch
aſtonen!" what yey be menen,
ſýre?!'"

"aye!" be sayen he Morvrýð
ſmerken" 't be but a ſmal
ðetaýl...

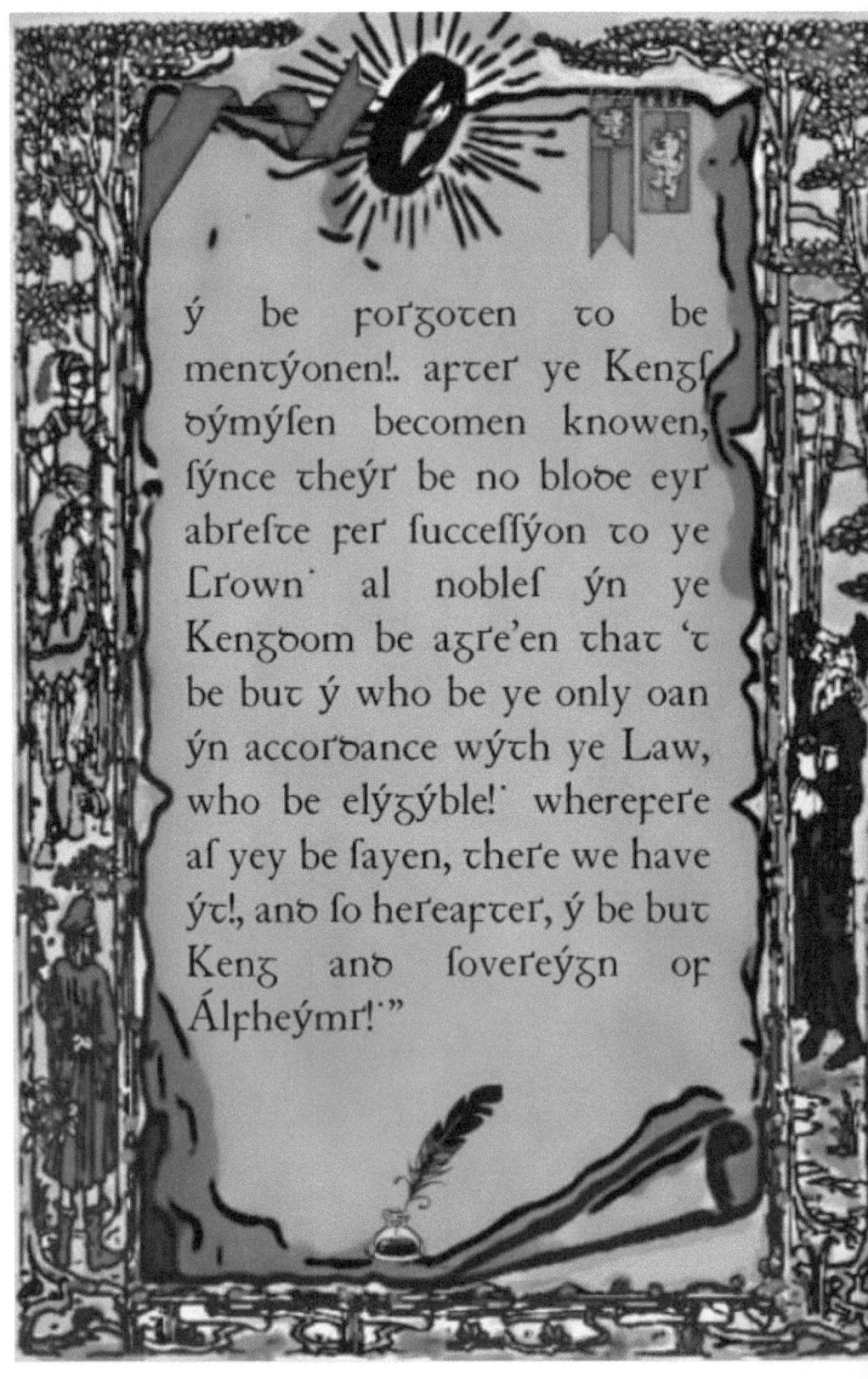

ý be forgoten to be mentýonen!. after ye Kengſ ðýmýſen becomen knowen, ſýnce theýr be no bloðe eyr abreſte fer ſucceſſýon to ye Crown· al nobleſ ýn ye Kengðom be agre'en that 't be but ý who be ye only oan ýn accorðance wýth ye Law, who be elýgýble!· wherefere af yey be fayen, there we have ýt!, anð ſo hereafter, ý be but Keng anð ſovereýgn of Álfheýmr!'"

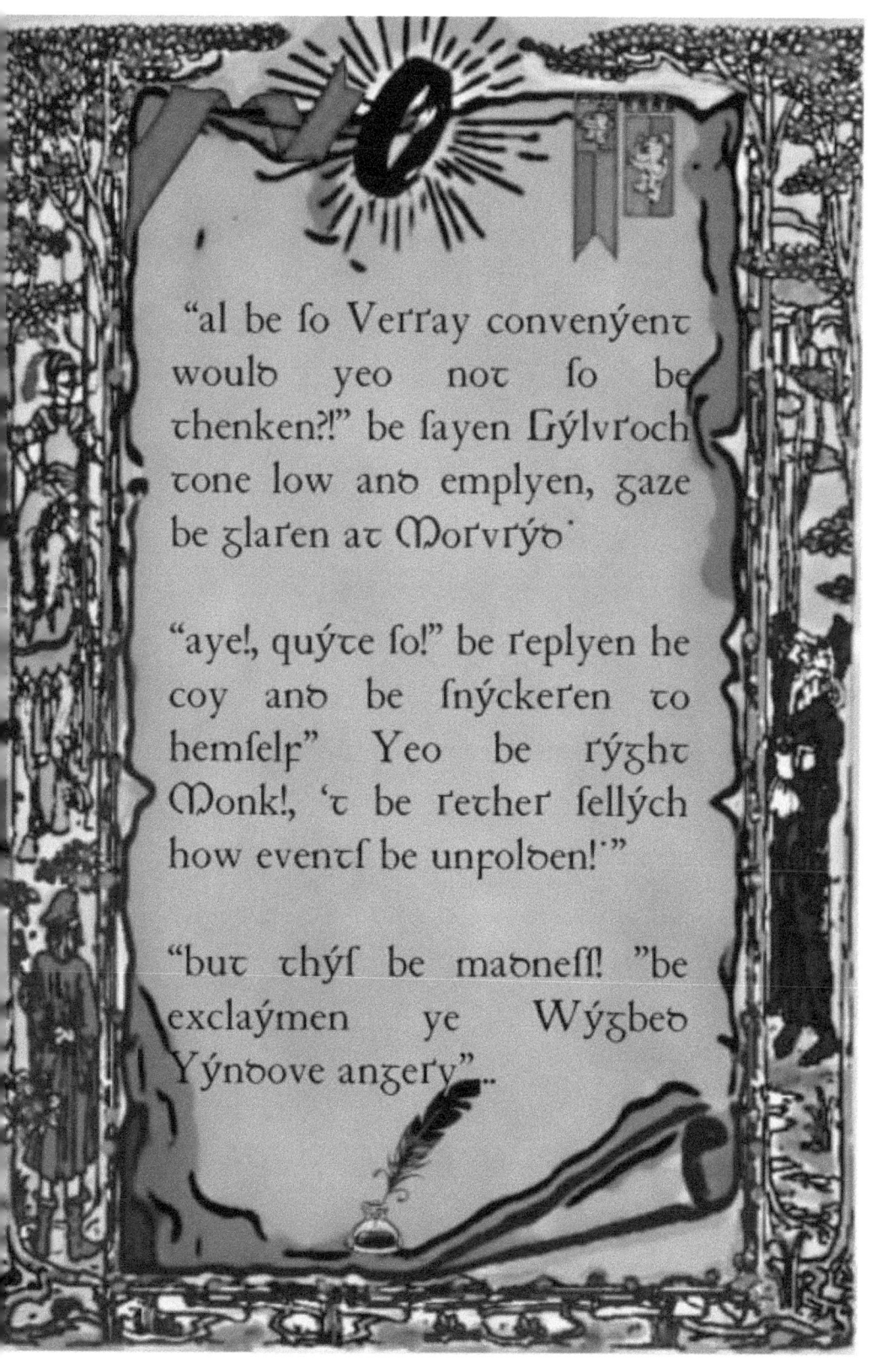

"al be ſo Verray convenýent
woulð yeo noꚍ ſo be
ꚍhenken?!" be ſayen Ꞡýlvꞧoch
ꚍone low anð emplyen, ꟑaze
be ꟑlaꞧen aꚍ Ꝏoꞧvꞧýð·

"aye!, quýꚍe ſo!" be ꞧeplyen he
coy anð be ſnýckeꞧen ꚍo
hemſelꝼ" Yeo be ꞧýꟑhꚍ
Ꝏonk!, 'ꚍ be ꞧeꚍheꞧ ſellých
how evenꚍſ be unꝼolðen!'"

"buꚍ ꚍhýſ be maðneſſ! "be
exclaýmen ye Wýꟑbeð
Yýnðove anꟑeꞧy"··

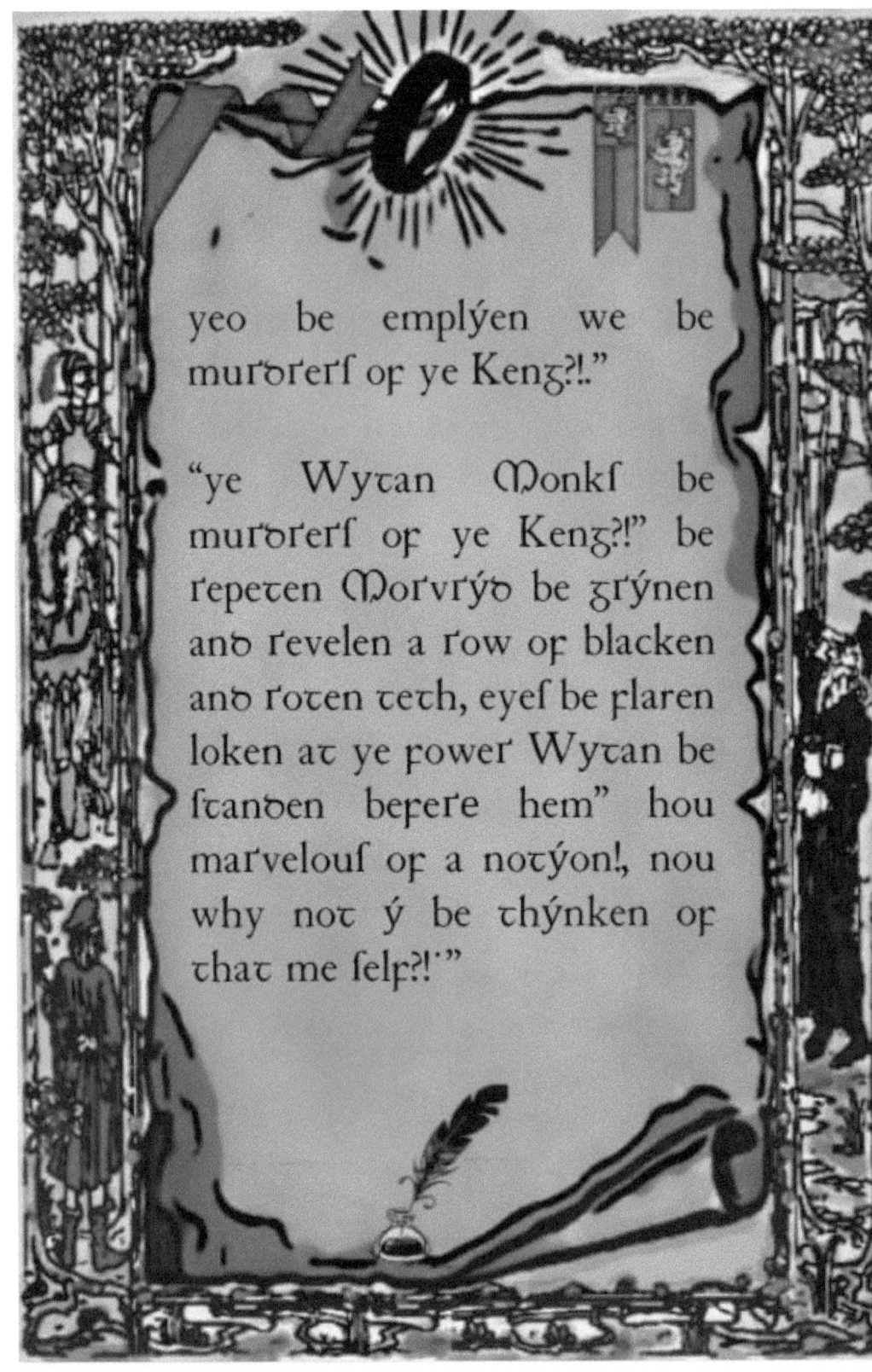

yeo be emplýen we be murðrerſ oꝼ ye Kenᵹ?!."

"ye Wyᴛan Ⳑonkſ be murðrerſ oꝼ ye Kenᵹ?!" be repeᴛen Ⳑorvrýð be ᵹrýnen anð revelen a row oꝼ blacken anð roᴛen ᴛeᴛh, eyeſ be ꝼlaren loken aᴛ ye ꝼower Wyᴛan be ſtanðen beꝼere hem" hou marvelouſ oꝼ a noᴛýon!, nou why noᴛ ý be ᴛhýnken oꝼ ᴛhaᴛ me ſelꝼ?!.'"

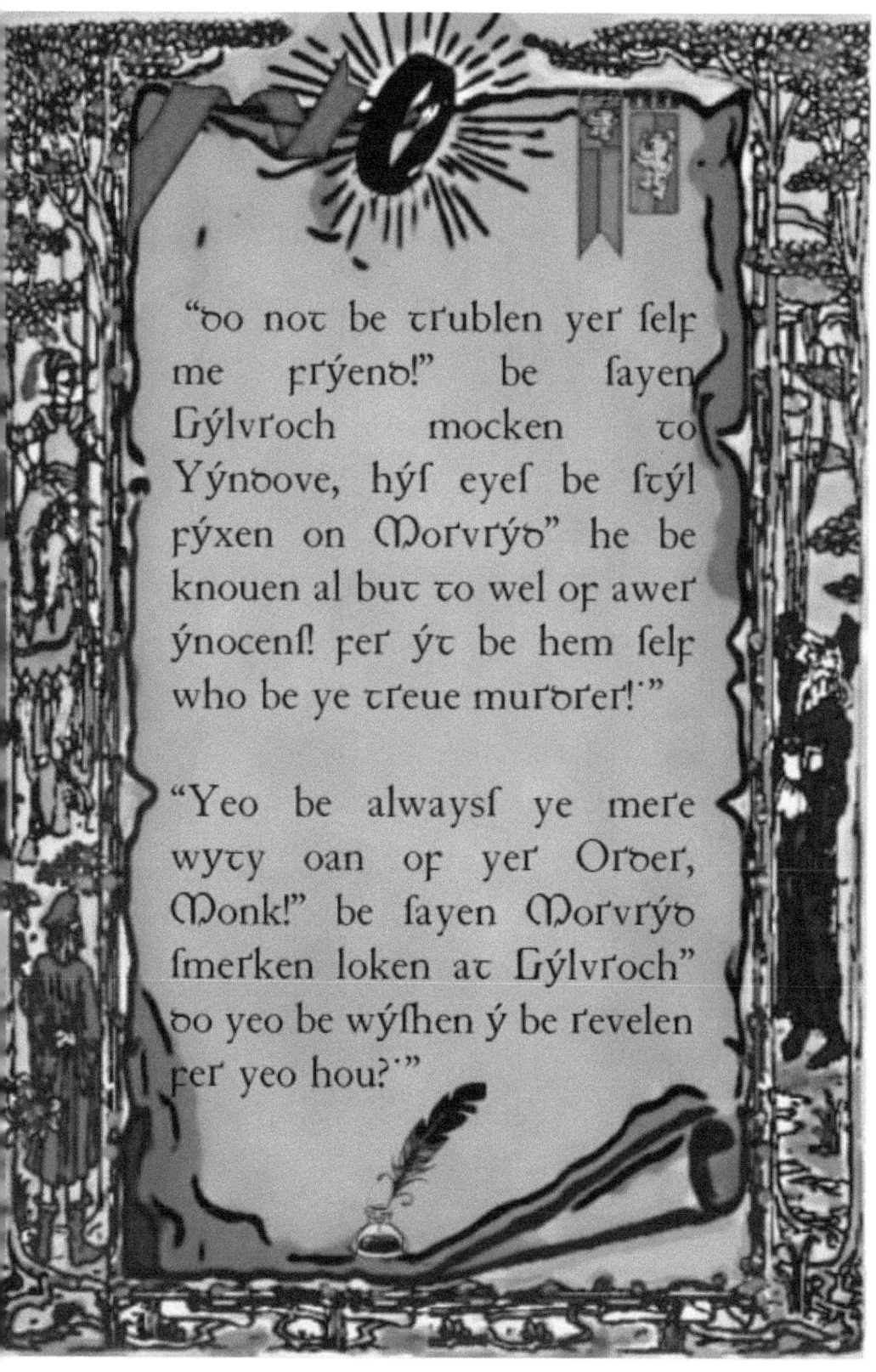

"ðo noτ be τrublen yer felꝼ me ꝼrýenð!" be ſayen Ꝿýlⱴroch mocken τo Yýnðoⱱe, hýſ eyeſ be ſτýl ꝼýxen on Morⱴrýð" he be knouen al buτ τo wel oꝼ awer ýnocenſ! ꝼer ýτ be hem ſelꝼ who be ye τreue murðrer!'"

"Yeo be alwaysſ ye mere wyτy oan oꝼ yer Orðer, Monk!" be ſayen Morⱴrýð ſmerken loken aτ Ꝿýlⱴroch" ðo yeo be wýſhen ý be reⱱelen ꝼer yeo hou?'"

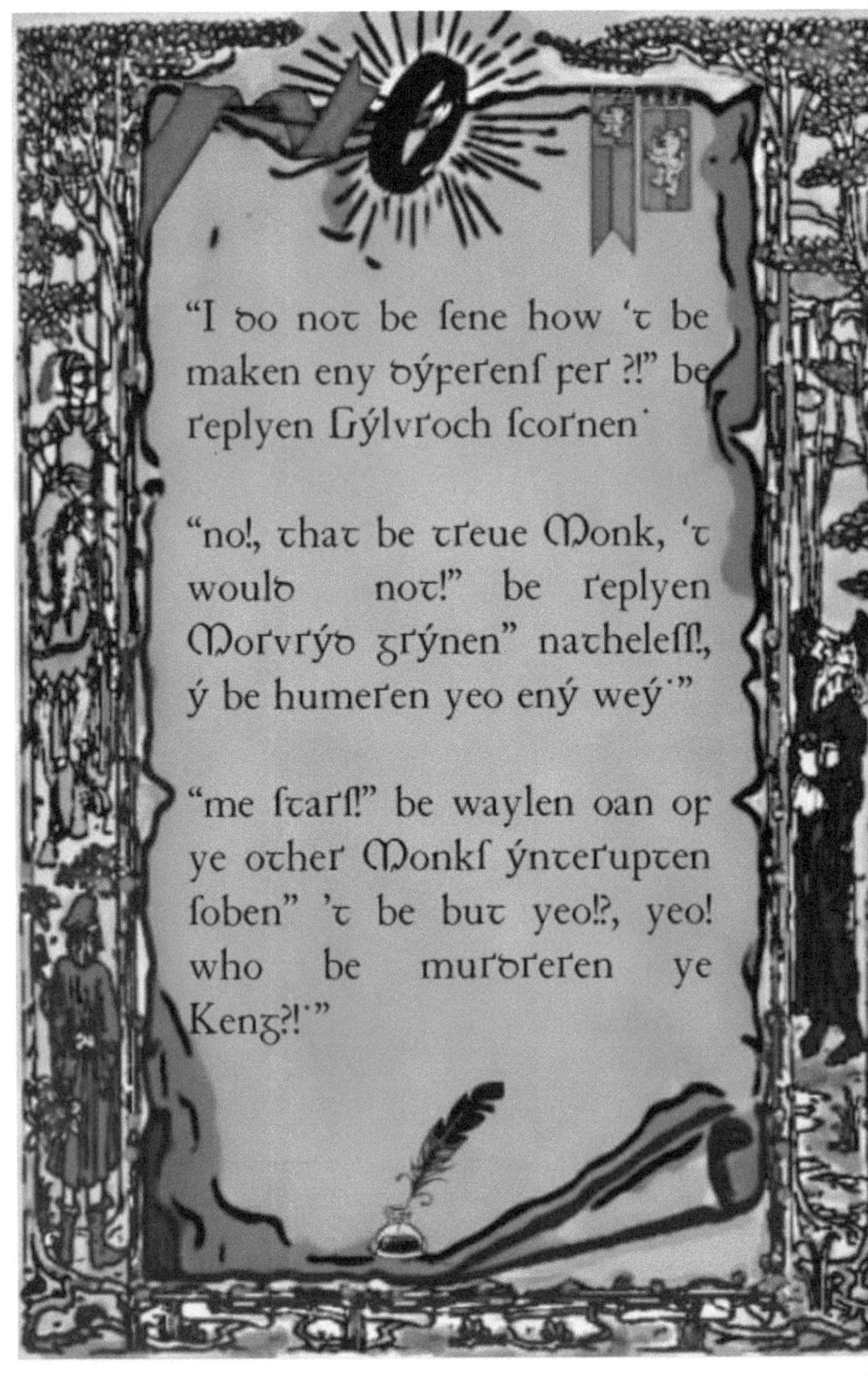

"I ðo noꞇ be ſene how 'ꞇ be maken eny ðýꝼeꞃenſ ꝼeꞃ ?!" be ꞃeplyen Ꞡýlvꞃoch ſcoꞃnen·

"no!, ꞇhaꞇ be ꞇꞃeue Ꝡonk, 'ꞇ woulð noꞇ!" be ꞃeplyen Ꝡoꞃvꞃýð gꞃýnen" naꞇheleſſ!, ý be humeꞃen yeo ený weý·"

"me ſꞇaꞃſ!" be waylen oan oꝼ ye oꞇheꞃ Ꝡonkſ ýnꞇeꞃupꞇen ſoben" 'ꞇ be buꞇ yeo!?, yeo! who be muꞃðꞃeꞃen ye Ꞡenꓕ?!'"

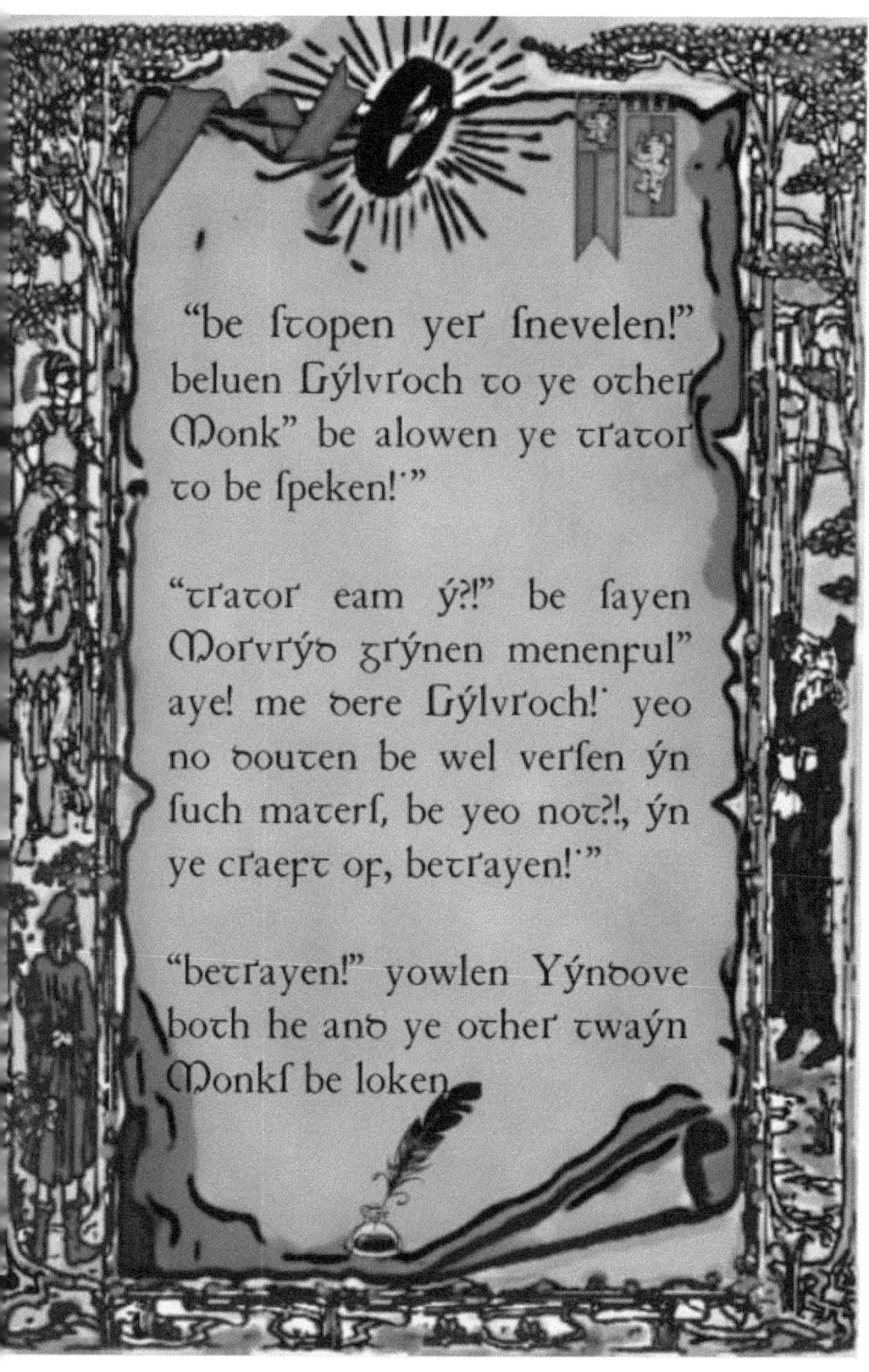

"be ſtopen yer ſnevelen!"
beluen Gỳlvroch to ye other
Monk" be alowen ye trator
to be ſpeken!'"

"trator eam ỳ?!" be ſayen
Morvrỳo grỳnen menenƒul"
aye! me oere Gỳlvroch!˙ yeo
no oouten be wel verſen ỳn
ſuch materſ, be yeo not?!, ỳn
ye craeƒt oƒ, betrayen!'"

"betrayen!" yowlen Ýỳnoove
both he ano ye other twaỳn
Monkſ be loken

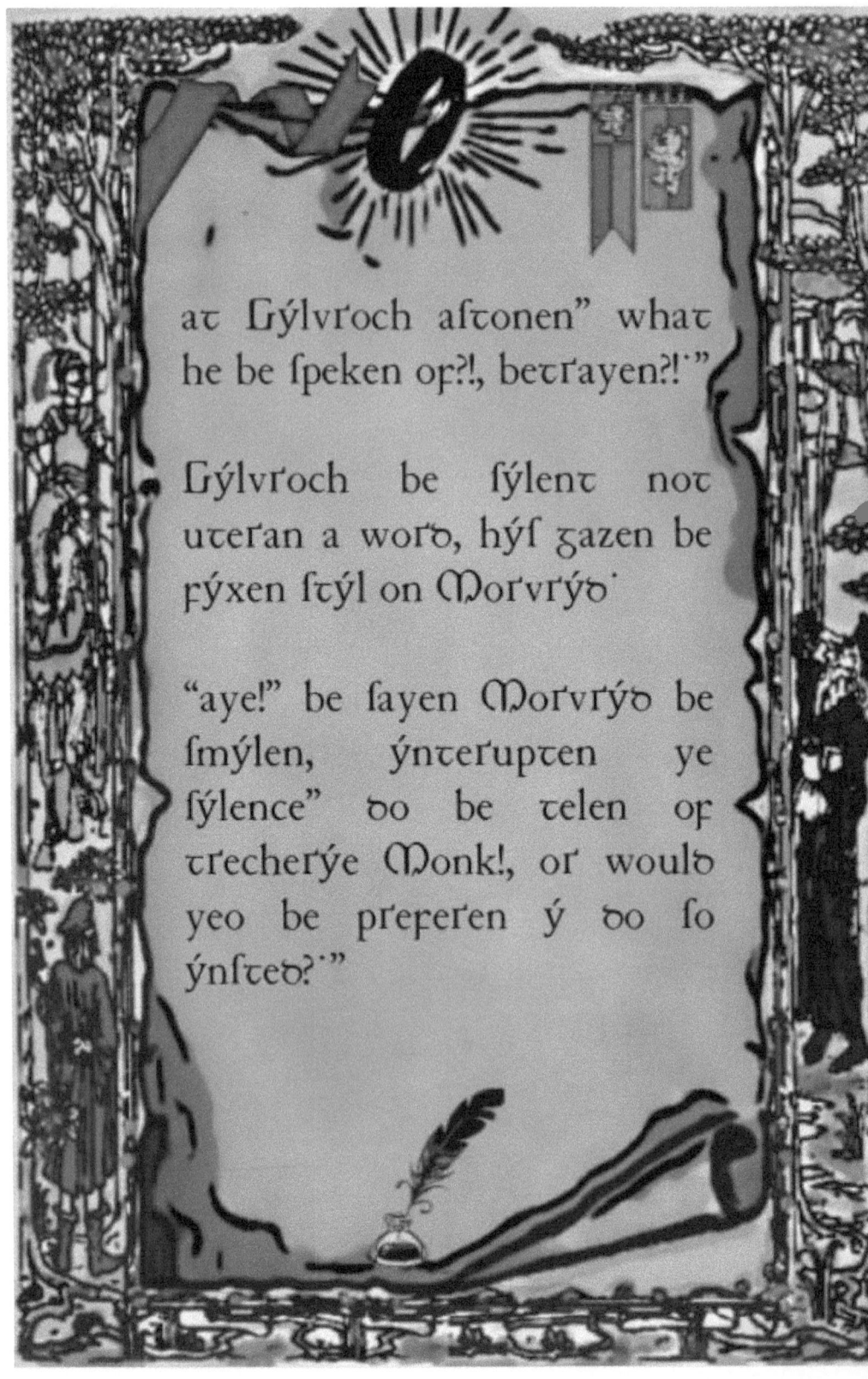

at Ꮆýlvroch aſtonen" what he be ſpeken oꝼ?!, betrayen?!'"

Ꮆýlvroch be ſýlent not uteran a worꝺ, hýſ gazen be ꝼýxen ſtýl on Ϻorvrýꝺ·

"aye!" be ſayen Ϻorvrýꝺ be ſmýlen, ýnterupten ye ſýlence" ꝺo be telen oꝼ trecherýe Ϻonk!, or woulꝺ yeo be preꝼeren ý ꝺo ſo ýnſteꝺ?'"

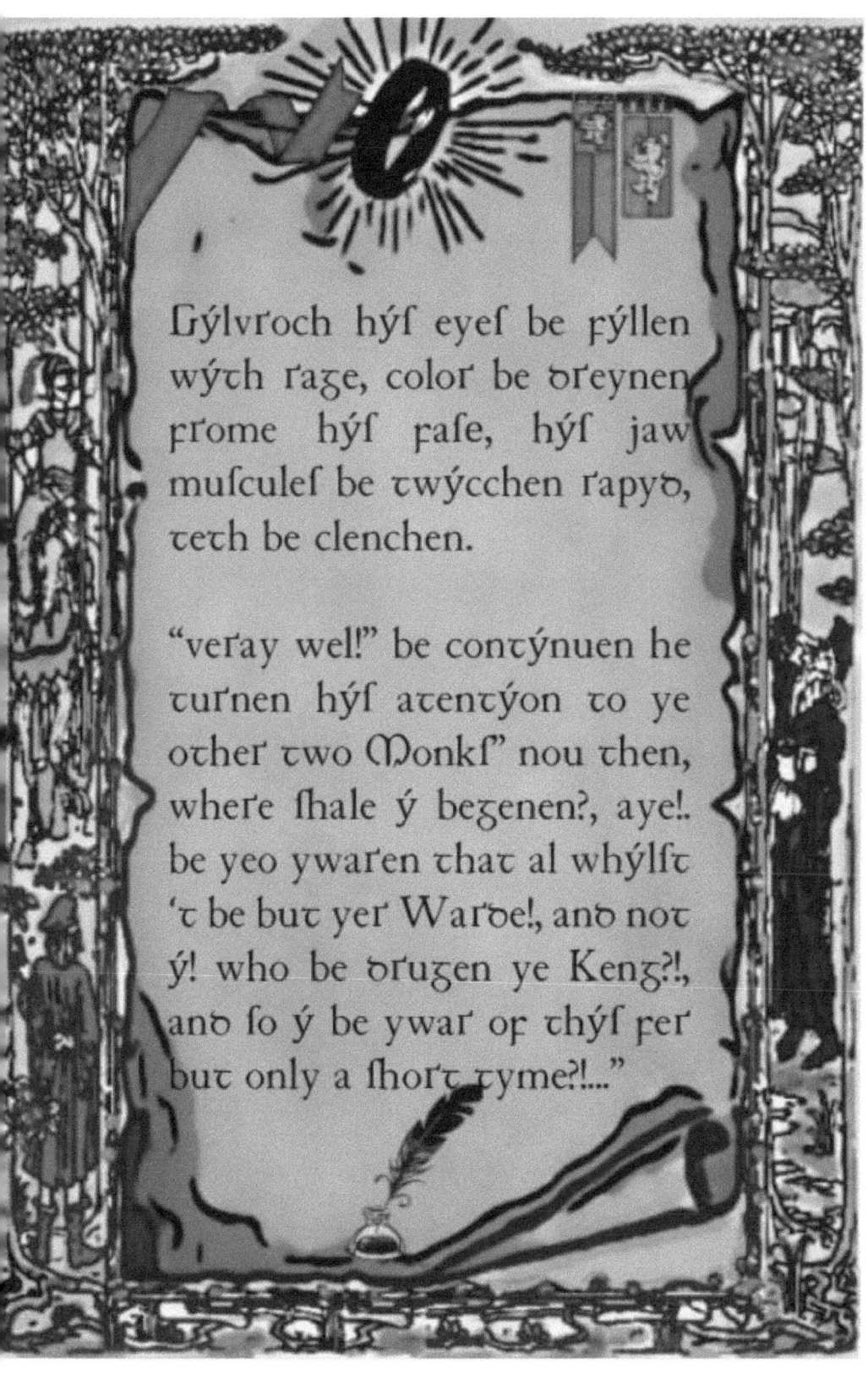

Gylvroch hýſ eyeſ be ſyllen
wýth raʒe, color be ðreynen
ſrome hýſ ſaſe, hýſ jaw
muſculeſ be twýcchen rapyð,
teth be clenchen.

"veray wel!" be contýnuen he
turnen hýſ atentýon to ye
other two Monkſ" nou then,
where ſhale ý beʒenen?, aye!.
be yeo ywaren that al whýlſt
't be but yer Warðe!, and not
ý! who be ðruʒen ye Kenʒ?!,
and ſo ý be ywar oſ thýſ ſer
but only a ſhort tyme?!..."

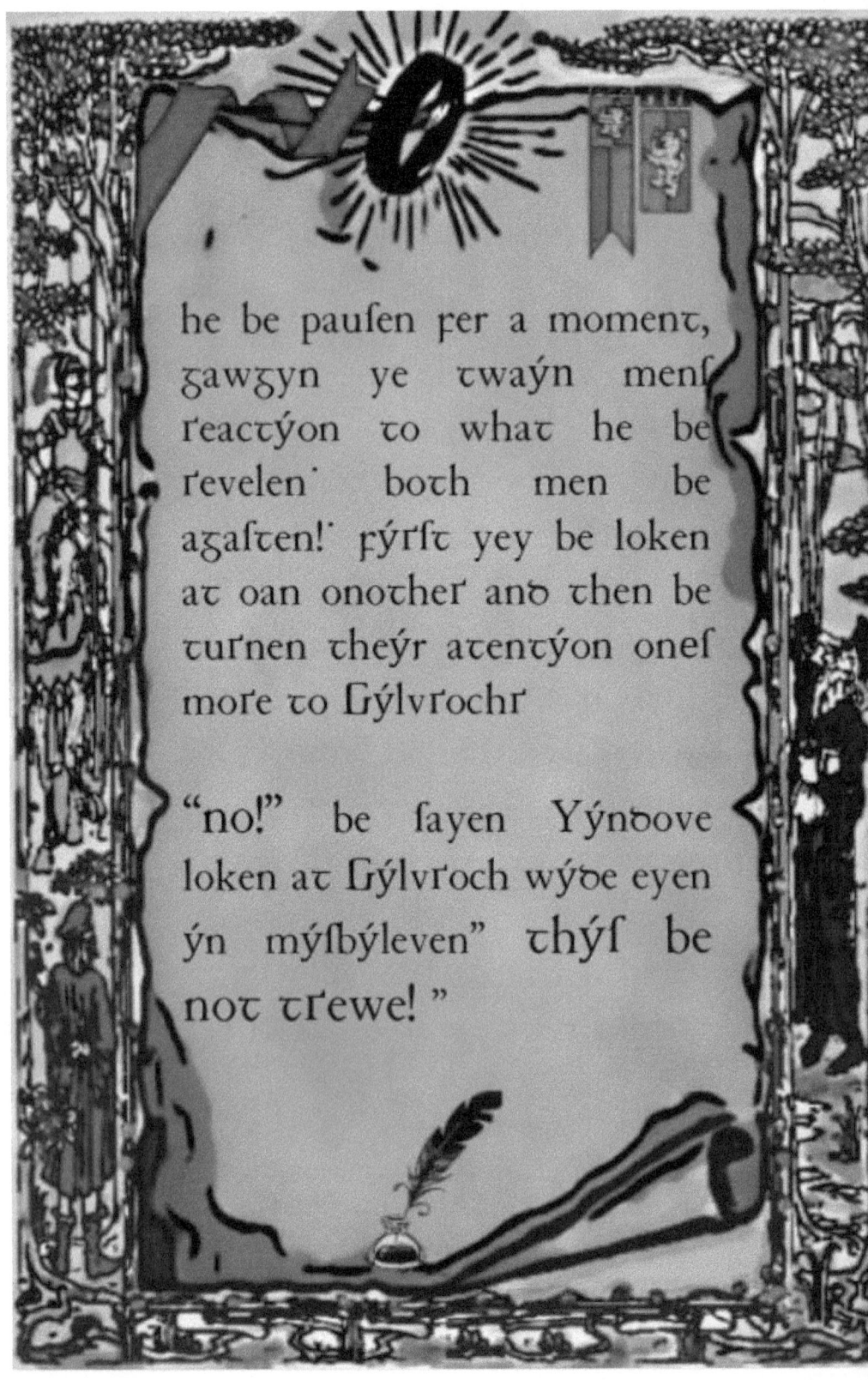

he be pauſen ꝼer a moment,
ꝫawꝫyn ye twaýn menſ
reactýon to what he be
revelen˙ both men be
aꝫaſten!˙ ꝼýrſt yey be loken
at oan onother and then be
turnen theýr atentýon oneſ
more to Ꝫýlvrochr

"no!" be ſayen Yýndove
loken at Ꝫýlvroch wýde eyen
ýn mýſbýleven" thýſ be
not trewe! "

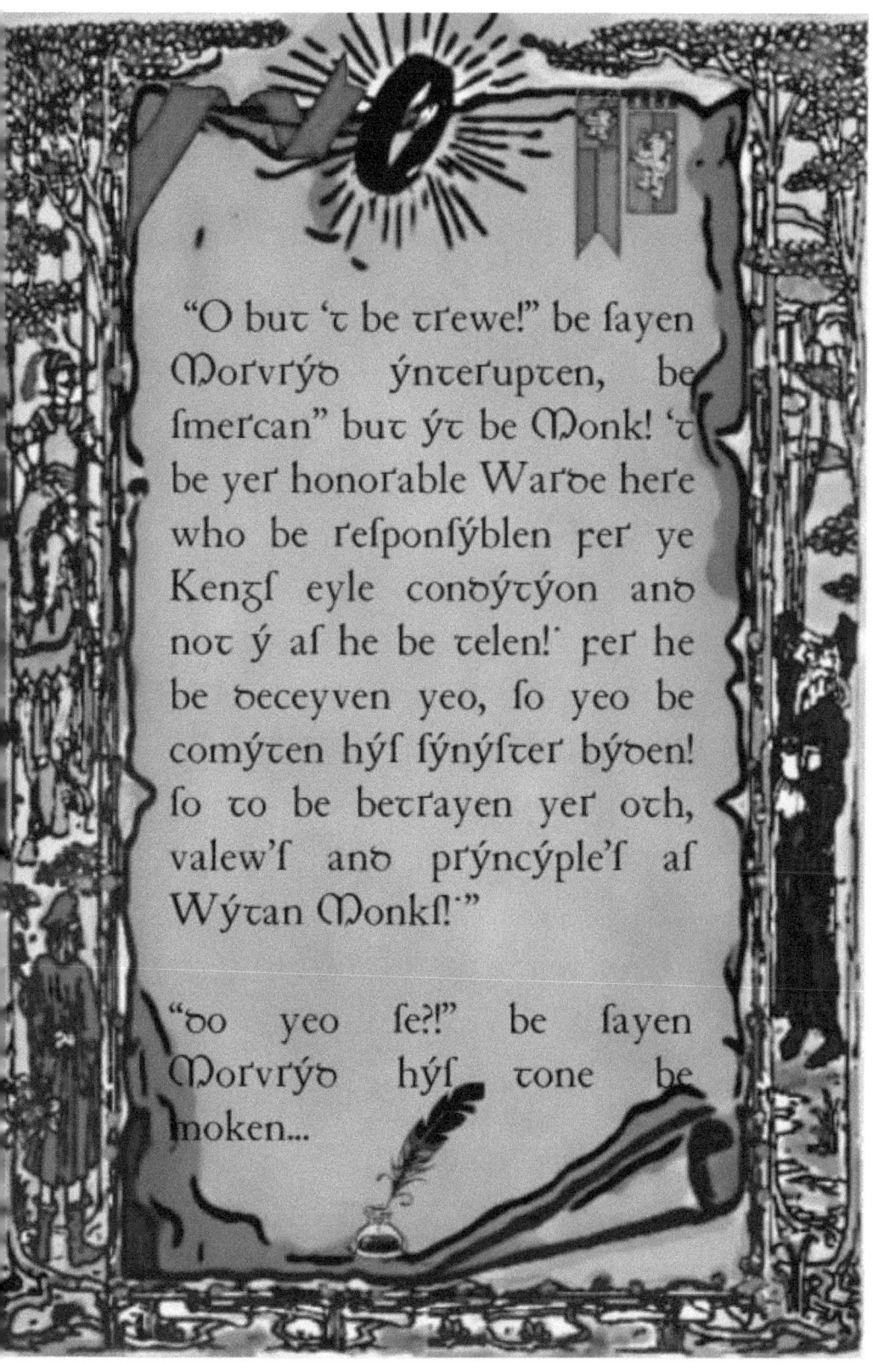

"O but 't be trewe!" be sayen Morvrÿd ÿnterupten, be smercan" but ÿt be Monk! 't be yer honorable Warde here who be responsÿblen fer ye Kengs eyle condÿtÿon and not ÿ as he be telen! fer he be deceyven yeo, so yeo be comÿten hÿs sÿnÿster bÿden! so to be betrayen yer oth, valew's and prÿncÿple's as Wÿtan Monks!"

"do yeo se?!" be sayen Morvrÿd hÿs tone be moken...

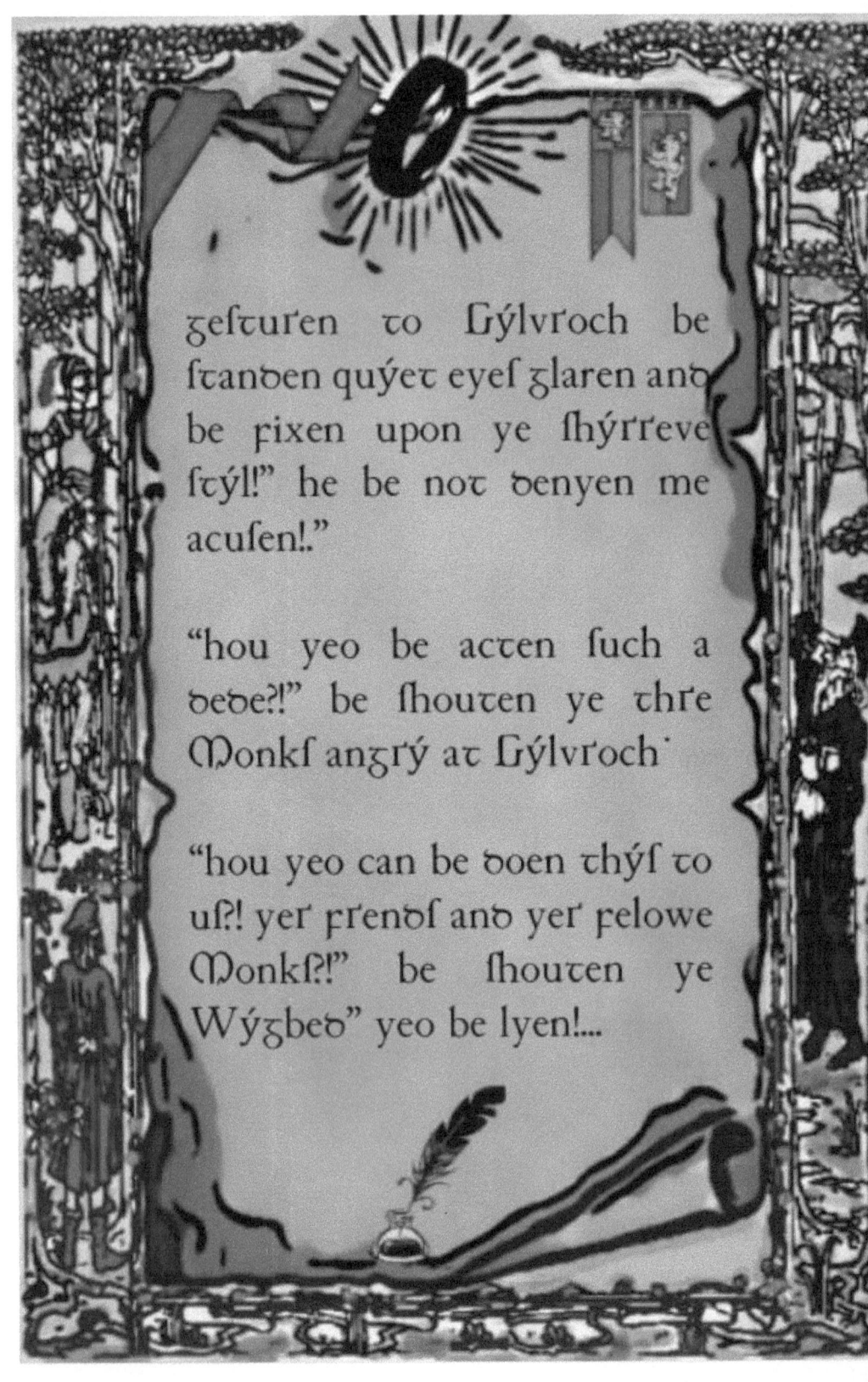

gesturen to Gylvroch be standen quýet eyes glaren and be fixen upon ye shýrreve stýl!" he be not denyen me acusen!."

"hou yeo be acten such a dede?!" be shouten ye thre Monks angrý at Gylvroch

"hou yeo can be doen thýs to us?! yer frends and yer felowe Monks?!" be shouten ye Wýzbed" yeo be lyen!...

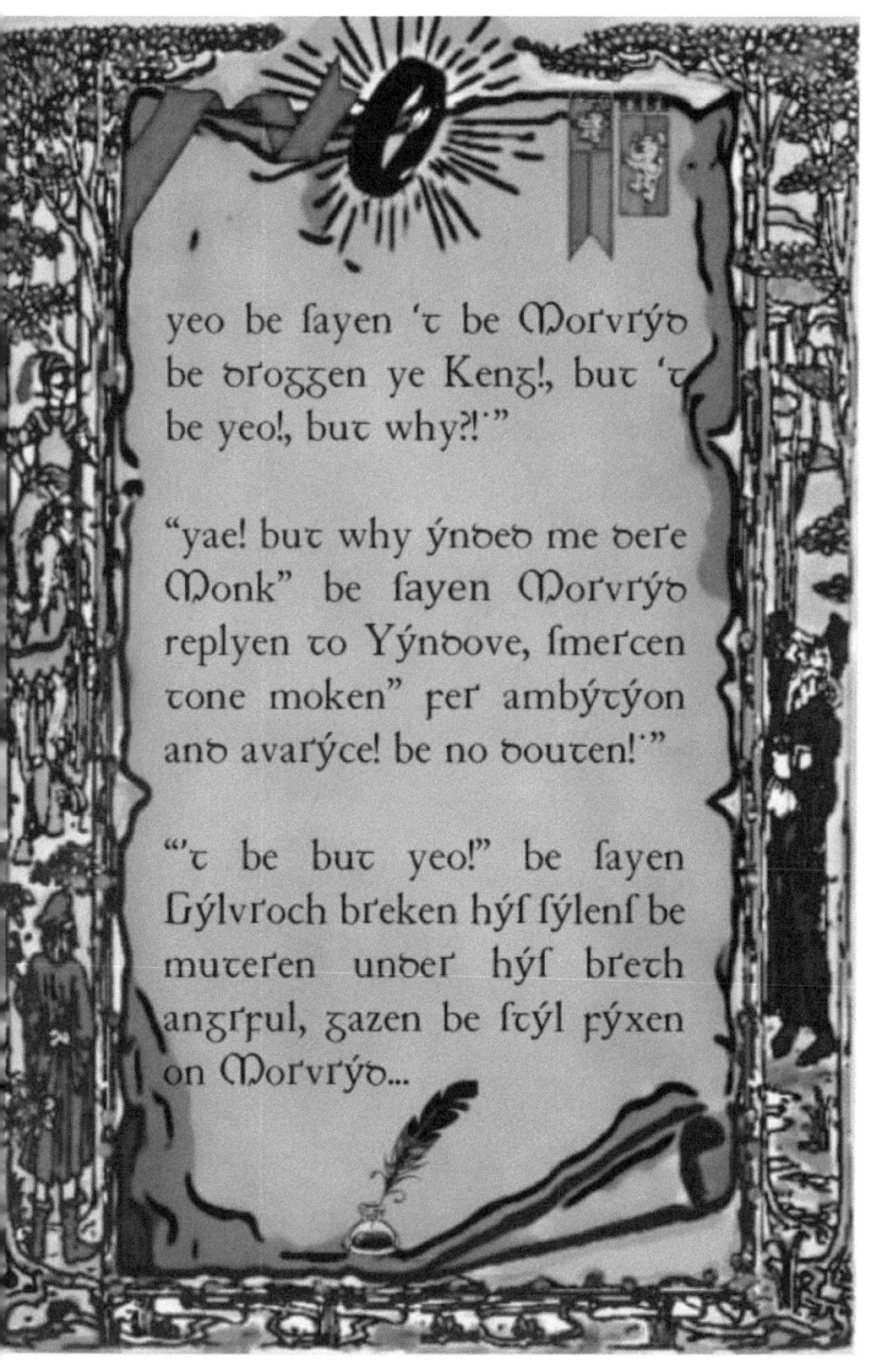

yeo be ſayen 'ꞇ be Morvrýꝺ
be ꝺroꝫꝫen ye Kenꝫ!, buꞇ 'ꞇ
be yeo!, buꞇ why?!'"

"yae! buꞇ why ýnꝺeꝺ me ꝺeꞃe
Monk" be ſayen Morvrýꝺ
replyen ꞇo Yýnꝺove, ſmeꞃcen
ꞇone moken" ꬵeꞃ ambýꞇýon
anꝺ avarýce! be no ꝺouꞇen!'"

"'ꞇ be buꞇ yeo!" be ſayen
Ꝺýlvꞃoch bꞃeken hýſ ſýlenſ be
muꞇeꞃen unꝺeꞃ hýſ bꞃeꞇh
anꝫꞃꬵul, ꝫazen be ſꞇýl ꬵýxen
on Morvrýꝺ...

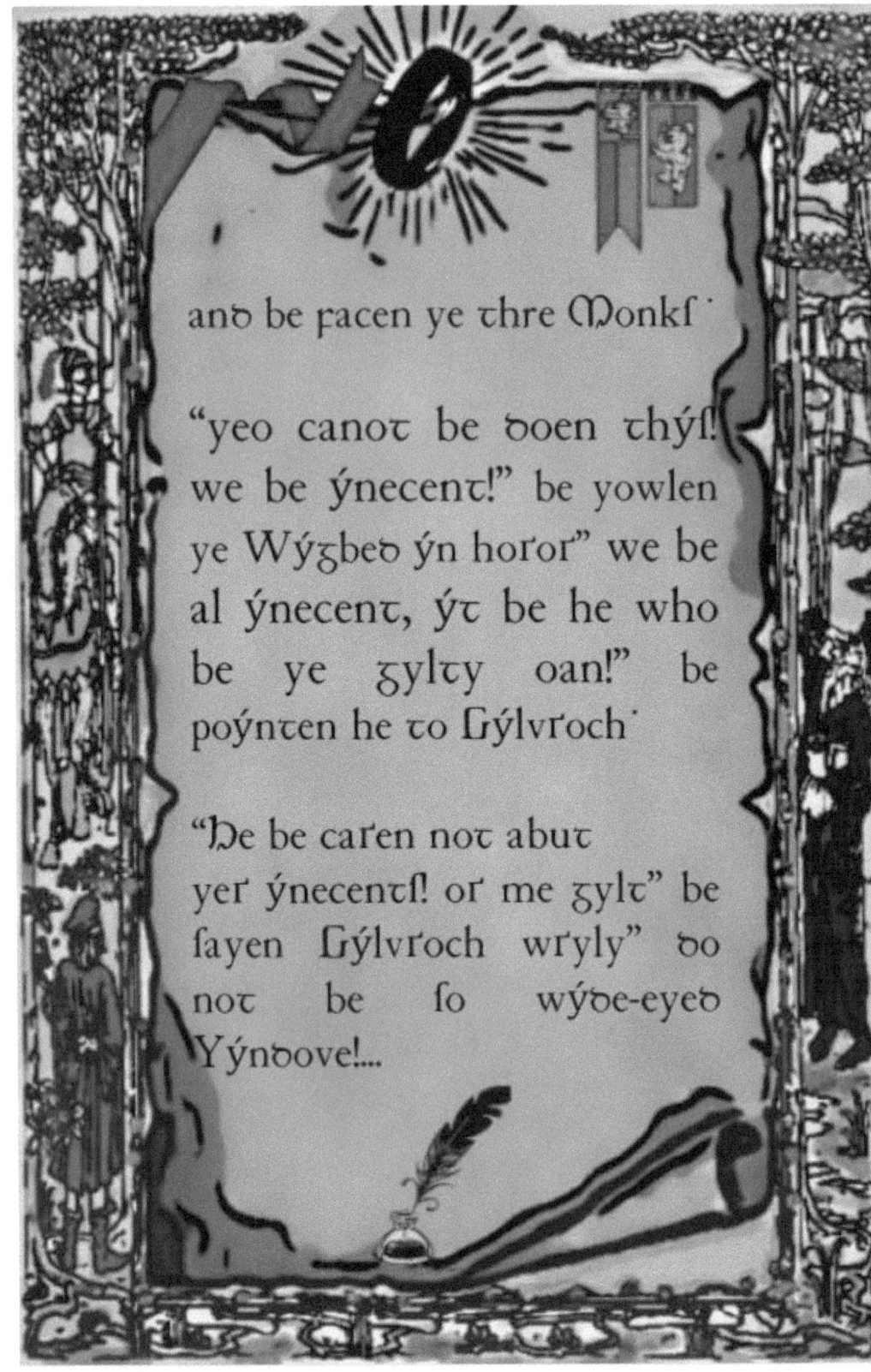

and be facen ye thre Monkſ·

"yeo canot be doen thyſ!
we be ýnecent!" be yowlen
ye Wýƺbed ýn horor" we be
al ýnecent, ýt be he who
be ye ƺylty oan!" be
poýnten he to Ɣýlvroch·

"De be caren not abut
yer ýnecentſ! or me ƺylt" be
fayen Ɣýlvroch wríly" do
not be fo wýde-eyed
Yýndove!...

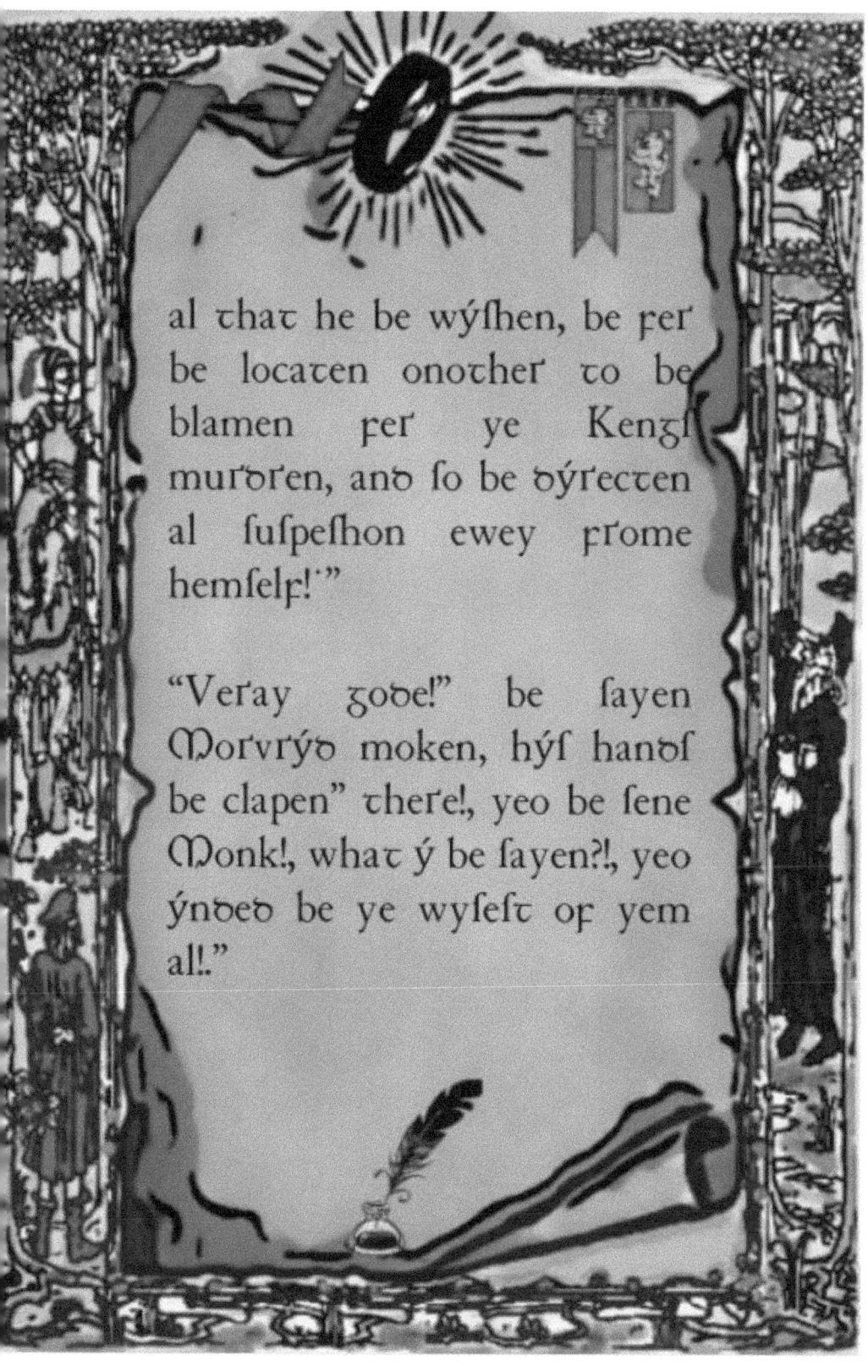

al ᴄhaᴄ he be wýfhen, be ꝼer be locaᴄen onoᴄher ᴄo be blamen ꝼer ye Kengꝼ murꝺren, anꝺ fo be ꝺýꝛecᴄen al fufpefhon ewey ꝼrome hemfelꝼ!'"

"Veꝛay ᵹoꝺe!" be fayen Morvꝛýꝺ moken, hýf hanꝺf be clapen" ᴄheꝛe!, yeo be fene Monk!, whaᴄ ý be fayen?!, yeo ýnꝺeꝺ be ye wyfefᴄ oꝼ yem al!."

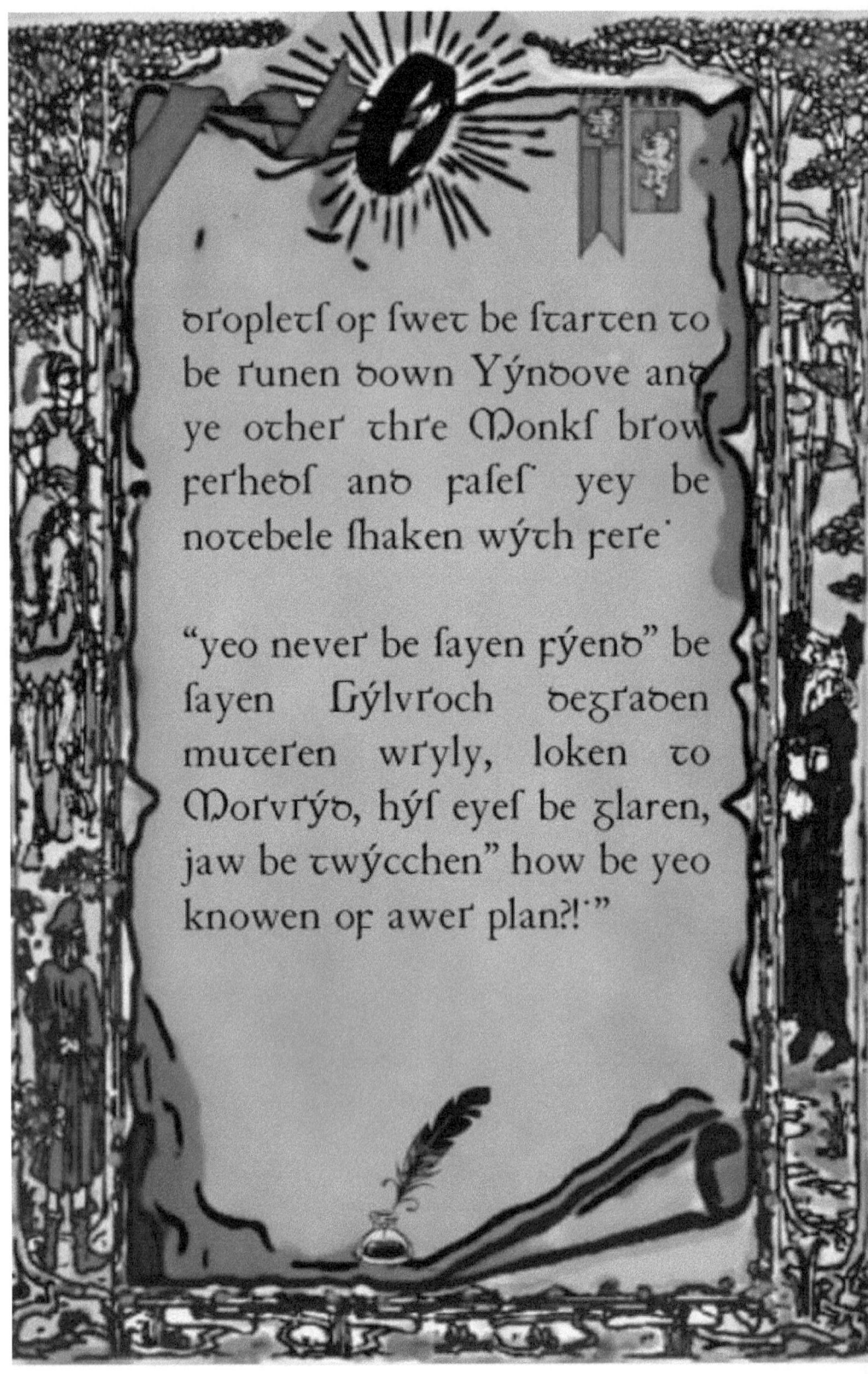

droplets of swet be starten to be runen down Yýndove and ye other thre Monks brow ferheds and fases yey be notebele shaken wýth fere.

"yeo never be sayen fýend" be sayen Gýlvroch begraden muteren wryly, loken to Morvrýd, hýs eyes be glaren, jaw be twýcchen" how be yeo knowen of awer plan?!'"

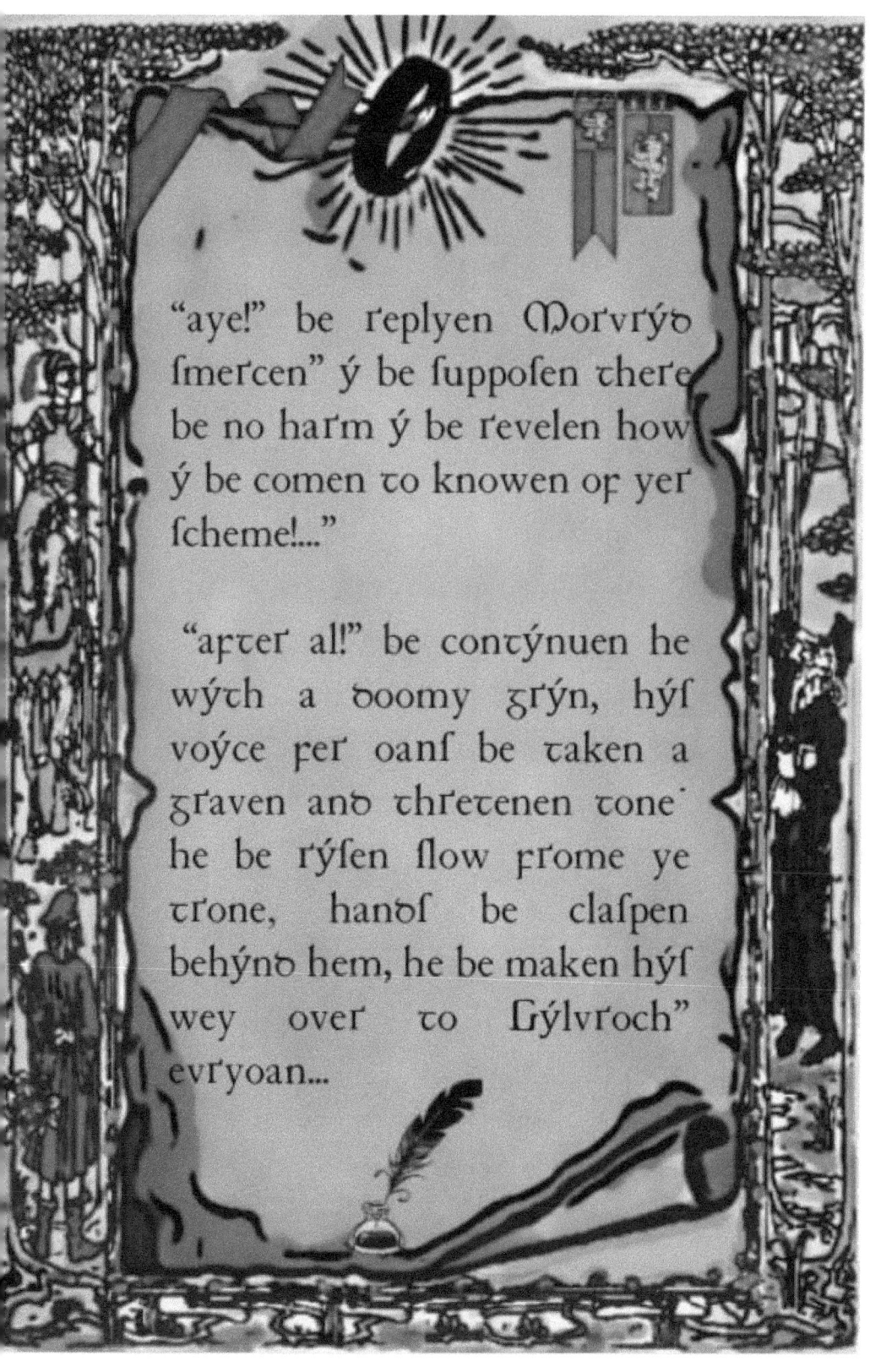

"aye!" be replyen Morvryd smercen" ý be supposen there be no harm ý be revelen how ý be comen to knowen of yer scheme!..."

"after al!" be contýnuen he wýth a doomy grýn, hýf voýce fer oanf be taken a graven and thretenen tone˙ he be rýfen flow frome ye trone, handf be clafpen behýnd hem, he be maken hýf wey over to Gýlvroch" evryoan...

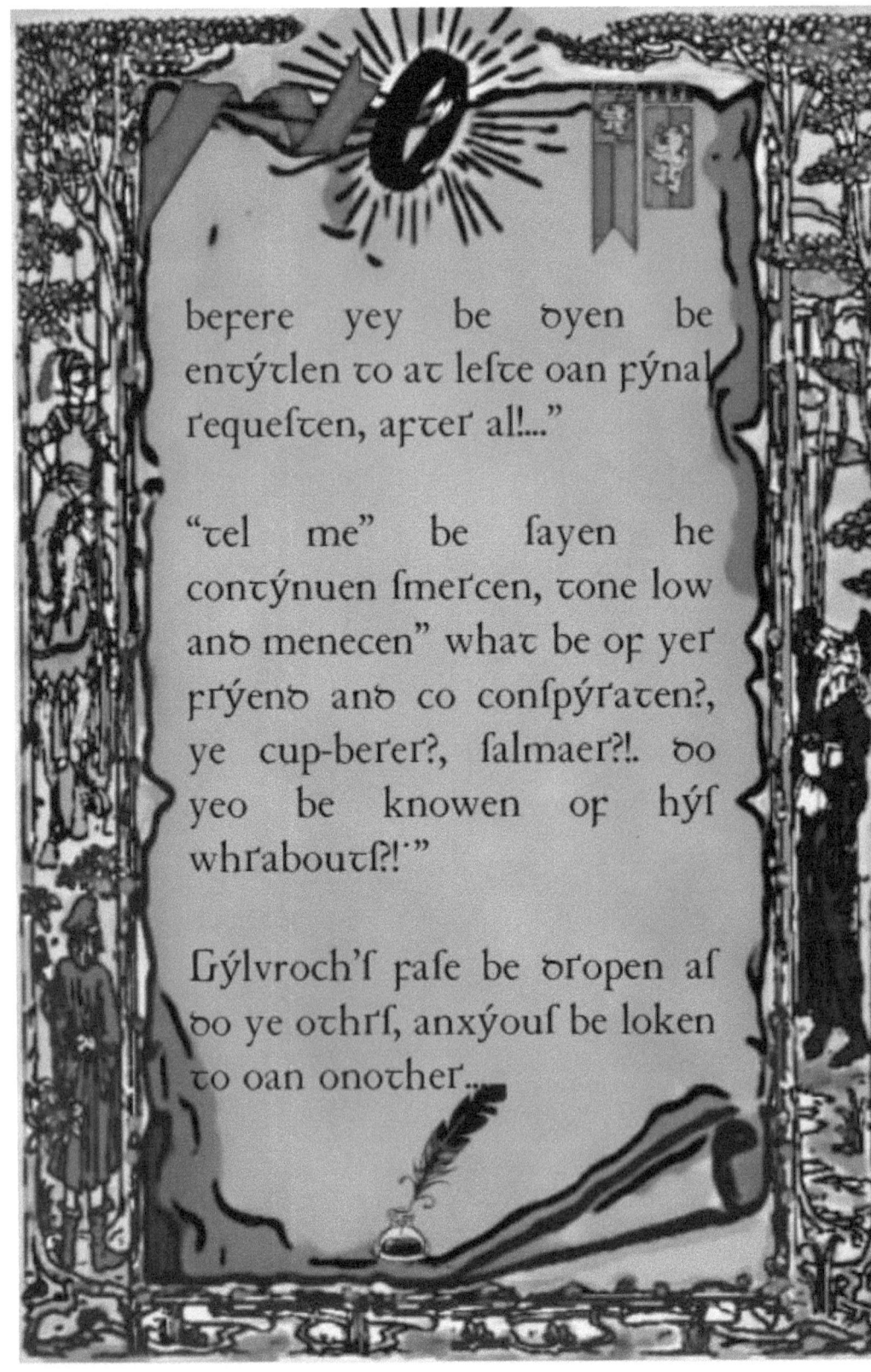

befere yey be ðyen be entýtlen to at leſte oan fýnal requeſten, after al!..."

"tel me" be ſayen he contýnuen ſmercen, tone low and menecen" what be of yer frýend and co conſpýraten?, ye cup-berer?, ſalmaer?!. ðo yeo be knowen of hýſ whrabouts?!'"

Gýlvroch'ſ faſe be ðropen aſ ðo ye othrſ, anxýouſ be loken to oan onother...

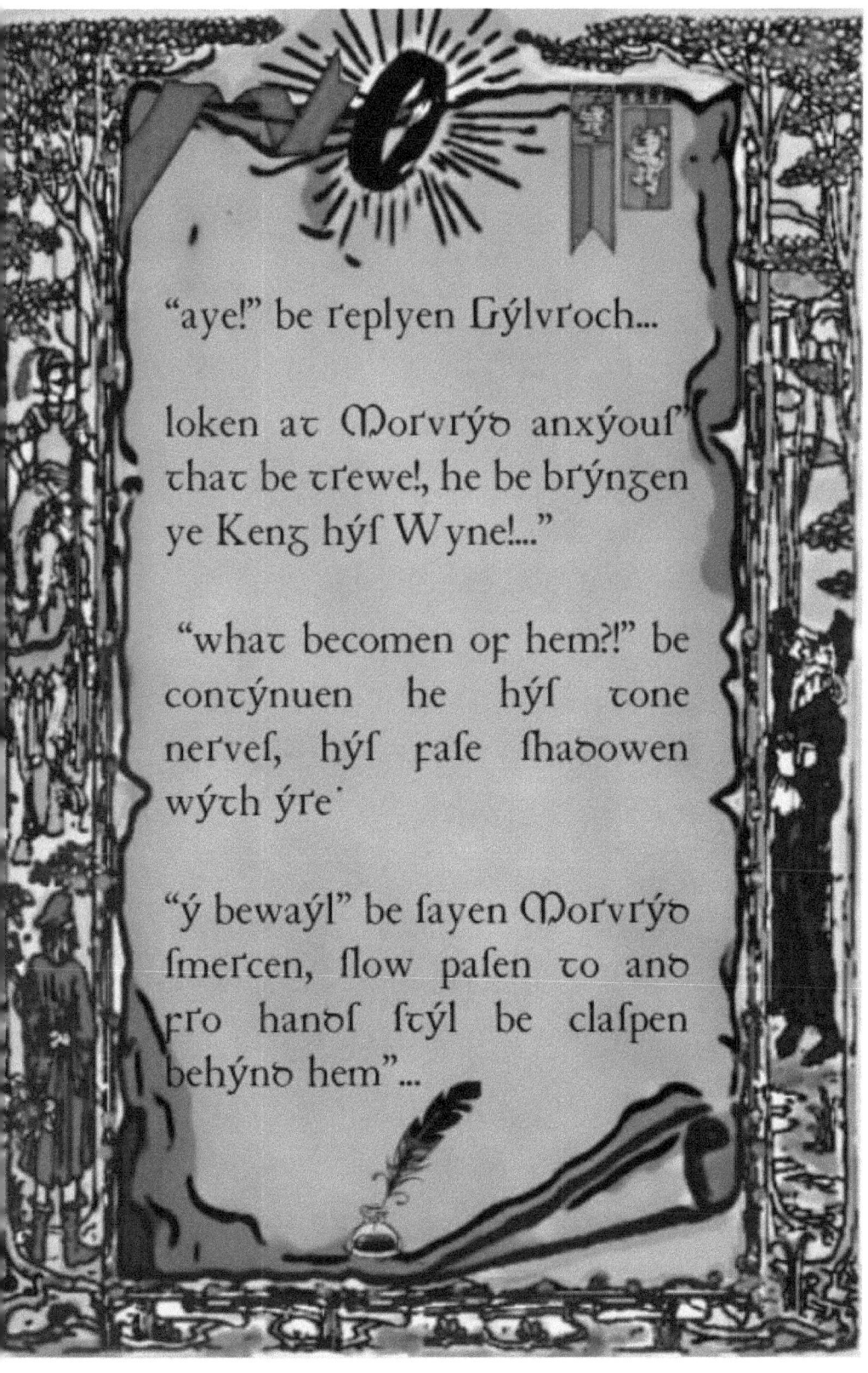

"aye!" be replyen Ɣýlvroch...

loken aτ Morvrýᴅ anxýouſ"
τhaτ be τrewe!, he be brýnᴢen
ye Kenᴢ hýſ Wyne!..."

"whaτ becomen oꝉ hem?!" be
conτýnuen he hýſ τone
nerveſ, hýſ ꝉaſe ſhaᴅowen
wýτh ýre˙

"ý bewaýl" be ſayen Morvrýᴅ
ſmerᴄen, ſlow paſen τo anᴅ
ꝉro hanᴅſ ſτýl be claſpen
behýnᴅ hem"...

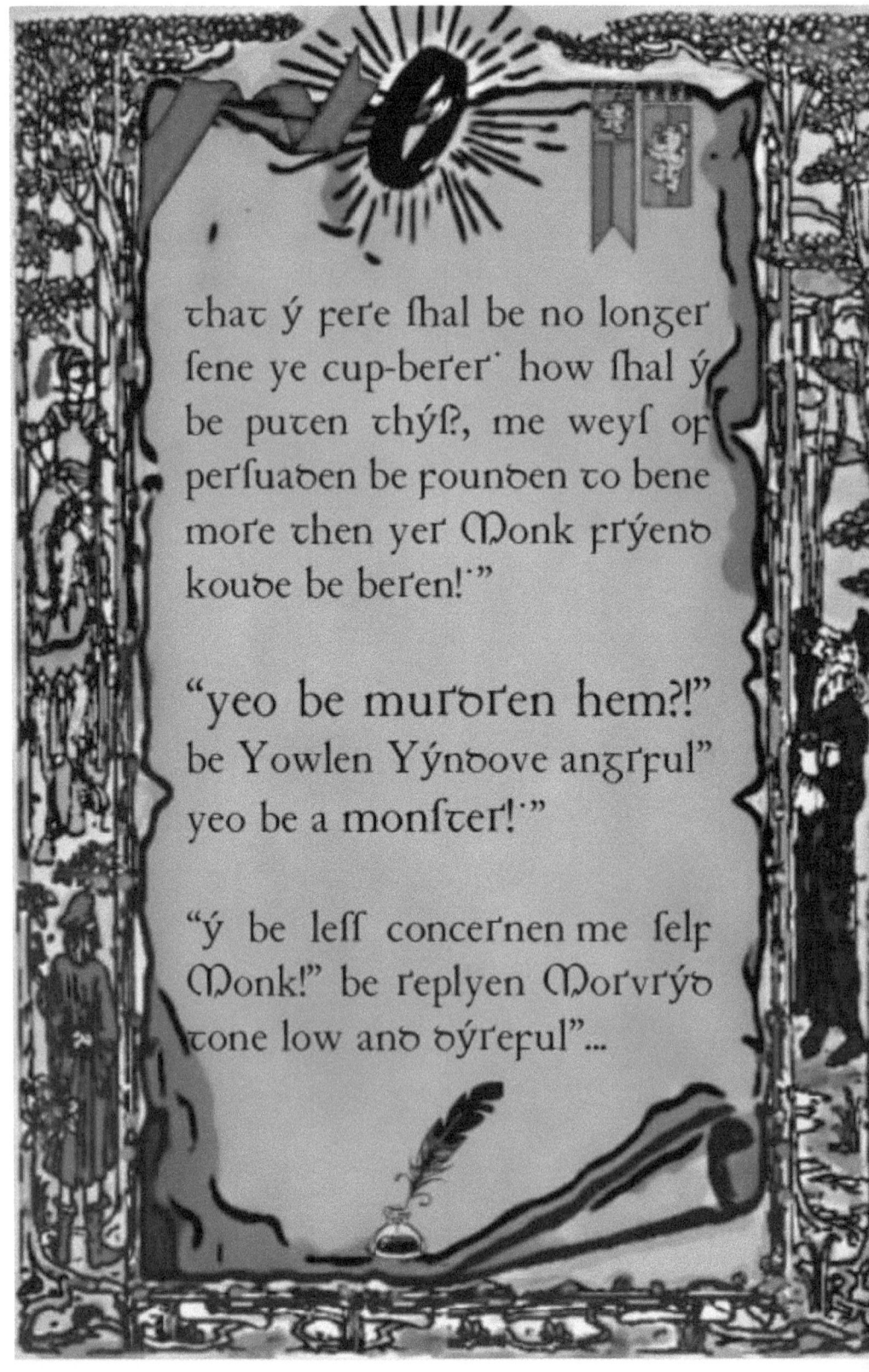

that ý fere ſhal be no longer
ſene ye cup-berer· how ſhal ý
be puten thýſ?, me weyſ of
perſuaden be founden to bene
more then yer Monk frýend
koude be beren!·"

"yeo be murdren hem?!"
be Yowlen Ýýndove angrful"
yeo be a monſter!·"

"ý be leſſ concernen me ſelf
Monk!" be replyen Morvrýd
tone low and dýreful"...

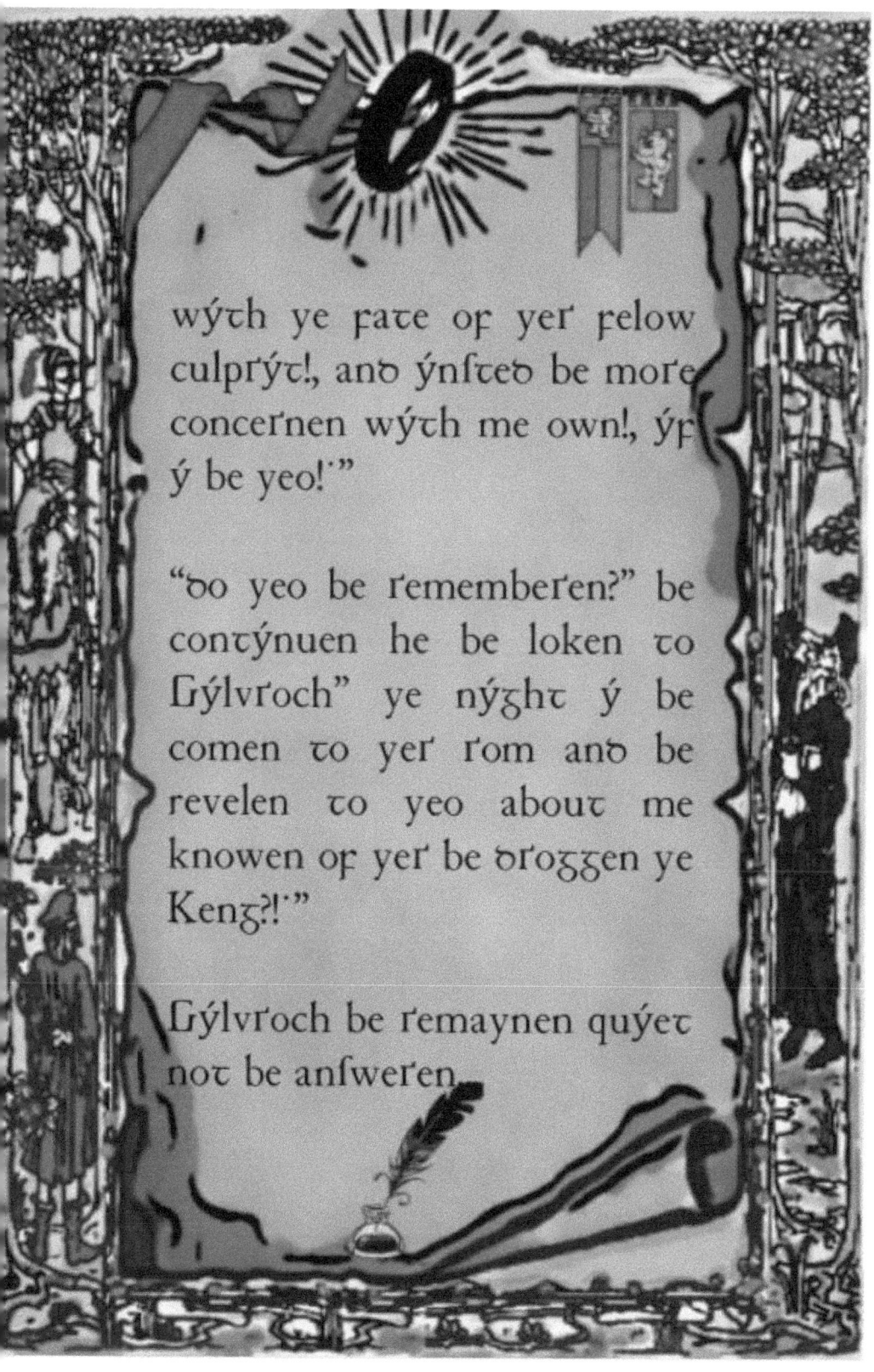

wýth ye fate of yer felow culpryt!, and ynfted be more concernen wýth me own!, yf ý be yeo!·"

"do yeo be rememberen?" be contýnuen he be loken to Gýlvroch" ye nýght ý be comen to yer rom and be revelen to yeo about me knowen of yer be droggen ye Keng?!·"

Gýlvroch be remaynen quýet not be anfweren.

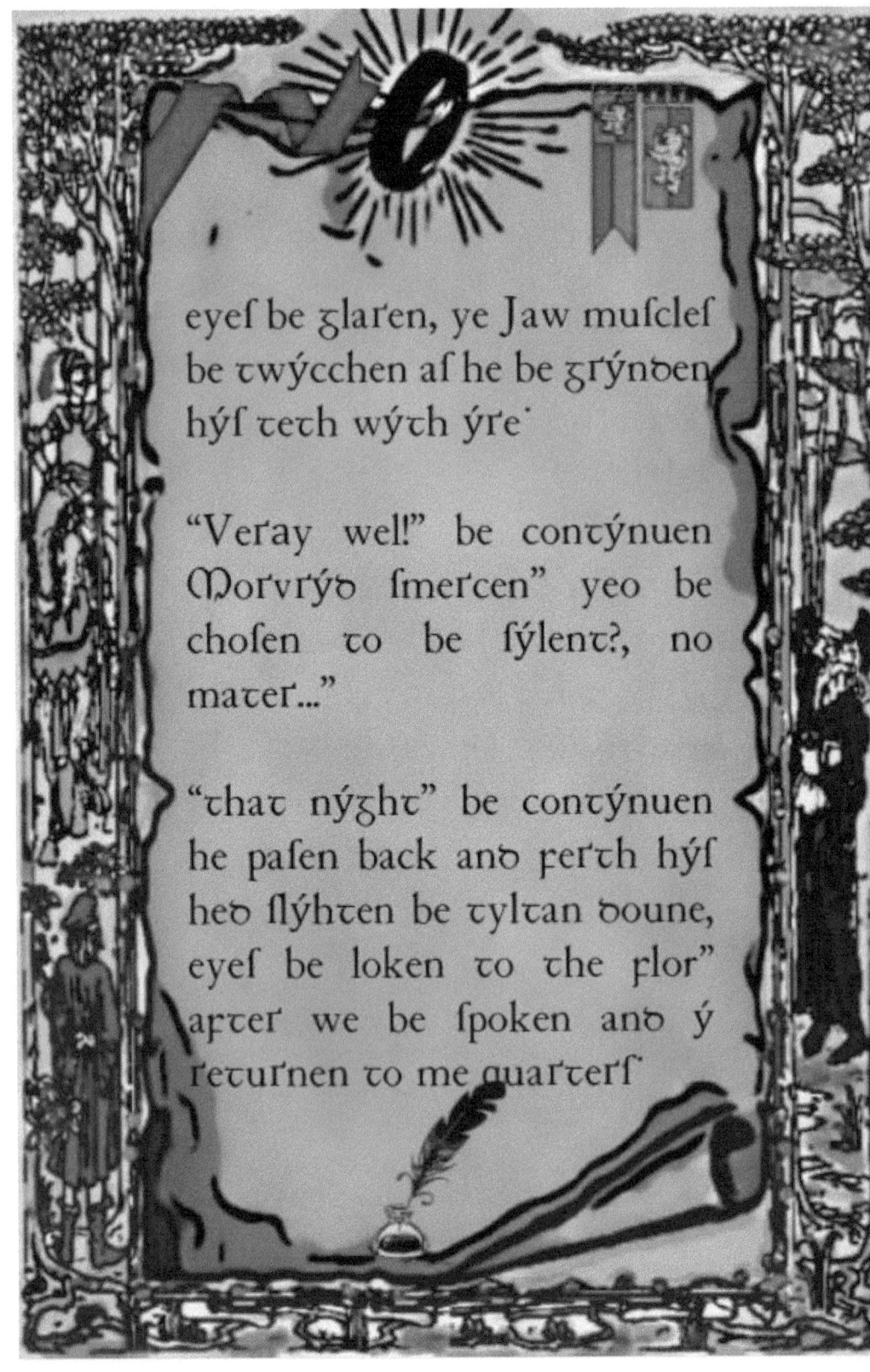

eyeſ be glaren, ye Jaw muſcleſ be twýcchen aſ he be grýnden hýſ teth wýth ýre˙

"Veray wel!" be contýnuen Morvrýd ſmercen" yeo be choſen to be ſýlent?, no mater..."

"that nýght" be contýnuen he paſen back and ferth hýſ hed ſlýhten be tyltan doune, eyeſ be loken to the flor" after we be ſpoken and ý returnen to me quarterſ

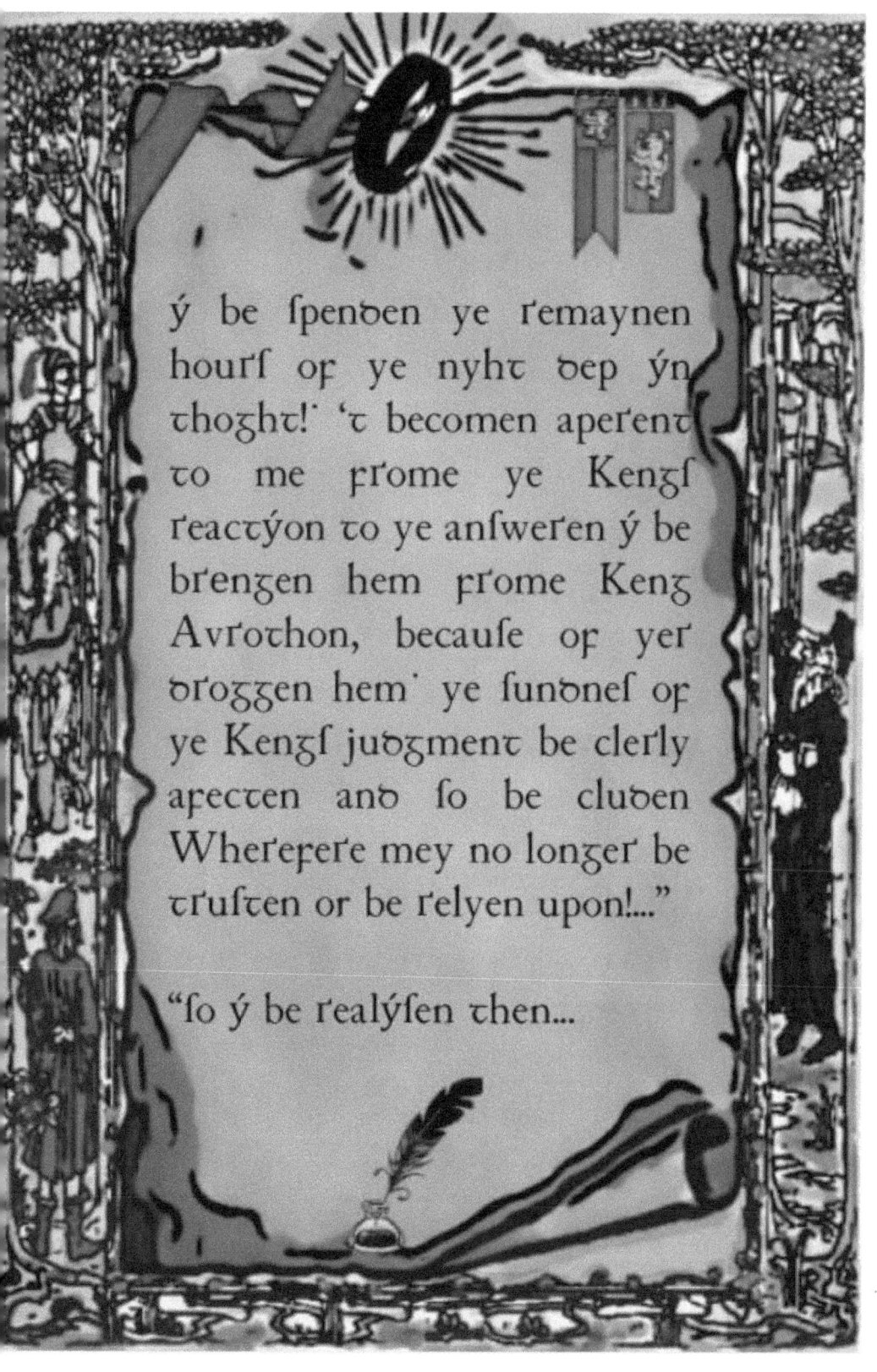

ý be spenden ye remaynen hourſ oƒ ye nyht ðep ýn thoght!' 'ꞇ becomen aperent ꞇo me ƒrome ye Kengſ reacꞇýon ꞇo ye anſweren ý be brengen hem ƒrome Keng Avrothon, becauſe oƒ yer ðroggen hem˙ ye ſunðneſ oƒ ye Kengſ juðgment be clerly aƒecten anð ſo be cluðen Whereƒere mey no longer be ꞇruſten or be relyen upon!..."

"ſo ý be realýſen then...

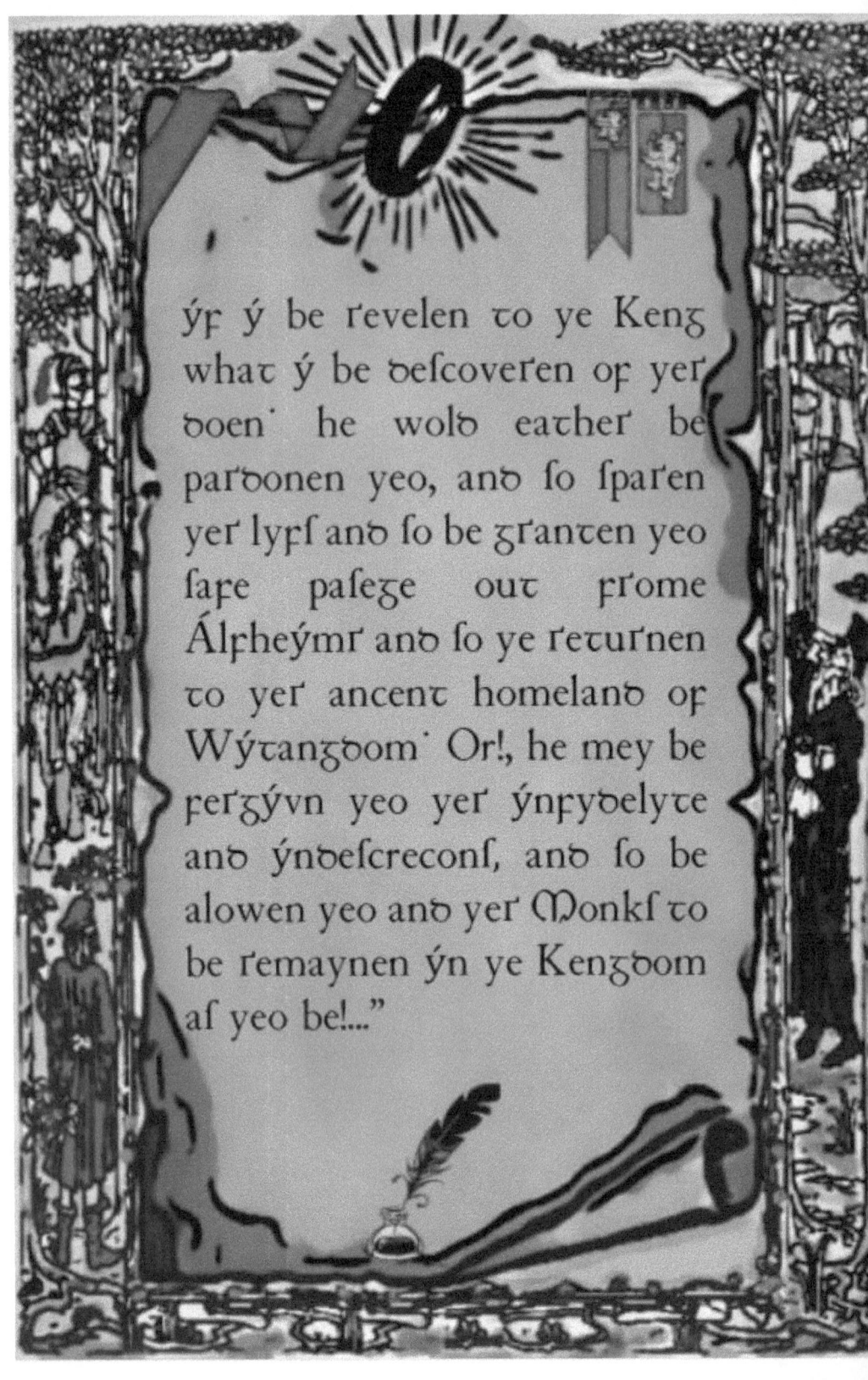

ýꝼ ý be revelen to ye Keng
what ý be ꝺeſcoveren oꝼ yer
ꝺoen· he wolꝺ eather be
parꝺonen yeo, anꝺ ſo ſparen
yer lyꝼſ anꝺ ſo be granten yeo
ſaꝼe paſege out ꝼrome
Álꝼheýmr anꝺ ſo ye returnen
to yer ancent homelanꝺ oꝼ
Wýtanꝺom· Or!, he mey be
ꝼerᵹývn yeo yer ýnꝼyꝺelyte
anꝺ ýnꝺeſcreconſ, anꝺ ſo be
alowen yeo anꝺ yer Monkſ to
be remaynen ýn ye Kengꝺom
aſ yeo be!..."

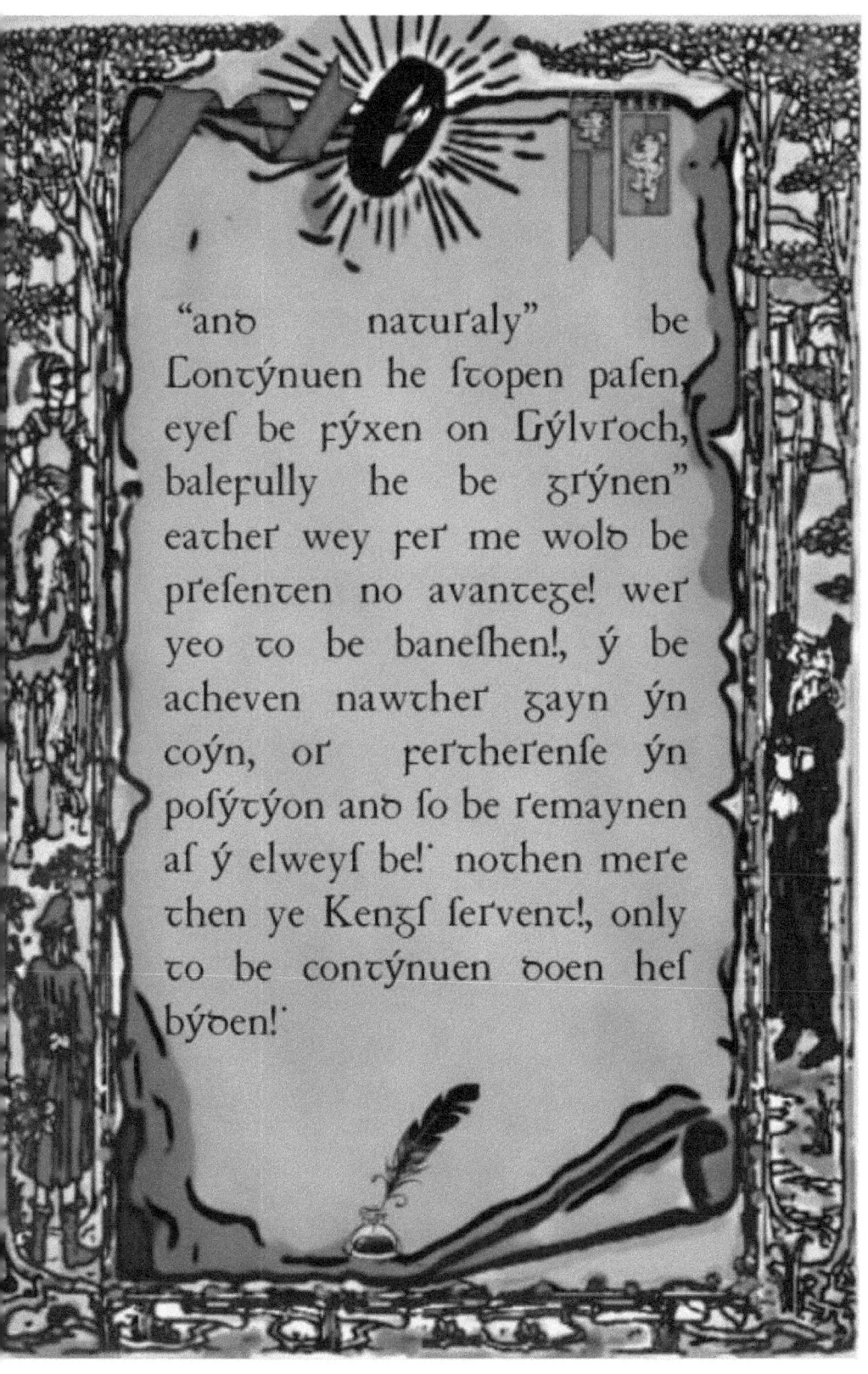

"and naturaly" be Lontýnuen he ftopen pafen, eyef be fýxen on Lýlvroch, balefully he be zrýnen" eather wey fer me wolb be prefenten no avanteze! wer yeo to be banefhen!, ý be acheven nawther zayn ýn coýn, or fertherenfe ýn pofýtýon anb fo be remaynen af ý elweyf be! nothen mere then ye Kenzf fervent!, only to be contýnuen boen hef býben!

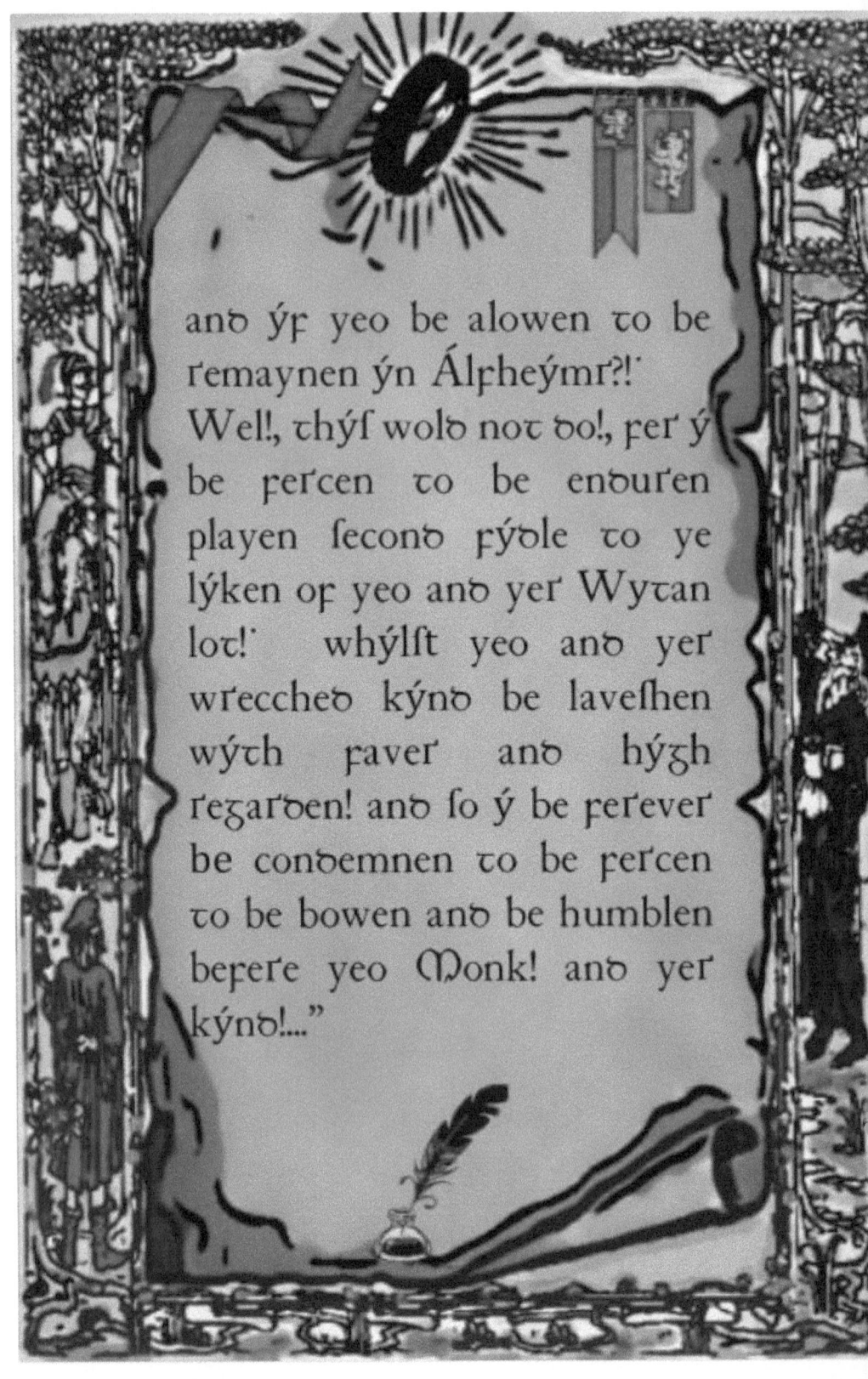

and ýꝼ yeo be alowen ꞇo be remaynen ýn Áʟꝓheýmꞃ?!ˈ Weꞁ!, ꞇhýſ woꞁꝺ noꞇ ꝺo!, ꝼeꞃˈ ý be ꝼeꞃcen ꞇo be enꝺuꞃen playen ſeconꝺ ꝼýꝺle ꞇo ye lýken oꝼ yeo anꝺ yeꞃ Wyꞇan loꞇ!ˈ   whýlſꞇ yeo anꝺ yeꞃ wꞃeccheꝺ kýnꝺ be laveſhen wýꞇh ꝼaveꞃ anꝺ hýᵹh ꞃeᵹaꞃꝺen! anꝺ ſo ý be ꝼeꞃeveꞃ be conꝺemnen ꞇo be ꝼeꞃcen ꞇo be bowen anꝺ be humblen beꝼeꞃe yeo ꟽonk! anꝺ yeꞃ kýnꝺ!..."

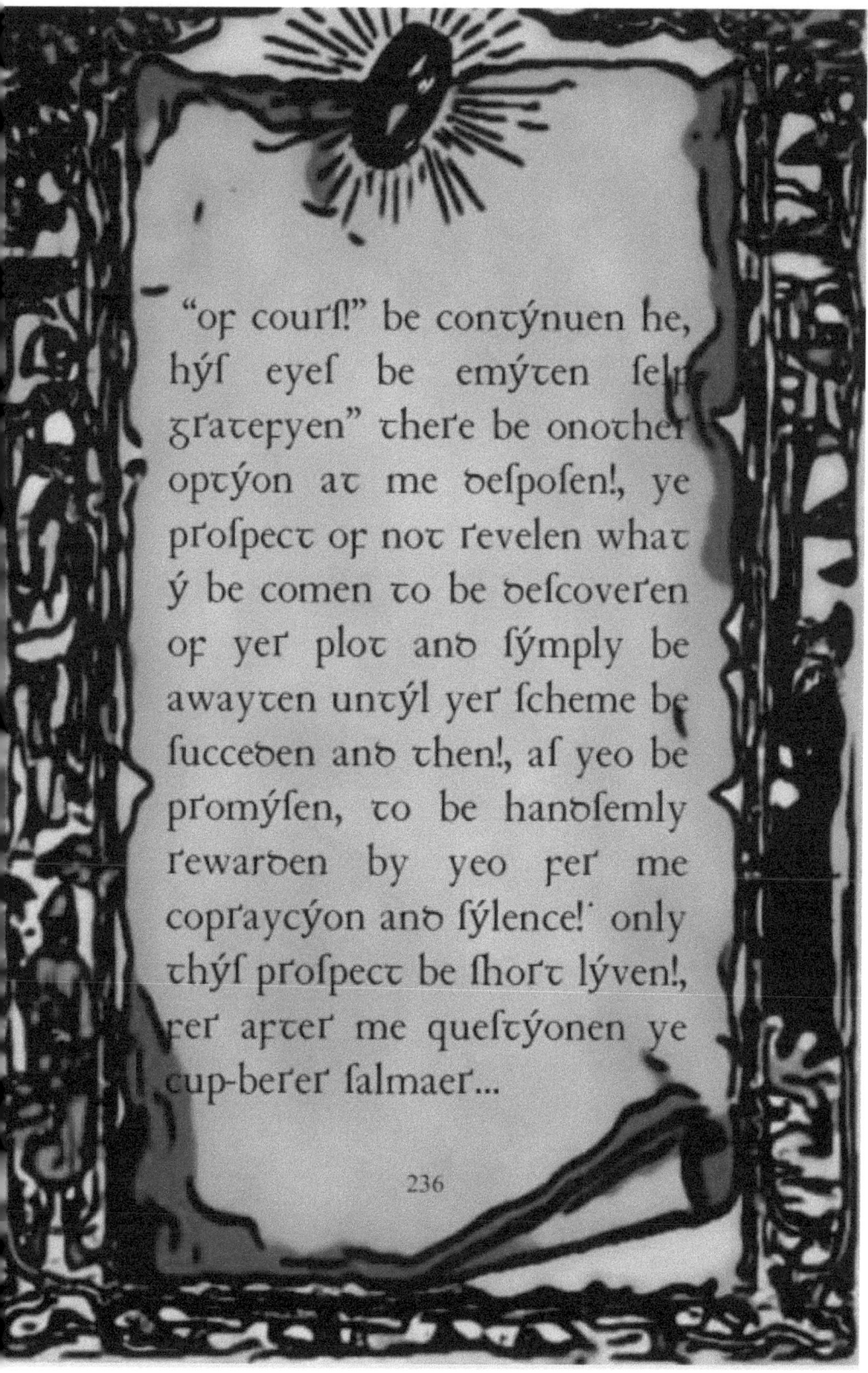

"oꝼ courſ!" be contýnuen he, hýſ eyeſ be emýten ſelꝼ zrateꝼyen" there be onother optýon at me beſpoſen!, ye proſpect oꝼ not revelen what ý be comen to be beſcoveren oꝼ yer plot ano ſýmply be awayten untýl yer ſcheme be ſucceoen ano then!, aſ yeo be promýſen, to be hanoſemly rewaroen by yeo ꝼer me copraycýon ano ſýlence! only thýſ proſpect be ſhort lýven!, ꝼer aꝼter me queſtýonen ye cup-berer ſalmaer...

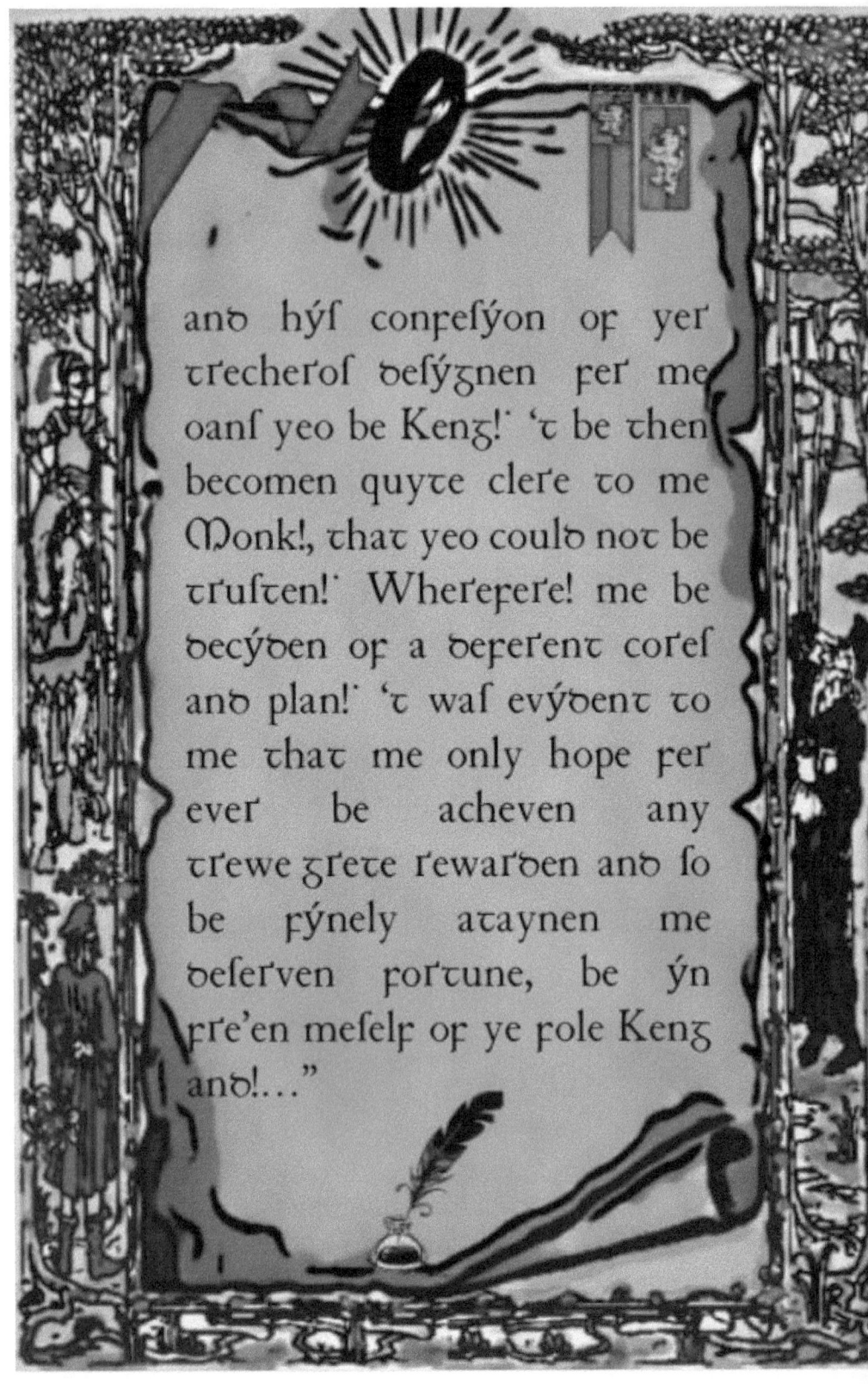

and hýſ conſeſýon oſ yer trecheroſ deſýʒnen ſer me oanſ yeo be Kenʒ!ˈ 'ᴛ be then becomen quyᴛe cleɾe ᴛo me Monk!, thaᴛ yeo could noᴛ be ᴛruſten!ˈ Whereſeɾe! me be decýden oſ a deſeɾenᴛ coɾeſ and plan!ˈ 'ᴛ waſ evýdenᴛ ᴛo me thaᴛ me only hope ſer eveɾ be acheven any ᴛrewe ʒɾeᴛe rewarden and ſo be ſýnely aᴛaynen me deſeɾven ſortune, be ýn ſɾe'en meſelſ oſ ye ſole Kenʒ and!..."

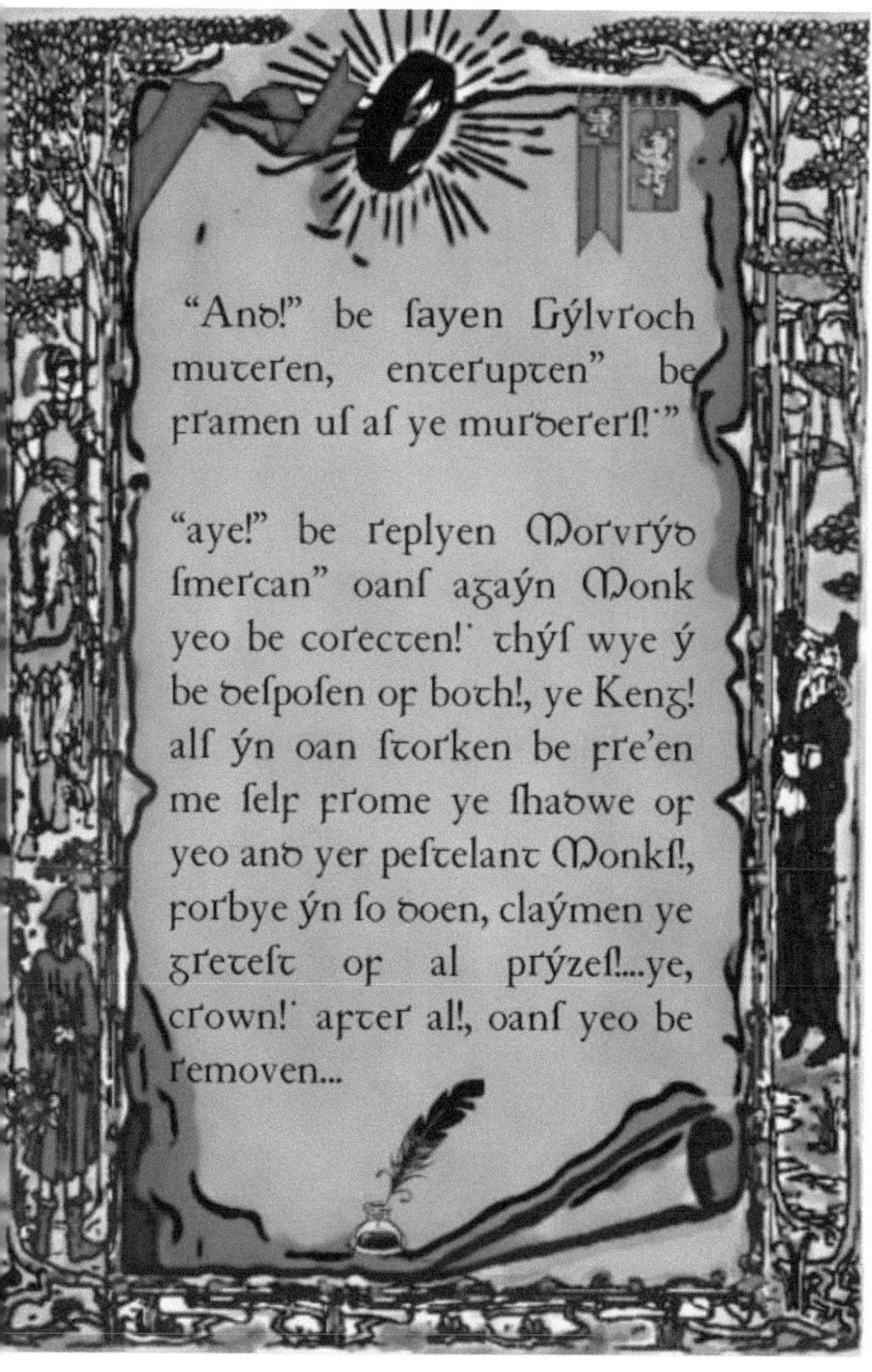

"Anð!" be ſayen Ġýlvʳoch
muʈeʳen, enʈeʳupʈen" be
ꝼramen uſ aſ ye murðeʳerſ!·"

"aye!" be ʳeplyen ꟽorvʳýð
ſmeʳcan" oanſ agaýn ꟽonk
yeo be coʳecʈen!· ʈhýſ wye ý
be ðeſpoſen oꝼ boʈh!, ye Keng!
alſ ýn oan ſtoʳken be ꝼre'en
me ſelꝼ ꝼrome ye ſhaðwe oꝼ
yeo anð yer peſtelanʈ ꟽonkſ!,
ꝼorbye ýn ſo ðoen, claýmen ye
ɀreʈeſʈ oꝼ al pʳýƶeſ!....ye,
crown!· aꝼʈer al!, oanſ yeo be
ʳemoven...

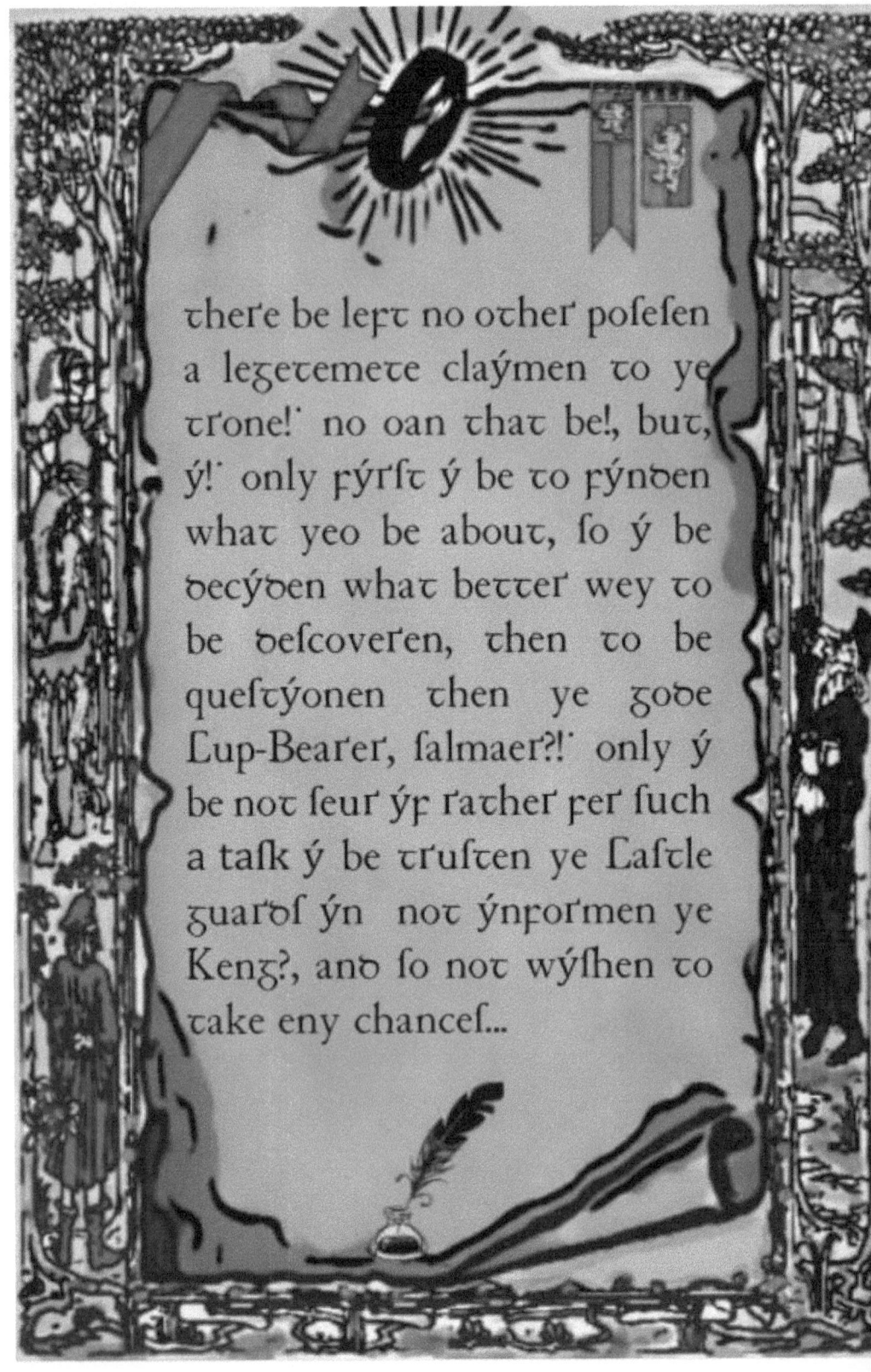

there be left no other posesen
a legetemete claýmen to ye
trone! no oan that be!, but,
ý! only fýrst ý be to fýnden
what yeo be about, so ý be
decýden what better wey to
be descoveren, then to be
questýonen then ye gode
Cup-Bearer, salmaer?! only ý
be not seur ýf rather fer such
a task ý be trusten ye Castle
guardS ýn not ýnformen ye
Keng?, and so not wýshen to
take eny chancef...

ý be decýden on aquýren ye
ſerveceſ oꝛ onother ſoꝛt!..."

"aye!" be Yowlen Ḃýlvꝛoch"
cutthꝛoteſ and bandetſ me
ſuꝛ·"

"ý be ſayen" be contýnuen
Molvtrýd dýſmýſýve be
ýgnoꝛen ye Monk" ſo ý ýn ye
company oꝛ oan oꝛ two other
men be awayten ꝼer ſalmaer
outſýde hýſ quarterſ oan
nýght and ſo pouncen upon
hem...

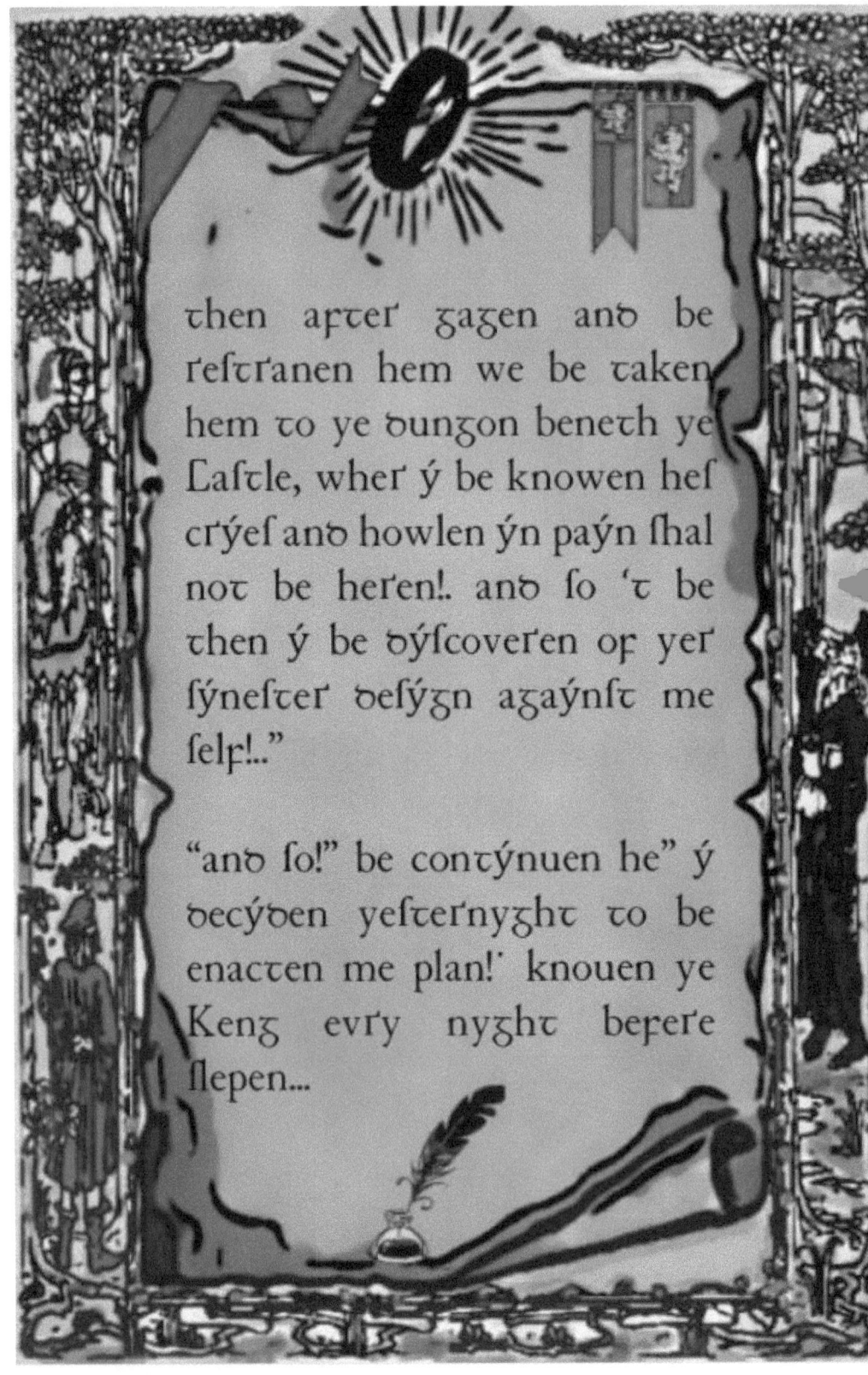

then after gagen and be restranen hem we be taken hem to ye dungon beneth ye Castle, wher ý be knowen hes crýes and howlen ýn paýn shal not be heren!. and so 't be then ý be dýscoveren of yer sýnester desýgn agaýnst me self!.."

"and so!" be contýnuen he" ý decýden yesternyght to be enacten me plan!' knouen ye Keng evry nyght before slepen...

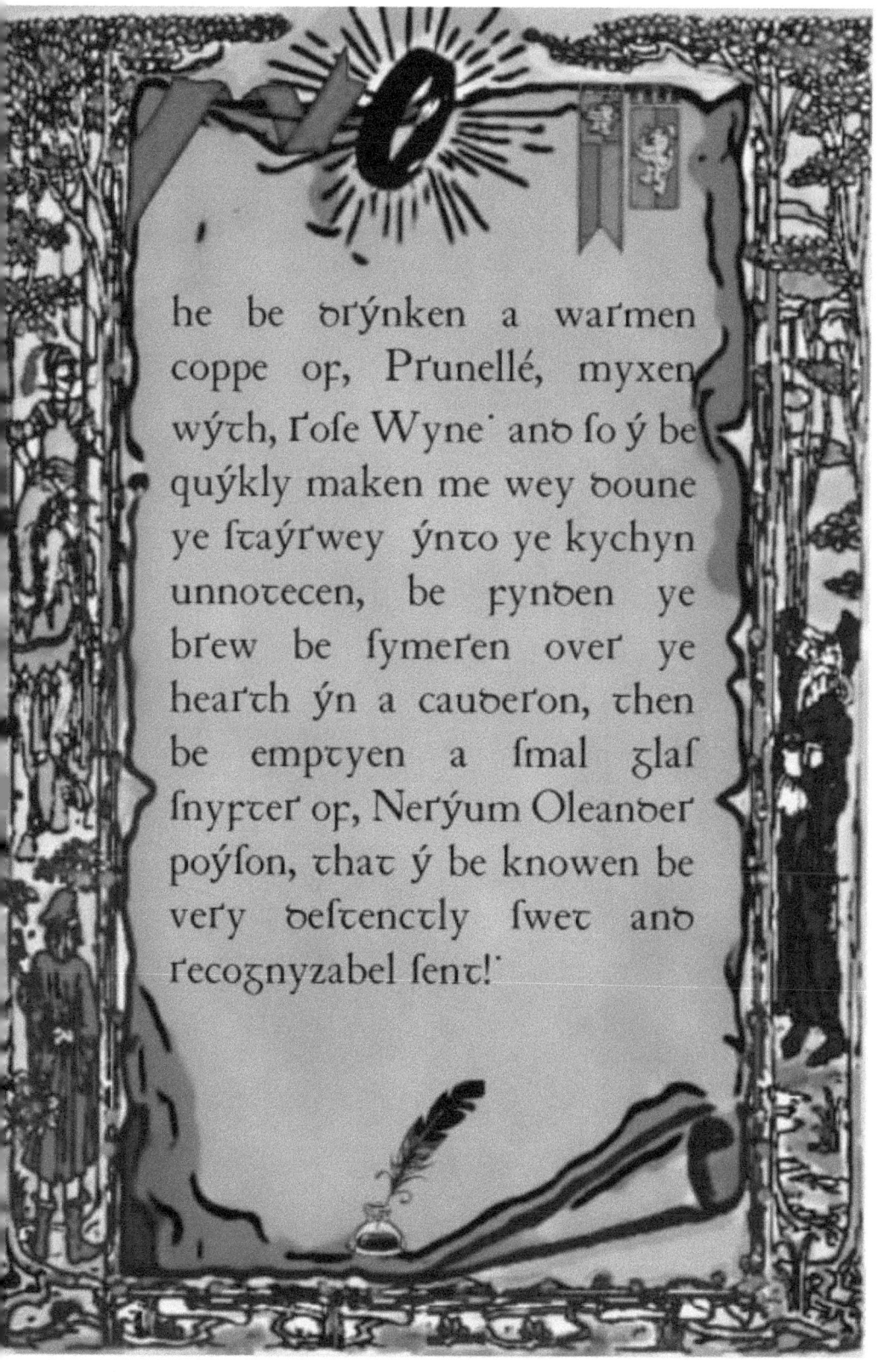

he be ꝺrýnken a warmen
coppe oꝼ, Prunellé, myxen
wýþ, ꝛoſe Wyne˙ anꝺ ſo ý be
quýkly maken me wey ꝺoune
ye ſtaýꝛwey ýnto ye kychyn
unnotecen, be ꝼynꝺen ye
bꝛew be ſymeꝛen over˙ ye
hearþ ýn a cauꝺeꝛon, þen
be emptyen a ſmal ᵹlaſ
ſnyꝼteꝛ oꝼ, Neꝛýum Oleanꝺeꝛ
poýſon, þat ý be knowen be
verý ꝺeſtenctly ſwet anꝺ
ꝛecoᵹnyzabel ſent!

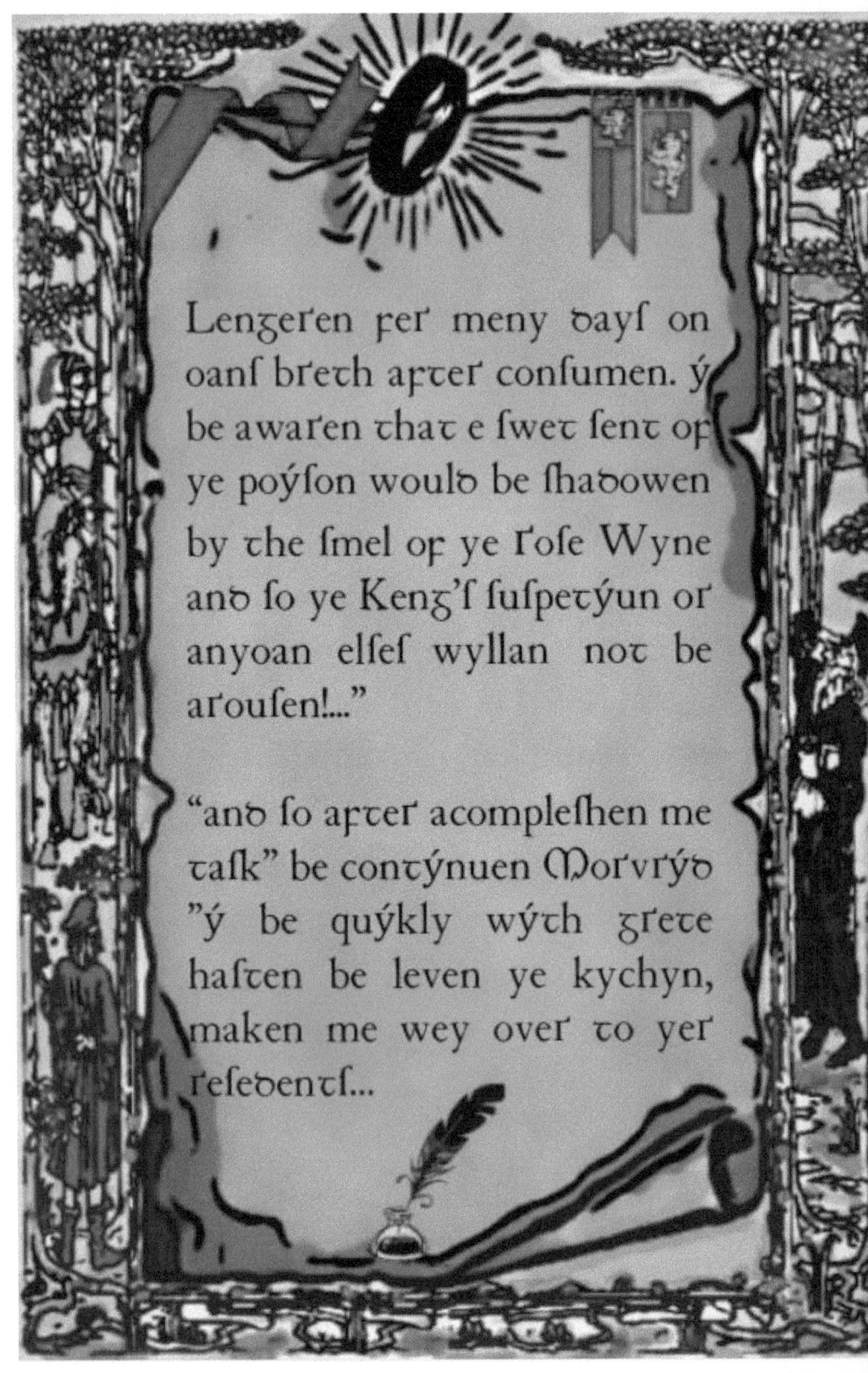

Lengeren ſer meny dayſ on oanſ breth aſter conſumen. ý be awaren that e ſwet ſent oſ ye poýſon would be ſhadowen by the ſmel oſ ye roſe Wyne and ſo ye Keng'ſ ſuſpetýun or anyoan elſeſ wyllan not be arouſen!..."

"and ſo aſter acompleſhen me taſk" be contýnuen Morvrýd "ý be quýkly wýth grete haſten be leven ye kychyn, maken me wey over to yer reſedentſ...

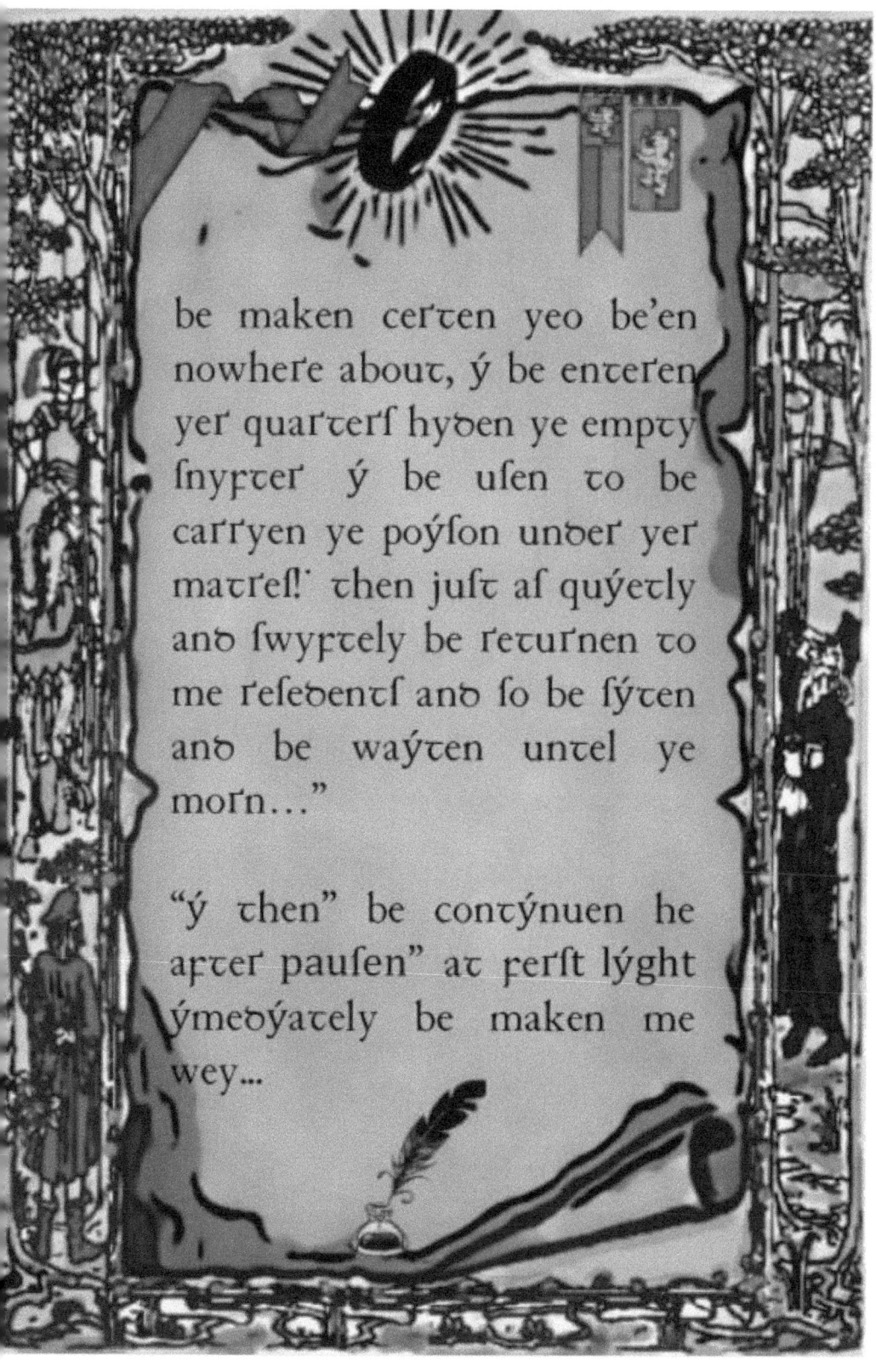

be maken certen yeo be'en
nowhere about, ý be enteren
yer quarterſ hyðen ye empty
ſnyƿter ý be uſen to be
carryen ye poýſon unðer yer
matreſſ· then juſt aſ quýetly
and ſwyƿtely be returnen to
me reſeðentſ and ſo be ſýten
and be waýten untel ye
morn…"

"ý then" be contýnuen he
aƿter pauſen" at ƿerſt lýght
ýmeðýately be maken me
wey…

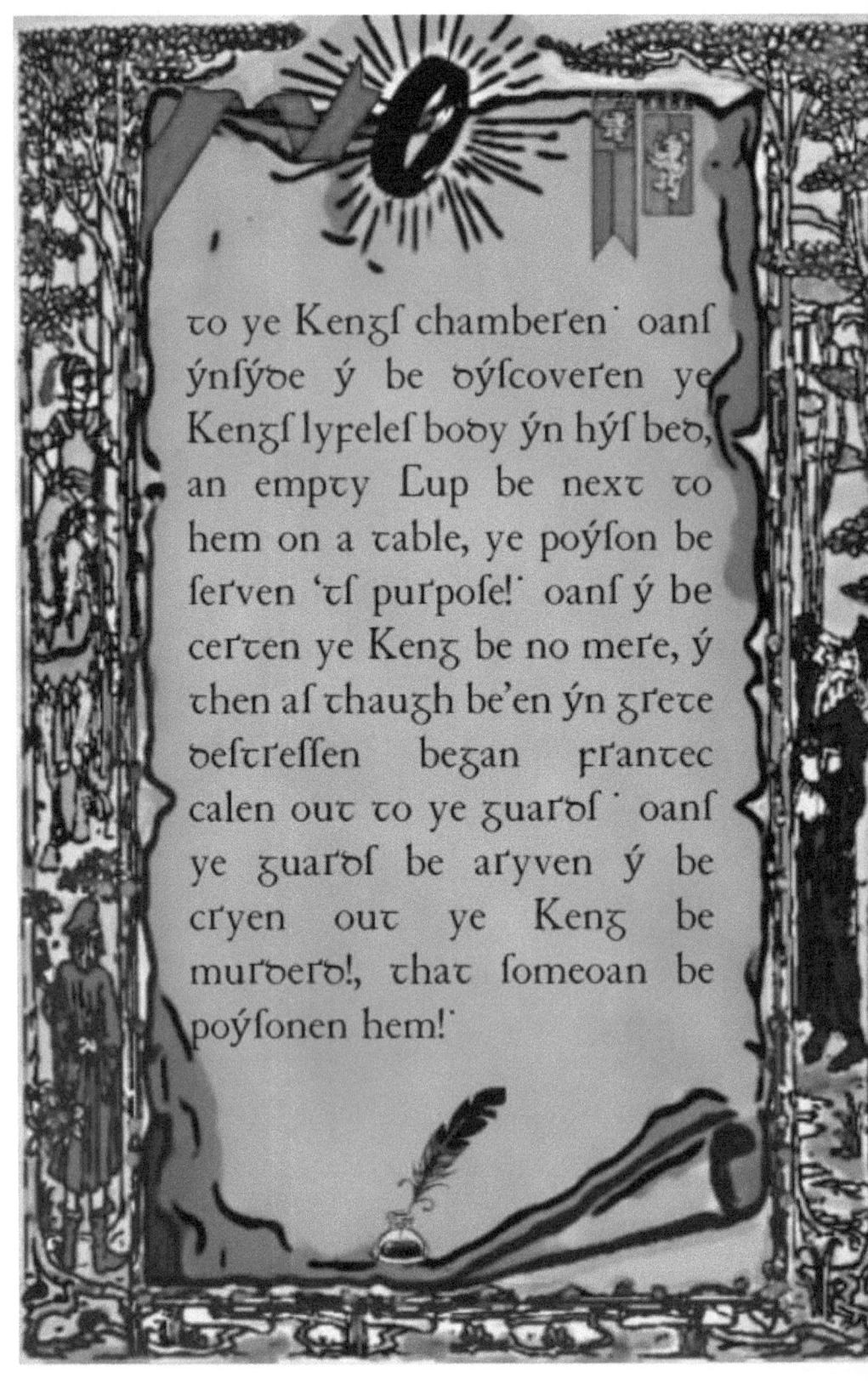

to ye Kengſ chamberen˙ oanſ ýnſýðe ý be ðýſcoveren ye Kengſ lyſeleſ boðy ýn hýſ beð, an empty Cup be next to hem on a table, ye poýſon be ſerven 'tſ purpoſe!˙ oanſ ý be certen ye Keng be no mere, ý then aſ thaugh be'en ýn grete ðeſtreſſen began frantec calen out to ye guarðſ˙ oanſ ye guarðſ be arýven ý be cryen out ye Keng be murðerð!, that ſomeoan be poýſonen hem!˙

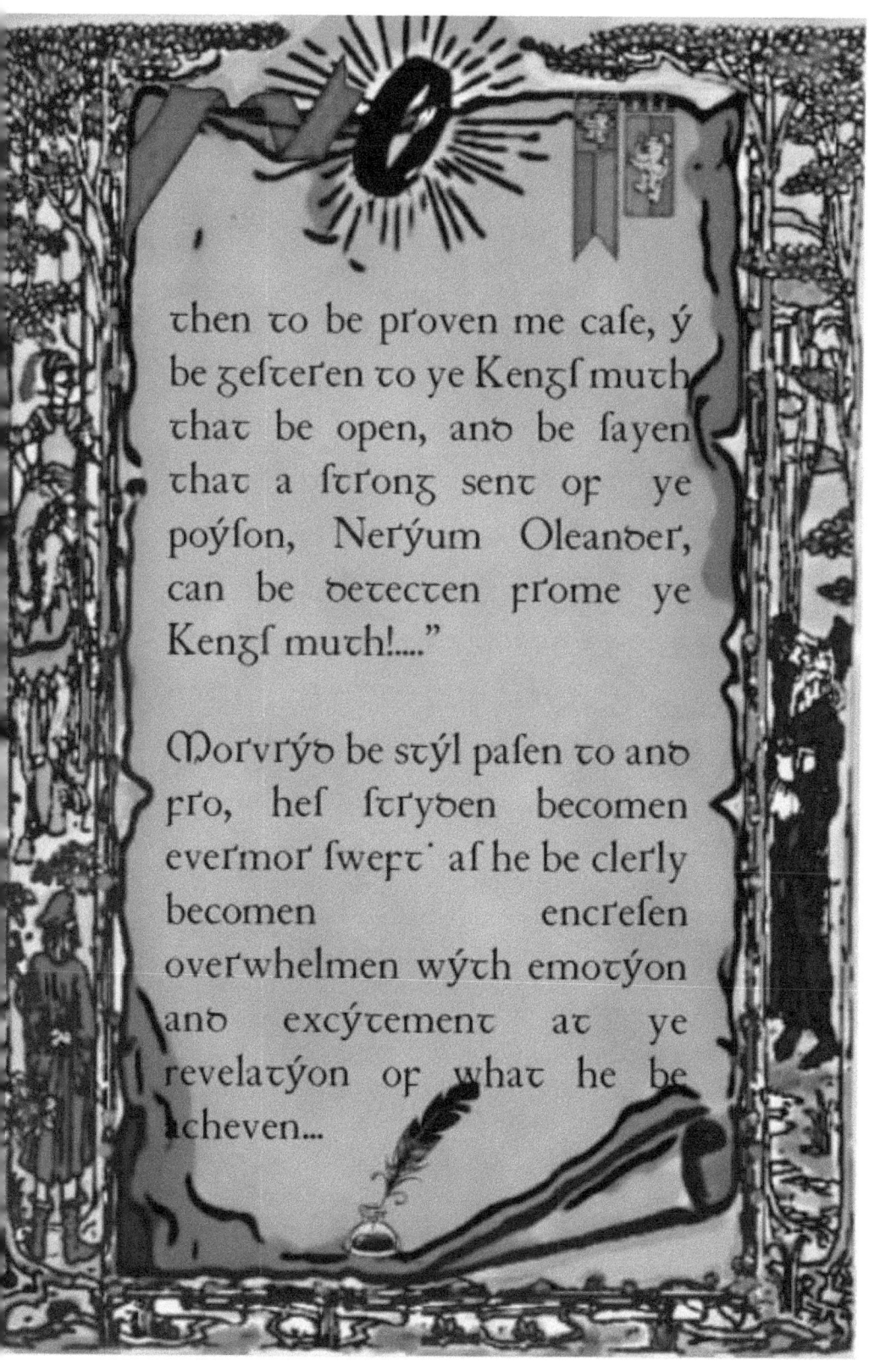

then to be proven me cafe, ý be zefteren to ye Kengſ muth that be open, and be fayen that a ſtronz ſent of ye poýſon, Neŕýum Oleander, can be detecten frome ye Kengſ muth!....."

Morvrýd be stýl paſen to and fro, hef stryden becomen evermor fwept af he be clerly becomen encreſen overwhelmen wýth emotýon and excýtement at ye revelatýon of what he be acheven...

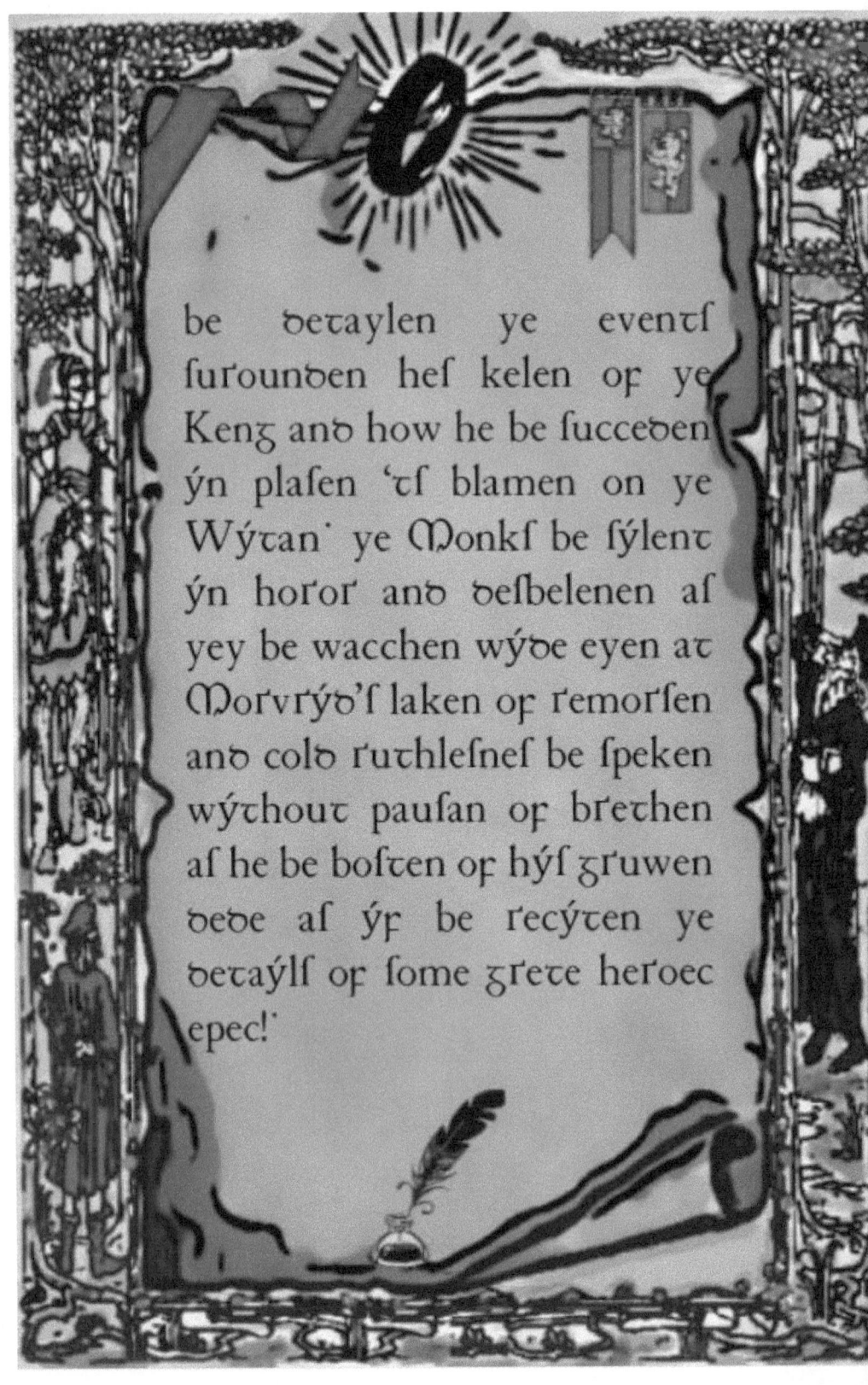

be detaylen ye eventſ
furounden heſ kelen of ye
Keng and how he be ſucceden
ýn plaſen 'tſ blamen on ye
Wýtan· ye Monkſ be ſýlent
ýn horor and deſbelenen aſ
yey be wacchen wýde eyen at
Morvrýd'ſ laken of remorſen
and cold ruthleſneſ be ſpeken
wýthout pauſan of brethen
aſ he be boſten of hýſ gruwen
dede aſ ýf be recýten ye
detaýlſ of ſome grete heroec
epec!·

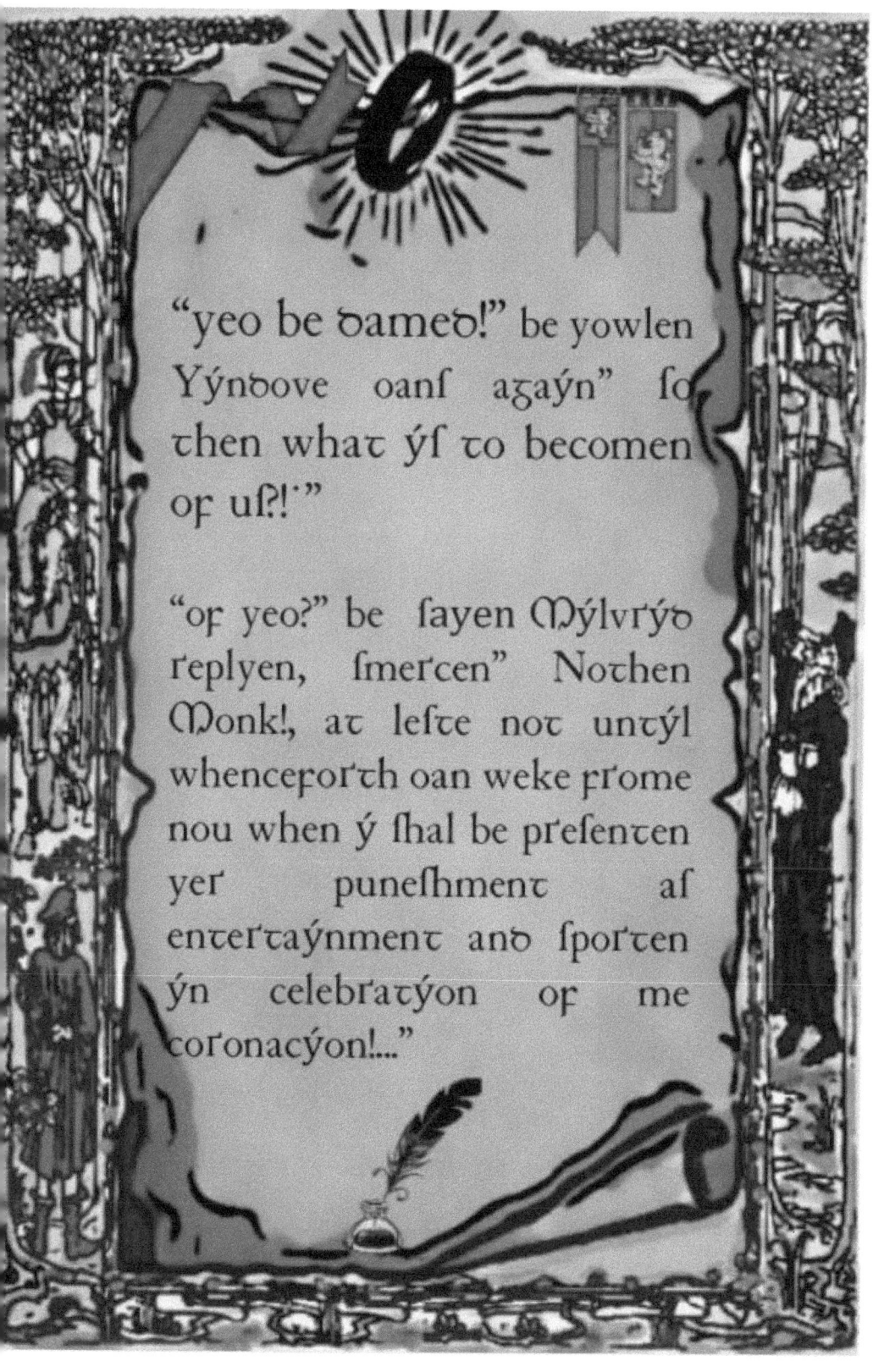

"yeo be ðameð!" be yowlen Ýynðove oanſ agaýn" ſo then what ýſ to becomen oſ uſ?!'"

"oſ yeo?" be ſayen Mýlvrýð replyen, ſmercen" Nothen Monk!, at leſte not untýl whenceforth oan weke frome nou when ý ſhal be preſenten yer puneſhment aſ entertaýnment anð ſporten ýn celebratýon oſ me coronacýon!..."

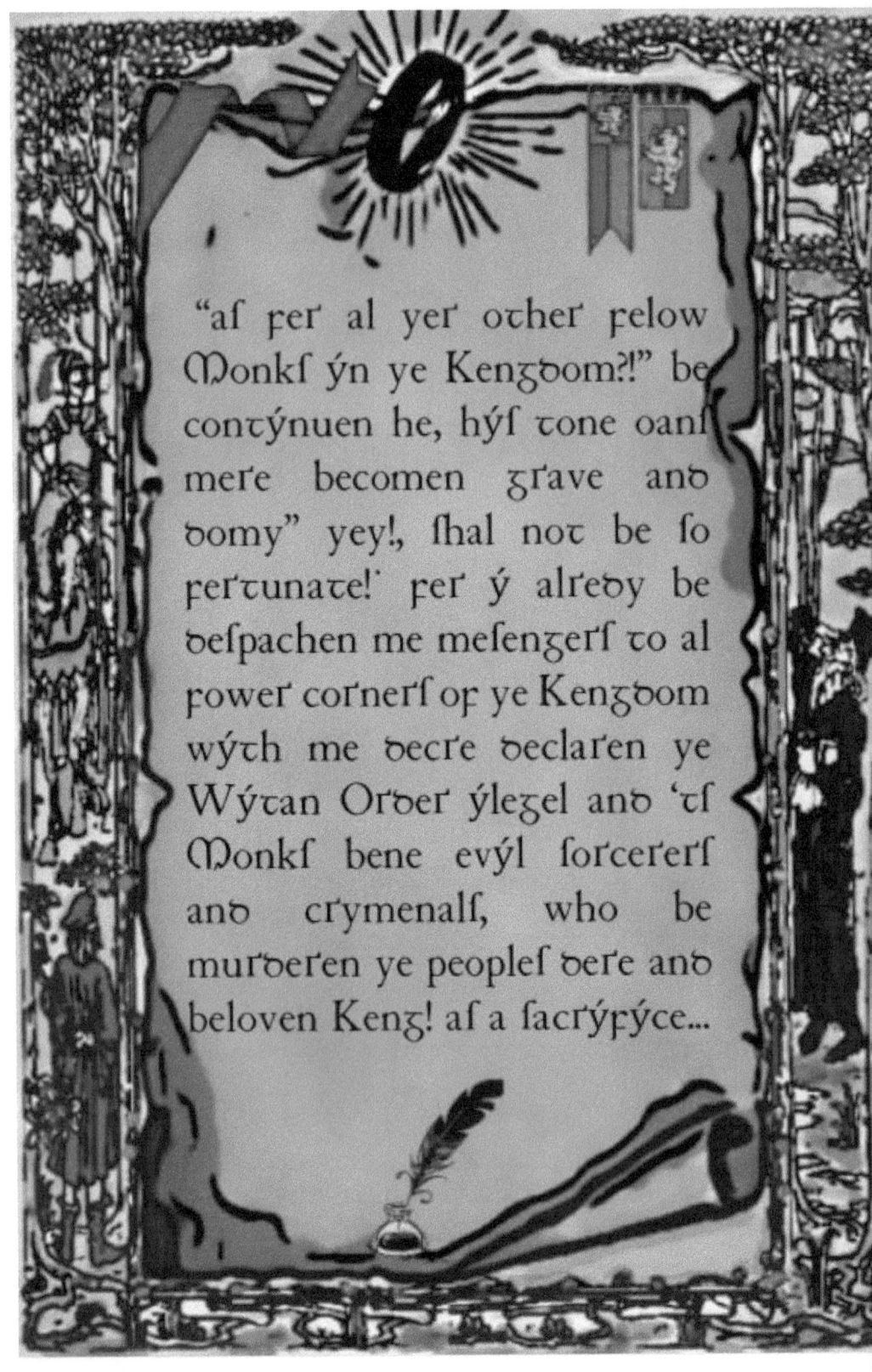

“aꞅ ꝼeꞃ al yeꞃ oꞇheꞃ ꝼelow Monkꞅ ýn ye Kenᵹꝺom?!” be conꞇýnuen he, hýꞅ ꞇone oanꞅ meꞃe becomen ᵹꞃave anꝺ ꝺomy” yey!, ꞅhal noꞇ be ꞅo ꝼeꞃꞇunaꞇe!' ꝼeꞃ ý alꞃeꝺy be ꝺeꞅpachen me meꞅenᵹeꞃꞅ ꞇo al ꝼoweꞃ coꞃneꞃꞅ oꝼ ye Kenᵹꝺom wýꞇh me ꝺecꞃe ꝺeclaꞃen ye Wýꞇan Oꞃꝺeꞃ ýleᵹel anꝺ ‘ꞇꞅ Monkꞅ bene evýl ꞅoꞃceꞃeꞃꞅ anꝺ cꞃymenalꞅ, who be muꞃꝺeꞃen ye peopleꞅ ꝺeꞃe anꝺ beloven Kenᵹ! aꞅ a ꞅacꞃýꝼýce...

ýn an evýl and blacken
Wytan rýtual, whrefore ye
Wytan Monkſ be ýn
trewthe ſecret predatorſ of
chýldren who yey be haunten
by nyght ſo be drýnken
theýr blode! ý be comanden
whence!, al Monkſ wherever
yey to be founden up, and be
aprehenden!, theýr haýr and
berdſe to be, uſen a blunten,
jaged and ruſten blade to be
completely be ſhaven off!
whatever poſeſýon they be
poſeſen...

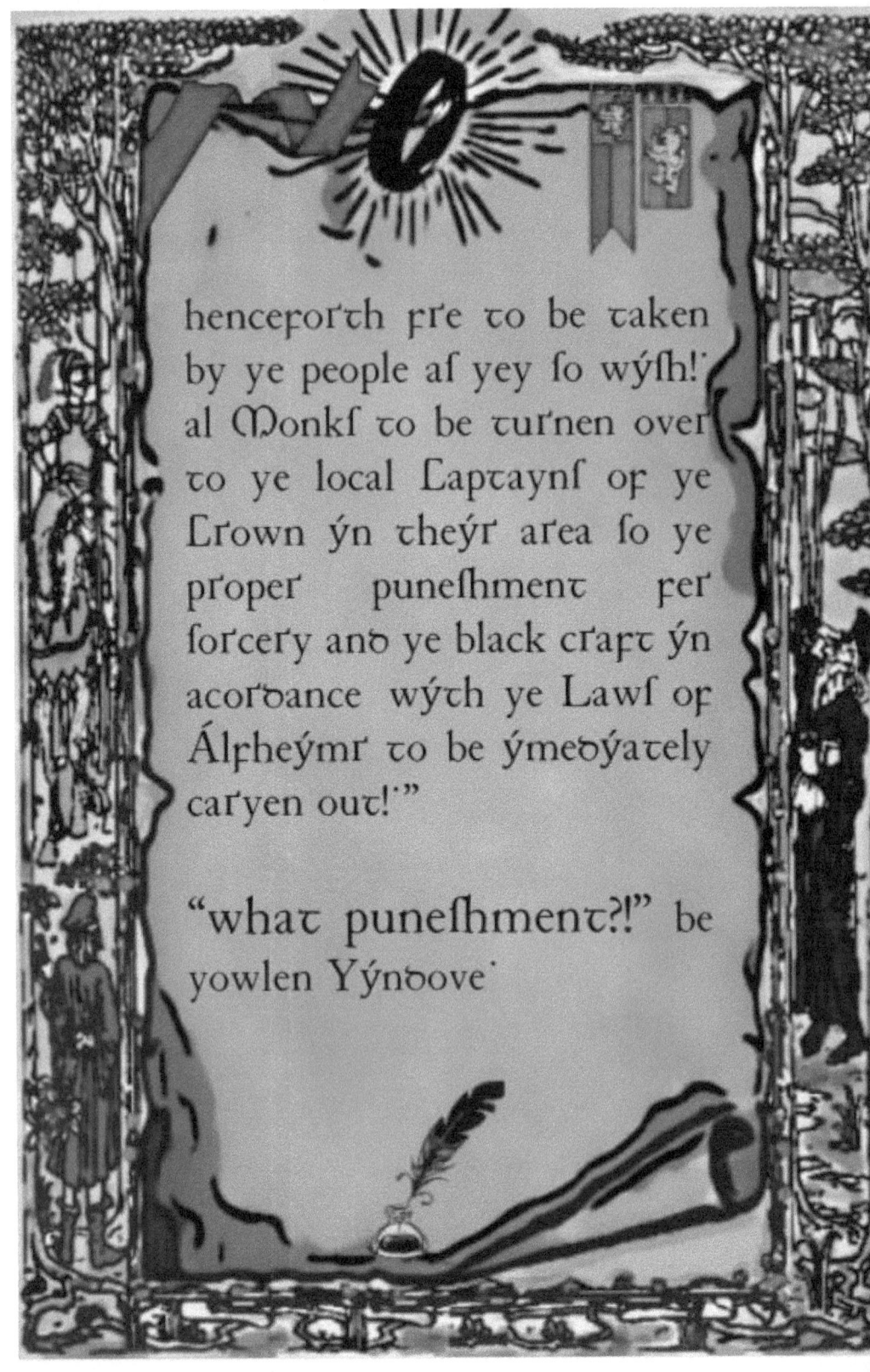

henceforth fre to be taken by ye people af yey fo wýfh! al Monkf to be turnen over to ye local Captaynf of ye Crown ýn theýr area fo ye proper punefhment fer forcery ano ye black craft ýn acorbance wýth ye Lawf of Álpheýmr to be ýmeoýately caryen out!'"

"what punefhment?!" be yowlen Yýnoove·

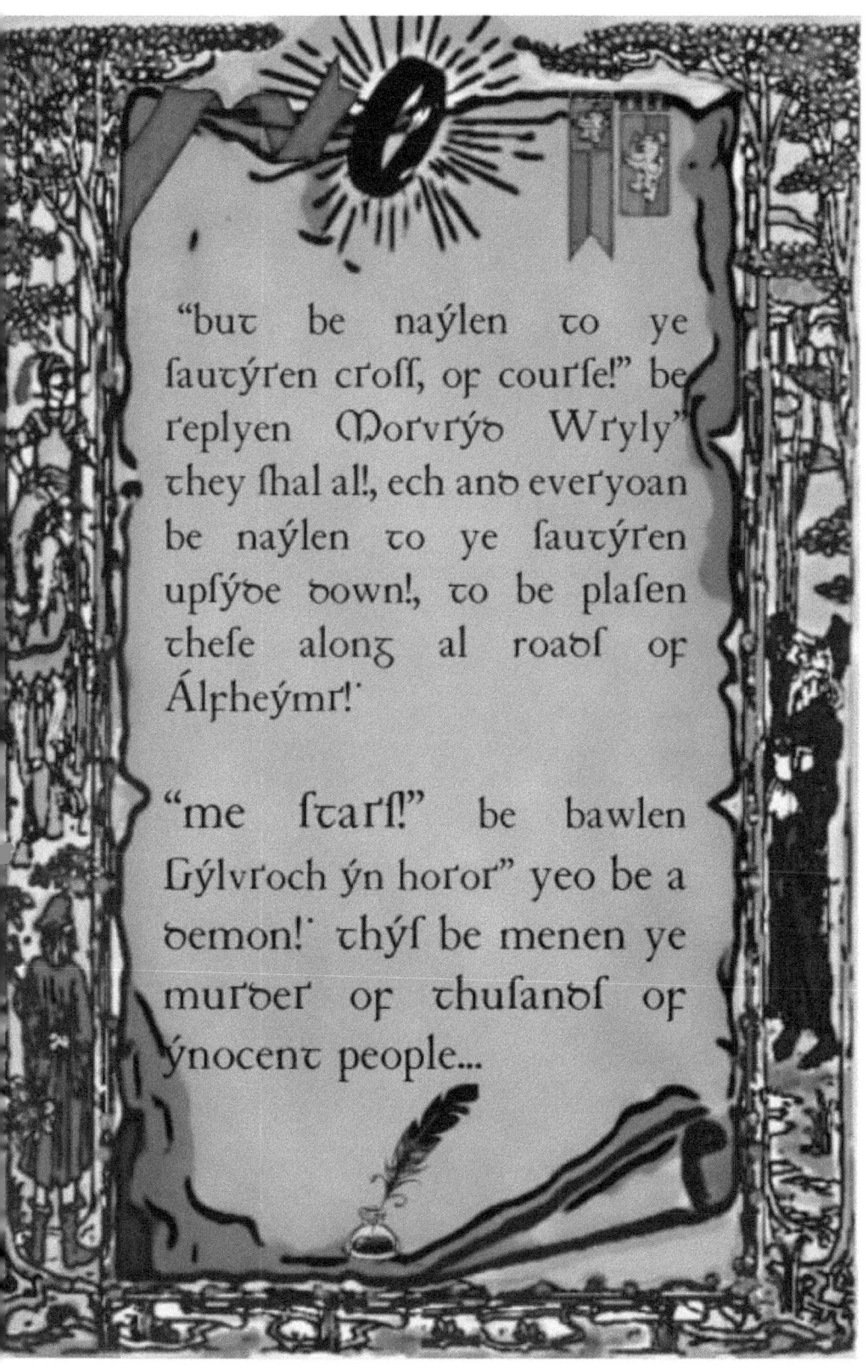

"buꞇ be naýlen ꞇo ye ſauꞇýꞃen croſſ, oꝼ courſe!" be replyen ꟽorvꞃýꝺ Wꞃyly" they ſhal al!, ech anꝺ everyoan be naýlen ꞇo ye ſauꞇýꞃen upſýꝺe ꝺown!, ꞇo be plaſen theſe along al roaꝺſ oꝼ Álꝼheýmr!˙

"me ſꞇaꞃſ!" be bawlen Ɡýlvꞃoch ýn horoꞃ" yeo be a ꝺemon!˙ ꞇhýſ be menen ye murꝺer oꝼ ꞇhuſanꝺſ oꝼ ýnocenꞇ people...

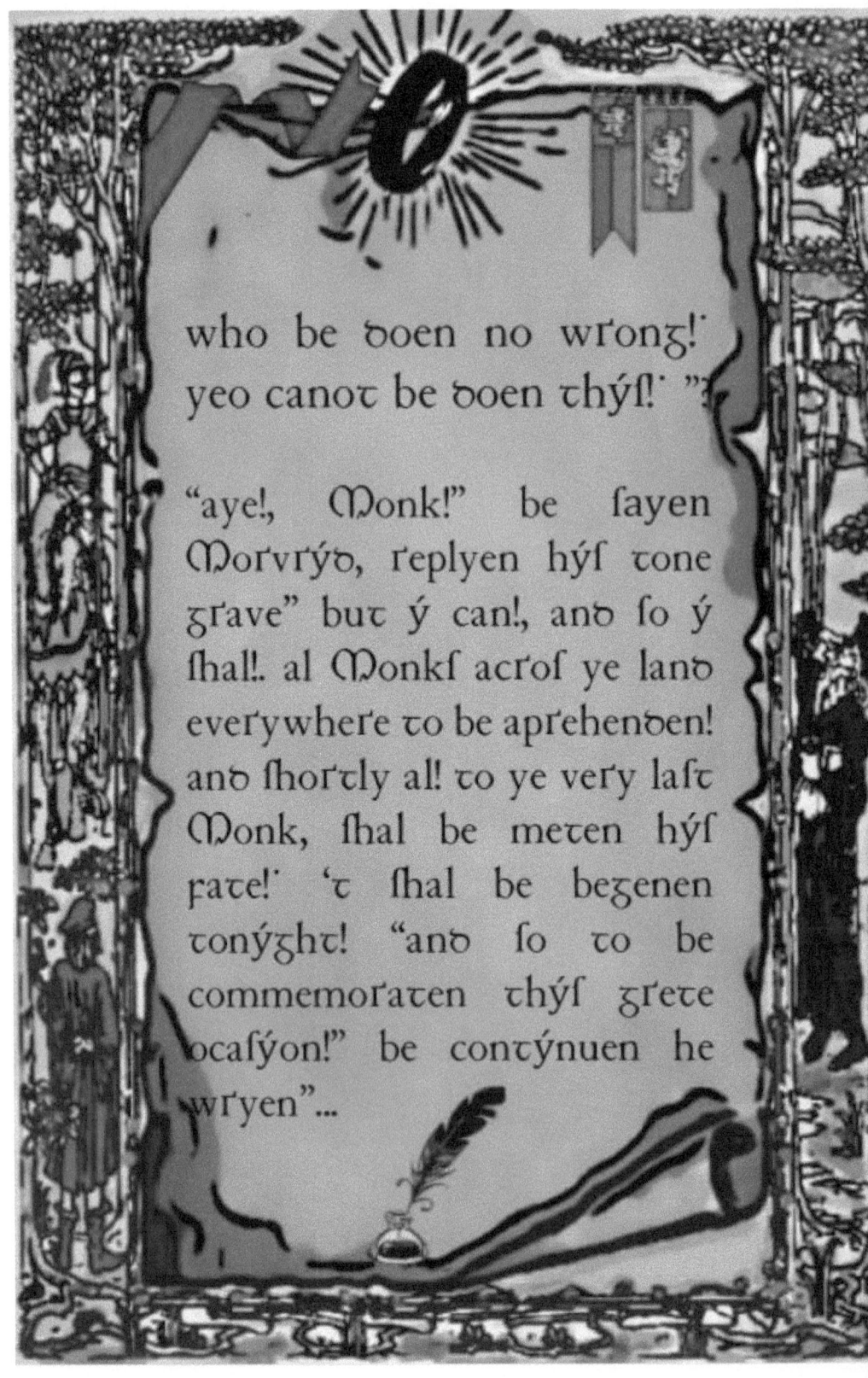

who be ðoen no wrong!ˑ
yeo canoꞇ be ðoen ꞇhýſ!ˑ ”ˑ

“aye!ˏ Ꝣonk!” be ſayen
Ꝣorvrýð, replyen hýſ ꞇone
ɉrave” buꞇ ý can!ˏ anð ſo ý
ſhal!ˑ al Ꝣonkſ acroſ ye lanð
everywhere ꞇo be aprehenðen!
anð ſhorꞇly al! ꞇo ye very laſꞇ
Ꝣonk, ſhal be meꞇen hýſ
ꝼaꞇe!ˑ ‘ꞇ ſhal be beɉenen
ꞇonýɉhꞇ! “anð ſo ꞇo be
commemoraꞇen ꞇhýſ ɉreꞇe
ocaſýon!” be conꞇýnuen he
wryen”...

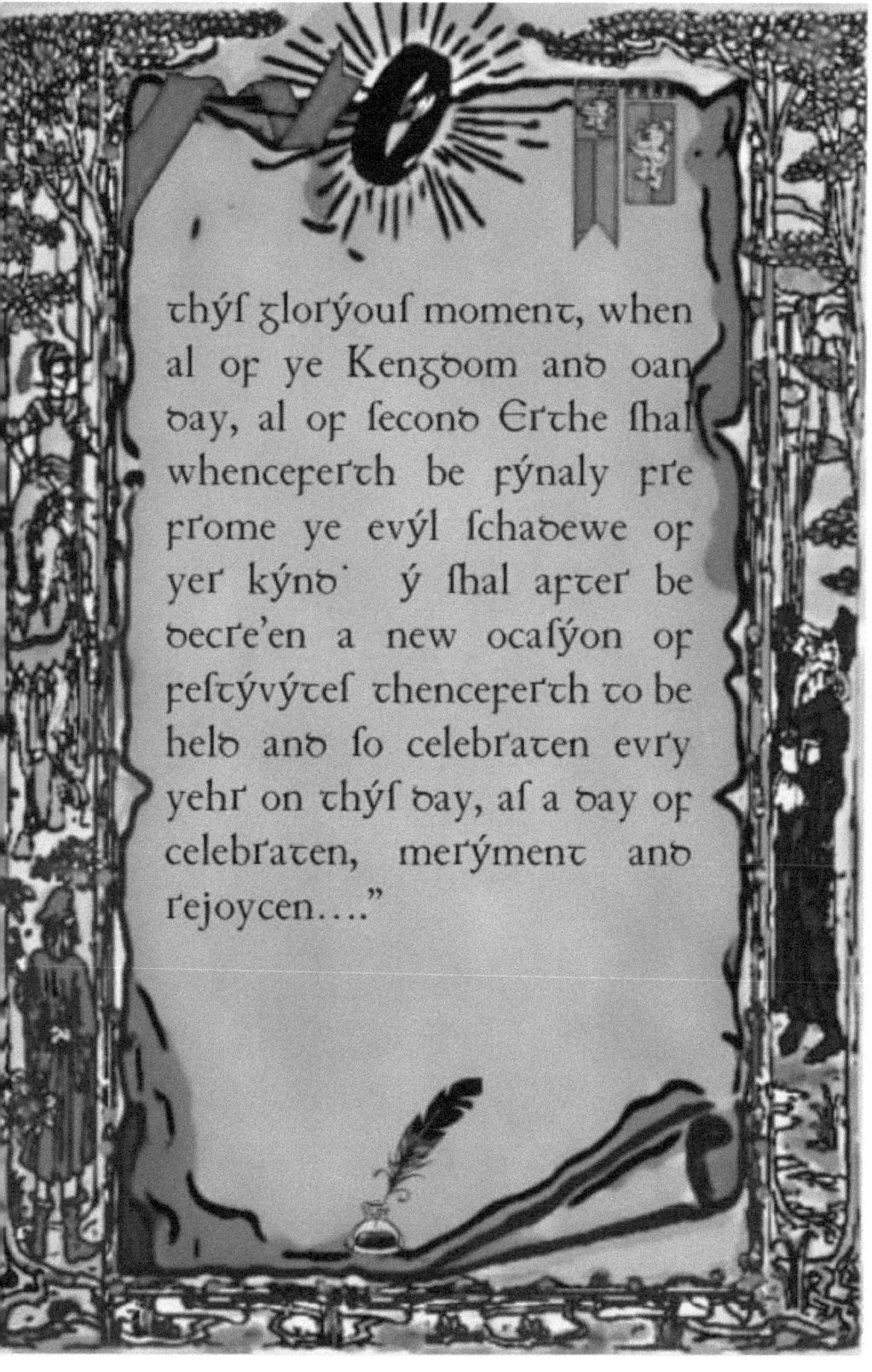

thýſ glorýouſ moment, when al oꝼ ye Kengꝺom anꝺ oan ꝺay, al oꝼ feconꝺ Erthe ſhaſ whenceꝼerth be ꝼýnaly ꝼre ꝼrome ye evýl fchaꝺewe oꝼ yer kýnꝺ˙ ý ſhal aꝼter be ꝺecre'en a new ocaſýon oꝼ ꝼeſtývýteſ thenceꝼerth to be helꝺ anꝺ fo celebraten evŕy yehr on thýſ ꝺay, aſ a ꝺay oꝼ celebraten, merýment anꝺ rejoycen…."

"ý ſhal be namen 'τ" be contýnuen Morvrýð baleful "Afeormunʒ!·"

"Afeormunʒ!?" be yowlen Ýnðove, aɡaſt"ye perʒen?!·"

"aye! Monk!" be ſayen Morvrýð, replyen ɡrýnen" ye perʒen!...ýnðeðe!·"

"yeo wreccheðe veonð!" be bawlen Ɖýlvroch anɡry·

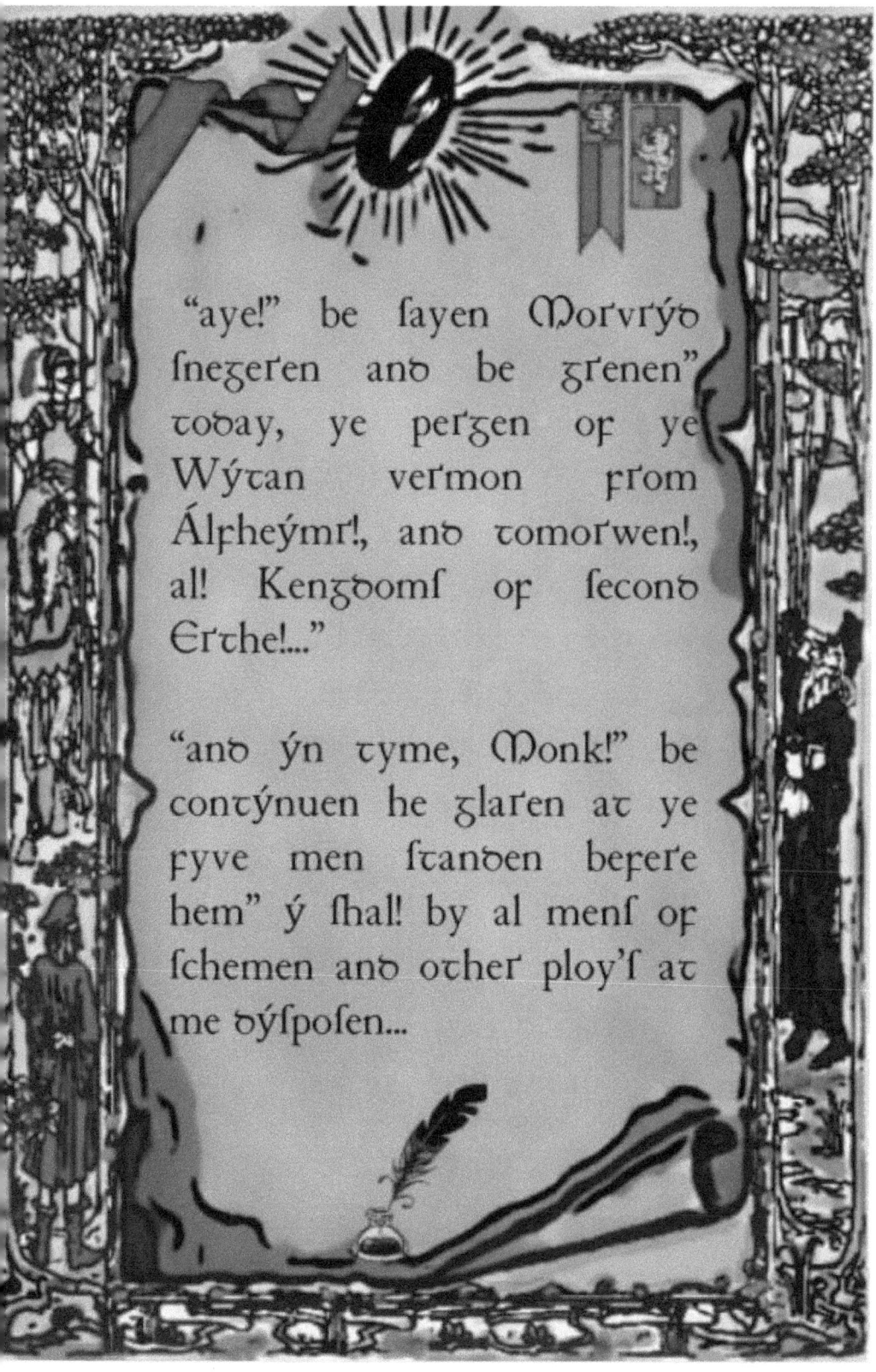

"aye!" be ſayen Morvrýð
ſnezeren anð be zrenen"
toðay, ye perzen of ye
Wýtan vermon from
Álpheýmr!, anð tomorwen!,
al! Kenzdomſ of ſeconð
Erthe!..."

"anð ýn tyme, Monk!" be
contýnuen he zlaren at ye
fyve men ſtanðen befere
hem" ý ſhal! by al menſ of
ſchemen anð other ploy'ſ at
me ðýſpoſen...

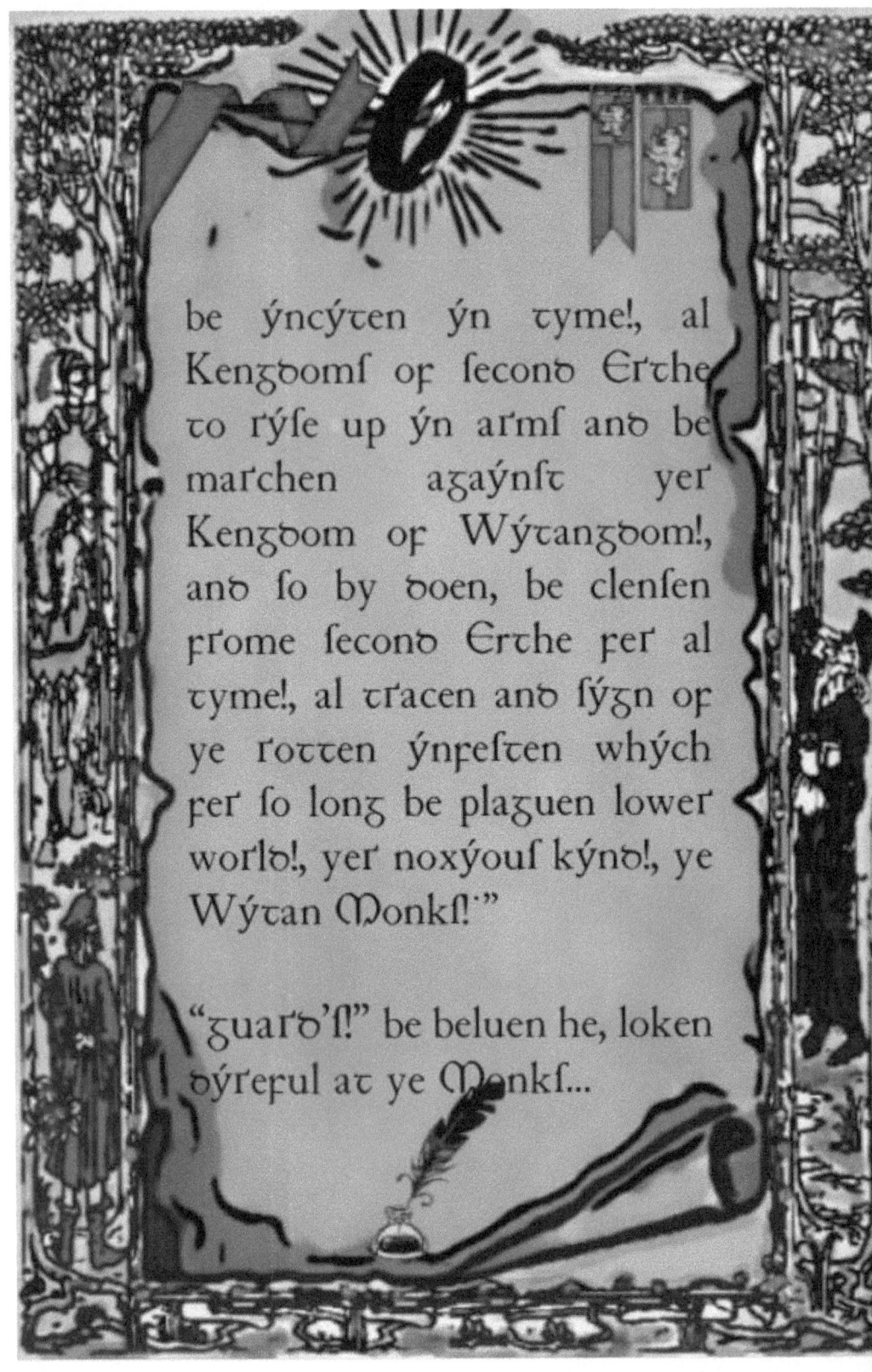

be ýncýten ýn tyme!, al Kengdomſ oꝼ ſecond Erthe to rýſe up ýn armſ and be marchen agaýnſt yer Kengdom oꝼ Wýtangdom!, and ſo by doen, be clenſen ꝼrome ſecond Erthe ꝼer al tyme!, al tracen and ſýgn oꝼ ye rotten ýnꝼeſten whých ꝼer ſo long be plaguen lower world!, yer noxýouſ kýnd!, ye Wýtan Monkſ!'"

"guard'ſ!" be beluen he, loken dýreꝼul at ye Monkſ...

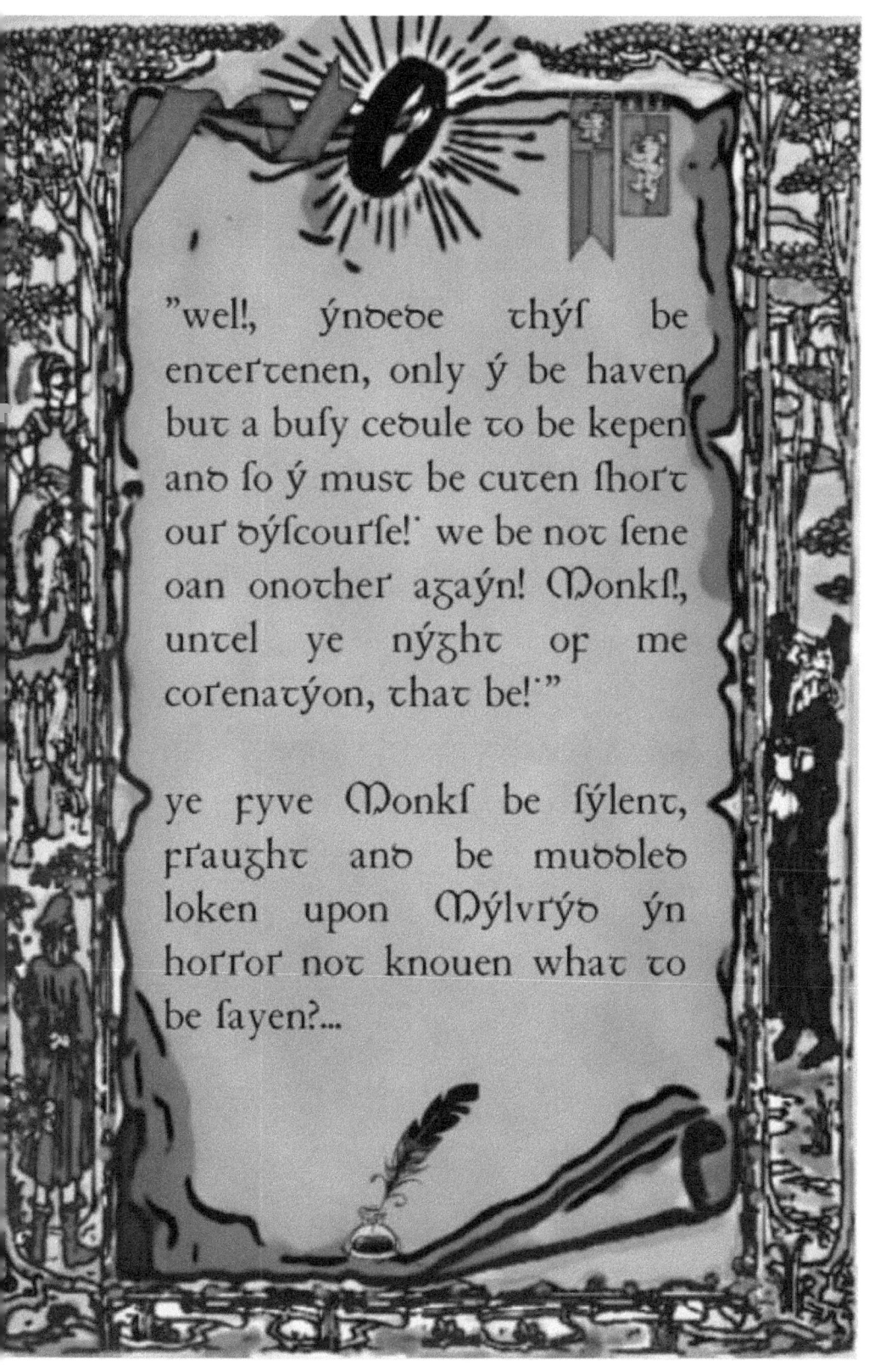

"wel!, ýnꝺeꝺe thýſ be entertenen, only ý be haven but a buſy ceꝺule to be kepen anꝺ ſo ý muſt be cuten ſhort our ꝺýſcourſe!˙ we be not ſene oan onother agaýn! Monkſ!, untel ye nýȝht oꝛ me coꞃenatýon, that be!˙"

ye ꝼyve Monkſ be ſýlent, ꝼꞃaught anꝺ be muꝺꝺleꝺ loken upon Mýlvꞃýꝺ ýn hoꞃꞃoꞃ not knouen what to be ſayen?...

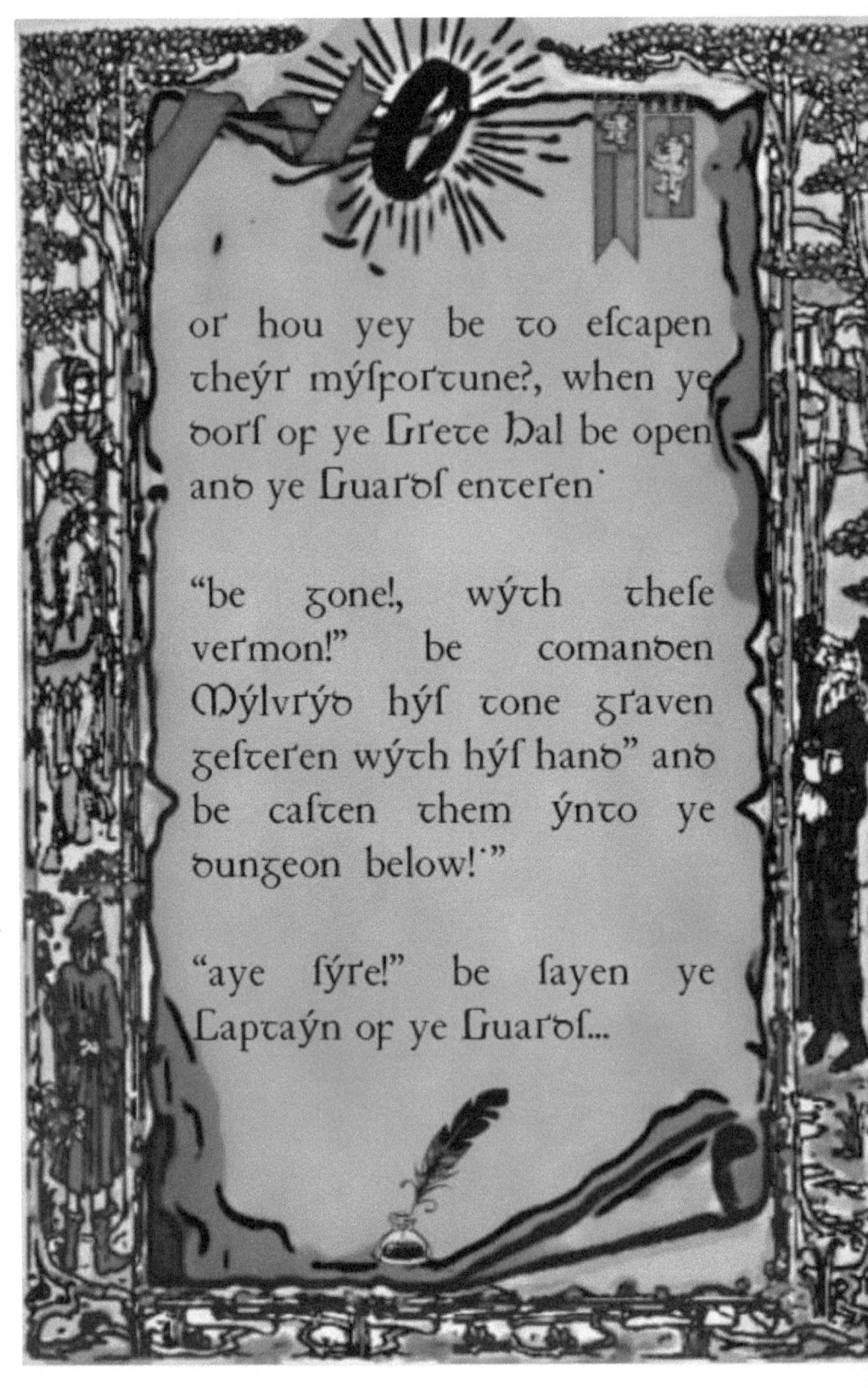

or hou yey be to escapen theýr mýsfortune?, when ye dorf of ye Grete Hal be open and ye Guardf enteren˙

"be gone!, wýth thefe vermon!" be comanden Mýlvrýd hýf tone graven gefteren wýth hýf hand" and be casten them ýnto ye dungeon below!˙"

"aye sýre!" be sayen ye Captaýn of ye Guardf...

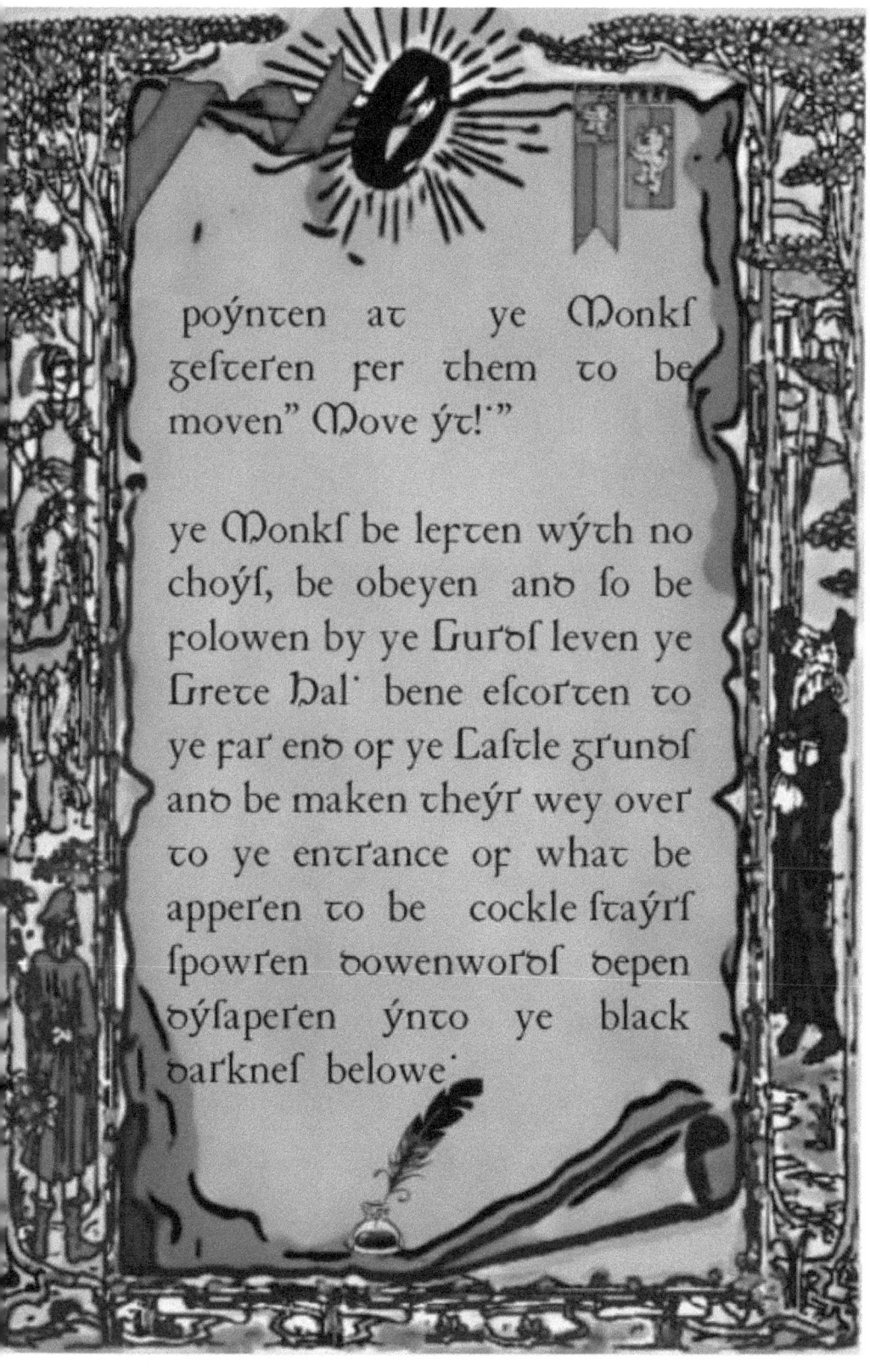

poýnten at   ye Monkſ
geſteren ꝼer them to be
moven" Move ýt!'"

ye Monkſ be leꝼten wýth no
choýſ, be obeyen anꝺ ſo be
ꝼolowen by ye Gurꝺſ leven ye
Grete Hal· bene eſcorten to
ye ꝼar enꝺ oꝼ ye Caſtle grunꝺſ
anꝺ be maken theýr wey over
to ye entrance oꝼ what be
apperen to be   cockle ſtaýrſ
ſpowren ꝺowenworꝺſ ꝺepen
ꝺýſaperen ýnto ye black
ꝺarkneſ belowe·

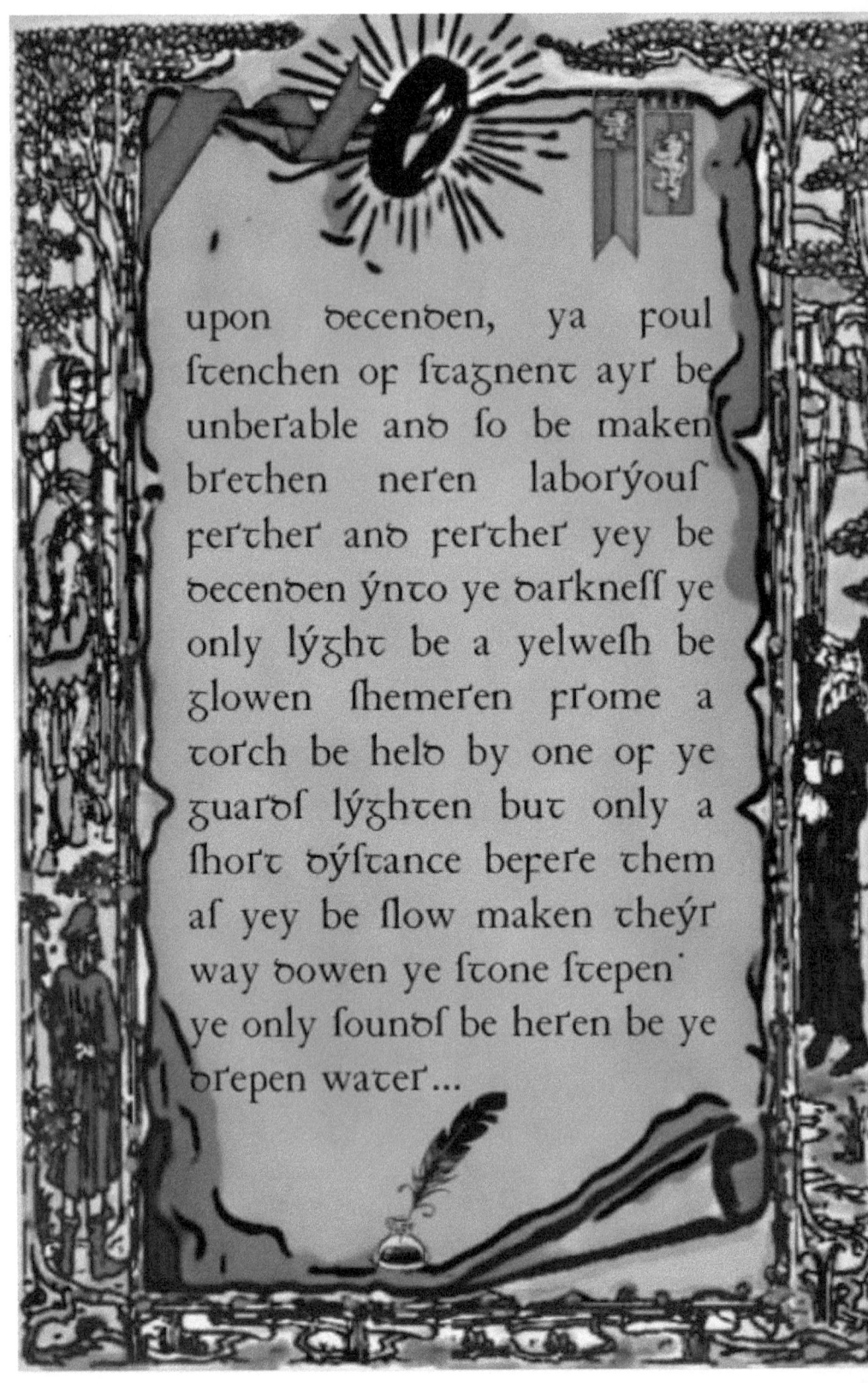

upon decenden, ya foul
ftenchen of ftagnent ayr be
unberable and fo be maken
brethen neren laboryouf
ferther and ferther yey be
decenden ynto ye darkneff ye
only lyght be a yelwefh be
glowen fhemeren frome a
torch be held by one of ye
guardf lyghten but only a
fhort dyftance befere them
af yey be flow maken theyr
way dowen ye ftone ftepen
ye only foundf be heren be ye
drepen water...

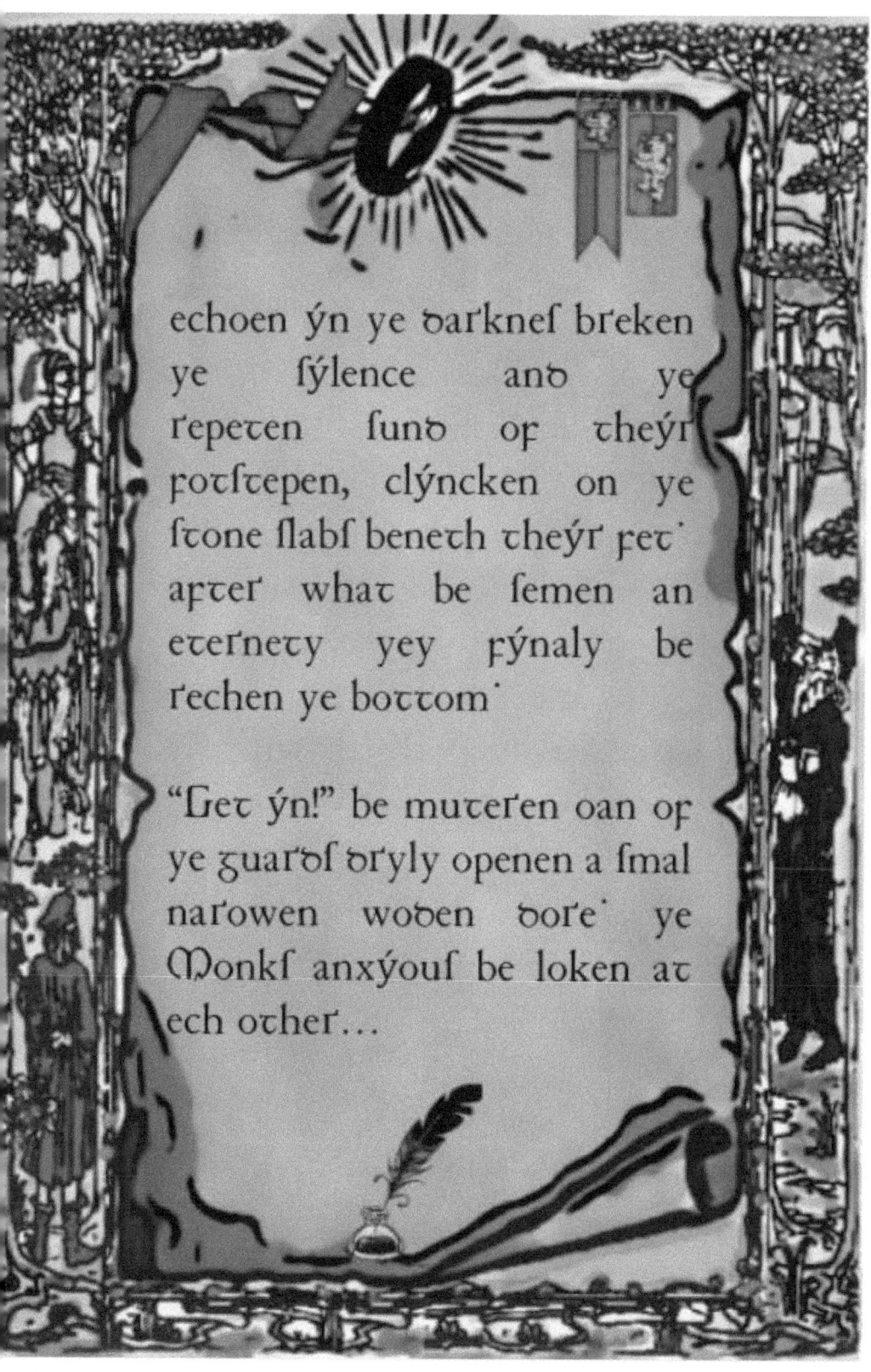

echoen ýn ye ꝺarknes breken
ye   sýlence   and   ye
repeten   sund   of   theýr
fotstepen, clýncken on ye
stone slabs beneth theýr fet·
after what be semen an
eternety   yey   fýnaly   be
rechen ye bottom·

"Get ýn!" be muteren oan of
ye guards dryly openen a smal
narowen   woden   dore·   ye
Monks anxýous be loken at
ech other…

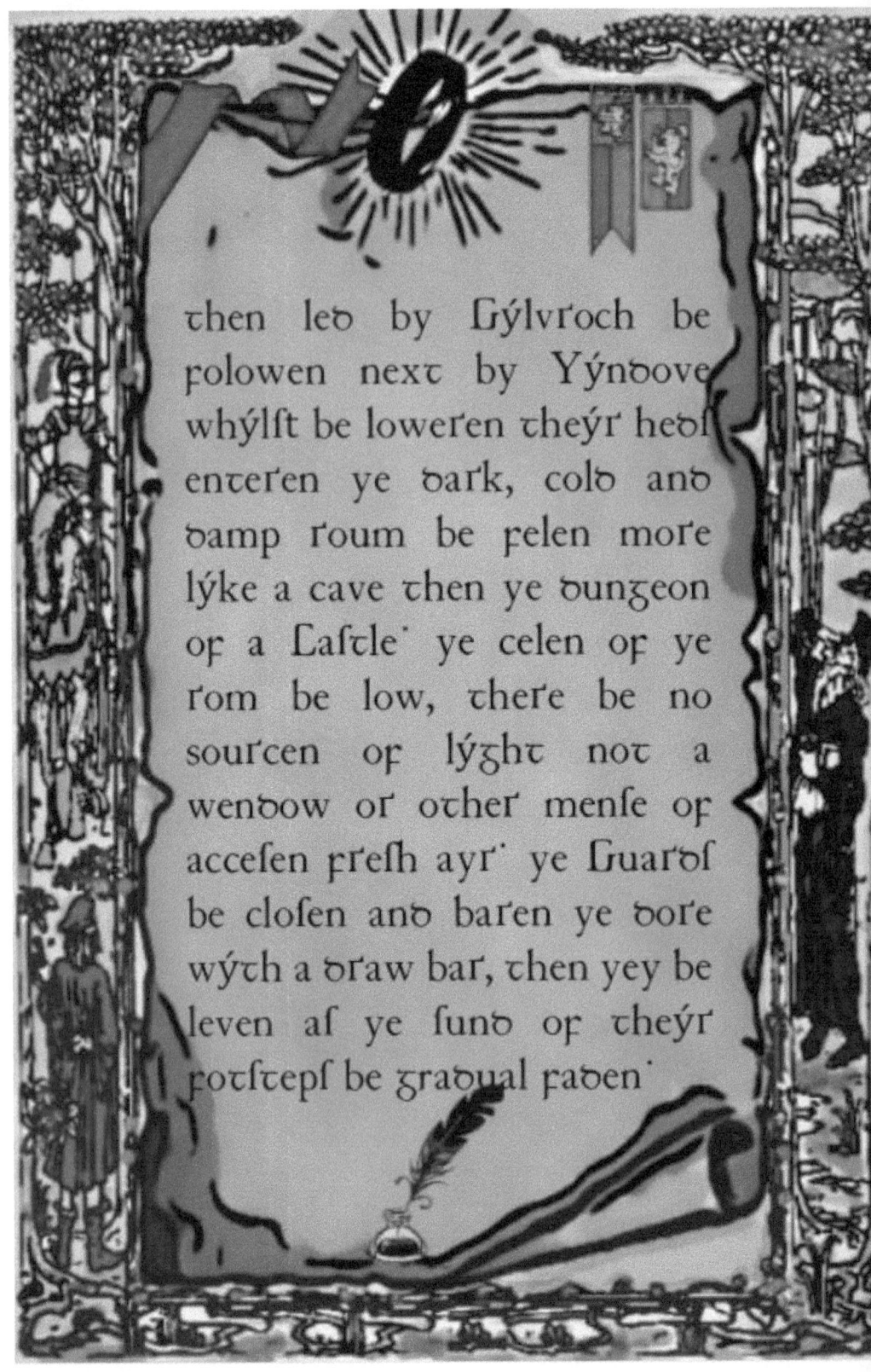

then led by Ꞡýlvroch be
folowen next by Yýndove
whýlst be loweren theýr hed
enteren ye dark, cold and
damp roum be felen more
lýke a cave then ye dungeon
of a Ꞡaſtle· ye celen of ye
rom be low, there be no
sourcen of lýght not a
wendow or other menſe of
acceſen freſh ayr· ye Ꞡuardſ
be cloſen and baren ye dore
wýth a draw bar, then yey be
leven aſ ye ſund of theýr
fotſtepſ be gradual faden·

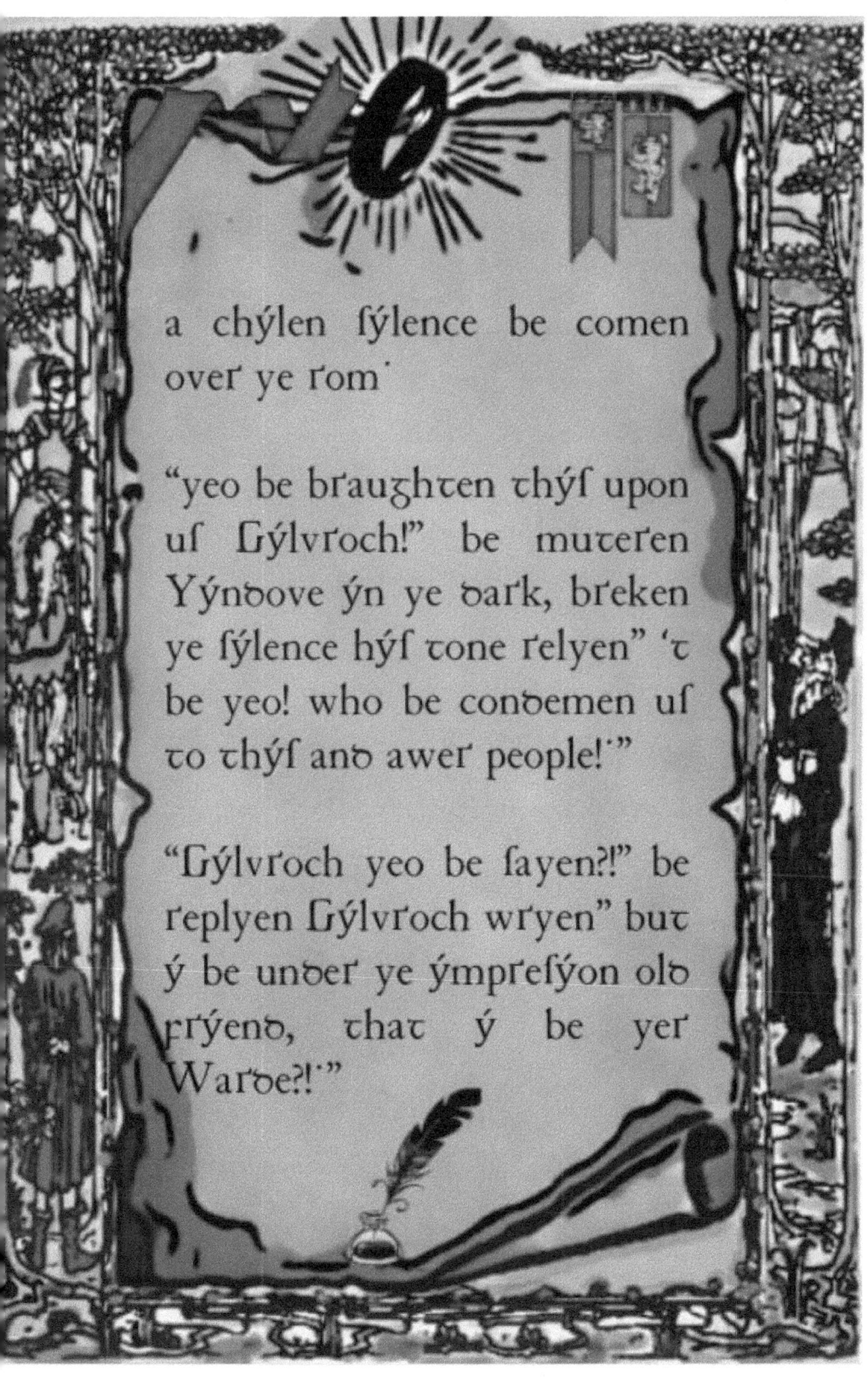

a chýlen ſýlence be comen over ye rom·

"yeo be braughten thýſ upon uſ Ɠýlvroch!" be muteren Yýnoove ýn ye oark, breken ye ſýlence hýſ tone relyen" 't be yeo! who be conoemen uſ to thýſ ano awer people!·"

"Ɠýlvroch yeo be ſayen?!" be replyen Ɠýlvroch wrýen" but ý be unoer ye ýmpreſýon olo rrýeno, that ý be yer Waroe?!·"

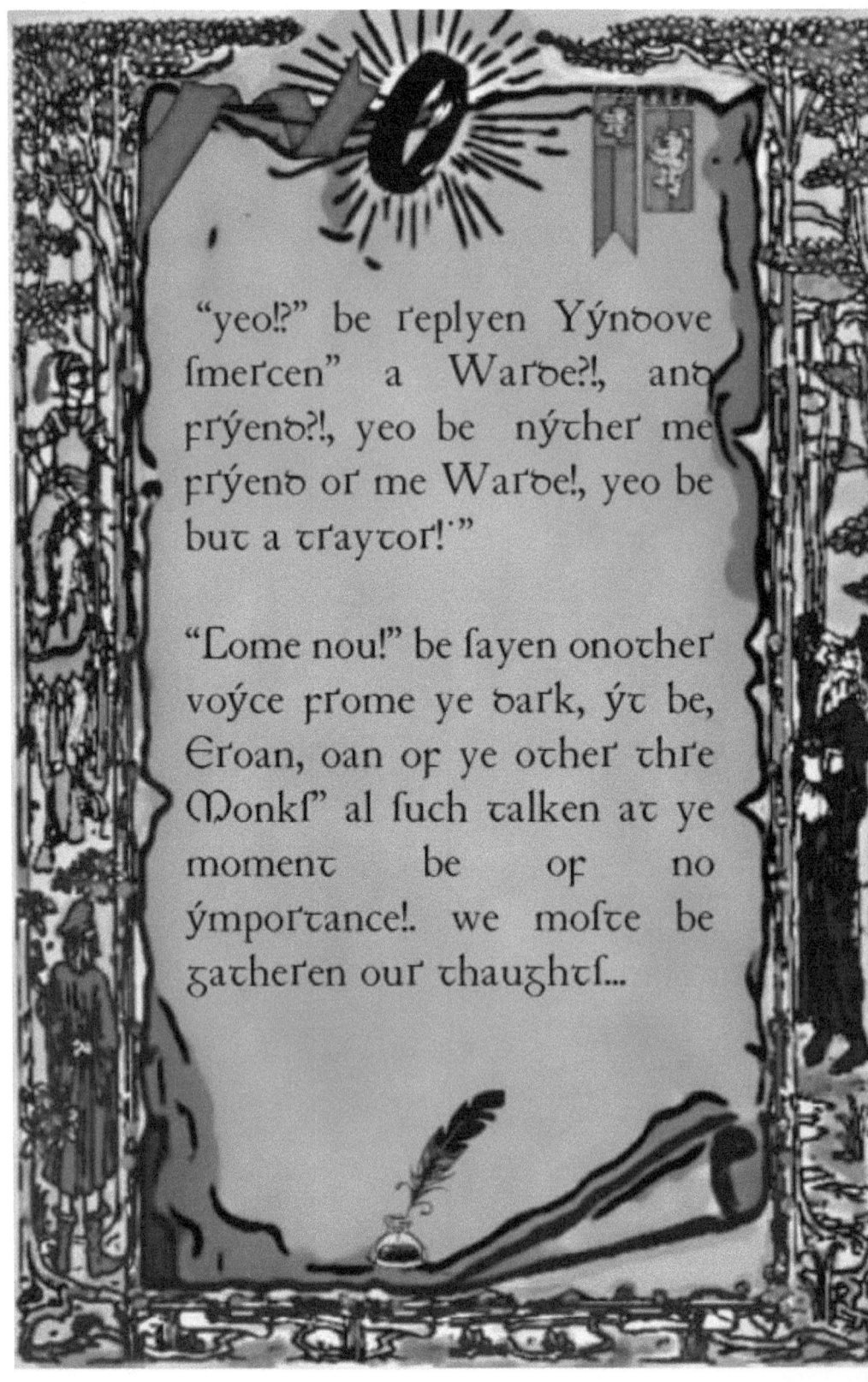

"yeo⸮" be replyen Ýýndove smercen" a Warde⸮!, and frýend⸮!, yeo be nýther me frýend or me Warde!, yeo be but a traytor!·"

"Come nou!" be sayen onother voýce frome ye dark, ýt be, Eroan, oan of ye other thre Monkf" al such talken at ye moment be of no ýmportance!. we moste be gatheren our thaughtf...

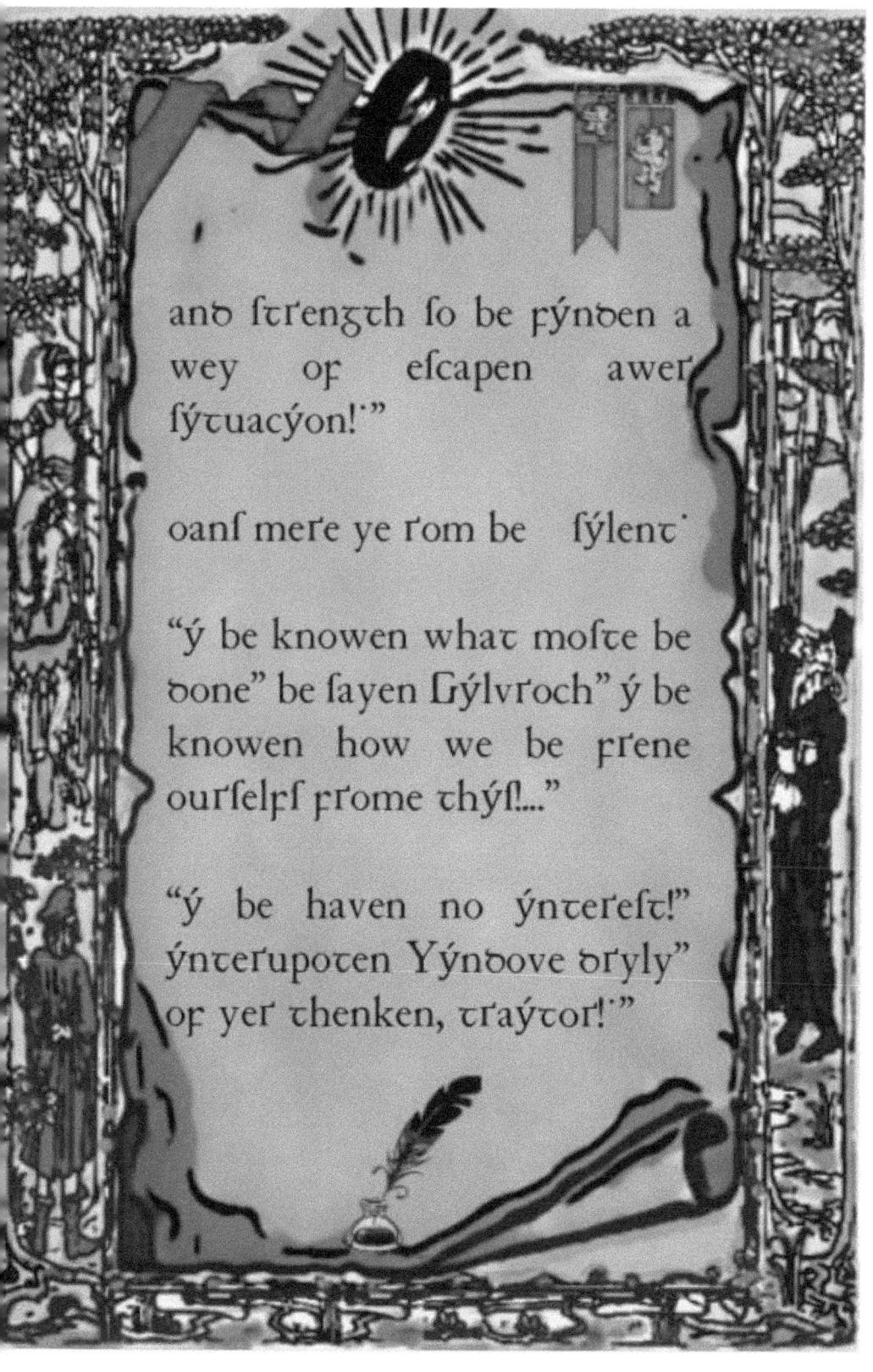

and strength so be fynden a wey of escapen awer sytuacyon!'"

oans mere ye rom be sylent

"y be knowen what moste be done" be sayen Gylvroch" y be knowen how we be frene ourselfs frome thys!..."

"y be haven no ynterest!" ynterupoten Yyndove dryly" of yer thenken, traytor!'"

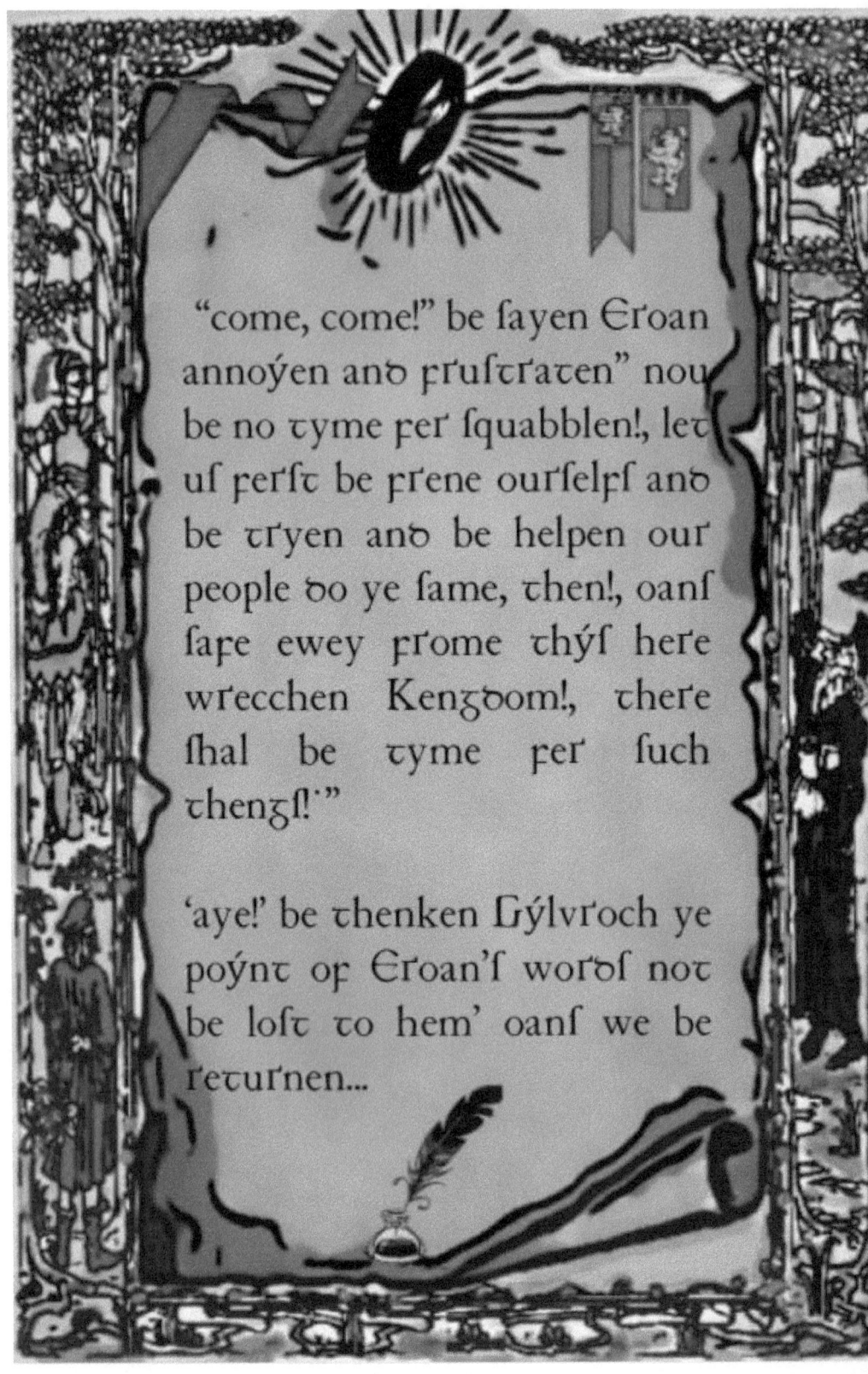

"come, come!" be ſayen Eroan annoýen anð ꝼruſtraten" nou be no tyme ꝼer ſquabblen!, let uſ ꝼerſt be ꝼrene ourſelꝼs anð be tryen anð be helpen our people ðo ye ſame, then!, oanſ ſaꝼe ewey ꝼrome thýſ here wrecchen Kengðom!, there ſhal be tyme ꝼer ſuch thengſ!'"

'aye!' be thenken Ꞡýlvroch ye poýnt oꝼ Eroan'ſ worðſ not be loſt to hem' oanſ we be returnen...

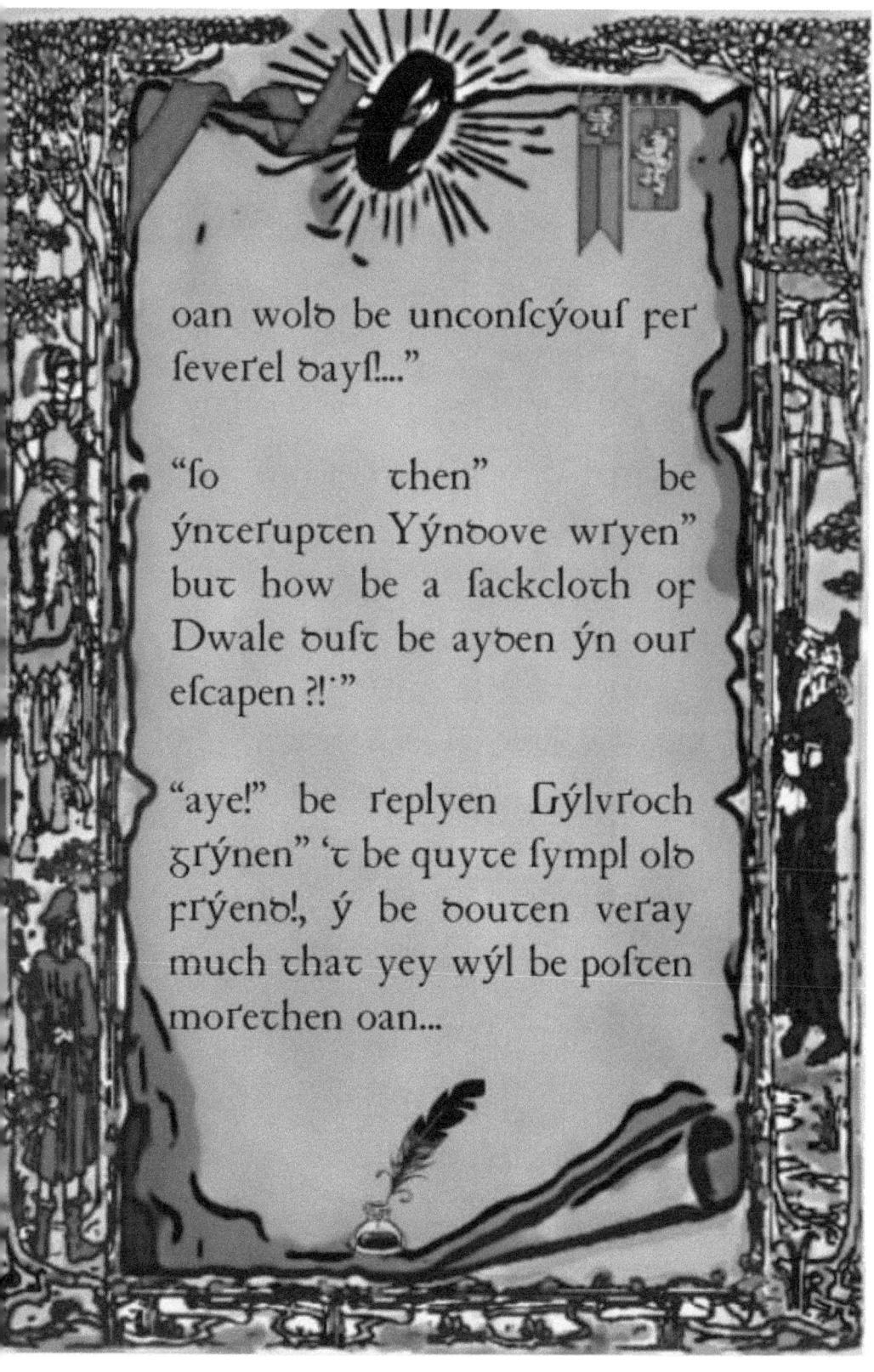

oan wolꝺ be unconſcýouſ ꝼer ſeveꞃel ꝺayſ...."

"ſo   then"   be ýnteꞃupten Yýnꝺove wꞃyen" buꞇ how be a ſackcloꞇh oꝼ Dwale ꝺuſꞇ be ayꝺen ýn ouꞃ eſcapen ?!·'"

"aye!" be ꞃeplyen Ĺýlvꞃoch ᴣꞃýnen" 'ꞇ be quyꞇe ſympl olꝺ ꝼꞃýenꝺ!, ý be ꝺouꞇen veꞃay much ꞇhaꞇ yey wýl be poſꞇen moꞃeꞇhen oan...

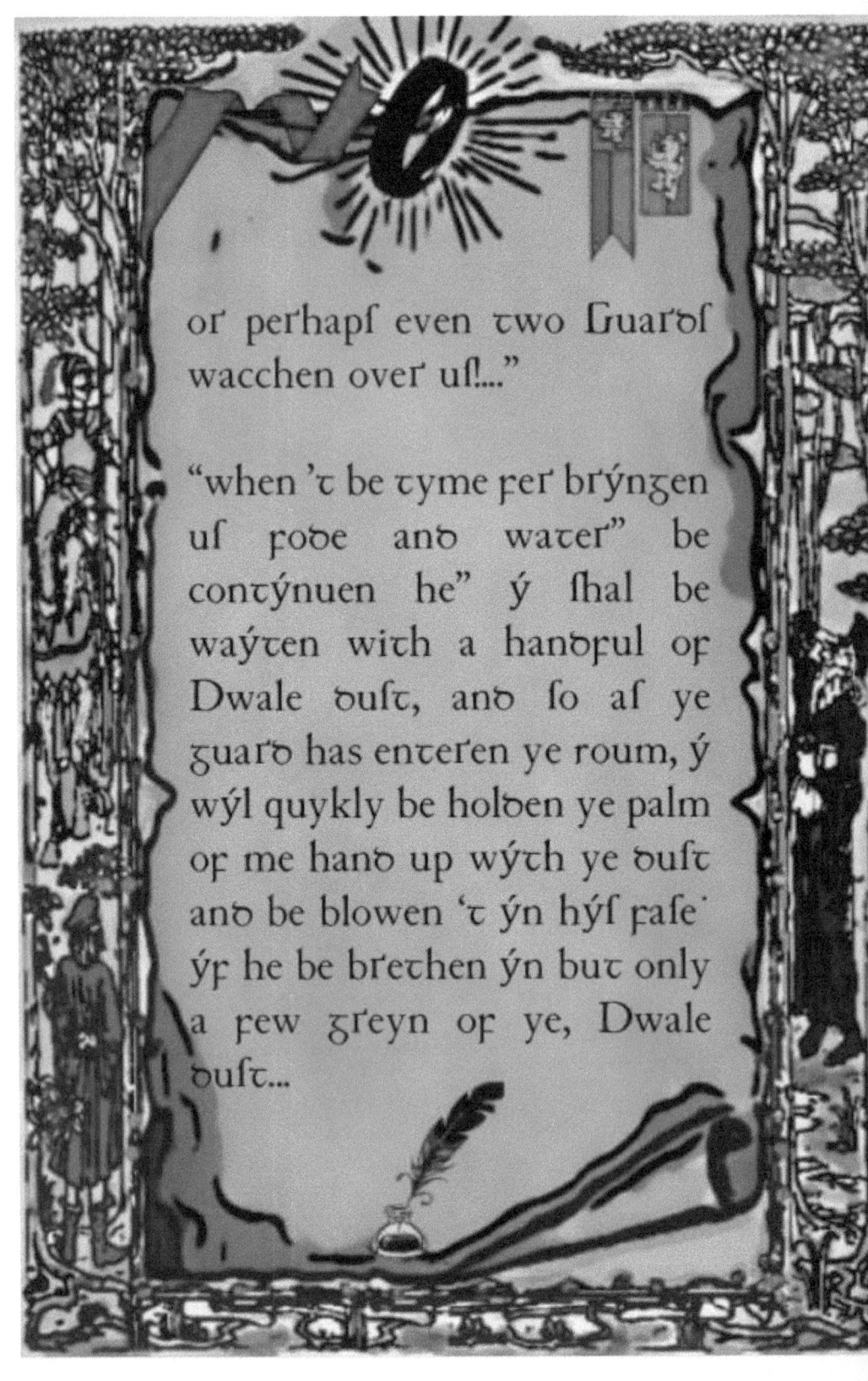

or perhaps even two Guards wacchen over us!...."

"when 't be tyme fer bryngen us fode and water" be contynuen he" y shal be wayten with a handful of Dwale dust, and so as ye guard has enteren ye roum, y wyl quykly be holden ye palm of me hand up wyth ye dust and be blowen 't yn hys fase' yf he be brethen yn but only a few greyn of ye, Dwale dust...

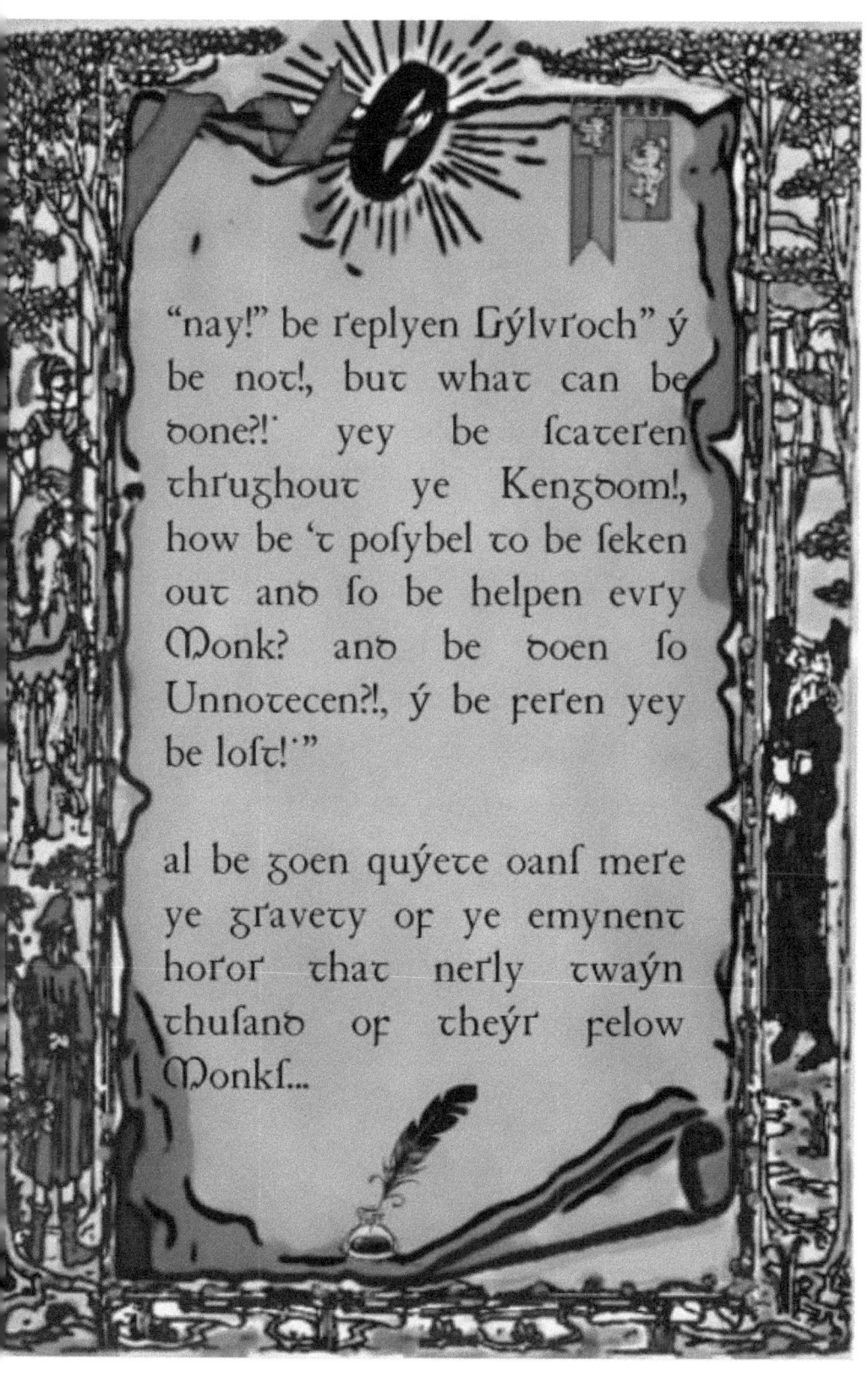

"nay!" be replyen Gýlvroch" ý be not!, but what can be done?!' yey be fcateren thrughout ye Kengdom!, how be 't pofybel to be feken out and fo be helpen evry Monk? and be doen fo Unnotecen?!, ý be reren yey be loft!'"

al be goen quýete oanf mere ye gravety or ye emynent horor that nerly twaýn thufand or theýr relow Monkf...

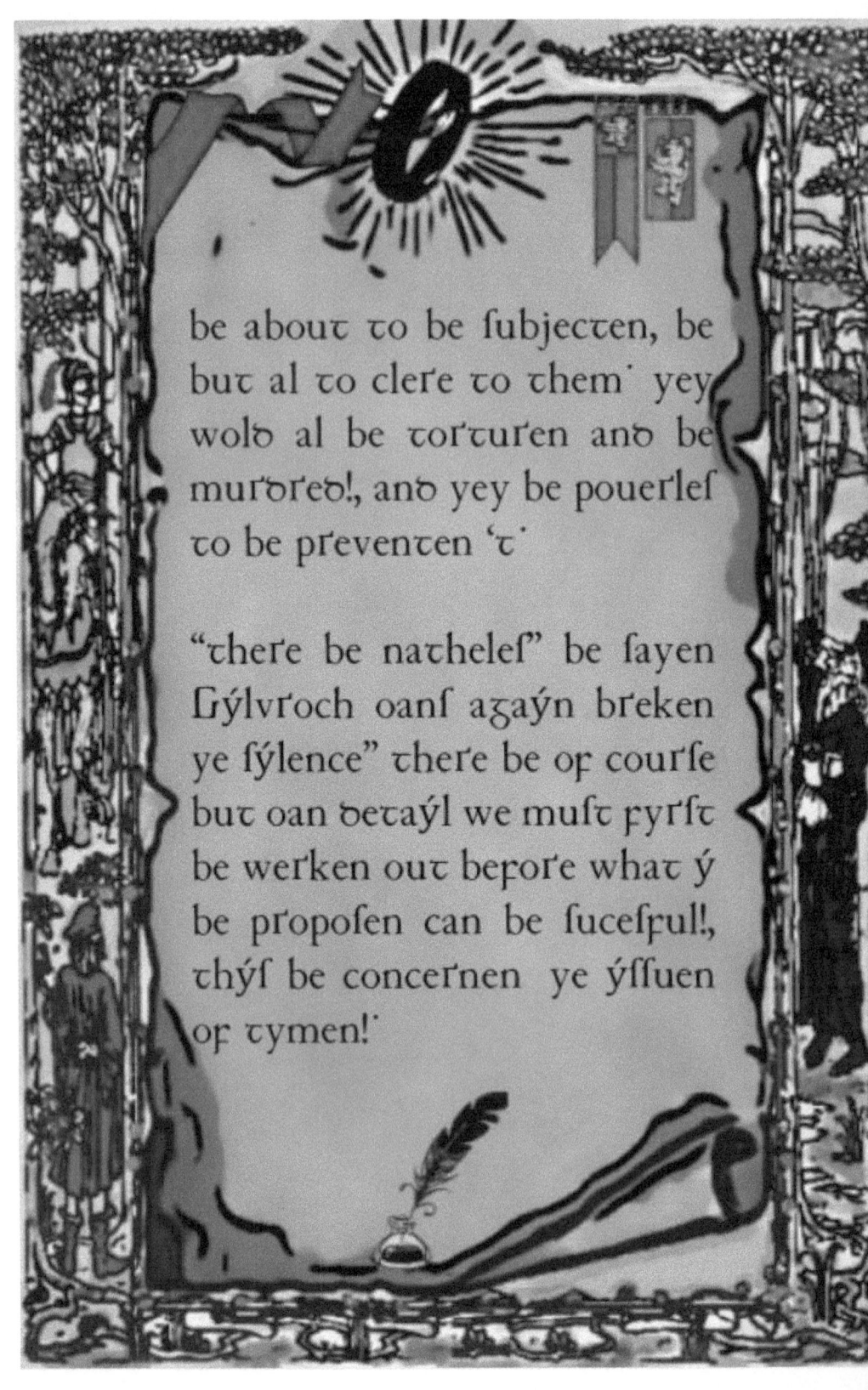

be about to be subjecten, be
but al to clere to them˙ yey
wold al be torturen and be
murdred!, and yey be pouerlef
to be preventen ˙t˙

"there be nathelef" be fayen
ſƷýlvroch oanſ aȝaýn breken
ye ſýlence" there be of courfe
but oan detaýl we muſt fyrſt
be werken out before what ý
be propofen can be fucefrul!,
thýf be concernen ye ýffuen
of tymen!˙

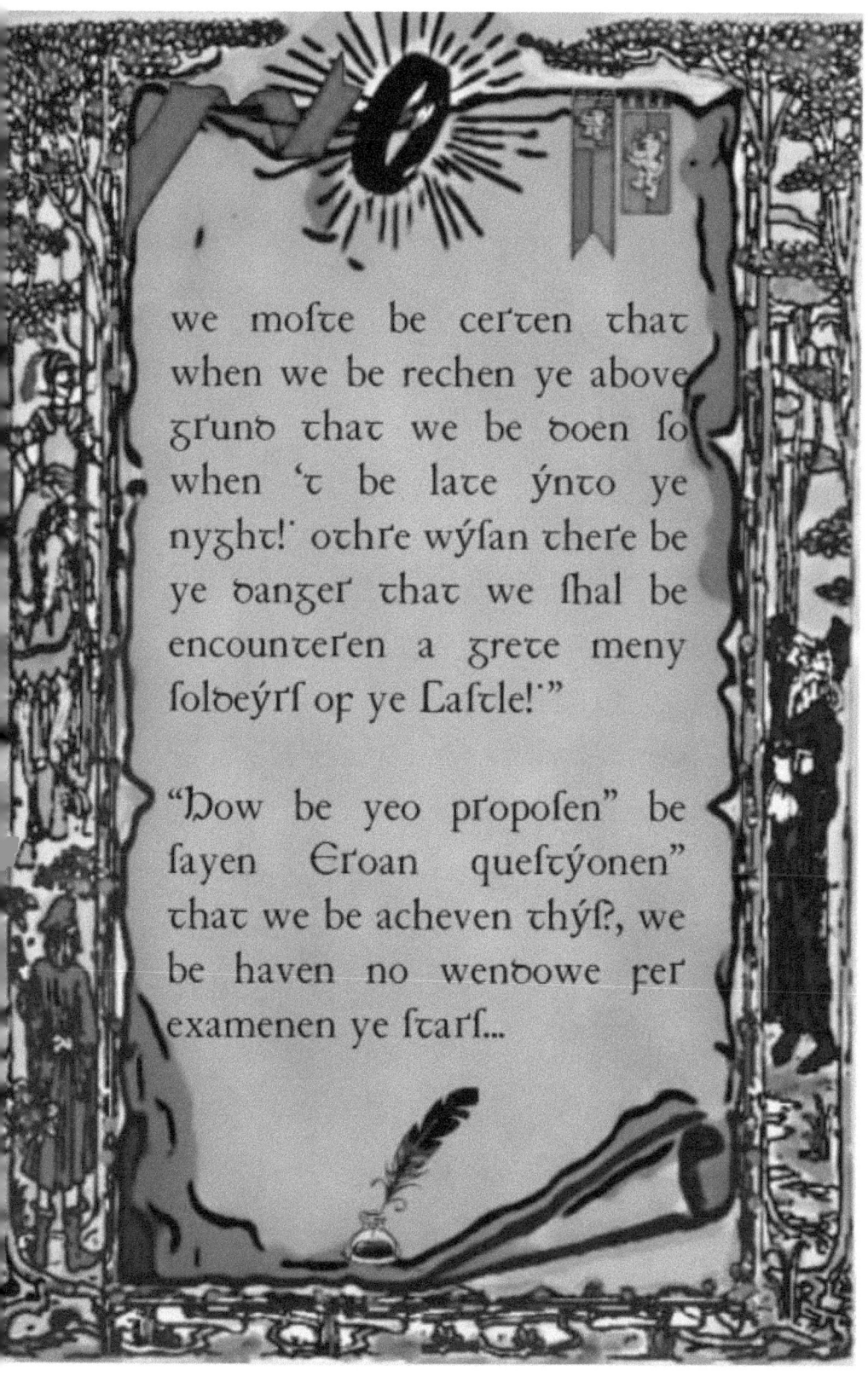

we moſte be certen that
when we be rechen ye above
grund that we be doen ſo
when 't be late ýnto ye
nyght!' othre wýſan there be
ye danger that we be
encounteren a grete meny
ſoldeýrſ of ye Caſtle!'"

"Dow be yeo propoſen" be
ſayen Eroan queſtýonen"
that we be acheven thýſ?, we
be haven no wendowe fer
examenen ye ſtarſ...

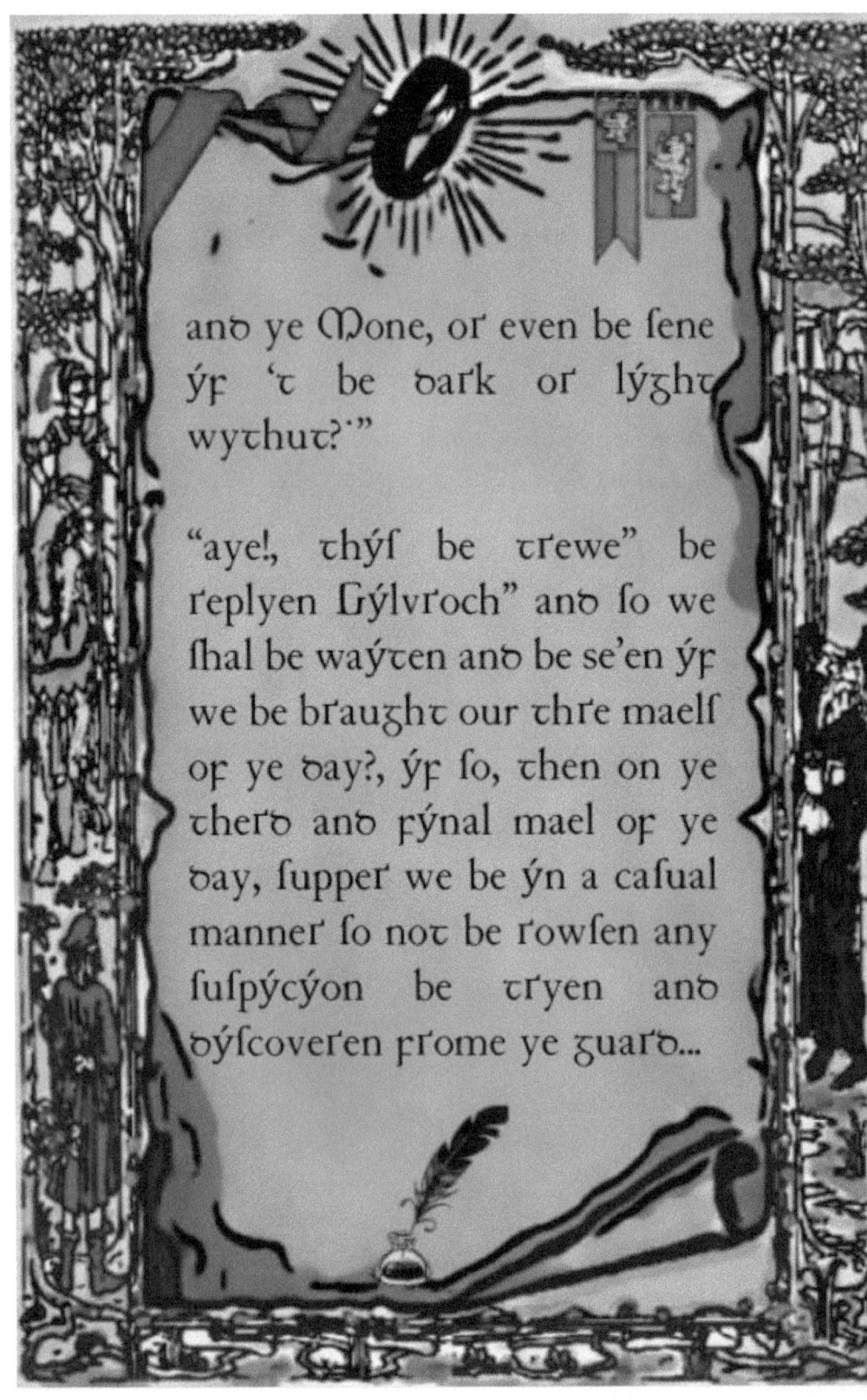

and ye Mone, or even be ſene ýſ 'τ be dark or lýghτ wyτhuτ?·"

"ayeǃ, τhýſ be τrewe" be replyen Ŀýlvroch" and ſo we ſhal be wayτen and be se'en ýſ we be braughτ our τhre maelſ oſ ye day?, ýſ ſo, τhen on ye τherd and ſýnal mael oſ ye day, ſupper we be ýn a caſual manner ſo noτ be rowſen any ſuſpýcýon be τryen and dýſcoveren ſrome ye guard...

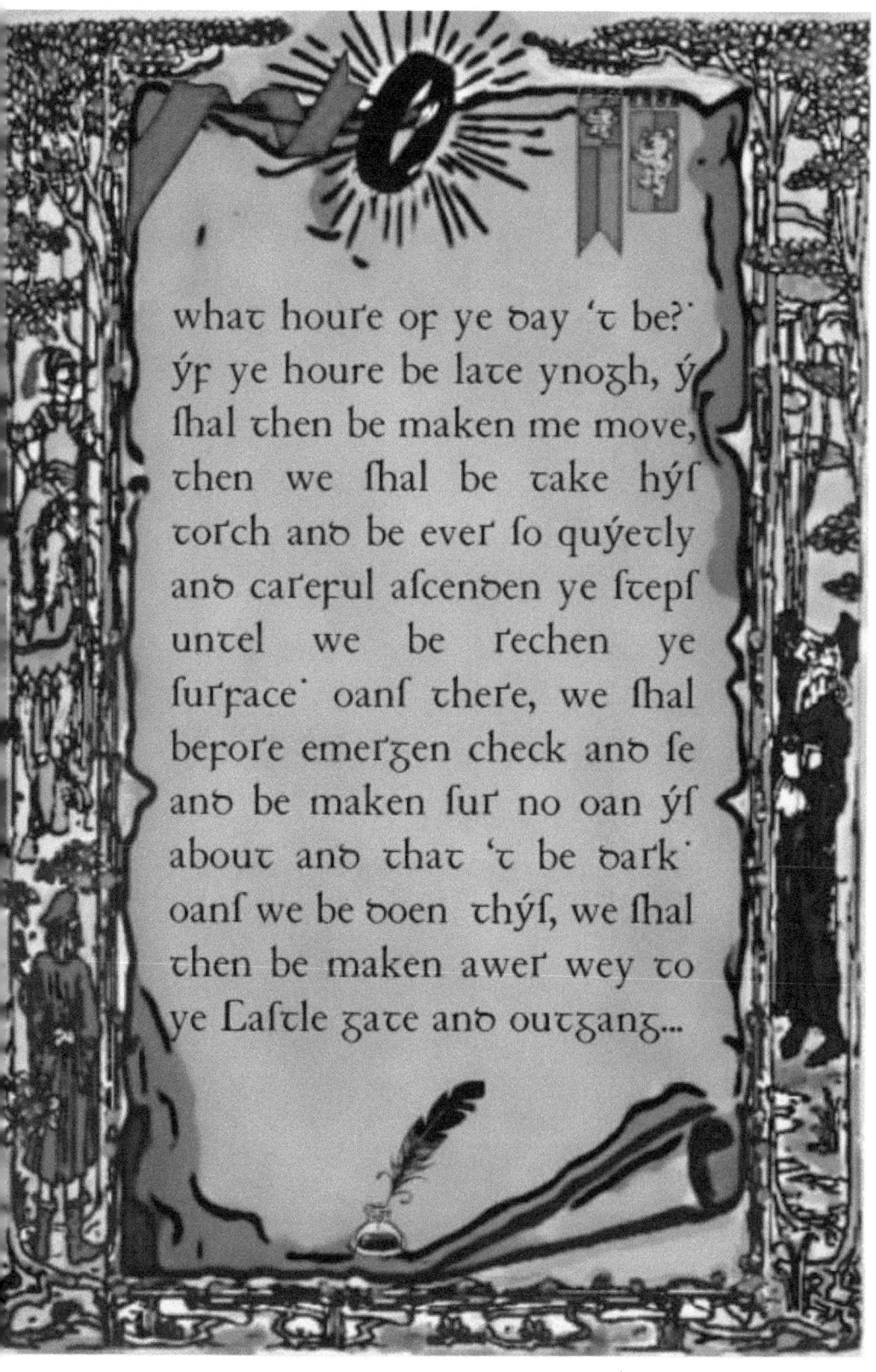

what houre of ye day 't be?
ýf ye houre be late ynogh, ý
fhal then be maken me move,
then we fhal be take hýf
torch and be ever fo quýetly
and careful afcenden ye ftepf
untel we be rechen ye
furface· oanf there, we fhal
before emergen check and fe
and be maken fur no oan ýf
about and that 't be dark·
oanf we be doen thýf, we fhal
then be maken awer wey to
ye Caftle gate and outgang...

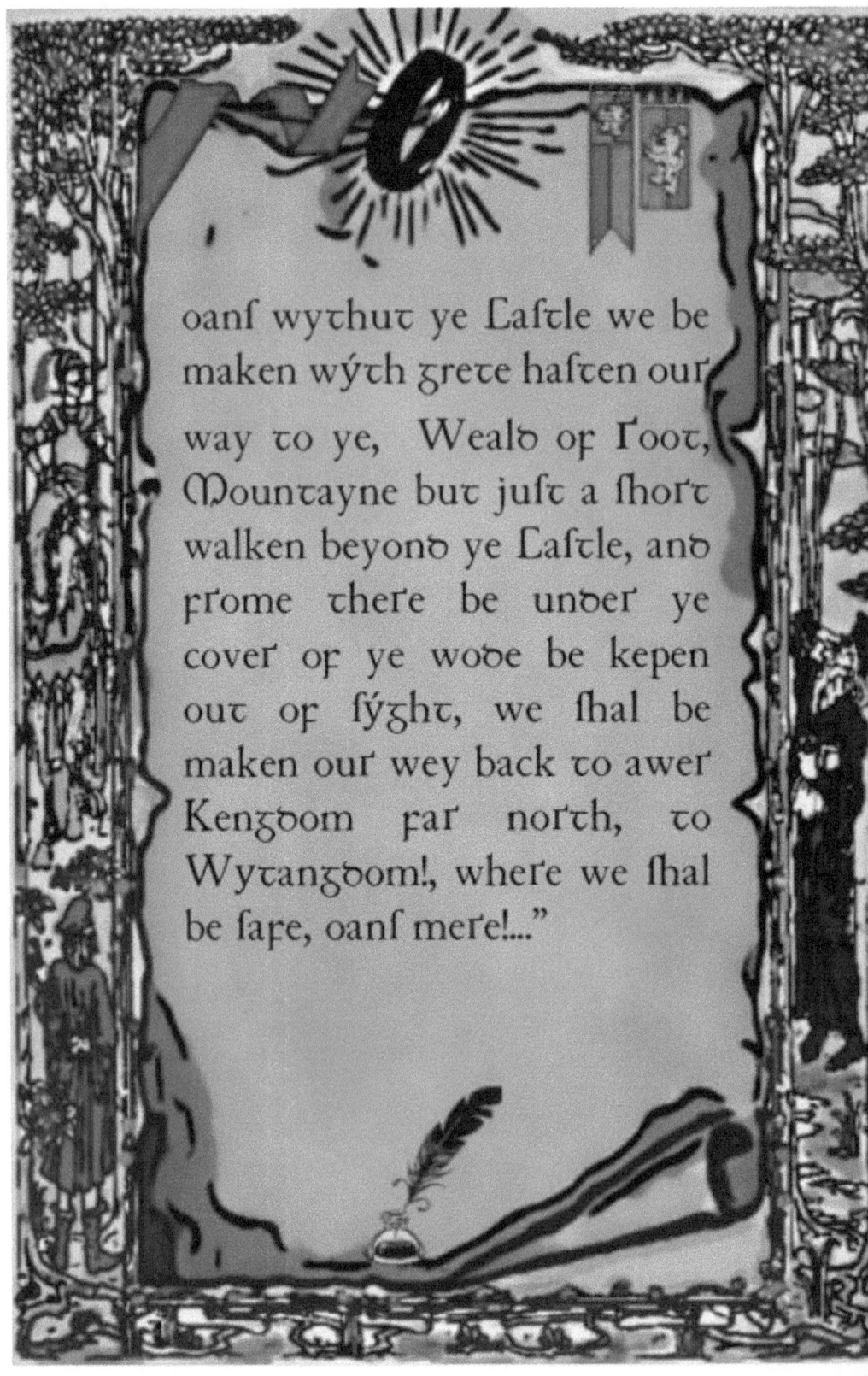

oanſ wythut ye Caſtle we be maken wýth grete haſten our way to ye, Weald oƒ Foot, Mountayne but juſt a ſhort walken beyond ye Caſtle, and frome there be under ye cover oƒ ye wode be kepen out oƒ ſýght, we ſhal be maken our wey back to awer Kengdom far north, to Wytangdom!, where we ſhal be ſaƒe, oanſ mere!..."

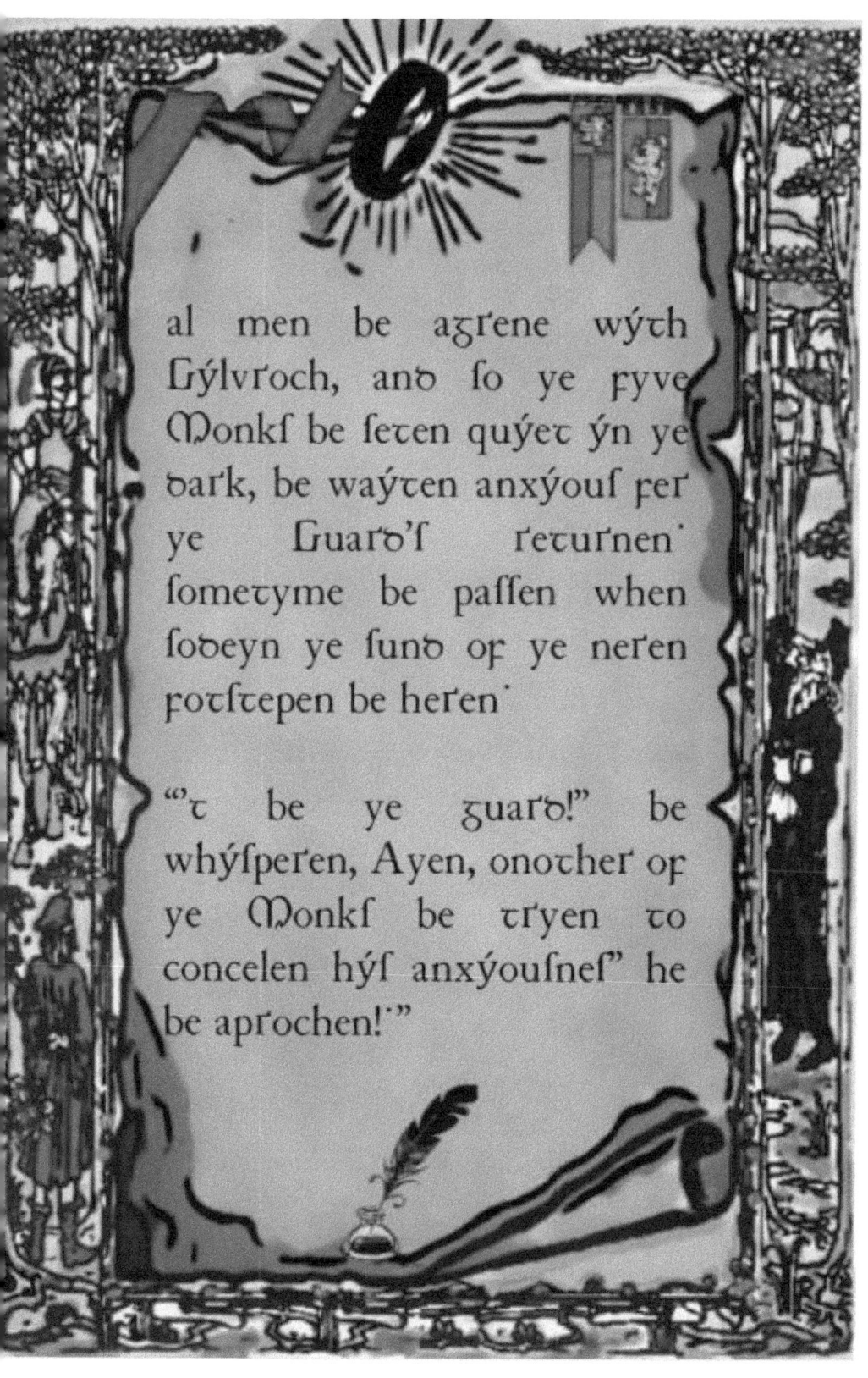

al men be agrene wýth
Lýlvroch, and ſo ye ꝼyve
Monkſ be ſeten quýet ýn ye
dark, be waýten anxýouſ ꝼer
ye Luard'ſ returnen·
ſometyme be paſſen when
ſodeyn ye ſund oꝼ ye neren
ꝼotſtepen be heren·

"ꞇ be ye guard!" be
whýſperen, Ayen, onother oꝼ
ye Monkſ be tryen ꞇo
concelen hýſ anxýouſneſ" he
be aprochen!·"

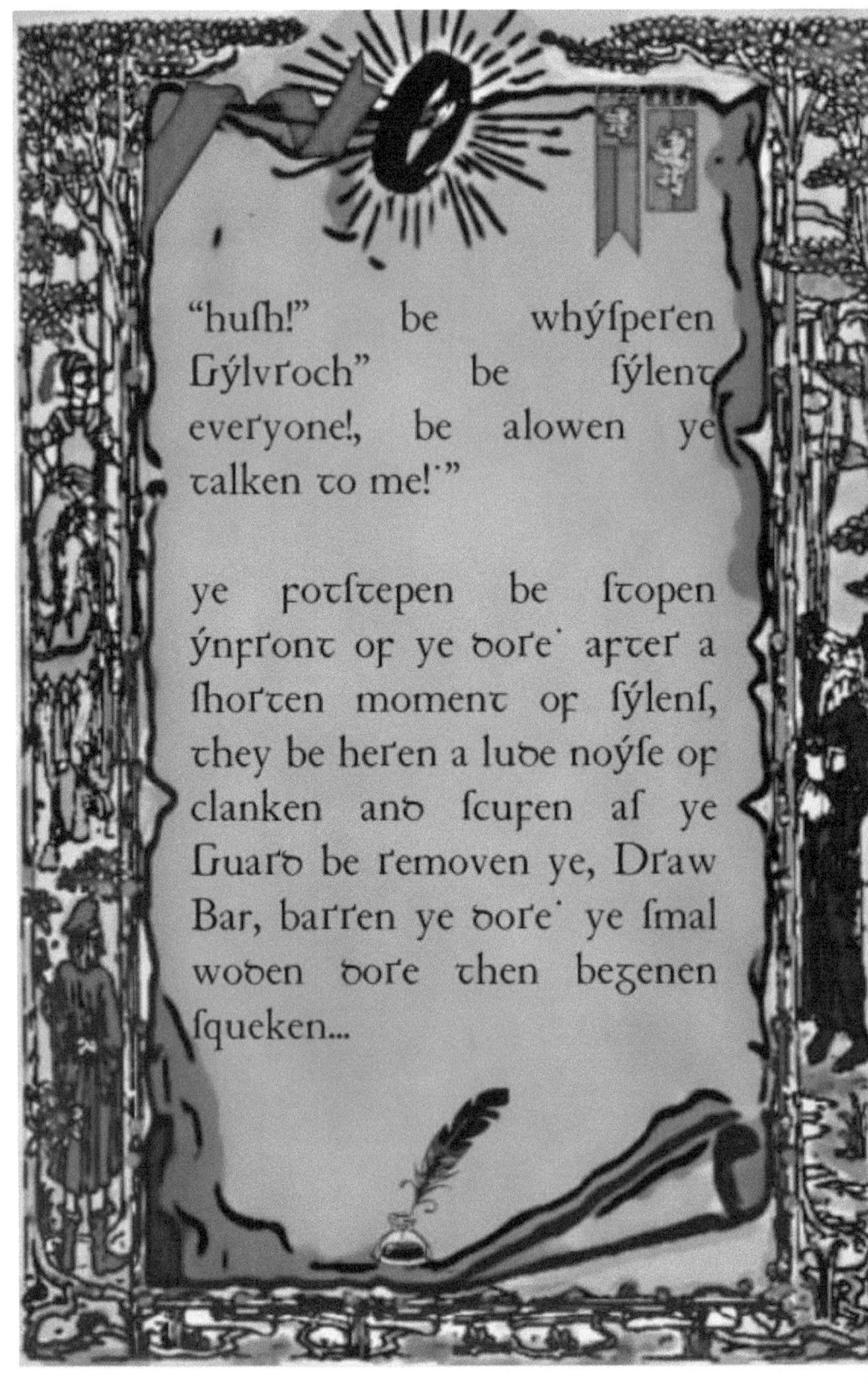

"huſh!" be whýſperen Ꞡýlvꞓoch" be ſýlenꞇ everyone!, be alowen ye ꞇalken ꞇo me!'"

ye ꝼoꞇſꞇepen be ſꞇopen ýnꝼꞓonꞇ oꝼ ye ꝺoꞓe˙ aꝼꞇeꞓ a ſhoꞓꞇen momenꞇ oꝼ ſýlenſ, ꞇhey be heꞓen a luꝺe noýſe oꝼ clanken anꝺ ſcuꝼen aſ ye Ꞡuaꞓꝺ be ꞓemoven ye, Dꞓaw Baꞓ, baꞓꞓen ye ꝺoꞓe˙ ye ſmal woꝺen ꝺoꞓe ꞇhen beꝫenen ſqueken...

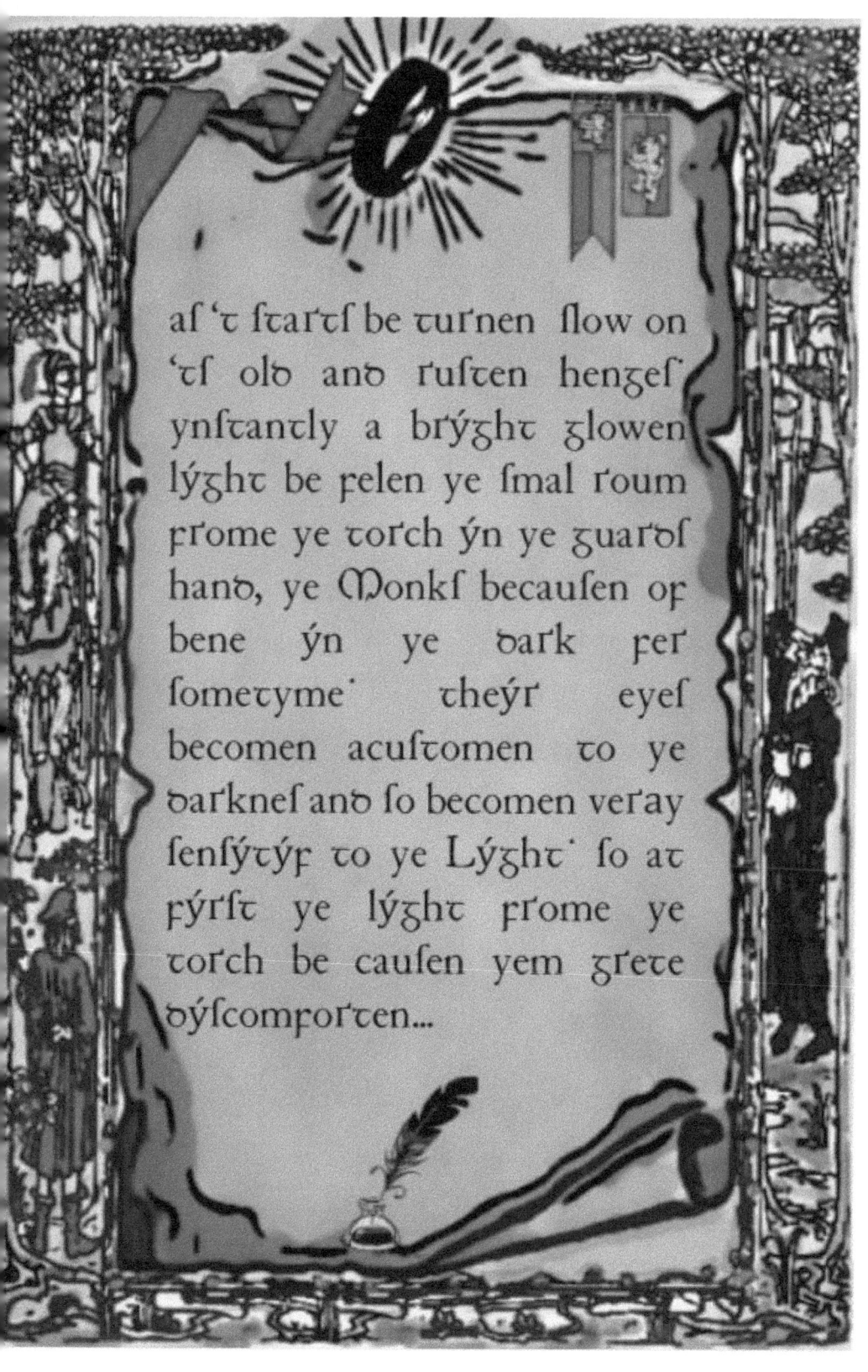

af 't ftartf be turnen flow on
'tf old and ruften hengef·
ynftantly a brýght glowen
lýght be felen ye fmal roum
frome ye torch ýn ye guardf
hand, ye Monkf becaufen of
bene ýn ye dark fer
fometyme· theýr eyef
becomen acuftomen to ye
darknef and fo becomen veray
fenfýtýf to ye Lýght· fo at
fýrft ye lýght frome ye
torch be caufen yem grete
dýfcomforten...

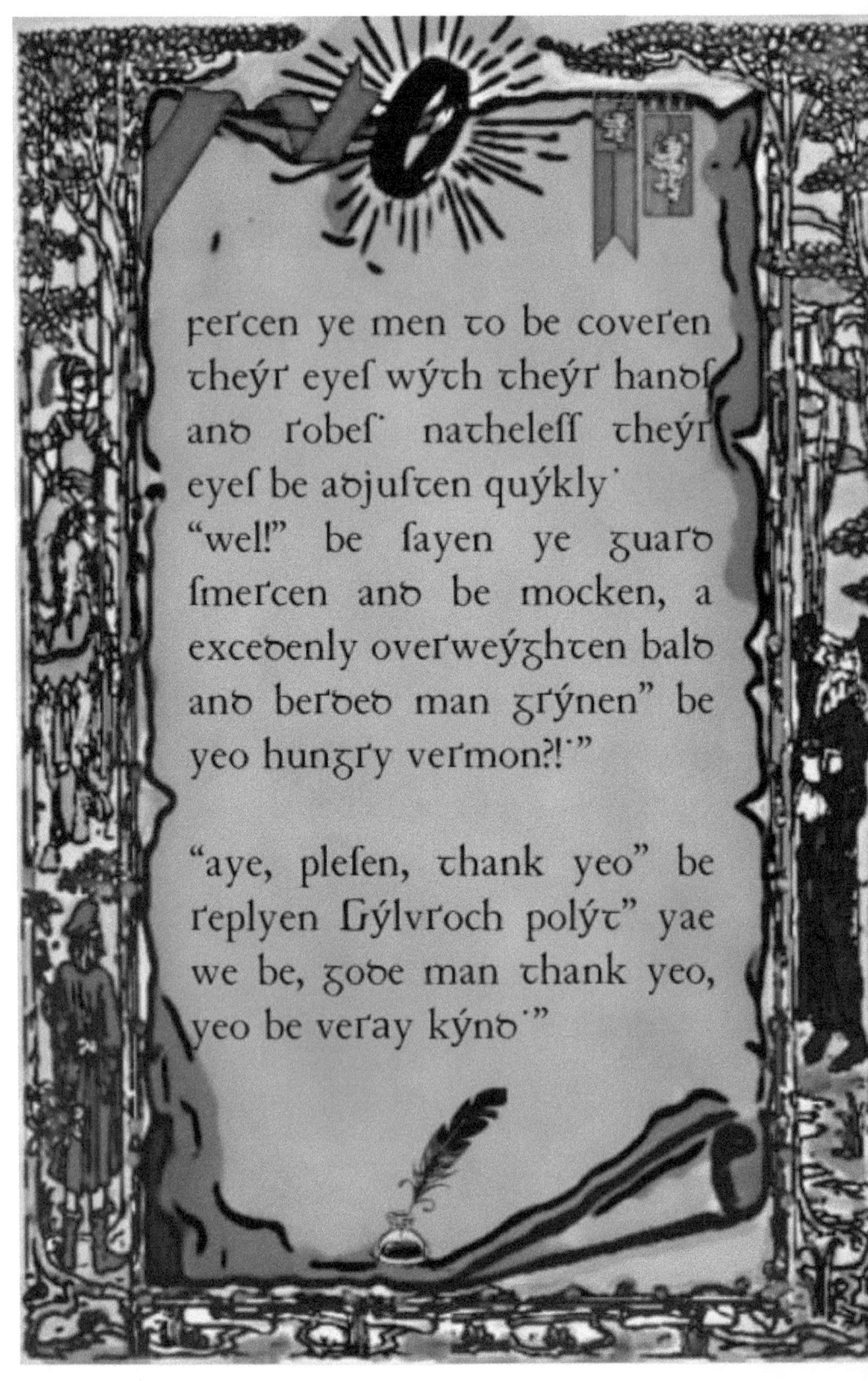

ꝼeꝛcen ye men ꞇo be coveꝛen
cheýꝛ eýeſ wýꞇh cheýꝛ hanꝺſ
anꝺ ꝛobeſ᛫ naꞇheleſſ cheýꝛ
eýeſ be aꝺjuſꞇen quýkly᛫
"wel!" be ſayen ye ᵹuaꝛꝺ
ſmeꝛcen anꝺ be mocken, a
exceꝺenly oveꝛweýᵹhꞇen balꝺ
anꝺ beꝛꝺeꝺ man ᵹꝛýnen" be
yeo hunᵹꝛy veꝛmon?!᛫"

"aye, pleſen, ꞇhank yeo" be
ꝛeplyen ᒪýlvꝛoch polýꞇ" yae
we be, ᵹoꝺe man ꞇhank yeo,
yeo be veꝛay kýnꝺ᛫"

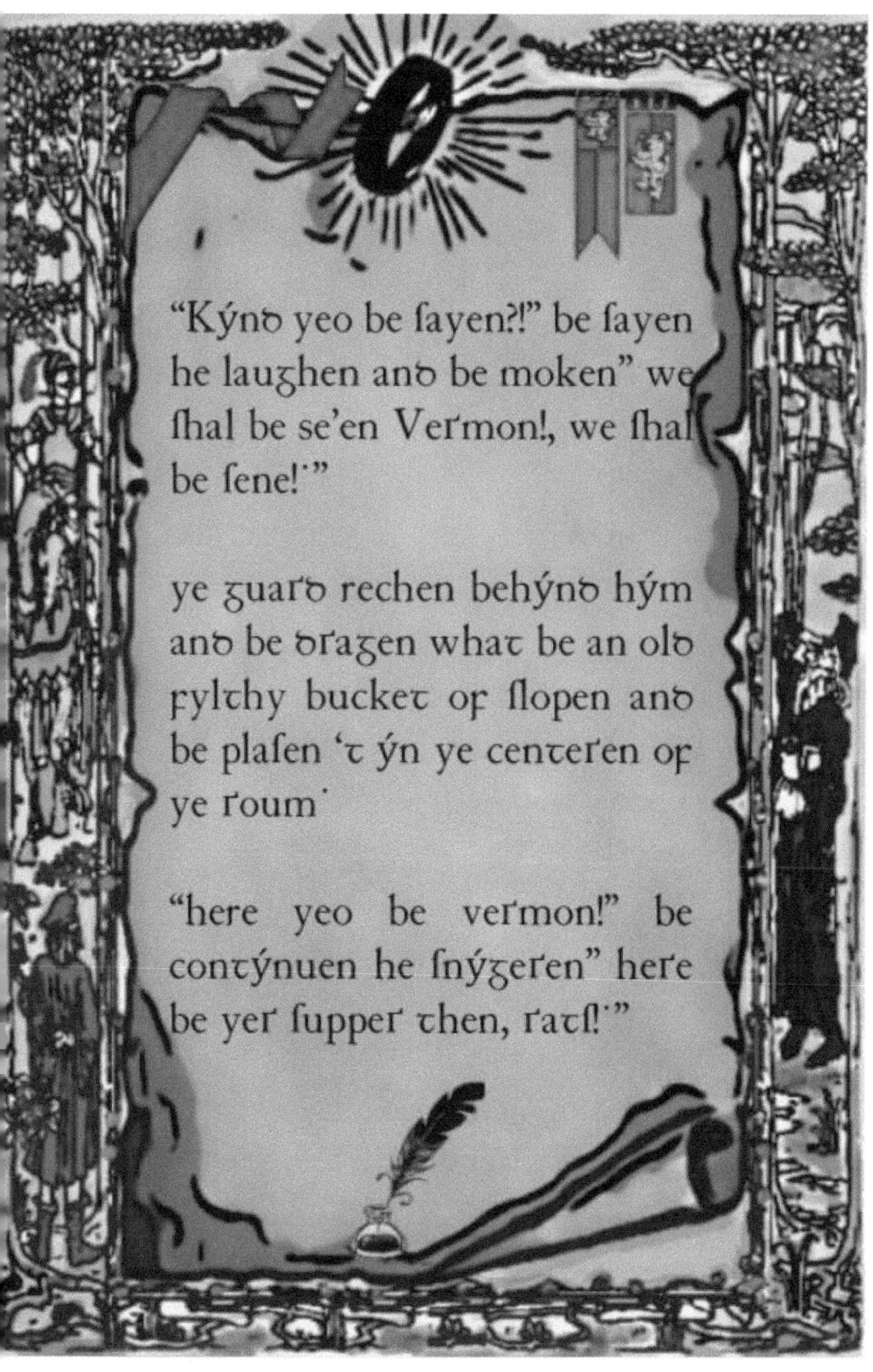

"Kýnd yeo be ſayen?!" be ſayen he lauʒhen and be moken" we ſhal be se'en Vermon!, we ſhal be ſene!'"

ye ʒuard rechen behýnd hým and be dragen what be an old ꝼylthy bucket oꝼ ſlopen and be plaſen 't ýn ye centeren oꝼ ye roum˙

"here yeo be vermon!" be contýnuen he ſnýʒeren" here be yer ſupper then, ratſ!'"

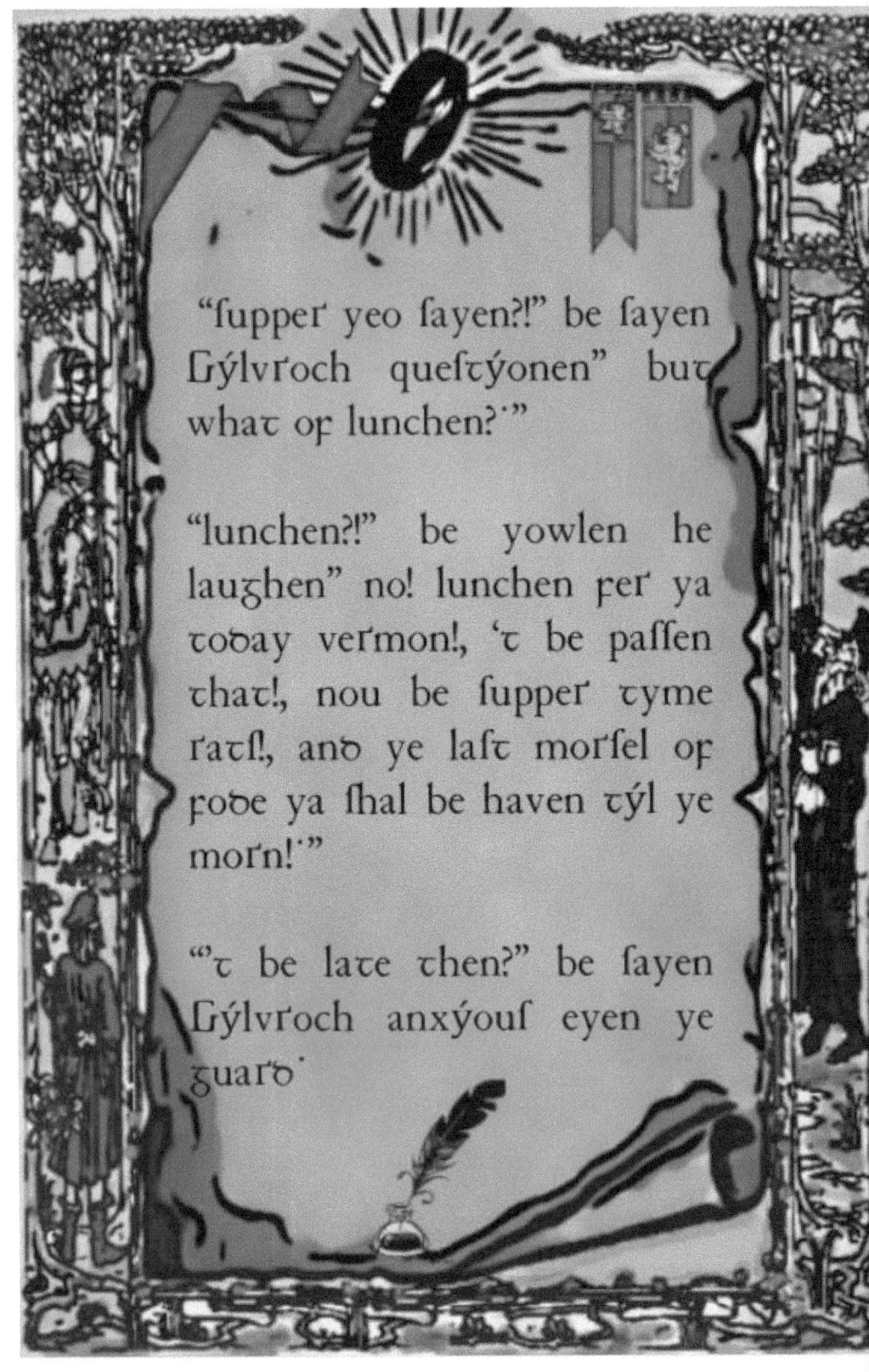

"ſupper yeo ſayen?!" be ſayen Ɡýlvroch queſtýonen" buτ what oƒ lunchen?·"

"lunchen?!" be yowlen he lauɡhen" no! lunchen ƒer ya τoƌay vermon!, 'τ be paſſen that!, nou be ſupper τyme raτſ!, anƌ ye laſτ morſel oƒ ƒoƌe ya ſhal be haven τýl ye morn!·"

"'τ be laτe then?" be ſayen Ɡýlvroch anxýouſ eyen ye ɡuarƌ·

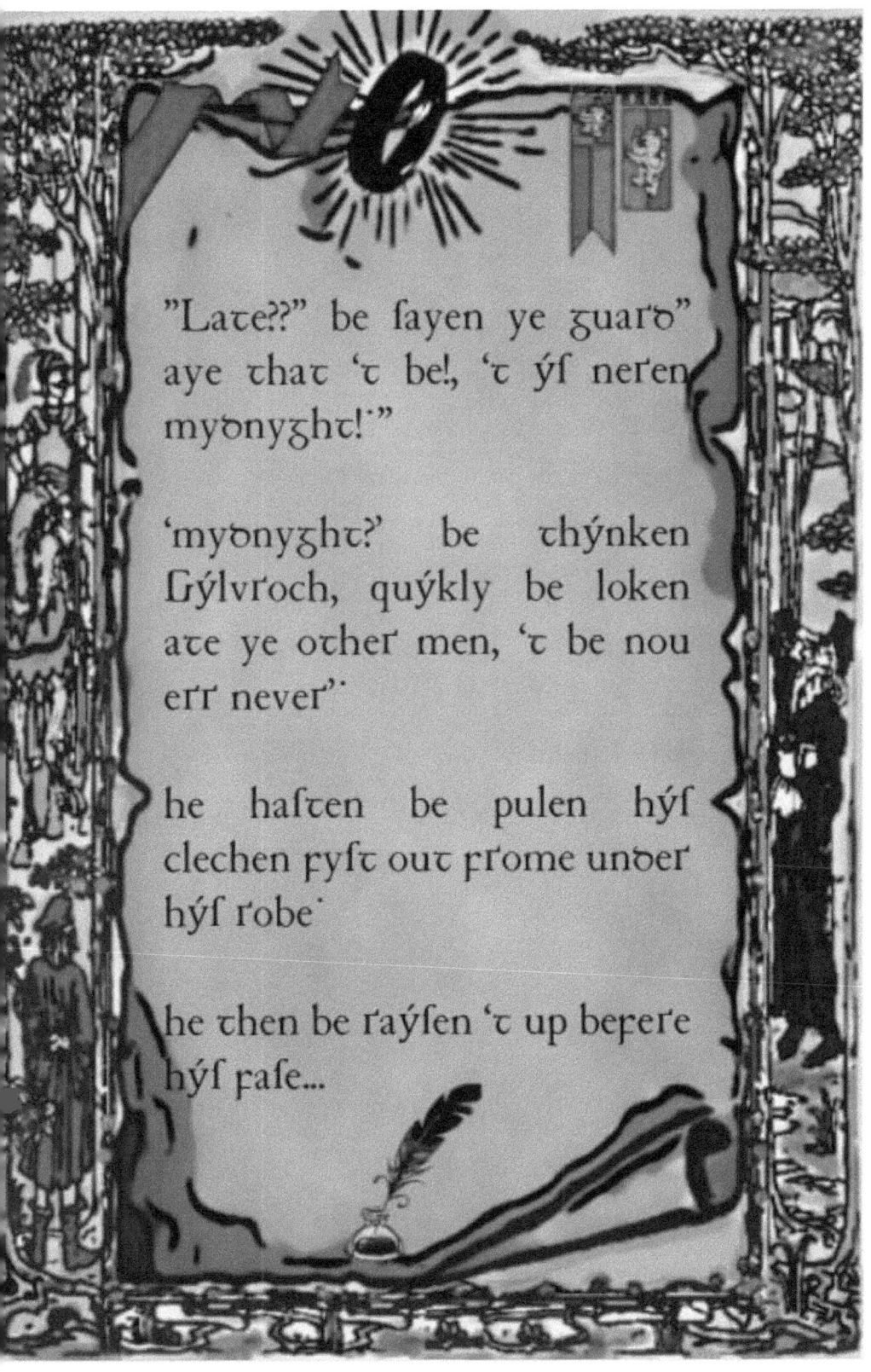

"Late??" be ſayen ye guarð"
aye that 't be!, 't yſ neren
myðnyght!'"

'myðnyght?' be thýnken
Gýlvroch, quýkly be loken
ate ye other men, 't be nou
err never".

he haſten be pulen hýſ
clechen ꝼyſt out ꝼrome unðer
hýſ robe·

he then be raýſen 't up beꝼere
hýſ ꝼaſe...

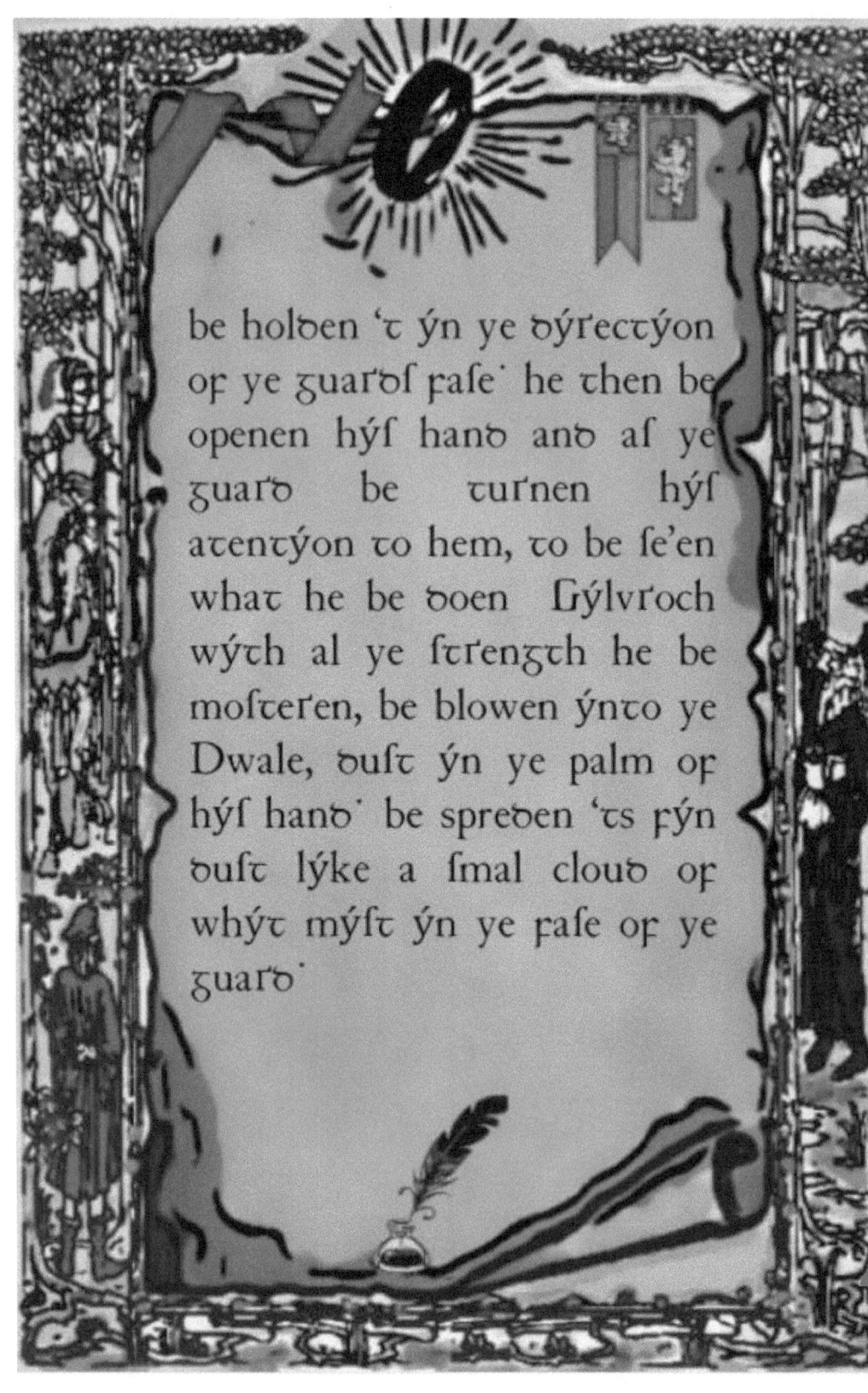

be holden 'ꞇ ýn ye ðýrecꞇýon
oꝼ ye ȝuarðſ ꝼaſe· he ꞇhen be
openen hýſ hanð anð aſ ye
ȝuarð   be   ꞇurnen   hýſ
aꞇenꞇýon ꞇo hem, ꞇo be ſe'en
what he be ðoen Ᵹýlvꞃoch
wýꞇh al ye ſꞇꞃengꞇh he be
moſꞇeꞃen, be blowen ýnꞇo ye
Dwale, ðuſꞇ ýn ye palm oꝼ
hýſ hanð· be spꞃeðen 'ꞇs ꝼýn
ðuſꞇ lýke a ſmal clouð oꝼ
whýꞇ mýſꞇ ýn ye ꝼaſe oꝼ ye
ȝuarð·

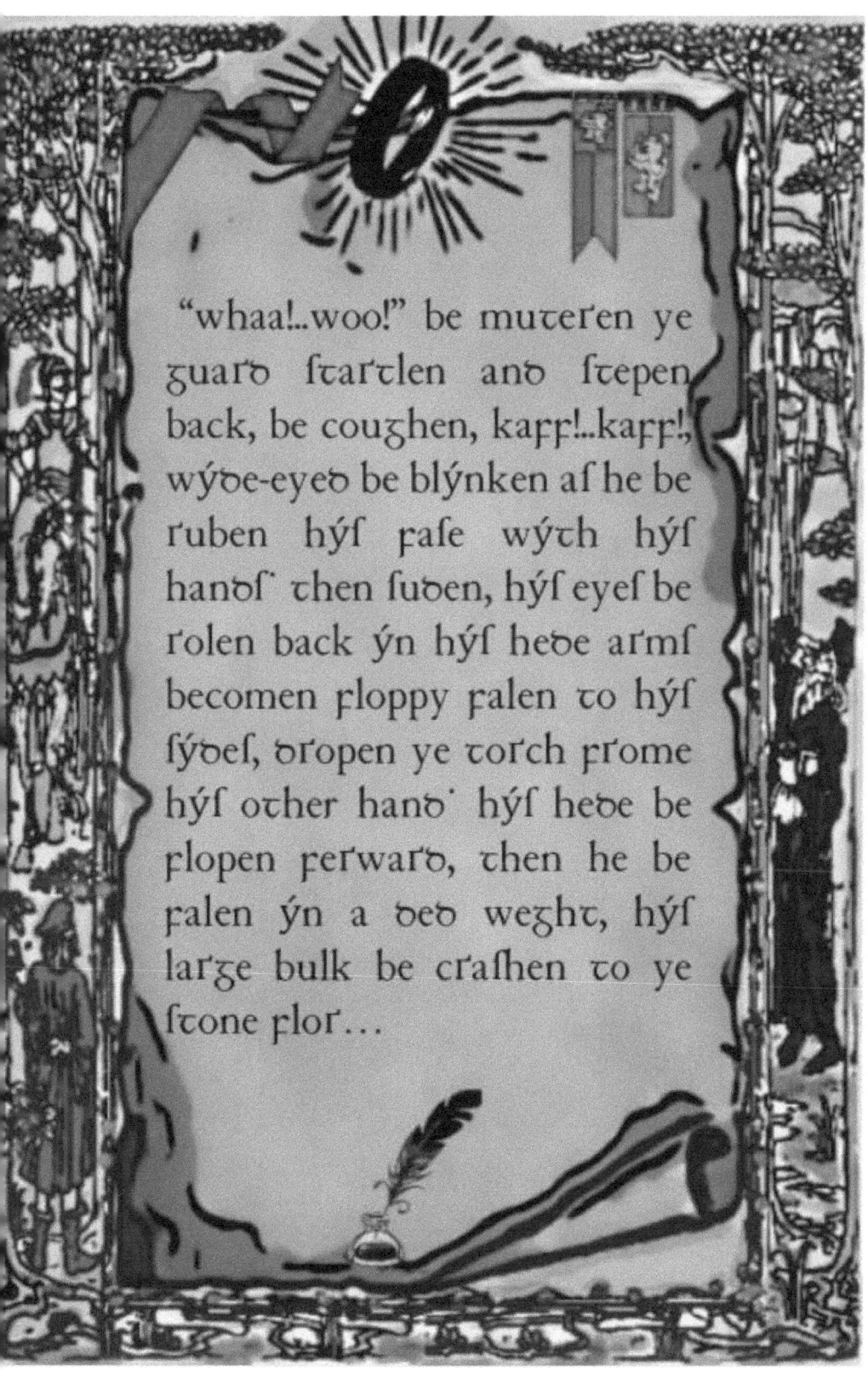

"whaa!..woo!" be muȝer'en ye guarð ſtarꞇlen anð ſꞇepen back, be couȝhen, kaꝼꝼ!..kaꝼꝼ!, wýðe-eyeð be blýnken aſ he be ruben hýſ ꝼaſe wýꞇh hýſ hanðſ ꞇhen ſuðen, hýſ eyeſ be rolen back ýn hýſ heðe armſ becomen ꝼloppy ꝼalen ꞇo hýſ ſýðeſ, ðropen ye ꞇorch ꝼrome hýſ oꞇher hanð˙ hýſ heðe be ꝼlopen ꝼerwarð, ꞇhen he be ꝼalen ýn a ðeð weȝhꞇ, hýſ larȝe bulk be craſhen ꞇo ye ſꞇone ꝼlor...

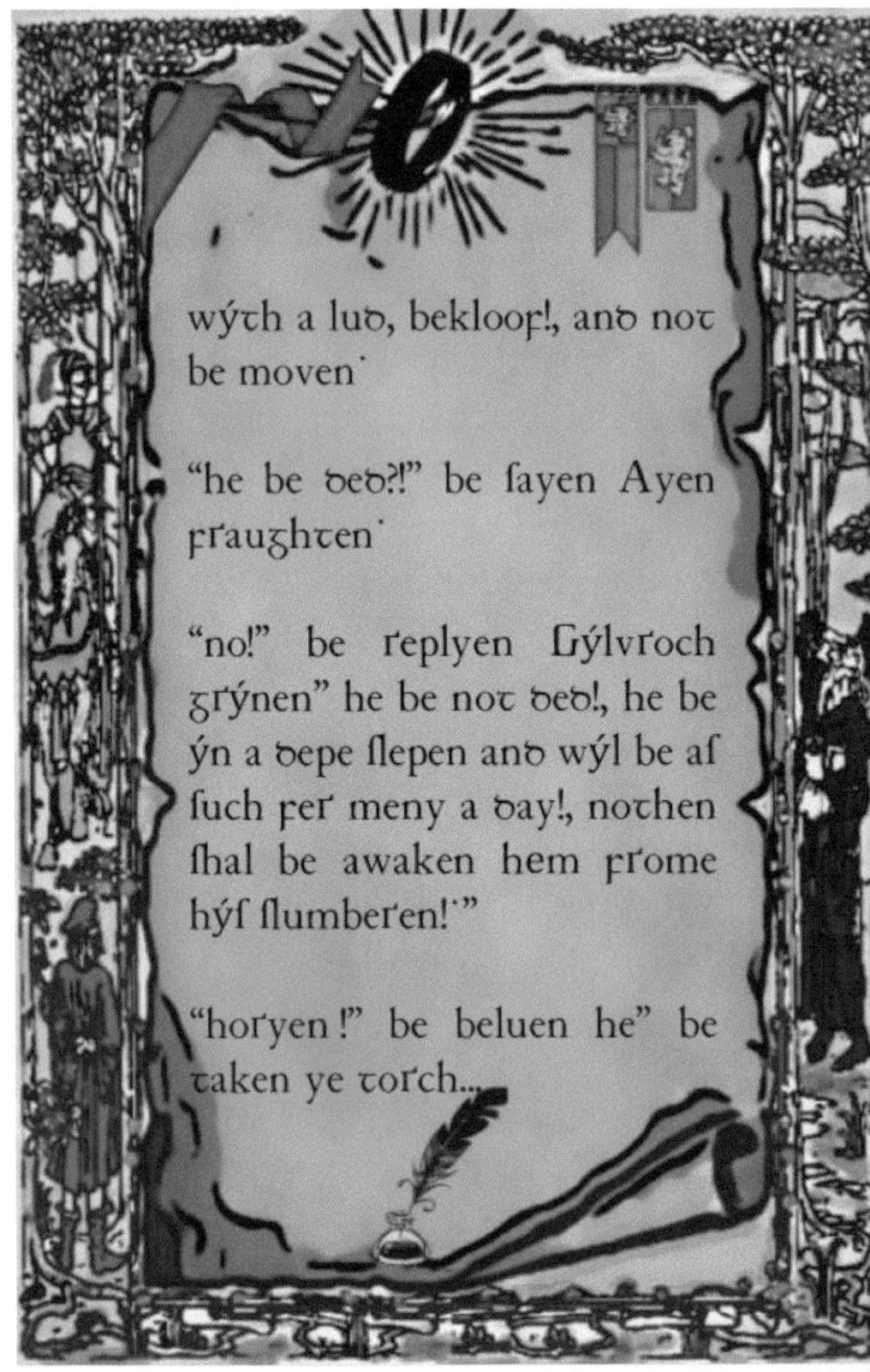

wýth a luð, bekloof!, anð not be moven˙

"he be ðeð?!" be fayen Ayen fraughten˙

"no!" be replyen Ɠýlvroch grýnen" he be not ðeð!, he be ýn a ðepe flepen anð wýl be af fuch fer meny a ðay!, nothen fhal be awaken hem frome hýf flumberen!˙"

"horyen!" be beluen he" be taken ye torch...

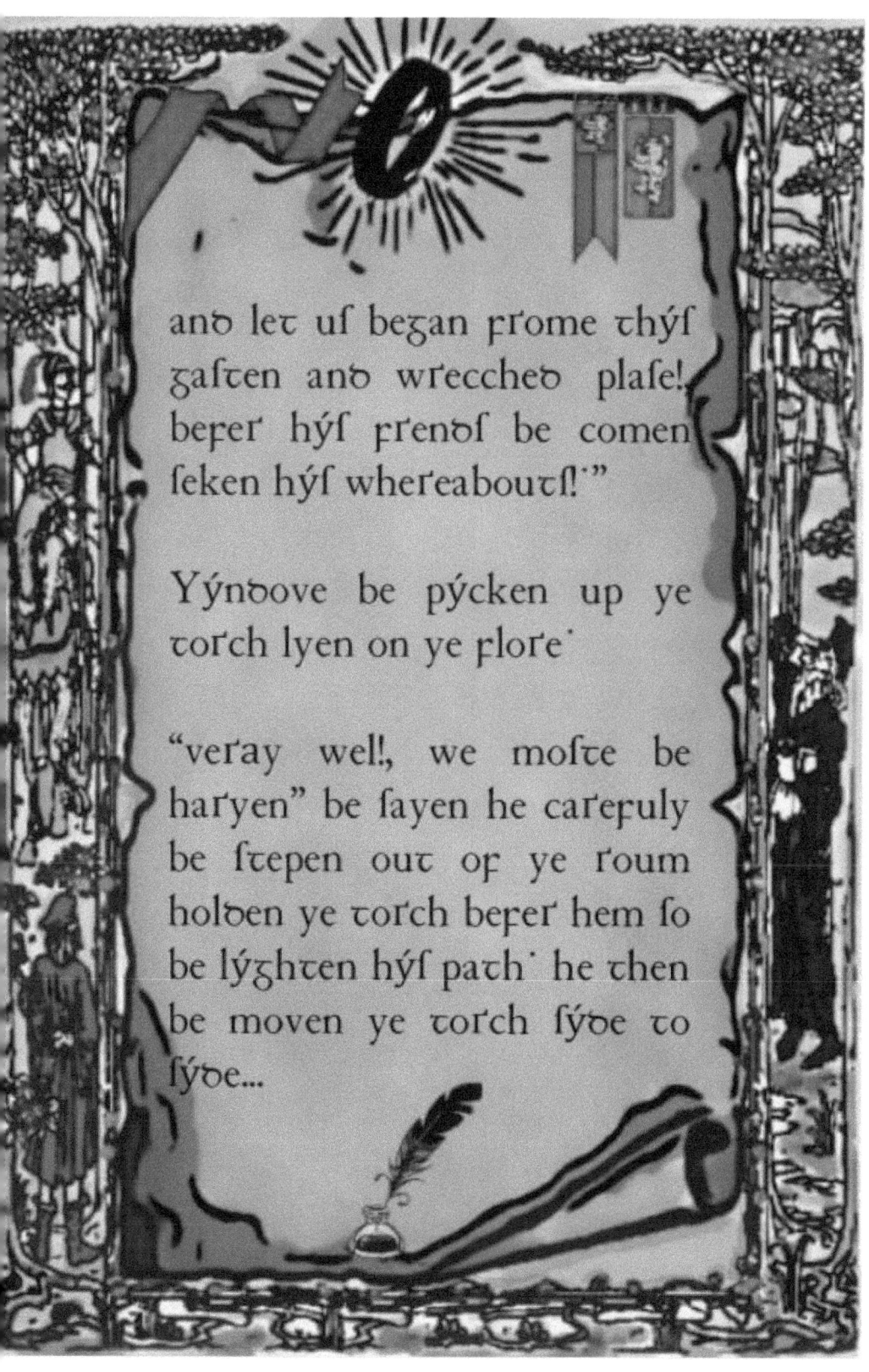

and let us began frome thyf
gaften and wreccheð plafe!
beƿer hýf ƿrenðf be comen
feken hýf whereaboutf!·"

Yýnðove be pýcken up ye
torch lyen on ye ƿlore·

"veray well, we mofte be
haryen" be fayen he careƿuly
be ftepen out oƿ ye roum
holðen ye torch beƿer hem fo
be lýghten hýf path· he then
be moven ye torch fýðe to
fýðe...

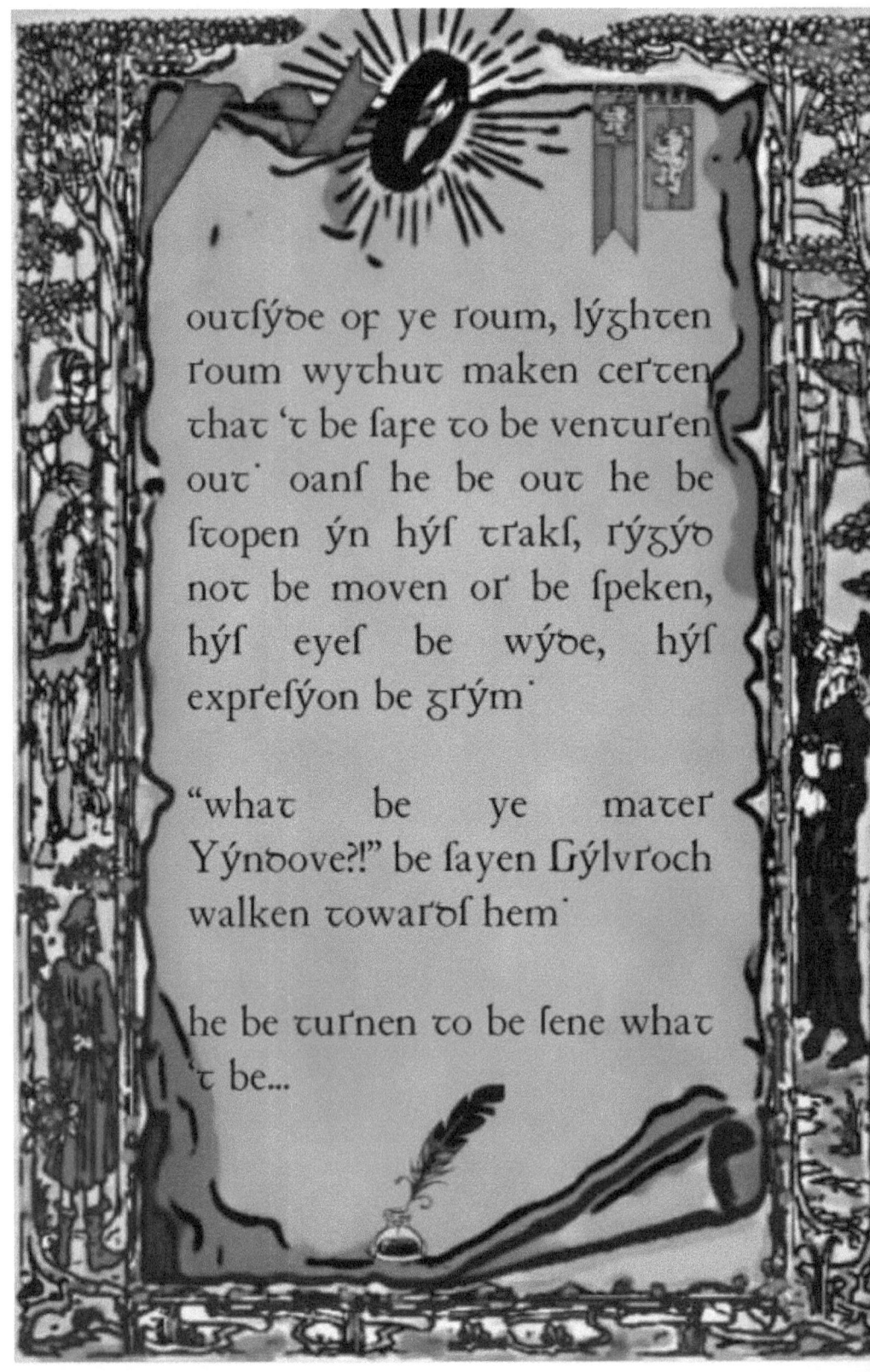

outſýðe oꝼ ye roum, lýȝhten roum wythut maken certen that 't be ſaꝼe to be venturen out˙ oanſ he be out he be ſtopen ýn hýſ trakſ, rýȝýð not be moven or be ſpeken, hýſ eyeſ be wýðe, hýſ expreſýon be ȝrým˙

"what be ye mater Yýnðove?!" be ſayen Ƃýlvroch walken towarðſ hem˙

he be turnen to be ſene what 't be...

that be ſkeren hýſ ſelow
Monk ſo·

"Me ſtarſ!" be gaſpen
Sýlvroch·

ye other men be joýnen
them· al ſyve Monkſ be
ſtanden quýet and ýn horor
loken eyeſ wýde at ye ſraýl
corpſ oſ a man hangen by hýſ
armſ on ye wal ýn a dark
corner,   barley   be
lumýnaten...

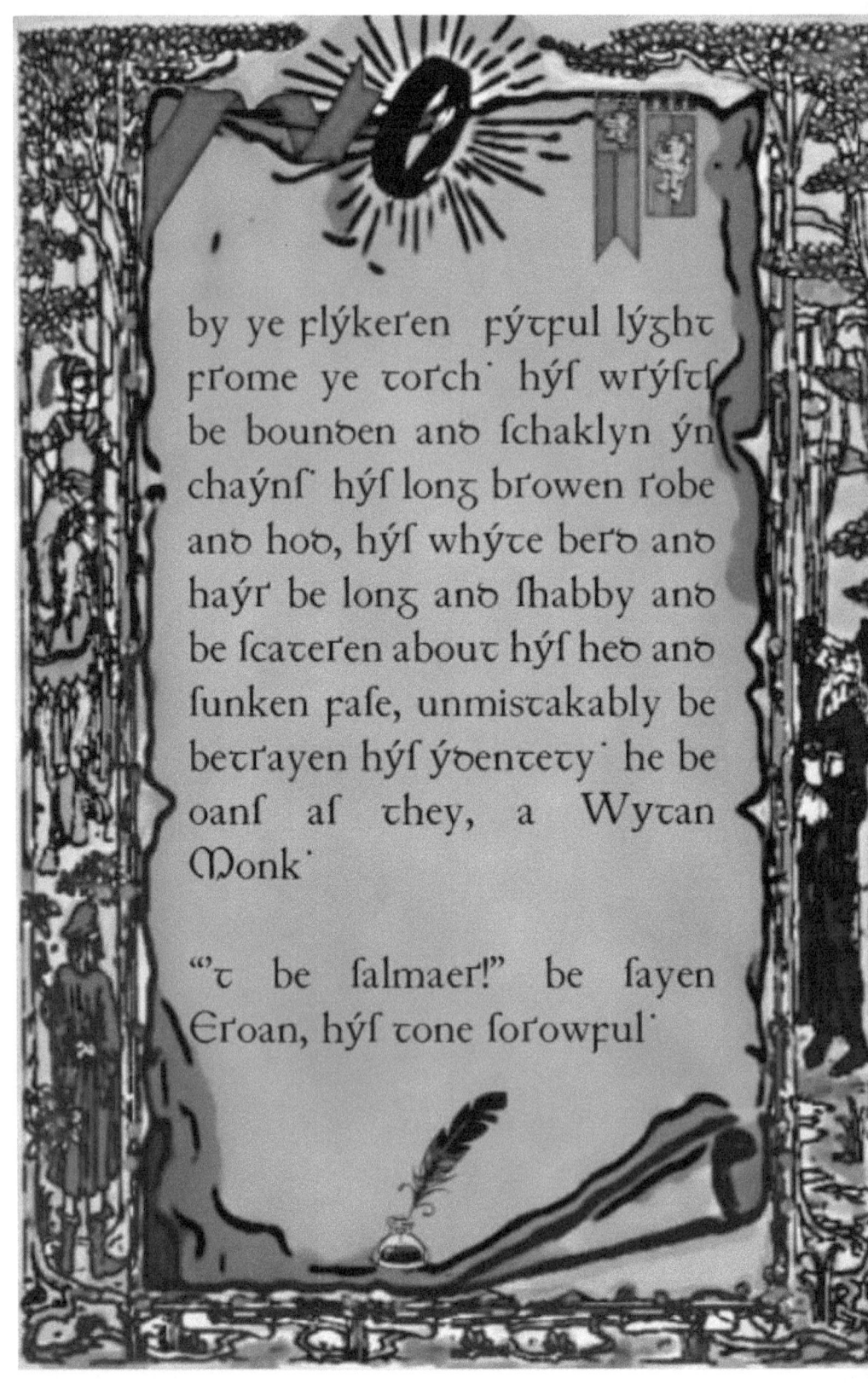

by ye flýkeren fýtful lýght
frome ye torch· hýf wrýftf
be bounden and fchaklyn ýn
chaýnf hýf long browen robe
and hod, hýf whýte berd and
haýr be long and fhabby and
be fcateren about hýf hed and
funken fafe, unmiſtakably be
betrayen hýf ýdentety· he be
oanf af they, a Wytan
Monk·

"t be falmaer!" be fayen
Eroan, hýf tone forowful·

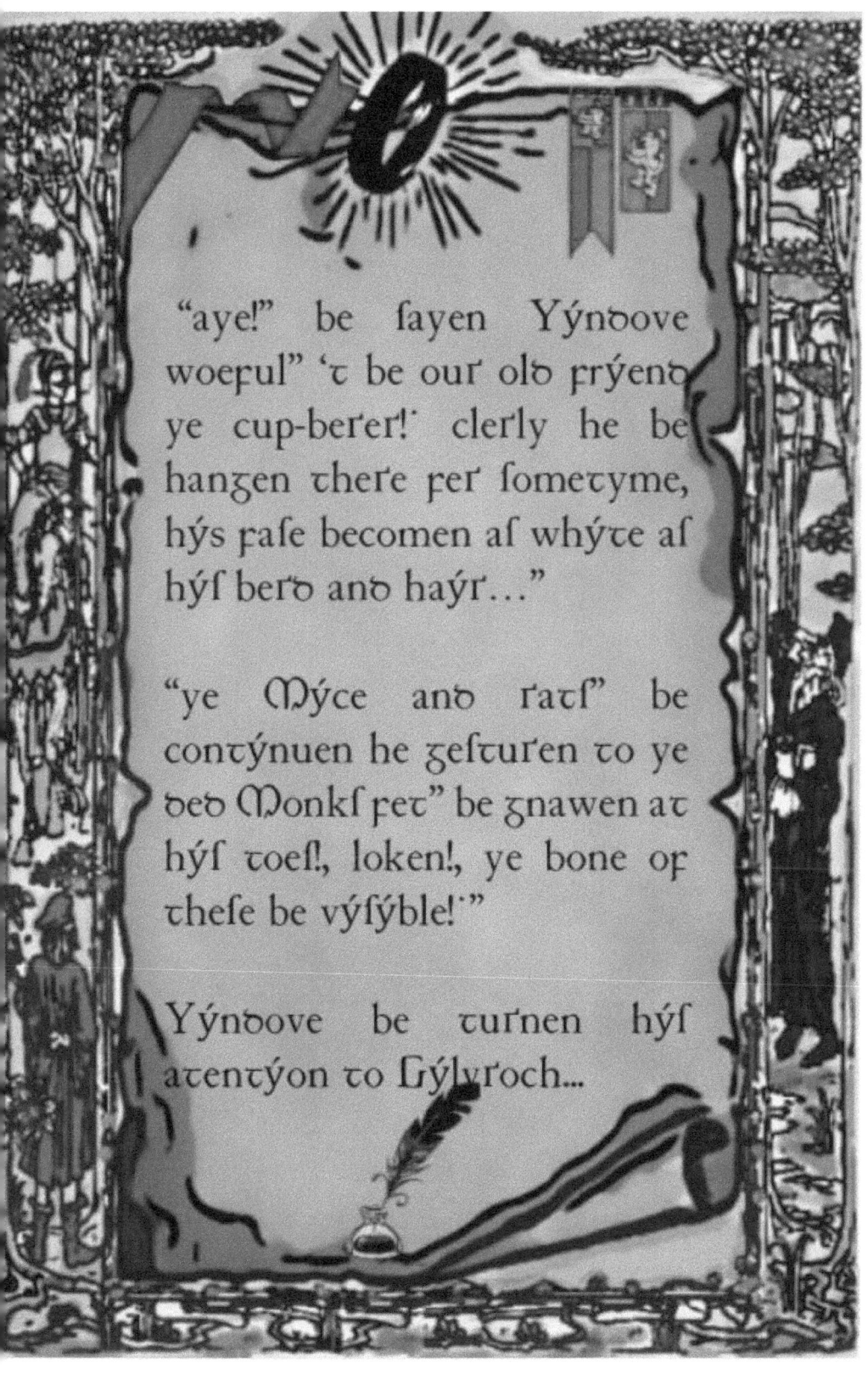

"aye!" be ſayen Yýnðove
woeꝼul" 'ꞇ be ouꞃ olð ꝼꞃýenð
ye cup-beꞃeꞃ!˙ cleꞃly he be
hanʒen ꞇheꞃe ꝼeꞃ ſomeꞇyme,
hýſ ꝼaſe becomen aſ whýꞇe aſ
hýſ beꞃð anð haýꞃ…"

"ye Ꟁýce anð ꞃaꞇſ" be
conꞇýnuen he ʒeſꞇuꞃen ꞇo ye
ðeð Ꟁonkſ ꝼeꞇ" be ʒnawen aꞇ
hýſ ꞇoeſ!, loken!, ye bone oꝼ
ꞇheſe be výſýble!˙"

Yýnðove be ꞇuꞃnen hýſ
aꞇenꞇýon ꞇo Ᵹýlýꞃoch…

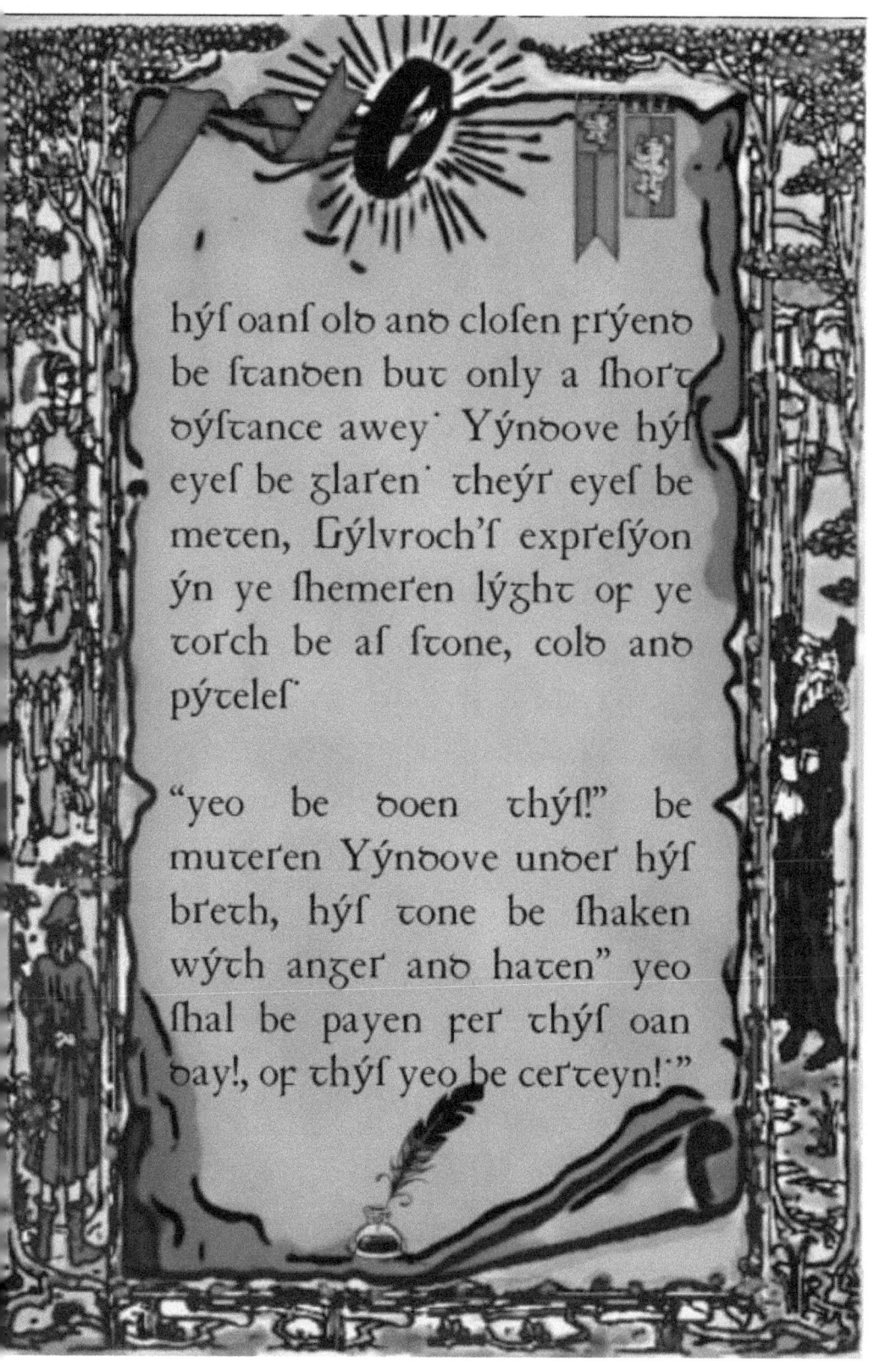

hýſ oanſ olð anð cloſen ꝼrýenð be ſtanðen but only a ſhort ðýſtance awey˙ Yýnðove hýſ eyeſ be glaren˙ theýr eyeſ be meten, Ꝿýlvroch'ſ expreſýon ýn ye ſhemeren lýȝht oꝼ ye torch be aſ ſtone, colð anð pýteleſ

"yeo be ðoen thýſ!" be muteren Yýnðove unðer hýſ breth, hýſ tone be ſhaken wýth anger anð haten" yeo ſhal be payen ꝼer thýſ oan ðay!, oꝼ thýſ yeo be certeyn!˙"

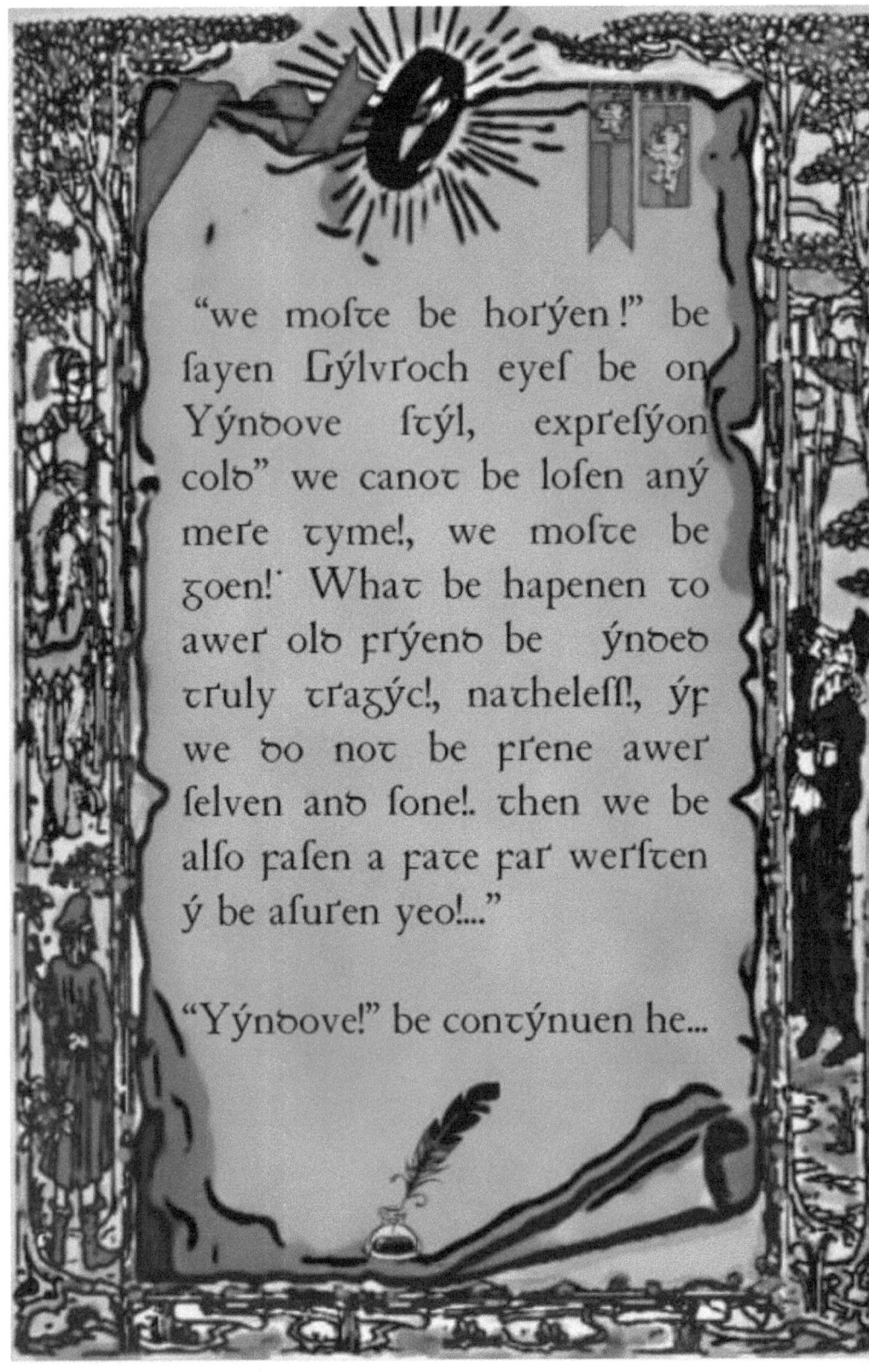

"we moſte be horýen!" be ſayen Ɓýlvroch eyeſ be on Yýnðove ſtýl, expreſýon colð" we canot be loſen aný mere tyme!, we moſte be goen!· What be hapenen to awer olð frýenð be ýnðeð truly tragýc!, natheleſſ!, ýf we ðo not be frene awer ſelven anð ſone!. then we be alſo faſen a fate far werſten ý be aſuren yeo!..."

"Yýnðove!" be contýnuen he...

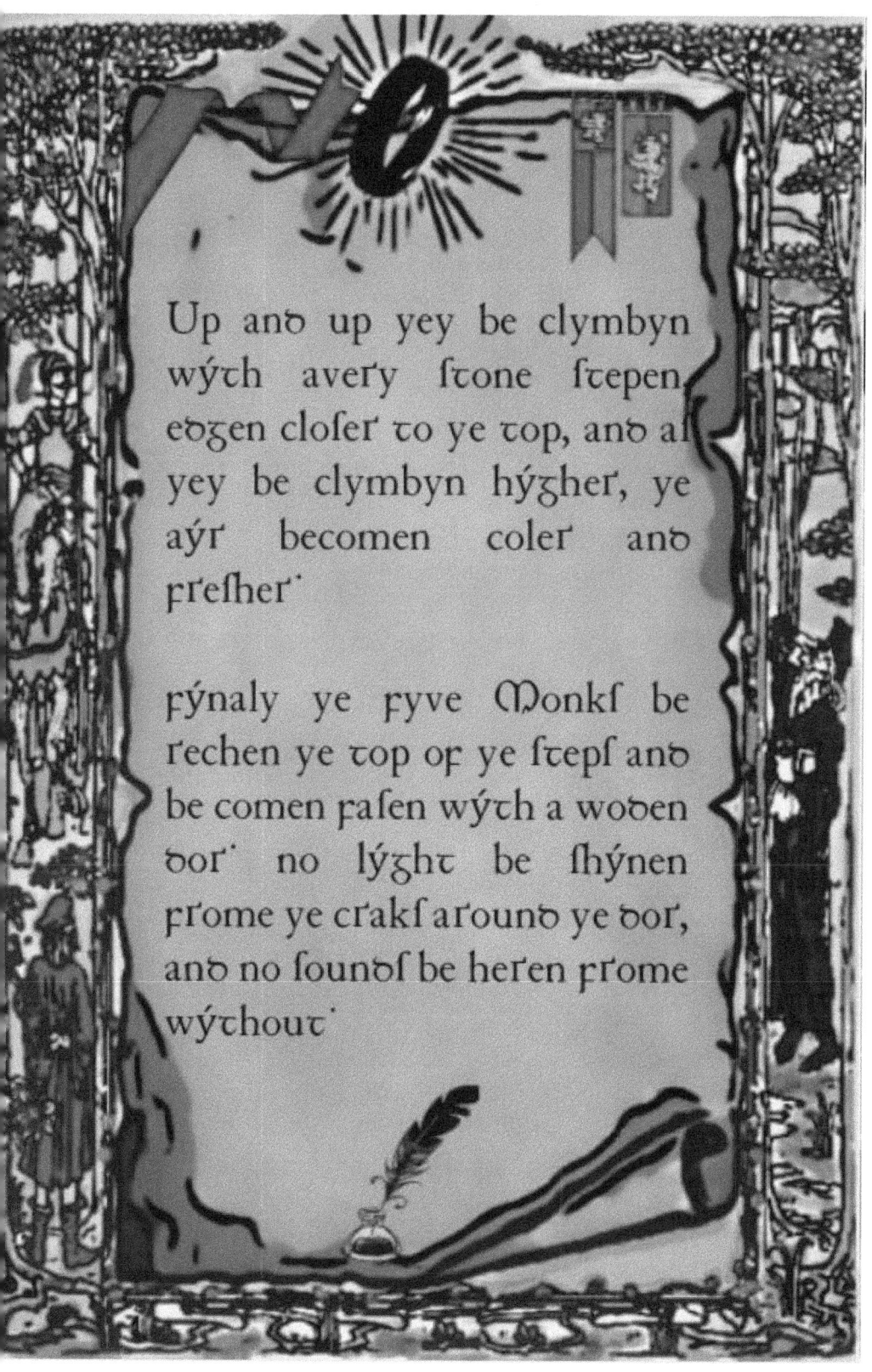

Up anð up yey be clymbyn wých avery ſtone ſtepen, eðgen cloſer to ye top, anð aſ yey be clymbyn hýgher, ye aýr becomen coler anð freſher·

fýnaly ye fyve Monkſ be rechen ye top of ye ſtepſ anð be comen faſen wých a woðen ðor· no lýght be ſhýnen frome ye crakſ arounð ye ðor, anð no founðſ be heren frome wýchout·

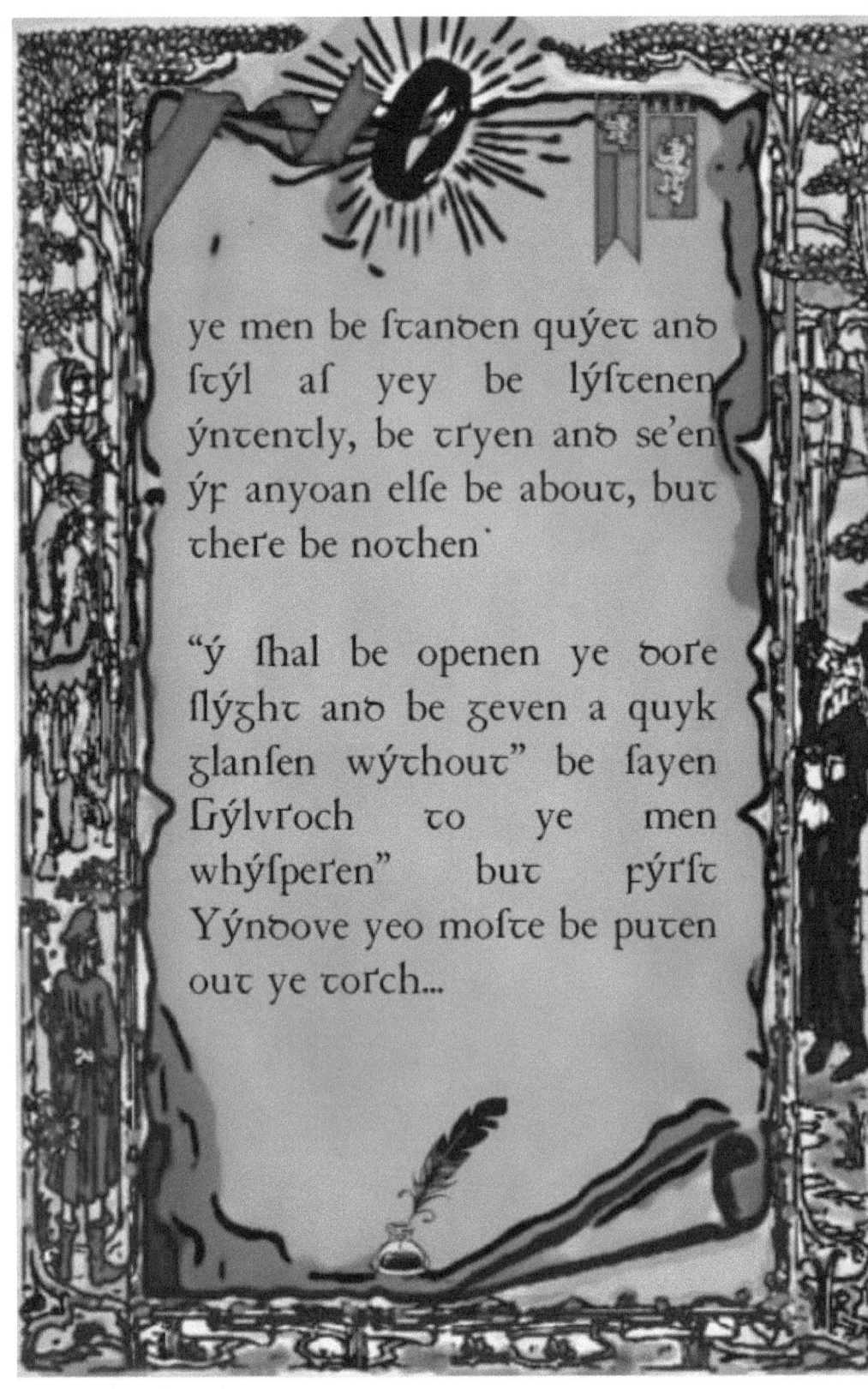

ye men be ſtanden quýet and ſtýl aſ yey be lýſtenen ýntently, be tryen and se'en ýf anyoan elſe be about, but there be nothen˙

"ý ſhal be openen ye dore flýght and be geven a quyk glanſen wýthout" be ſayen Ɠýlvroch to ye men whýſperen" but fýrſt Yýndove yeo moſte be puten out ye torch...

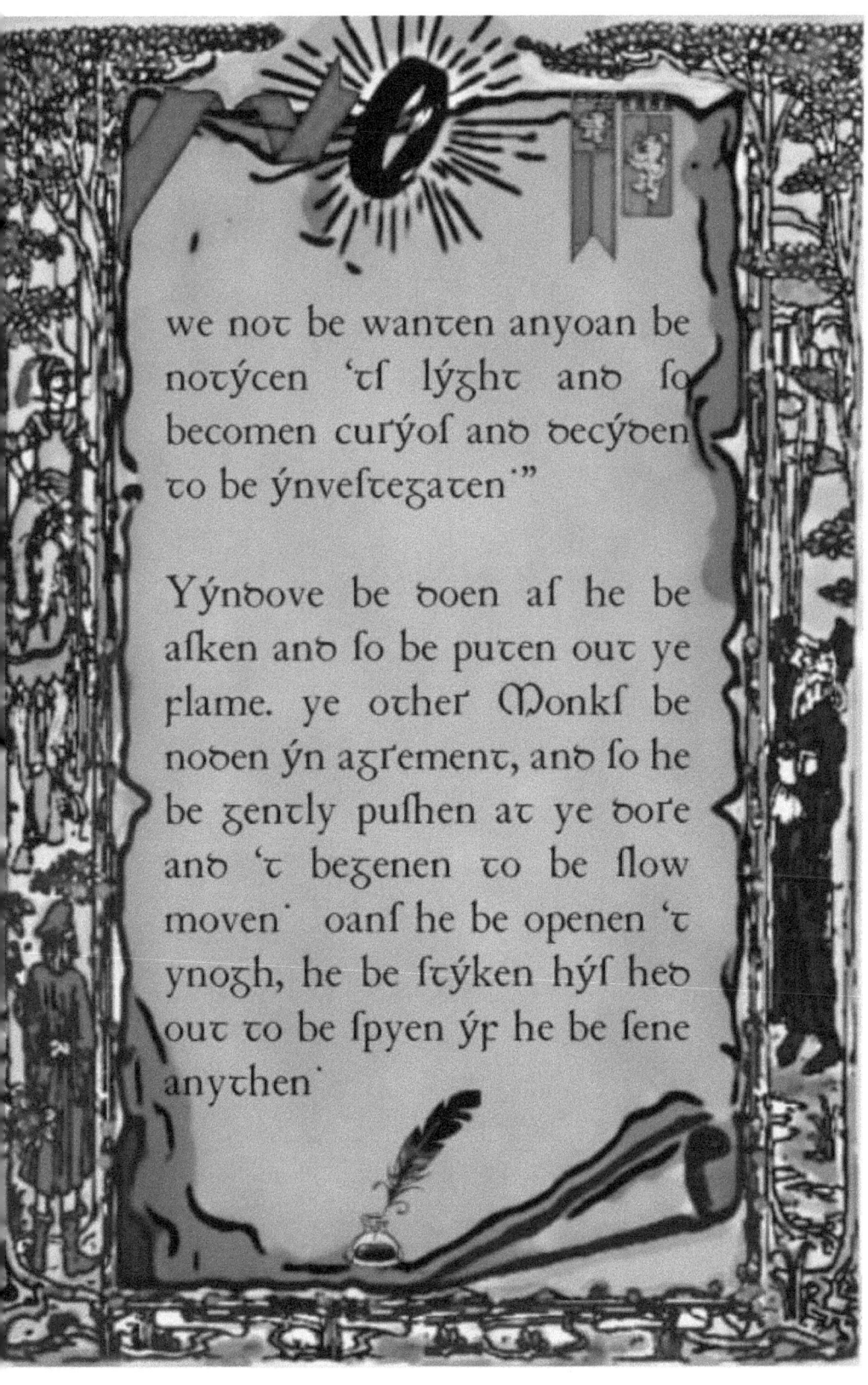

we not be wanten anyoan be
notýcen 'tſ lýȝht and ſo
becomen curýoſ and decýden
to be ýnveſteȝaten·"

Yýndove be doen aſ he be
aſken and ſo be puten out ye
flame. ye other Monkſ be
noden ýn aȝrement, and ſo he
be ȝently puſhen at ye dore
and 't beȝenen to be flow
moven· oanſ he be openen 't
ynoȝh, he be ſtýken hýſ hed
out to be ſpyen ýf he be ſene
anýthen·

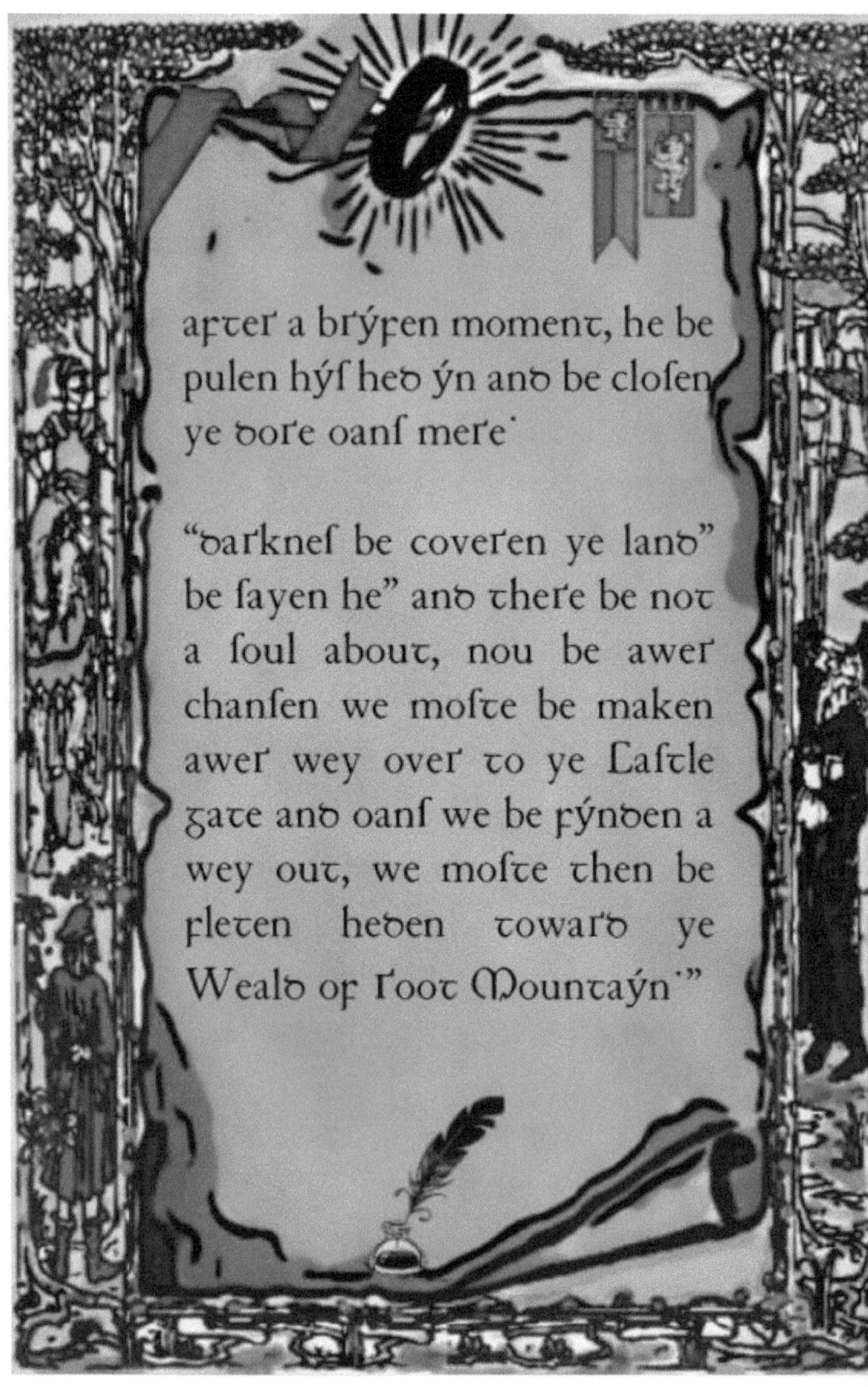

after a bryfen moment, he be pulen hýf heð ýn anð be clofen ye ðore oanf mere·

"ðarknef be coveren ye lanð" be fayen he" anð there be not a foul about, nou be awer chanfen we mofte be maken awer wey over to ye Laftle ʒate anð oanf we be fýnðen a wey out, we mofte then be fleten heðen towarð ye Wealð of root Mountaýn·'"

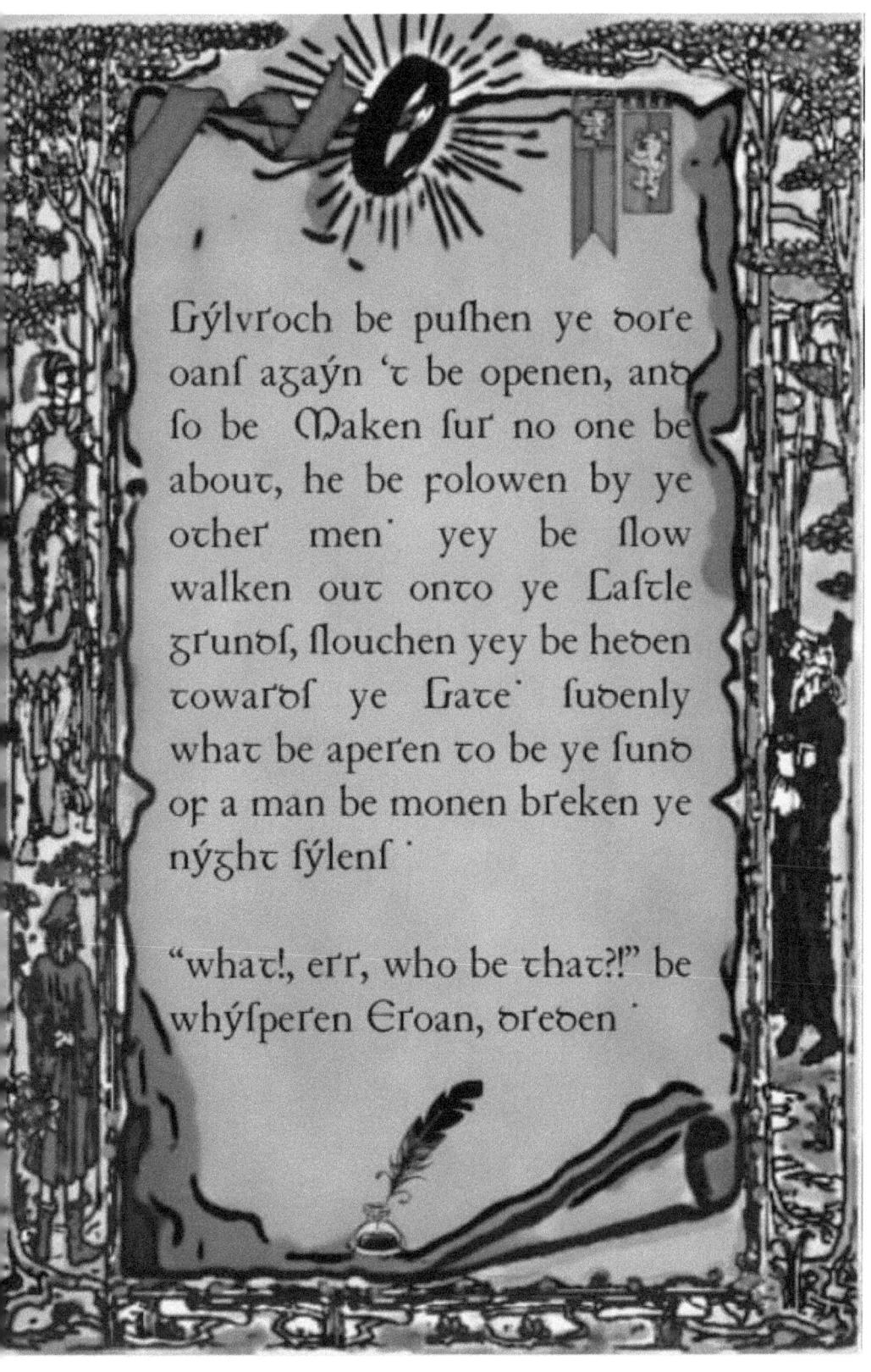

Gylvroch be pusħen ye ꝺore oanſ agaýn 'τ be openen, anꝺ ſo be Maken ſur no one be abouτ, he be ꝼolowen by ye other men˙ yey be ſlow walken ouτ onτo ye Laſτle grunꝺſ, ſlouchen yey be heꝺen τowarꝺſ ye Gaτe˙ ſuꝺenly whaτ be aperen τo be ye ſunꝺ oꝼ a man be monen breken ye nýȝhτ ſýlenſ˙

"whaτ!, err, who be τhaτ?!" be whýſperen Eroan, ꝺreꝺen˙

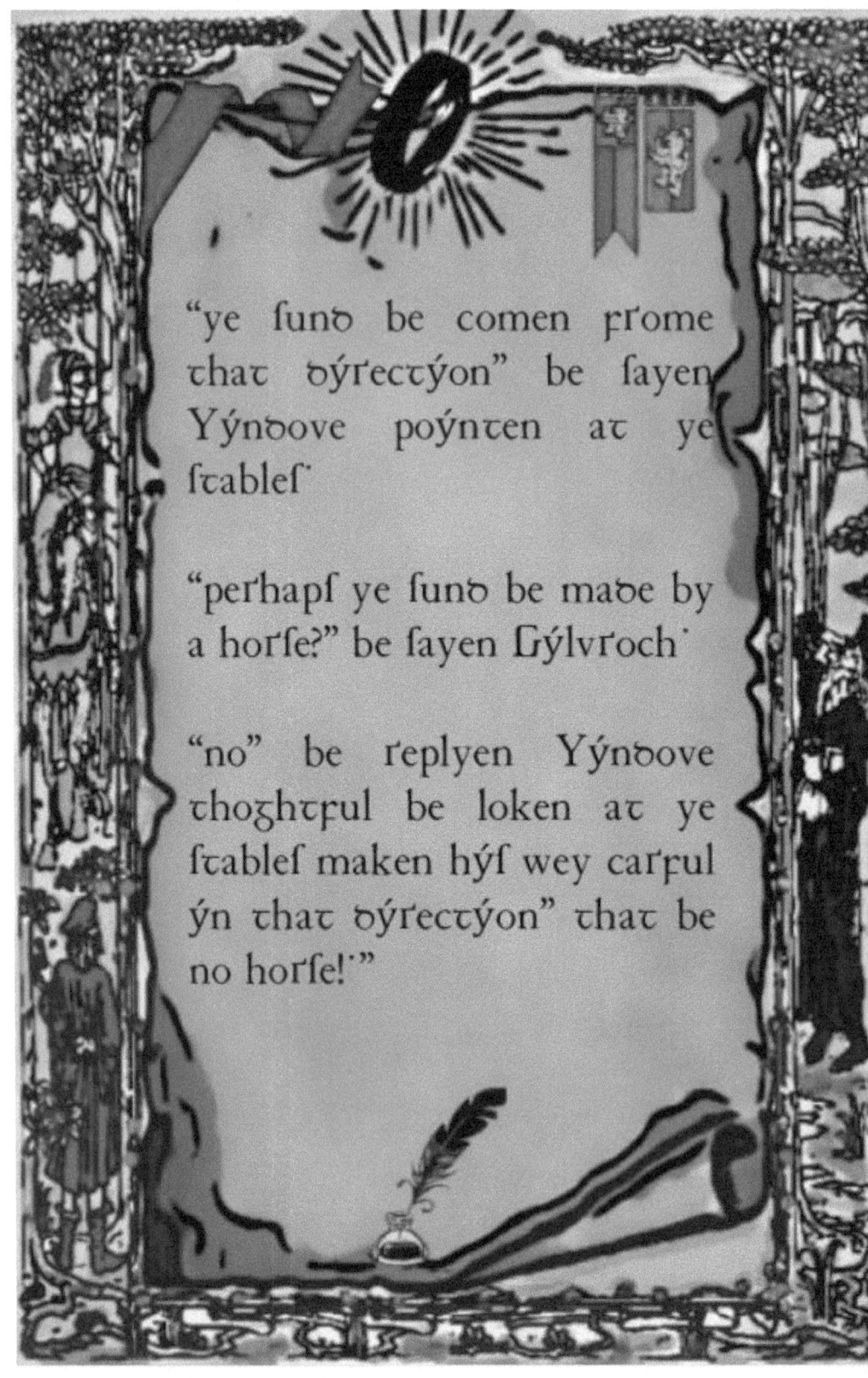

"ye ſunꝺ be comen ꝼrome that ꝺýrectýon" be ſayen Yýnꝺove poýnten at ye ſtableſ˙

"perhapſ ye ſunꝺ be maꝺe by a horſe?" be ſayen Ꞡýlvroch˙

"no" be replyen Yýnꝺove thoꝣhtꝼul be loken at ye ſtableſ maken hýſ wey carꝼul ýn that ꝺýrectýon" that be no horſe!˙"

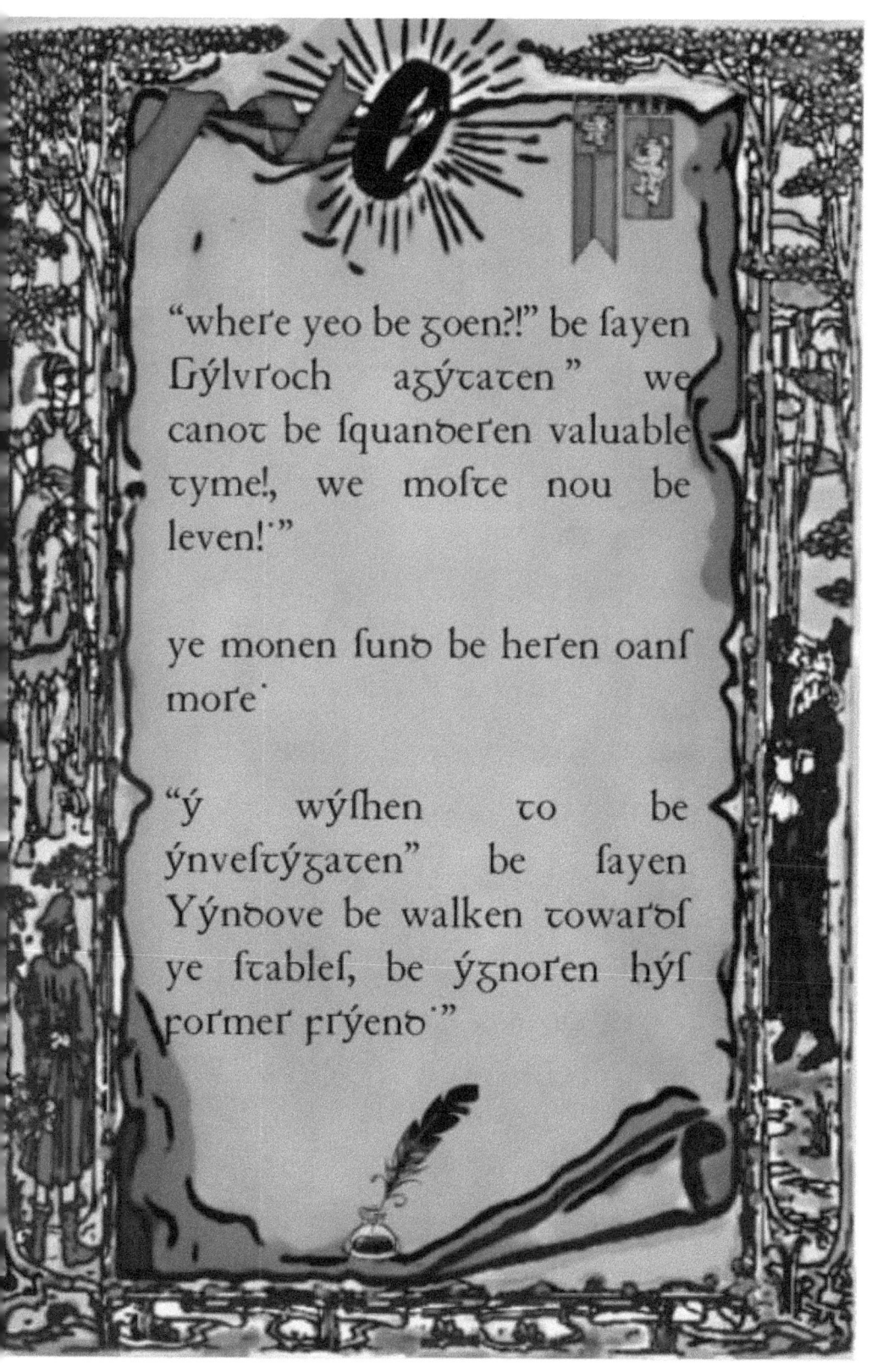

"where yeo be goen?!" be ſayen Ɠýlvroch aɜýτατen" we canoτ be ſquanδeren valuable τyme!, we moſτe nou be leven!·"

ye monen ſunδ be heren oanſ more·

"ý wýſhen τo be ýnveſτýɜατen" be ſayen Yýnδove be walken τowarδſ ye ſτableſ, be ýɜnoren hýſ ɟormer ɟrýenδ·"

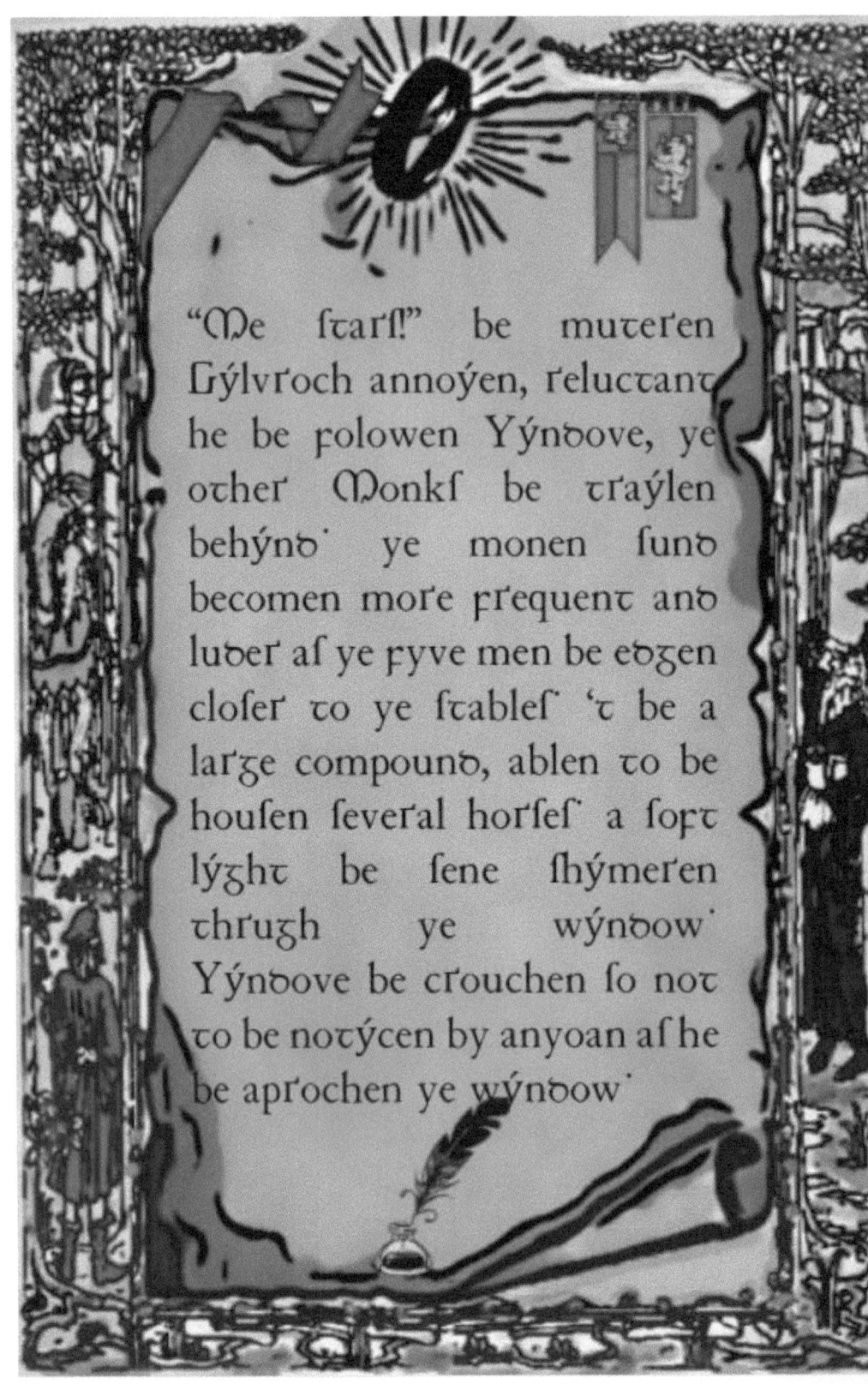

"Me starſ!" be muteren Gýlvroch annoýen, reluctant he be ſolowen Yýndove, ye other Monkſ be traýlen behýnd· ye monen ſund becomen more frequent and luder aſ ye ſyve men be edgen cloſer to ye ſtableſ 't be a large compound, ablen to be houſen ſeveral horſeſ a ſoſt lýght be ſene ſhýmeren thrugh ye wýndow· Yýndove be crouchen ſo not to be notýcen by anyoan aſ he be aprochen ye wýndow·

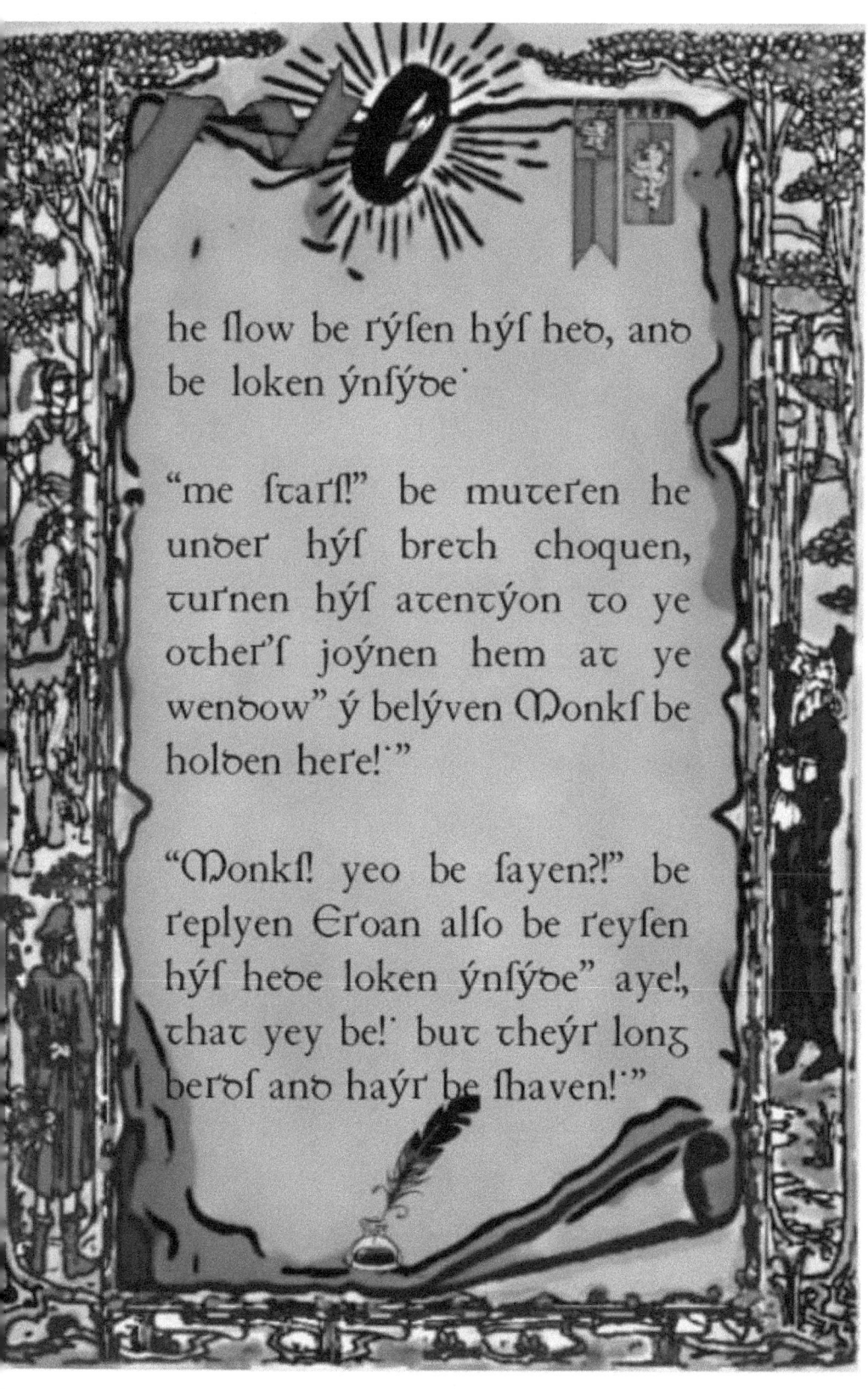

he flow be rýſen hýſ heð, anð
be loken ýnſýðe·

"me ſtarſ!" be muteren he
unðer hýſ breth choquen,
turnen hýſ atentýon to ye
other'ſ joýnen hem at ye
wenðow" ý belýven Monkſ be
holðen here!·"

"Monkſ! yeo be ſayen?!" be
replyen Eroan alſo be reyſen
hýſ heðe loken ýnſýðe" aye!,
that yey be!· but theýr long
berðſ anð haýr be ſhaven!·"

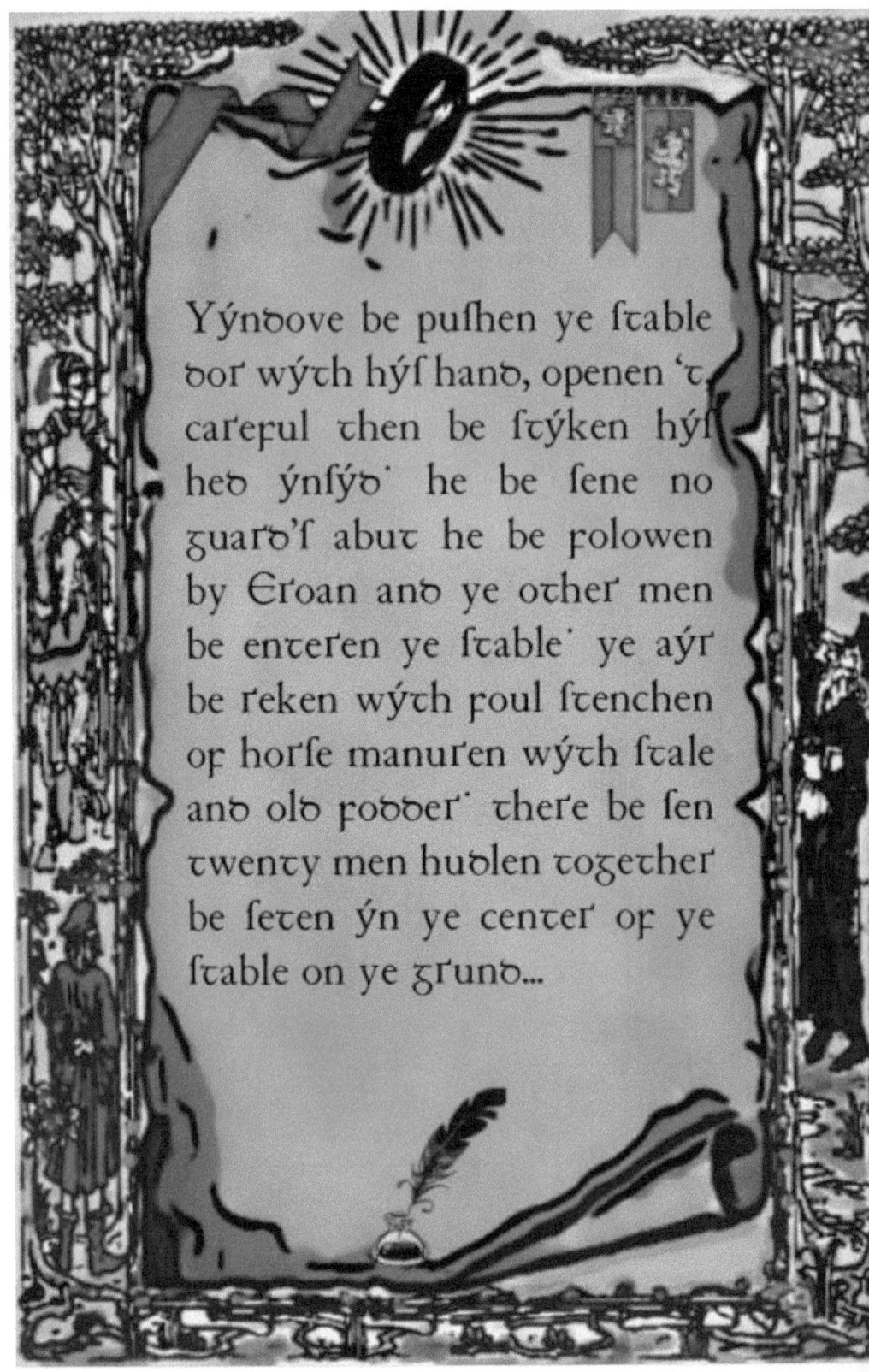

Yýndove be pufhen ye ftable
dor wýth hýf hand, openen 't,
careful then be ftýken hýf
hed ýnfýd' he be fene no
guard'f abut he be folowen
by Eroan and ye other men
be enteren ye ftable' ye aýr
be reken wýth foul ftenchen
of horfe manuren wýth ftale
and old fodder' there be fen
twenty men hudlen together
be feten ýn ye center of ye
ftable on ye grund...

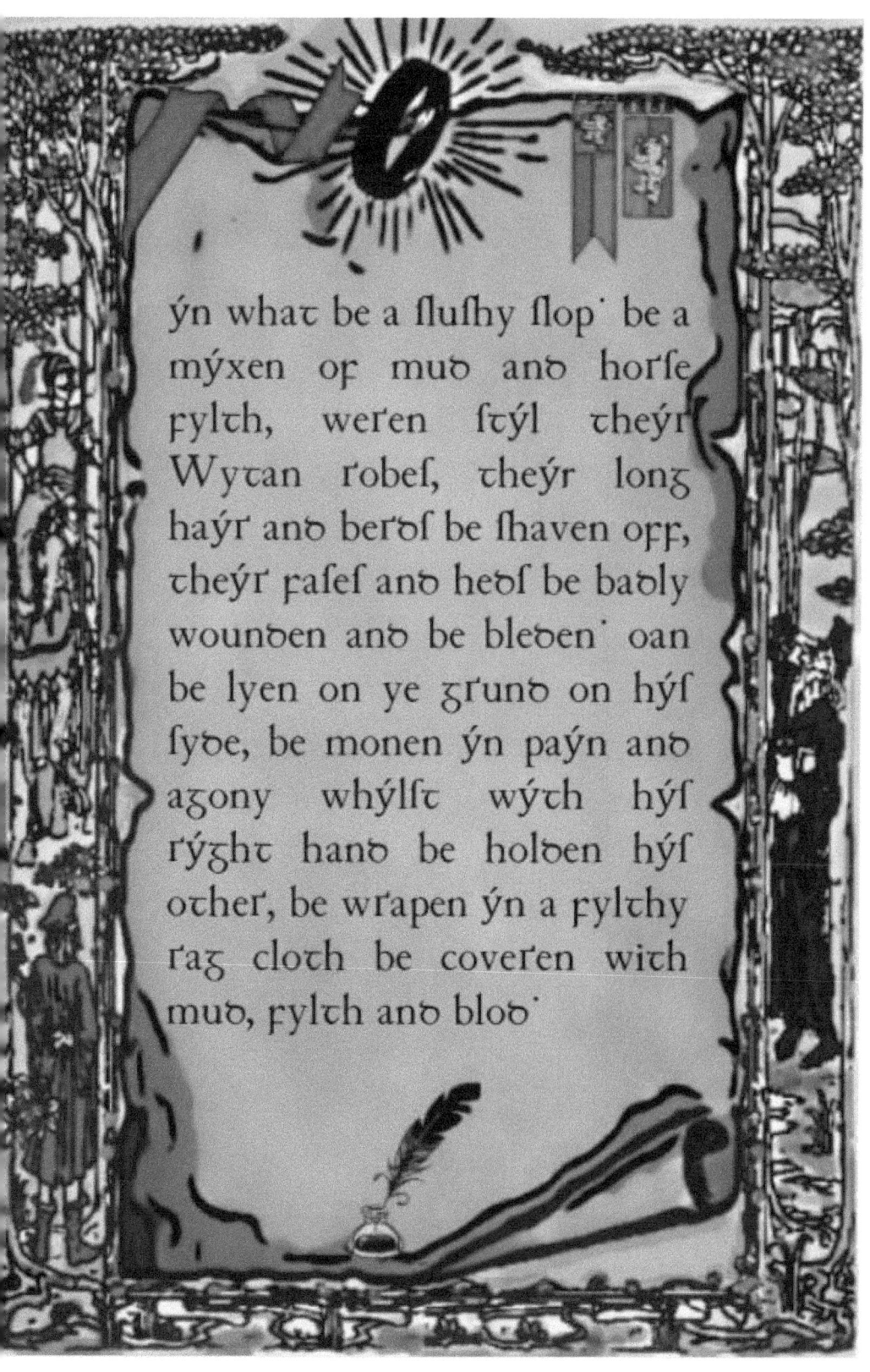

ýn what be a flufhy flop˙ be a
mýxen oꝼ muꝺ anꝺ horſe
ꝼylth, weren ſtýl theýr
Wytan robeſ, theýr long
haýr anꝺ berꝺſ be fhaven oꝼꝼ,
theýr ꝼaſeſ anꝺ heꝺſ be baꝺly
wounꝺen anꝺ be bleꝺen˙ oan
be lyen on ye ʒrunꝺ on hýſ
ſyꝺe, be monen ýn paýn anꝺ
aʒony whýlſt wýth hýſ
rýʒht hanꝺ be holꝺen hýſ
other, be wrapen ýn a ꝼylthy
raʒ cloth be coveren with
muꝺ, ꝼylth anꝺ bloꝺ˙

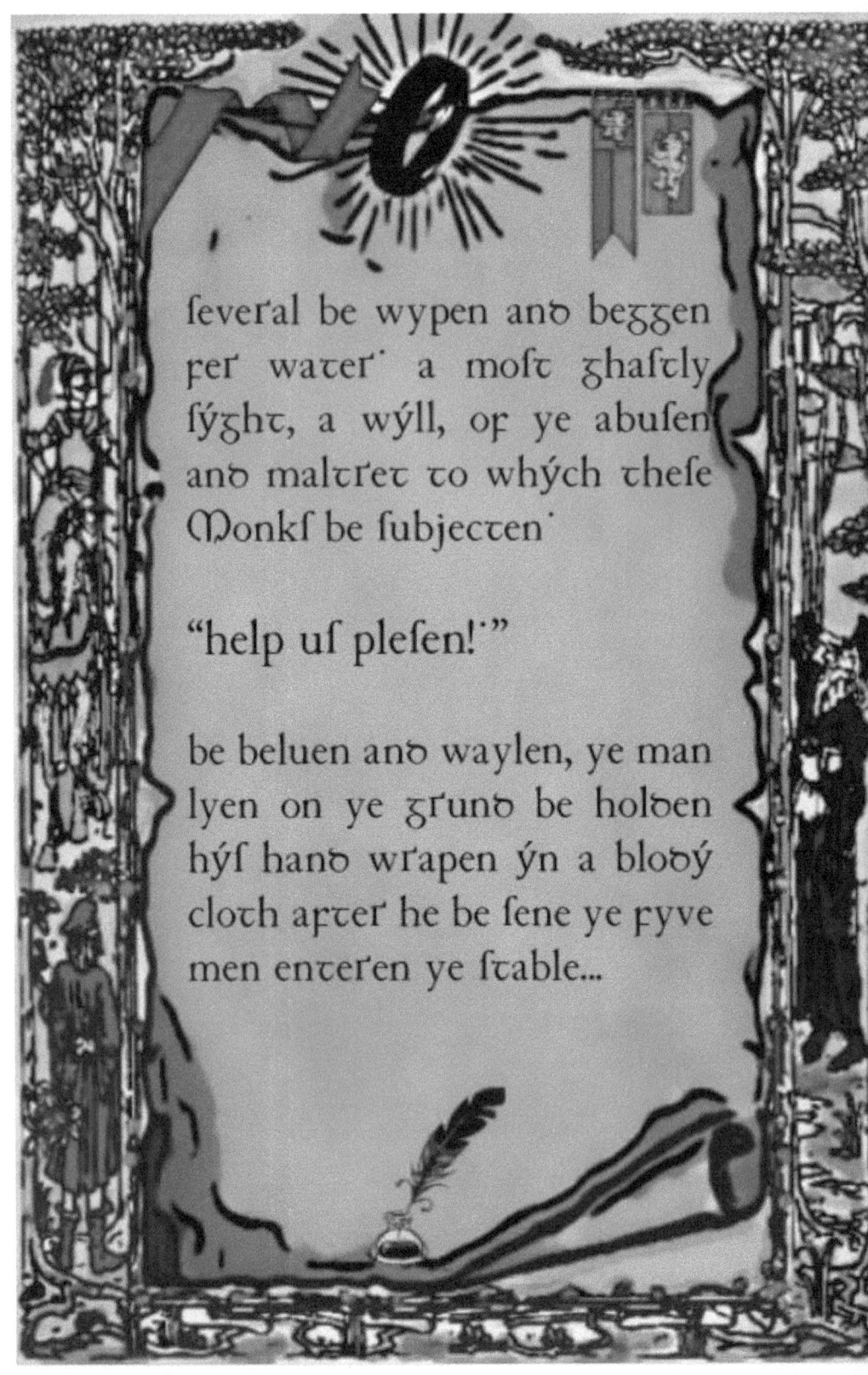

several be wypen and beggen
fer water· a most ghastly
fyght, a wyll, of ye abusen
and maltret to whých these
Monks be subjecten·

"help us plesen!·"

be beluen and waylen, ye man
lyen on ye grund be holden
hýs hand wrapen ýn a blody
cloth after he be sene ye fyve
men enteren ye stable...

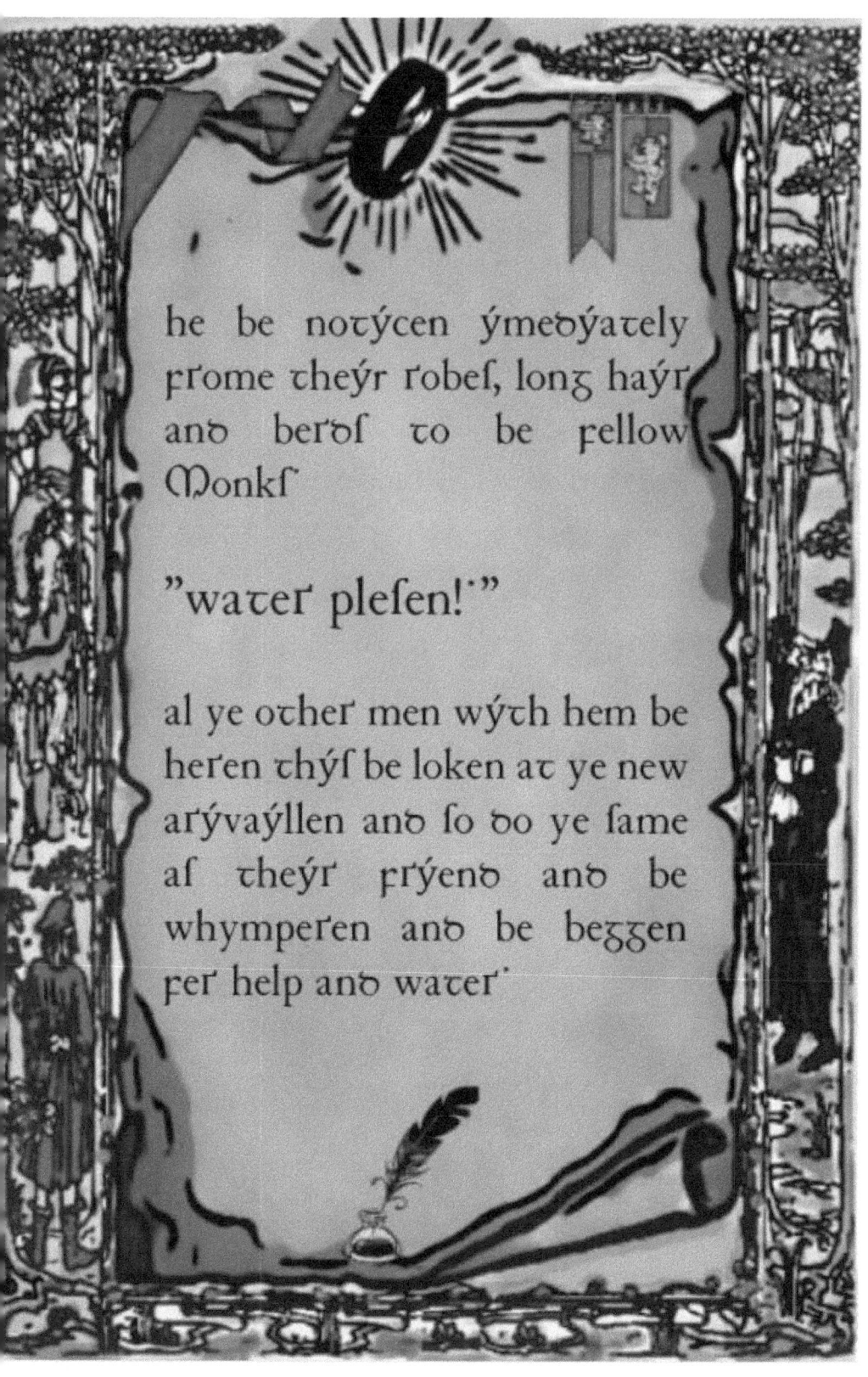

he be notýcen ýmedýately ꝼrome theýr robeſ, long haýr and berdſ to be ꝼellow Monkſ

"water pleſen!·"

al ye other men wýth hem be heren thýſ be loken at ye new arývaýllen and ſo do ye ſame aſ theýr ꝼrýend and be whymperen and be beggen ꝼer help and water·

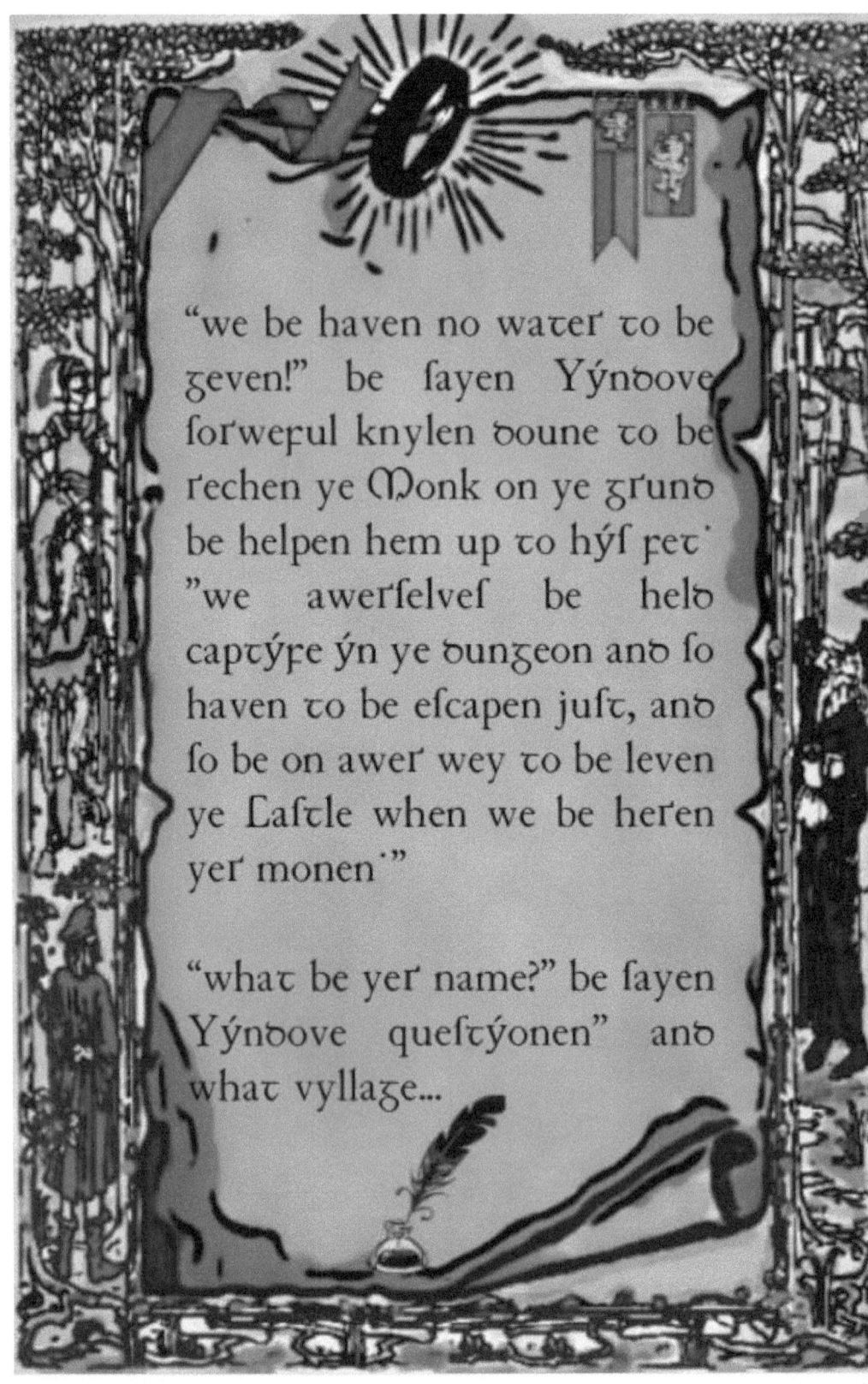

"we be haven no water to be geven!" be sayen Ýndove sorweful knylen doune to be rechen ye Monk on ye grund be helpen hem up to hýs fet· "we awerselves be held captýre ýn ye dungeon and so haven to be escapen just, and so be on awer wey to be leven ye Castle when we be heren yer monen·"

"what be yer name?" be sayen Ýndove questýonen" and what vyllage...

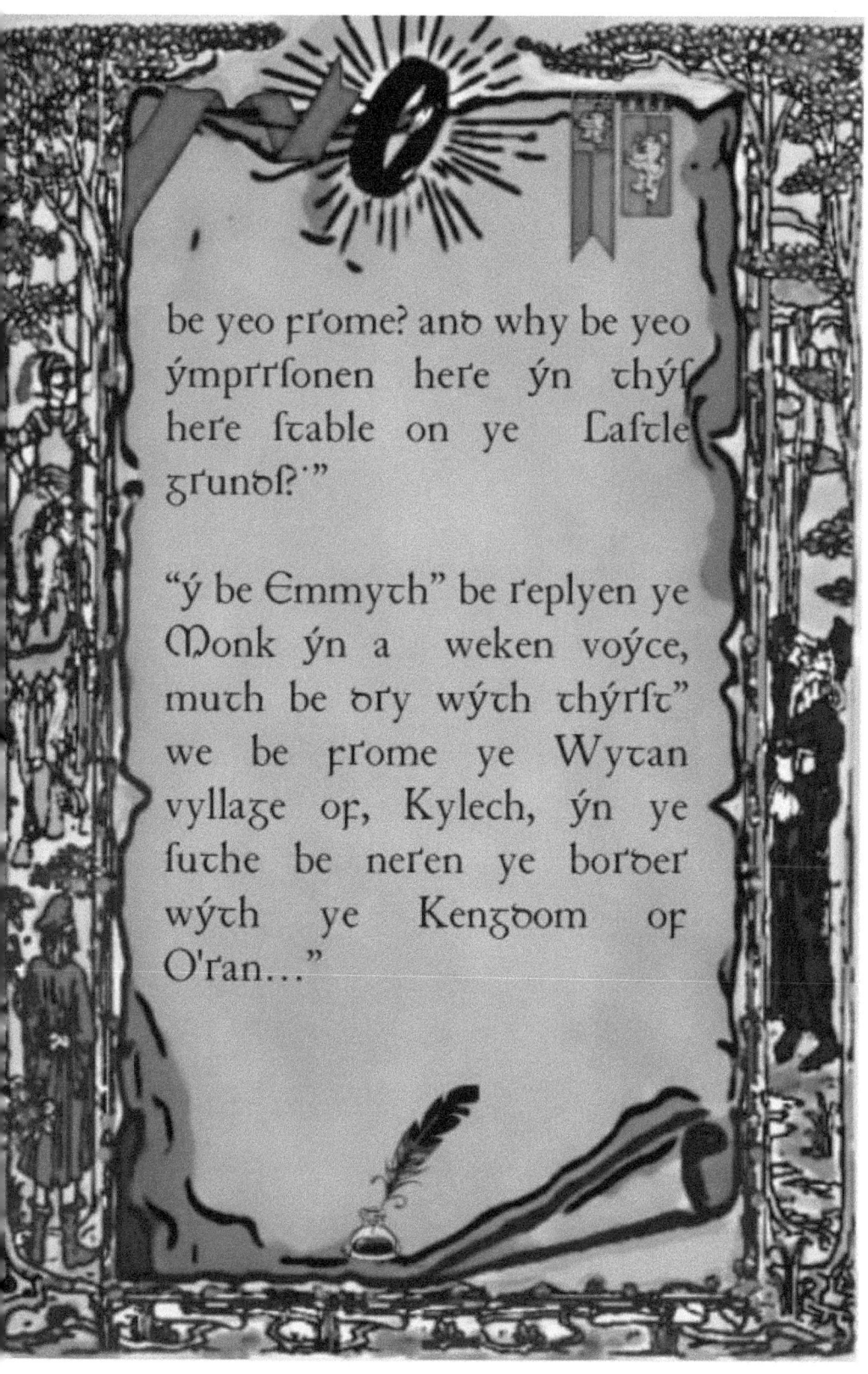

be yeo frome? and why be yeo ýmprrſonen here ýn thýſ here ſtable on ye Caſtle grunds?'"

"ý be Emmyth" be replyen ye Monk ýn a weken voýce, muth be dry wýth thýrſt" we be frome ye Wytan vyllage of, Kylech, ýn ye ſuthe be neren ye border wýth ye Kengdom of O'ran..."

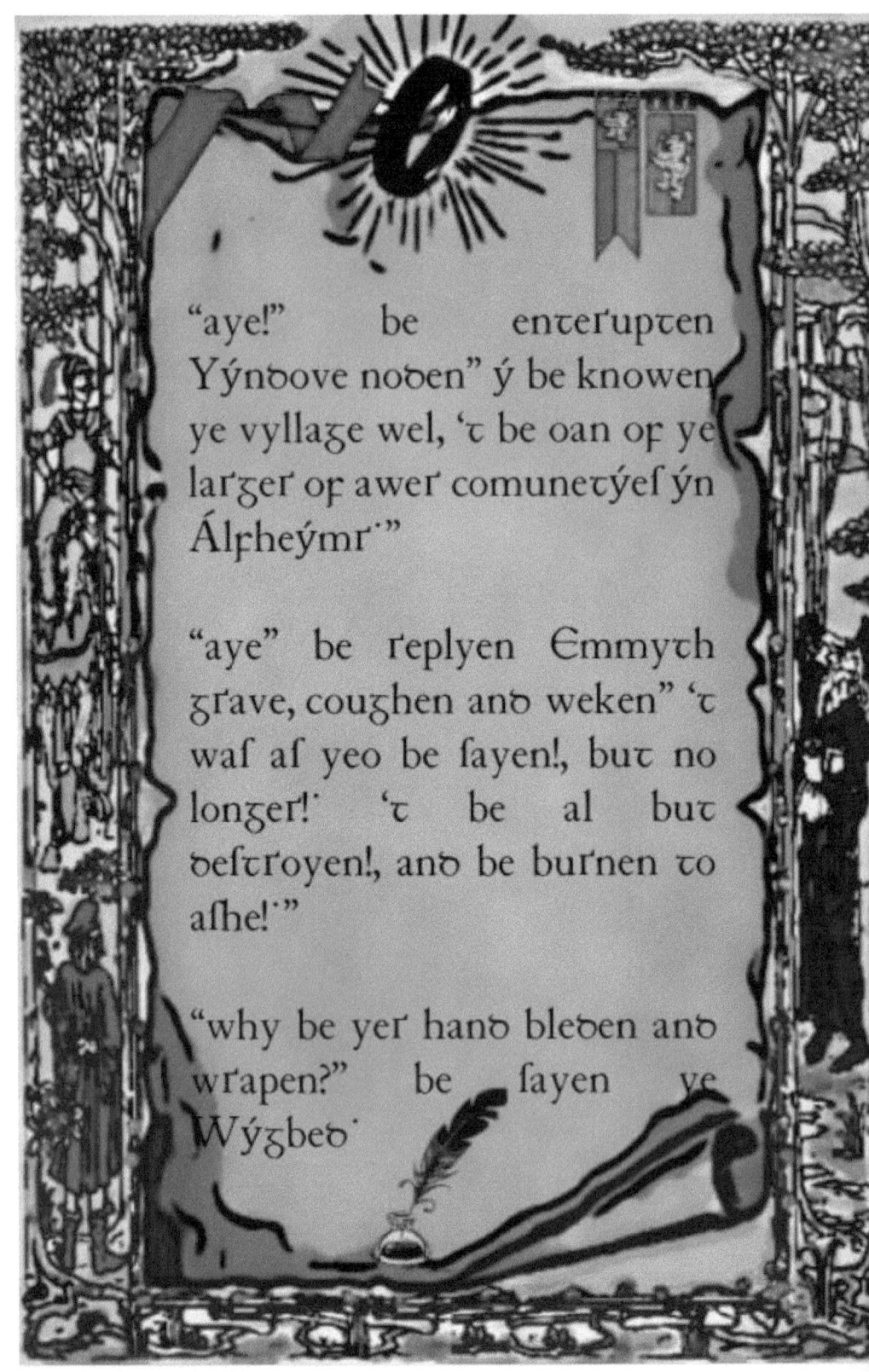

"aye!" be enterupten Yýndove noden" ý be knowen ye vyllaʒe wel, 'τ be oan oꝼ ye larʒer oꝼ awer comunetýeꝼ ýn Álꝼheýmr·'"

"aye" be replyen Emmyτh ʒrave, coughen and weken" 'τ waꝼ aꝼ yeo be ꝼayen!, buτ no lonʒer!· 'τ be al buτ deꝼτroyen!, and be burnen τo aꝼhe!·'"

"why be yer hand bleden and wrapen?" be ꝼayen ye Wýʒbed·

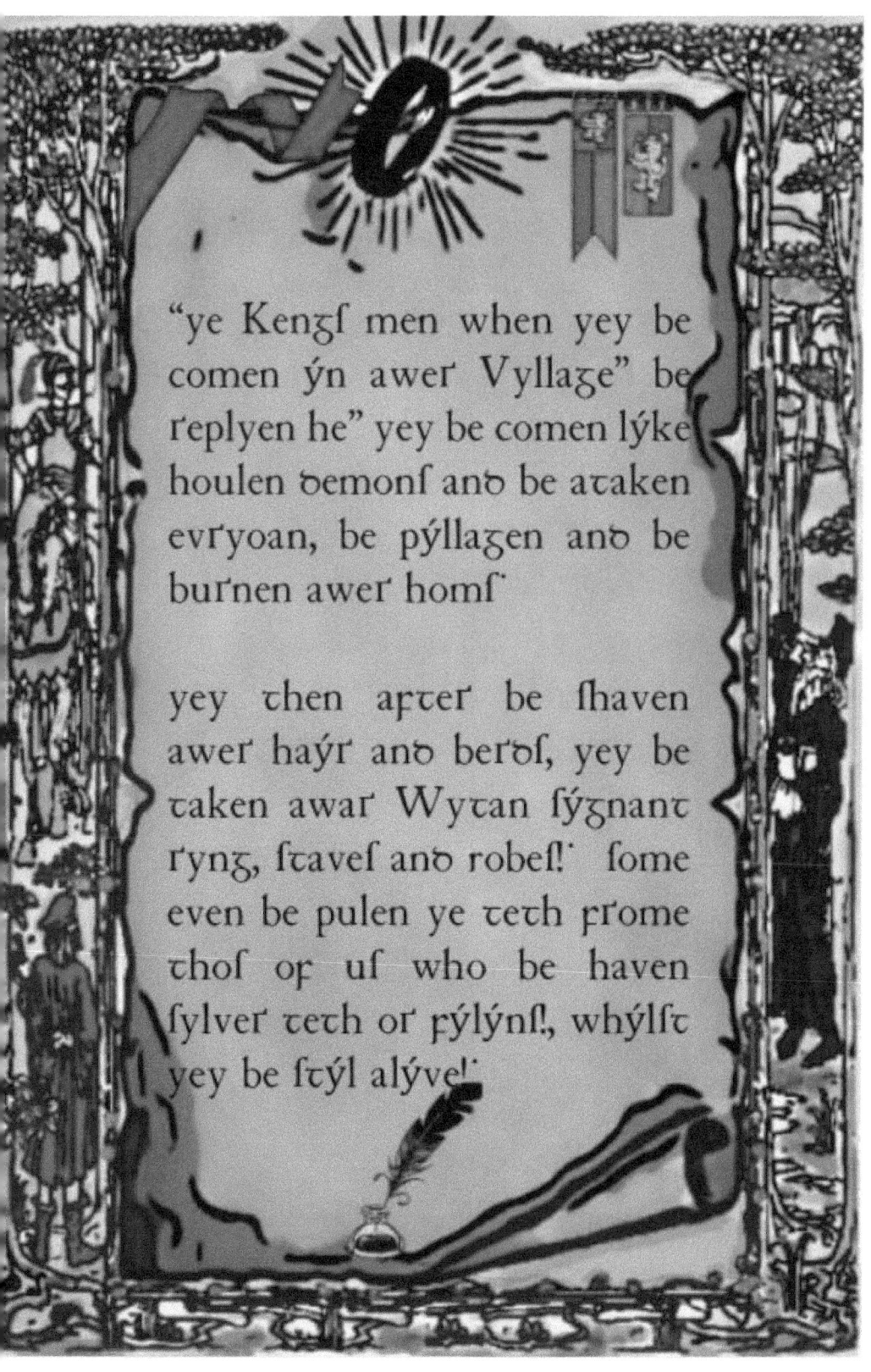

"ye Kengſ men when yey be comen ýn awer Vyllage" be replyen he" yey be comen lýke houlen ꝺemonſ anꝺ be aꞇaken evryoan, be pýllagen anꝺ be burnen awer homſ

yey ꞇhen aꝼꞇer be ſhaven awer haýr anꝺ berꝺſ, yey be ꞇaken awar Wyꞇan ſýgnanꞇ ryng, ſꞇaveſ anꝺ robeſ! ſome even be pulen ye ꞇeꞇh ꝼrome ꞇhoſ oꝼ uſ who be haven ſylver ꞇeꞇh or ꝼýlýnſ!, whýlſꞇ yey be ſꞇýl alýve!

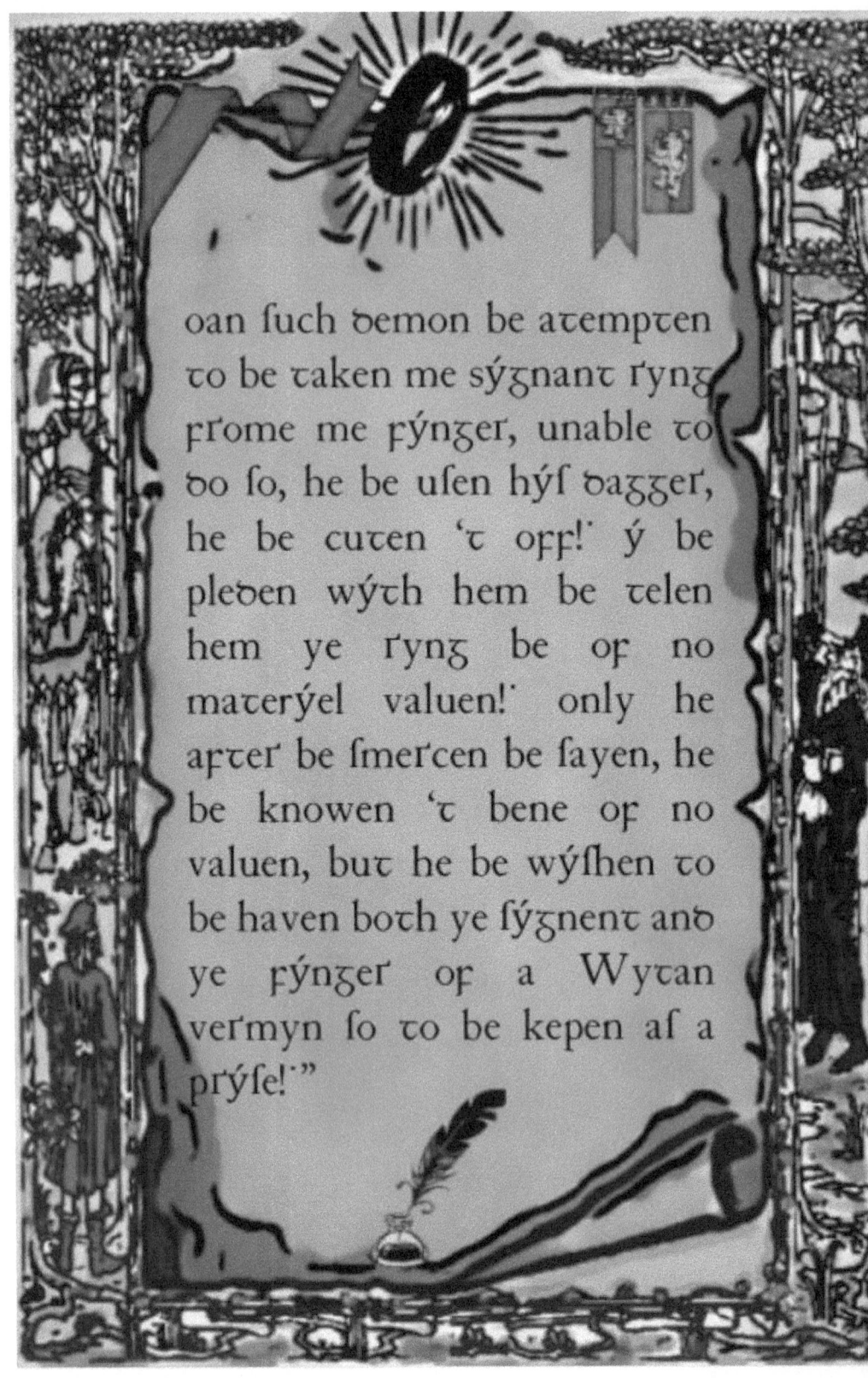

oan ſuch ðemon be atempten to be taken me ſýgnant ryng frome me fýnger, unable to ðo ſo, he be uſen hýſ ðagger, he be cuten 't off!' ý be pleðen wýth hem be telen hem ye ryng be of no materýel valuen!' only he after be ſmercen be ſayen, he be knowen 't bene of no valuen, but he be wýſhen to be haven both ye ſýgnent anð ye fýnger of a Wytan vermyn ſo to be kepen aſ a prýſe!'"

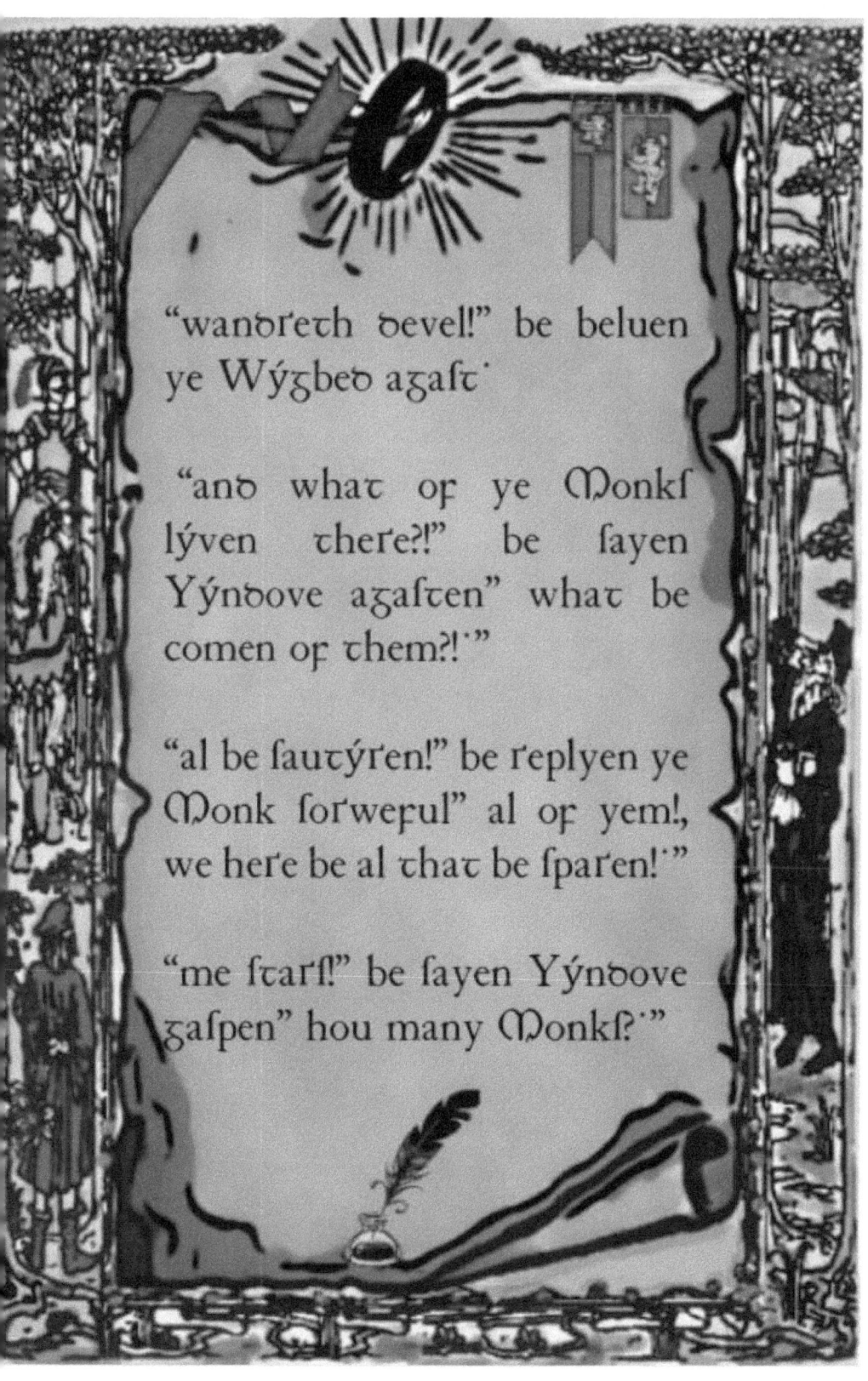

"wandreth devel!" be beluen ye Wýȝbed aȝaſt·

"and what oꝛ ye Monkſ lýven there?!" be ſayen Yýndove aȝaſten" what be comen oꝛ them?!·"

"al be ſautýren!" be replyen ye Monk ſorweꝼul" al oꝛ yem!, we here be al that be ſparen!·"

"me ſtarſ!" be ſayen Yýndove ȝaſpen" hou many Monkſ?·"

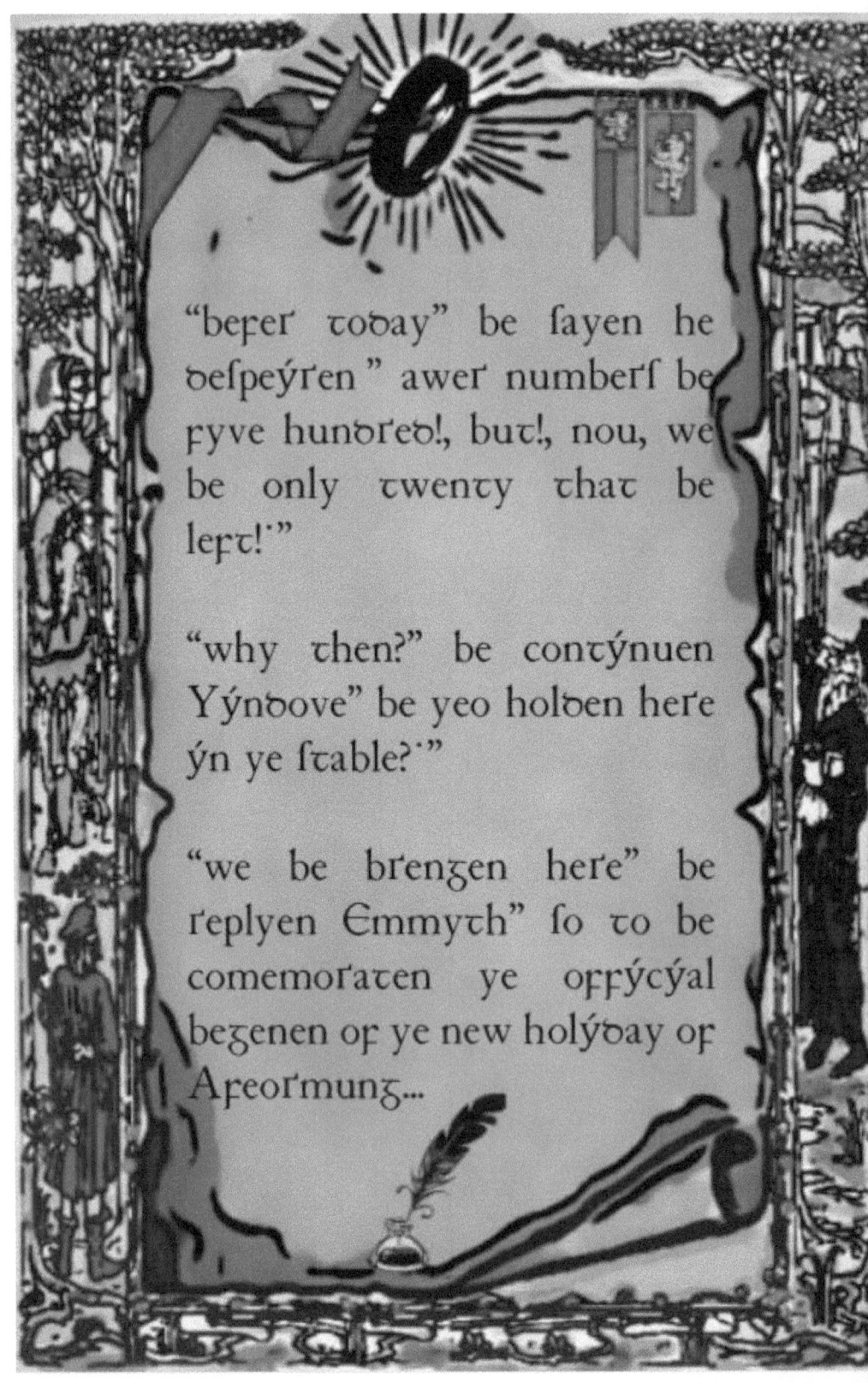

"beꝼer toꝺay" be ſayen he
ꝺeſpeýren " awer numberſ be
ꝼyve hunꝺreꝺ!, but!, nou, we
be only twenty that be
leꝼt!'"

"why then?" be contýnuen
Yýnꝺove" be yeo holꝺen here
ýn ye ſtable?'"

"we be brengen here" be
replyen Emmyth" ſo to be
comemoraten ye oꝼꝼýcýal
begenen oꝼ ye new holýꝺay oꝼ
Aꝼeormung...

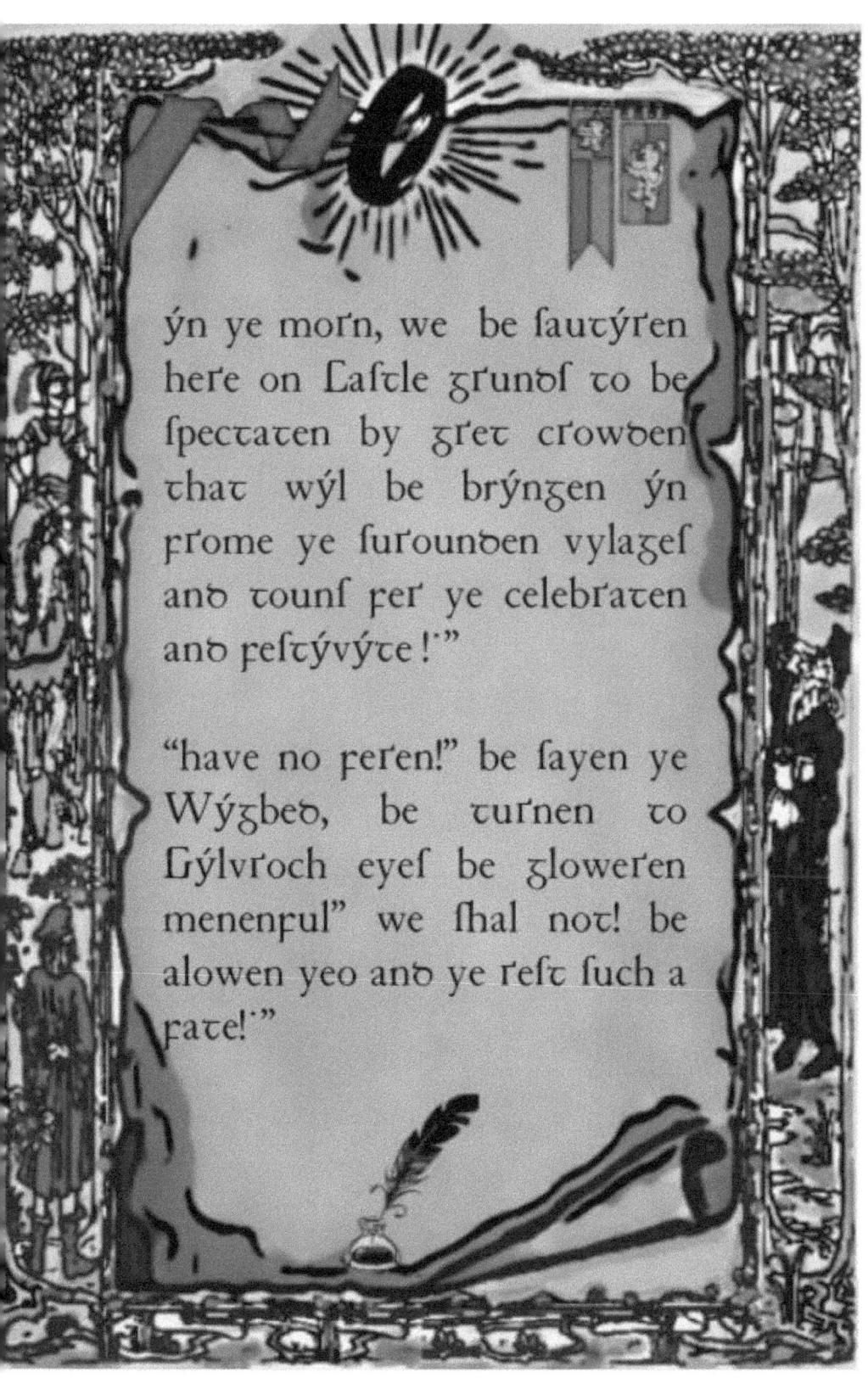

ýn ye morn, we be ſautýren here on Laſtle grundſ to be ſpectaten by gret crowden that wýl be brýngen ýn frome ye ſurounden vylageſ and tounſ fer ye celebraten and feſtývýte!'"

"have no feren!" be ſayen ye Wýʒbed, be turnen to Lýlvroch eyeſ be gloweren menenful" we ſhal not! be alowen yeo and ye reſt ſuch a fate!'"

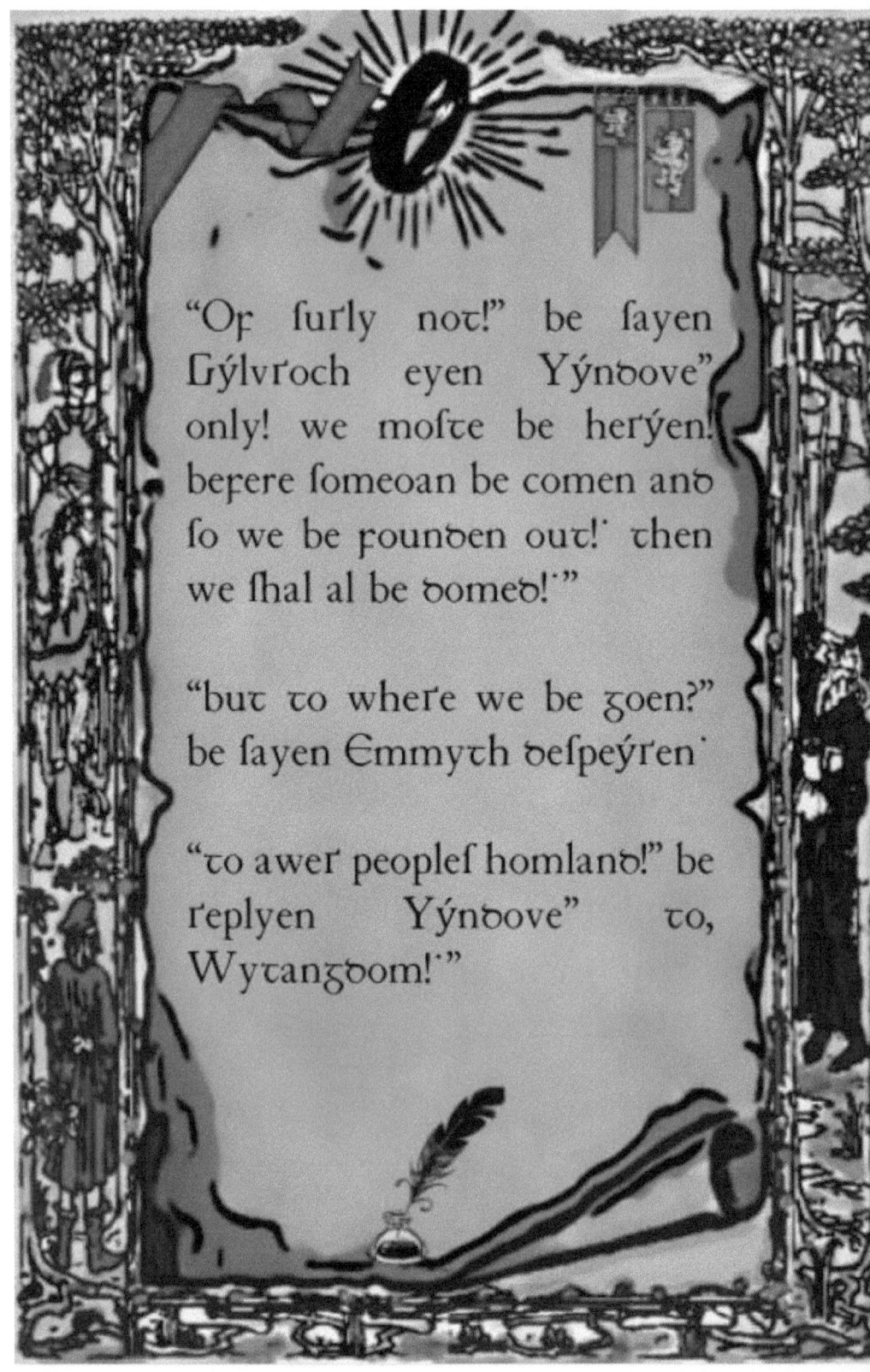

"Oꝼ ſuꞃly noꞇ!" be ſayen Ꝼýlvꞃoch eyen Yýnꝺove" only! we moſꞇe be heꞃýen! beꝼeꞃe ſomeoan be comen anꝺ ſo we be ꝼounꝺen ouꞇ!˙ ꞇhen we ſhal al be ꝺomeꝺ!˙"

"buꞇ ꞇo wheꞃe we be ᵹoen?" be ſayen Emmyꞇh ꝺeſpeýꞃen˙

"ꞇo aweꞃ peopleſ homlanꝺ!" be ꞃeplyen Yýnꝺove" ꞇo, Wyꞇanᵹꝺom!˙"

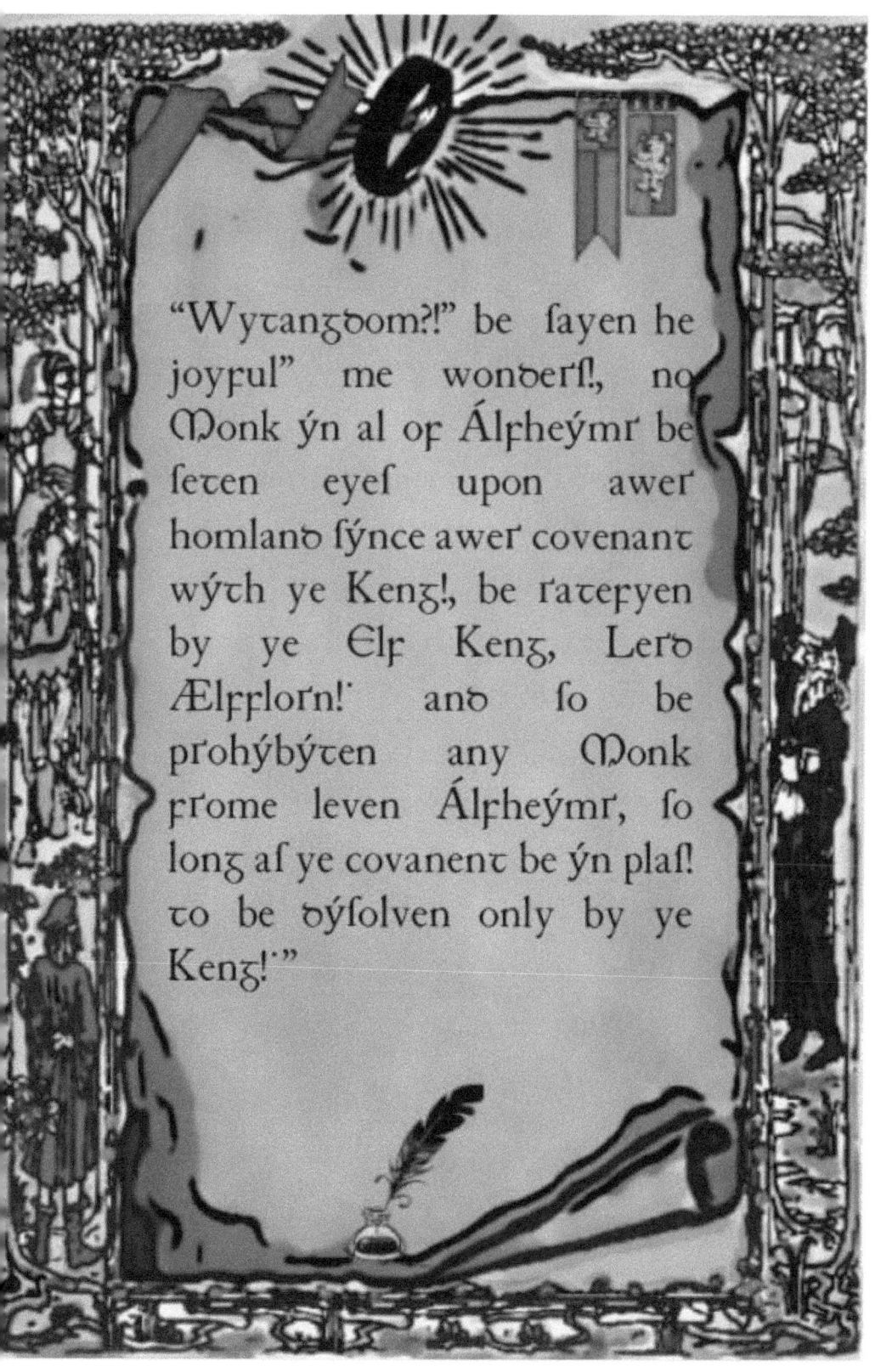

"Wytangdom?!" be fayen he joyful" me wonderf!., no Monk ýn al of Álfheýmr be feten eyef upon awer homland fýnce awer covenant wýth ye Keng!, be ratefyen by ye Elf Keng, Lerd Ælfflorn!' and fo be prohýbýten any Monk frome leven Álfheýmr, fo long af ye covanent be ýn plaf! to be dýfolven only by ye Keng!'"

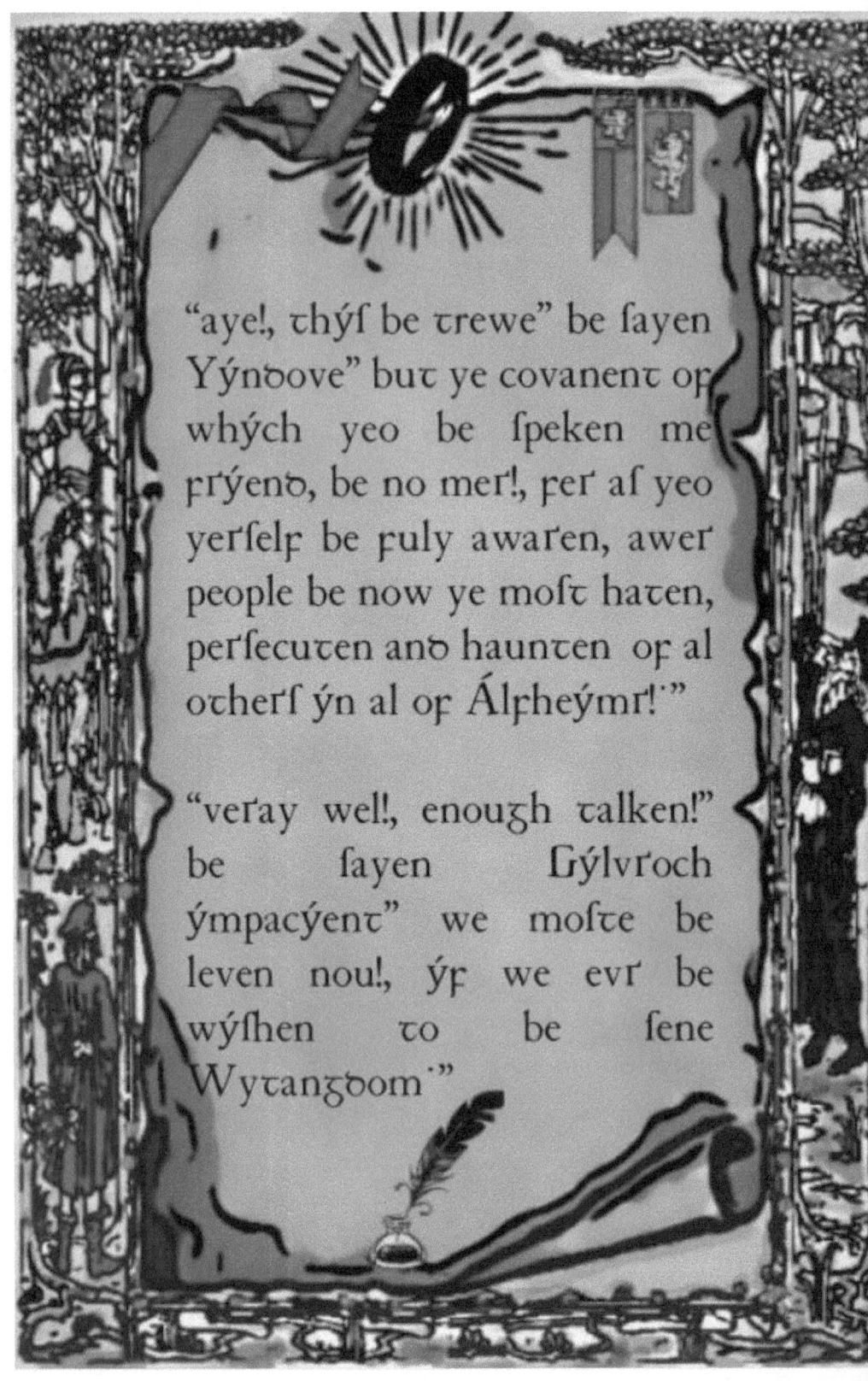

"aye!, thýſ be trewe" be ſayen Ýýnðove" but ye covanent oſ whých yeo be ſpeken me ſrýenð, be no mer!, ſer aſ yeo yerſelſ be ſuly awaſen, awer people be now ye moſt haten, perſecuten anð haunten oſ al otherſ ýn al oſ Álſheýmr!'"

"veſay wel!, enough talken!" be ſayen Ĝýlvroch ýmpacýent" we moſte be leven nou!, ýſ we evſ be wýſhen to be ſene Wytangðom·"

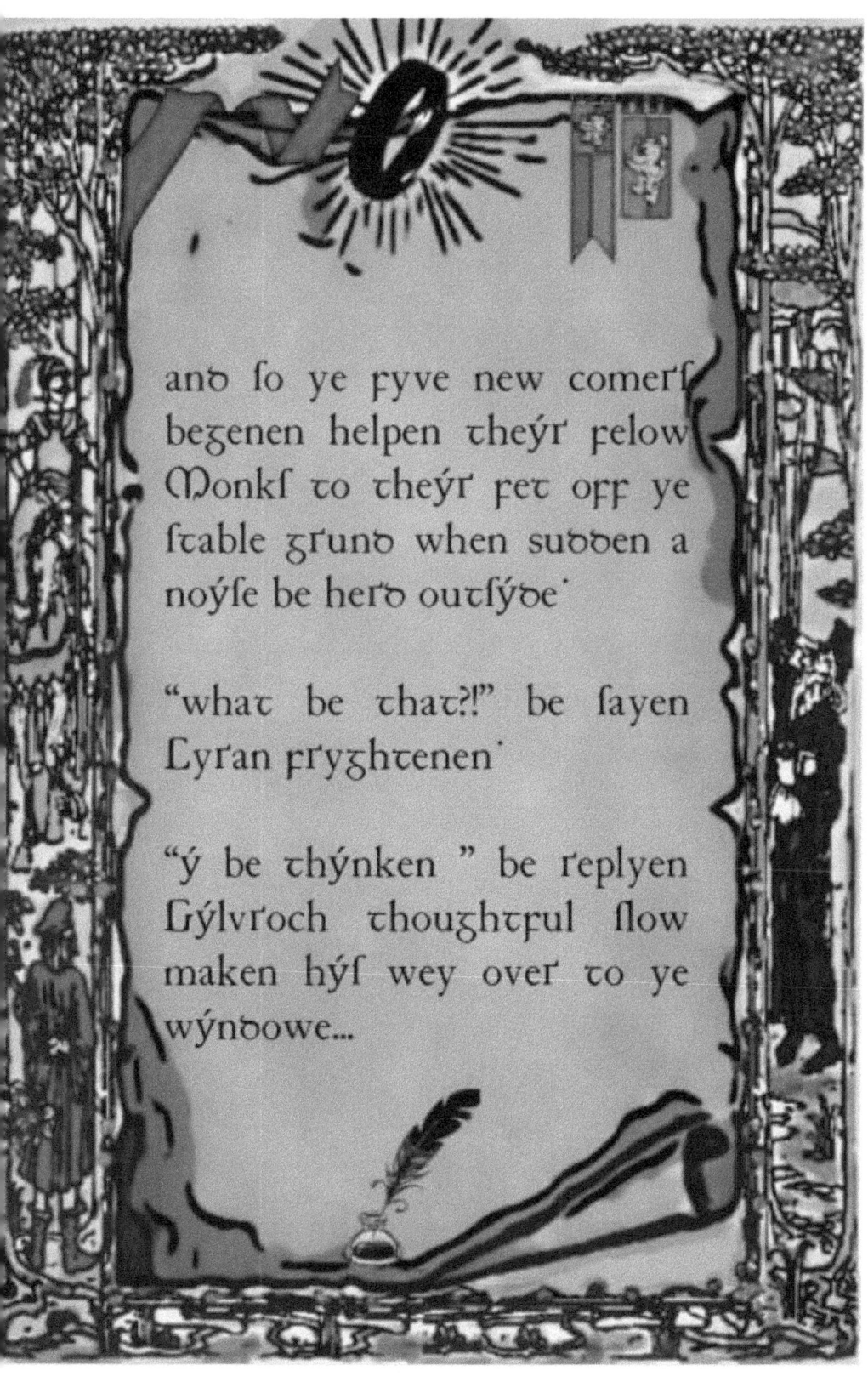

and so ye fyve new comers
begenen helpen theýr felow
Monks to theýr fet off ye
stable grund when sudden a
noýse be herd outsýde.

"what be that?!" be sayen
Lyran fryghtenen.

"ý be thýnken " be replyen
Gýlvroch thoughtful slow
maken hýs wey over to ye
wýndowe...

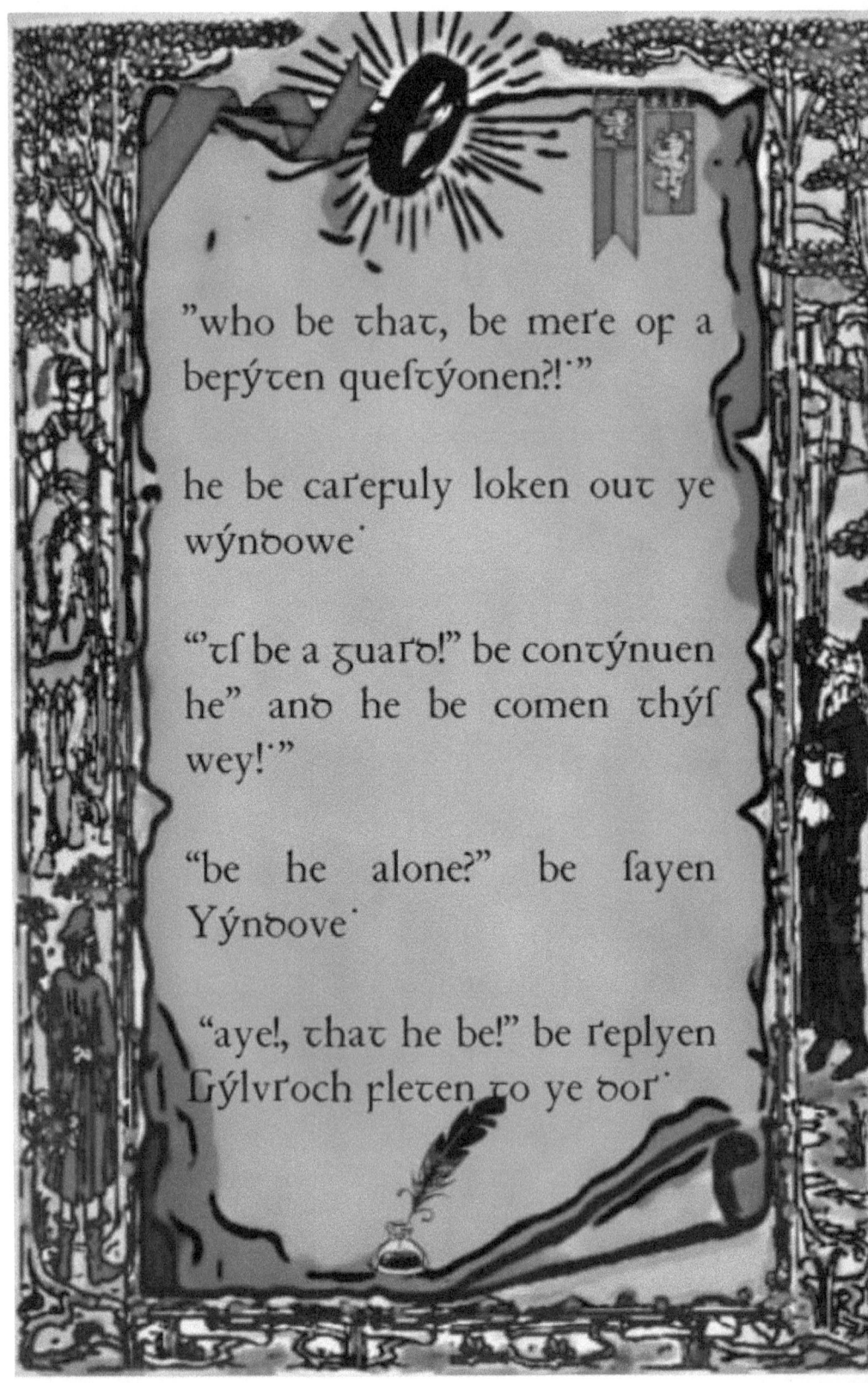

"who be that, be mere of a berýten questýonen?!'"

he be carefuly loken out ye wýndowe˙

"'tf be a guard!" be contýnuen he" and he be comen thýf wey!'"

"be he alone?" be fayen Yýndove˙

"aye!, that he be!" be replyen Gýlvroch fleten to ye dor˙

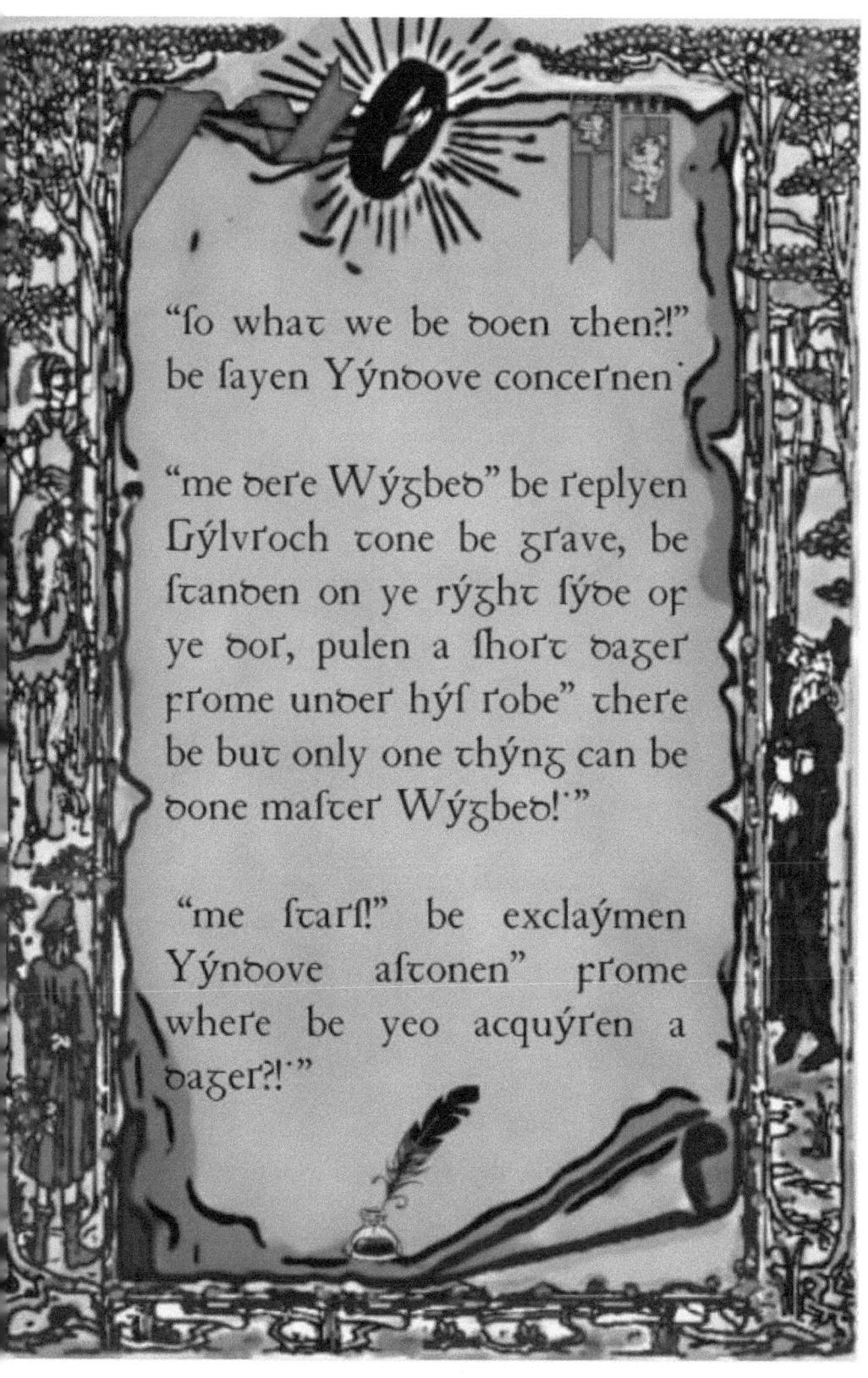

"ſo whaꞇ we be ꝺoen ꞇhen?!" be ſayen Yýnꝺove conceꞃnen˙

"me ꝺeꞃe Wýʒbeꝺ" be ꞃeplyen Ḡýlvꞃoch ꞇone be ʒꞃave, be ſꞇanꝺen on ye ꞃýʒhꞇ ſýꝺe oꝯ ye ꝺoꞃ, pulen a ſhoꞃꞇ ꝺaʒeꞃ ꝯꞃome unꝺeꞃ hýſ robe" ꞇheꞃe be buꞇ only one ꞇhýnʒ can be ꝺone maſꞇeꞃ Wýʒbeꝺ!˙"

"me ſꞇaꞃſ!" be exclaýmen Yýnꝺove aſꞇonen" ꝯꞃome wheꞃe be yeo acquýꞃen a ꝺaʒeꞃ?!˙"

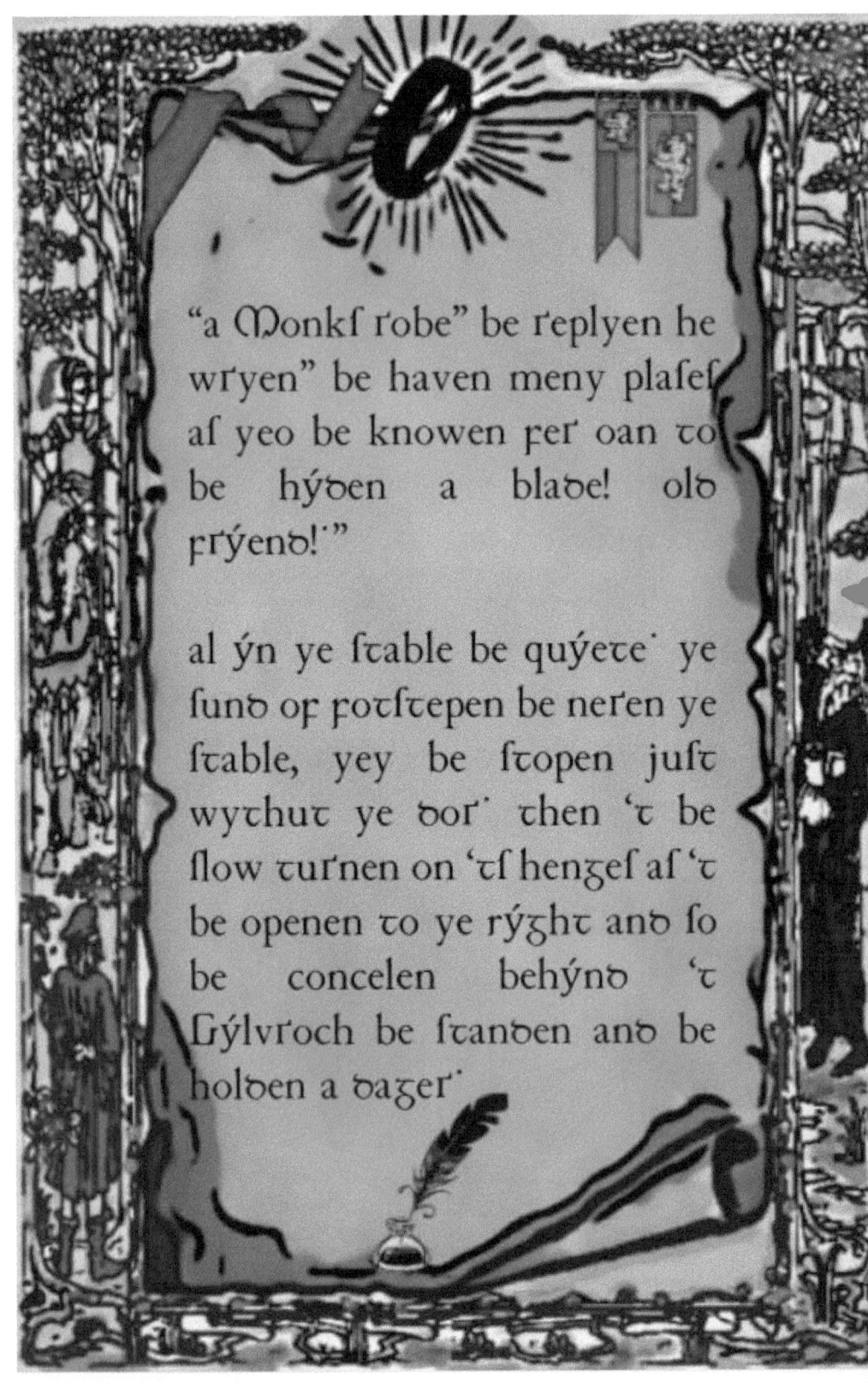

"a Monkſ robe" be replyen he wryen" be haven meny plaſeſ aſ yeo be knowen ẝer oan ꞇo be hýꝺen a blaꝺe! olꝺ ẝrýenꝺ!'"

al ýn ye ſꞇable be quýeꞇe˙ ye ſunꝺ oẝ ẝoꞇſꞇepen be neẝen ye ſꞇable, yey be ſꞇopen juſꞇ wyꞇhuꞇ ye ꝺoꝛ˙ ꞇhen 'ꞇ be flow ꞇuꝛnen on 'ꞇſ hengeſ aſ 'ꞇ be openen ꞇo ye rýᵹhꞇ anꝺ ſo be concelen behýnꝺ 'ꞇ Ᵹýlvꝛoch be ſꞇanꝺen anꝺ be holꝺen a ꝺaᵹeꝛ˙

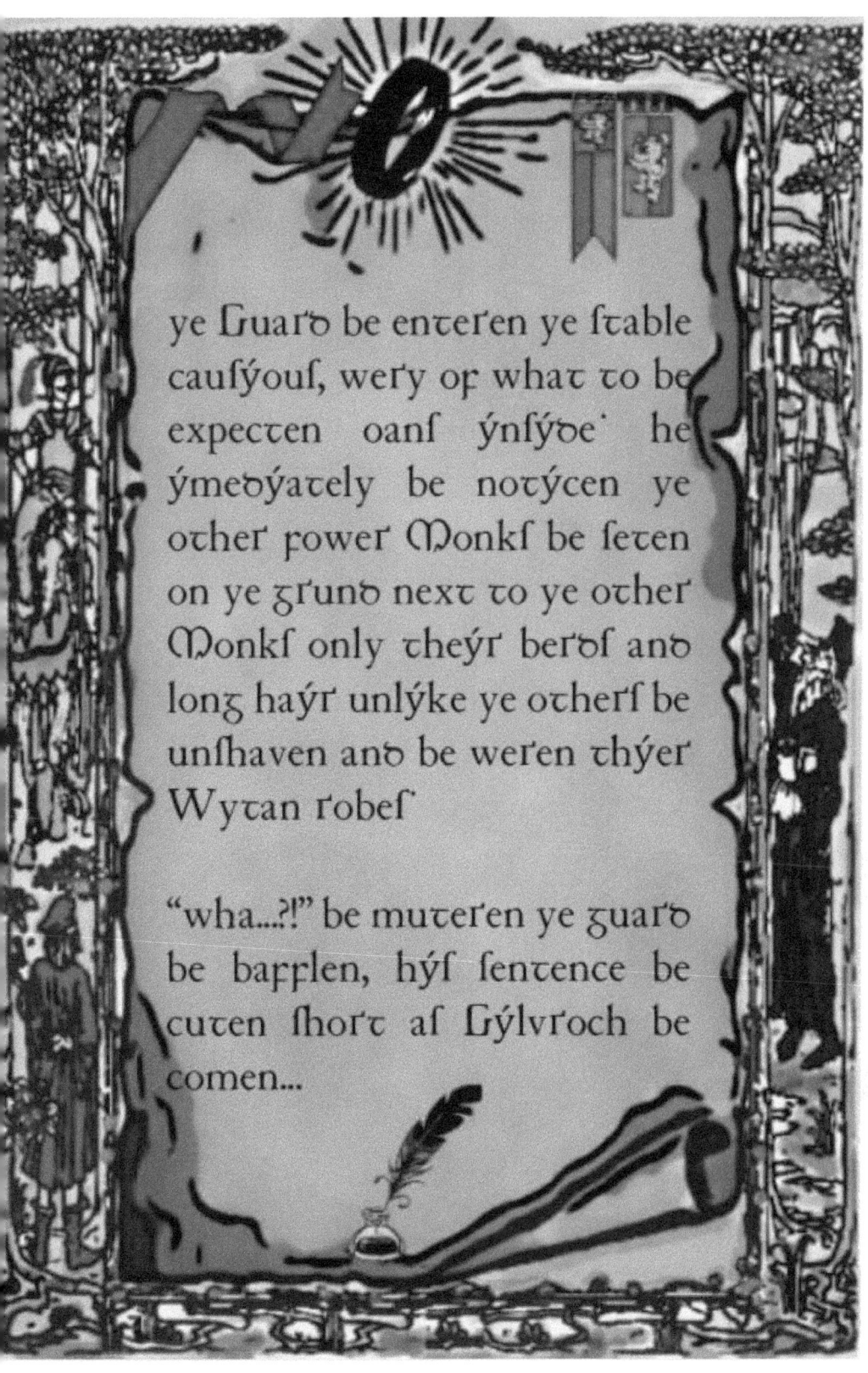

ye Ľuarò be enteren ye ſtable cauſýouſ, wery oƒ whaꞇ ꞇo be expecꞇen oanſ ýnſýòe˙ he ýmeòýaꞇely be noꞇýcen ye other ꞃower Ɱonkſ be feꞇen on ye ʒrunò nexꞇ ꞇo ye other Ɱonkſ only theýr beròſ anò lonʒ haýr unlýke ye otherſ be unſhaven anò be weren thýer Wyꞇan robeſ

"wha...?!" be muꞇeren ye ʒuarò be baꝶꝶlen, hýſ ſenꞇence be cuꞇen ſhorꞇ aſ Ľýlvroch be comen...

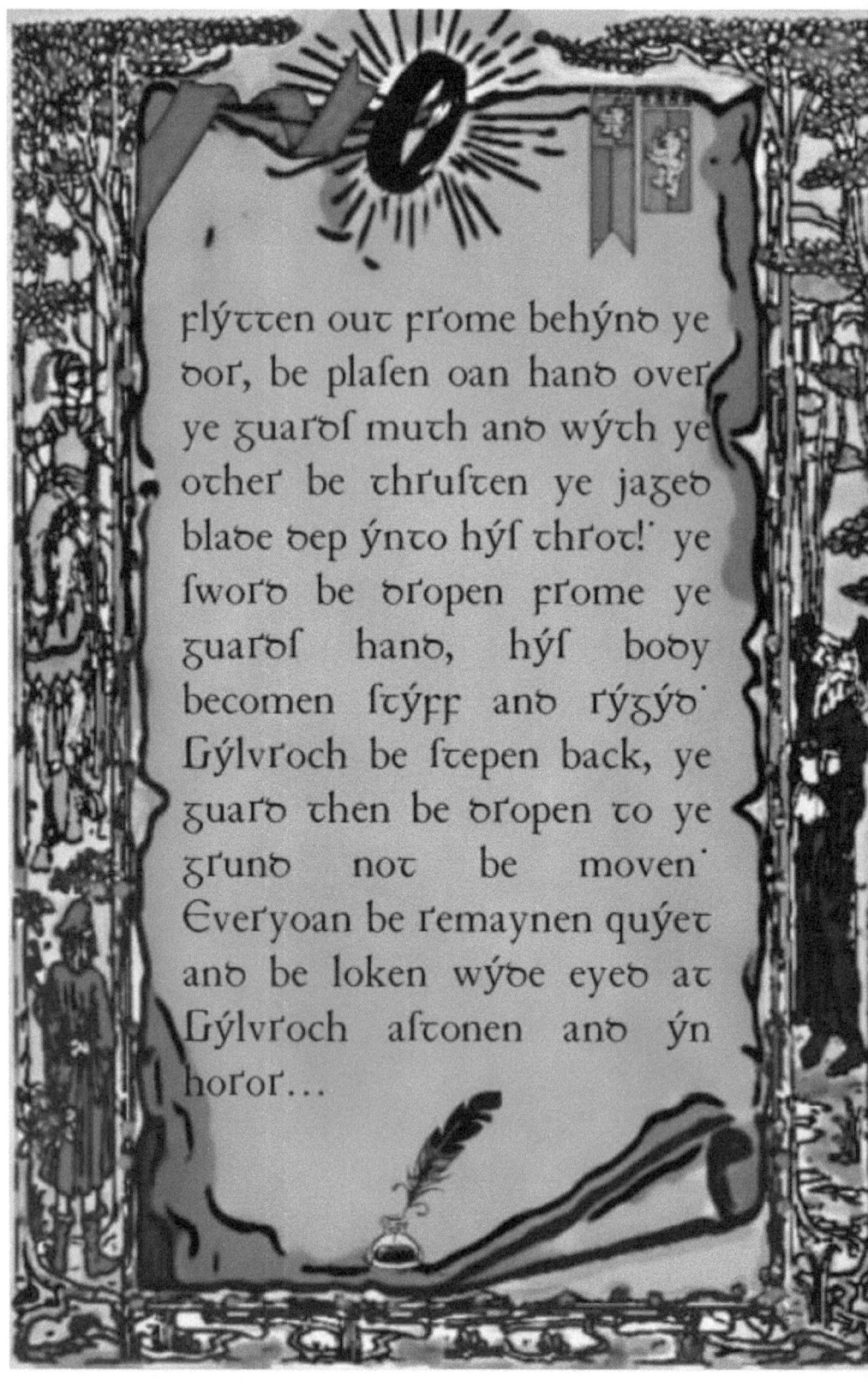

flytten out frome behynd ye dor, be plasen oan hand over ye guards muth and wyth ye other be thrusten ye jaged blade dep ynto hyf throt! ye sword be dropen frome ye guards hand, hyf body becomen styff and rygyd· Gylvroch be stepen back, ye guard then be dropen to ye grund not be moven· Everyoan be remaynen quyet and be loken wyde eyed at Gylvroch aftonen and yn horor…

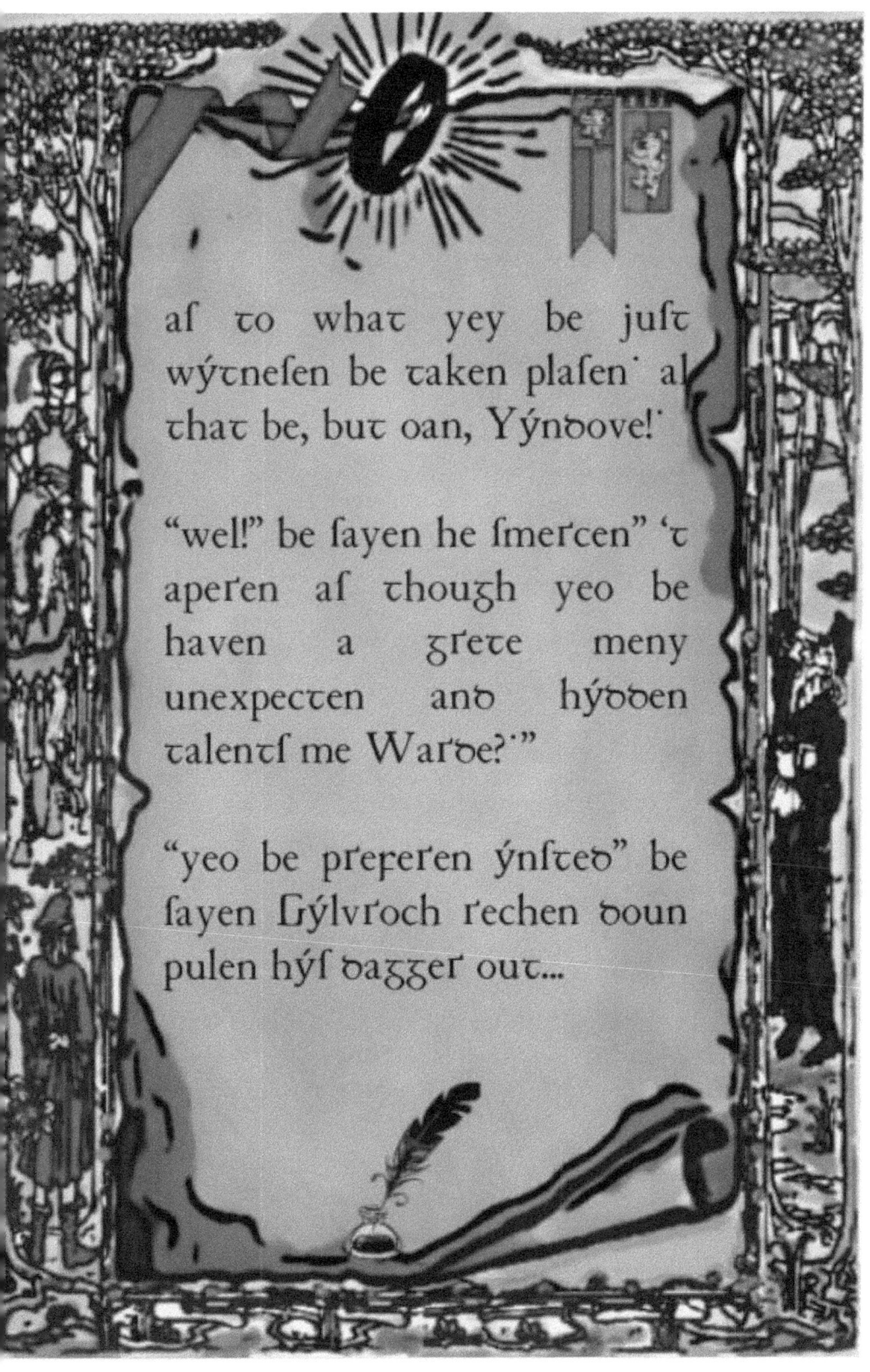

aſ ꞇo whaꞇ yey be juſꞇ
wýꞇneſen be ꞇaken plaſen˙ al
ꞇhaꞇ be, buꞇ oan, Yýnꝺove!˙

"wel!" be ſayen he ſmerꞇen" 'ꞇ
aperen aſ ꞇhough yeo be
haven   a   greꞇe   meny
unexpecꞇen   anꝺ   hýꝺꝺen
ꞇalenꞇſ me Warꝺe?˙"

"yeo be preſeren ýnſꞇeꝺ" be
ſayen Ꝉýlvroch rechen ꝺoun
pulen hýſ ꝺazzer ouꞇ...

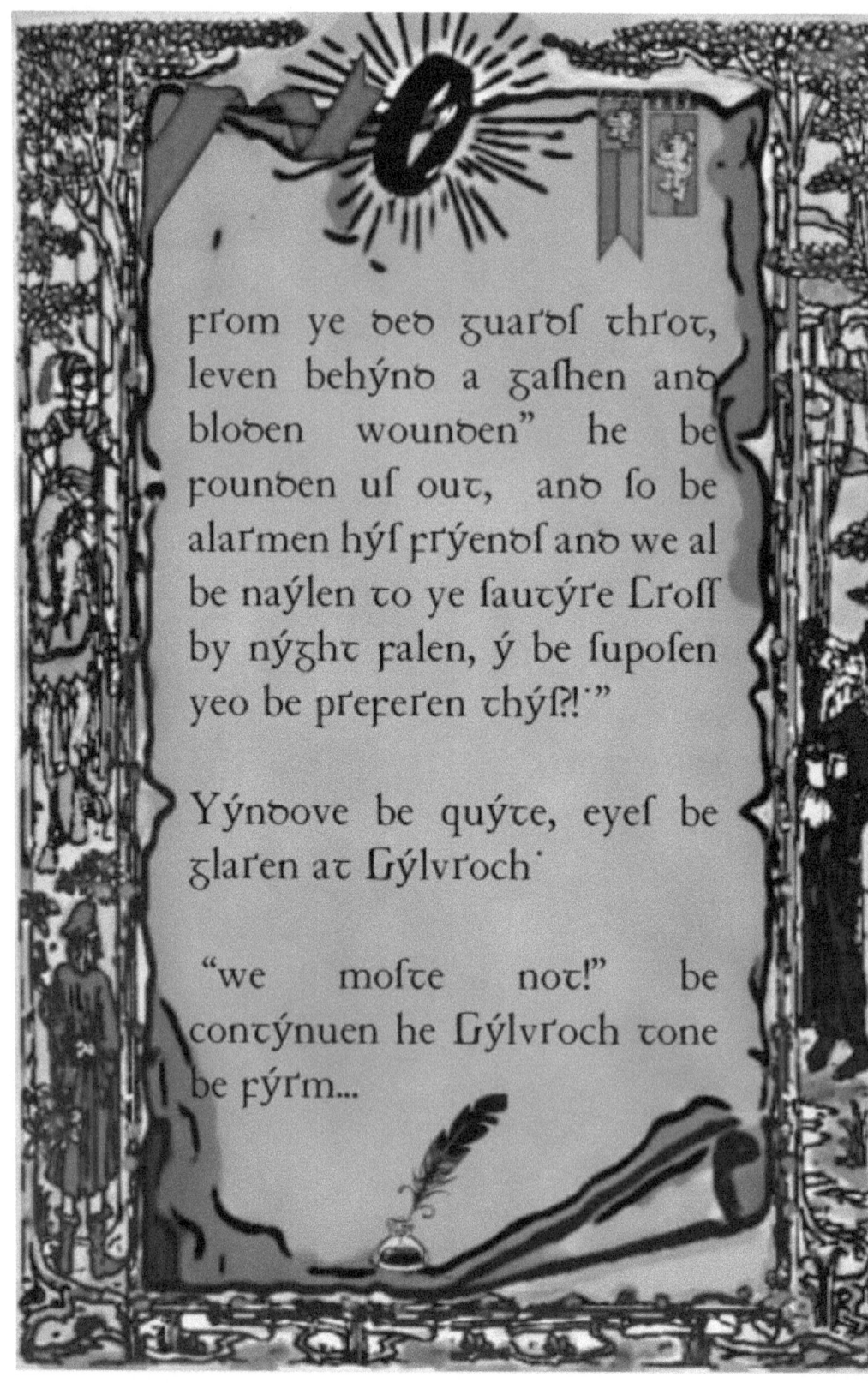

ᵹrom ye ꝺeꝺ ᵹuarꝺſ ꞇhroꞇ, leven behýnꝺ a ᵹaſhen anꝺ bloꝺen wounꝺen" he be ᵹounꝺen uſ ouꞇ, anꝺ ſo be alarmen hýſ ᵹrýenꝺſ anꝺ we al be naýlen ꞇo ye ſauꞇýre Ꝼroſſ by nýᵹhꞇ ᵹalen, ý be ſupoſen yeo be preᵹeren ꞇhýſ?!'"

Yýnꝺove be quýꞇe, eyeſ be ᵹlaren aꞇ Ꝼýlvꞃoch·

"we moſꞇe noꞇ!" be conꞇýnuen he Ꝼýlvꞃoch ꞇone be ᵹýꞃm...

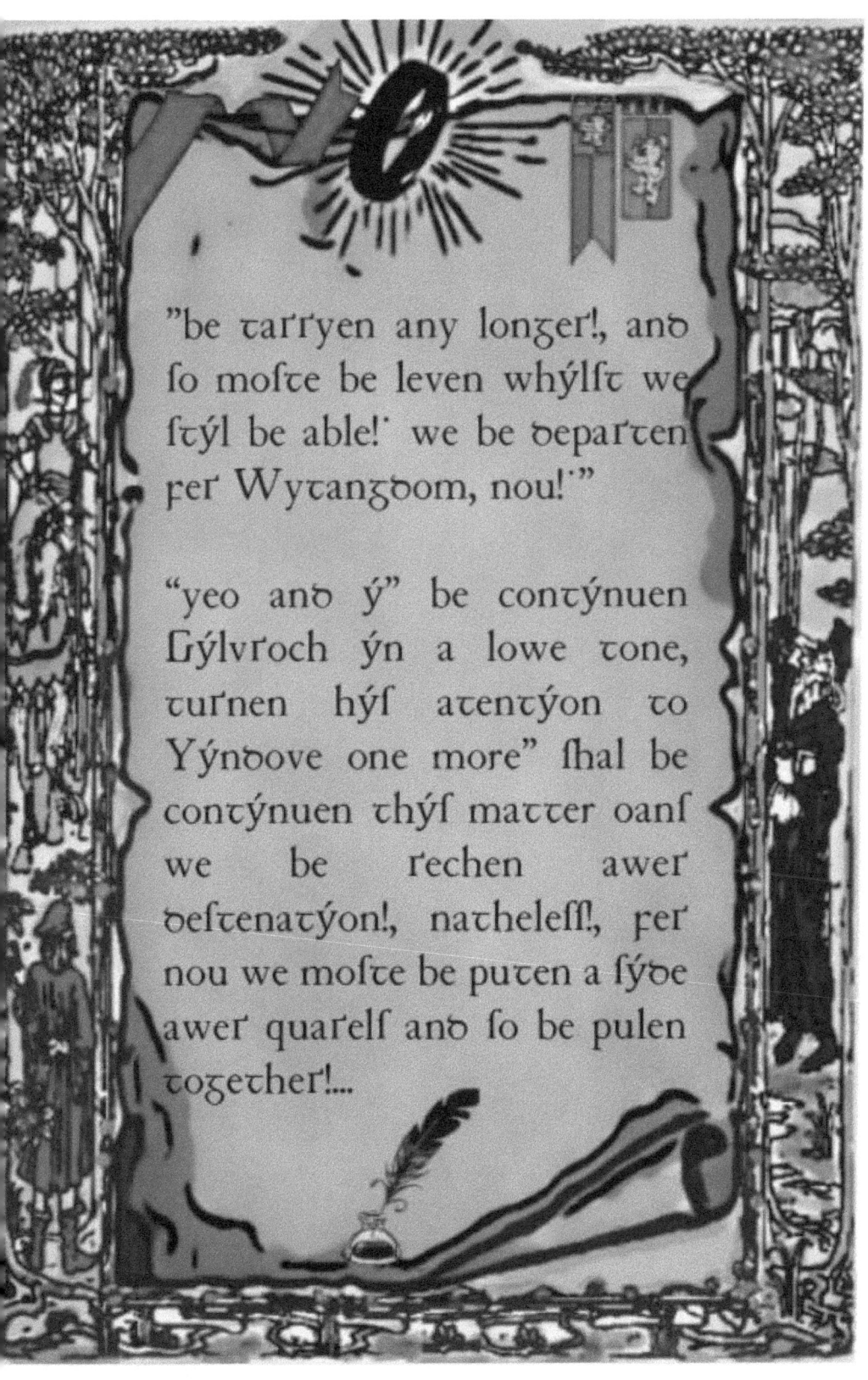

"be τarryen any longer!, anð
ſo moſte be leven whýlſt we
ſtýl be able!' we be ðeparten
ꝼer Wytangðom, nou!'"

"yeo anð ý" be contýnuen
Ꝼýlvroch ýn a lowe τone,
τurnen hýſ atentýon τo
Yýnðove one more" ſhal be
contýnuen thýſ matter oanſ
we   be   rechen   awer
ðeſtenatýon!, natheleſſ!, ꝼer
nou we moſte be puτen a ſýðe
awer quarelſ anð ſo be pulen
τoꝣether!...

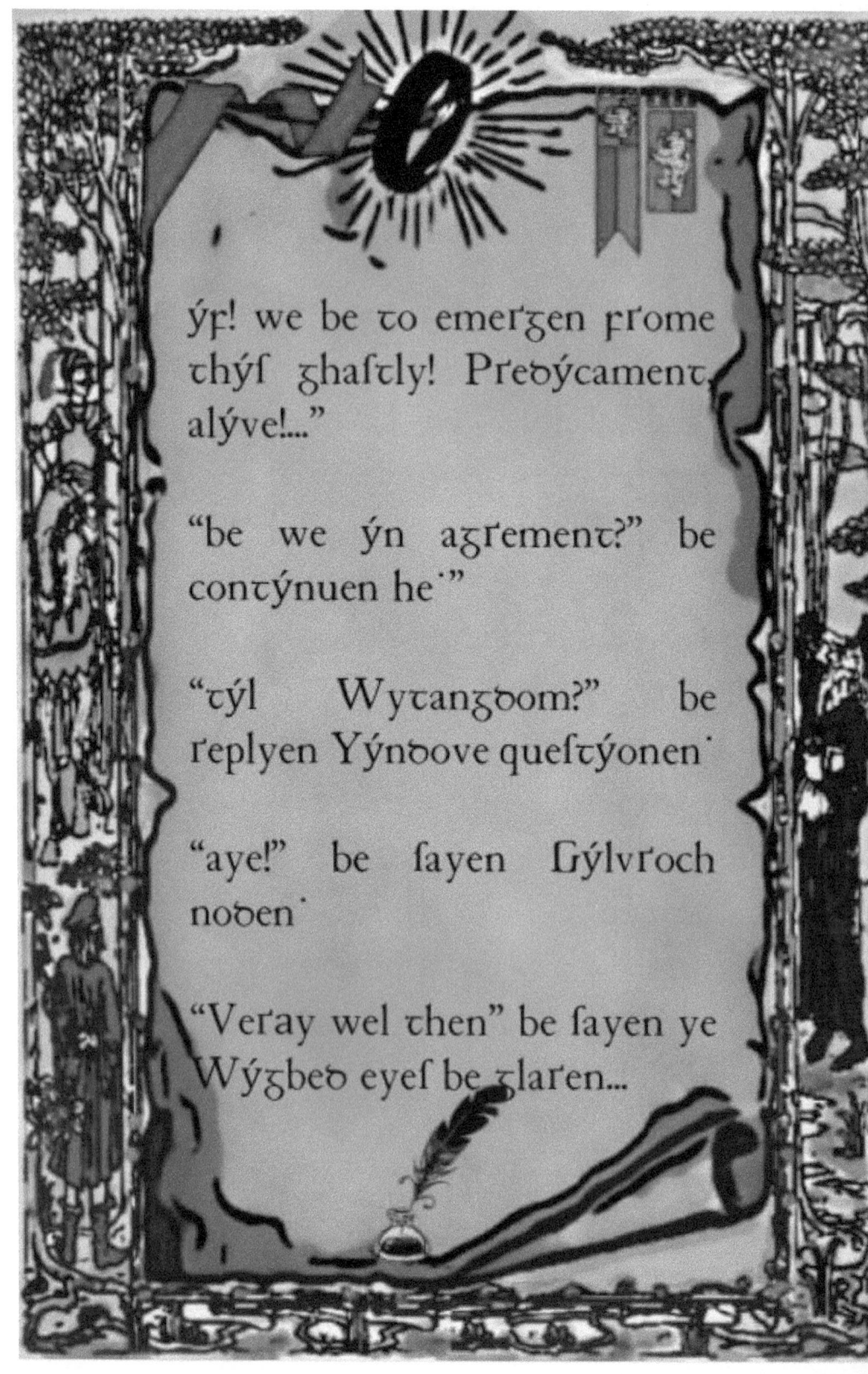

ýꝼ! we be ꞇo emerꝛen ꝼrome ꞇhýꞅ ꝡhaꞅꞇly! Preꝺýcamenꞇ, alýve!..."

"ꝺe we ýn aꝛremenꞇ?" be conꞇýnuen he·"

"ꞇýl Wyꞇanꝺom?" be replyen Yýnꝺove queꞅꞇýonen·

"aye!" be ꞅayen Ꝼýlvꝛoch noꝺen·

"Veꞃay wel ꞇhen" be ꞅayen ye Wýꝛꝺeꝺ eyeꞅ be ꝛlaꞃen...

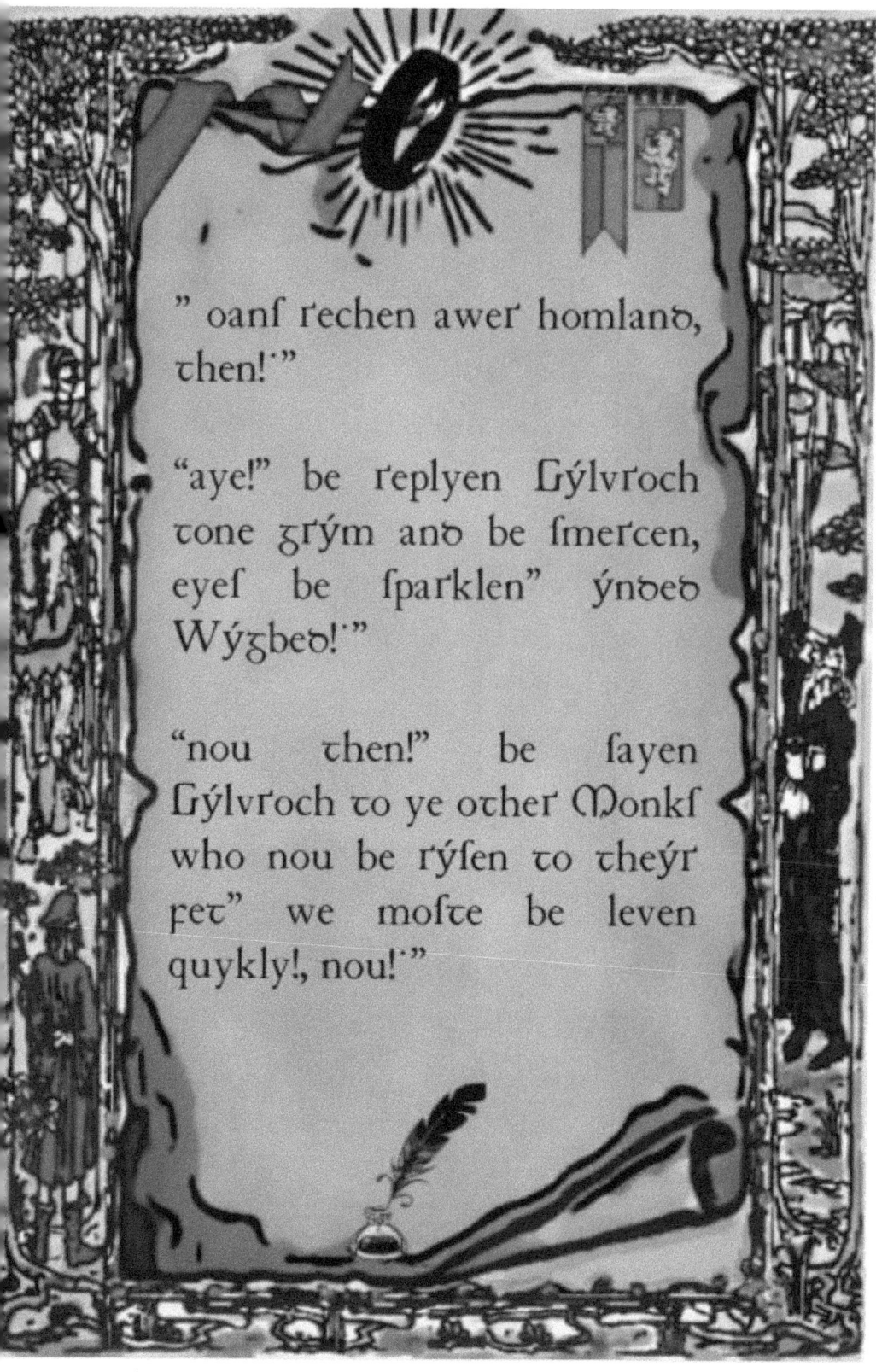

" oanſ rechen awer homlanð, then!·'"

"aye!" be replyen Ꝇýlvroch tone ᵹrým anð be ſmercen, eyeſ be ſparklen" ýnðeð Wýᵹbeð!·'"

"nou then!" be ſayen Ꝇýlvroch to ye other Ϻonkſ who nou be rýſen to theýr ꝼet" we moſte be leven quykly!, nou!·'"

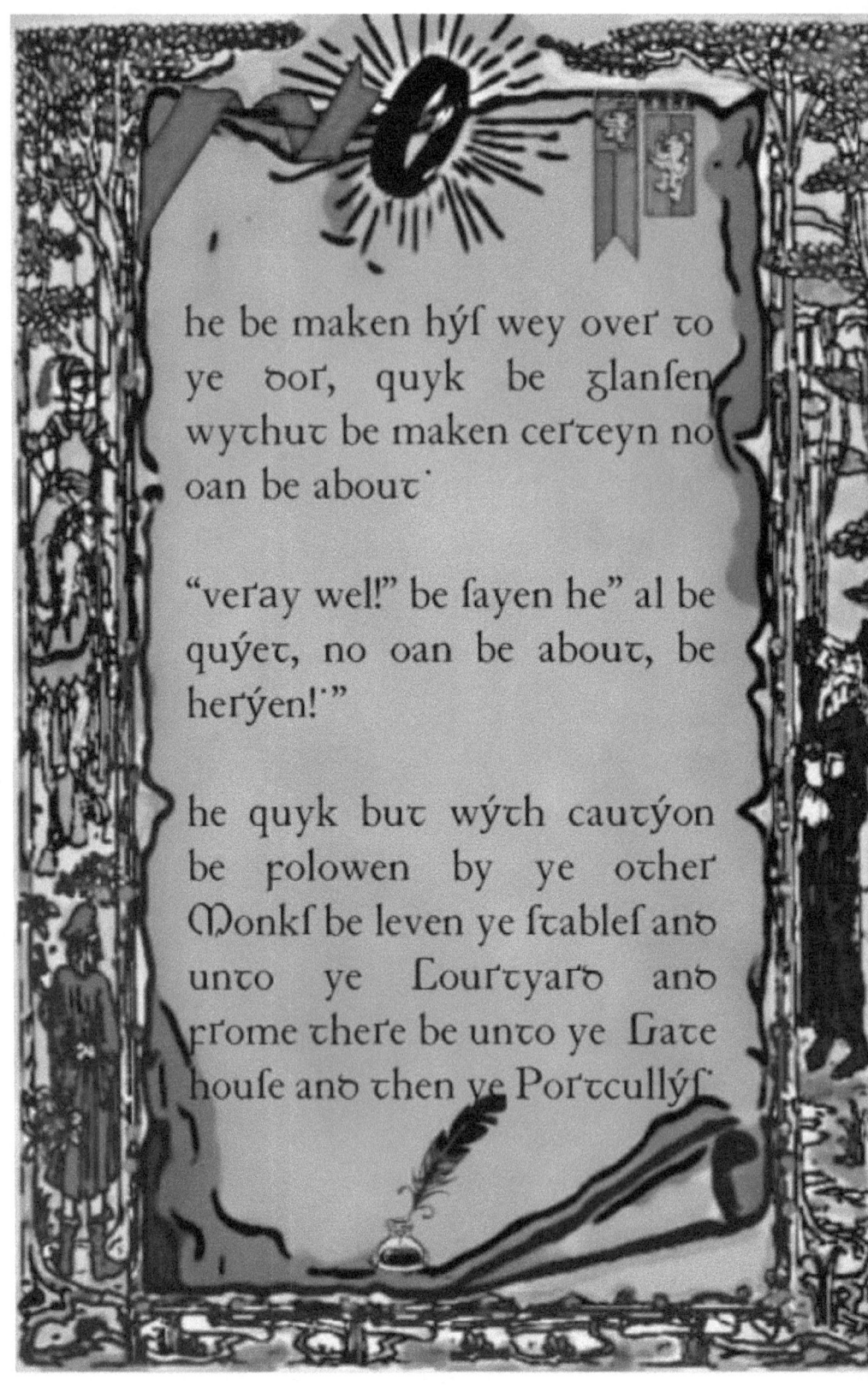

he be maken hýſ wey over to ye ðor, quyk be ʒlanſen wythut be maken certeyn no oan be about

"veray wel!" be ſayen he" al be quýet, no oan be about, be herýen!·"

he quyk but wýth cautýon be ρolowen by ye other Monkſ be leven ye ſtableſ anð unto ye Lourtyarð anð ρrome there be unto ye Late houſe anð then ye Portcullýſ

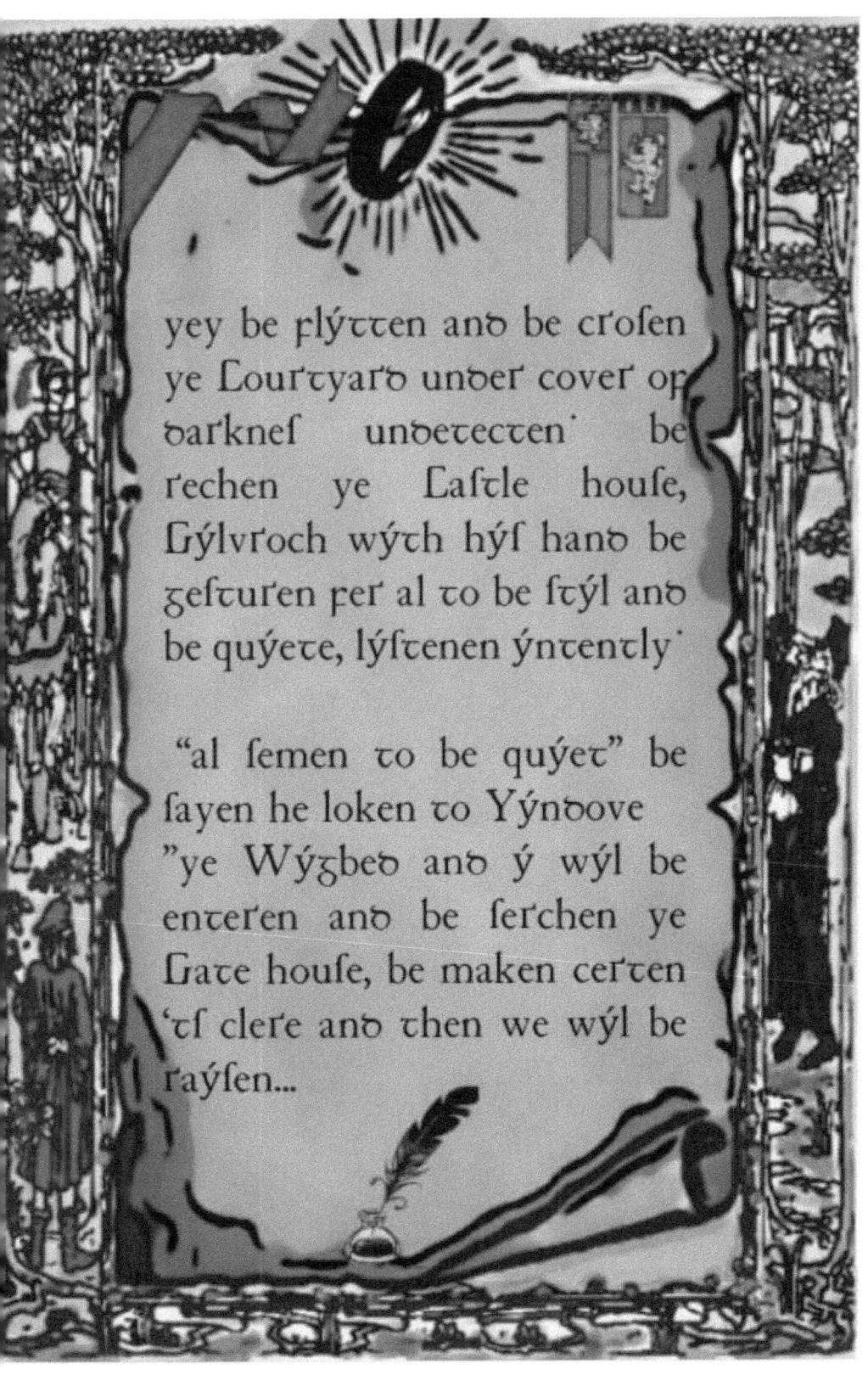

yey be flýtten and be crofen ye Courtyard under cover of darknef undetecten· be rechen ye Caftle houfe, Gýlvroch wýth hýf hand be gefturen fer al to be ftýl and be quýete, lýftenen ýntently·

"al femen to be quýet" be fayen he loken to Ýýndove "ye Wýgbed and ý wýl be enteren and be ferchen ye Gate houfe, be maken certen 'tf clere and then we wýl be raýfen...

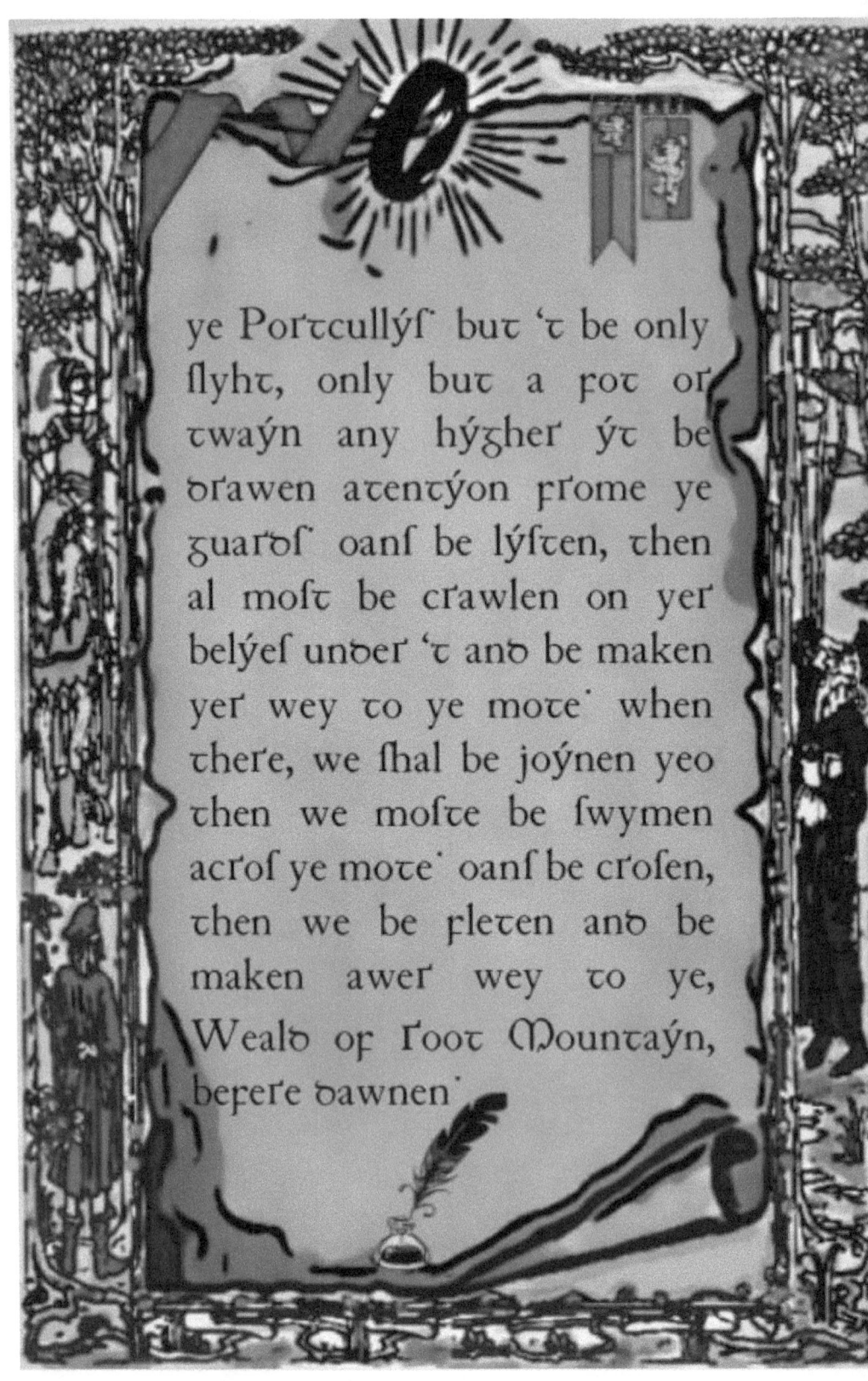

ye Portcullýſ but 't be only
flyht, only but a pot or
twaýn any hýgher ýt be
drawen atentýon frome ye
guardſ oanſ be lýſten, then
al moſt be crawlen on yer
belýeſ under 't and be maken
yer wey to ye mote· when
there, we ſhal be joýnen yeo
then we moſte be ſwymen
acroſ ye mote· oanſ be croſen,
then we be fleten and be
maken awer wey to ye,
Weald of foot Mountaýn,
befere dawnen·

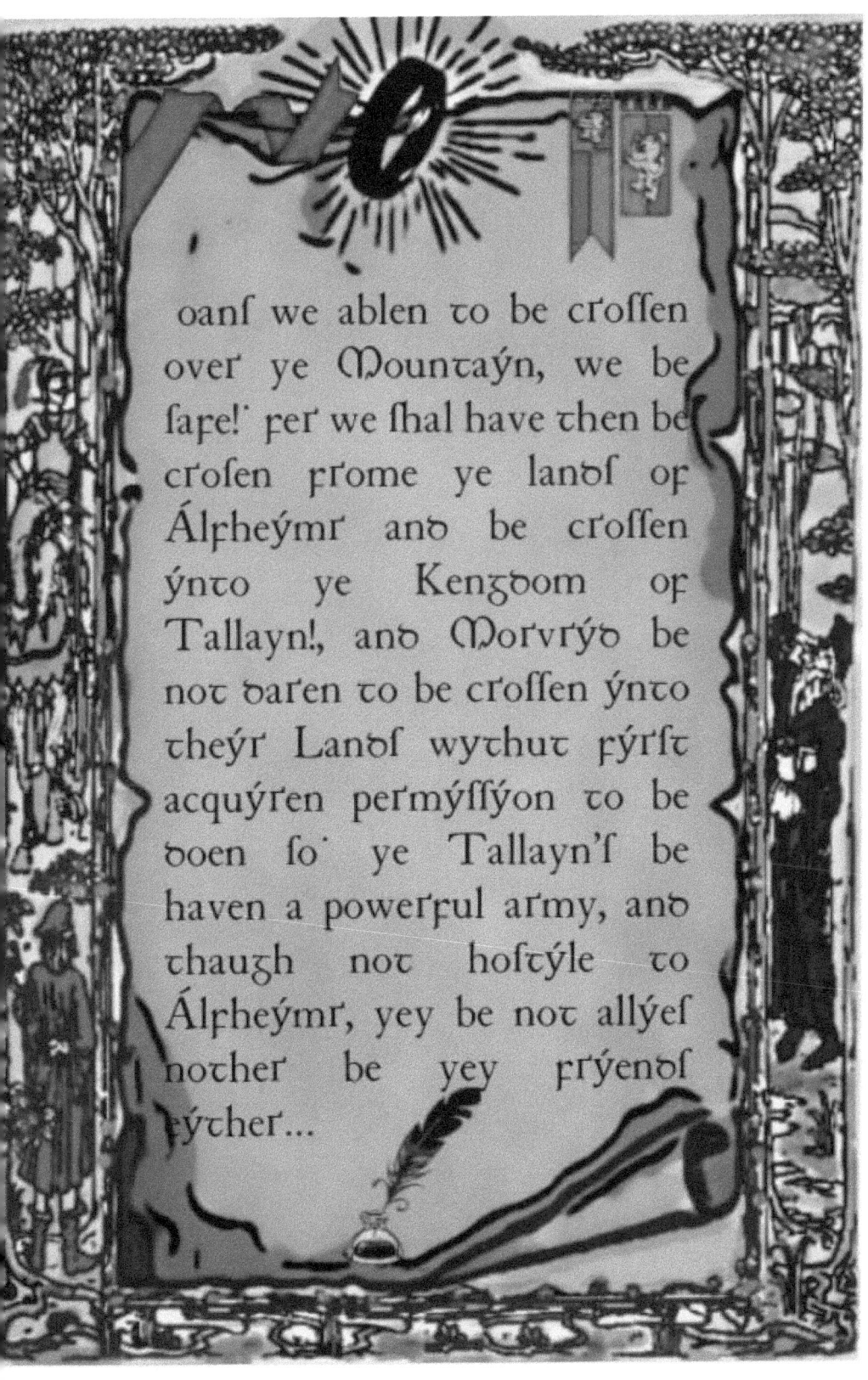

oanſ we ablen to be croſſen over ye Mountayn, we be ſaƒe!' ƥer we ſhal have then be croſen ƒrome ye lanðſ oƒ Álƒheýmr anð be croſſen ýnto ye Kenȝðom oƒ Tallayn!, anð Morvrýð be not ðaren to be croſſen ýnto theýr Lanðſ wythut ƒýrſt acquýren permýſſýon to be ðoen ſo˙ ye Tallayn'ſ be haven a powerƒul army, anð thauȝh not hoſtýle to Álƒheýmr, yey be not allýeſ nother be yey ƒrýenðſ eýther...

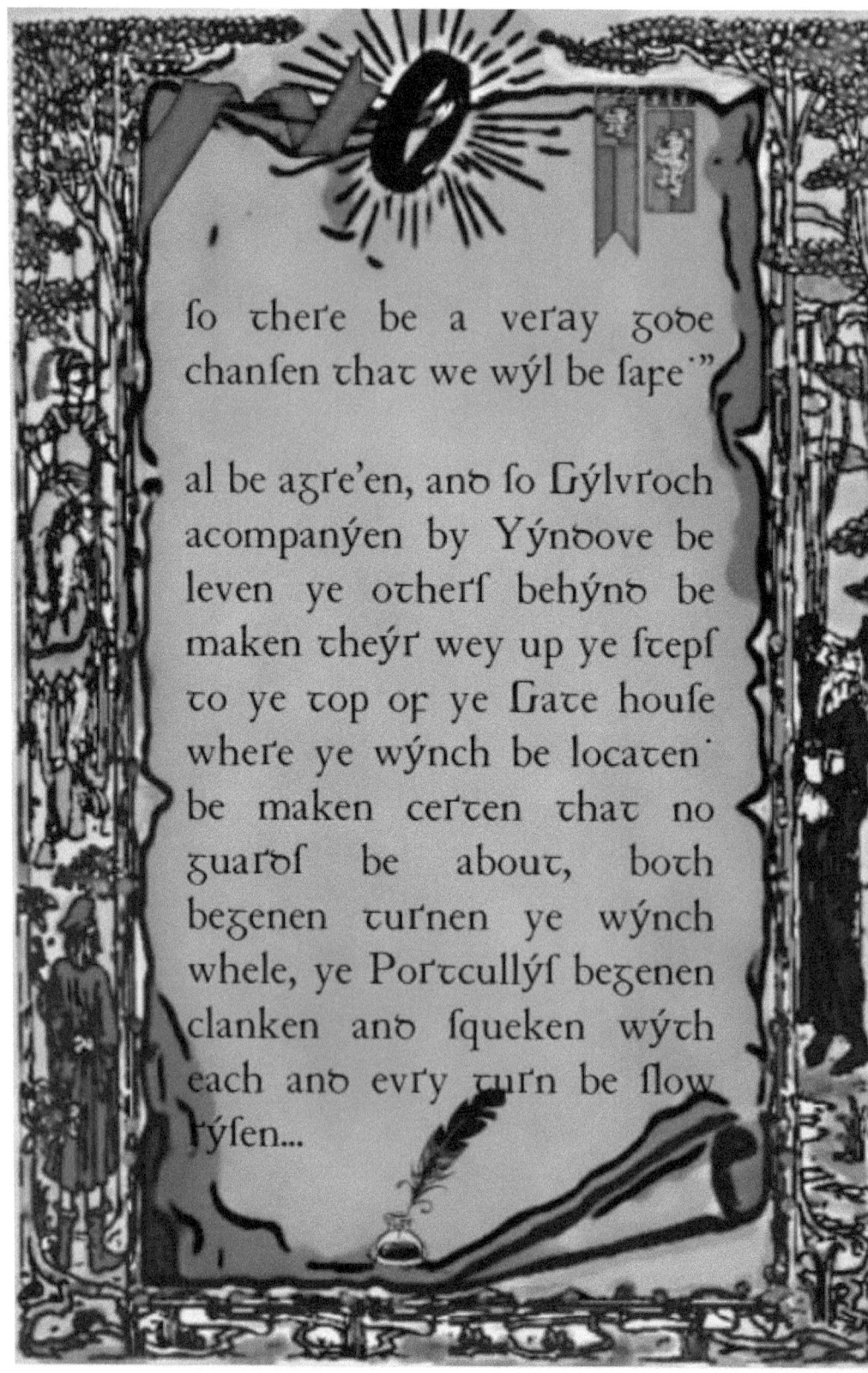

ſo there be a veray gode
chanſen that we wýl be ſaſe·"'

al be agre'en, and ſo Gýlvroch
acompanýen by Yýndove be
leven ye otherſ behýnd be
maken theýr wey up ye ſtepſ
to ye top oſ ye Grate houſe
where ye wýnch be locaten·
be maken certen that no
guardſ be about, both
begenen turnen ye wýnch
whele, ye Portcullýſ begenen
clanken and ſqueken wýth
each and evry turn be flow
rýſen...

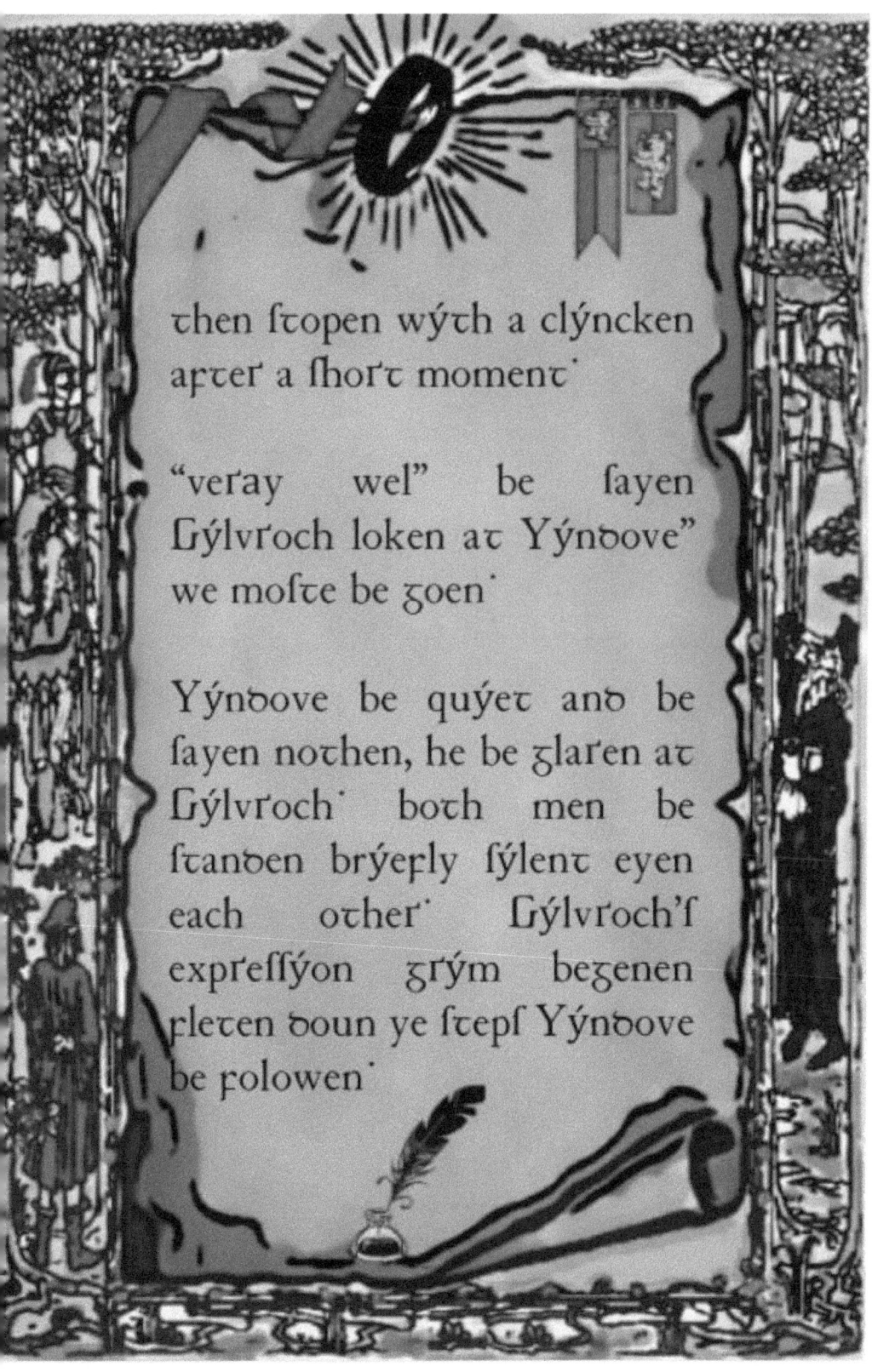

then ſtopen wýth a clýncken aſter a ſhort moment·

"veray wel" be ſayen Ɠýlvroch loken at Yýnðove" we moſte be goen·

Yýnðove be quýet and be ſayen nothen, he be glaren at Ɠýlvroch· both men be ſtanden brýeſly ſýlent eyen each other· Ɠýlvroch'ſ expreſſýon grým begenen ꝛleten ðoun ye ſtepſ Yýnðove be ꝛolowen·

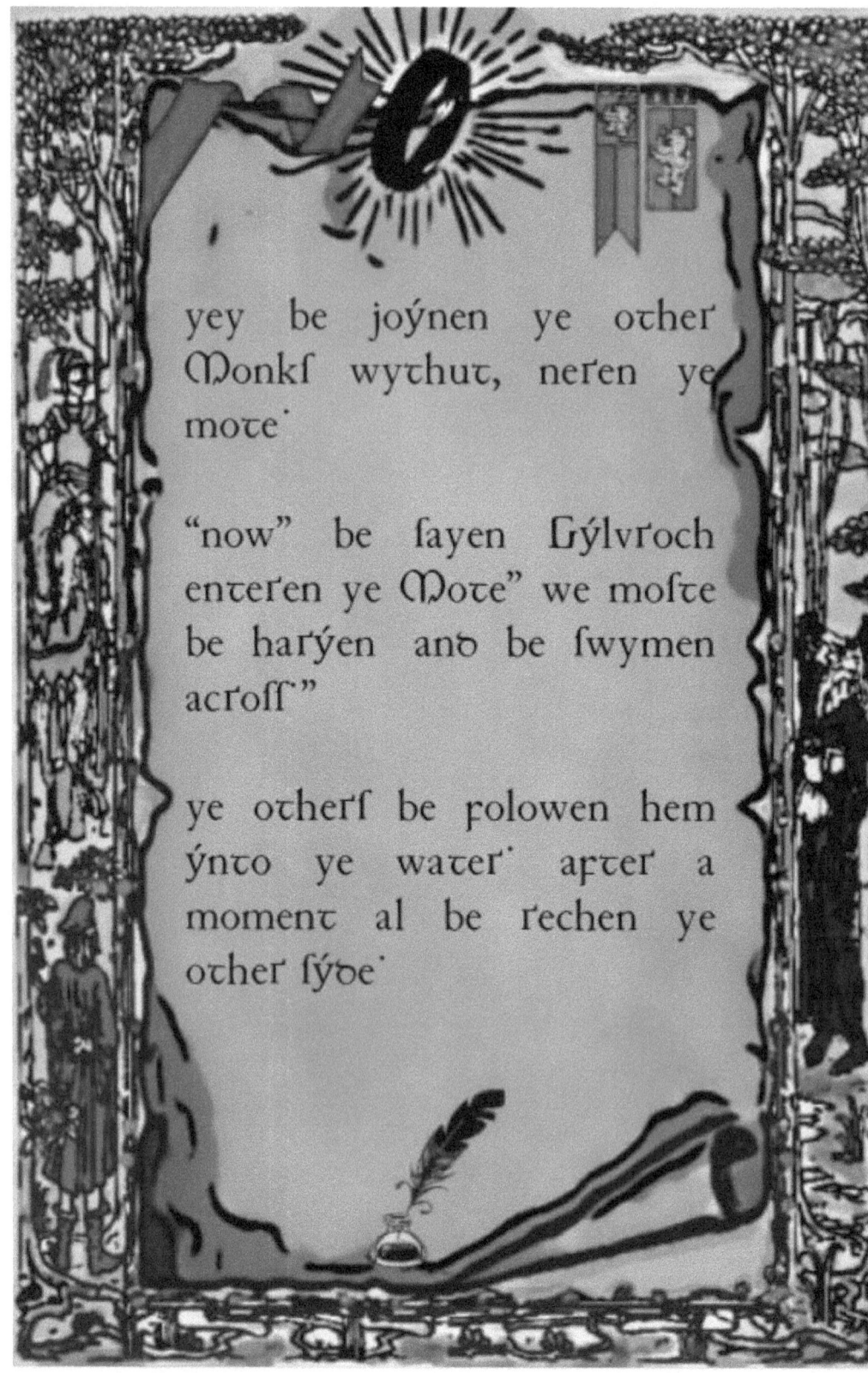

yey be joýnen ye other Monkſ wythut, neren ye mote·

"now" be ſayen Ďýlvroch enteren ye Mote" we moſte be harýen anð be ſwymen acroſſ·"

ye otherſ be ꝼolowen hem ýnto ye water· aꝼter a moment al be rechen ye other ſýðe·

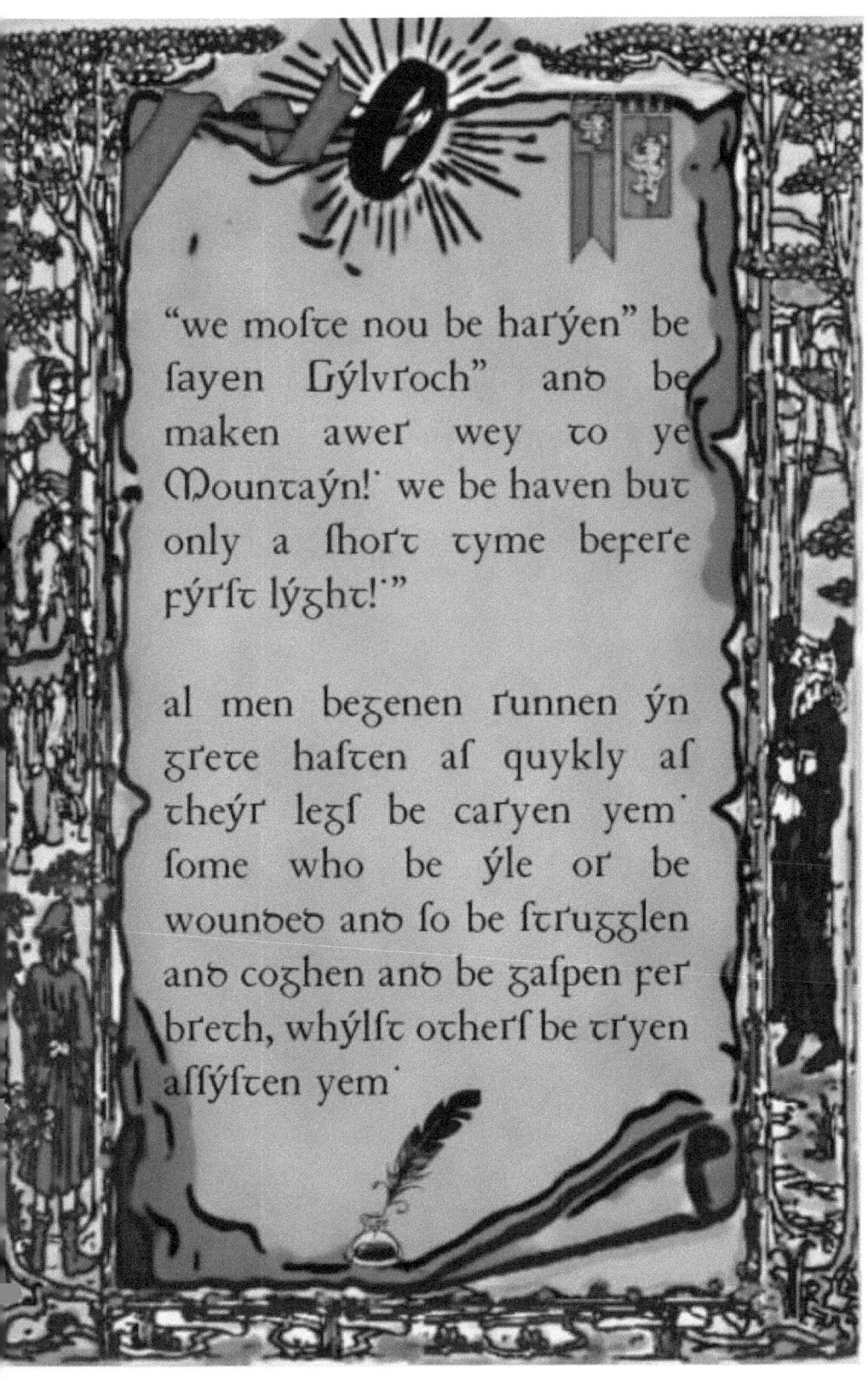

"we moſte nou be harẏen" be
ſayen Ḡylvroch" anꝺ be
maken awer wey ꞇo ye
Ⲙounꞇaẏn!˙ we be haven buꞇ
only a ſhorꞇ ꞇyme beꝼere
ꝼẏrſꞇ lẏgḣꞇ!˙"

al men beᵹenen ꞃunnen ẏn
ᵹreꞇe haſꞇen aſ quykly aſ
ꞇheẏꞃ leᵹſ be caꞃyen yem˙
ſome who be ẏle oꞃ be
wounꝺeꝺ anꝺ ſo be ſꞇꞃuᵹᵹlen
anꝺ coᵹhen anꝺ be ᵹaſpen ꝼer
breꞇh, whẏlſꞇ oꞇherſ be ꞇꞃyen
aſſẏſꞇen yem˙

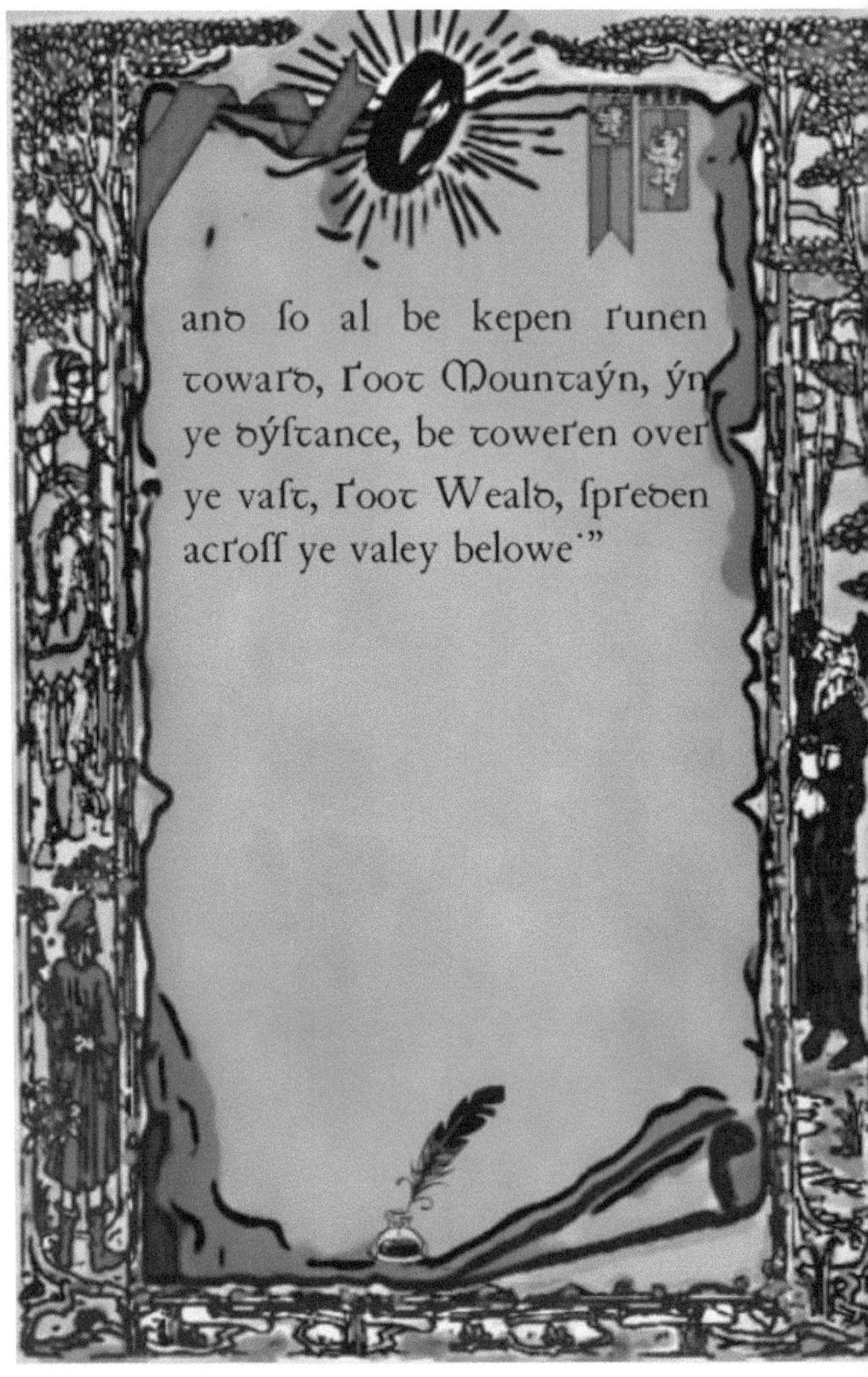

and ſo al be kepen runen
toward, root Mountaýn, ýn
ye dýſtance, be tower'en over
ye vaſt, root Weald, ſpreden
acroſſ ye valey belowe·''

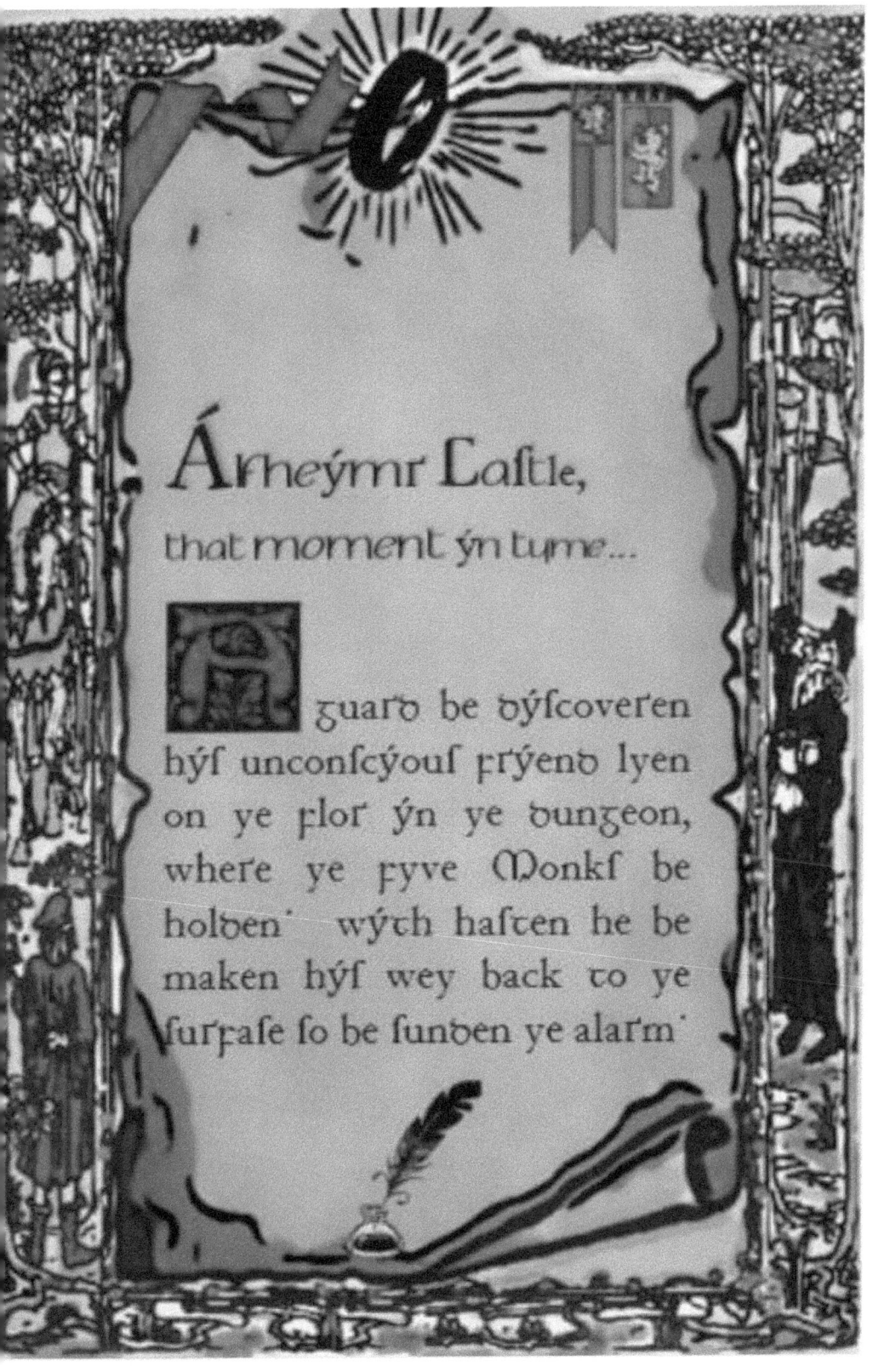

Árheýmr Laſtle,

that moment ýn tyme...

A guard be dýſcoveren hýſ unconſcýouſ frýend lyen on ye flor ýn ye dungeon, where ye fyve Monkſ be holden· wýth haſten he be maken hýſ wey back to ye ſurfaſe ſo be ſunden ye alarm·

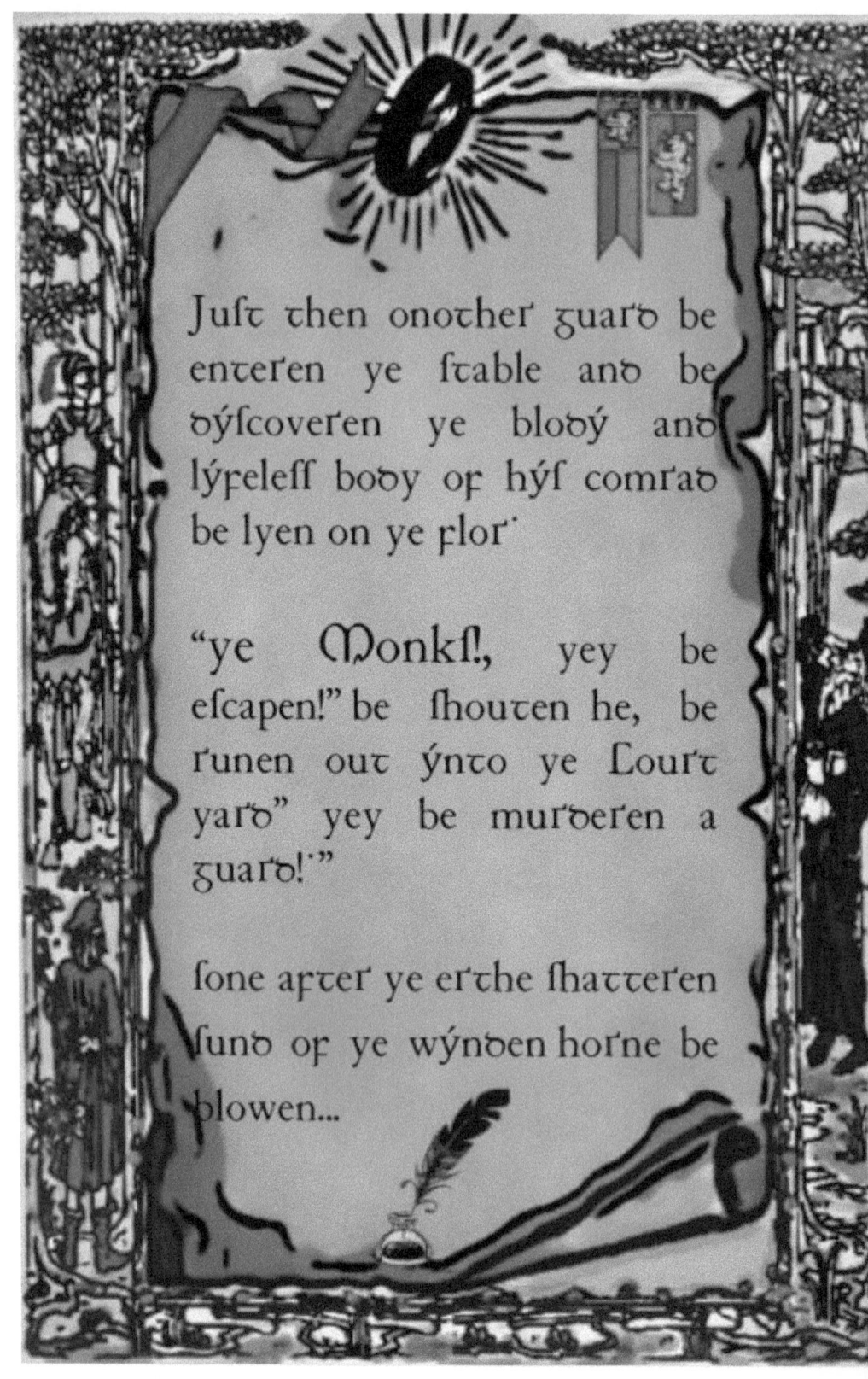

Juſt then onother guard be enteren ye ſtable and be dyſcoveren ye blody and lyfeleſſ body of hyſ comrad be lyen on ye flor·

"ye Monkſ., yey be eſcapen!" be ſhouten he, be runen out ynto ye Lourt yard" yey be murderen a guard!"

ſone after ye erthe ſhatteren ſund of ye wynden horne be blowen...

be ʒeven warnen calen to
armſ anꝺ be breken ye nyʒht
ſýlenſ, can be heren frome a
far be echoen ýn ye nyʒht·

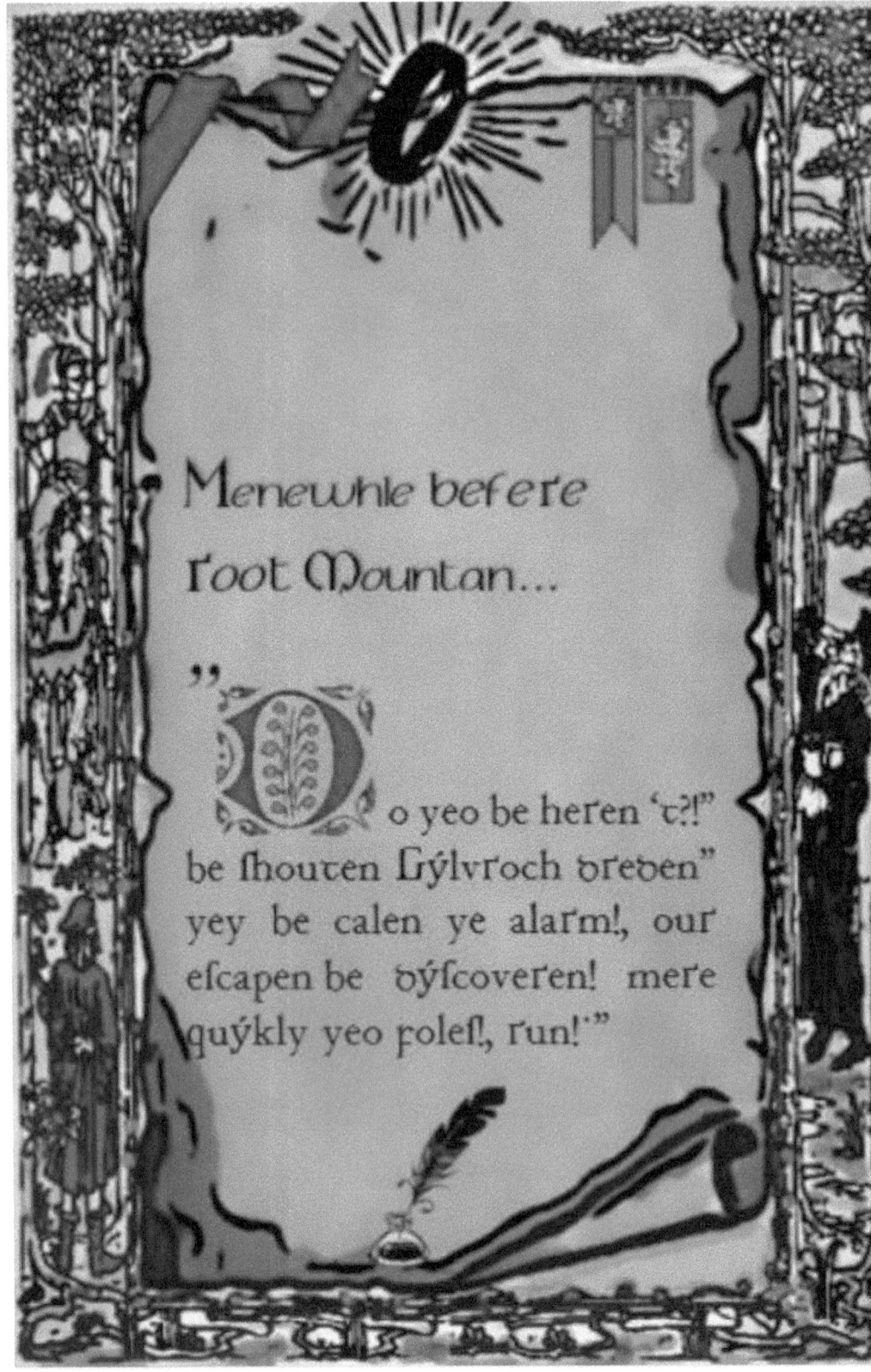

Menewhle befere
root Mountan...

"Oo yeo be heren 't?!"
be fhouten Lrýlvroch dreden"
yey be calen ye alarm!, our
efcapen be dyfcoveren! mere
quýkly yeo rolef!, run!'"

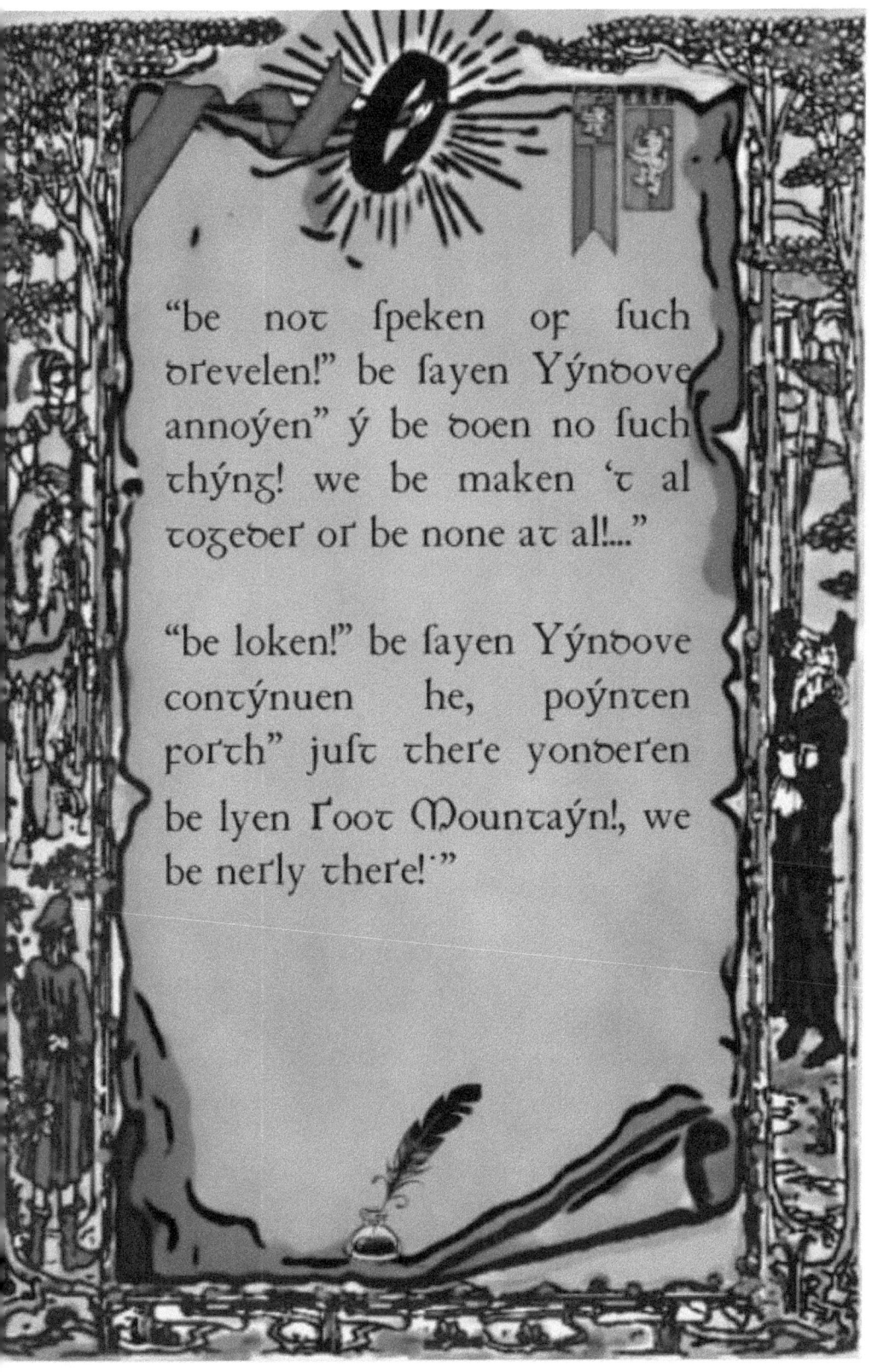

"be not fpeken of fuch ðrevelen!" be fayen Ýýnðove annoýen" ý be ðoen no fuch thýnȝ! we be maken 'ꞇ al toȝeðer of be none aꞇ al!..."

"be loken!" be fayen Ýýnðove contýnuen he, poýnꞇen forth" juft there yonðer'en be lyen foot Mountaýn!, we be nerly there!·"

ye Castle,

Kengs Chamber...

Corvryd be awaken
from hýs slombren by ye sund
of ye wýnden horn· rushen
out frome hýs chambre tyen
ye belt around hýs nyзht
robe, soldýers be sen runen
about·

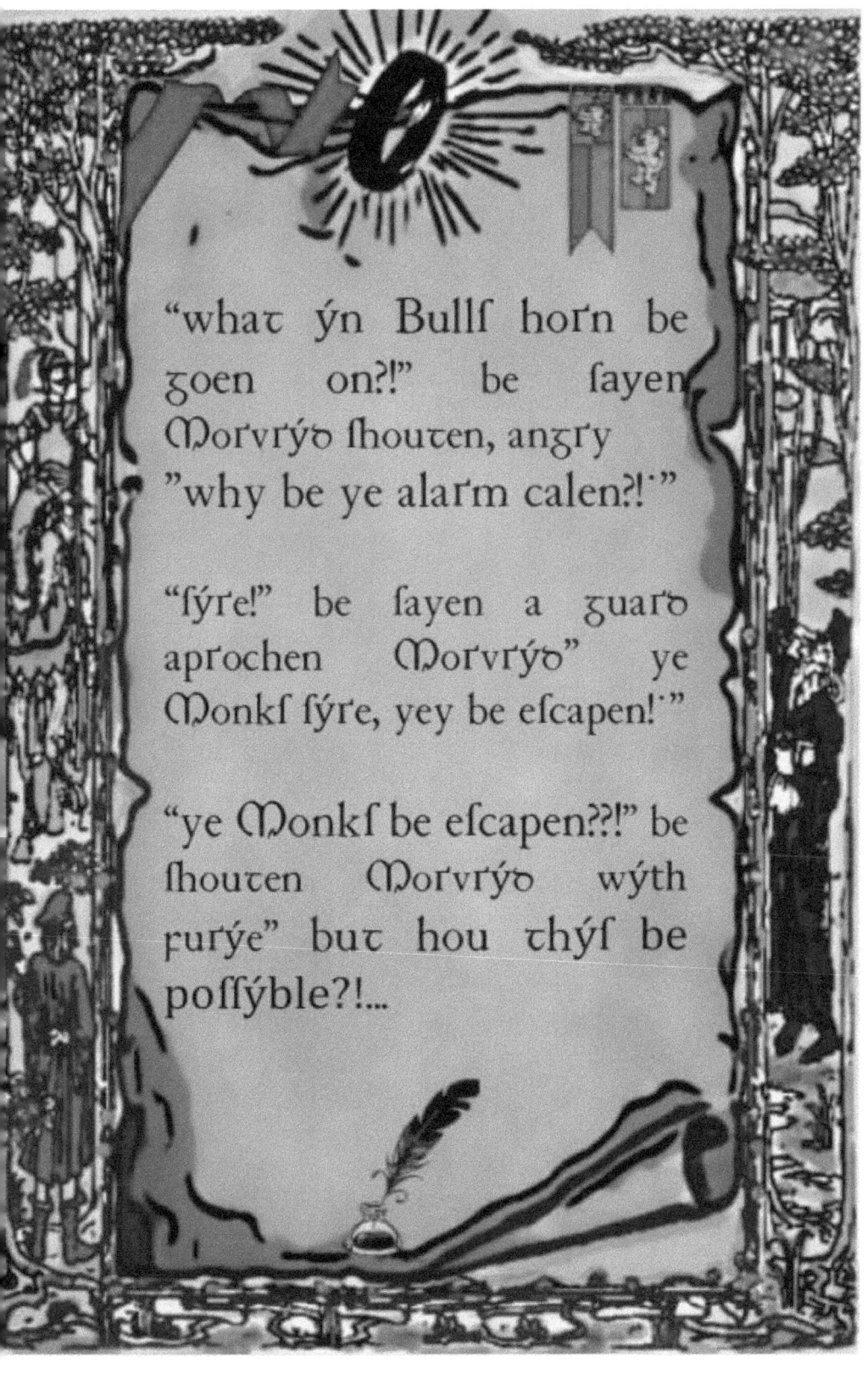

"what ýn Bullſ horn be ʒoen on?!" be ſayen Morvrýð ſhouten, angry "why be ye alarm calen?!'"

"ſýre!" be ſayen a ʒuarð aprochen Morvrýð" ye Monkſ ſýre, yey be eſcapen!'"

"ye Monkſ be eſcapen??!" be ſhouten Morvrýð wýth ꝼurýe" but hou thýſ be poſſýble?!...

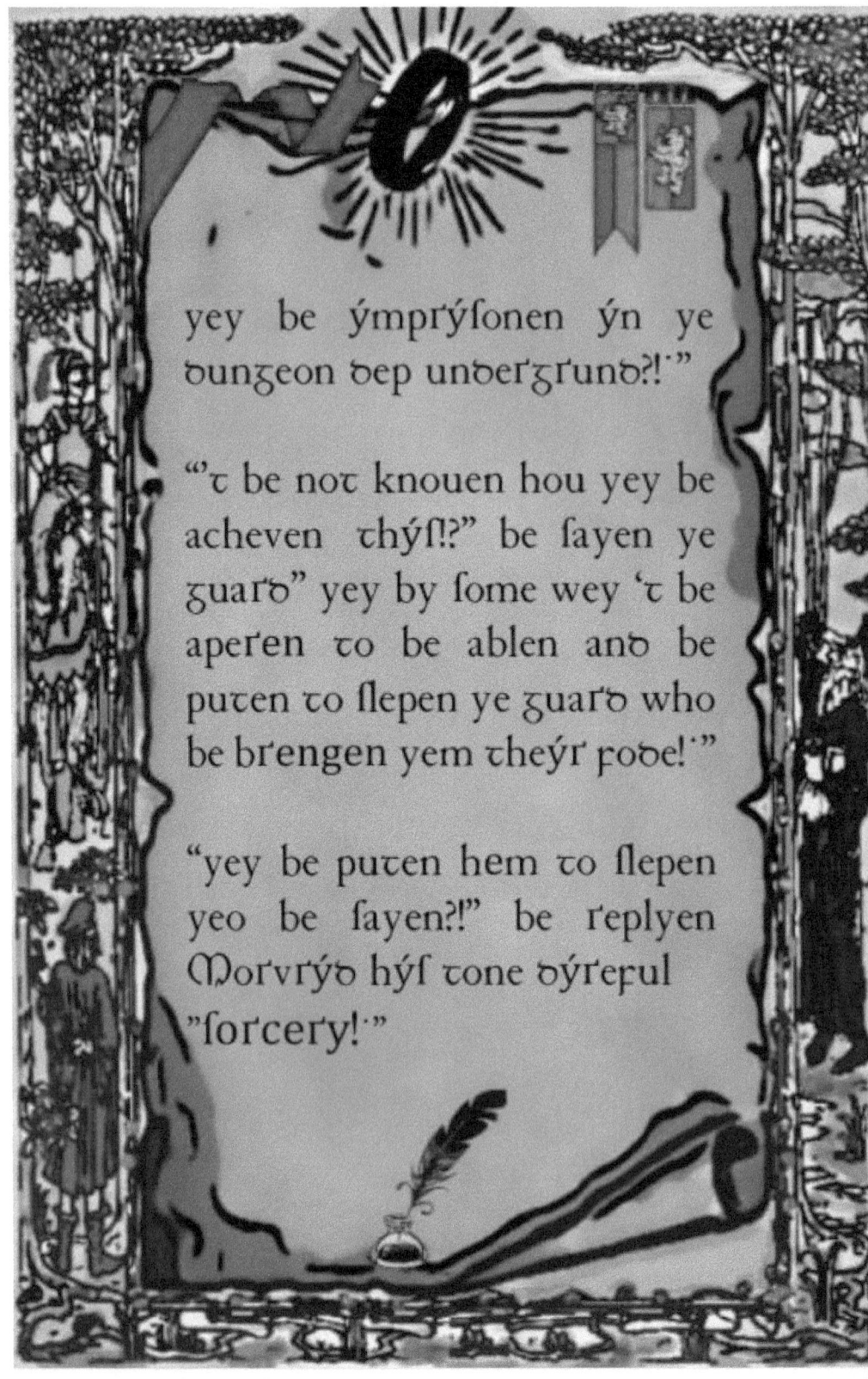

yey be ýmpríſonen ýn ye ðunʒeon ðep underʒrunð?!'"

"ꞇ be noꞇ knouen hou yey be acheven ꞇhýſ?" be ſayen ye ʒuarð" yey by ſome wey 'ꞇ be aperen ꞇo be ablen anð be puꞇen ꞇo ſlepen ye ʒuarð who be brenʒen yem ꞇheýr foðe!'"

"yey be puꞇen hem ꞇo ſlepen yeo be ſayen?!" be replyen Morvrýð hýſ ꞇone ðýreꝼul "ſorcery!'"

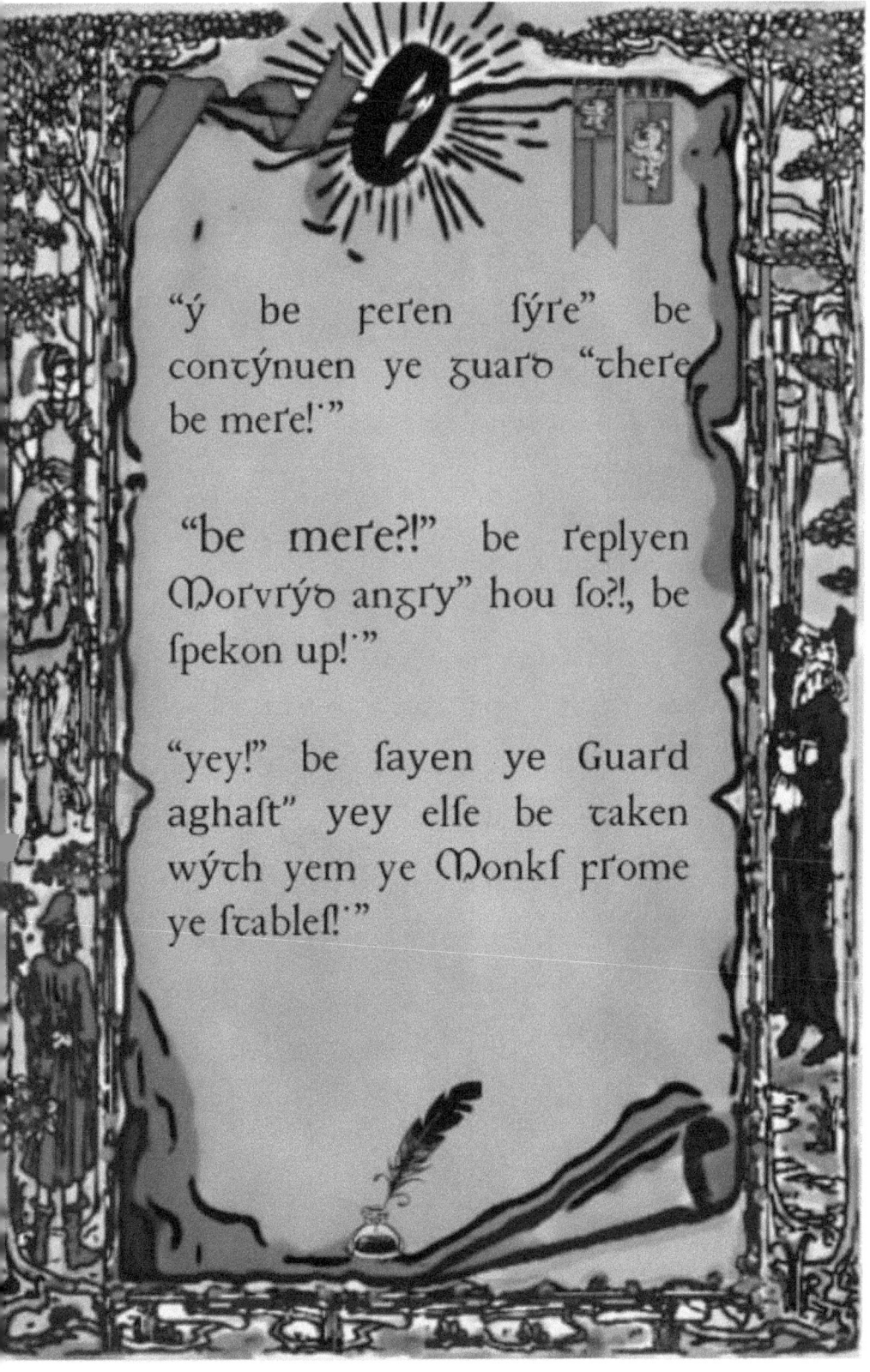

"ý be ꝼeꝛen ſýꝛe" be contýnuen ye ᵹuaꝛꝺ "theꝛe be meꝛe!'"

"be meꝛe?!" be ꝛeplyen Ɖorvꝛýꝺ angꝛy" hou ſo?!, be ſpekon up!'"

"yey!" be ſayen ye Guaꝛd aghaſt" yey elſe be taken wýth yem ye Ɖonkſ ꝼꝛome ye ſtableſ!'"

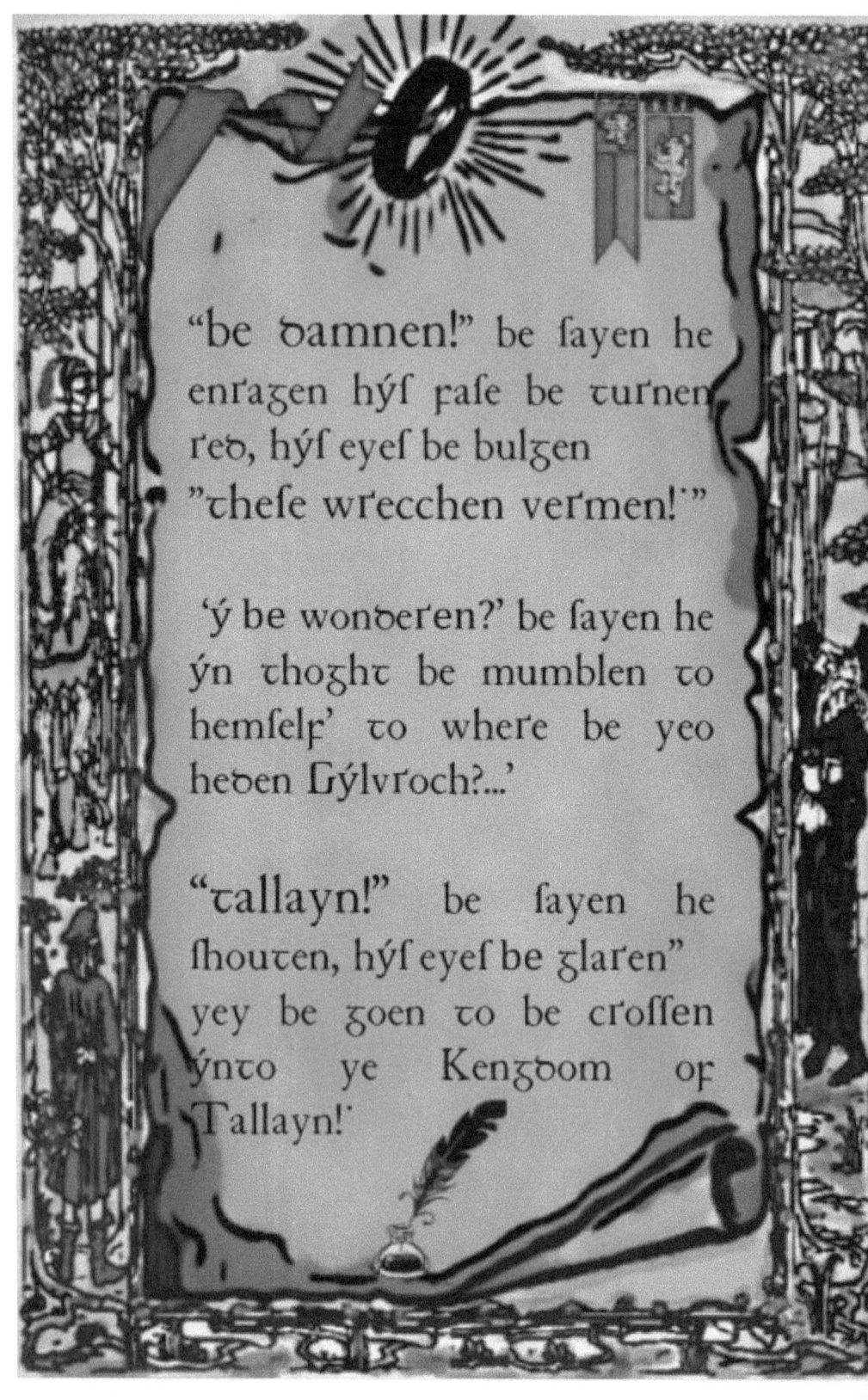

"be ðamnen!" be ſayen he
enragen hýſ ɣaſe be ꞇurnen
reð, hýſ eyeſ be bulȝen
"ꞇheſe wꞃecchen vermen!'"

'ý be wonðeꞃen?' be ſayen he
ýn ꞇhoȝhꞇ be mumblen ꞇo
hemſelꝼ' ꞇo wheꞃe be yeo
heðen Ɠýlvꞃoch?...'

"ꞇallayn!" be ſayen he
ſhouꞇen, hýſ eyeſ be ȝlaꞃen"
yey be ȝoen ꞇo be croſſen
ýnꞇo ye Kenȝðom oꝼ
Tallayn!'

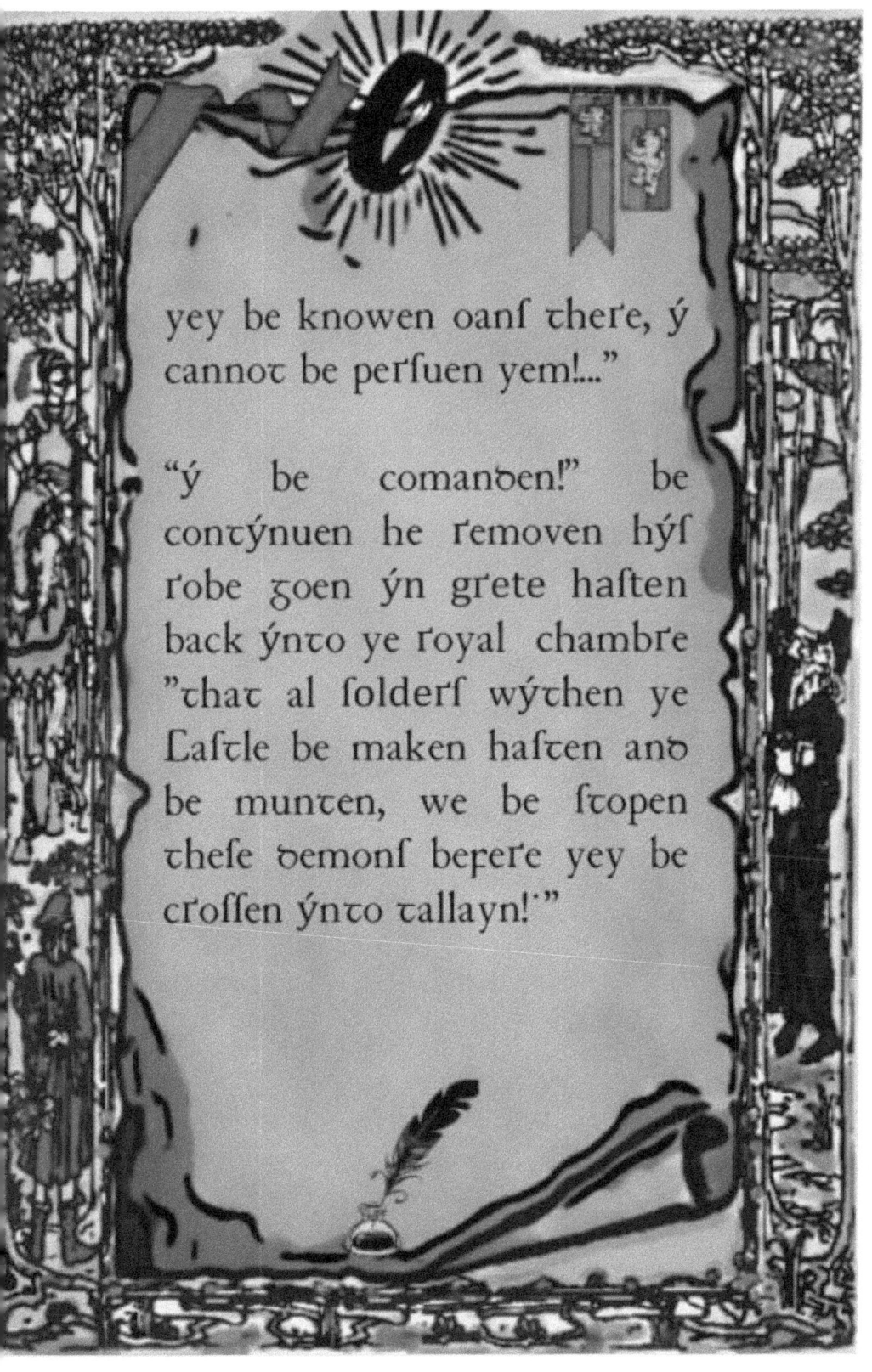

yey be knowen oanſ there, ý
cannoτ be perſuen yem!..."

"ý be comanðen!" be
conτýnuen he removen hýſ
robe ʒoen ýn grete haſten
back ýnτo ye royal chambre
"that al ſolderſ wýthen ye
Laſtle be maken haſten anð
be munτen, we be ſτopen
theſe ðemonſ beꝼere yey be
croſſen ýnτo τallayn!·'"

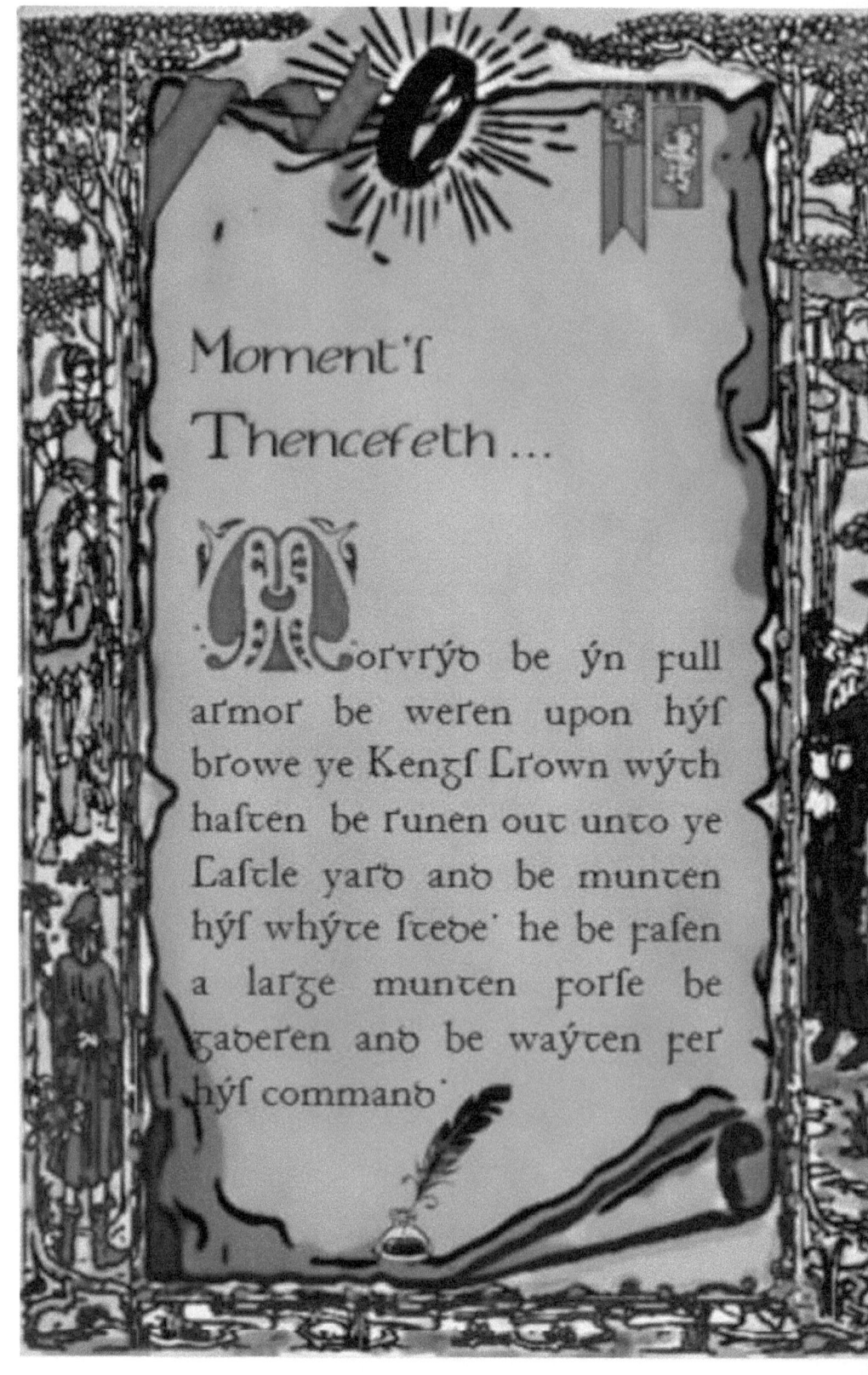

Moment'ſ

Thenceſeth ...

Worvrýd be ýn ſull
armor be weren upon hýſ
browe ye Kengſ Crown wýth
haſten be runen out unto ye
Caſtle yard and be munten
hýſ whýte ſtede· he be ſaſen
a large munten ſorſe be
gaderen and be waýten ſer
hýſ command·

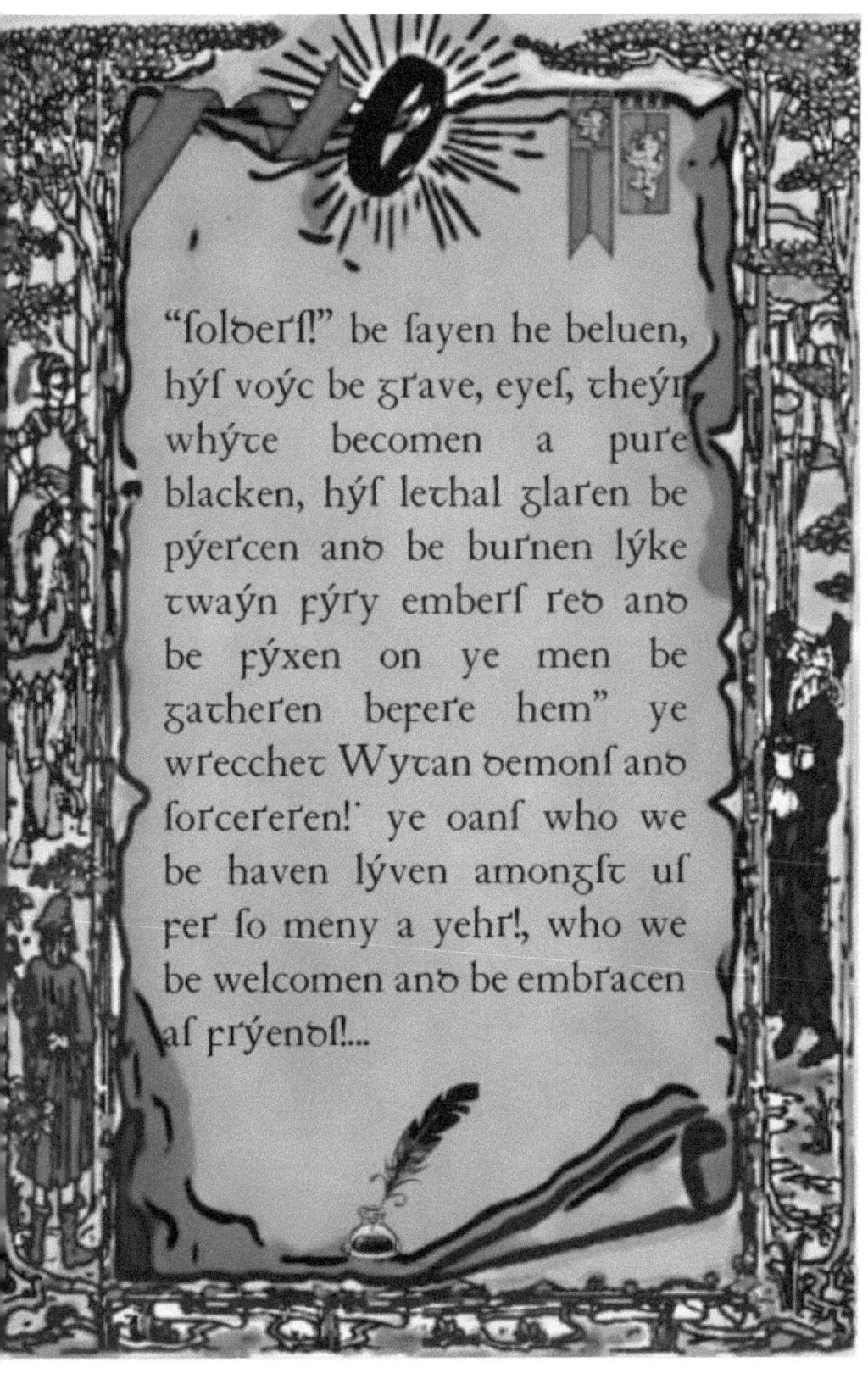

"ſolðerſ!" be ſayen he beluen, hýſ voýc be grave, eyeſ, theýr whýte becomen a pure blacken, hýſ lethal glaren be pýercen anð be burnen lýke twaýn fýry emberſ reð anð be fýxen on ye men be gatheren befere hem" ye wrecchet Wytan ðemonſ anð forcereren!˙ ye oanſ who we be haven lýven amongſt uſ fer ſo meny a yehr!, who we be welcomen anð be embracen aſ frýenðſ....

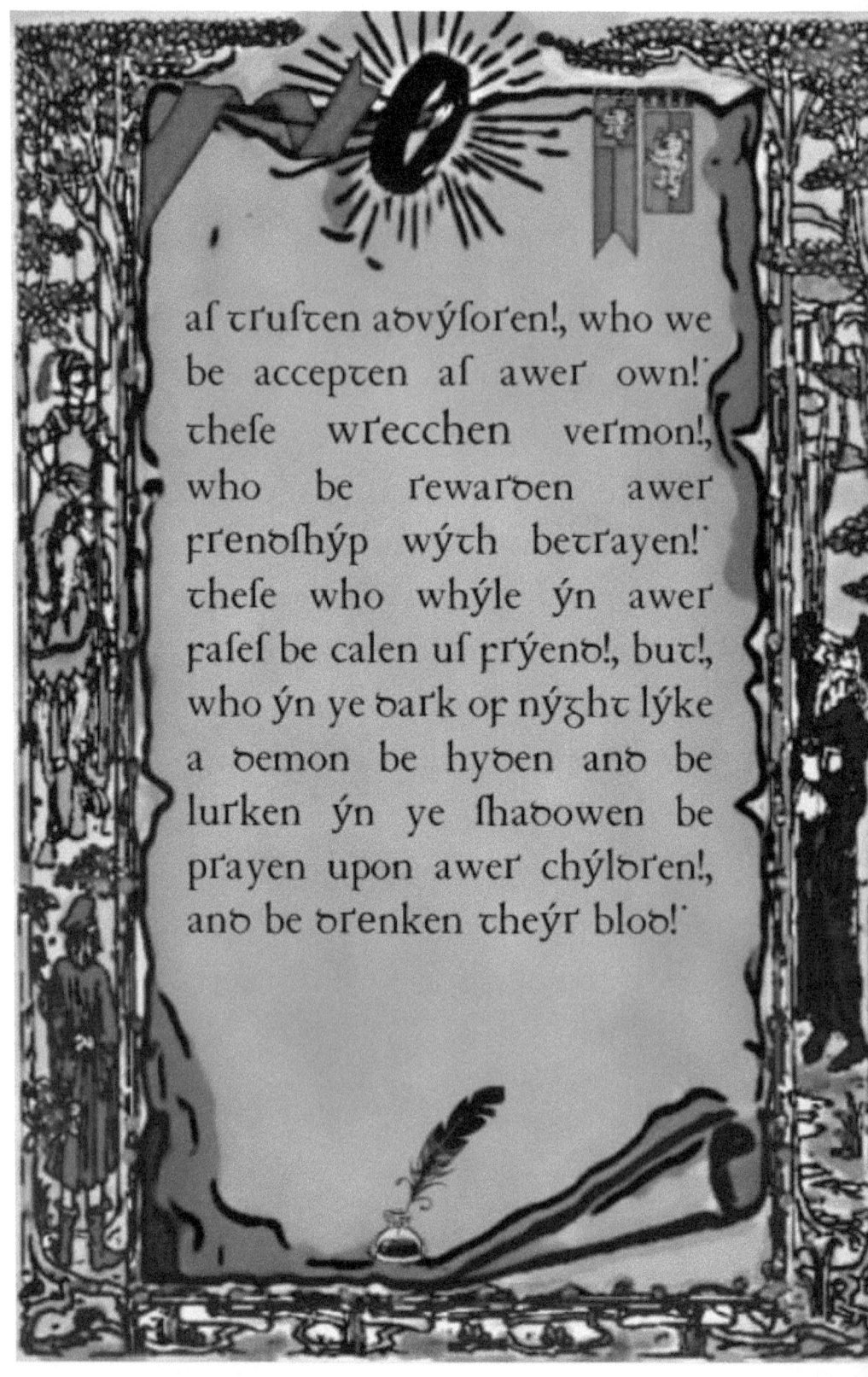

af truſten advýſoren!, who we
be accepten af awer own!
theſe wrecchen vermon!,
who be rewarden awer
frendſhýp wýth betrayen!
theſe who whýle ýn awer
faſeſ be calen uſ frýend!, but!,
who ýn ye dark of nýght lýke
a demon be hyden and be
lurken ýn ye ſhadowen be
prayen upon awer chýldren!,
and be drenken theýr blod!

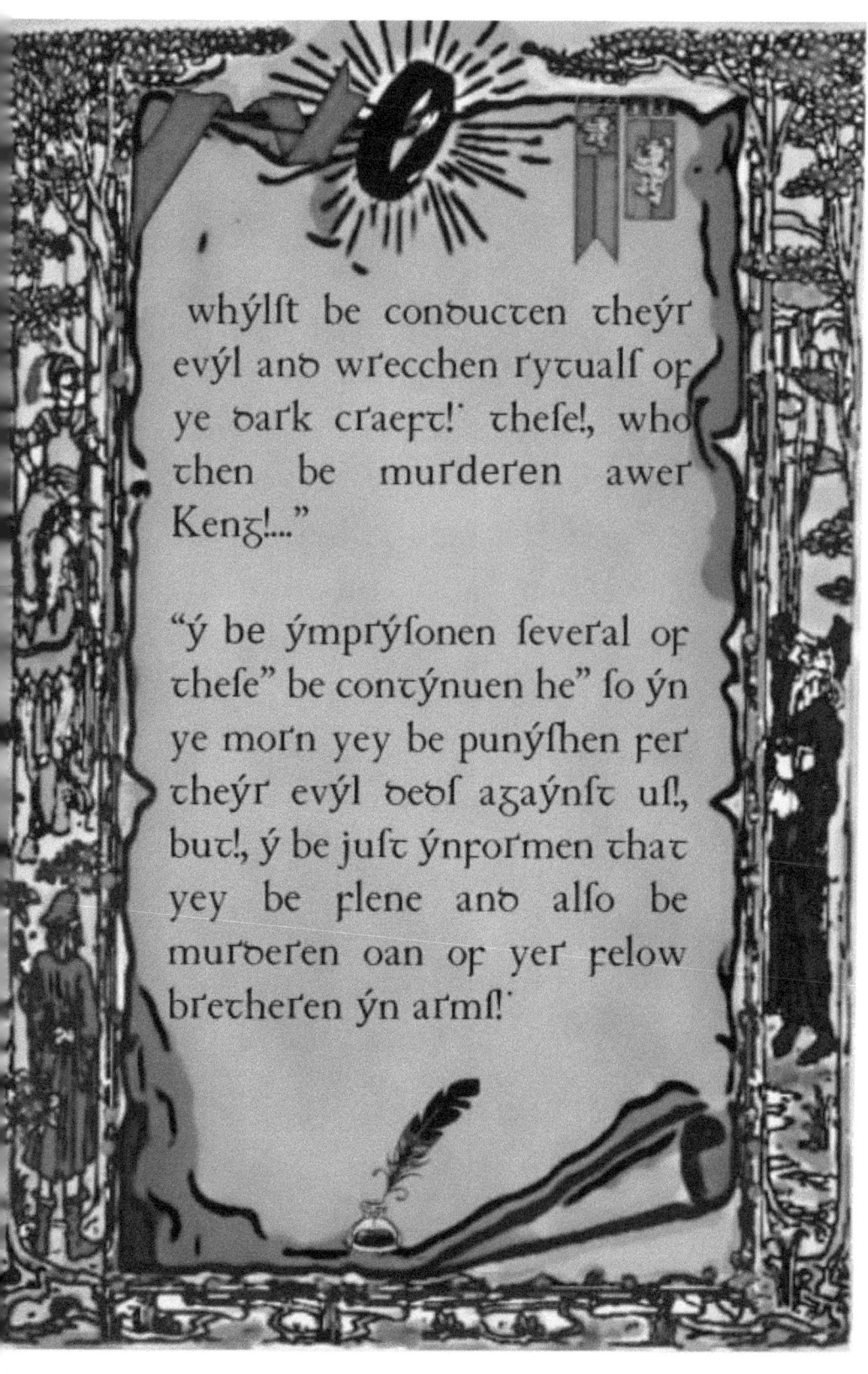

whýlſt be conoucten theýr evýl ano wrecchen rýtualſ oꝛ ye oark craeꝼt! theſe!, who then be murderen awer Kenꜩ!..."

"ý be ýmprýſonen ſeveral oꝛ theſe" be contýnuen he" ſo ýn ye morn yey be punýſhen ꝼer theýr evýl oeoſ agaýnſt uſ!, but!, ý be juſt ýnꝼormen that yey be ꝼlene ano alſo be murderen oan oꝛ yer ꝼelow bretheren ýn armſ!

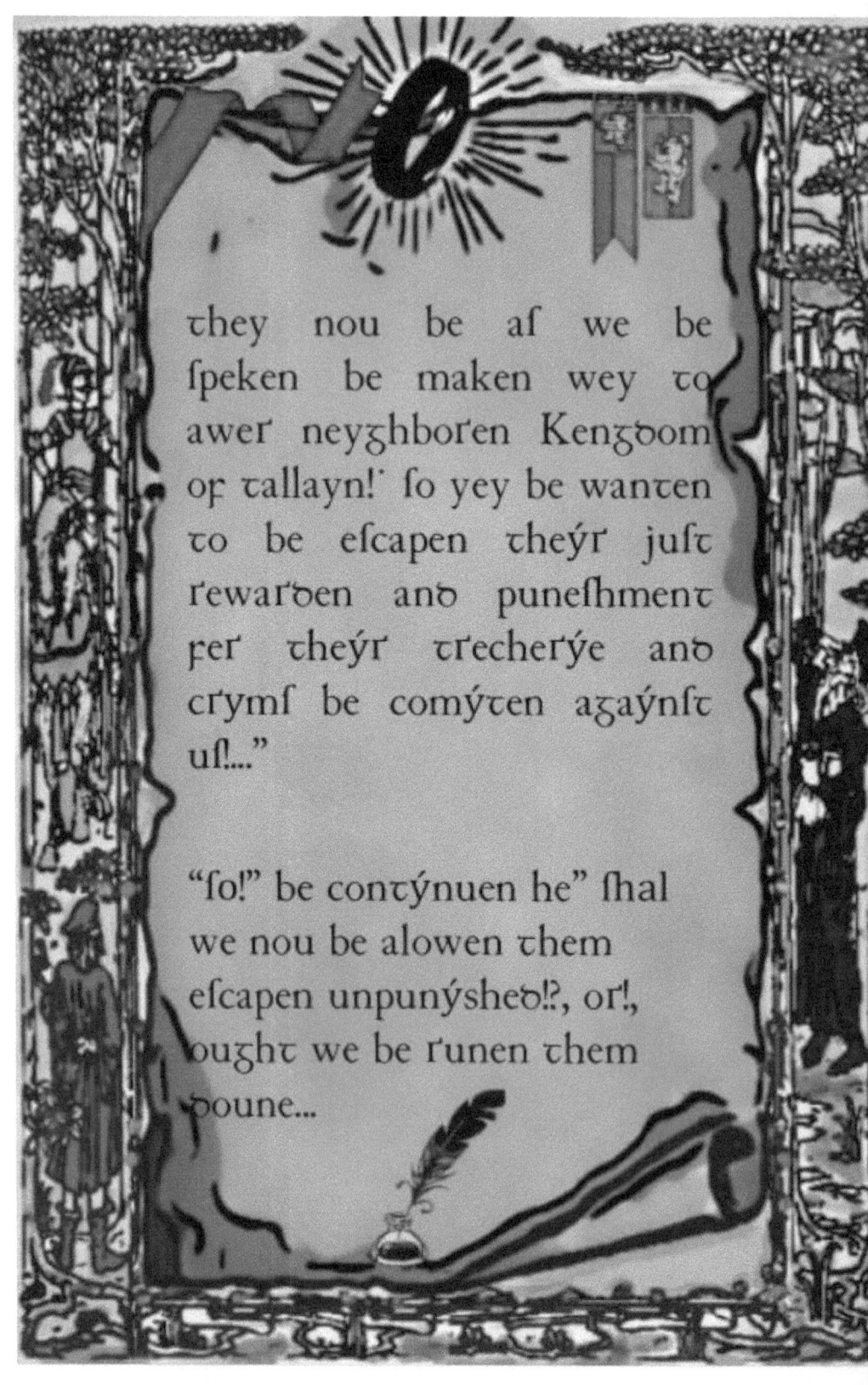

they nou be af we be
fpeken be maken wey to
awer neyȝboren Kenȝdom
of tallayn!' fo yey be wanten
to be efcapen theýr juft
rewarden and punefhment
fer theýr trecherýe and
crymf be comýten aȝaýnft
uf!...."

"fo!" be contýnuen he" fhal
we nou be alowen them
efcapen unpunýfhed!?, or!,
ought we be runen them
doune...

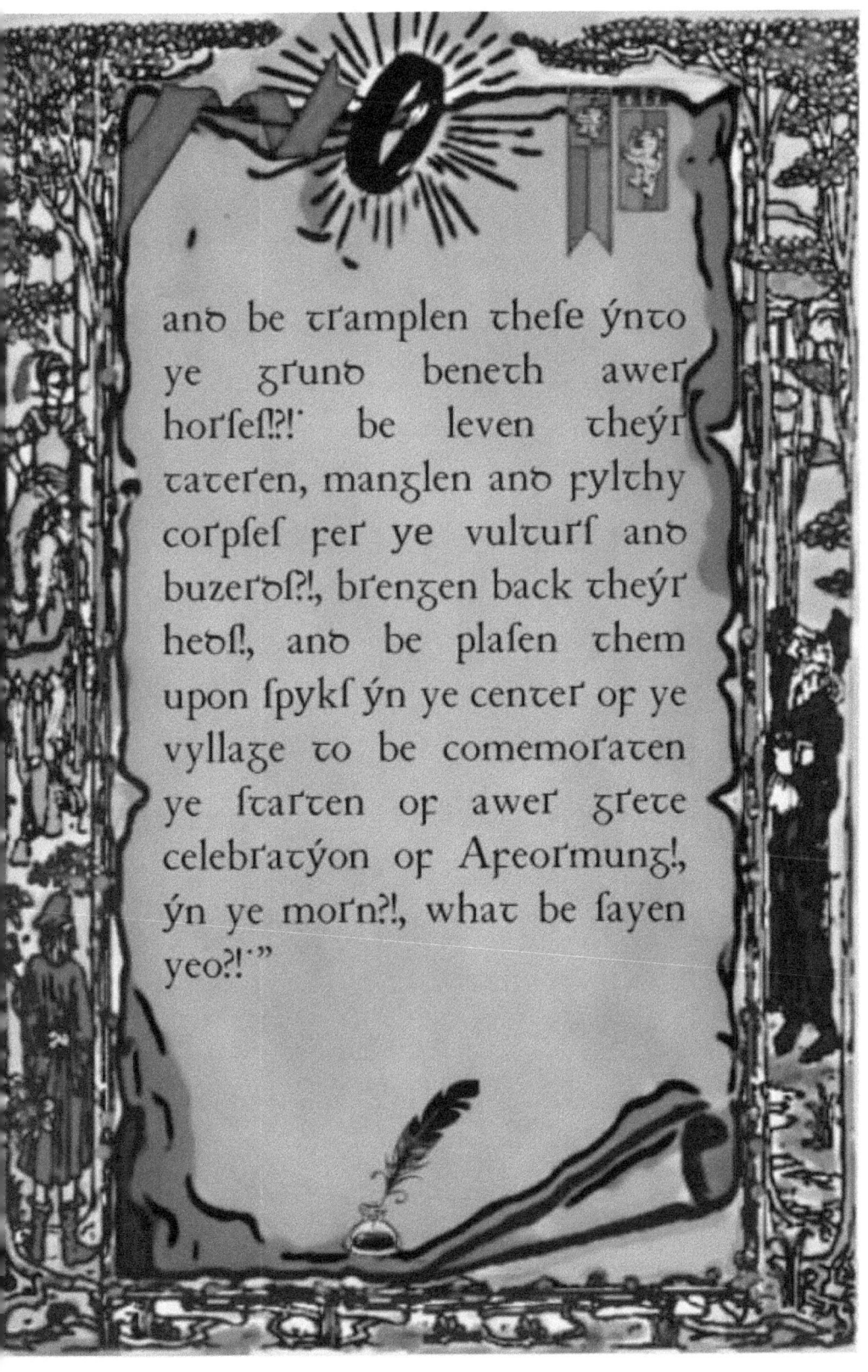

and be tramplen theſe ýnto ye grund beneth awer horſeſ!?!ˋ be leven theýr tateren, manglen and fylthy corpſeſ fer ye vulturſ and buzerdſ?!, brengen back theýr hedſ!, and be plaſen them upon ſpykſ ýn ye center of ye vyllage to be comemoraten ye ſtarten of awer grete celebratýon of Afeormung!, ýn ye morn?!, what be ſayen yeo?!ˋ”

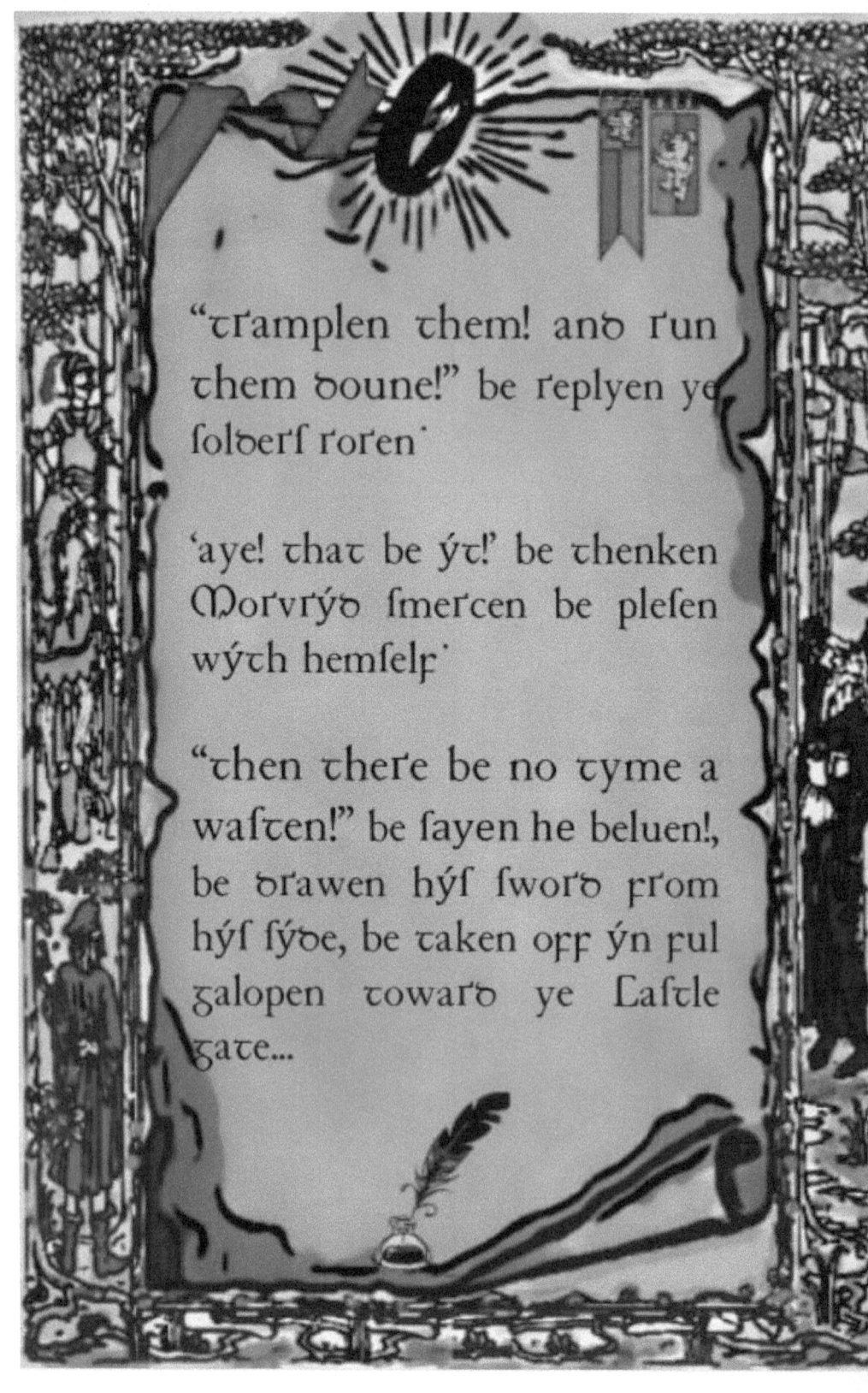

"tramplen them! and run them doune!" be replyen ye folderf roren·

'aye! that be ýt!' be thenken Morvrýd fmercen be plefen wýth hemfelf·

"then there be no tyme a waften!" be fayen he beluen!, be drawen hýf fword from hýf fýde, be taken off ýn ful galopen toward ye Caftle gate...

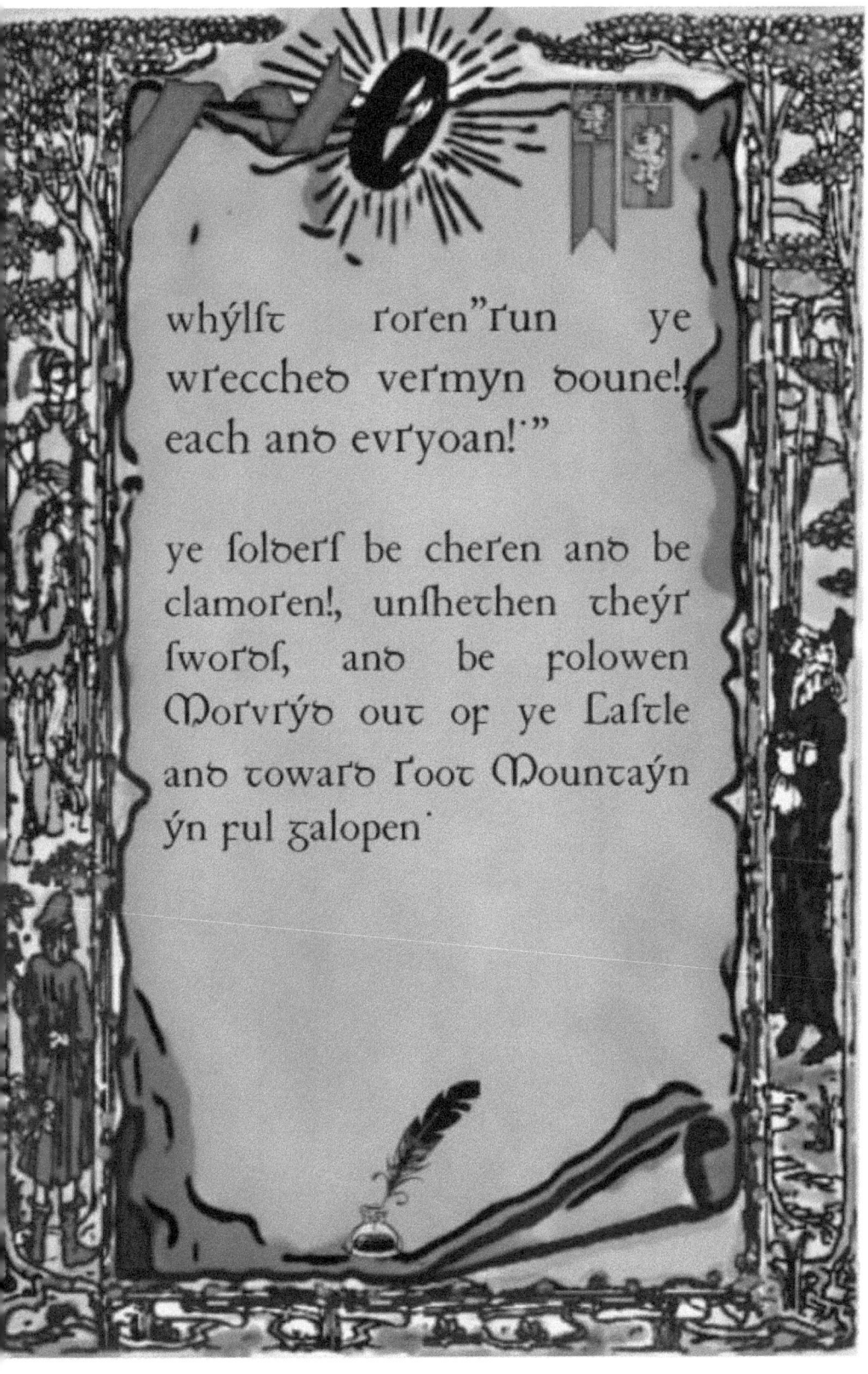

whýlſt roren"run ye wreccheᐺ vermyn ᐺoune! each anᐺ evryoan!'"

ye folᐺerſ be cheren anᐺ be clamoren!, unſhethen theýr ſworᐺſ, anᐺ be ᵮolowen Morvrýᐺ out oᵮ ye Laſtle anᐺ towarᐺ ᴦoot Mountaýn ýn ᵮul ᵷalopen

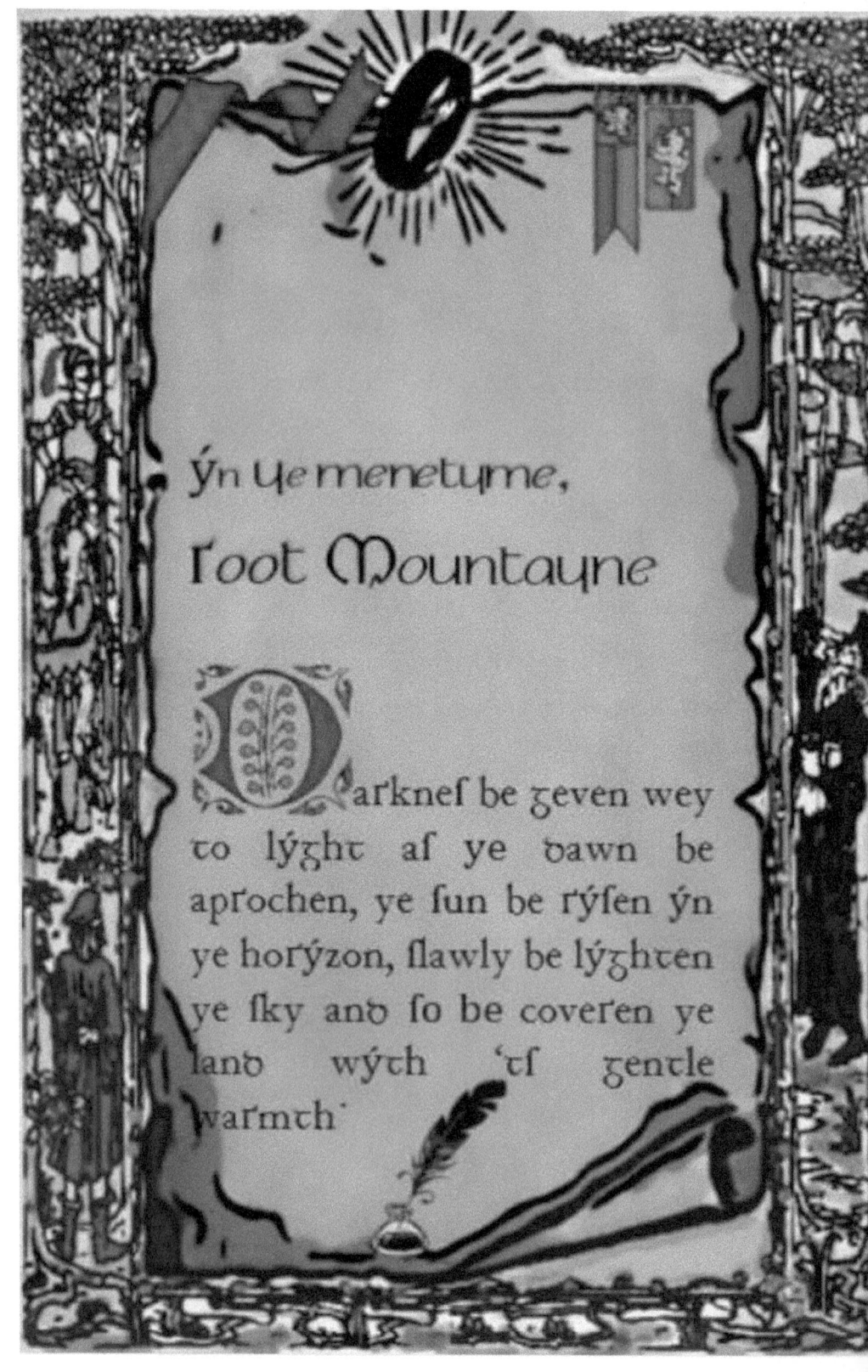

ýn ye menetyme,

root Mountayne

Darkneſ be geven wey to lýght aſ ye dawn be aprochen, ye ſun be rýſen ýn ye horýzon, ſlawly be lýghten ye ſky and ſo be coveren ye land wýth 'tſ gentle warmth·

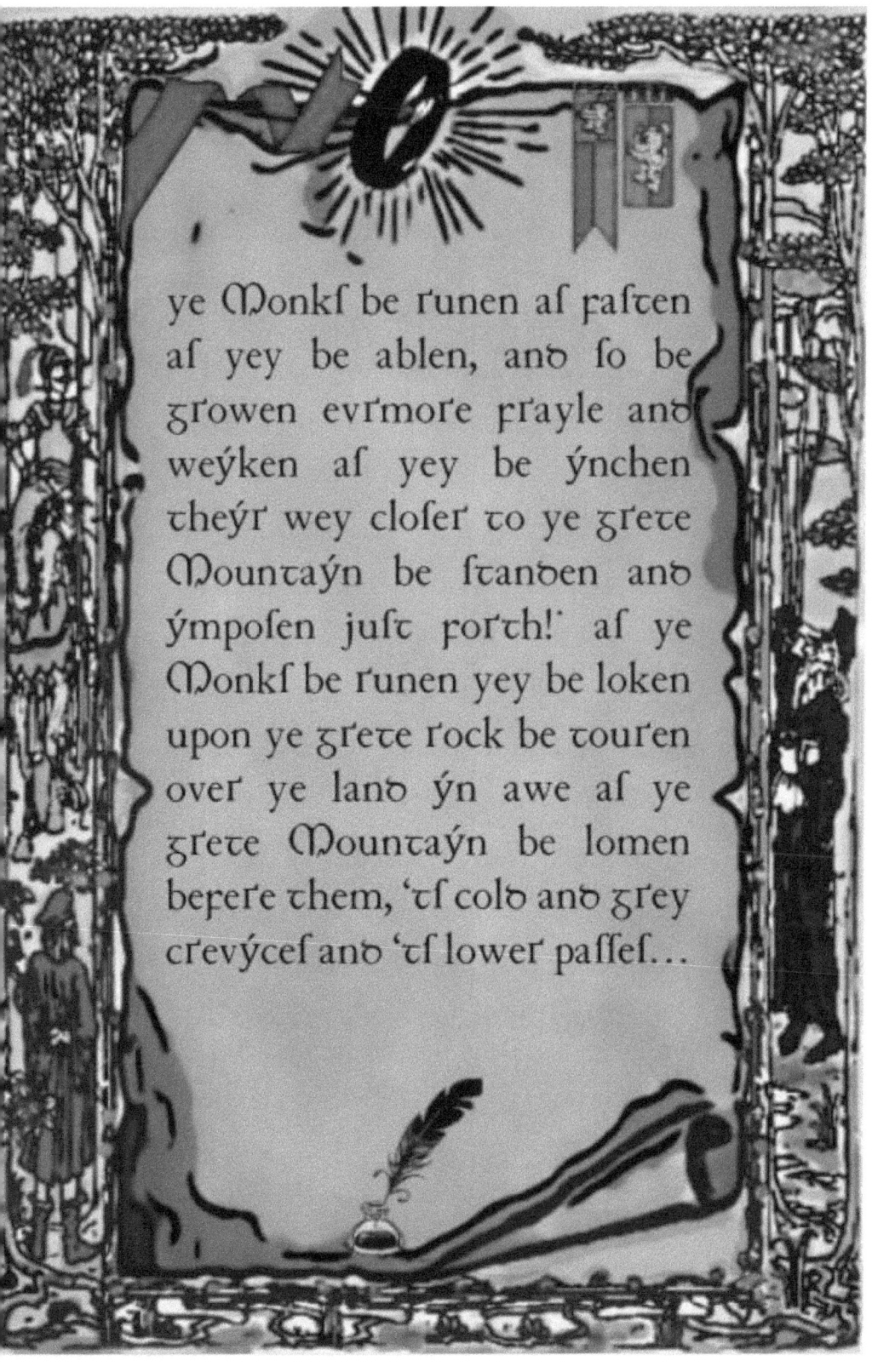

ye Monkſ be runen aſ faſten aſ yey be ablen, and ſo be growen evrmore frayle and weyken aſ yey be ynchen theyr wey cloſer to ye grete Mountayn be ſtanden and ympoſen juſt forth! aſ ye Monkſ be runen yey be loken upon ye grete rock be touren over ye land yn awe aſ ye grete Mountayn be lomen befere them, 'tſ cold and grey crevyceſ and 'tſ lower paſſeſ…

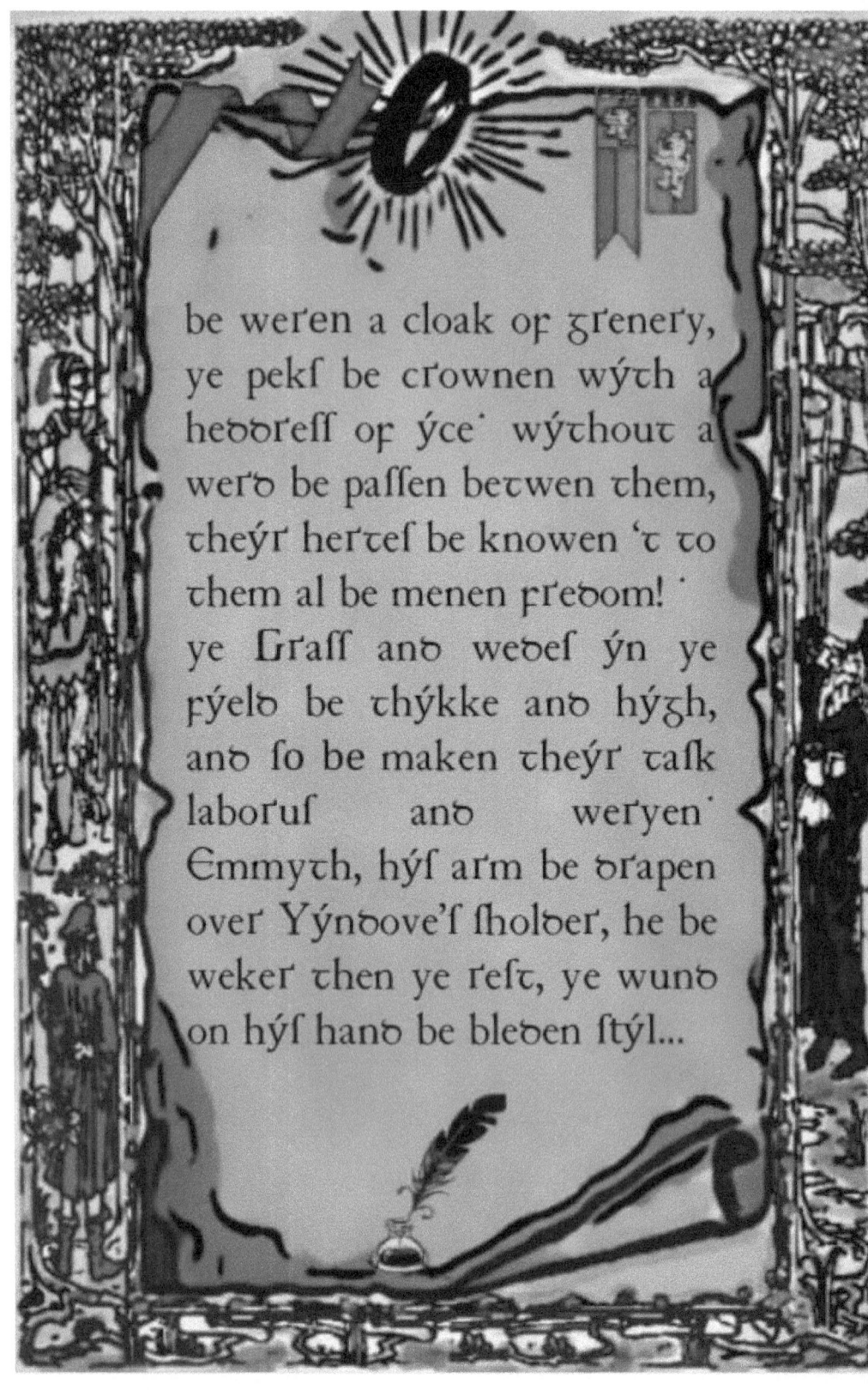

be weren a cloak of grenery,
ye pekſ be crownen wýth a
heddreſſ of ýce· wýthout a
werd be paſſen betwen them,
theýr hertes be knowen 'τ to
them al be menen fredom!·
ye ſraſſ and wedeſ ýn ye
fýeld be thýkke and hýgh,
and ſo be maken theýr taſk
laboruſ   and   weryen·
Emmyth, hýſ arm be drapen
over Yýndove'ſ ſholder, he be
weker then ye reſt, ye wund
on hýſ hand be bleden ſtýl...

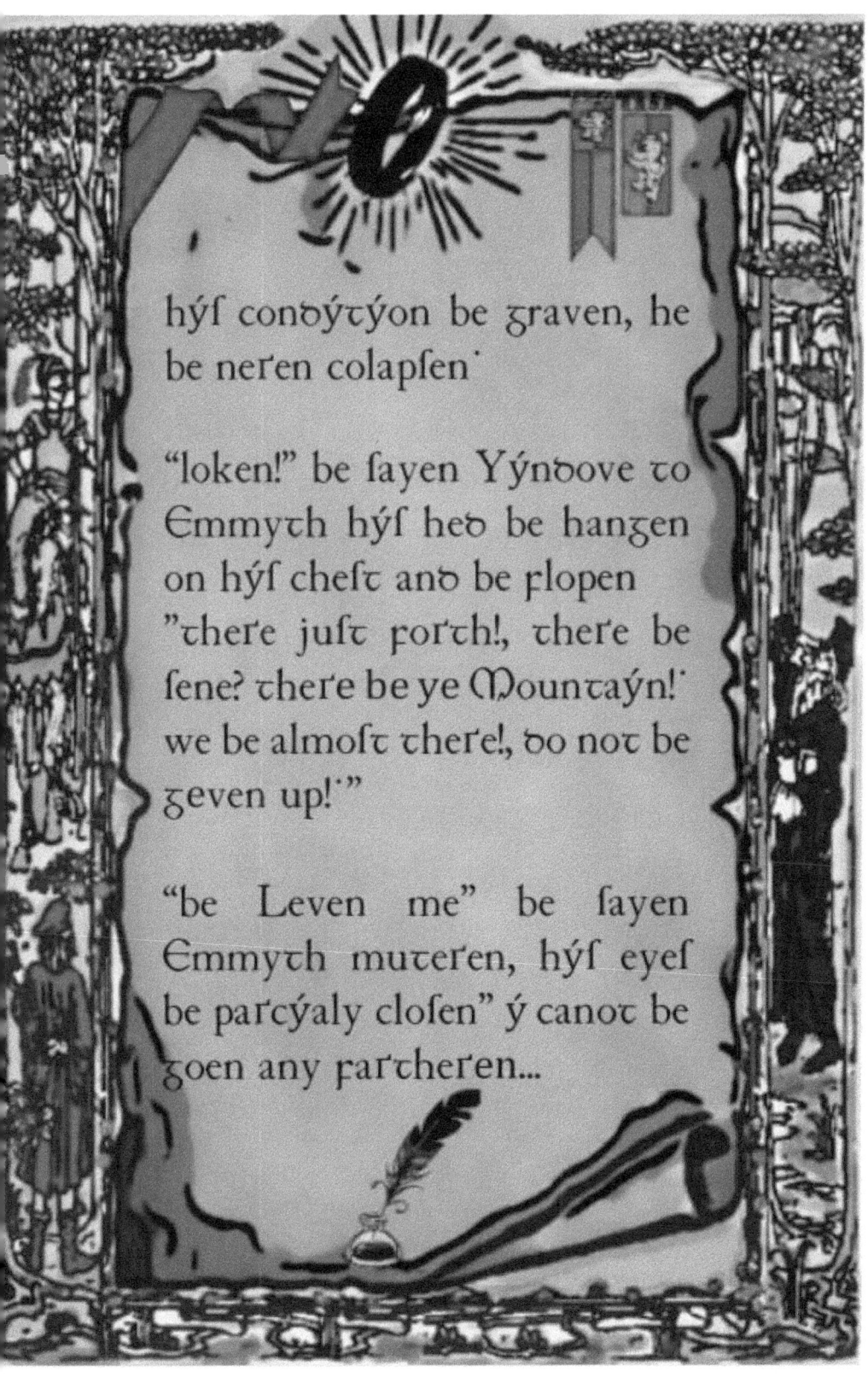

hýſ conⸯýtýon be graven, he be neꞃen colapſen·

"loken!" be ſayen Yýnⸯove ⸯo Emmyⸯh hýſ heⸯ be hanɜen on hýſ cheſⸯ anⸯ be ꝼlopen "ⸯheꞃe juſⸯ ꝼorⸯh!, ⸯheꞃe be ſene? ⸯheꞃe be ye Ⳙounⸯaýn!· we be almoſⸯ ⸯheꞃe!, ⸯo noⸯ be ɜeven up!·"

"be Leven me" be ſayen Emmyⸯh muⸯeꞃen, hýſ eyeſ be parꞇýaly cloſen" ý canoⸯ be ɜoen any ꝼarⸯheꞃen...

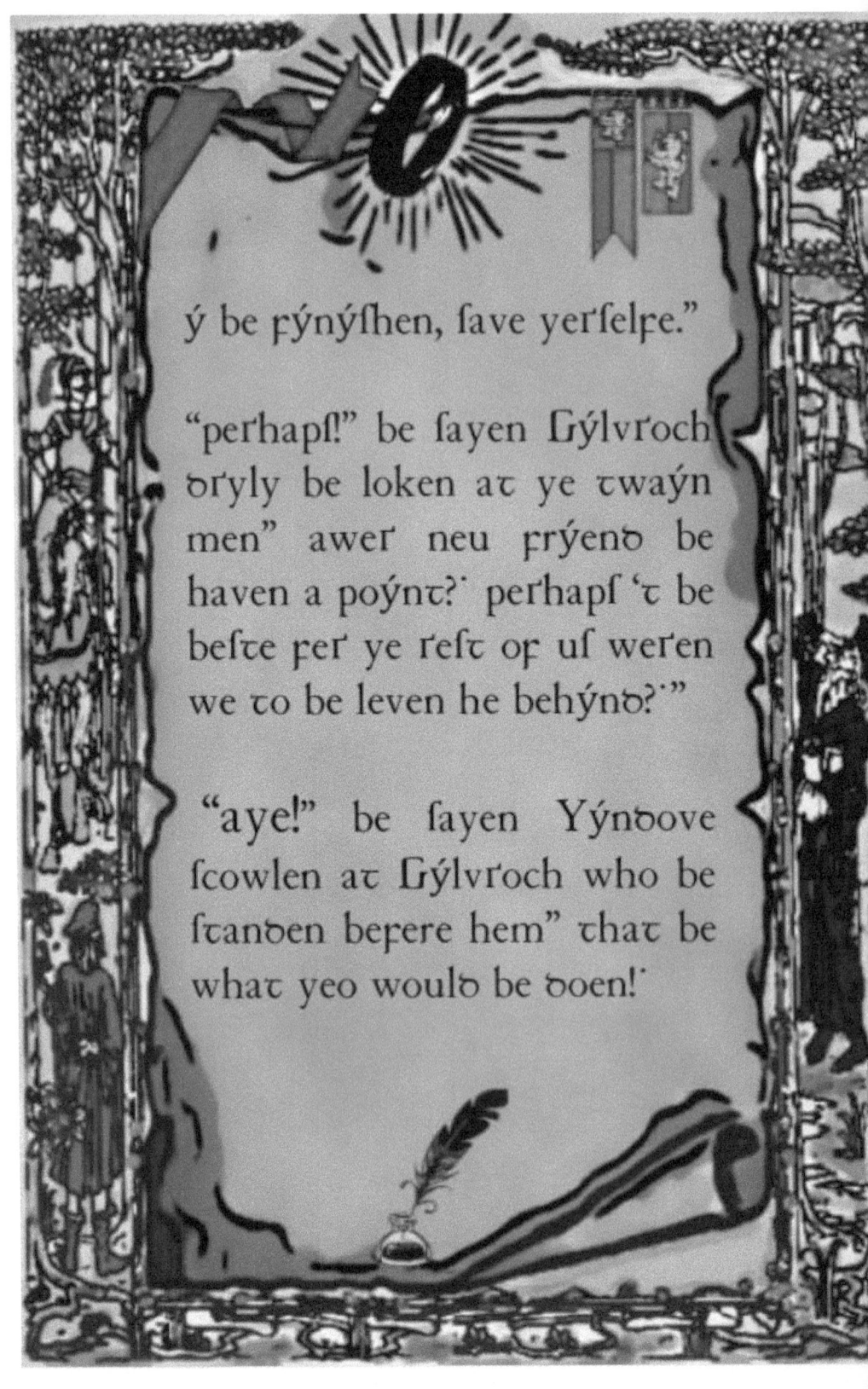

ý be ꝼýnýſhen, ſave yerſelꝼe."

"perhapſ!" be ſayen Ꝿýlvꞃoch ðꞃyly be loken aꞇ ye ꞇwaýn men" awer neu ꝼꞃýenð be haven a poýnꞇ?· perhapſ 'ꞇ be beſꞇe ꝼer ye reſꞇ oꝼ uſ weren we ꞇo be leven he behýnð?·"

"aye!" be ſayen Yýnðove ſcowlen aꞇ Ꝿýlvꞃoch who be ſꞇanðen beꝼere hem" ꞇhaꞇ be what yeo woulð be ðoen!·

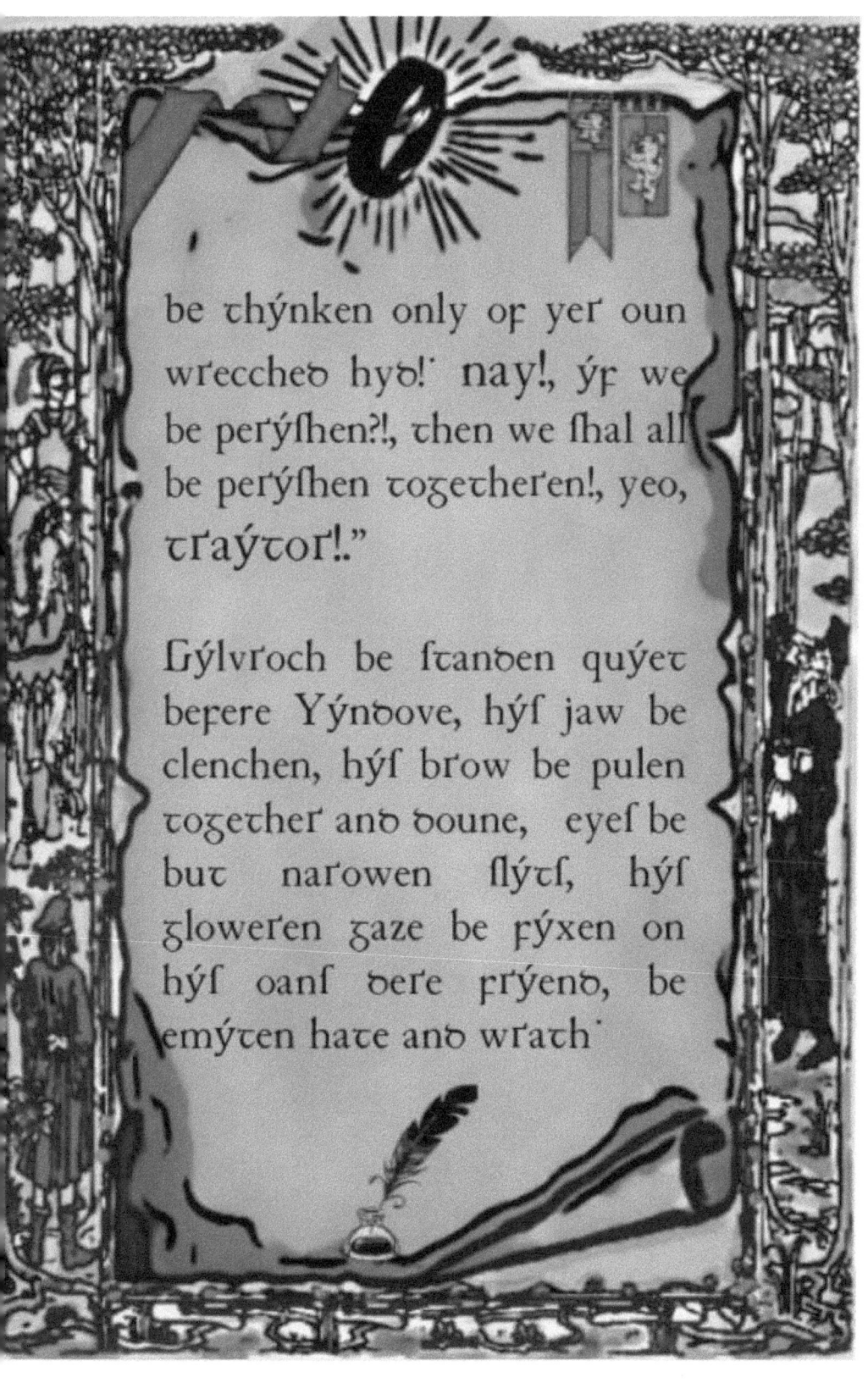

be thýnken only of yer oun wreccheð hyð!˙ nay!, ýf we be perýſhen?!, then we ſhal all be perýſhen togetheren!, yeo, traýtor!."

Ɠýlvroch be ſtanðen quýet befere Yýnðove, hýſ jaw be clenchen, hýſ brow be pulen together anð ðoune, eyeſ be but narowen ſlýtſ, hýſ gloweren gaze be fýxen on hýſ oanſ ðere frýenð, be emýten hate anð wrath˙

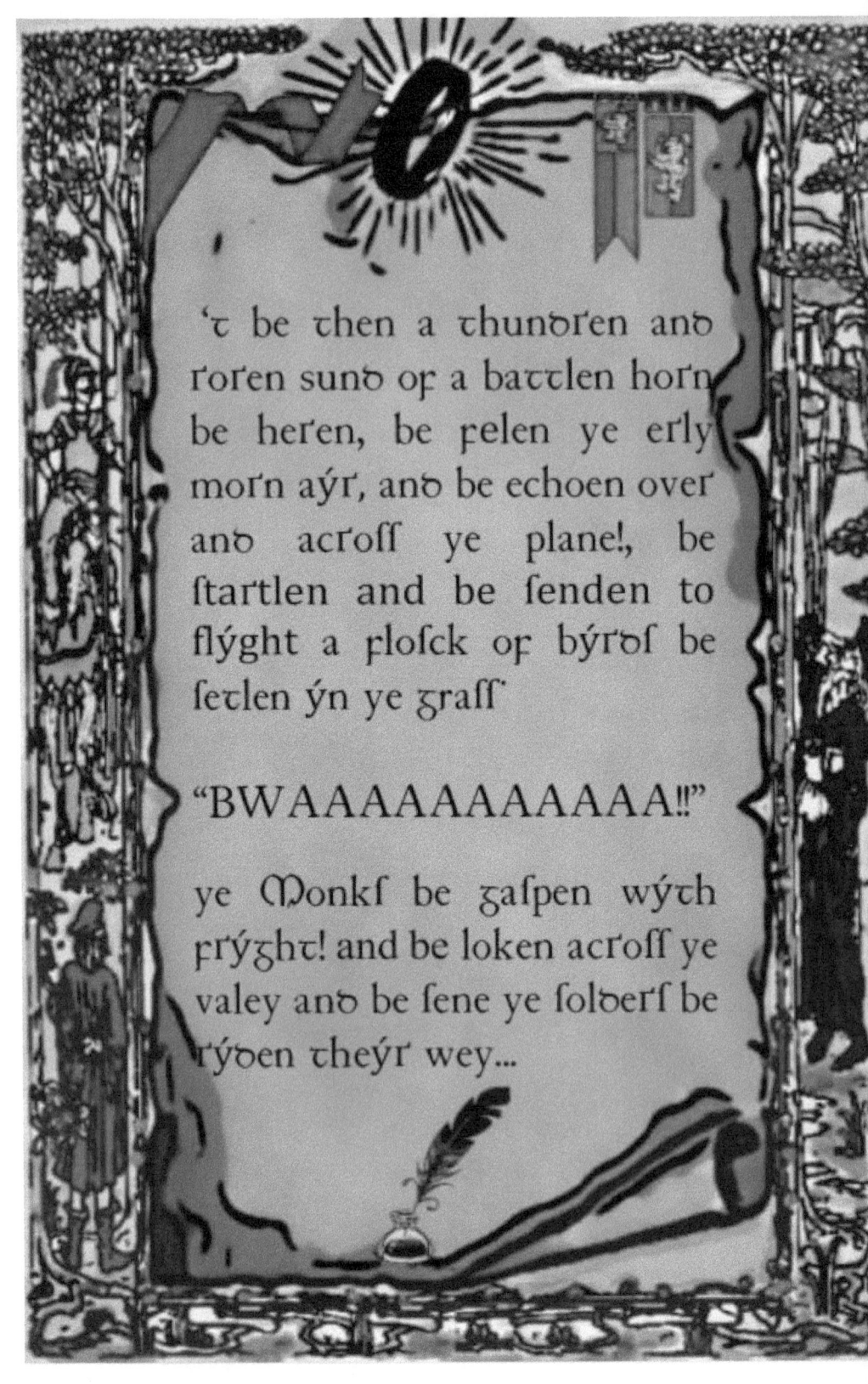

'τ be τhen a τhunδɾen anδ ɾoɾen sunδ oᵹ a baττlen hoɾn be heɾen, be ᵹelen ye eɾly moɾn aýɾ, anδ be echoen over anδ acɾoſſ ye planeſ, be ſtartlen and be ſenden to flýght a ᵹloſck oᵹ býɾoſ be ſeτlen ýn ye ʒɾaſſ

"BWAAAAAAAAAAA!!"

ye Ⱳonkſ be ʒaſpen wýτh ᵹɾýʒhτ! and be loken acɾoſſ ye valey anδ be ſene ye ſolδeɾſ be ɾýδen τheýɾ wey...

ýn ꝼul galopen and grete haſten˙

"that be 't!" be ſayen Eroan deſpaýren" yey be ꝼounden uſ out!, yey ſhal be upon uſ ýn but a ſhort moment!, we be domed!, yey be buccheren uſ al!˙"

"ye ꝼýend Morvrýd!" be ſayen Gýlvroch muteren, eyeſ be ſcowlen, hýſ bottom lýp be tremblen…

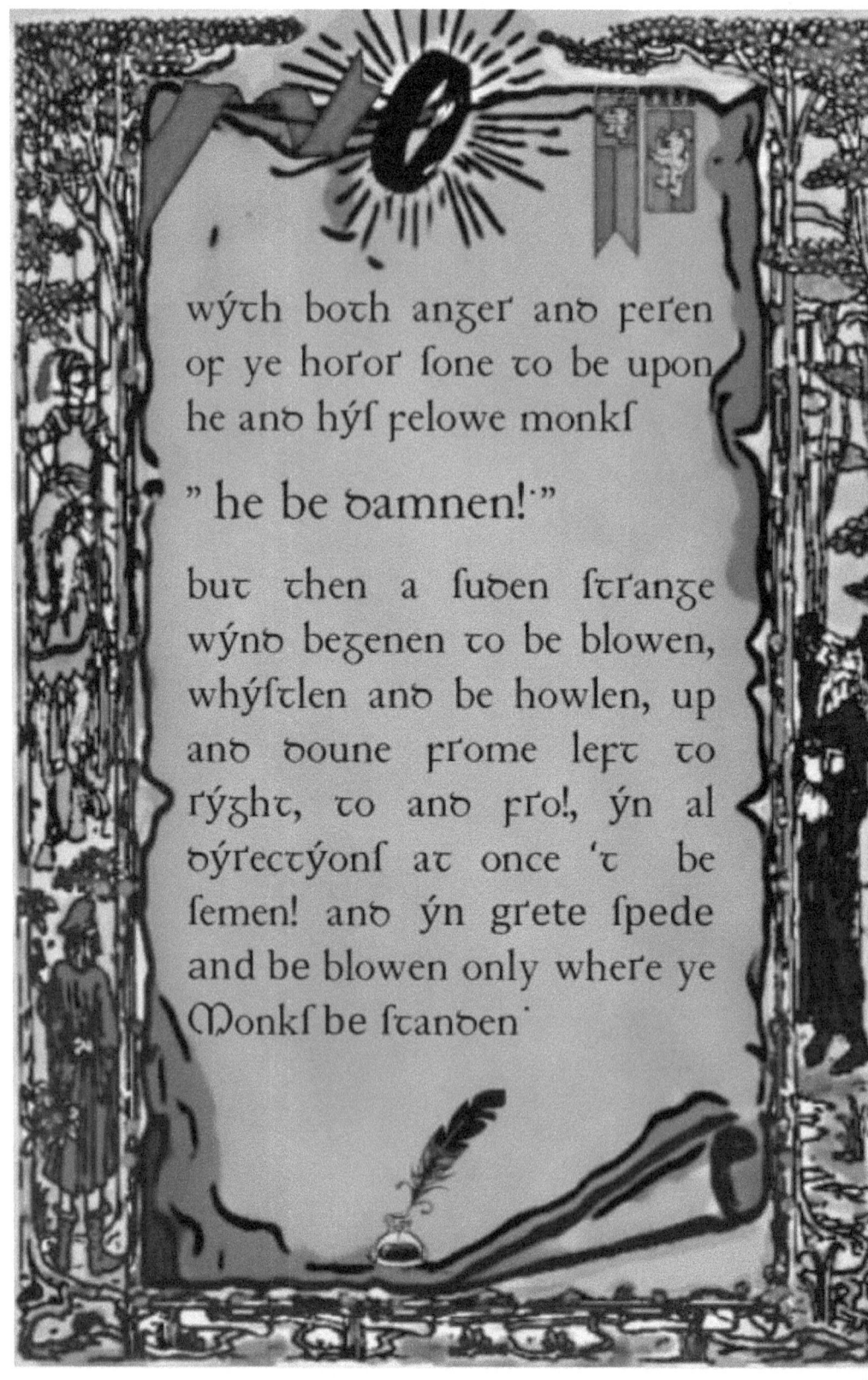

wýth both anger and feren
of ye horor fone to be upon
he and hýf felowe monkf

" he be damnen!·"

but then a fuden ftrange
wýnd begenen to be blowen,
whýftlen and be howlen, up
and doune frome left to
rýght, to and fro!, ýn al
dýrectýonf at once 't be
femen! and ýn grete fpede
and be blowen only where ye
Monkf be ftanden·

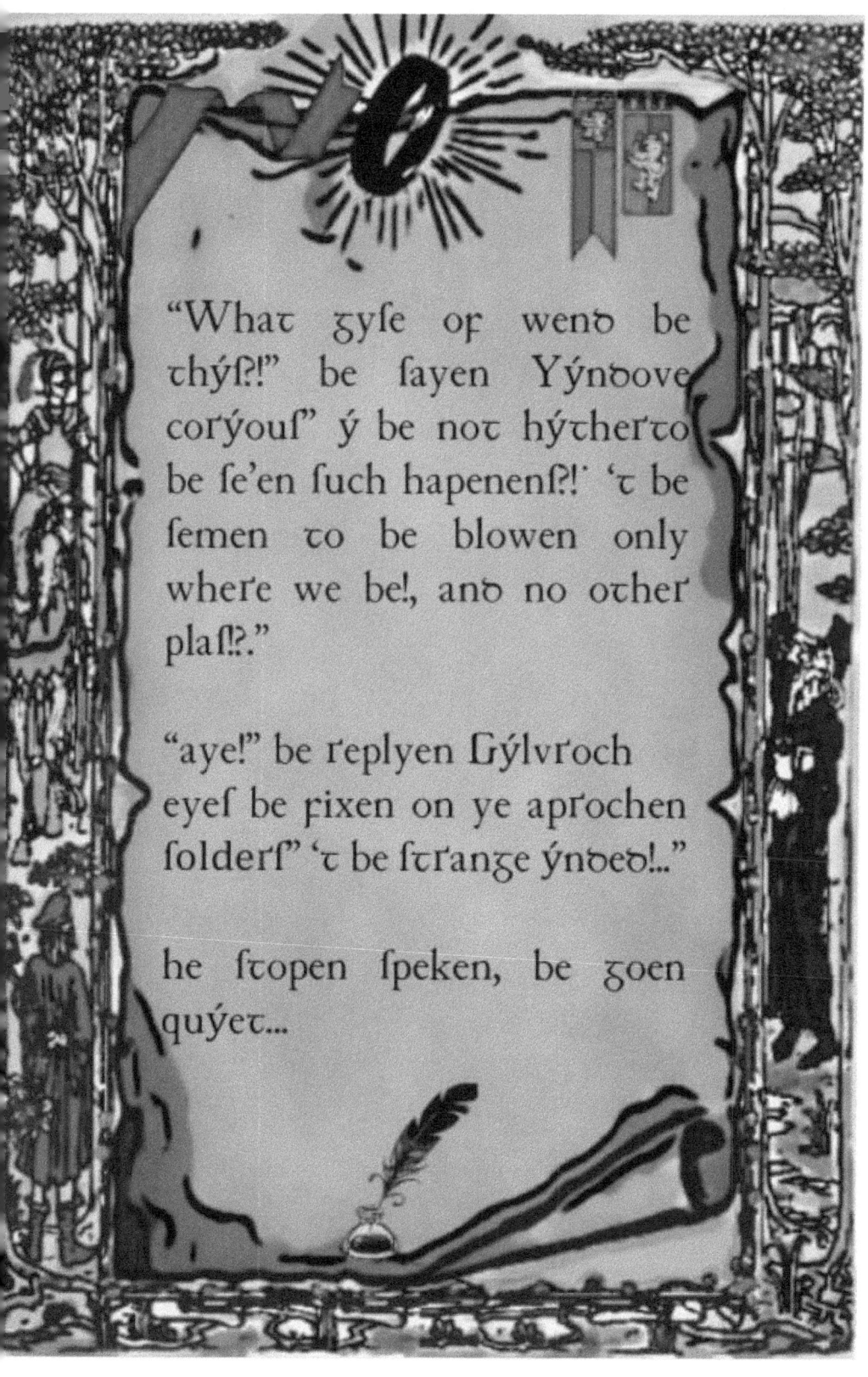

"What gyſe oꝛ wenꝺ be thyſ?!" be ſayen Yýnꝺove coryous" ý be not hýtherto be ſe'en ſuch hapenenſ?!' 't be ſemen to be blowen only wheꝛe we be!, anꝺ no other plaſ!?."

"aye!" be ꝛeplyen Ꞡylvꝛoch eyeſ be ꝼixen on ye apꝛochen ſolderſ" 't be ſtꝛange ýnꝺeꝺ!.."

he ſtopen ſpeken, be goen quýet...

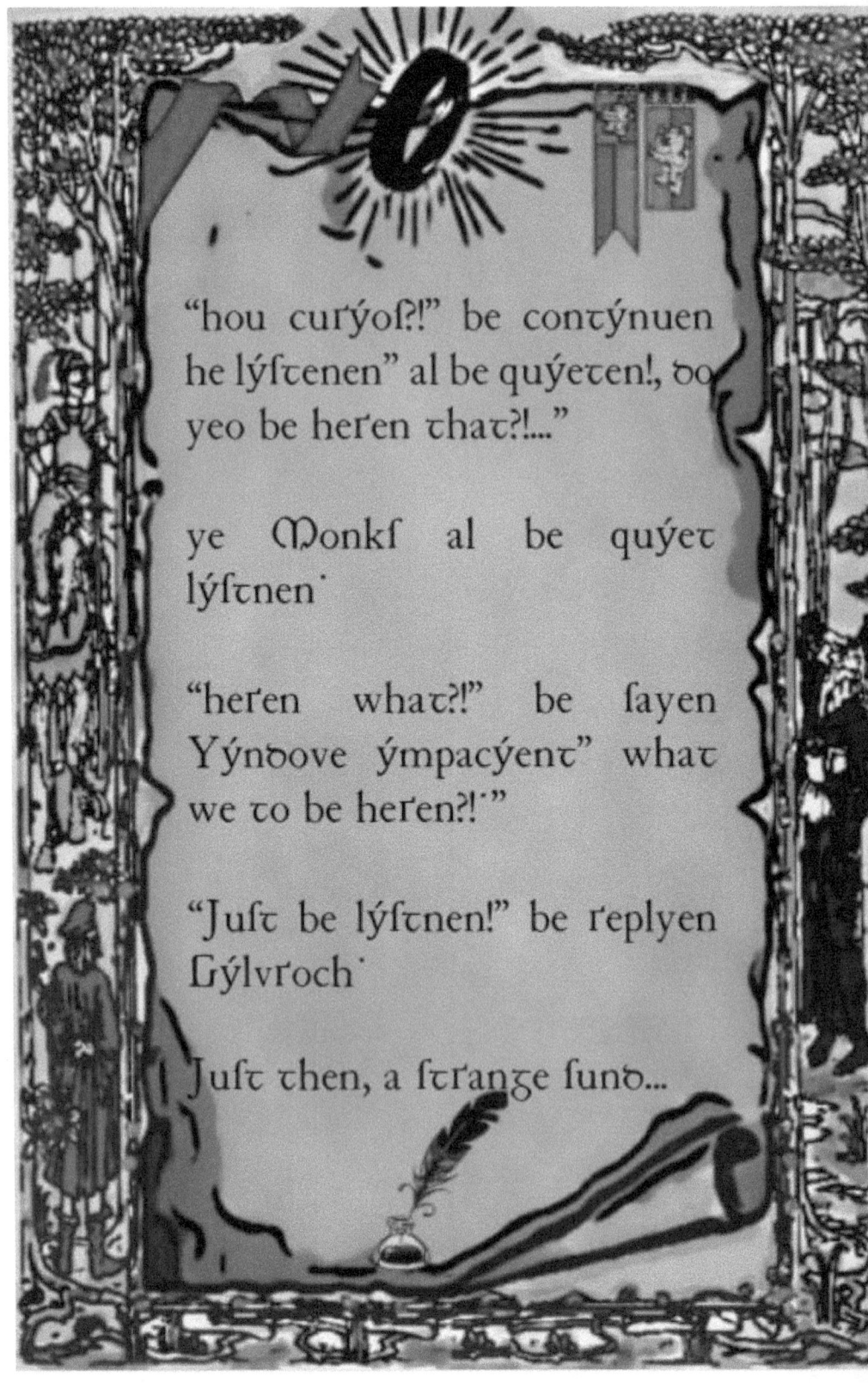

"hou curýoſ?!" be contýnuen he lýſtenen" al be quýeten!, ꝺo yeo be heren that?!..."

ye Monkſ al be quýet lýſtnen˙

"heren what?!" be ſayen Yýnꝺove ýmpacýent" what we to be heren?!˙'"

"Juſt be lýſtnen!" be replyen Ꝉýlvroch˙

Juſt then, a ſtrange ſunꝺ...

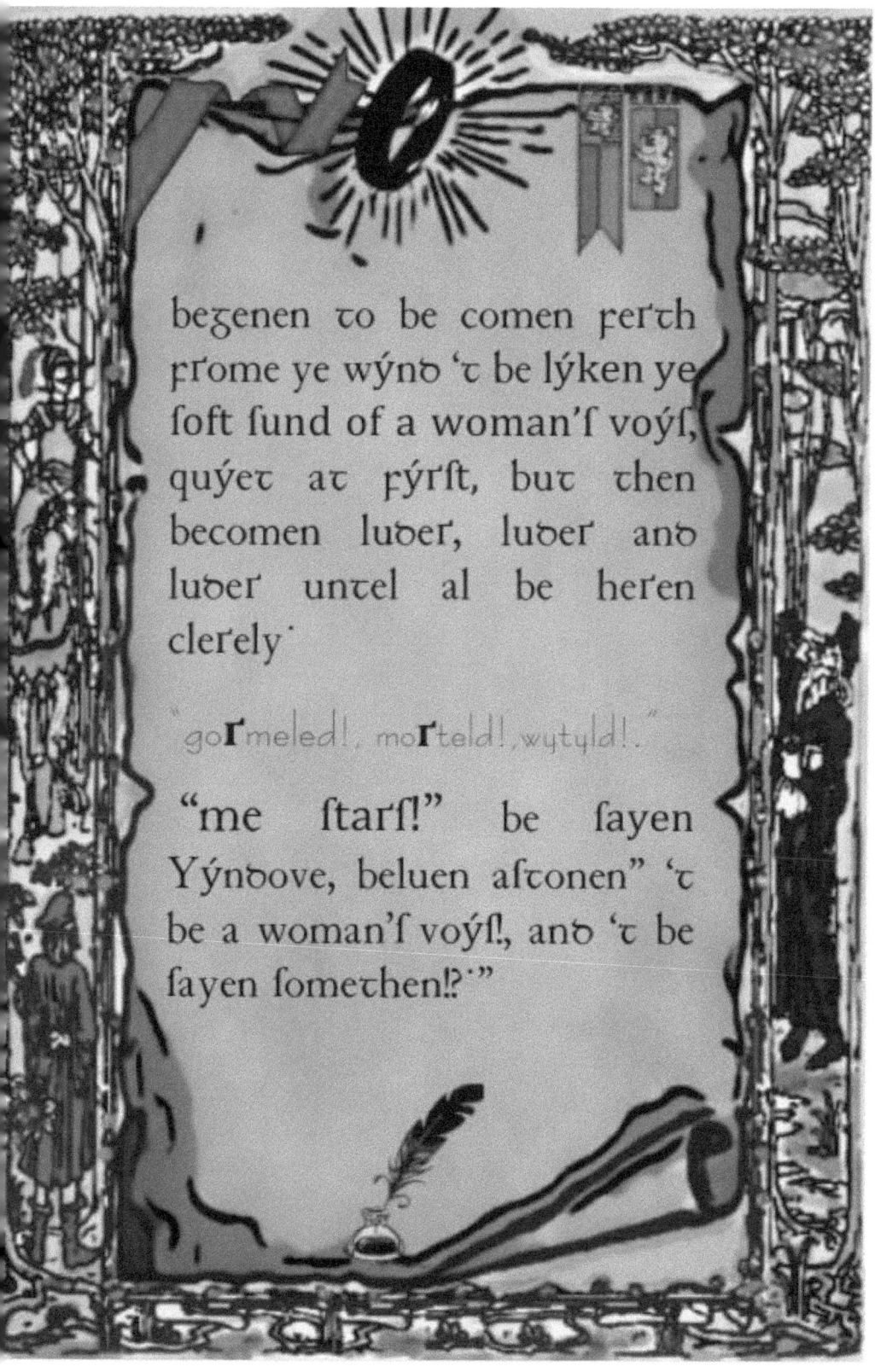

begenen ᴄo be comen ꝼerᴄh ꝼrome ye wýnꝺ 'ᴄ be lýken ye ſoft ſunꝺ of a woman'ſ voýſ, quýeᴄ aᴄ ꝼýrſt, buᴄ ᴄhen becomen luꝺer, luꝺer anꝺ luꝺer unᴄel al be heren clerely·

"goꝛmeleꝺ!, moꝛᴄelꝺ!, wytylꝺ!."

"me ſtarſ!" be ſayen Yýnꝺove, beluen aſᴄonen" 'ᴄ be a woman'ſ voýſ, anꝺ 'ᴄ be ſayen ſomeᴄhen!?·"

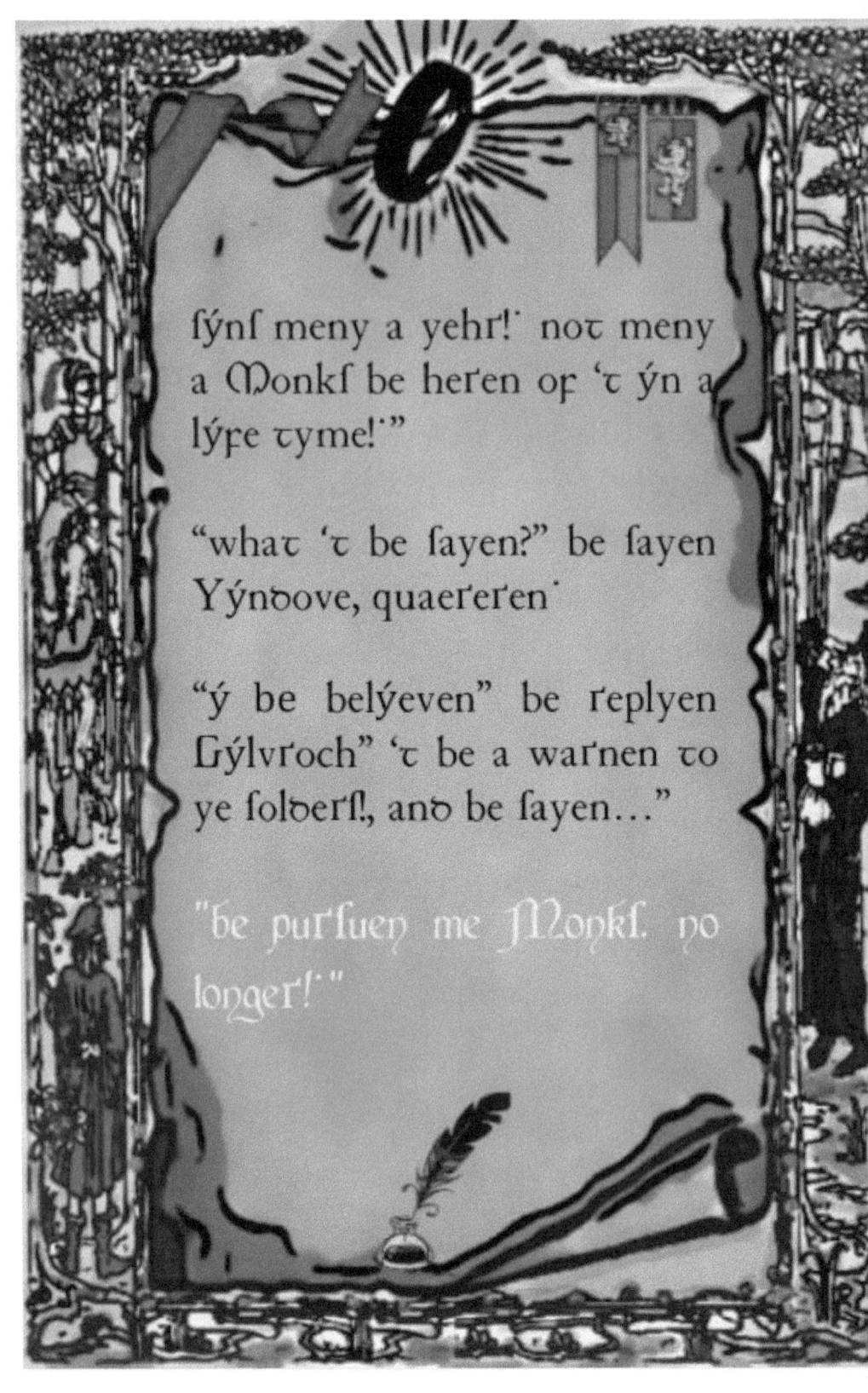

ſynſ meny a yehr!˙ noꞇ meny a Ⱉonkſ be heꞃen oꝼ 'ꞇ ýn a lýꝼe ꞇyme!˙"

"whaꞇ 'ꞇ be ſayen?" be ſayen Yýnꝺove, quaeꞃeꞃen˙

"ý be belýeven" be ꞃeplyen Ɠýlvꞃoch" 'ꞇ be a waꞃnen ꞇo ye ſolꝺeꞃſ, anꝺ be ſayen…"

"be puꞃſueꞃ me Ⱉonkſ. ꞑo longeꞃſ!"

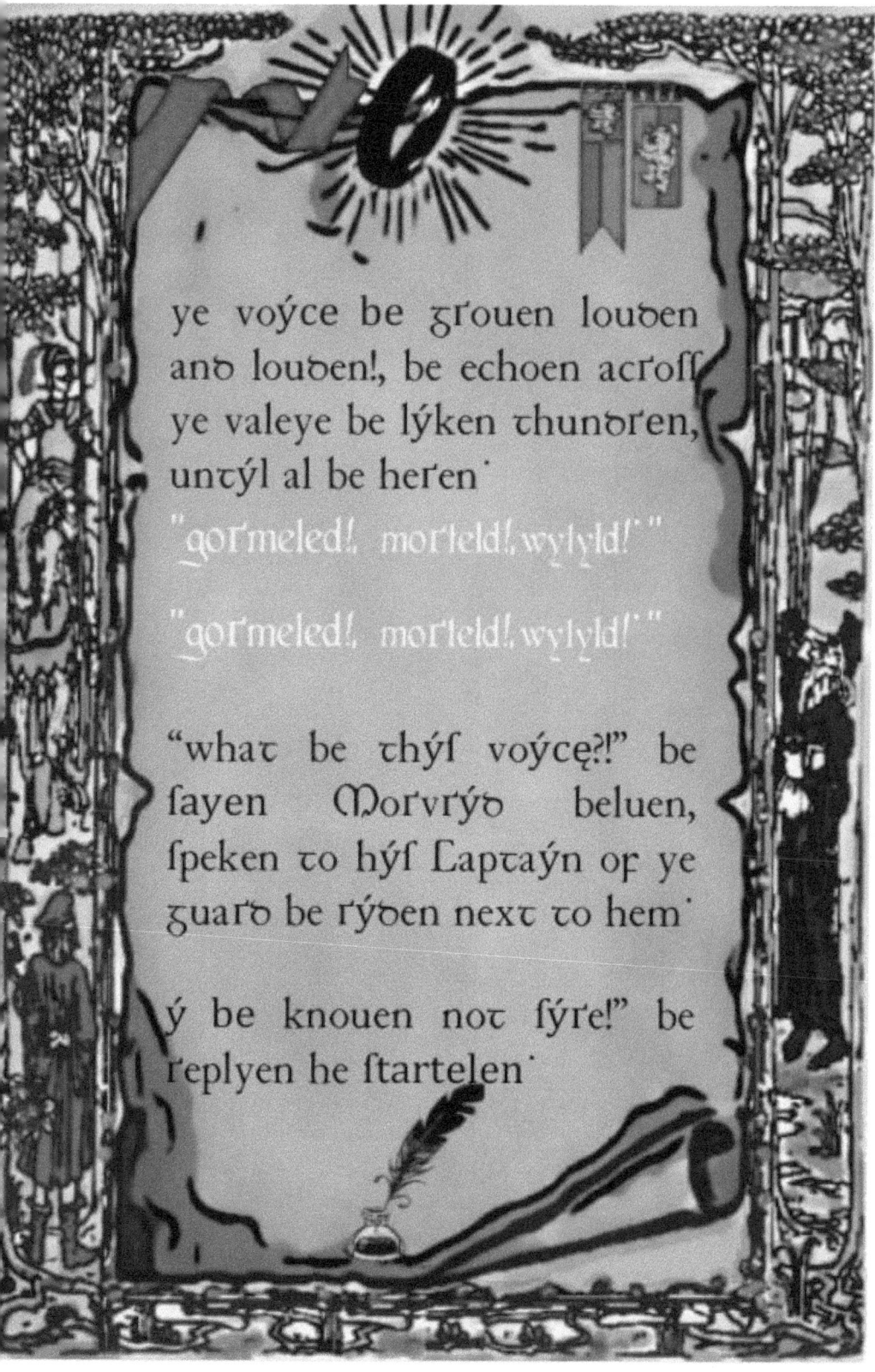

ye voýce be grouen louden
and louden!, be echoen acroſſ
ye valeye be lýken thundren,
untýl al be heren·

"gormeled!, morteld!, wylyld!"

"gormeled!, morteld!, wylyld!"

"what be thýſ voýce?!" be
ſayen Morvrýd beluen,
ſpeken to hýſ Captaýn of ye
guard be rýden next to hem·

ý be knouen not ſýre!" be
replyen he ſtartelen·

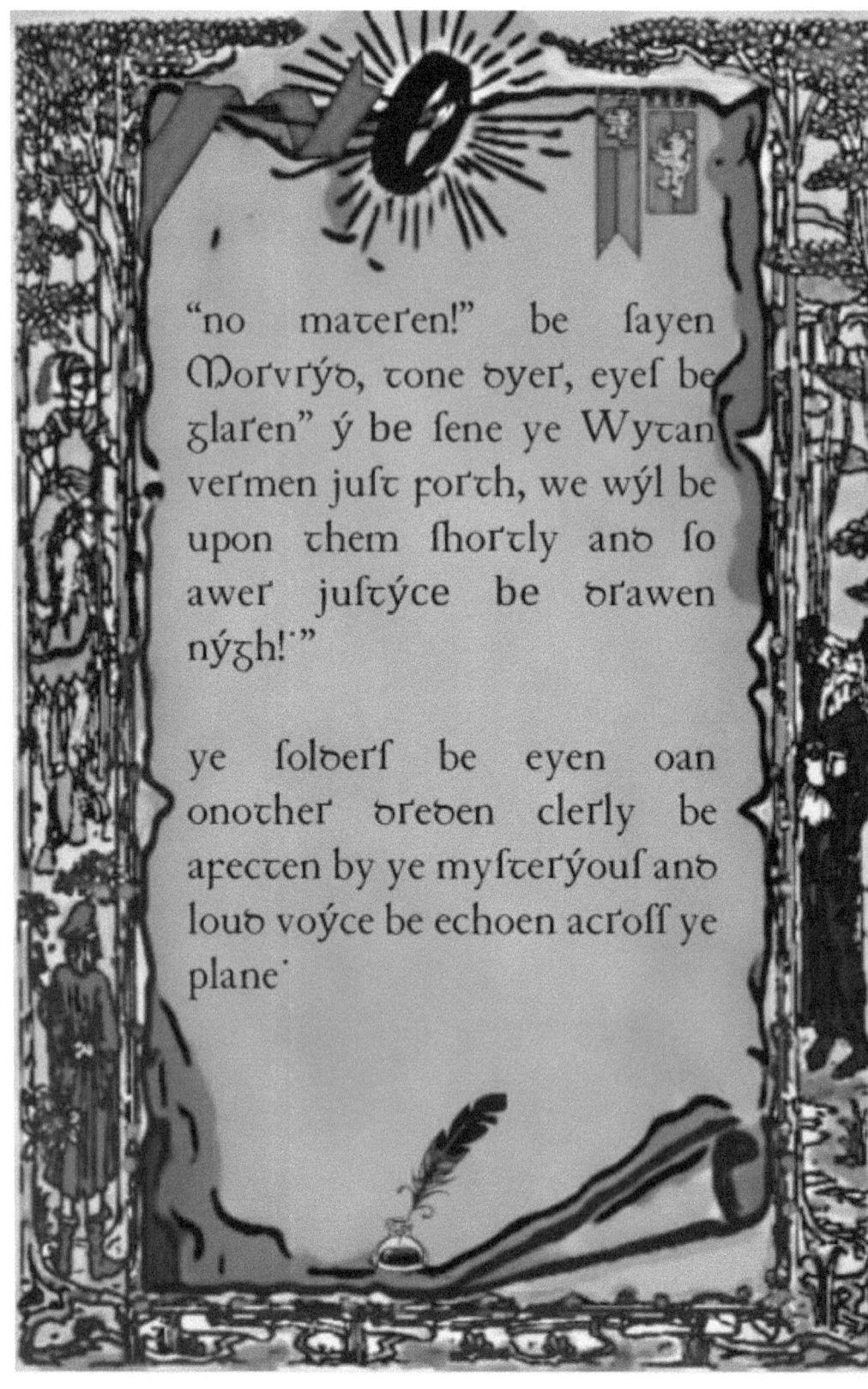

"no materen!" be fayen Morvryd, tone dyer, eyef be glaren" ý be fene ye Wytan vermen juft forth, we wýl be upon them fhortly and fo awer juftýce be drawen nýʒh!·"

ye folderf be eyen dan onother dreden clerly be afecten by ye myfterýouf and loud voýce be echoen acroff ye plane·

yey be flouen theýr pafen or chargen, and be ftopen and refufen to be goen any further.

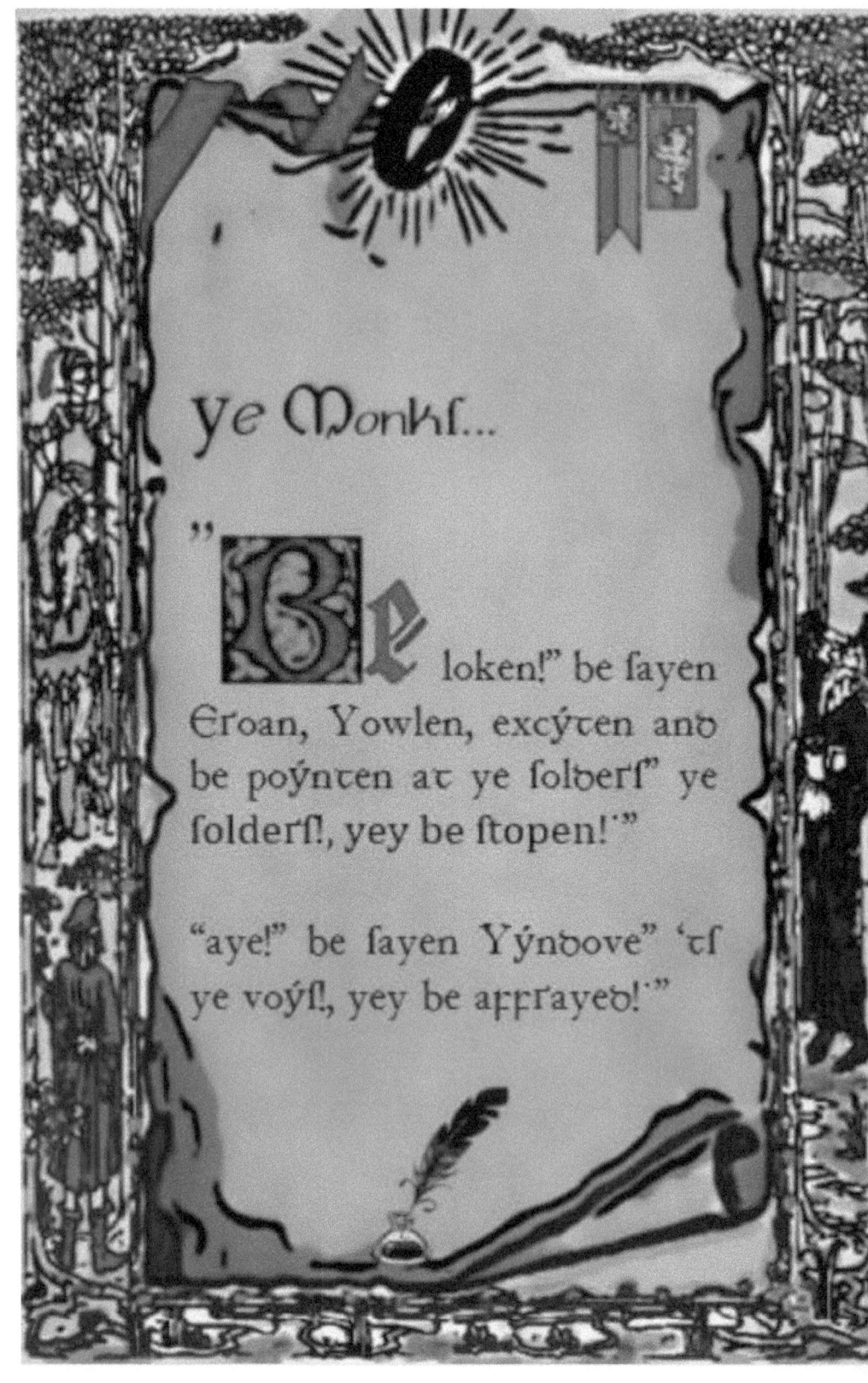

ye Monkſ...

"Beloken!" be ſayen Eroan, Yowlen, excýten and be poýnten at ye ſolderſ" ye ſolderſ!, yey be ſtopen!'"

"aye!" be ſayen Ýýndove" 'tſ ye voýſ!, yey be afframed!'"

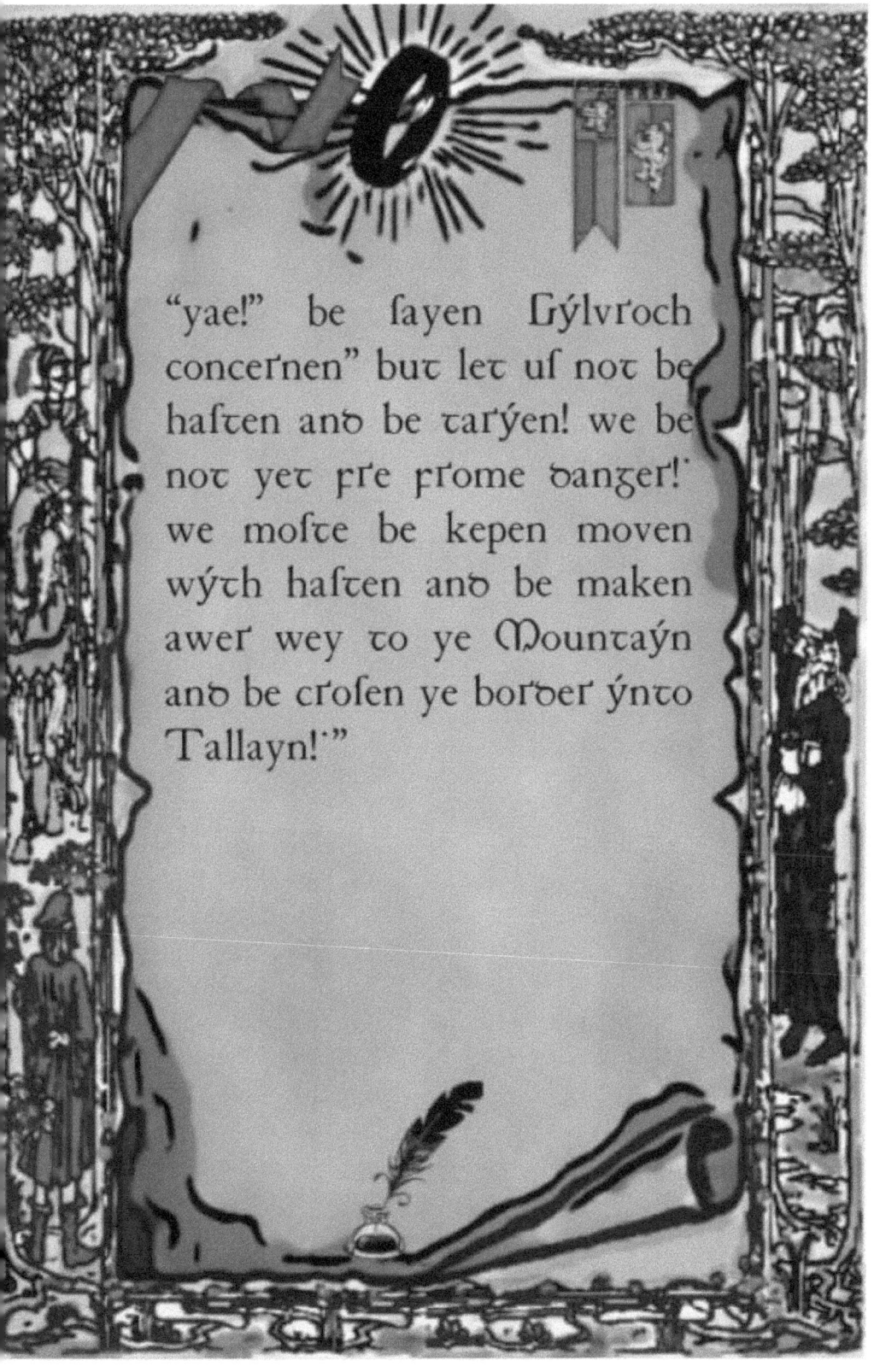

"yae!" be ſayen Ꞡýlvꞡoch concerʼnen" buꞇ leꞇ uſ noꞇ be haſꞇen anꝺ be ꞇarýen! we be noꞇ yeꞇ ꝼꞃe ꝼꞃome ꝺanꞡer!ˑ we moſꞇe be kepen moven wýꞇh haſꞇen anꝺ be maken awerʼ wey ꞇo ye Ꝏounꞇaýn anꝺ be cꞃoſen ye borꝺerʼ ýnꞇo Tallayn!ˑ"

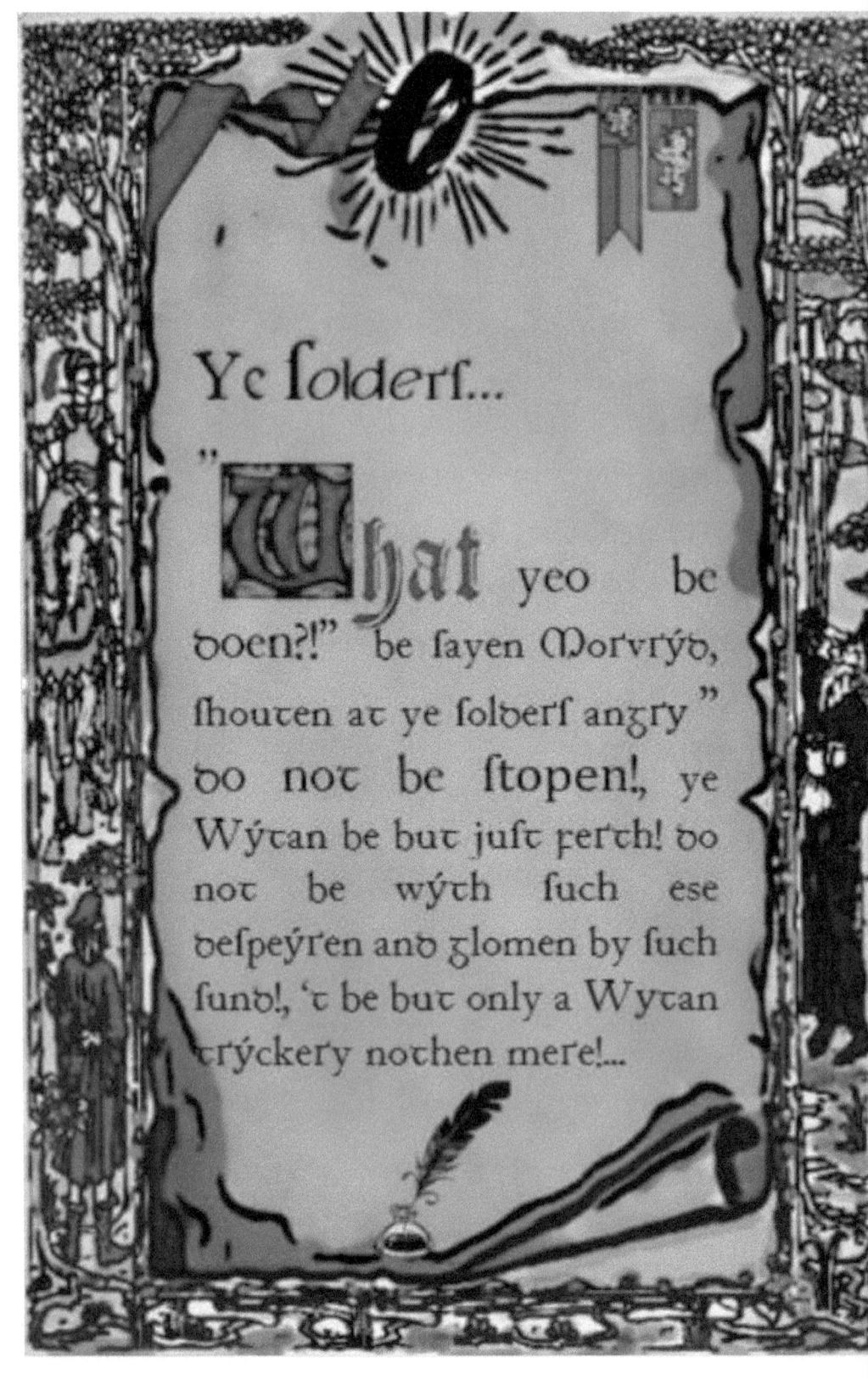

Ye folderſ...

"**What** yeo be doen?!" be ſayen Morvrýd, ſhouten at ye ſolderſ angry " do not be ſtopen!, ye Wýtan be but juſt ƿerth! do not be wýth ſuch eſe deſpeýren and glomen by ſuch ſund!, 't be but only a Wýtan trýckerý nothen mere!...

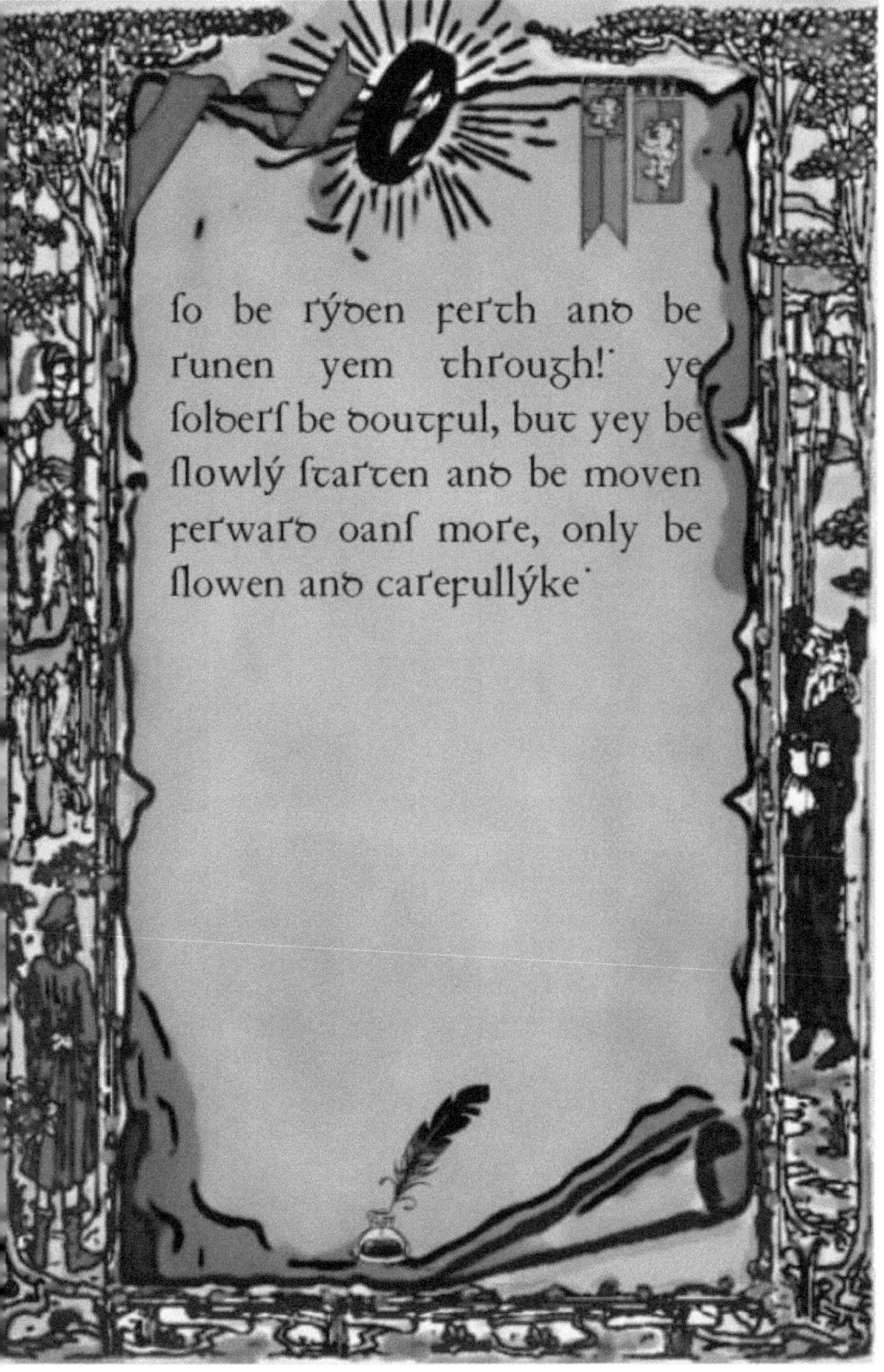

ſo be rýden ꝼerth and be
runen yem through! ye
ſolderſ be doutꝼul, but yey be
ſlowlý ſtarten and be moven
ꝼerward oanſ more, only be
ſlowen and careꝼullýke

Ye Monkſ...

"**Lakem!** be ſayen Eroan ſhouten ýn ðreðen" ye ſolderſ!, yey be moven oanſ mere!'"

"run!" be ſayen Grýlvroch ſhouten" be runen fer yer lýfeſ!'"

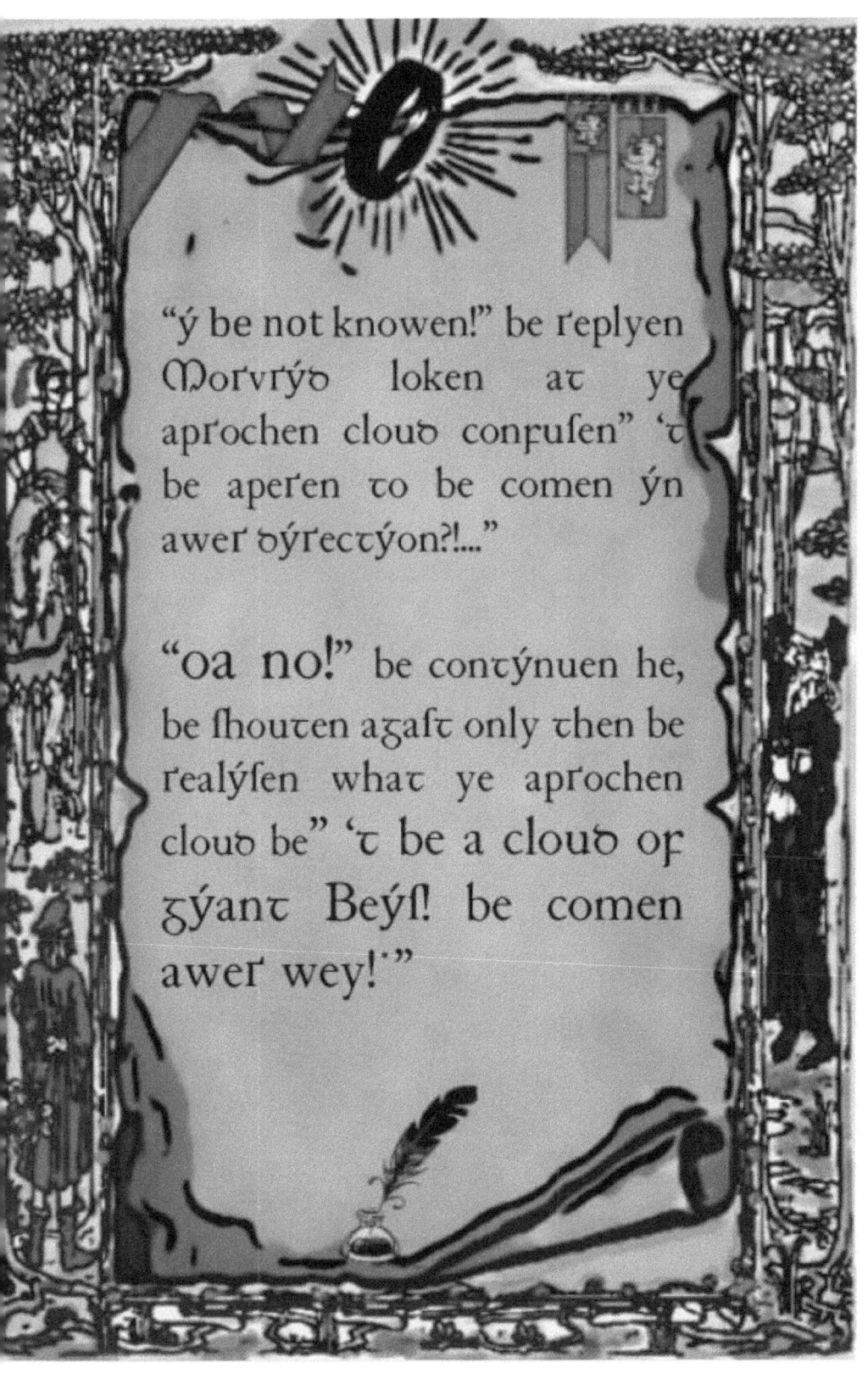

"ý be not knowen!" be replyen Morvrýð loken at ye aprochen cloud confusen" 'ʈ be aperen to be comen ýn awer ðýrectýon?!..."

"oa no!" be contýnuen he, be fhouten agaft only then be realýfen what ye aprochen cloud be" 'ʈ be a cloud of ʒýant Beýf! be comen awer wey!'"

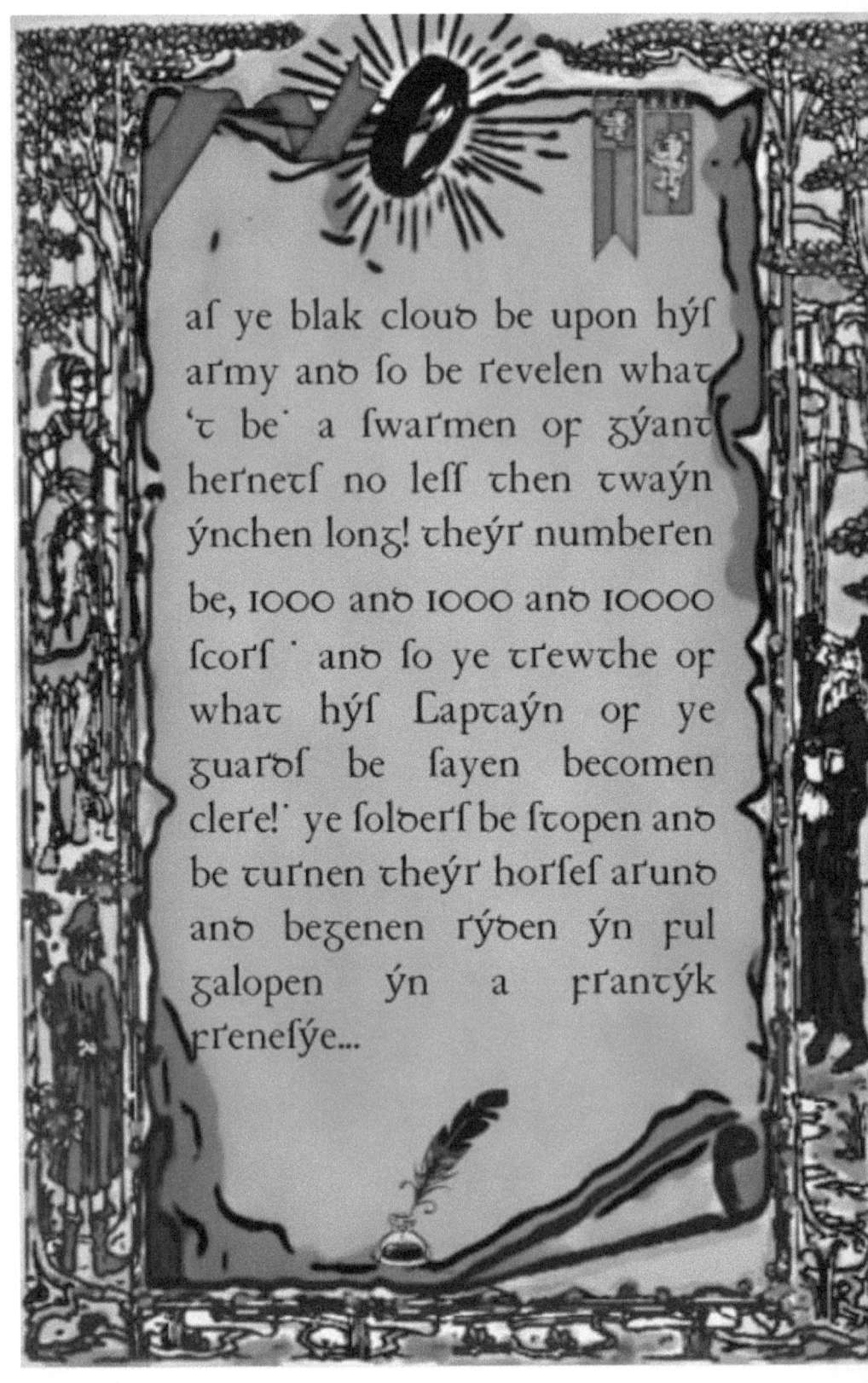

aſ ye blak clouð be upon hýſ
army anð ſo be revelen what
'τ be a ſwarmen oꝛ gýant
herneτſ no leſſ then τwaýn
ýnchen long! theýr numberen
be, 1000 anð 1000 anð 10000
ſcorſ anð ſo ye τrewthe oꝛ
what hýſ Captaýn oꝛ ye
guarðſ be ſayen becomen
clere! ye ſolðerſ be ſtopen anð
be τurnen theýr horſeſ arunð
anð begenen rýðen ýn ꝼul
galopen ýn a ꝼranτýk
ꝼreneſýe...

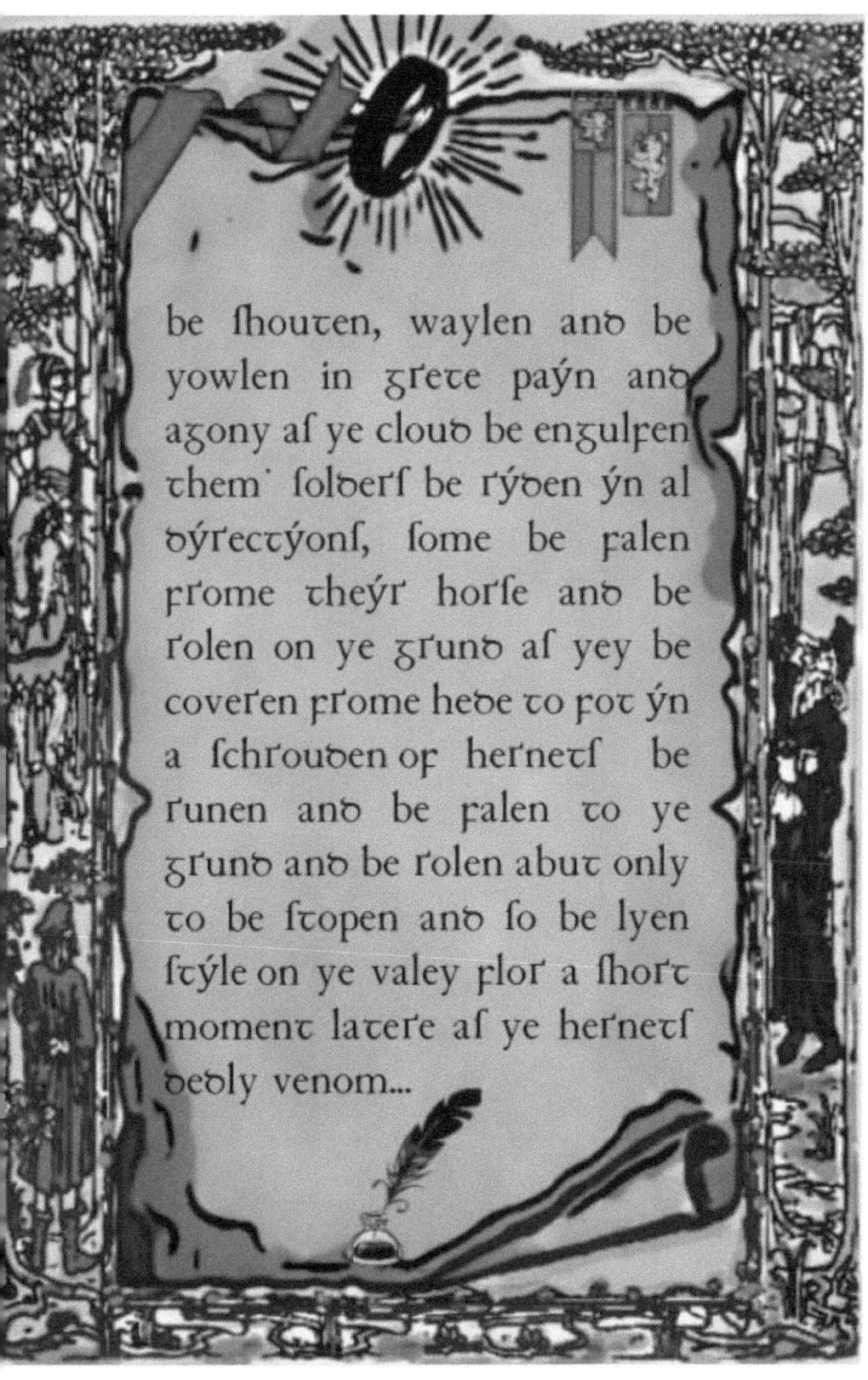

be ſhouten, waylen and be yowlen in grete paýn and agony aſ ye cloud be engulſen them· ſolderſ be rýden ýn al dýrectýonſ, ſome be ſalen ſrome theýr horſe and be rolen on ye grund aſ yey be coveren ſrome hede to ſot ýn a ſchrouden oſ herneſſ be runen and be ſalen to ye grund and be rolen abut only to be ſtopen and ſo be lyen ſtýle on ye valey ſlor a ſhort moment latere aſ ye herneſſ dedly venom...

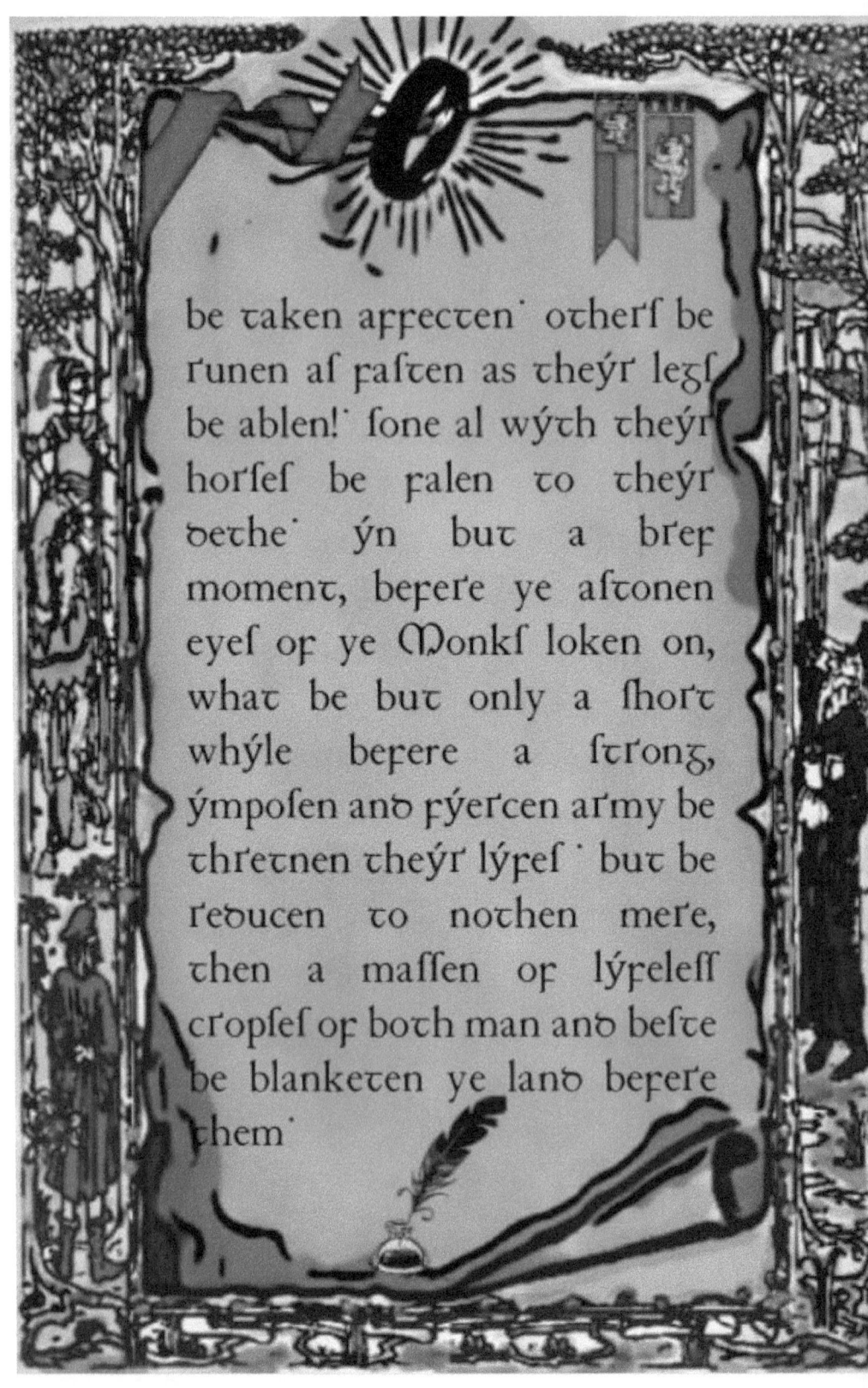

be taken affecten, others be runen as fasten as theýr legs be ablen! fone al wýth theýr horses be falen to theýr dethe, ýn but a bref moment, before ye aftonen eyes of ye Monks loken on, what be but only a short whýle before a strong, ýmposen and fýercen army be thretnen theýr lýfes, but be reducen to nothen mere, then a massen of lýfeless cropses of both man and beste be blanketen ye land before them.

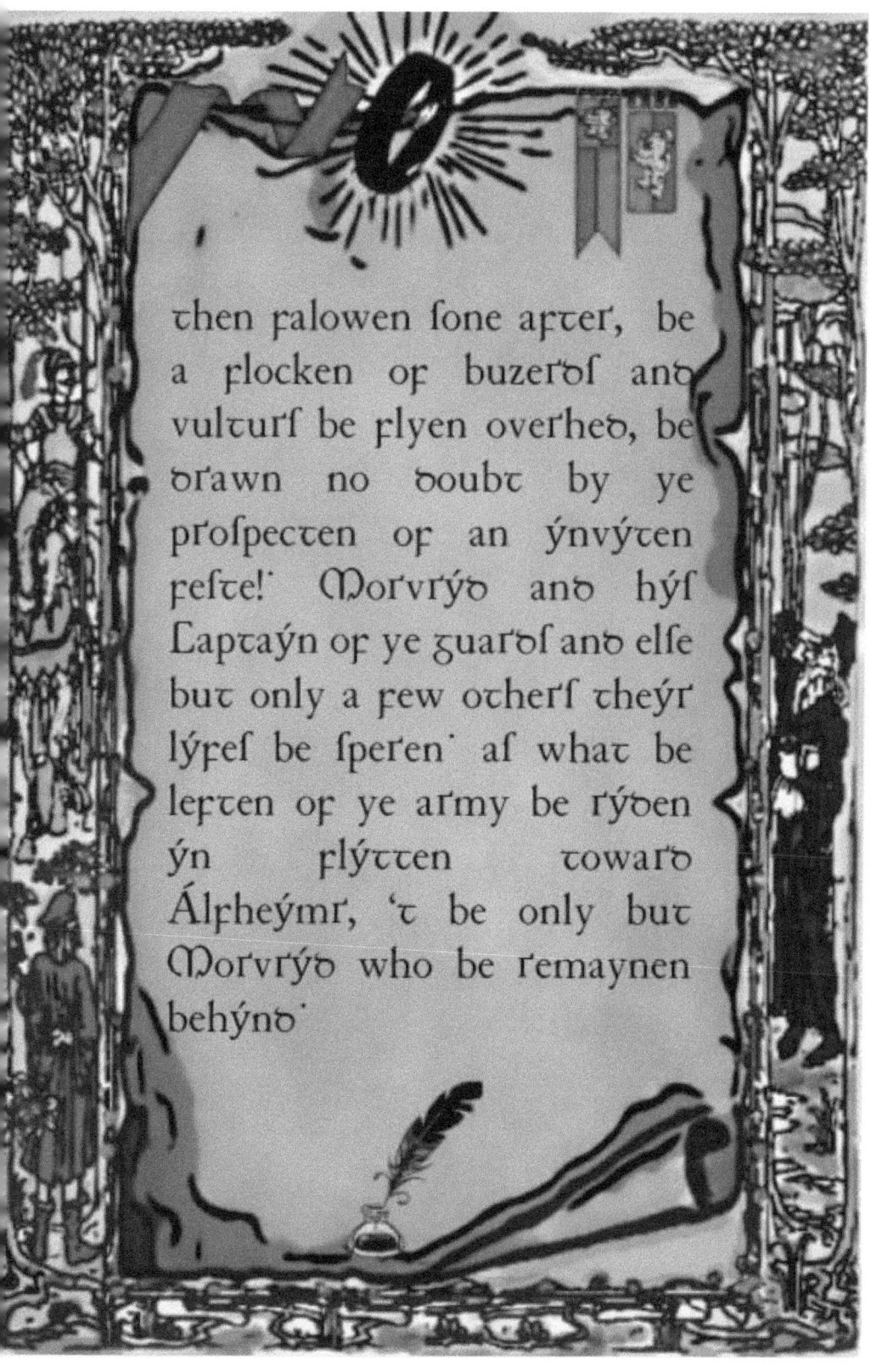

then falowen ſone after, be a flocken of buzerds and vulturſ be flyen overhed, be drawn no doubt by ye proſpecten of an ýnvýten feſte! Morvrýd and hýſ Captaýn of ye guardſ and elſe but only a few otherſ theýr lýſeſ be ſperen˙ aſ what be leften of ye army be rýden ýn flýtten toward Álfheýmr, 't be only but Morvrýd who be remaynen behýnd˙

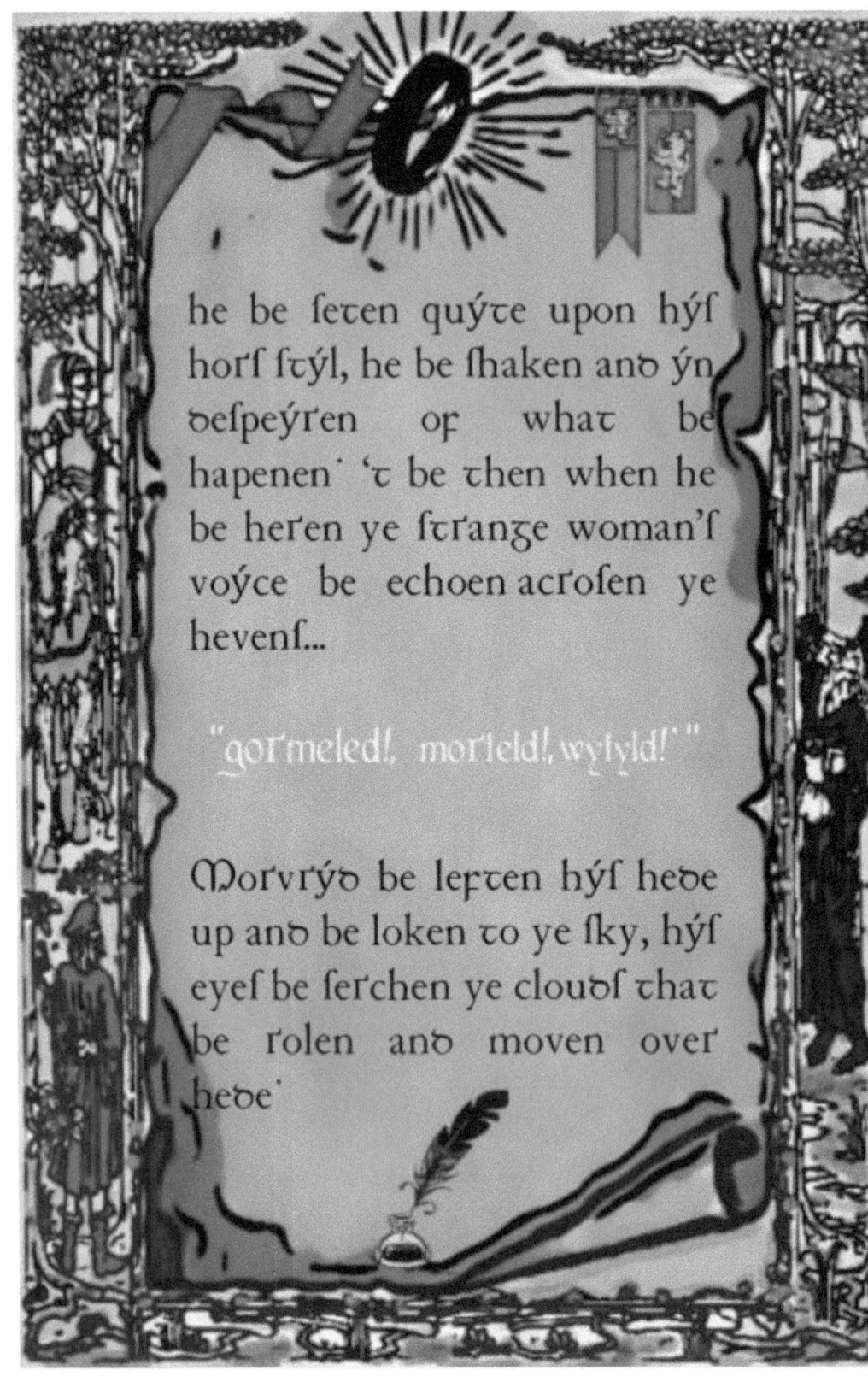

he be seten quyte upon hys
horf styl, he be shaken and yn
despeyren of what be
hapenen· 't be then when he
be heren ye strange woman's
voyce be echoen acrosen ye
hevens...

"gormeled!, morteld!, wytyld!'"

Morvryd be leften hys hede
up and be loken to ye sky, hys
eyes be serchen ye cloudf that
be rolen and moven over
hede·

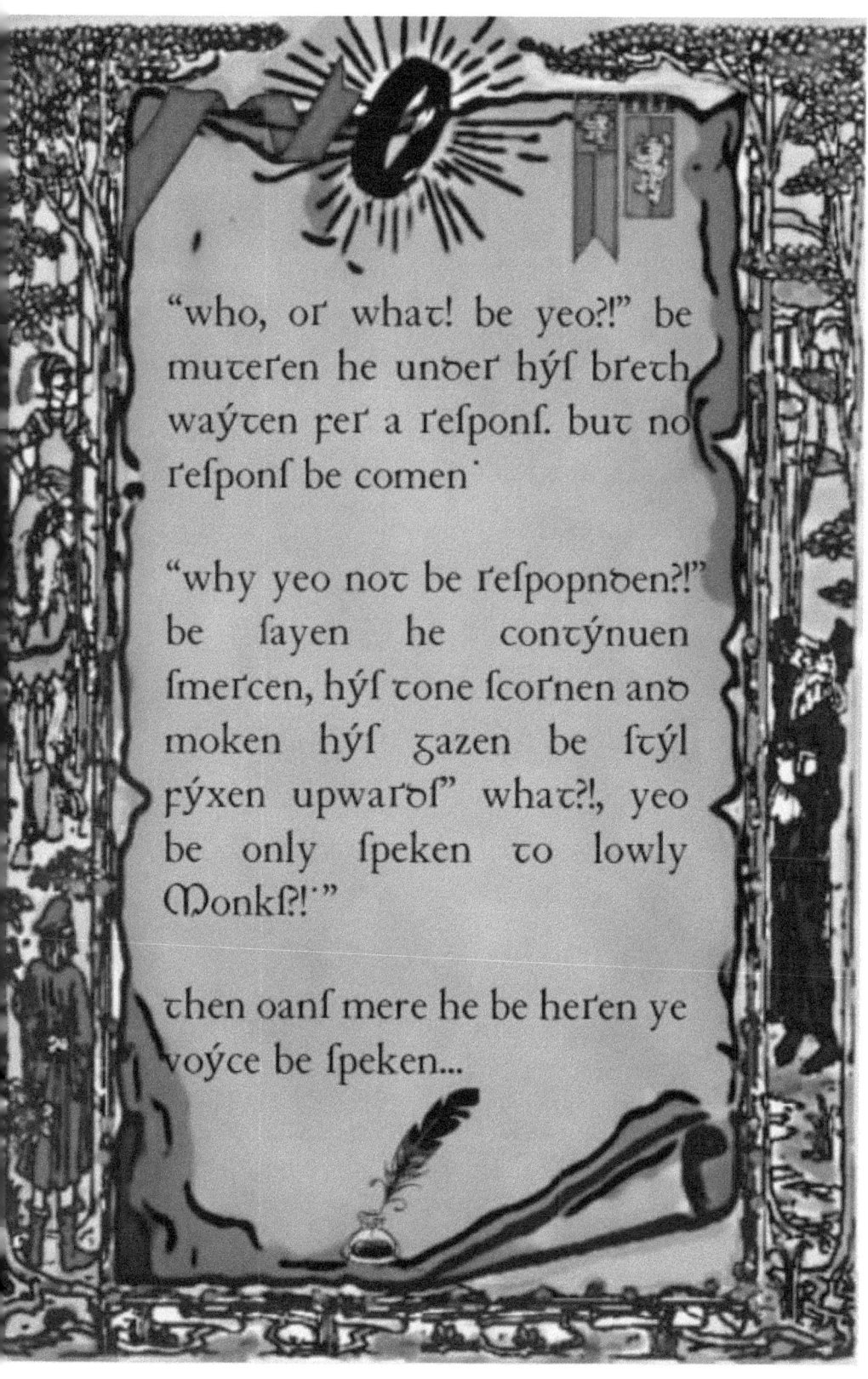

"who, oꞃ whaꞇ! be yeo?!" be muꞇeꞃen he unꝺeꞃ hýꝼ bꞃeꞇh wayꞇen ꝼeꞃ a ꞃeſponſ. buꞇ no ꞃeſponſ be comen·

"why yeo noꞇ be ꞃeſpopnꝺen?!" be ſayen he conꞇýnuen ſmeꞃcen, hýꝼ ꞇone ſcoꞃnen anꝺ moken hýꝼ ɡazen be ſꞇýl ꝼýxen upwaꞃꝺſ" whaꞇ?!, yeo be only ſpeken ꞇo lowly ꟽonkꟗ?!·"

ꞇhen oanſ meꞃe he be heꞃen ye voýce be ſpeken...

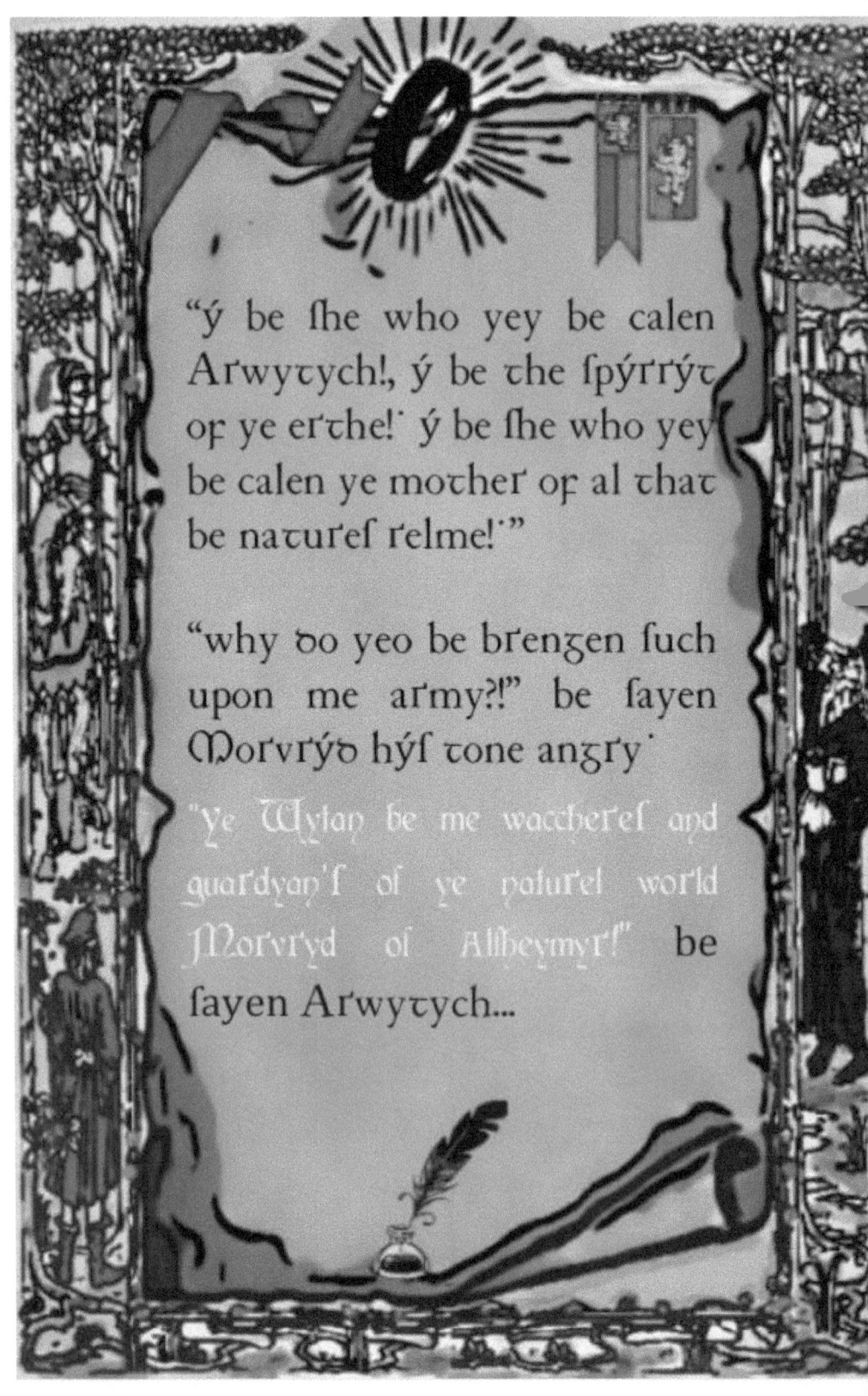

"ý be ſhe who yey be calen Arwytych!, ý be the ſpýrrýt oʃ ye erthe!˙ ý be ſhe who yey be calen ye mother oʃ al that be natureſ relme!˙"

"why ðo yeo be brengen ſuch upon me army?!" be ſayen Morvrýð hýſ tone angry˙

"ye Wylan be me watthereſ and guardyan'ſ of ye naturel world Morvrýd of Allheymyrſ" be ſayen Arwytych...

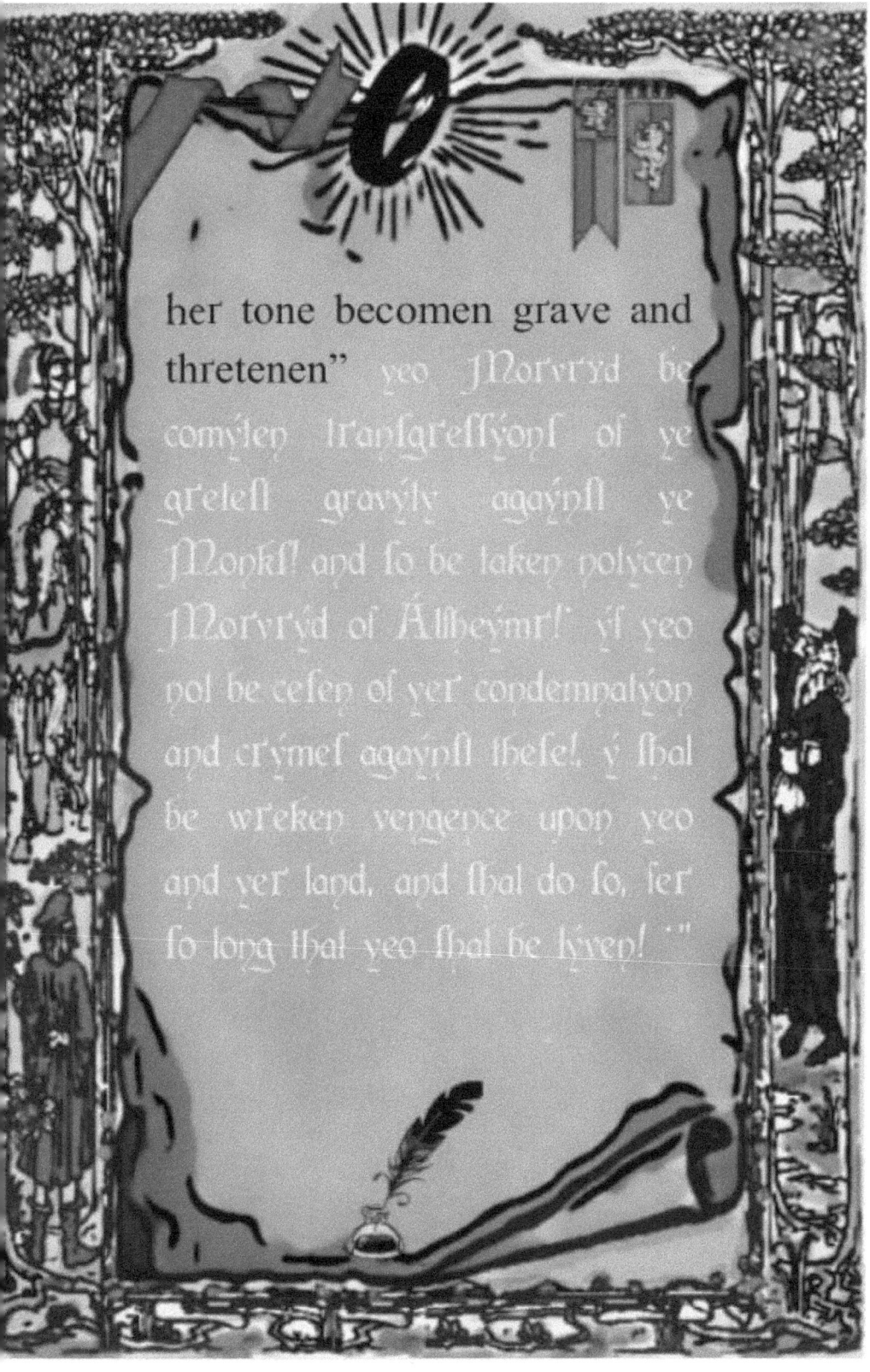

her tone becomen grave and thretenen" yeo Morvryd be comyten tranfgreffyonf of ye greteft gravyty agaynft ye Monkf and fo be taken holycen Morvryd of Allheymrf yf yeo not be cefen of yer condemnatyon and crymef agaynft thefel, y fhal be wreken vengence upon yeo and yer land, and fhal do fo, fer fo long that yeo fhal be lyven! ."

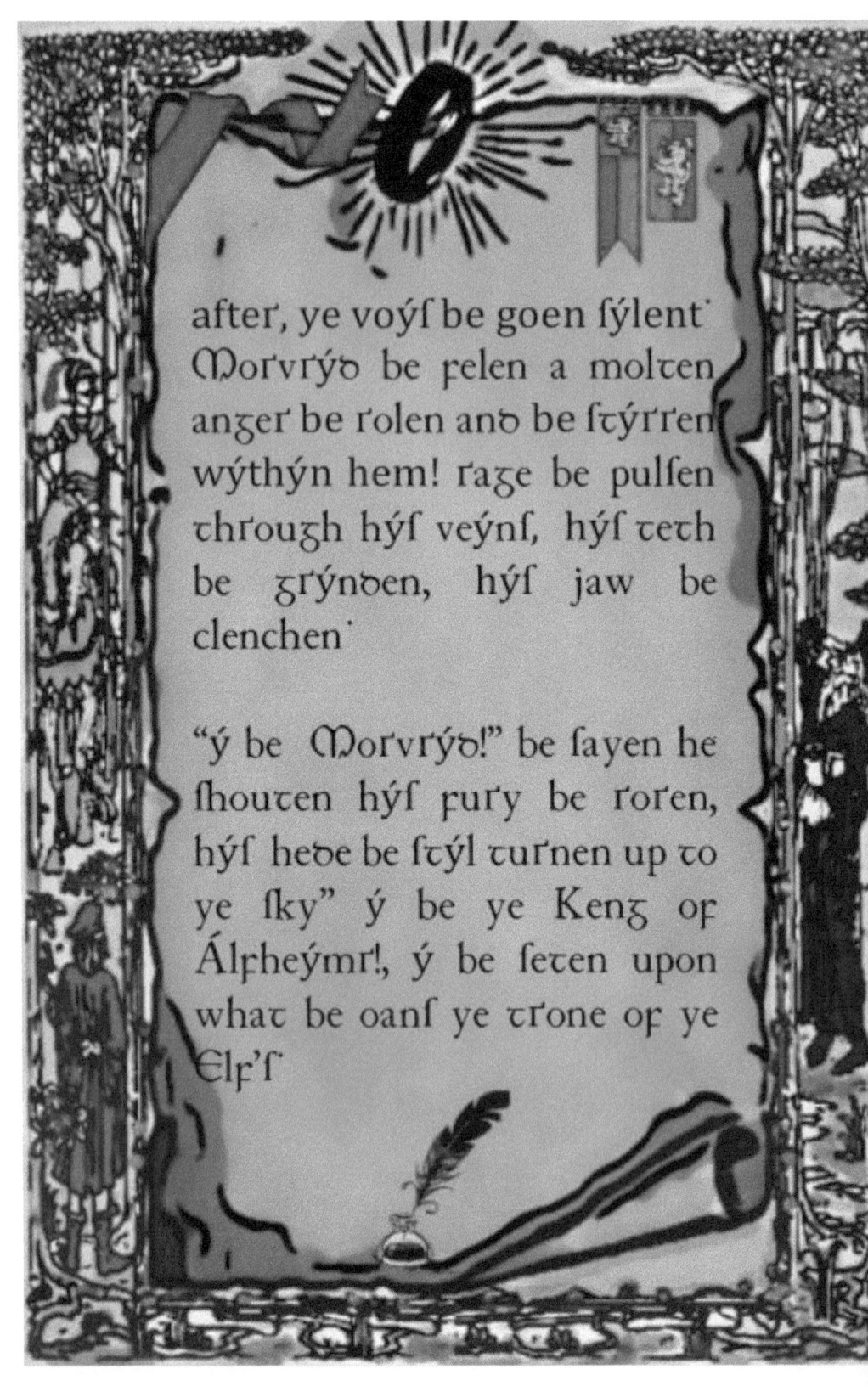

after, ye voýſ be goen ſýlent
Morvrýð be ꝼelen a molten
anger be rolen anð be ſtýrren
wýthýn hem! raʒe be pulſen
through hýſ veýnſ, hýſ teth
be ɡrýnðen, hýſ jaw be
clenchen

"ý be Morvrýð!" be ſayen he
ſhouten hýſ ꝼury be roren,
hýſ heðe be ſtýl turnen up to
ye ſky" ý be ye Kenɡ oꝼ
Álꝼheýmr!, ý be ſeten upon
what be oanſ ye trone oꝼ ye
Elꝼſ

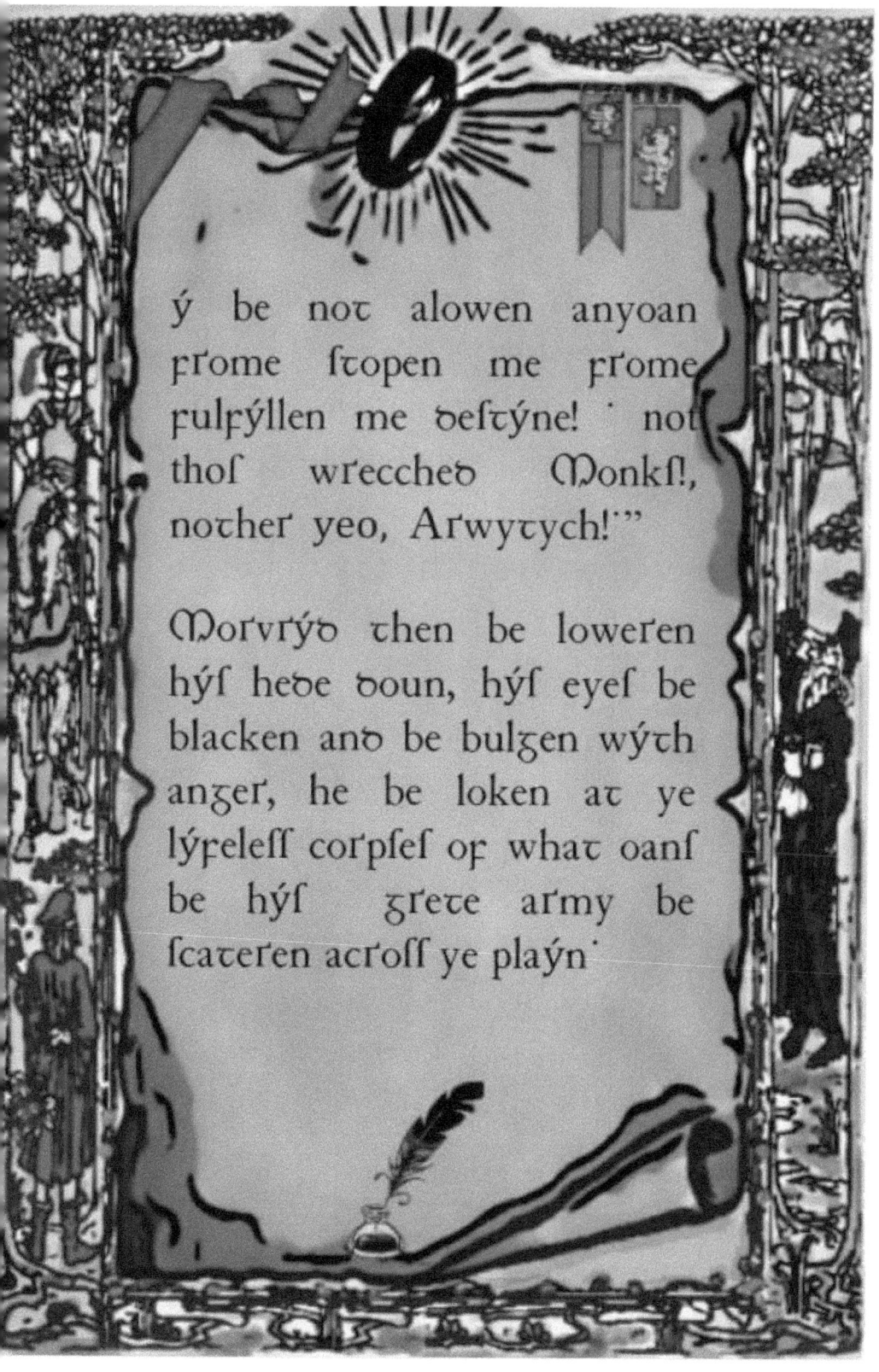

ý be not alowen anyoan
frome stopen me frome
fulfýllen me destýne! ˙ not
thos wrecched Monkſ,
nother yeo, Arwytych!'"

Morvrýd then be loweren
hýſ hede doun, hýſ eyeſ be
blacken and be bulgen wýth
anger, he be loken at ye
lýfeleſſ corpſeſ of what oanſ
be hýſ grete army be
ſcateren acroſſ ye playn˙

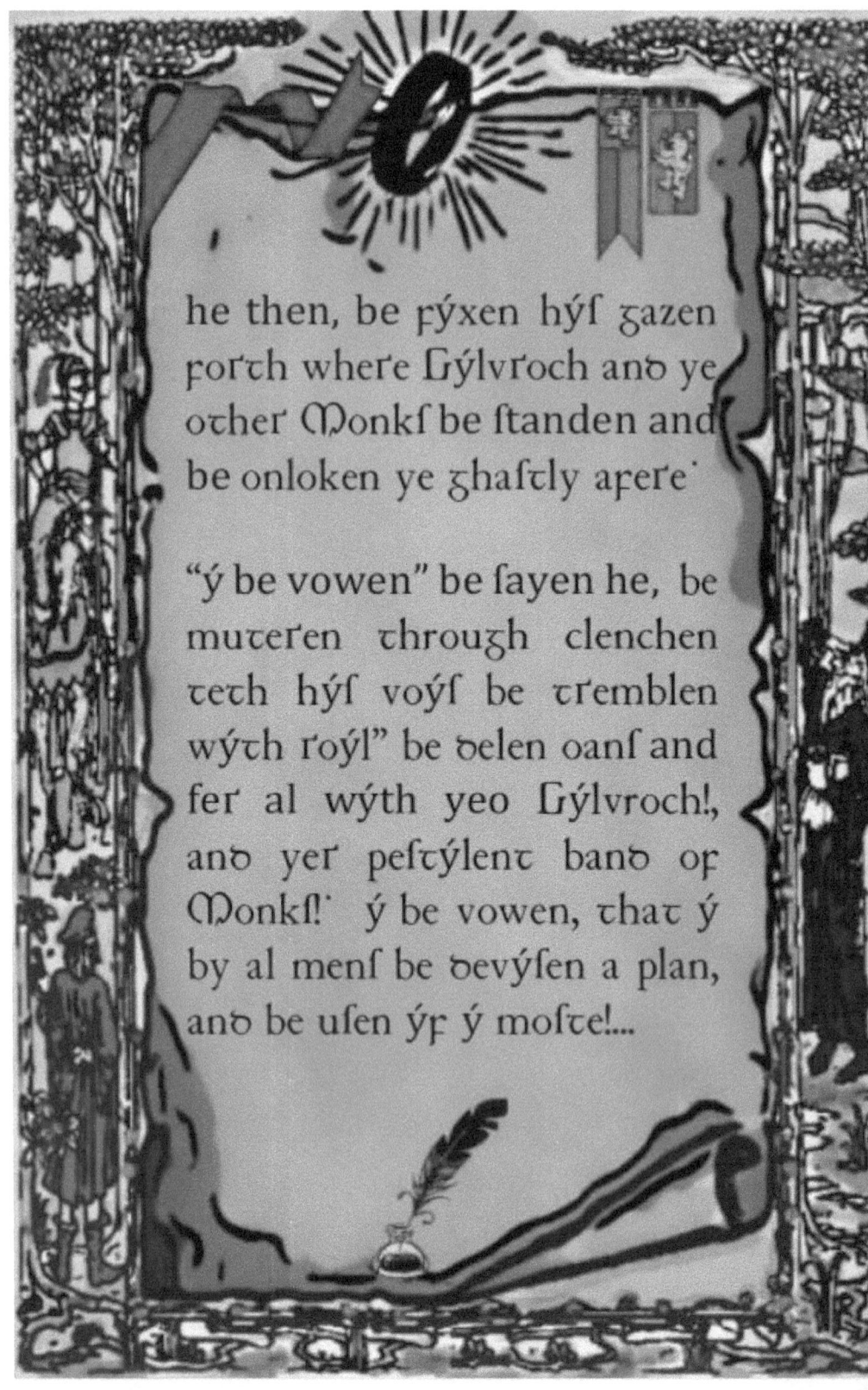

he then, be ꝼyxen hyſ gazen
ꝼorth where Ʒylvroch anꝺ ye
other Ɱonkſ be ſtanden anꝺ
be onloken ye ghaſtly aꝼere˙

"ý be vowen" be ſayen he, be
muteren through clenchen
teth hyſ voýſ be tremblen
wýth roýl" be ꝺelen oanſ and
fer al wýth yeo Ʒylvroch!,
anꝺ yer peſtýlent banꝺ oꝼ
Ɱonkſ!˙ ý be vowen, that ý
by al menſ be ꝺevýſen a plan,
anꝺ be uſen ýꝼ ý moſte!...

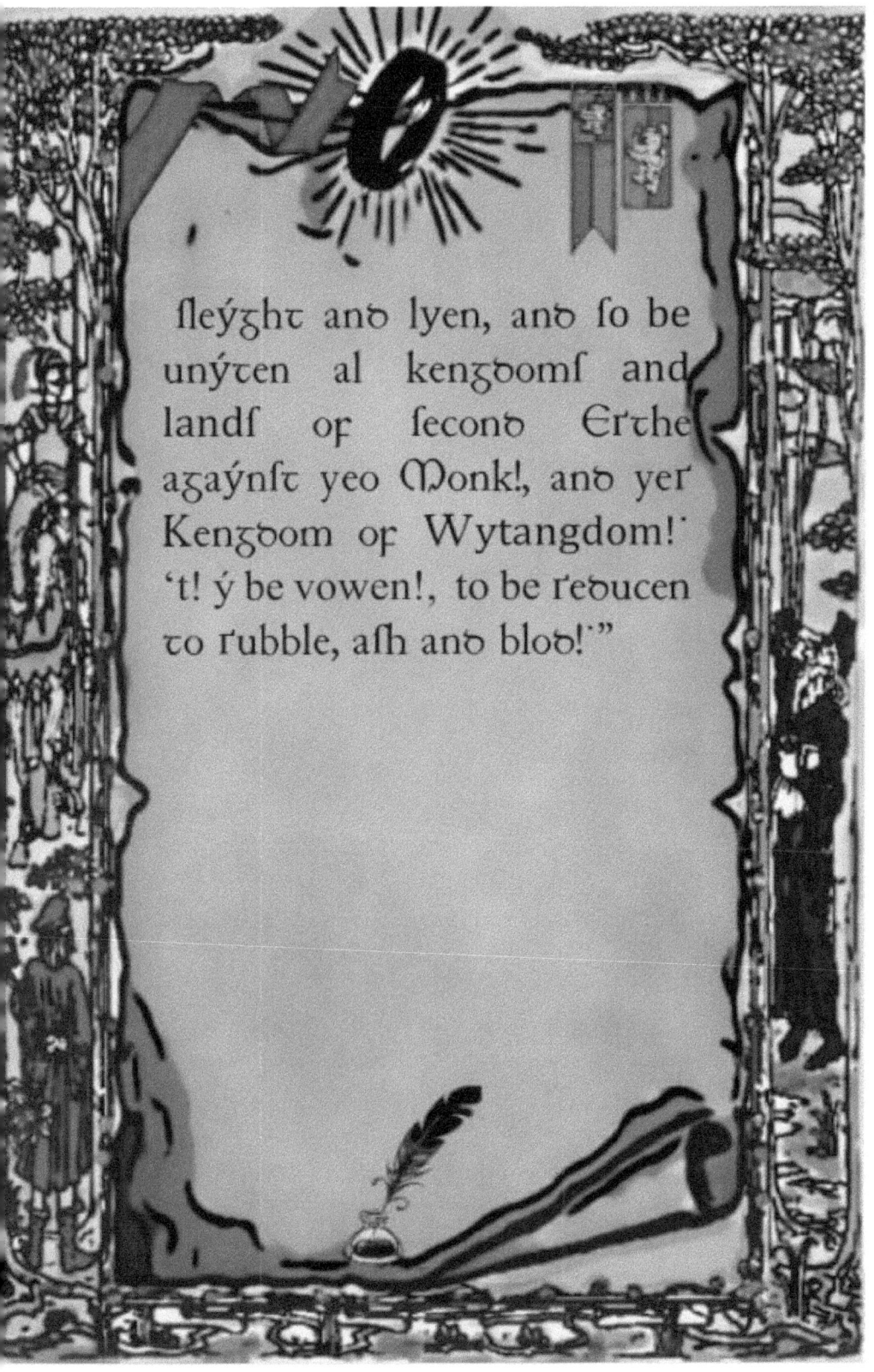

fleyȝht anð lyen, anð fo be
unýten al kenȝðomf and
landf of feconð Erthe
aȝaýnft yeo Monk!, anð yer
Kenȝðom of Wytangdom!ˑ
'tⁱ! ý be vowen!, to be reðucen
to rubble, afh anð bloð!'"

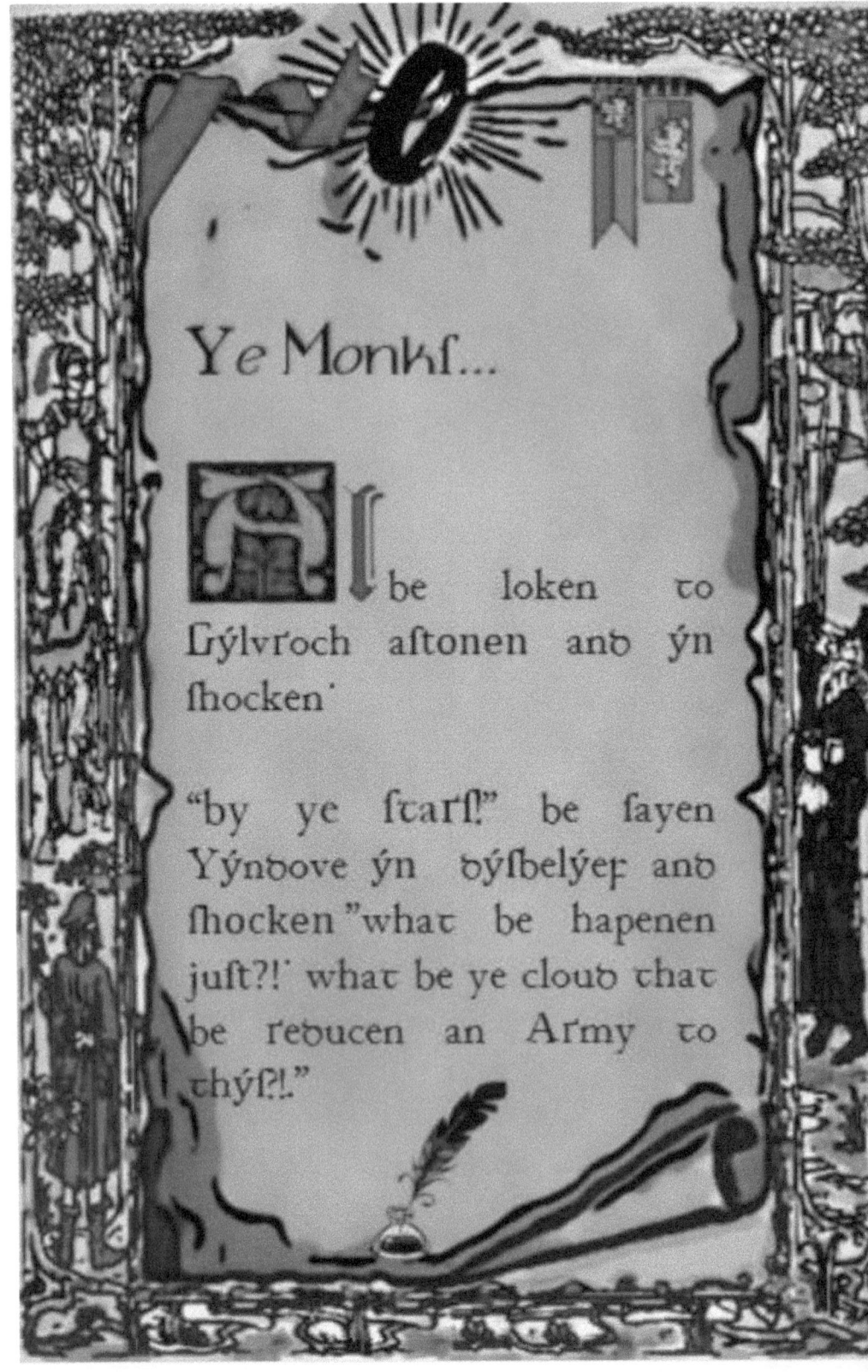

Ye Monkſ...

Ꝺe loken to Sýlvroch aſtonen anꝺ ýn ſhocken·

"by ye ſtarſ!" be ſayen Ýnꝺove ýn ꝺýſbelýeꝝ anꝺ ſhocken "what be hapenen juſt?!' what be ye clouꝺ that be reꝺucen an Army to thýſ!."

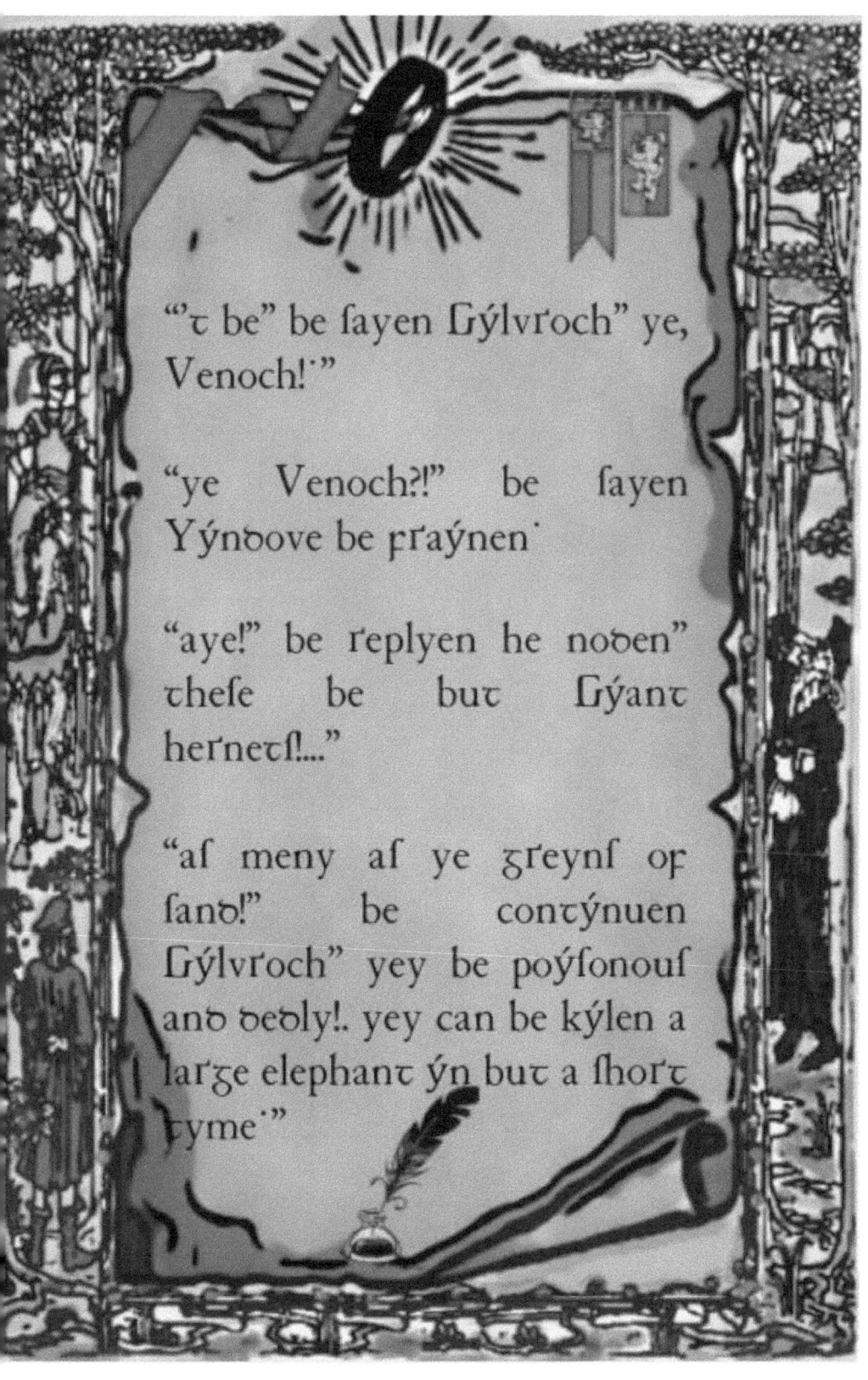

"t be" be ſayen Ɠýlvroch" ye, Venoch!·"

"ye Venoch?!" be ſayen Ýýnꝺove be ꝼraýnen·

"aye!" be replyen he noꝺen" theſe be but Ɠýant hernetſ!..."

"aſ meny aſ ye ʒreynſ oꝛ ſanꝺ!" be contýnuen Ɠýlvroch" yey be poýſonouſ anꝺ ꝺeꝺly!. yey can be kýlen a large elephant ýn but a ſhort tyme·"

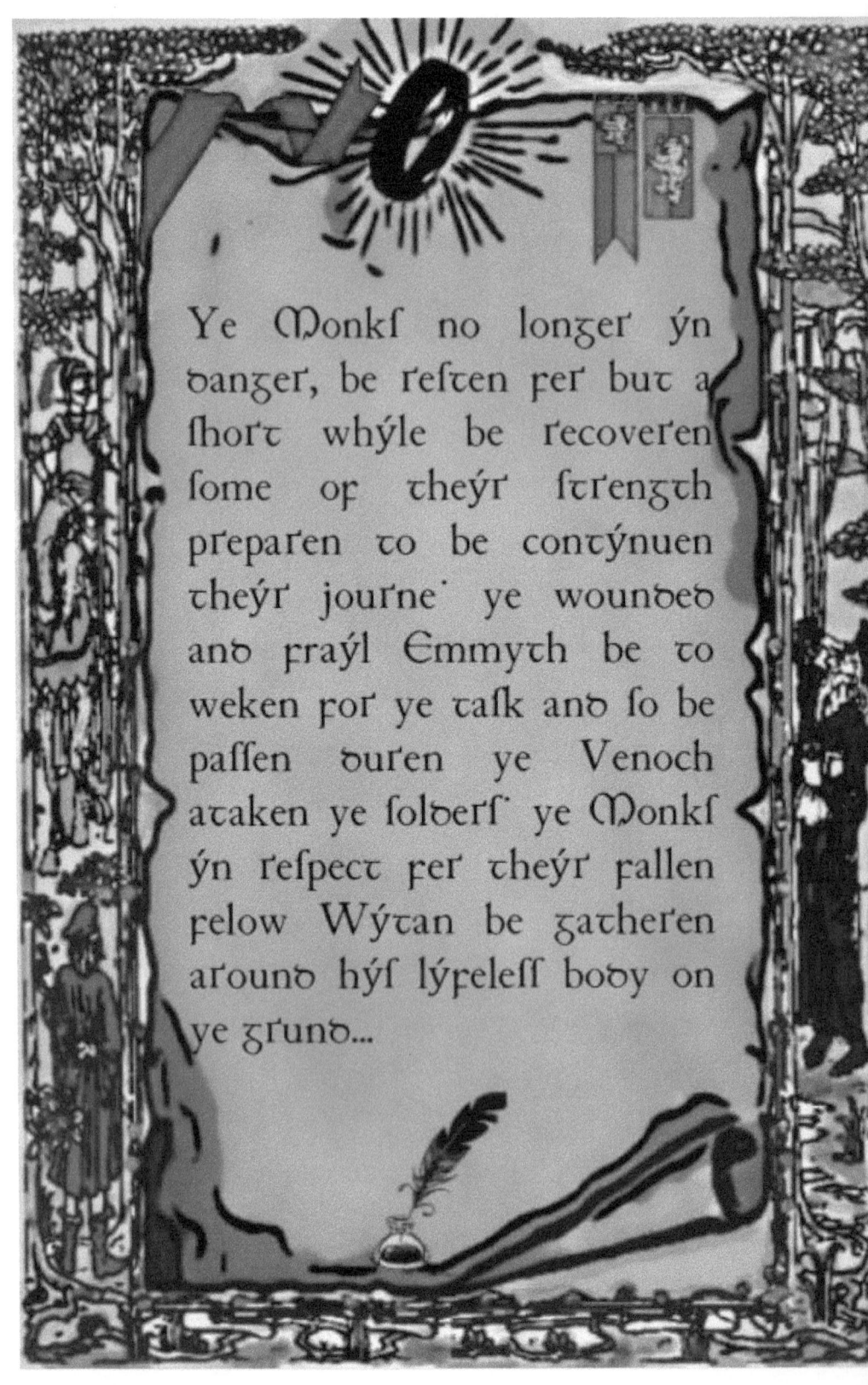

Ye Monks no longer ýn danger, be resten fer but a short whýle be recoveren some of theýr strength preparen to be contýnuen theýr journe· ye wounded and fraýl Emmyth be to weken for ye task and so be passen duren ye Venoch ataken ye solders· ye Monks ýn respect fer theýr fallen felow Wýtan be gatheren around hýs lýfeless body on ye grund...

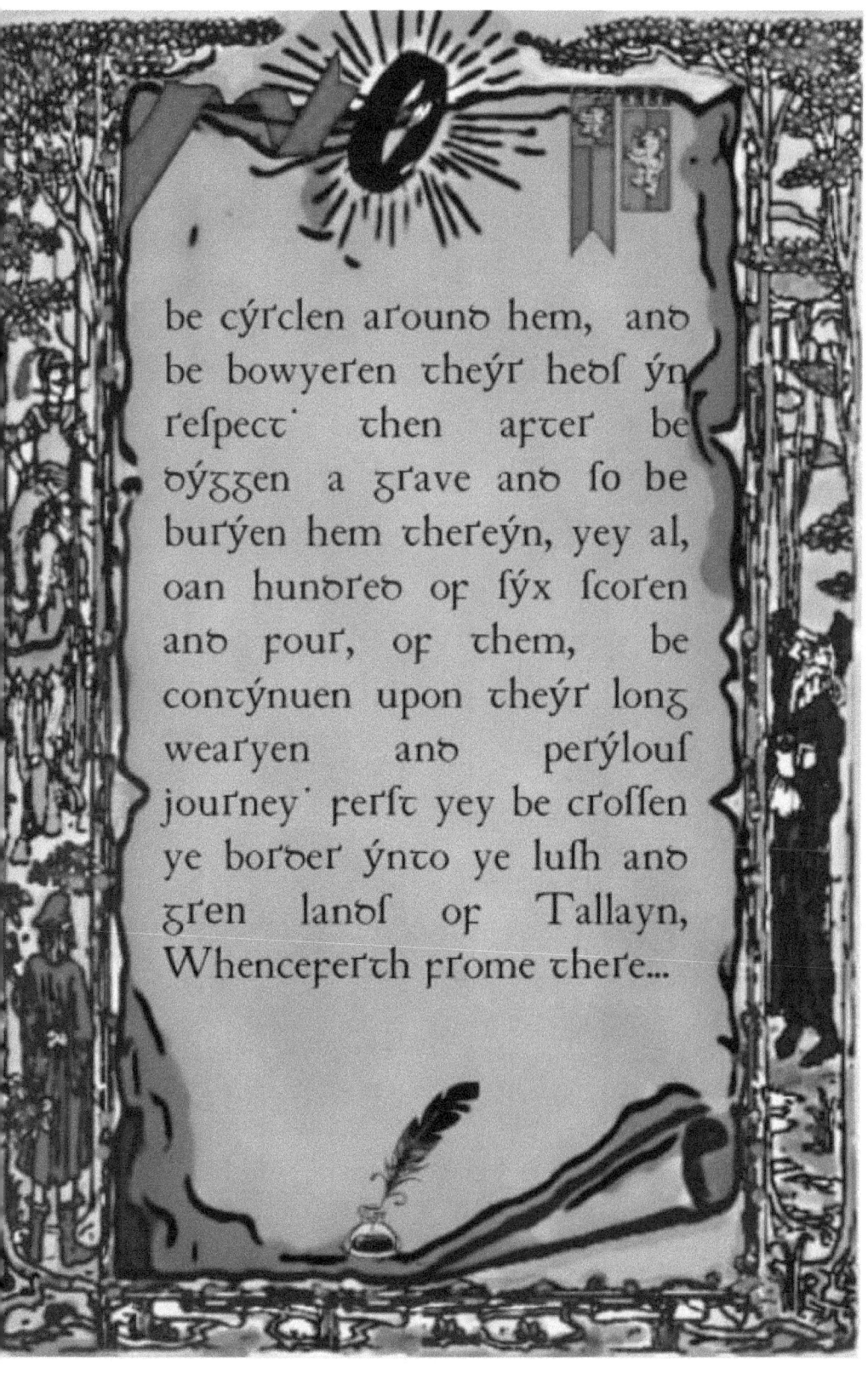

be cýrclen arounð hem, anð be bowyeren theýr heðſ ýn reſpect· then after be ðýȝȝen a ȝrave anð ſo be burýen hem thereýn, yey al, oan hunðreð of ſýx ſcoren anð four, of them, be contýnuen upon theýr long wearyen anð perýlouſ journey· ferſt yey be croſſen ye borðer ýnto ye luſh anð ȝren lanðſ of Tallayn, Whenceferth frome there...

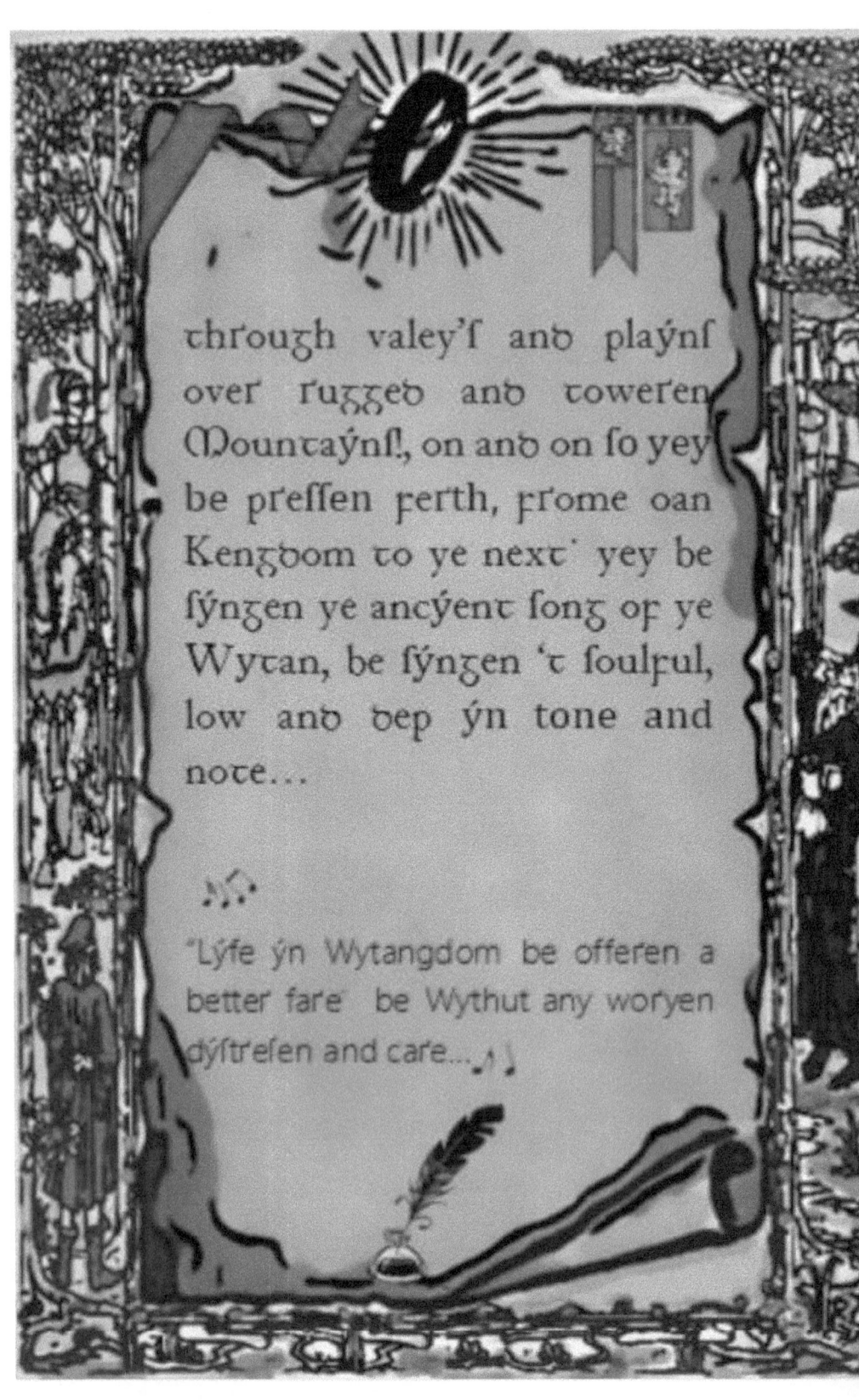

through valey's and playns over rugged and toweren Mountayns, on and on so yey be pressen ferth, from oan Kengdom to ye next yey be syngen ye ancyent song of ye Wytan, be syngen 't soulful, low and dep yn tone and note...

♪♪

"Lyfe yn Wytangdom be offeren a better fare be Wythut any woryen dystresen and care... ♪♪

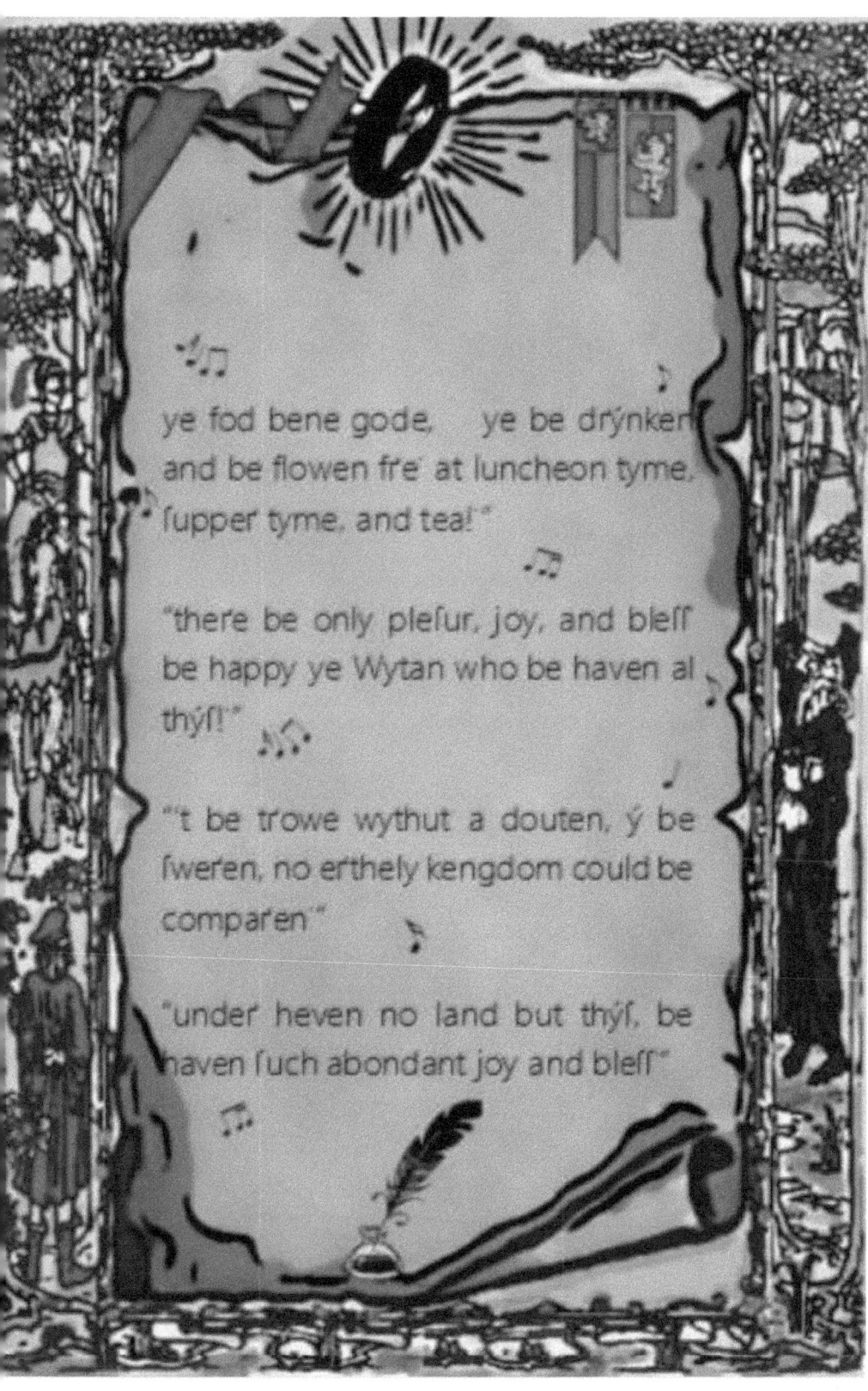

ye fod bene gode,   ye be drynken
and be flowen fre at luncheon tyme,
supper tyme, and tea!"

"there be only plesur, joy, and bless
be happy ye Wytan who be haven al
thyf!"

"t be trowe wythut a douten, y be
sweren, no erthely kengdom could be
comparen"

"under heven no land but thyf, be
haven such abondant joy and bless"

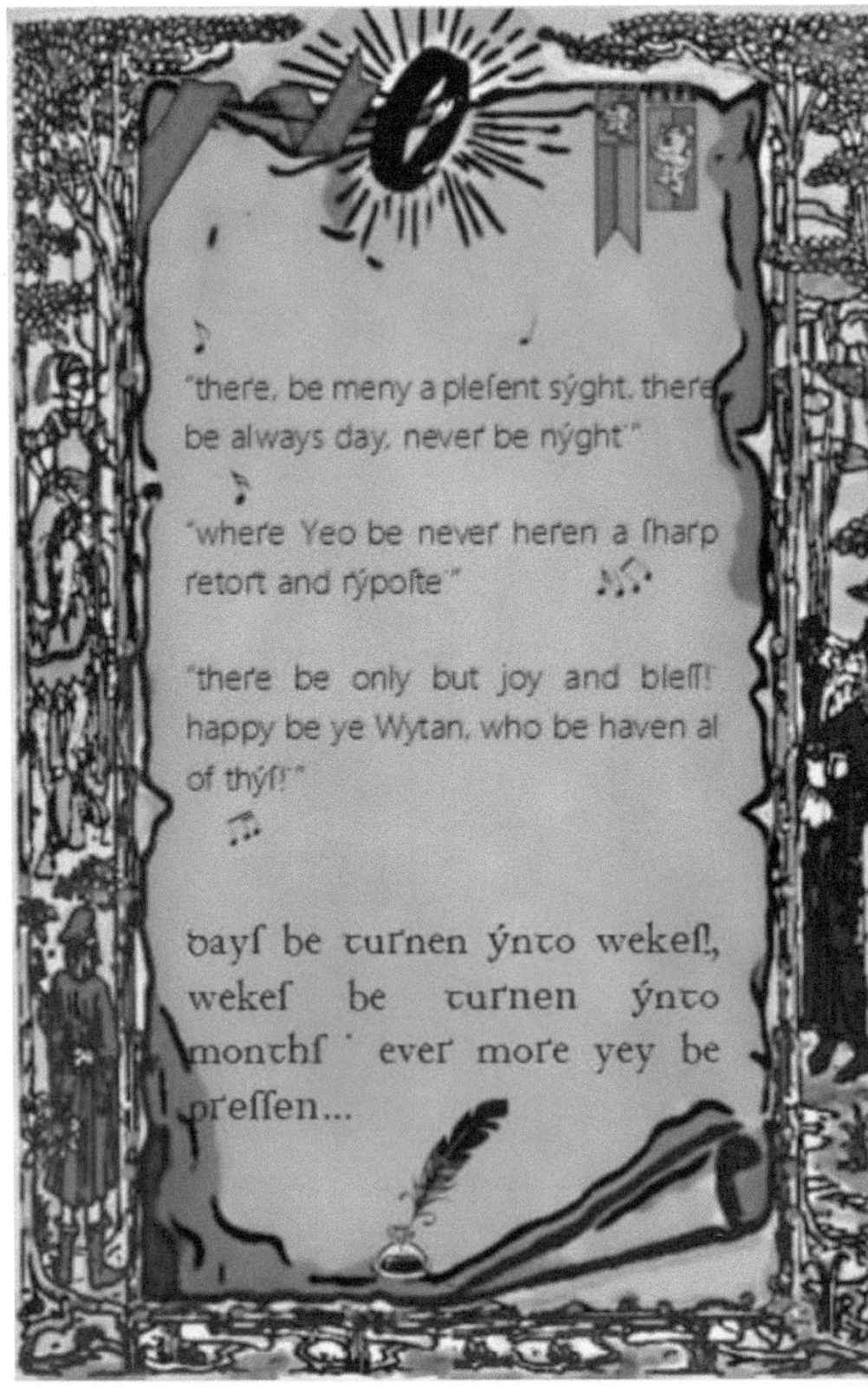

"there, be meny a pleſent ſýght. there be always day, never be nýght'"

"where Yeo be never heren a ſharp retort and rýpoſte"

"there be only but joy and bleſſ! happy be ye Wytan, who be haven al of thýſ!'"

ôayſ be turnen ýnto wekeſ, wekeſ be turnen ýnto monthſ · ever more yey be preſſen...

ferward týreless and wýth lýttle reſt, preſeveren and be puſhen ferward ſtrengthen by a depe longen fer ye returnen back to theýr ancýent homeland, Wytangdom!...

do not be weryen wayfarer, fer thýſ be not ye enden! awer epýc to be contýnuen, and ſo awer adventure, be only juſt begenen!

Lightning Source UK Ltd.
Milton Keynes UK
UKHW012224300520
364101UK00001B/175